MW01440711

Living in an Eldritch Neighborhood: A Suspenseful and Gripping Sci-Fi Alien Invasion Novel

By: Regolith42

Table of Contents

Part One: Life in Serenity

Chapter 1: An Average Day In the Neighborhood 1

Chapter 2: Recovering From Meeting the Neighbors 10

Chapter 3: Intruder! - Mortal (John) Fragment of Memory 14

Chapter 4: Uncomfortable Small Talk - Mortal John Fragment of Memory 17

Chapter 5: Interrogation By The Authorities 20

Chapter 6: Finally Back Home 25

Chapter 7: A Nostalgic Memory 29

Chapter 8: Preparation for the Weekend 36

Chapter 9: Assault Charges Will be Brought 40

Chapter 10: The Destiny of Fulcrum 49

Chapter 11: Form Versus Function 53

Chapter 12: Kaiju Attack on the Neighborhood 58

Chapter 13: To Battle in the Neighborhood 63

Part Two: The New Neighbors Are Everywhere

Chapter 14: Neighborhood Watch, Here to Help! - Prime Mortal (Bill) Fragment 73

Chapter 15: A Thoughtful Gift with Puppet Strings Attached - Beholder Fragment 78

Chapter 16: Betrayal Most Foul - Infiltrator of Authority Fragment 85

Chapter 17: Polite Disagreements within the Neighborhood Watch - Prime Mortal Fragment 90

Chapter 18: Never Pay a Lawyer Upfront - Beholder Fragment 95

Chapter 19: Outside The Bubble of the Neighborhood - Beholder Fragment 101

Chapter 20: Neighborhood Watch Has a Meeting - Prime Mortal Fragment 111

Chapter 21: The Neighbor Goes to the Hospital - Prime Mortal Fragment 115

Chapter 22: Under Arrest - Prime Mortal Fragment 124

Chapter 23: Party in The Streets - Mortal (Francis) Fragment 129

Chapter 24: Trying to Leave the Party Early - Mortal Francis Fragment 137

Chapter 25: Escaping the Partygoers - Mortal Francis Fragment 142

Chapter 26: Chaos at the Hospital - Infiltrator of Authority Fragment 147

Chapter 27: A New Club in The Neighborhood - Mortal (Ryan) Fragment 153

Chapter 28: Safehouse for the Club - Mortal Ryan Fragment 161

Chapter 29: Presentation to the Club - Mortal Ryan Fragment 167

Part Three: The Neighborhood Watch Steps In

Chapter 30: Story Time in Safehouse Nine - Mortal Francis Fragment 173

Chapter 31: Meeting the Leader of the Neighborhood Watch - Mortal (Alice) Fragment 180

Chapter 32: Entering the Ranch - Mortal Alice Fragment 183

Chapter 33: Tour of the Ranch - Mortal Francis Fragment 188

Chapter 34: Francis Before the Neighborhood - Mortal Francis Fragment 193

Chapter 35: Francis Before the Neighborhood Continued - Mortal Francis Fragment 198

Chapter 36: Visiting the Club - Mortal Alice Fragment 204

Chapter 37: Suspicious Activity at the Ranch - Mortal Alice Fragment 211

Chapter 38: Escaping the Neighborhood Watch - Mortal Alice Fragment 215

Chapter 39: Long Walk Out of the Bubble - Mortal Alice Fragment 220

Chapter 40: Up the Chain of Command - Multiple Fragments of Memory 228

Chapter 41: Appeasing the Guest - Beholder Fragment 233

Chapter 42: A Gift for the Visitor - Beholder Fragment 237

Chapter 43: Negotiating with the Visitor - Multiple Fragments of Memory 245

Chapter 44: Touring the Visitor's Collection - Beholder Fragment 252

Chapter 45: The Visitor Returns to Earth - Multiple Fragments of Memory 256

Chapter 46: Missing Person in the Neighborhood - Infiltrator of Authority Fragment 264

Chapter 47: Assault on the Club - Prime Mortal Bill Fragment 272

Chapter 48: Escaping the Assault on the Club - Mortal Ryan Fragment 279

Chapter 49: The Neighborhood Watch Revealed to the World - Multiple Fragments of Memory 285

Part Four: War Against the New Neighbors

Chapter 50: Messenger to the New Club - Mortal Ryan Fragment 294

Chapter 51: Club to Battle - Mortal Ryan Fragment 300

Chapter 52: Fighting off the Swarm - Mortal (Augustus) Fragment 305

Chapter 53: Suspicions - Mortal Ryan Fragment 309

Chapter 54: The Growing Threat - Mortal Ryan Fragment 313

Chapter 55: Parting Ways with the Club - Multiple Fragments of Memory 319

Chapter 56: The Army meets the Cult - Multiple Fragments of Memory 323

Chapter 57: Escaping the Neighborhood Watch - Mortal Francis Fragment 328

Chapter 58: Scouting - Mortal Francis Fragment 332

Chapter 59: The Plan Revealed - Mortal Francis Fragment 338

Chapter 60: Joining the Army - Mortal Francis Fragment 344

Chapter 61: Opening a Doorway to the World Outside of the Bubble - Mortal Francis Fragment 349

Chapter 62: Assault on the Backlines - Infiltrator of Authority Fragment 354

Chapter 63: Escaping the Horde - Mortal Francis Fragment 360

Chapter 64: Holding the Line - Mortal Ryan Fragment 364

Chapter 65: An Aerial Perspective - Mortal Francis Fragment 368

Chapter 66: Breach! - Mortal Francis Fragment 374

Chapter 67: War in the Neighborhood - Mortal (Emily) Fragment 380

Chapter 68: Failure is not an Option - Mortal Francis Fragment 385

Chapter 69: Destined for a Greater Purpose - Multiple Fragments of Memory 391

Chapter 70: Self-imposed Duty - Nameless Amalgamation Fragment 397

Part Five: An Oddly Familiar World

Chapter 71: A New World for Fulcrum 404

Chapter 72: A New Friend for Fulcrum? 412

Chapter 73: A New Acquaintance for Fulcrum? 418

Chapter 74: Enjoying the Appetizers - Seed of the Eldest's Fragment of Memory 423

Chapter 75: Welcome and Goodbye - Multiple Fragments of Memory 431

Chapter 76: Where Have You Been? - Multiple Fragments of Memory 436

Chapter 77: Back After a Long Absence - Mortal Steven Fragment 442

Chapter 78: Coming Clean - Steven Fragment 448

Chapter 79: A Recurring Dream - Steven Fragment 453
Chapter 80: Preparations for the Feast - Multiple Fragments of Memory 459
Chapter 81: A Nightmare With the Ones You Love - Multiple Fragments of Memory 466
Chapter 82: What Have You Done with Her? 472
Chapter 83: The Dream Continues for Fulcrum 477
Chapter 84: Making Friends in the Dream - Mortal (Jessica) Fragment 486
Chapter 85: A New Life in the Dream - Multiple Fragments of Memory 491
Chapter 86: Sneaking Past the Guard - Multiple Fragments of Memory 499
Chapter 87: Blind Rage - Squirrel Fragment of Memory 505
Chapter 88: A Blessing from Above - Multiple Fragments of Memory 510
Chapter 89: The Final Assault - Multiple Fragments of Memory 514
Chapter 90: The Final Choice 519
Chapter 91: The Escape - Multiple Fragments of Memory 527
Chapter 92: Epilogue - Multiple Fragments of Memory 534
Afterword

Part One: Life in Serenity

Chapter 1: An Average Day In the Neighborhood

It was a sunny day and the sky was bright blue in Serenity. There wasn't a cloud in sight and it was a beautiful day to go to the park, or just absorb some summer sun. Too bad everyone else was missing it. Here in Serenity, the days were always beautiful. Always the same.

Here I was, on my own personal eighth day of the week, nestled between the Saturday and Sunday of everyone else on Earth. Every Saturday at midnight, I am transported into this silent world.

A perfect mimicry of Earth without all the people or most of the animals. All the objects are frozen in midair, frozen in time, only to drop to the ground when I touch them. Leaves, cars, trees. All still. All waiting in the air and frozen if I didn't touch them.

At first, I thought that this place was hell, but eventually I came around. Especially when I figured out how to get the TV working. Figuring out how to get one to work in Serenity had taken me years. But here I was now, able to enjoy it all at my leisure. Serenity was a place away from the franticness and responsibilities of my everyday life. Somewhere calm and… Serene. The place I was always meant to be.

I yawned and curled up on the couch trying to distract myself with the show on the TV.

The downloaded show I am watching is just terrible, but not quite bad enough to make me reach for the remote. It was surprisingly relaxing to just watch something I wasn't overly engaged with. To just let the words wash over me without wondering what they could mean. To let my mind fuzz over so I could think about nothing at all for a little while.

I can feel the hum of the generator through the floor as it provides power to my house. I'm glad I figured that one out. I had to reassemble that thing every time I came in here so I'm a pro at it by now. I can rebuild it in five minutes flat now.

I remember back to when it took over an hour. I had to touch every little part inside or it wouldn't be unfrozen while I was in Serenity. Just one little part frozen in time on the insides would make the whole thing not work properly…

Suddenly, there was a rhythmic knocking at the door. The end of every knock was punctuated by a loud ripping sound like tape being peeled back from the wood. Probably stripping the paint again like it did almost every time. I turned off the TV, grumbling to myself a bit as the knocks continued, and made my way to the front door.

People on Earth kept bothering me about the stripped paint and bare wood at the door, saying it was an eyesore. But where were they now huh? Paint's expensive, you know.

A few years ago, I gave up trying to make it look perfect every week. Now I just do what I like to call the hard slam test. Every Sunday after I return to Earth I open my front door and slam it shut as hard as I can, and if there are no visible holes and the door handle stays on then I'm good.

Otherwise, I get a new door. Any visible wood gets a little dab of paint to cover it up. And even with that half-assed system you would be surprised how much I spend on replacing the door still.

"Clack *rrrrririiiiip*. Clack *rrrrrrip*, Clack *rrrririippppp,*"

There it is again, the sound not stopping the slightest as I walk to the door. I wish it would skip a week for just once. But I had to do the stupid routine every time, otherwise it would just keep knocking all day.

Well, sometimes it would stop for a while and leave if I waited. But it always would return within an hour or two to continue knocking again. Over and over until I responded to it... I waited for a few seconds and paused by the door for the moment the thing outside would hit the door open again.

"Clack rrrrrii......"

I flung open the door to witness the shambling horror falling flat on its face and blinked dumbly at the ground. With all thirty of its eyeballs in sync. Well around thirty. They changed size and position sometimes so it was hard to tell the exact count. It's surprising how well they could express dumb confusion so perfectly with such an alien body.

A small smile of amusement twitched at the corner of my lips. It lay there for a few more seconds with only a flicker of interest in me.

A few eyes on its humanoid back met mine for a moment before they started blankly staring into the sky again. The eyes facing the ground started darting around as they focused on the dirt below. The eyes on the creature gained intense focus and I nearly groaned. It was going to be one of those days, wasn't it?

s

I felt a tinge of remorse as it kept ignoring me. I just wish I could tell it to just not knock so hard every time. It had been years at this point and we were the only ones that were here.

It could be a little more considerate. But it wasn't really its fault, it just didn't understand I think. Well, I'm not entirely sure, maybe it really is doing it just to annoy me.

Fifteen minutes later there was no change, and I was annoyed despite telling myself to just be patient. Usually, it just stumbled a bit and looked at me in shock when I started doing this prank a few months ago. I actually had never seen it fall all the way over like that before.

It had surprisingly good balance for what appeared to be the mass of exposed muscle and overly large bones that lined its frame. There was the occasional reddish chitinous plating covering some sections, especially the articulating interlocking bone or chitin looking plates covering the hands and feet. Those parts almost looked like some elaborate chainmail gloves. I call it Red in my mind, named after the color of its plating. Not very original I know, but it didn't seem to care either way... Not like it could speak normally anyway.

Red finally looked up and the set of eyes I met flashed with a light of unknowable depths for a second. I felt my memories of the earth, warm soil, ground, a pile of rotting leaves. All of it flashed by and the images consumed my mind for a moment as the mental probe from Red scanned my thoughts.

"Fshhhulllllll ka ka ka GRRRRRROUUUUUUnnn— ka —-AN—-ka---ANDA. GRUND?"

The beak clacked with each sound and the tentacles flapped as it stood. I shook my head a bit to shrug off the mental probe. I thought about the images I had seen looking for a common theme.

"Ground?" I asked hesitantly.

I put my hand to my temple as I felt a twinge of pain as the wave of images filling my thoughts resumed, but now a repeating loop of 'ground' in my voice playing over and over beneath it. I shook off the mental probe a little harder this time before replying,

"Eh, Close enough," I say, shrugging at it.

Red seemed to get the message and clicked its beak in satisfaction before standing to its feet and ambling off farther down the empty street. I closed the door to my house and went back to the stupid shows on the TV. The street went silent once more. I needed some time to clear the headache I had coming on. The telepathy with Red was always the worst part of this place.

———O—o—O———

After a few more minutes of watching, I turned off the TV again and stood up with restless energy. I always felt a little off balance after the mental probes. I just needed to do something with my hands to take my mind off things. I could barely watch TV anymore with the headache I was nursing anyway. Even for mindless shows like the one I had been watching.

Hm, but what should I do? I think I should finish building the birdhouse. That should keep Red interested for a while. I was actually a little surprised it had left with just that one tidbit drawn from my mind.

Maybe it got a little of the concept of death when I thought of the soil? Especially when it focused on the rotting leaves near the end. Compost? Yeah, that must be it. Leaves that decompose and leave fresh soil for new growth. That was a meatier concept than normal. Maybe that's why it was staring at the dirt for so long?

It always got confused about stuff like that. Big concepts even for us natives to grasp let alone for aliens from whatever crazy reality Red must come from.

Wetness on my upper lip. I reached up and felt something wet dripping from my nose. Ah shit, I almost forgot. I lifted my hand and put my hand to my nose before inspecting it. Yep, there it is. Sure enough, there was a trickle of blood flowing down my hand. Bloody nose.

I went to the bathroom and looked at the mirror. Alright, looks pretty mild. I tapped the corners of my eyes and my ears and was pleasantly surprised when my finger came back dry. That was good.

Blood from your nose was pretty easy to explain to people. From your ears and tear ducts? Much more concerning. Not normal, worthy of investigation. I quickly washed off from the bucket I had filled up on Saturday since none of my plumbing would work while everything was frozen in Serenity. My bleeding nose's leaking slowly petered to a stop after a few minutes.

I only made the mistake of attempting to explain my bleeding to the neighbors once. I shuddered as I remembered how Bill across the street had called the ambulance anyway over my protests at the time.

I suppose my explanation of random nosebleeds with no cause had sounded concerning. Especially when I had been bleeding from my eyes too at the time which was not something I could as easily explain. Even for the nosebleeds, I knew that I wouldn't be able to explain myself to the doctors.

After I first came to Serenity the first few times, I took all of their tests, and they couldn't determine what was going on. After spending most of my money on various specialists, I eventually was just prescribed some blood thickeners and moved on with my life. And told to come back if anything changed.

I never used the drugs, even the worst of the bleeding seemed to stop within a day or two of leaving Serenity. Supernatural nosebleeds deserved supernatural recovery from them as well it seems. I shook my head at the old vague memories swirling around my head from the beginning of my time at Serenity as I entered my garage.

I feel a little proud of myself as I took out my tools and started looking at some of the sections of wood that I had already measured and marked in pencil before this. Near the beginning of my time at Serenity, that telepathic exchange with Red earlier would have knocked me out for hours but now it was barely a nosebleed. Not worth more than a quick wash up before being able to move along with my day. It made me feel proud of how far I had come since then.

Suddenly with a lurch in my gut, I feel the shrouded memories from my past rise, struggling against their cage with sudden ferocity. I stop mid motion reaching for another piece of wood and frowned as the memories were suppressed brutally and decisively. No need to push my luck, the past was the past. Best to stay in the here and now instead.

As the conflict died down, my hand resumed its motion as I entered a sort of blank trance as I worked. Time passed in a blur and I hummed a little tune to myself unconsciously. I startle awake when I reach for the bench and see there are no more pieces to cut. I blink a few times and struggle for a second to remember what I was doing.

My eyes scan the workbench, and eventually, my eyes catch on the box full of nails. Aha, the birdhouse! I grabbed the little bucket of nails and the hammer and began assembling the slanted roof and square walls. Putting all the pieces together and nailing them into place so it would be steady and secure. Finally, I screwed the metal hook into the top for the whole birdhouse to hang from and it was ready to go.

I had already set the pole into the ground in the backyard ready to hang the completed birdhouse on last week. Taking it outside, I put the birdhouse out to hang on it. I stepped back to admire my work. The birdhouse swung in the soft wind gently and the hot sun beat down on my back.

Yeah, there was a day-night cycle here. And no, I had no idea how that was possible. I smiled as I thought about how Red would react to see its newest toy. Despite its horrifying appearance, it had surprisingly human body language. If I ordered my thoughts and aligned them with the right concepts when it came next week then the birdhouse should hold its interest for a while.

It was totally fascinated with even the most mundane things, but after a while, it would lose interest in that object for seemingly forever. It was like giving it a guided tour rather than letting it rifle through a cluttered cabinet filled with interesting objects. More controlled and less chance for chaos or strange surprises.

And having something new would give the front door a break. Red would still knock at the back if I stayed on that side of the house but it might spend a few hours inspecting the birdhouse on its own before it did so.

Over the years I had gotten a sense of what would interest it and I had a good feeling in my gut about the potential of the birdhouse to catch its interest. It is surprisingly relaxing to be able to meet the eldritch creature on my own time rather than right on the dot every week.

It took a lot of work to set up sometimes, but was a nice break from routine even if just in a small way. If I stood outside my door and waited for Red then it wouldn't appear. It was only when I went back inside that it would approach from the street and knock on my door.

That's why I waited for it to knock inside. If it missed its appointment then its arrival was far more unpredictable and the door got even more damaged if I wasn't ready to meet it or became distracted with something on the other side of the house.

I was surprised I hadn't thought of making a birdhouse before this after all these years. I kept admiring my handiwork. There it was with a triangular roof and a little stick poking out from the entrance. The unpainted wood swung from the post.

When Red began to lose interest I would paint it to get its attention again. I needed to give myself time to wrack my brain for something else to do after all this. After all, the more I can prepare myself the less chance I get blasted with a surprisingly complicated concept like what happened today.

———O—o—O———

It was late and the shadows grew long as the sun dipped below the horizon. I sat on the sofa reading a well worn book under the glaring light of the nearby battery powered lamp that I had just turned on. I looked up as I heard loud thumps from the front door for the second time today.

How strange.

The knocking came with heavy slams and growls. The creature let out a loud screech and clicking from behind the door, sounding angry. I frowned as I inserted my bookmark and shut the book with one hand with a click.

I stretched and put the book on the side table as I stood from my chair. What could be wrong? Why was it back again today? I tried to think of what it could be.

I knew Red was still vaguely upset about that squirrel it mentally probed too hard last year. Little guy practically vanished when he entered the Serenity realm even if I occasionally saw him during the week on Earth. The squirrel ran for the hills whenever he saw the eldritch creature, which made Red's shoulders slump a little whenever it happened.

That squirrel was the only other animal I had ever seen in this place besides just the two of us. That I could remember at least.

And yes I could tell it was the same squirrel in the real world because she had a distinctive black diamond pattern of fur on her back on her otherwise gray coat. I didn't even realize squirrels could have clear shapes in their fur like that. I chuckled a bit. I bet the other squirrels were amazed at how much extra food she stored for the winter with an extra day a week with no predators hunting her down.

I knew for a fact that she ran around like a madman whenever I saw her. I frowned at myself as I realized I was getting distracted. I've been daydreaming a lot more these days, haven't I? I blinked in slight confusion as I suddenly found myself standing in front of the main door. Shadows flickered in the corners of the room like dark flames as I stood there in confusion.

Maybe Red, no Ally, wanted help with the new creature and be its friend this time? It wasn't too uncommon but it hadn't had much luck even with my help. It was one of the few topics the creature actively tried to get me to help it with.

Ally's shoulders had hunched and its face tentacles had hung loosely from its face for months after the squirrel started running from it. I could just feel its visceral disappointment as most of its eyes pointed dejectedly at the ground.

It had taken the introduction of trampolines to fix that one. That one had kept its interest for over a year. It just had taken one of its fingers and pressed down on various points of the trampoline a month or two before I finally demonstrated jumping up and down for on the trampoline.

Ally was enthusiastic but I did wince when it landed directly on a few of its eyes a few times when it bounced too high back then. The injured eyes looked pretty gruesome and deflated for a few minutes while leaking a disgusting whitish fluid. After that, they formed what looked like a rough scab.

Less than ten minutes later the scab had fallen off, leaving a fully healed eyeball. The freshly healed eyeballs would dart around frantically as if to make up for lost time to look at everything possible. Ally screeched pitifully a little after the injury but after it scabbed over later it promptly forgot and just resumed merrily jumping on the trampoline before eventually injuring itself again.

"Thump Thump Thump SCRREEEEECH"

Oh right, I should just answer the door. I had just been standing there with my hand on the door handle without moving for a few seconds as I spaced out. Maybe Re— Ally just found composting really interesting and wanted more information? It began its loud slams and screeching at the door again as I resumed walking to the door.

Wait, but wasn't my hand just on the door handle? Why was I back in the kitchen? Something just didn't feel right... Why was it slamming the door so hard? And it almost never screeched unless it was scared or upset. Why would it be upset?

As I approached the door again I frowned and decided to divert slightly to peek out the window to see in front of the door at an angle. I froze. This... This wasn't my eldritch neighbor.

Its posture is totally different, its multitude of eyes focused and narrowed in anger. Its posture was tight and its shoulders stiff. The face tentacles are thrashing around in agitation and its carapace plates are corn yellow with black splotches rather than dark red. I felt visceral disgust build in my gut. This is the *ENEMY*!

One of the eyes on its shoulders drifted from the door it was pounding on and met my own. I felt a mental probe enter my mind, but this wasn't the gentle one I was used to. It was barbed and pointed with malice as it attempted to fragment my positive memories and reinforce the negative ones.

The waves of raw malice of sharp edged images contained in the attack were almost as stunning as the damage itself. It was built to savagely wound and maim the mind.

I was stunned by the sudden vicious assault. I only snapped out of the spell as the foreign *ENEMY* outside moved, I pushed back at the mental assault, and it was... easy? The sharp images penetrated but then it felt like a wave of energy pushed out from the back of my mind to help me. The attack was instantly washed from my mind leaving me with nothing but faint pressure from behind my eyes.

As the creature rushed to the window it launched another mental attack, its face tentacles thrashing even more wildly now. I brushed the assault back preemptively as I imagined walls in my mind. Everything felt fluid and easy compared to normal and I marveled at the strength of my quickly erected mental defenses.

They were like the stone walls of an ancient castle. Thick and sturdy. The pressure behind my eyes builds and I feel a slight headache coming on. But my confidence seemed misplaced after a few seconds. Endless wave after wave of psychic assaults follows the first attack one after another with seemingly no end. The headache builds more and I feel myself begin to sweat.

Those barriers that felt like mountains are now crumbling more every second, my misplaced confidence turned to fear as my defenses were stripped away bit by bit. I look away to the ground but I can feel the *ENEMY* forcing the mental connection open even without eye contact.

Thousands of attacks and sharpened images launched each second into my mental walls. Each was weaker without eye contact to strengthen the telepathic connection, but even with that the attacks were still wearing me down slowly. After nearly ten seconds of being mentally assaulted my headache has transitioned into a full-blown migraine and I clutch my head in pain.

I desperately tried to counterattack but only formed a few distorted and lumpy images that barely even crossed the divide between our minds before dissolving. My weak counterattack came at the cost of my crumbling barriers. As my assault petered out, one strong barbed image suddenly pierced my mind and sent me reeling back in pain.

A woman with a caved in chest, blood leaking from her slack mouth... She was familiar. The image of her hurt was painful, horrible, the end of my world.

I stumbled backward away from the window but tripped as the gap in my mental defenses widened under another wave of mental attacks. The window shattered and a yellow carapace coated arm reaches through the broken glass… Only to pause and retreat in a hiss of pain and the sizzling of flesh.

The frequency of the mental attacks quickly slows until suddenly, the bridge between our minds snaps with an elastic twang. I lay sprawled face down on the floor and my head was fuzzy as I reeled from the backlash of the mental bridge snapping. I'm pretty sure the warmth underneath my chin is blood. It's sticky and I can smell something metallic as my face was pressed against the floor. I try to push myself up but my arms are weak and violently tremble when I put weight on them.

I collapse to the ground bonelessly, not even to lift my head up anymore with my failing strength. Everything swims around me as shadows begin twisting in the corner of my vision.

The pool of liquid beneath me grows and I feel something warm and metallic on my lips that are kissing the floor. Blood. My blood. In the distance, I hear a challenging screech followed by another louder one outside the window, and I close my eyes for just a moment…

———O — o — O———

Another pair of screeches sends a sharp burst of pain through me and jolts me back awake. I must have fallen unconscious because I hear the thumps and grunts of battle farther down the street now. I hear more eldritch screeching and wet slaps of flesh on flesh and flesh on exoskeleton as the fight continues.

The shadows around me wobble. Finally, after what seems like an eternity, the sounds die down and I hear one of them whimpering and shambling away with what sounds like a limp, while the other lets out a triumphant screech of victory.

I can't tell which one came out on top of the battle. Ally or *ENEMY*? I flip myself onto my back and cough as some blood runs into my mouth from my running nose. I tuck in my chin and barely manage to sit up so I can see the shattered frame of the window leading out into the night, the whole bottom portion of the frame in a pile of wooden splinters.

A cold wind blew through the shattered fragments of glass clinging to the bits of wood left. The cold air stung my watering eyes as I blinked hard to see. I waited with baited breath and my shoulders tensed as I heard the winner of the battle shuffling toward the shattered window from out on the street.

After a moment, a familiar red form appeared framing the window shadowed by the street lamps behind it and I let out my held breath in a sigh of relief. Ally's visible eyes appeared worried and it put its right hand up as if to reach for me. But before it could finish its motion it paused before its hand would have reached through the shattered window.

For a moment it looked indecisive; it returned its hand to its sides and just stood there silently and watched me. I meet one of its eyes and a mental connection begins to form. But as soon as it connects my headache flares and I wince in pain. The channel is quickly severed by Red and the eldritch lets out a loud decisive click from its beak.

Red got a determined look in its eyes and began to turn. Its back merged into the darkness of the street and my wobbling vision grew even blurrier. I heard the warbling of the eldritch across the street before a crash of a shattered window broke the silence.

My mind grew fuzzy and I could barely focus. Another crash of a shattered window. This time to my neighbor on my right. Everything faded as the crashes continued. I had one last ridiculous woozy thought before passing out,

"Hopefully I don't have to pay for the neighbors windows too now…"

Chapter 2: Recovering From Meeting the Neighbors

I hear the soft babble of voices in the background and the electric buzz of equipment as I manage to open my eyes. The blurry figures around me approach and babble a little louder than before but I can't understand them.

I try to say something but the words come out as if I was underwater. Warbled and distorted.

My vision faded in and out before a wave of cold rushed into my veins from the IV needle attached to my wrist. I looked down, surprised that I hadn't noticed it earlier. But even as I traced my eyes up from the tube taped to my wrist my eyes began to droop. I see a white coat and hear a feminine voice before I quickly slip back into unconsciousness again.

―――O―o―O―――

My consciousness faded in and out as I woke up and fell back unconscious several times. My memories were fuzzy and everything blurred together into a soupy mess in my mind as I faded in and out. I still couldn't understand anyone or tell if anyone could understand my slurred speech. Everything was still faded and distorted all around me.

The time I was awake was getting longer each time and my mind became a little sharper though.

Each time I felt like I was thinking fine until I woke up again and realized how slow my mind had been before. Until it happened again and again as my mind reconstructed itself each cycle as I recovered.

I still couldn't speak to the hospital staff, but I felt I could almost understand their words when they spoke to me now. Exhausted from the effort of thinking so hard trying to understand them, I lay back on my pillow and fell asleep again ready to begin another cycle.

―――O―o―O―――

All of a sudden I was startled awake at something. I looked around at the empty hospital room. Everything felt so clear now, unlike the muddled waters of my memories at the hospital so far. The faded and blurred still swimming in the back of my thoughts like a half forgotten dream.

The curtains were drawn in what I could see was a hospital room. The room was dark.

My head was still fuzzy, but at least I could string some of my thoughts together now. I strained my ears for a second before realizing what had startled me awake.

The silence. The low conversation and shuffling of feet in the hallway heard through the walls had cut off and left only Serenity. Silence. But maybe I was wrong?

I weakly lift my arms and press the call button on the side of the hospital bed. At least I vaguely remembered one of the nurses pointed at it after looking at me for a bit and making some noises with a concerned expression.

Yeah, it made sense she would make sure I was awake for something like that. I waited. And waited. And waited some more.

Nothing happened

———O—o—O———

Eventually after waiting for some more time, I just laid back and tried to go back to sleep.

It seems that no one was coming.

Why was I here again? Let's see… I watched some TV, finished the birdhouse, then Red came to the door… Wait but hadn't it come earlier at the usual time? No, so it came twice? I reached the door twice?

But that didn't make any sense… But then something bad happened… But what? My eyebrows furrowed as I tried harder to remember. My headache grew a fraction stronger as I thought deeper.

Finally, after a few minutes of disjointed flashes of memory, it all came rushing back as all the scattered memories cobbled themselves together into a more coherent picture. I remember most of it now, the foreign eldritch, Enemy, the mental assaults, and how my eldritch, Ally, apparently fought it off while I was passed out.

My head pulsed as I thought of each of their names. Something seemed strange about them, but I couldn't place it for the life of me. Weird that Ally didn't show up until the other one's hand was already through the window though…

I sat and thought over the past day for a second before the reason for the silence came over me. Shit, it had been a whole week! I was in Serenity!

Everyone in the hospital had disappeared as usual when I entered Serenity, waking me up presumably. I flopped around in my hospital gown for a moment on the bed, but weakly. Okay yeah, I'm definitely not walking anywhere. I sighed and slumped back into the hospital bed. Damn, this was going to be hard to explain to the staff tomorrow given I could barely move my arms let alone stand to open the hospital room door. Especially if Ally ended up showing up to damage the door knocking on it so much…

It was strange. I had only fully been awake since what was presumably sometime just after midnight in Serenity yet I could feel my mental recovery improve by the second. I had slept fitfully through the night as it was still dark out, and each time I woke my thoughts felt clearer and clearer as my headache receded. Was being in Serenity healing me?

By the time the sun filtered through the blinds of the room, I only had a slight headache like what I'd get after a cold. Even that was fading quickly after a few more hours and it reached late morning. Yet my body remained weak as ever and despite my mental recovery, I could still barely move my arms, which led to the next issue. I was bored. There was nothing to read, no one to talk to, nothing to watch. I counted the pits in the ceiling and specks of dirt on the tiles, but even that can only last you so long.

Absolutely none of the entertainment in the modern world was available to me. I couldn't even go back to sleep as the sun was shining directly through the window into my face now. I had to weakly shade my face with my hands and squint as I did my duty and counted whatever I could within sight to stave off the boredom.

Occasionally I strained my legs and arms a little to test them but made no progress on that front either. They moved shakily, but at least they were moving in the direction my brain told them to move now. Maybe a little more motion each time as morning turned to afternoon, but not enough to even attempt walking or leaving the bed. I didn't really want to try taking out the IV or, uh, other tube they installed in my current state either. I'm almost glad I didn't jump out of bed initially and rip either of those tubes out. Especially the lower one.

I shuddered and quickly shifted focus back to counting the wrinkles in the bedsheet if I didn't move. Anytime I finished I would just shift around a bit to reset the board. Genius! Hah, as if… Around five extremely boring hours later by my reckoning I tensed as I heard something approaching the door from the outside. With bated breath, I stared hard at the door as the footsteps stopped outside. Then I heard a familiar knock at the door and sighed in relief. A calm one and not a rage fueled assault.

It was my eldritch neighbor, Ally. Ally knocked again when I didn't respond and open the door. Then again. Then dozens more. Or even a hundred. It felt like that at least. "Clack rrrriippp. Clack rririiiipp". Constant, over and over without pause as it waited for me to answer as I lay here trapped in this hospital bed. I shifted slightly in the bed knowing I was in this for the long haul. Ally wouldn't stop knocking anytime soon…

— — — O — o — O — — —

"Clack rrrriippp. Clack rririiiiipp. Clack rrrrrriiiippp, clatter clunk clunk".

Oh, looks like the metal lock finally fell from the door due to the continuous pounding from Ally. With one final knock, the door swung open with a splintering of wood. There standing in the shattered doorway was Ally with its red plating. Something at seeing the color of them sparked something in my memories.

Several of its eyes were scabbed over and one of its little tentacles below its mouth was hanging limp. Battle wounds The feeling of familiarity rushed over me for a moment before I remembered what I had forgotten as I stared at Ally's red plating. I had named it Red in my mind. I had always called it that. How could I have forgotten…

I met one of the big eyes on its skull and one of the weakest mental connections I had ever felt from it formed between us. I think it was trying to not injure me more? That was considerate. I didn't even think it knew how to do that. It skimmed my thoughts, not delving deeply into any particular topic. As I thought of the other creature that attacked me I felt the eldritch's probe hit the thought and snag on it.

Red brought the memory of my encounter to the forefront of my mind again and scanned through it several times slowly and with focus. I could sense a little frustration from it and it seemed to be struggling to make sense of the memory through my senses directly. After a minute it withdrew and clicked softly.

"Click caaaa. Ennnnneeee. Cla… ennaaaaaamiiiiiii".

I did a mental doubletake. Wait, 'enemy'? Did I hear that right? I opened my mouth to say something despite knowing the futility of speaking, but before I could say anything it just turned around and left.

I could hear the crunch from the splinters of wood scattered across the floor as it stepped back through the shattered door hanging loosely off its frame, its metal lock sitting on the floor.

I closed my open mouth and settled back on my bed. Well, Enemy wasn't exactly a name, was it? I think I'll be creative again. I'll call it Yellow after the color of its plating. My naming system has worked well so far, I think. No reason to change it up too much.

— — — O — o — O — — —

Ten minutes later I startled and sat up as I heard crashing and screeching out the window in the parking lot below. The fight between what must have been Red and Yellow felt like it lasted a long time as they screeched and fought below.

There were loud crashed and the signature crashes of smashed windows and crumpling windows as I realized they must be wrecking the cars around them as they fought each other. The screeches and crashes from the two of them parking lot below faded into the distance as the fight continued and migrated away from the hospital. I waited for what felt like hours as I strained my ears in the silence, listening for either of them coming back.

It was hard to tell the exact time in Serenity without a working clock in the room though. The sun went down and Red didn't come back, but neither did the other one. As I started to drift off to sleep one thought kept rattling through my mind.

"Yellow," I muttered to myself, "It's going to keep coming back until it gets me, isn't it? What am I going to do when it can bring me to this state with one look? I have to prepare for the next time it comes the best I can…"

Chapter 3: Intruder! - Mortal (John) Fragment of Memory

John was in the middle of his night shift and it was a slow day. He was mostly just filling out paperwork right now, the boring forms as dull as usual. The patients were mostly asleep and the other staff of the hospital had already distributed the nightly medications and left only John and a few others left in the subdued halls of the hospital.

The paperwork needed to be done but he almost wished something would happen so he could do anything else. He didn't know how he always somehow got saddled with this crap.

John crushed that thought quickly. Exciting things at hospitals were almost never good news. Stab wounds were exciting. ER cases were exciting. This paperwork was nice and boring.

He was saddled with the mountain of paperwork because he accidentally put the wrong medical chart out for that brain injury patient last week. Usually nothing much, but they almost injected him with something he was allergic to before they realized the chart was wrong. The doctors were always supposed to check to make sure the chart matches too, but John got chewed out anyway.

He just felt lucky they followed procedure. He knew sometimes they barely even glanced at them. Who knew what would have happened otherwise? He would take grunt work over getting fired from his residency.

With a flourish, John finished scribbling out the last form on the stack before putting down his pencil and cracking his knuckles as he leaned back in his chair. Hmmm. The chair creaked and he glanced around.

Didn't seem like he was needed anywhere at the moment. Several other nurses met his gaze and distractedly nodded but none diverted their path to ask him for something.

He stood and glanced at his watch. 11:57. About halfway through his shift. John made his way to the bathroom and did his business. Feeling lighter and reinvigorated, he made his way back toward the main desk.

As he rounded the corner, he stopped in shock. The door to his right was hanging off its hinges and visibly battered. Impacts that looked like they came from a giant fist covered the whole top section of the door. Splinters covered the floor and as he stood there the shattered remnants of the door slowly swung open with a loud squeal and groan of splintered wood.

John looked around in stupefaction for a moment as if to subconsciously check for the hidden cameras. Like someone would come out and announce that it was all a prank soon. But when his eyes turned back, the door remained in its very destroyed state.

What in the world? He thought as he took a step forward. As he took another step he paused. He was being an idiot, this is the kind of thing police are for, weren't they? He's not going in there by himself.

John looked up and met Rachel's eyes as she suddenly turned the other corner across the way. Her bored expression quickly morphed into shock as she took in the state of the door and John standing there.

Her eyes quickly widened and after a moment quickly backpedaled while keeping one eye on the open door. John was unnerved by her sudden fear.

Usually, she was the calm and collected type even with all the stress they dealt with at the hospital. Then a thought struck him that sent chills down his neck.

What if the maniac who beat down the door was still in there? That thought broke his inaction. He followed Rachel's lead and turned to run as silently as he could looking for a hospital officer.

Thirty seconds of running later, he finally found two of them idly chatting near the elevator. When they heard the thudding of his squeaky shoes on the tile floor they turned and immediately put their hands on their holstered pistols upon seeing the expression on John's face.

One of them was a towering man with jet black hair and a thick mustache. The other was shorter and heavyset with straw blonde hair that was slicked back like he used too much hair product. John gestured wildly behind him and panted as he slid to a quick stop.

"Come quick, I think someone broke into Room 311! They kicked in the door and probably are still in there! Whole thing was shattered into pieces!"

The officers glanced at each other and shared a look before simultaneously drawing their guns and jogging past John. John ran behind them not sure what to do now as the shorter officer began rapidly talking into his radio. He found it odd how calm the two seemed despite the situation.

The taller officer stopped him with his free arm as the officers suddenly stopped at the corner closest to room 311. His other hand held his gun as he poked his head around the corner.

— — — O — o — O — — —

"Step back."

The tall mustached officer's voice carried a no nonsense tone to it that led John to instinctively follow his instructions without a second thought. As his rational mind kicked in, John decided to take a few more steps backward. The officers' radios began squawking back at the pair rounded the corner.

John couldn't make out the tinny words from this distance over the sound of his beating heart in his ears as the two rounded the corner.

But the intensity and volume of the radio seemed to be increasing as time went by after the taller man's deep voice gave an inaudible reply into the device.

John spread the message to anyone he saw nearby until people started getting the hind and the hallways were quickly abandoned as quickly as they could. The two officers were around the corner and now John could hear them approaching the broken door. The crunch of splinters crushed under their boots sounded with each of their footsteps as they walked.

The taller officer demanded something in a harsh tone, and there were a few seconds of tense silence as John stood around the corner, unsure why he hadn't fled outside yet. But the muffled reply from the room seemed calm enough.

The shorter officer barked out something aggressive in reply. The delayed response from within the room caused both officers to tense for a moment as they spoke before their voices relaxed fractionally again.

The two carefully entered the room and their voices became even more muffled than before. John wrung his hands for a few minutes and wondered if he should leave. But his curiosity was getting the better of him now. And he had already stuck around for this long, after all.

—— O — o — O ——

John sighed in relief when the two officers emerged no worse for wear from the room after a few minutes. The black haired man was talking into his radio while the shorter man looked a little lost and was glancing around as if the intruder would suddenly appear at any moment around the corner, guns blazing. He kept glancing back into the room with thinly veiled looks of disgust and irritation.

Two more officers appeared from the direction Rachel retreated from and the four officers had a brief conversation before the other two left again. Both of the officers that had arrived were extremely calm, almost bored as they spoke. After the conversation they casually strolled away as if nothing was amiss.

Well, seems they at least didn't think they were in danger. John peeked around the corner to see before entering the hallway after seeing the coast seemed clear.

The two officers both stared at John in disbelief as he walked towards them. The taller officer just shook it off and kept talking into his radio while still keeping his eyes fixed on John. John still felt a little nervous still being here, but he felt safer near two cops than taking his chances right now. Especially with all the strangeness happening around town recently. No one wanted to be out on the streets at night anymore. Or even the day, really.

John also knew the patient in room 311 was a severe case so maybe he could help keep the patient stable until the doctor could get there if there was a problem. That would be a great thing to put as a work experience where he helped a patient above and beyond his job.

John leaned forward as he whispered to the shorter blonde officer and stepped slightly to the side so as not to interrupt the larger man on the radio.

"Is the patient in there okay? Should I go check on him?" He whispered.

The shorter officer grumbled inaudibly under his breath, but glanced at the taller man for confirmation. John thought he was quiet but apparently the other officer heard him anyway. The tall man's mustache twitched as he nodded back and dismissively waved at the two of them into Room 311 before stepping further away to keep speaking into the radio.

John followed the shorter blonde officer into the room and carefully tried to avoid stepping on the larger wooden splinters covering the floor. He stepped to the various machines in the room and checked the patient's vitals at a glance.

Nothing seemed out of order. He gave an internal sigh of relief. The patient was stable, and all vitals looked fine. He'd be able to help even if he wasn't a doctor yet if it was just basic patient care rather than a real emergency situation.

Chapter 4: Uncomfortable Small Talk - Mortal John Fragment of Memory

John turned to the patient and expected the same watery dull gaze he had seen intermittently for the last week. But the patient's eyes were full of life and surprisingly alert as their eyes met.

The patient seemed to be straining to sit up as he opened his mouth to speak but his arms trembled and barely lifted him off the pillow. John looked at him and quickly assessed him for any injuries.

Nothing looked out of place. No scratches or bruises that would indicate some kind of fight. John wasn't sure what to think of him though.

For some reason, he had difficulty focusing on the patient's features. The patient's build was... well. He was... John looked at his face. His face looked like... Well, it wasn't really that important anyway.

It was rude to judge people by their appearances. John should probably check the machines again to make sure they're really working. He looked up as the patient shifted in place as John fiddled with the machines. The shorter officer at the door gave John a strange look before returning to face the hallway.

"What is going on here? Why are there police here?" The patient asked.

The patient looked around the room and his eyes caught on the shattered door to the room for a second.

His brows furrowed for a split second before he seemed to realize something and coughed awkwardly. He tilted his head to the door and continued in a much flatter tone.

"And uh... the door. What happened to the door?"

The officer in the hallway heard the patient speaking and turned to walk into the room. His partner stepped to the side to let him through. John realized just now that he didn't know either of the officers' names.

Everything had just happened so fast that he hadn't thought to ask. He opened his mouth to say something before the taller officer cut in, seeming to forget John was even there.

"Sir, that's what we would like to know. Did you see or hear anything when you woke up?"

The patient's expression was carefully blank as he answered. He spoke clearly with clear eyes on the tall officer.

"No sorry officer, I only woke up when your partner called out from the hallway. I was asleep before that."

The patient shifted a bit in the bed as he maintained his neutral expression as they all stared at him. The tall officer frowned and gestured towards the door as his mustache twitched.

John looked at the patient incredulously. Even he could tell the man was hiding something! He guessed the man didn't have much time to think of a better lie though. A faint note of suspicion entered the officer's voice.

"So you slept while that happened..." He gestured toward the door, "But our voices are what woke you up?"

The man in the hospital bed just shrugged helplessly and seemed indifferent to the officer's suspicion as far as John could tell.

The officer just let out a frustrated huff and stared the patient down with his arms crossed across his chest as he silently took in the patient's response.

The patient met the tall officer's gaze and an apparent staring contest started. John sighed as he finished his checks on the equipment. How childish. He thought the officer was coming across as a little aggressive here, grilling a man in the hospital bed like this but the patient seemed to be responding well enough.

John wasn't sure why the patient would lie though, there was no way he didn't hear *something* given the state of the door. It seemed obvious just based on his response that he had to know more than he was telling.

What really surprised John was how lucid the patient was right now. Just a few hours ago when the patient last woke up he babbled nonsense and had just blankly stared at John when he spoke without any coherent response.

But now the patient had miraculously recovered and was studiously ignoring one of the officer's blatant hostility towards him. John wasn't sure he would have done as well himself given the tense atmosphere building in the room.

The shorter blonde officer had stood back in the doorway, just silently glowering in their direction during the whole exchange.

The larger officer had taken a step forward while maintaining eye contact as the staring contest continued. John was feeling uncomfortable and shifted his feet nervously, not sure what to do about the building tension between the taller officer and the patient.

John had finished his equipment check but pretended to check again so he wouldn't draw too much attention to himself.

Finally, the officer blinked and the patient let a slight smile slip out through his mask at his small victory. Something that led to the momentary frown of the officer who had lost. The shorter officer barked out a derisive laugh from the doorway.

"So that's really it? Not some crazy ghost doing it like last time? I thought you would try again, it seems like it worked well enough last time." he spat out.

The patient's face twisted in anger as his neutral mask broke and he opened his mouth and twitched his arm upward to weakly point at the officer.

"You know that I never would hurt her."

The other officer exploded into rage.

"WELL LOOK WHAT HAPPENED! ALWAYS SO COLLECTED. I SHOULD HAVE STOPPED YOU WHEN I HAD THE CHANCE! YOU'RE JUST TRYING TO WRIGGLE OUT OF THIS LIKE YOU ALWAYS DO! WHAT DID YOU DO!?"

The man was quivering in rage and seemed about to lunge at the patient. He stood there breathing heavily after his loud rant. His partner seemed stunned and unsure of what to do about the sudden outburst. But John could see this was clearly going too far.

He could see the patient gearing up to respond in kind and tensing up. And no matter their past history, the patient yelling at a police officer wouldn't do him any favors. John raised his voice to cut off the flushed officer in the doorway.

"Hey, cut it out! I'm not sure about the history between you two but this isn't the time or place. This man was likely just attacked and you're yelling at him like some kind of criminal! This is hardly the time for arguments! Get control of yourself!"

The patient's mouth remained open and his expression remained angry, but after a few seconds his arm lowered and his mouth shut. He nodded at John, seeming to realize he had almost said something that he would have regretted later.

The short blonde officer almost seemed as if he was about to protest John's words, still quivering in place from his anger, but stopped at a piercing look from his partner. The angry officer stormed out muttering under his breath while the patient's stare drilled into his back.

It seemed the taller officer was just as surprised about the sudden outburst as John was.

But as the blonde officer left John saw a flicker of something underneath the patient's anger. Was that... Guilt? But the emotion was gone before John could be sure and the patient's blank mask returned with full force.

The patient slumped back, looking even more wrung out than before as the intense emotions seemed to drain from the room leaving everyone tired and emotionally drained.

John adjusted the IV bag and noticed the fluids inside were low. He'd get it changed after the chaos died down some more. There seemed to be enough fluid left for an hour or two based on the current flow rate. He shook his head. Seems it wasn't refilled properly, the bag should have been replaced last shift if it had gotten so low.

John looked down at the patient who had fallen into a deep sleep the instant they relaxed and sat back. His eyes were closed. It was like he was fully alert one moment when John looked away, and when John looked back in a deep sleep the next.

John reached down and adjusted the thin blanket to cover the man after it had been knocked back by his feeble motions earlier.

After an uncomfortable amount of time standing in silence with the remaining officer and the sleeping patient, Rachel came in the door with one of the doctors on shift in tow.

John helped them transfer the patient to a new room as more police and forensics began to muddle around the hospital and take pictures of the crime scene and shattered door.

Most of the officers were quiet and seemed rather bored as they took photos and went about collecting evidence, clearly not happy to be there. Probably just not happy to have to wake up and work in the middle of the night.

All the hospital staff worked frantically as patients woke and were shifted as police locked down the building. It was one of the busiest shifts John had ever experienced, day or night.

When he got home in the morning he collapsed directly into bed without even changing as all the stress drained out of him all at once, and slept better than he had in months. He never even noticed the expressionless figure that followed him the whole way home from the hospital...

Chapter 5: Interrogation By The Authorities

I woke in the morning as an unfamiliar nurse walked in. I went to sit up and was surprised to see that I was much stronger than before. My core muscles burned and my heart rate accelerated a little, but my arms were able to hold my weight enough to leverage myself into a sitting position on the hospital bed.

The nurse came over and changed the IV bag hanging above me. The old one was deflated and nearly empty. Hopefully, they don't find it too suspicious that I took an extra day's worth of fluids as it kept running to keep me hydrated while I was in Serenity.

The nurse stepped back after she was done and nodded at me before going to leave. I called out to her as she began to turn.

"Wait! Um… Did they catch whoever broke into my room last night?"

She turned and seemed a little shocked for a moment before a look of realization came over her face.

"Oh, there's a manhunt going on right now. I guess you've probably slept through all the chaos here for the last few hours. The police are still working to find whoever it is, but they have officers guarding your room for your protection now. In case they try to come back again."

She paused a moment before seeming to remember something else.

"Actually, they wanted to ask you some questions about last night. John reported that officer's behavior to the police sergeant, and the sergeant sent that officer home. He assured the staff that he wouldn't be on the case so you won't have to deal with him disturbing your rest. We understand if you would feel uncomfortable, so you can make your statement later if you don't feel up to it right now."

"John was the nurse who was here last night?" I clarified, to which she nodded. Huh, well that was a relief, at least I wouldn't have to deal with Officer Smith for the foreseeable future.

I'm glad Officer Smith got reported though. I don't think I could think properly with him hovering about waiting to pounce on some parking fine he could pin on me. I felt a twinge of grief as my thoughts turned to the past and my mistake that led to his blatant hostility towards me. But the wispy memory quickly drifted away again and I realized I'd drifted off to stare into space again.

"Do you need anything else?" The nurse asked, "I was actually just going to fetch Doctor Gupta so you could discuss your health situation and make choices on any further medical treatment now that we can discuss it with you. You seem well enough to make informed medical decisions, so the doctor will sit down and explain everything to you moving forward."

I nodded at her, "No, no, that's fine go ahead. That would be good."

She smiled, "That's great. I'll go and get him now."

―――O―o―O―――

Doctor Gupta ordered various tests to attempt to explain my 'miraculous' recovery in his words. He said it like it was some kind of curse, like anything unexplained was bad somehow. As the morning bled into the afternoon I felt stronger and stronger physically.

By the time I decided to give my statement to the police in the afternoon, I felt almost back to my normal strength.

The doctor ran the tests and I came back clear, with no brain tumors or unforeseen side effects to my recovery so far. After that, the doctor seemed to accept the miraculous nature of my recovery a little easier. But even still he seemed a little disappointed in the unsolved mystery after he was done.

I heard footsteps in the hallway, a group gathering together and stopping just outside of my room door. The group of four entered together one after the other as the door opened.

First entered the tall officer with the imposing mustache from last night, the new partner to Officer Smith it seems. Behind him was an unfamiliar officer and the nurse from this morning who had called Doctor Gupta. Finally following behind was a man in a charcoal suit and tie that looked important based on the way the others were treating him.

The taller officer looked very uncomfortable. From the way the nurse from this morning was fidgeting and shooting the suited man her nervous glances too, I guessed that he probably worked for the hospital.

The officer from last night seemed to choose his words carefully, speaking slowly in whispers with the man in the suit. The unfamiliar officer seemed calm but shot indecipherable glances at the suited man when he thought the man wasn't looking.

After a moment, the man in the suit turned to me, "Mr. FuLcRuM?" I blinked. His lips moved strangely and his voice changed briefly as he spoke. The words felt strange like they didn't describe me somehow. But it was just my name, wasn't it? I tried to feel the cause of my unease, but after a moment I shrugged it off. Probably just the stress getting to me. Fulcrum was my name, of course. What else would it be?

"Mr. FulcRum?" The man in the suit continued, "I'm here representing the hospital board given the events of last night. We want to know the full scope of events the best we can given the breach in our security. I can leave if you wish."

I was startled as I finally began registering the man's words. "Oh no. sorry! I'm ready for the statement now. You can stay, I guess." After a moment of silence, the suited man just nodded and stepped back. The two officers stepped forward in unison to replace him.

Given their prompting, I began to explain to my audience how I was enjoying my late Saturday night when something came through the window and hit my head. True enough without diving into the supernatural.

Couldn't afford to look too crazy after all. I am only going to make that mistake once. Officer Smith was the result whenever I tried too hard to convince people about Serenity. I was still feeling the waves of that mistake today obviously.

I continued my story with how I woke to the officers outside and the following 'conversation' with Officer Smith and his partner.

The two officers seemed to wince a little at my account of him shouting at me immediately after I woke up. Especially the unfamiliar officer that hadn't been present. The man in the suit's lips turned down into a slight disapproving frown as his eyes shifted between the two officers, barely looking at me as I spoke.

The officer on the right was scratching into his notepad the whole time trying to avoid his gaze. He seemed to be using it as a shield so the man from the hospital wouldn't ask him to do anything.

He let the familiar officer ask me leading questions or minor clarifications on my story even if it was pretty simple. I heard nothing, saw nothing. Suddenly something hit me on the head and I woke up here. Invisible tension filled the room as the suited man stared down Officer Smith's partner especially as I finished my full version of events of last night.

"Do you have any enemies, anyone you think would attempt to hurt you? This is twice now you've been attacked. Any information you give us will help us track down whoever is doing this." The officer with the notepad asked. At his words, everyone in the room turned to me in interest to see my response. Just as I was about to respond, the officer cut back in. "I'm Officer Nick, if I didn't already say." He held his pad expectantly, looking pleased with himself at the clarification. Everyone looked at him strangely. I shook it off and considered his question.

I thought of Yellow's hand reaching through the window at my house. Not sure how they would see that one if I told them. But surely they must have security footage showing no one entered the room?

Why did they think the person was after me anyway? The door breaking was weird but surely this being caused by an attacker wouldn't be their first thought without evidence?

As my thoughts rushed onward I blurted out a quick response to stall for time, "Did you at least see whoever it was on the security cameras? For the hospital?"

I collected my thoughts a little and restarted, "I can't really think of anyone that hates me that much but Officer Smith, but it would probably be pretty obvious if it was him I'd think."

At my statement, the man in the suit looked slightly uncomfortable while Officer Smith's partner paused for a moment as if considering how much he should tell me. After a short pause Officer Nick jumped in to speak, not appearing affected by my half-accusation of Officer Smith at all.

———O — o — O———

"For your first question, no," Officer Nick said, "The security footage was tampered with and someone with a backdoor into the hospital system came in and deleted all the footage for the last week.

"All the medical records of the patients that were admitted too. It's causing chaos for everyone around here for obvious reasons. Last night we saw someone fleeing from the parking lot but they got away."

Officer Nick continued, "They were wearing some kind of mask, so no one could ID them before they escaped. In the ten minutes they were in the building, they knocked out several officers that attempted to arrest them starting on this floor and trailing down back to the underground parking lot.

"After that, they drove off in a car with no plates and shook off the police pursuit. Luckily no one was seriously hurt except for a few minor cuts and concussions."

Officer Nick adjusted his grip on his notepad and I noticed there was no corporate brands or labels on it. It's bindings were completely blank, "We're still figuring out who this person is, but they clearly have resources to pull something like this off," Officer Nick said with a slight frown, "Most apparent right now would be some kind of organized crime. That's why we wanted to talk with you as soon as possible.

"Any detail you think of could help us track this person down. Any debts from the wrong people someone came to collect? Someone who attempted to blackmail you? Anything suspicious that's happened to you recently at all."

I thought for a moment, but honestly didn't know what I should say. There were people after me on Earth too?

Were they connected to the attack by Yellow? I mean it could be a coincidence but I don't think I did anything to warrant that kind of attention in my normal life. I looked up and replied honestly that I wasn't involved with anything like that that would get me in trouble.

The officer nodded and silently moved on from my denial, but I thought he seemed a bit skeptical at my claim. He kept speaking, seeming to be almost absentmindedly talking to himself at this point rather than asking a question at this point.

"The oddest thing about his case was the stealth involved. Whoever broke into your room somehow demolished your door without anyone nearby hearing a thing, apparently including you.

"You seem unharmed and nothing from the room seemed disturbed when we arrived, which makes the goal of this intruder even more mysterious. Why destroy the door to such a degree as well? Seems excessive and unneeded given the competence otherwise shown."

Now, I knew the door was broken in Serenity by Red. But something caught in my mind as the officer spoke. It seemed like a little too much of a coincidence now.

This person showed up almost exactly at midnight. Someone who could take out several officers at once like some kind of secret agent. Someone with those abilities would be highly sought after by criminals and governments alike. Which showed the power of whatever organization was potentially behind whatever happened to the hospital on Earth.

Whoever it was showed up at the same time I would enter Serenity. Maybe they wanted to finish the job Yellow started in Serenity? To kill me?

I started freaking out internally as my thoughts raced at the implications of that. The others in the room perked up as they took in my reaction.

"Think of something?" Officer Nick with the notepad emerged from behind his clipboard as he seemed to notice the sweat beading on my forehead.

The officer had his pen hovering over the paper. The other two men leaned in as I tried to control my reaction. I took a few seconds to compose myself and take a few shaky breaths before I replied.

"No, I really don't know who would do this. I think the situation is hitting me all at once. It's like something from a spy film. Just hitting me now that it's all happening for real. Whoever did this seems important and they seem to be gunning after me. Anything else?"

The officers' eyes met and the one without a notepad gave a subtle shake of his head before turning back to me.

"Well, I think that will be all sir. Thank you for answering our questions. We hope you have a speedy recovery and just let the officers outside know if you think of anything else at all. Remember your friend Officer Nick when you become somebody important, FulCrUm."

I blinked, "Huh? Did you say something?" I said.

"Yes, have a good day Fulcrum," Officer Nick said pleasantly, "Best wishes for your recovery."

"Oh, well thank you then. Thought you said something else."

As the group went to leave, Officer Nick pulled out a little business card from the top of a stack pinned with a clip to the side of his notebook.

He turned to the suited man from the hospital, "Here, take this. It has information on which officers the department has assigned to the case. I filled in the relevant names and numbers for you."

The man accepted the card and slipped it in his pocket without question. I sat there as the two officers and suited man left the room together, leaving only the silent nurse behind. She stepped forward and checked the equipment again before leaving without speaking as well.

Huh, that was strange. For a second I thought I saw a glimmer of triumph pass into Officer Nick's eyes as he passed over the card. But the next moment his face reverted back into a placid smile.

The nurse left. That night as I drifted off, I dreamed of secret agents and cackling villains fighting over boiling pits of magma as the events of the day gradually bled into my insane and irrational dream state.

Chapter 6: Finally Back Home

The next few days were tense for me. I was walking within the day of the incident in Serenity, but they held me for another day even after I said I felt fully recovered. The manhunt for the hospital intruder was ongoing, but without any information the police seemed to be at a loss on catching them.

I had seen the important man from the hospital around, discussing things in a low voice, seemingly still concerned about the hospital security. The hospital was in chaos as they attempted to notify the people whose medical files had been deleted along with the security footage.

They seemed very understaffed, and lots of people seemed depressed for some reason. Well, hospitals weren't very happy places so that one probably made some sense though.

Two officers were stationed outside my door as guards against any further attempts to attack me. I was very bored in being confined to my bed as the doctors ran even more tests on me.

But by Wednesday afternoon they decided I was healthy enough to release from the hospital without having me drop dead after taking a step out of the hospital. I thanked the bored officers guarding at the door and walked through the hospital to the reception desk.

The receptionist walked through the massive bill from my stay at the hospital as I looked down in dismay. My insurance covered some of it but not nearly as much as I thought it would. After she was done, I shoved the bill in my left pocket and turned around only to stop as I saw a familiar face.

There in the waiting room was the officer with the clipboard from when I gave my statement. Officer Nick. He was wearing casual clothes and was talking with two teenage guys, one who looked heavily concussed.

As I walked past, the officer chuckled and took two cards from the stack he had on his clipboard. I frowned and slowed my pace as I walked by to try to listen in as the officer said something.

"...best skating park in the area. It's all on the card there. And one for your friend too. Make sure he's more careful this time haha." He handed one to the concussed guy's friend who looked at the card with interest.

Out of the corner of my eye, I saw the officer hold out the card to the concussed guy as well who dreamily took it and slipped it into his pocket without seeming to see anything around him at all.

I noticed that I had stopped walking and was just blatantly staring at the scene. I quickly shifted my gaze to the left as if just scanning the room. I looked back as I saw the officer walking straight toward me, a smile plastered on his face.

I opened my mouth to say something only to notice him looking over my shoulder. I turned to look behind me but no one behind me seemed to be looking in our direction.

Oof. I fell forward a little as the officer bumped into my shoulder and brushed right passed me without sparing me a look. He glanced over his shoulder behind him, but his eyes skidded right past me before he turned back around. "Wha.. Hey!" I said.

The officer ignored me. I stared in disbelief as he focused on a woman in her thirties coughing into her cloth mask. The officer struck up conversation, and the woman perked up and seemed interested even as she coughed.

I drifted a little closer, still in disbelief, he hadn't taken just one step to the side to avoid me in the wide open room!

"...Best delivery in town I say! Used it last year when I was quarantining myself! Better than my wife's cooking, but don't tell her that!" The man said. The woman took the card and thanked him before releasing another hacking cough. He nodded at her before taking a decisive step back.

Officer Nick turned and walked to the other side of the room again, but I was smart enough to dodge him this time. I slow walked toward the exit and witnessed him hand out another three cards to people.

It was strange. It was as if he had the exact card for whatever that person needed. The last one must have been a wild guess. He offered the information to a knitting society to an eighty year old man with a cane. The old man just accepted it and said he would tell his wife about it. How she had recently complained that she missed her old group.

Every person he approached accepted a card. It was like some kind of magic trick. I stood by the door for another moment and tried to catch the officer's eye as he crossed the room again.

But I was completely ignored again. How strange, I'm not sure what I ever did to him to deserve this. He seemed decent enough when he was questioning me last Sunday.

I guess I didn't imagine him as some kind of super salesman on his own time either. Well, whatever was going on there, I was just happy to finally be able to go home at last.

$———O-o-O———$

As I walked back into my house I could see the glass shards and dried blood covering the floor. Tiny red flakes had spread across the room in all the nooks and crannies of the floorboards.

As I stood there, I could feel a cool breeze at my back through the broken window. I went into the garage and got a tarp and some duct tape. I heaved it with my still slightly weak arms and put it over the window to fix the hole in my house as best as I could.

I got a dustpan and started cleaning out the glass shards from where they'd fallen. Eventually, I reached the caked mass of blood where my head had been when I passed out over a week ago.

I got a bucket of water and a mop out but then just looked down. I paused and just stared at the circle of dried blood. Just thinking about the attack. The sudden snap of the tarp behind me snapped me awake and brought me back into motion as I began to scrub. It wouldn't clean all of it, but I could scrape off the majority of it at least.

As I cleaned, I realized that I hadn't been prepared. After all these years, I had subconsciously viewed Serenity as some kind of safe space. Sure, things were strange there.

Red had definitely been frightening initially. But I had never been attacked in Serenity before. Even the pain from the telepathy was something I considered as little more than an inconvenience at this point. Something more like a splinter or a stubbed toe. But the hostile creature was still out there. And potentially hostile humans too based on the stranger's fight with the police at the hospital.

So I needed to prepare so something like this didn't catch me unaware again. It would only take one wrong glance out the window to initiate a psychic battle after all. I had to be more prepared for the next time so I could protect myself properly.

———O—o—O———

After finishing fixing the damage and cleaning up as best I could, it was time to make an alarm system. As I cleaned I had considered what I could do based on the rules of the strange realm of Serenity. I had a basic idea of how I could set up the system, but it would require a lot of maintenance.

One basic rule I discovered early on is that every object not touching a person on Earth froze in place. It was the influence of living things in the realm that whatever I or Red, and now Yellow, touched slowly returned to life and acted normally like they would on Earth.

Everything directly touching a person besides me like clothes or a wallet would disappear along with them, staying on Earth. So if I threw something that would make a loud sound into the air at exactly midnight then it would freeze in place midair until something interact with it.

That would be my perfect alarm system as it would make its normal sound if it unfroze. But would be perfectly silent when it was frozen and no one had interacted with it in Serenity. That Yellow hadn't interacted with it.

I needed something easier to use and set up than that system though, the timing would be too precise for even one object, let alone dropping a whole perimeter of objects at once around my house. So I decided that my best bet on short notice would be the use of wind chimes.

Red only approached from the front path so I had to cover the other directions to give me a warning of Yellow's approach. The alarm system couldn't be too obvious either for the watching police and neighbors. Well, it could be strange and odd but not something so out of place I couldn't explain it away if I was questioned about it.

Police cars were uncommon in my suburban neighborhood yet there was one setting a speed trap on the main road suspiciously close to the street as I drove by. They were likely standing by in case I got attacked again. Maybe I was bait for whatever organization was after me? I'm not sure I liked that thought. Hopefully, they would keep me safe from attackers on Earth at least. That was a big if though…

I bought lots of twine, a few windchimes, and high visibility ribbons at the store. I strung up the twine around the perimeter of the roof after getting my ladder out of the garage.

Near each of the ground level windows I had a dangling piece of twine attached to a windchime on the outside. I also dangled some high visibility ribbons on the bottom of the windchimes so I could see their movement if they unfroze as well as hear them.

Finally, I ran a line from the roof and looped it through the grass and over the edge of the tree line. I didn't have a fence or anything so I just draped it over branches of the nearby trees so the line would end up at roughly knee height around most of the property. I also snaked part of the line through the grass for extra security.

Each window had one uninterrupted piece of twine for the whole setup so any contact would unfreeze the whole assembly. That should let me know what direction someone is coming from as well because the portions for each window would trigger independently and so I should know what window Yellow would be approaching from when it arrived.

I also set up a similar windchime system on the backdoor, making it a little awkward to open and close the door through the looping twine. I planned to use the front for Red's visits, so I shouldn't have to go through the back in Serenity at least.

I made sure the path to the front door would be clear for when Red came. I would have to rig something up after he left since Yellow had come later than Red every time so far.

As the sun began to set, I finally finished and walked around my house to inspect my work. The twine was visible to me, but thin enough to miss unless you were looking for it.

The windchimes and high visibility ribbon hanging in front of every ground floor window definitely was a little stranger. I couldn't really explain the looping twine over the back door, but it wasn't visible from the street so I should be fine.

But If I had to explain the windchimes, I could just say I liked the sound. No reason to think of some overcomplicated lie, sometimes people just do weird stuff because they want to

.

Chapter 7: A Nostalgic Memory

It was Thursday afternoon, and I sat in the kitchen looking at the giant hole in the wall. It looked like someone had thrown a singular punch full force and left a hole in the plaster wall.

I felt like that wasn't really an important issue to fix right now, but I couldn't help but keep staring at it. It reminded me that I wasn't safe here. Yellow had created that hole, how strong must it be to be able to do something like that? I looked up as I heard a soft pattering at my kitchen window.

There outside, I could see the squirrel that had entered Serenity standing pressed against my kitchen window. Its front paws were splayed against the glass as it stood on its hind legs while it cocked its head at me as it saw me turn.

Its fur was gray with the signature black diamond of fur on its back. I blinked as it chittered at me for a moment before leaping out of sight to the ground.

Slightly confused, I went to the window and peered out to see the squirrel nowhere in sight. I wonder if it was more intelligent than normal? I mean it did enter Serenity after all so there must be something special about it. It wouldn't be the strangest thing that's happened to me in the last few years. I stepped outside for a bit into the backyard, but it seems the squirrel was gone.

Already outside, I decided to check on the security system for when I reentered Serenity this weekend. The sound of the windchimes was annoying and a few hours after I had first set it up, I had to make it stop. I had muffled the hanging windchimes by stuffing some fabric inside each of them.

After a few minutes of standing in the backyard looking around for the squirrel, I finally saw a familiar animal perched in a tree staring down at me. It jumped down to the ground and reared back on its hind legs with its two front limbs curled inwards. Its tail was erect straight out, and it seemed to eye me warily as it stood in place motionless.

We both stood there, man and squirrel for a moment staring at one another. That is until I almost fell backward as I felt a faint mental probe reach out for me and touch my mind. I reflexively slapped it away. My head whipped around, searching for the culprit, but it was just me and the squirrel. It shifted on its feet for a moment before stilling. The probe tentatively reached out again. I turned back and looked down at the squirrel for a second before accepting the connection cautiously.

The squirrel fell back down on all fours and sent a series of images to me. They were all distorted, like they were taken on a wide angle lens, and everything looked massive. Before I could make sense of an image, another would take its place.

I forcefully slowed down the deluge by focusing on one image. It wavered as the stream of other images passed by at the corner of my focus like a flowing stream, trying to draw my attention. It took a moment, but I finally interpreted why the perspective was so strange.

The images were captured from the squirrel's point of view. It was wide angled because squirrels have eyes on the sides of their head while humans have their eyes pointed forward. It could see almost completely around its head while I could only look mostly forward as a human.

And the squirrel was obviously way smaller than I am! After interpreting the first image, I moved on and grabbed the next from the stream flowing by.

The stream gradually slowed as the connection between the two of us grew thicker and the squirrel seemed to realize I could only focus on a few images at a time. I considered the images I had examined so far.

They were all images of different angles of my house.

For some reason, all the views of the interior were blurry and distorted. I was in all of the images as a grayish blob caught through a window. It showed different times, and different weather. Rain and shine, myself as a blurry figure captured around my home. But these images were followed by images of me outside with perfect clarity. I tried to understand why it would show me that. I think I understood.

Maybe it was some form of greeting, showing its view of me? So the proper response would be to send back my view of it? I packaged some of my memories of the squirrel outside and the few times I spotted it in Serenity and sent them back along the mental bridge, even if at a much slower pace than the squirrel's deluge.

It wasn't so much as me doing something actively but more like I focused really hard on the images I wanted to summon and send over and willing the squirrel to see them. And then letting them drift along the connection over to the animal.

The squirrel chittered happily for a moment as it received my stream of images. It tucked its head into its chest and wiped at its face with its little paws. I stood there, unsure what was happening as the telepathic bridge sat there unused by both of us for several seconds.

I shuffled in place and scratched my arm. Both of us stood there for a second longer before the squirrel's tail drooped a bit. It sent another stream of images at me, this time much more slowly.

This time underneath the stream of images were emotions as well. Seemingly the same images of my house but more attention was given to the blur behind the windows. Caution, wariness, flee.

Then all of a sudden, the perspectives shifted again to a larger hunched figure that was similarly blurred. The images began to come in sequence. It played like a jittery video.

At the end of the street, the blurred figure seemed to pop into existence mid-stride. It would walk a few steps before the perspective shifted and it was suddenly farther down the street than before. Like the video was buffering and skipping ahead after reloading.

The longer the video played in my mind, the smoother it became. The blurred figure made its way to a familiar house before banging on the door with its similarly blurred fist. Recognition finally hit me. It was Red! Sure enough, I saw the door open into the distorted interior of the house and there was my blurred silhouette standing in the doorway.

The video faded away and now it felt like there was a pane of glass separating me from the events happening in front of me. I took a step forward and as soon as my foot touched the glass, I was sucked inwards into the illusory world.

It felt like my body suddenly snapped into high definition. Taste, smell, temperature. It all came rushing back. I floated there as some kind of ghost as I saw the blurry figure in my house answering the door. What I knew now as my past self stared at Red's blurry figure for a minute or two before stepping back into the doorway like it was some kind of portal and shutting the door behind him with a slam.

I frowned. The same emotions from the squirrel pulsed throughout the whole encounter when I focused on either of the blurred figures. Unease. Fear. Wrongness.

I sent the squirrel comfort and affirmation back. Images of me in the house reading a book, or weathering out a storm. Burrowing into the ground for the winter. I thought that was an analogy a squirrel would understand more. It sent skepticism back. I sent affirmations back. I understood it was frightened, but Red just wanted to be its friend, not hurt it!

And the weird distortions, well it was… it was… Really, the best explanation... My telepathic messages faltered for a moment as I considered… Red didn't want to hurt it, and I certainly didn't want to either and I sent affirmations again. The squirrel now looked more tense as it shifted the illusory world to show another scene.

It showed the same interaction as before. Red approached, and my past self answered the door, Red tripped and lay there for a while, then left. The world stuttered and jumped.

The sun was now at the horizon. It was twilight. That was when Yellow appeared. There it was framed in perfect clarity, with narrowed eyes, yellow plating, thrashing tentacles on its face.

There at the end of the street, it stood. I recoiled as the squirrel pulsed acceptance and comfort along with the figure. I watched as it beat on the door with massive force. But a few inches from the wood its fist slowed, as if suddenly pushing through molasses. It turned the titanic blows into something weaker than one of my average punches.

After a moment I saw its eyes snap to my blurry figure standing there behind the window. The interiors of the house were impossible to discern. Anything beyond the window seemed to shimmer and waver as if caught in a mirage.

I winced as my blurry shadow collapsed out of sight as Yellow shifted to the nearby window and began hitting it instead of the door. For some reason the fists weren't slowed as much as before and the wood splintered and glass shattered as it reached its arm through the broken window into the house.

But the distortions shifted behind the window and condensed into a thick dark smoke tendril the width of a thumb that latched onto the creature's arm, sending it reeling back in pain as its arms reached through the window.

I felt warm and fuzzy inside at seeing the smoke protect my past self. I gasped in dismay as the smoke grew a little less dense after the creature withdrew its arm with a hiss of pain.

The smoke was growing weaker! The yellow creature collected itself for a moment before smashing the base of the window as the smoke condensed around its fist to reduce its blows.

Its downward stomps were able to push through the smoke and open a gap large enough for it to enter through. Each blow made the smoke lighter and lighter. The lighter the smoke became, the better I could see into the room as the strange distortions through the squirrel's vision decreased.

The invading creature finished widening the hole before stepping through the gap. It screeched in pain but began taking slow steps forward as dark tendrils burst from the neighboring rooms and began latching onto it and burning its flesh.

It shielded its face with its arms and slowly stepped forward even as an enraged shriek sounded in the far distance. Red coming back to help me and fight off the intruder.

I turned by head, but the street was empty. Red was still far away. I looked back into the house. Wherever the smoky tendrils the invading creature touched, the creature's skin sizzled as it burned as if being soaked in acid.

I instinctively held my breath, even if I was just a mental projection of some kind, as I approached what I recognized as my prone body inside the house. Yellow was approaching my past self, barreling through as it swatted at the rapidly fading tendrils trying to fight off.

I clutched my chest as it raised its foot over my image's body… only to step over me without even a second glance. It continued its battle with the smoke tendrils into the next room, ignoring my past self's prone body like it wasn't even there.

I heard it move into the kitchen and begin smashing the floor with mighty blows. I could see my past self's body shift and the furniture shift slightly at the power of the blows coming from the kitchen vibrated the whole house like an earthquake.

Another heavy blow.

Another scream of rage in the distance from Red, this time far closer than before.

Before the invading creature could land another heavy blow, Red burst through the breach to the house with a scream of rage. It barely touched the ground as it launched into the kitchen and began to fight the other creature out of sight. I tried to shift to look, but my feet were rooted in place.

I looked around and spotted a familiar squirrel squatting on my front lawn. I tried for another look, but it was no use. It seems I could only see what the squirrel had seen at the time. I was locked outside of the kitchen.

After a series of heavy blows from the kitchen that shook the whole house and loud angry inhuman screeches and growls, the battle between the two eldritch creatures returned to the main room. They shifted and punched violently until they were practically fighting on top of my past self's limp form.

Red was pushing the other creature back, assisted by dark tentacles emerging from the kitchen doorway that was as thick as an arm now and were pitch black. Every time the tendrils would dim, they would retreat to the kitchen before returning darkened once more a few seconds later.

The yellow plated creature jumped over my body and retreated to the window as the counterattack by Red and the strange shadowy tentacles both grew overwhelming. I shouted out in horror at the illusionary world as Red lifted its foot over my body, wholly focused on the retreating creature and the battle. Not even looking down as it remained wholly focused on fighting Yellow.

My eyes widened in fear and my ghostly projection dived forward as Red's foot descended and stomped directly on my prone past self body's right shoulder.

I felt like vomiting as I heard the snap of bone and saw blood and gore spread from the wound where the right half of my body was crushed. My past self twitched and woke with a scream as the red carapace creature continued the chase outside, paying my body no mind. I stared as my past self writhed in pain and clutched his shoulder.

Snot and tears ran down his face as I saw the dark tendrils loop around his torso. Still thrashing, my past self began to cough up blood as he was roughly dragged into the kitchen by the tendrils. The battle between the two angry creatures continued outside unabated.

I heard my screams from the other room and the ripping and tearing of flesh. Thousands of babbling voices assaulted me from every direction, all shouting into my ears, asking for attention. I felt a phantom pain in my shoulder and my head began throbbing.

After what seemed like forever, my past self fell silent. The ripping and gurgling sounds from within the kitchen continued. The sounds from the kitchen stopped before my prone form was dragged back into the main room and thrown roughly onto the floor face down.

I leaned down to inspect my prone body's shoulder, only to see smooth unblemished skin. Only my tattered shirt on one side remained of the injury.

The dark tendrils began waving, emerging from the kitchen and diffusing in the room as a dark mist, distorting my view of the room. I was drawn back out of the house as the distortion and twisting view grew greater and greater over time.

The mirage beyond the threshold reasserted itself into it was once more indistinct blobs in my vision. As I floated over the front lawn, I turned to see a familiar squirrel sitting on a tree branch nearby. It seemed to have moved out of the way of the fighting.

As soon as our gazes met the illusory world dissolved into white motes of light until there was only me and the squirrel in silence in a white void. The light grew brighter and brighter until even the squirrel disappeared.

I shuddered as the mental bridge was suddenly severed, and I returned to my body.

——— O — o — O ———

I woke up staring up at the darkening sky. Sitting up, the squirrel was nowhere in sight. I stood and considered what I had seen, feeling slightly sick. The red carapace creature had just stepped on me!

The yellow carapace one actually had been the one to take pains to avoid stepping on me despite launching the telepathic assault earlier.

Why would the squirrel show me all of this? How would I not remember something that traumatic? However, despite my whirling thoughts, one thing stuck out in my thoughts. The yellow carapace creature had been smashing the floor in the kitchen. I was sure based on the vibrations on the floor it must have done serious damage.

The emotions underlying the illusory world also constantly blared the kitchen's importance despite my inability to look inside of it. The kitchen was also where I had been dragged off to when I was injured. That's where those black tendrils had returned to to refill their color.

Something important was there. I rushed to the back door and hesitated for a moment at the door handle getting a feeling of foreboding.

Finally, I threw open the door and peered into the kitchen but didn't step inside, suddenly afraid. As I watched, the shadows seemed to lengthen. I shivered as I remembered the tendrils and took a step back from the doorway.

A dark spot began growing in the middle of the floor, and I began to feel a pull towards it. My eyes widened and I turned to run. I only made it a few steps before something grabbed my ankle.

I tripped and looked down, but there was nothing there. I sat up and tried to grab where I could feel something wrapped around my ankle, but my hand passed through whatever it was like it wasn't even there. I started to panic and started tearing at where I could feel the thing wrapped around me.

In a moment of clarity, I remembered. The dark tendrils! I must just not be able to see them like the squirrel.

The invisible tendril began dragging me toward the doorway that now began to look like a cavernous mouth of a beast as I was dragged towards it with inexorable force. I struggled and grabbed at the grass but it gave way in great clumps as I was dragged back.

As I drew closer to the door, I felt more and more tendrils latched onto me increasing the pull and throwing me faster and faster towards the cavernous mouth into my house.

Finally with a final burst of force I flew off the ground and through the doorway and floated in the middle of the room. The back door slammed shut behind me and I stared down in horror at the pool of liquid shadow that was quickly growing beneath my feet.

I twisted and shouted as the shadow grew over my legs and began working its way up my torso. It felt cool, and wherever the shadows touched, I lost all sensation. As I struggled, the tendrils held firm and my protests fell on deaf ears as the shadow reached my neck.

I strained for one final effort, but now I could only move my head, losing sensation in the rest of my body. I let out one final scream as the liquid shadow began pouring into my mouth as I twitched and looked towards the sky.

———o — O — o ———

I startled awake at the kitchen table. I had slumped over and started drooling all over the tablecloth. I sat up and looked around. It was nearly dark, the sky tinged a deep red as the last rays of light fled. I remembered I had a strange dream.

Something about the attack on the house, then a big shadow… healed me? Something like that. I just remembered the shadows had helped me somehow. I strained at the memory for a second, but the details were already fading away as dreams tend to do.

Had Enemy and Ally been involved somehow? I flipped on the light to the room and squinted as I looked at my feet. Was my shadow darker than normal? Pretty sure my shadow shouldn't be a perfect circle below my feet…

The shadow pulsed and I remembered I had forgotten to put a cloth inside of the last windchime by the backdoor earlier. That's what I had forgotten. I went outside and did it quickly before it got too dark.

I went down my mental checklist before nodding to myself. Alright, all my chores were done, time to make myself some dinner. Never could go wrong with some pasta.

Chapter 8: Preparation for the Weekend

It was Friday, and I was planning for the next assault. The first thing I did was unstopper the windchimes. I didn't want to leave unstoppering them to the last minute just because they were a little annoying. All my other preparations should be last resorts to running and hiding until Ally came to bail me out again.

One of Enemy's most dangerous weapons it had shown by far was its telepathic assault. In a physical fight, all it needed to do was make eye contact before the battle was over.

It also had a large amount of strength, given it pounded a hole in the wall with just its fists in a few seconds. Excluding the coloring, Ally and Enemy looked almost identical in form.

Enemy's attack had happened too fast, but based on my interactions with Ally it wasn't too speedy in general. Assuming they were similar, I was fairly confident in being able to outrun Enemy if need be. But a telepathic assault would mean as soon as it spotted me it was over.

I would be essentially paralyzed while it seemed to be able to move as well during the telepathic battle. That's if my mind wasn't almost instantly overpowered like how it had been during its first attack.

So even if I could somehow win the telepathic battle it could catch up to me even with its slow pace and crush me into paste with its fists anyway.

The last time Enemy attacked I had fallen unconscious before it even reached me, but presumably Ally had fought it off before it could attack me physically and crush me.

I took out several recently bought handheld mirrors and placed them on the table in front of me. I already knew that once the mental bridge was formed the eldritch didn't need eye contact to keep the connection active. Whenever I interacted with Ally, the bond had been cut as soon as either of us broke eye contact.

I wasn't sure why Enemy would be able to maintain the connection while Ally could not. Or maybe Ally could? Now that I think of it, it always tried to communicate with me for short bursts only so I wouldn't be hurt too much.

Maybe Ally was just being polite and manually cut the connection each time? But I do remember the connection weakening when I broke eye contact with Enemy, even if it wasn't completely severed.

Hmmmm.

So clearly eye contact was important to the telepathic connection in some way? I sat down and reevaluated, shocked at the revelation. In the back of my mind, a distant feeling wafted to the surface. I had telepathically communicated with something else too...

Through a series of images with little backlash... I thought for a moment trying to place what it could have been. Ally, Enemy, and... Oh! From that strange dream with the shadows! It was just a dream, it wasn't real. What a strange thought to have. I sighed in relief as the answer came to me.

I shook my head and returned back to my planning. I couldn't daydream right now, I had work to do. I turned back to the table and looked at the mirrors again. I wasn't sure if the mirrors would protect me from that initial eye contact to form the mental bridge initially, as I apparently didn't know as much about it as I thought I did.

I wasn't sure what limitations I knew were real or simply Ally being considerate of my health. Was eye contact even needed to open the connection, or did it just make it easier?

It was possible the connection could be established through reflections just as easily as direct eye contact. But tomorrow night when I entered Serenity I could test it on Ally, as it had arrived earlier than Enemy both times so far.

That was assuming I was attacked again, which seemed reasonable given it had attacked again outside in the hospital parking lot last weekend.

I went out front to unload several coils of steel cable, long nails, and other supplies I had just bought and lugged them into the house where I dropped them to the side in the main room.

When I drove out to shop, the town had seemed strangely empty.

There were few cars on the road and not many people walking around. A few seemed drunk, stumbling side to side as they walked.

I didn't often go out into town without going directly to the highway on Friday mornings though, so maybe it was always like that and I just never noticed.

Maybe.

People getting drunk in broad daylight was definitely odd though. Some kind of party last night? Was there a holiday that I had missed? Also my phone wasn't working for some reason, it didn't have any signal. Next week I'd have to take it to the store for my provider and see if I could get it fixed up.

But anyway, I already knew that mobility was probably Enemy's greatest weakness. Ally hadn't arrived until I was already nearly unconscious in the initial attack. So my best bet would be to delay Enemy's approach and trip it where possible.

Give enough time for Ally to rush in and save me. This afternoon I would fix the steel cable to the walls with the nails and stretch them from wall to wall to impede its path. Create layers of traps inside the house that I could hide behind.

The freezing effect of Serenity would assist me here too. If I stayed back, Enemy would be forced to wait a moment to unfreeze each cable rather than just barreling straight through them.

I had spent all of yesterday marking the spots for the nails with tape and planning out how to cover all the routes in to the little spot I'd decided I would remain for my time in Serenity.

I had scanned the wall with my stud finder to make sure the nails I would put in the walls would remain secure as well. The walls would be all torn up and have holes in them after I mangled them. But... Eh. That was a low priority right now.

I had to do all the heavy lifting at the last moment though in the construction of my wire traps, as I couldn't risk the police coming back for questioning and seeing my insane setup. I didn't have a good explanation for it, so

I was worried it would make me look even more suspicious than I did right now for their investigation. I don't think I would last long if I entered Serenity and was attacked while trapped in a prison cell.

I had no doubt that Enemy would be able to deal with some prison bars if it had enough time to do so.

Based on their questions so far, the police might think that I was somehow involved with whatever criminal conspiracy that broke into the hospital. What with my vague and suspicious answers to all of their questions. I tried my best, but even I could recognize that I hadn't exactly provided the clearest answers to their pointed questions.

So I thought once they got more information, they probably would return to ask me more questions about it. After getting more information from the officers observing me from the car down the street who were also probably waiting for the people who came to the hospital to come to attack/talk to me.

I didn't know when the police would actually try to talk to me to get more information, but the hospital case seemed like it must be a pretty important given the fallout from all those people's medical records being deleted. So I thought they probably would come back sooner rather than later.

I went back outside to get the axe from the tool bin from behind the house. I walked over and grabbed the plastic lid and flipped it upward. As I opened the lid, a squirrel burst from inside startling me.

I jumped back and fell on my butt in surprise, but the squirrel just jumped onto the rim of the open bin and stared at me without running for a moment. I looked with interest and surprise back at it. It had a gray fur coat, but on its back was a black diamond pattern. After we stared at each other for a few seconds, I started to get a faint headache.

I looked away and blinked. After a moment the squirrel scurried off into a tree, scrambling as if the last few moments never happened. I stared after it. Something about it seemed familiar… but it was just a squirrel, I had to get started on the cable setup soon if I wanted to get done today.

Defend myself and the kitchen as best I could…

I stood back up and brushed myself off before retrieving the long hafted fire axe from the bin.

I returned inside before considering what else I could use. A spear might be better than an axe to give me some extra reach. A gun? No, it would take too long to get for this weekend, and it wouldn't even work in Serenity anyway.

I didn't own a gun already so I'd have to go get a license and get it approved and everything… Yes, it would take too long for this weekend at least. Also it wouldn't work in Serenity. There was that too.

The gunpowder was enclosed in the bullet casing, so it wouldn't ignite when the gun was fired. I knew because when I tried to pour myself some salt for food, each grain was frozen individually.

So I had to reach inside and slather my finger around inside to unfreeze them and grind them out onto my food. So the gunpowder inside the bullet likely would be frozen and not react in the same way as normal.

For complicated mechanisms I had to touch each component for it to unfreeze, so anything electronic like a Taser or cattle prod was out too.

I didn't know enough about them to be able to disassemble and reassemble them inside of Serenity fast enough, especially not in the next few days.

Not that I even knew where someone could buy a cattle prod. Could normal people even buy those? There was another concern too. What about the humans on earth that might be after me? I had to be ready in case they came to attack me on Earth too.

I resolved to try to buy a gun next week just for my defense on Earth, even if it wouldn't be useful in Serenity. Oh, and learn how to shoot a gun and all that too. Probably should know how to use it so I don't end up shooting myself by accident or something.

But back to combat in Serenity. Another thing I needed in combat was reach if I had to fight Enemy in the future. The axe was a good weapon, but given its strength I wanted to stay as far from its reach as possible. It would probably take one solid blow from Enemy to take me out if I had to fight.

I knew that the spear would probably be the best medieval weapon for me to use in this case. Not only would it be able to strike from farther away, but it also was apparently easier to learn than blades would be.

Maybe I could make a basic spear tomorrow on Saturday. I could use it to strike through the cables I would set up. Maybe strap a kitchen knife to a sturdy stick to make the spear?

Something like that. I'd figure it out.

I thought about it for a moment, then pulled out my laptop to do some research on makeshift spears, only to frown when the screen stayed black when I pressed the power button.

I pressed it again to no response and sat up as I realized something was wrong.

I rushed to the door and flung it open and looked around wildly. Leaves were frozen in midair. The wind didn't move the blades of grass around me. The windchimes of my alarm system were silent.

No sounds from nature or the animals. Everything around me was silent as the grave. My heartbeat accelerated and my breathing grew heavier.

Panting and sweating, I rushed back inside and grabbed the axe as I reached one inescapable conclusion.

I was in Serenity.

My knuckles were white as I gripped the axe handle with all my strength and glanced around warily.

I was in Serenity.

Early. There was no more time to prepare.

The attack was coming now.

Chapter 9: Assault Charges Will be Brought

Sweat burned in my eyes as I gripped the axe. I stood there. For what felt like hours, I just stood there waiting in the silence. I nervously shifted and adjusted my sweaty grip, straining my ears for any sound. Eventually, I started to relax as nothing else happened.

Just at that moment, I heard the faint thuds of footsteps from the street. In a burst of motion, I retreated to the kitchen and put my back to the interior wall, breathing heavily. I picked a handheld mirror and angled it so I could see around the corner to the front door. It was too early! I was supposed to have more time! I wasn't ready! I hadn't even set up any of the wire traps I had planned to slow down Enemy!

The footsteps grew closer and closer. I lost my grip on the axe as my sweaty and trembling fingers and slipped and dropped it on the floor. I leaned down and fumbled to retrieve it with one hand, mirror gripped in the other. I pointed my eyes to the floor in case the eldritch was close by and could see me.

I wasn't sure if it was Ally or Enemy just yet. Hopefully Ally. The footsteps stopped in front of my front door and paused. Nothing happened. I strained my ears again, but everything was silent as the figure stood there without shifting an inch.

Finally, I heard the figure take a few slow, heavy steps to its right. I nearly jumped out of my skin as the wind chime started clanging as it suddenly unfroze as the creature touched one of their connected twine.

I sat there tensely peering through the mirror, trying to shift the angle so I could see where Enemy was. The next windchime in line unfroze. I could see the high visibility ribbon begin to dance in my view through the mirror. The figure passed by the window and I only got a glimpse of yellow plating before I hastily looked away and withdrew the mirror.

Shit, it was Enemy!

As Enemy continued to circle the house, I now realized my mistake. Now that I knew that Enemy was in the area, the windchimes were hurting me. I couldn't hear Enemy's steps over the loud clanging chimes. If it doubled back then I would be screwed. With its muffled steps, I was now blind to what direction it would come from and what it was doing!

I froze in place, unsure of what to do. I wiped my forehead with my forearm with the hand holding the axe. I stood with the mirror in one hand and the axe gripped in the other. I wanted to move but I was frozen in fear that it had stopped and was just waiting for me to look.

It only needed to catch me with a passing glance and a little focus to eliminate me. I stuck my hand back out around the corner and scouted out the main room with the mirror, but I couldn't see Enemy anywhere no matter how much I shifted the mirror every which way.

Crash! I whirled around as the back door shattered into splinters and a thick arm burst through it. I fell to the side as little chunks of wood sprayed all over, several bigger pieces embedding themselves into the wall next to my head.

I lay on the floor and instinctively curled inwards. I hastily shifted the mirror so I could see, forcing myself to not instinctively look toward the source of the chaos. Another crack sounded out as Enemy pushed its way through the shattered frame of the door. As it stepped through it seemed to pause for a moment to take stock of the room. It stayed stationary as it glared into the mirror.

I let out an internal sigh of relief as nothing seemed to happen even as it stared me down through the mirror. I tilted the mirror in my hand to get a better look even as I scrambled to my feet.

It took a step towards me but suddenly stumbled onto one knee as it went for another step to my surprise. It struggled in place for a moment, until in frustration it released an unearthly screech.

The pressure wave from its mouth emerged like a grenade blast and the shockwave lifted me off my feet and blew me out of the kitchen and out into the main room. I dropped the mirror, which shattered into little pieces as it landed on the floor behind me.

The axe lay in front of me on the floor. Dust rained down from the ceiling and loose chunks torn loose from the force of the blast fell down.

— — — O — o — O — — —

Dazed, I stood and instinctively looked back into the kitchen, leaving the shattered mirror on the ground. Luckily Enemy was preoccupied and didn't punish my mistakes or meet my gaze with any of its dozens of eyes.

It was being pushed every which way, being battered by some kind of invisible blows from every angle as if from invisible fists.

Eyeballs popped and chitin cracked under the rain of invisible blows. But even as I watched, Enemy shook itself and drew its foot into the air and leaned forward with all its body weight.

The blows continued, but Enemy accepted the hits from the invisible force as its foot descended. With a thunderous stomp, Enemy shattered the tile of the kitchen floor and cracked the concrete beneath. I stumbled and began to feel a sense of crimson tinted anger invade my thoughts. More rubble fell from the ceiling and I coughed as the dust irritated my lungs.

I ran forward and scooped the axe from the ground from where it lay among the rubble. I charged into the kitchen as the Enemy winded up for another stomp. The invisible blows seemed weaker than before, barely causing the Enemy to shift at all at this point.

As I charged, I began a large overhand swing blindly. The axe plummeted toward Enemy and sliced off one of the oversized fingers as it hit a gap in the chitin plates from the arm raised to ward off my blow.

Not expecting the lack of resistance, I overextended and stumbled forward past Enemy, even as it screeched in pain behind me. I continued my motion until I caught myself on the wall in front of me.

I turned around to see Enemy raising its foot for another stomp, ignoring its injuries and bleeding finger stump. I braced myself against the wall and drunkenly stumbled to my right as the floor shook as Enemy's stomp landed.

I coughed and turned back around as I readjusted my grip on my axe. Enemy's leg was already lifting for another stomp even as I turned. Underneath its foot, I saw an unnatural red glow shining through the gaps of the shattered concrete.

Suddenly the invisible force came back with a vengeance and held Enemy's leg in midair as it burst into motion again. Enemy struggled and pushed with its leg still raised mid-air. The invisible force released it resulting in a lackluster impact.

Enemy raised its foot again.

The invisible force stopped the blow at the last instant. The two forces struggled, but as time passed the invisible force slowly weakened, each of Enemy's stomps growing stronger and stronger as the invisible force weakened and couldn't fully hold back its blows on the floor anymore.

Enemy's foot raised for one final time and stomped, but this time the invisible force was barely able to slow the blow at all.

The world shook as the blow landed.

I looked through the gaps in the concrete, and saw something beneath the shattered concrete. As soon as I saw it, my world narrowed to only the intruder and defending the Seed. Red fog filled my mind and animal rage pulsed deep in my chest. A faint screech in the distance echoed my rage.

An eye on Enemy's chest met mine and a mental bridge tried to form. The rage severed the connection as soon as it formed with a mental slap and screech in the back of my mind. The bridge formed and dissolved several times a second as I charged the Enemy, hardly aware of what I was doing.

The remaining eyes on the creature all narrowed at once in frustration as it focused on me. As I approached, it swung its arm at me even while still winding up for what I knew would be the final stomp.

I ducked to dodge its clumsy off-balance swipe and whipped my axe upwards in retaliation. It leaned back to avoid the blow, but I managed to slice off several of the whipping tentacles on the bottom of its face that didn't withdraw fast enough.

It hissed in pain.

I shifted the axe in my grip and brought it behind me to follow up with an overhand blow. Just as the blow was about to land, I fell to the floor as Enemy's foot slammed into the floor and shook the world again and threw me from my feed.

With a screech of triumph, Enemy stared down at the Seed exposed for the whole world to see. Enemy kicked me with its foot as I lay on the floor, punting me into the closest wall at high speed. As I flew through the air, the axe slipped from my grip and flew away.

As I impacted the wall, I felt something snap in my chest, and as I took a breath something clicked. I stiffened and hit the floor hard as I fell to the ground roughly.

I leveraged myself upwards into a sitting position. I took a few more shallow breaths each accompanied by the click of shifting bone. I tried to stand but my legs were weak and my head was fuzzy. My left leg was twisted the wrong way, with sections of bone piercing the skin.

There was blood everywhere.

I was bleeding.

But the rage pushed me onward with growing intensity as Enemy stooped over and reached its arm down toward the exposed Seed.

I weakly reached out and felt my right hand weakly brush part of the axe handle next to me. I looked and it was just out of reach. My fingers, slick with blood couldn't find purchase on it as I went to grab it. With a grunt, I leaned over and fell to the floor again, finally close enough to get a good grip. My fingers curled around the axe handle.

I could hear the impacts as the Enemy hit the floor over and over in the center of the house to clear the final few concrete chunks between it and its prize.

One chunk of concrete was sent flying and went through the wall next to me. I rolled to my side and coughed as I used my free arm to crawl closer to Enemy.

Behind me, I dragged the axe. It scraped and jumped as it moved over the uneven floor, and I struggled to keep my grip on it with one arm. As Enemy went to throw concrete pieces away they would occasionally stick like glue as the invisible force held them down.

I heard the enraged screech from outside again, this time from the end of the street. I was right behind Enemy now crawling and weakly pushing with my good leg for maximum speed. But not fast enough.

Another blow and one last concrete chunk was thrown to the side, and the black chitin was exposed.

NO!

I scrunched into a ball and slightly sat up into a squat with my bad leg dragging behind me. With my good leg bunched under me, I pushed upward with all my might and desperately swung the axe, burying it in the invader's leg. With a screech, it toppled to the side.

It flailed out with its injured arm as it fell and pulverized my other leg in mid-air and sent me spinning away. My vision blackened at the corners. By now, I barely felt the pain as my mind only fixated on my goal.

I rolled over as Enemy crawled forward and reached for the Seed, the axe still embedded in its leg. I reached out as if to plead with it.

NO!

Enemy reached the edge. It raised its fist.

NOOOooOOoO!

Its fist came down and the black chitin of the Seed shattered and gave way to the pink flesh beneath. The blow punched through and little pink chunks went flying every which way, splattering the ceiling above the hole and Enemy's face.

The little chunks quivered like little pieces of gelatin. Sharp agony shot through my whole body and I spasmed in the wave of pain that immediately followed.

Through the waves of pain, I barely took note as the front door shattered behind me. Ally burst into the house and rushed into the kitchen. My thoughts were fuzzy.

With amazing speed, Ally rushed forward with an agonized screech and leaped over me. The running kick impacted Enemy just as it twisted around to inspect the axe embedded in its leg.

With a meaty *Thwap*, Enemy went flying. It smashed through the walls and went flying into the backyard, leaving a massive hole behind it. As I lay there, the ceiling of the kitchen began collapsing around me as the exterior wall began to give out.

Ally leaped out through the hole in the wall to follow Enemy outside. My vision faded more at the corners as chunks of rubble rained down around me.

Everything felt so distant.

So cold…

———O—o—O———

I snapped back awake, the burning anger and purpose still ingrained in my mind as I realized that I had just fallen unconscious for a few seconds.

I crawled toward the hole in the floor unconsciously where the exposed Seed sat as a cataclysmic fight continued outside. It just felt like it was the right thing to do.

Everything dimmed, and my world narrowed as I dragged myself forward on my arms over the rubble. My mangled legs dangled uselessly behind me.

As the screeches and crashes continued outside, I reached the pit in the floor exposing the Seed. I turned my head and saw a glimpse of the fight outside in flashes. Ally was now smaller than the invader somehow. Enemy had swelled in size, looming over Ally now.

However, Enemy still seemed heavily injured. It limped on its leg and seemed uncoordinated. Its blows unfocused. Most of its eyes were punctured except near its head and one of its arms moved stiffly at its side.

In the short exchange I watched, Ally kept piling on the blows and Enemy was continuously pushed back.

Just as I thought the fight was won, Enemy pushed back with a second wind. With a surge of strength, the battered invader pushed past its opponent, throwing it to the side by shoulder checking it, and rushed toward me.

The rubble from the back wall and collapsed roof stood in piles blocking its route. One blow of its fist shook the ground and sent the rubble in its way flying in every direction, clearing its path toward me.

It barely slowed.

Ally was in hot pursuit but it wouldn't reach us in time. Enemy just had too much momentum by now. I tipped myself inside the pit with the Seed and rolled down the slope. I shifted so my body laid over the Seed protectively.

I lay there for a fraction of a second, in pain, until some instinct prompted me to stick my left arm into the exposed pink flesh below me. Pink strings like long thin worms peeled off and implanted themselves into my arm as I watched my doom approach. Watched Enemy's approach.

The longer I watched the more pink worms entered me until the flesh of my arm roiled like boiling water. Worms emerged and leaped from the limb before diving back into the flesh, leaving my skin rippling like it was water in their wake.

I knew I should be disturbed, but it just felt like the right thing to do. I was sure that if I had some time to think about it I'd come up with a reason why it wasn't bothering me at all as I watched the roiling flesh of my arm.

Enemy's head became visible from within the pit for a moment before it slammed full force into the slope of the pit behind me, unable to stop its momentum from the leap.

As it slid down the rubble, momentarily stunned, I struck. With a burst of strength, I rolled over and pointed my left arm writhing with the pink worms at Enemy's face. With the crunch of bone and flesh, my arm exploded into tiny chunks, and the mass of worms was blasted directly into Enemy's face in a solid cylinder.

The worms went into a feeding frenzy as they landed and burrowed into Enemy's flesh. After a moment, each worm would reemerge in a spray of gore before diving back in to feast again.

Enemy swatted them and twisted around to smack them all as they dived in and out of its body, but it was almost totally out of functioning eyes now. Its blows were uncoordinated and clumsy.

It protectively lifted its arms to protect the four or five remaining eyes on its head. But it was almost fully blinded and thrashed drunkenly as it attempted to stand.

I looked at the stump where my arm used to be.

It wasn't bleeding. How odd.

Enemy began twitching as it stumbled towards me, collapsing when it was only a few steps away, worms still burrowing through it. I let out a sigh of relief.

Wait! My eyes widened as the twitching grew more intense and Enemy rolled forward down the slope toward me. The worms all pushed out of its flesh and crawled away in every direction.

Enemy thrashes grew more intense like it was having a seizure and I felt waves of heat begin to waft from its direction. Ally rushed in and leaped into the pit between Enemy and the Seed and me.

Ally took a step toward Enemy, whose waves of heat were growing more and more intense by the second. With both hands, Ally reached out and grabbed Enemy by the ankles.

A large chunk of wet flesh like a long snake fell from Enemy's chest and squirmed on the ground below.

I felt my skin feeling like it was about to burn under the heat around me.

With a heave, Ally spun around and in perfect hammer throw form launched Enemy out of the pit and back outside. With a deep 'WHummmmmfffff' that I could feel in my chest, Enemy exploded into an intense fireball that consumed the backyard.

The flames washed off the frozen neighbors' houses like water off a duck's back, barely affecting them in their frozen state. The wall of flame approached us as the grass burned and unfrozen soil from the yard went flying with the pressure wave, scraping the earth clean.

The flames reached the walls and began to consume everything in the kitchen in moments.

For a moment, the fire passed over us, not sinking into the pit. But after a moment, a wave of darker reddish flames formed above us and rushed down into the pit all at once towards us. Ally took a step forward and held out an arm and all its eyes squinted at once.

To my shock, the flames roaring towards us suddenly diverted away as if there were a bubble-shaped invisible barrier around us.

The reddish flames flowed around us until it raged all around us. Tongues of Flame would suddenly jab inwards, only to twist away after Ally glared at them.

After several seconds, Ally dropped to its knees but kept its arms raised. Finally, like it was being crushed by a giant fist it slammed into the ground face first. The barrier cut off and all I could hear was the roaring of flame in my ears as the raging Flame seemed to pause for a moment before rushing inwards all at once.

Ally stood and screeched with all its might. The sound wave scattered the reddish flames away from us. The evil flames seemed to scream somehow as huge chunks of it were scattered and destroyed.

For a moment, I thought Ally had won. But from above us, a wisp of flame survived and struck out toward the Seed. But as it made its way rapidly toward the Seed, Ally threw itself in the way. The fiery blow landed on Ally's chest. The flame took its rage out on Ally and burned up its way up its chest, to its shoulder in a line of flame.

As Ally thrashed, the flame unnaturally leaped down and burned Ally's calves and ankles until Ally fell over and began rolling on the floor.

The fire suddenly gave off less heat than before.

Ally screeched in pain.

The flames looped over Ally's back while the creature continued to thrash and roll in pain.

The fire grew dimmer and colder as time went on.

Finally, the flame gathered in one spot on Ally's shoulder, leaving charred lines behind as it gathered.

Ally rolled again, and as soon as Ally was at the right angle, the flame launched itself as a fireball directly toward the exposed Seed. All the remaining flames that burned on Ally snuffed themselves in an instant, joining with the fireball as it left.

The fireball flew as if in slow motion. It was going to be a direct hit.

At the last moment, the pink worms I had thought had fled revealed themselves. They had crawled back and regrouped in a ring near the Seed amongst the rubble.

As one, they emerged and threw themselves into the fireball as it approached the Seed. As each sacrificed themselves, the fire maintaining the fireball grew ever more dim and cold. The fireball sputtered weakly, the flames flickering now.

But there were no more worms to weaken it now.

It kept moving, growing closer to the Seed by the second. Somehow I knew that if the flame reached the Seed then the flames would burst into renewed life and consume us all.

The flame grew closer and closer… then with a blast of air, a chunk of concrete flew over my head and blasted through the ball of flame.

The fireball dispersed into a cloud of floating embers.

The small cloud of dispersed flecks of flame was less than ten feet from the Seed now. With a whoosh of air, the floating flecks recondensed back into the fireball.

But the flame had grown weaker.

The fireball lurched into motion, moving toward the Seed slowly in short bursts of movement. It lurched side to side as it moved like someone stumbling to the finish line after a marathon.

Wham! Ally threw another chunk of concrete through it and dispersed it again. The fireball condensed again, now smaller and barely bigger than my thumb. It floated almost directly above the Seed now.

The thumb-sized flame drifted down, floating this way and that in the wind. It almost resembled a candle flame now. I watched as it danced above me. Ally threw another chunk of concrete.

The fire dimmed until it was barely visible, barely giving off any light, but managed to dodge enough to avoid the projectile.

The flame moved closer.

Five feet away now. *Whoosh*! This time the concrete chunk missed. I could barely see the flame through my rapidly narrowing vision. The flame was descending still.

Four feet.

Three feet.

I glanced over at Ally and met one of its eyes. A telepathic connection formed. I looked back at the small ember two feet above the Seed. I couldn't believe this was how it would all end.

I sensed dull triumph emanating from the spark as it made its final plunge to the Seed. I felt Ally pull on our connection before it released one final projectile. The triumph of the spark quickly morphed into panic as the spark used its last energy to blast downwards.

But it was too late for the wisp. The concrete chunk blasted through the flame, blasting it into oblivion. The projectile carried on and shattered into a million pieces as it blasted into another pile of rubble, sending up a cloud of dust.

The dust suffused the area like fog. I sensed the will of the flame struggle for a moment as it struggled to reform before it finally failed and was snuffed out forever.

Above me, the mundane flames merrily consumed everything around us. They danced and laughed in the ruins of my home. The smoke wafted upward into the open sky as I lay there, feeling numb.

I glanced over at Ally, the Eldritch's eyes were all closed as if it was asleep. It lay there bonelessly, limbs splayed and covered in severe burns.

I thought I saw movement for a moment, but I saw that Ally was still, so it probably was just a shifting rock or something.

As I looked away, the unnatural focus of the last few minutes faded away and my vision began cutting in and out again. My thoughts became more muddled. The darkness closed in. I rolled back over and stared down into the pink flesh of the seed for a moment.

Something washed over me, and in a moment of clarity, I stuck my remaining arm into the pink flesh again. This time there were no worms. The flesh pressed inward like it was taking a firm grip on me. A firm handshake for a business meeting. Or like compression socks for my arms…

As my consciousness finally faded, I could dimly feel myself being pulled down into the Seed. After a moment I was now surrounded by warmth on every side. It was comforting, like a warm blanket. I felt safe.

I relaxed and began to drift off to sleep. I felt a wave of melancholy wash over me. Because I somehow knew that this would be the end of Serenity.

And despite the horror… I had good memories here too. A sense of wonder at the world frozen in time. Spending hours just watching the arrangement of falling leaves unmoving.

Laughing as I ran around and unfroze everything around him and watched them fall to the ground.

Watching Ally's joy at me presenting it with utensils. Just relaxing in relative peace after a long week at work.

I realized that I was sad to see it go. After all of these years of subtle resentment, I had forgotten my initial wonder. How ironic, that I could truly only appreciate it now that it was too late…

The darkness took me, the Seed having survived with the Enemy having been finally defeated…

Chapter 10: The Destiny of Fulcrum

I woke up slowly to the feeling of warm and moist air blowing on my face. It felt like a sauna. I was naked. I was relaxed, my body completely relaxed as it felt like I was waking up from a pleasant dream. Like everything was all right.

I opened my eyes and sat up to inspect my surroundings. All around me was a dome of reddish flesh that curved over me to at least three times my height above at the highest point.

Soft vibrations rippled through the dome, causing it to look like it was quivering like it was a living thing. The far edge of the dome started only twenty or so feet from where I was sitting in the center.

The vibrations in the interior surface of the dome grew larger. A deep thumping like a heartbeat sounded out as the dome of flesh pressed inward for a moment before returning to its original size. I felt another blast of warm moist air blast me from all sides.

I twisted around while still sitting to inspect my surroundings. There was no entrance or exit that I could see, just a uniform dome and a flat floor. Steam rose from tiny holes perforating the floor. The floor was hard and smooth, white and perfectly flat.

I noticed that a soft glow of light suffused through the fleshy walls around me from all sides. I lifted my hand to my face and inspected it for a moment. I tried to remember how I got here.

The vibrations quickened and the walls pulsed inwards again. I sat and thought. What had I been doing before I woke up in this strange place?

I was in some kind of fight I think? I stood and approached the walls of the dome as I struggled to remember. I think I should be more frightened than I am of this situation.

Everything felt distant and detached as I walked toward the edge of the fleshy dome. I walked forward and put my hand on the warm red flesh of the walls. It was slimy and wet.

The walls beat inward again and my hand was pushed back. Another blast of warm air hits my face. For some reason this place made me feel like I was wrapped in a warm blanket, that I was safe.

I tried to remember the fight, whatever it was before I woke up here. Steam curled from the holes in the floor with a quiet hiss. The walls beat inwards again. I frowned as I tried to remember. I felt I was close. The faded memories swirled around in my mind.

I think I was protecting something. Something important to me. That thing had been hurt. I had been hurt and then ended up here. I unconsciously rubbed my left arm with my right as I tried to remember. But I feel fine now. No pain now.

If anything I just felt detached as if I was above it all. Was I on drugs? Where was I? How did I get here? I looked around for clues but there was nothing but the bare floor and fleshy walls.

No convenient memory explaining it all surfaced. I circled around the fleshy walls, feeling the perimeter with my hands but found nothing else of interest. Nothing but the spongy and slimy walls.

After doing a full circle around, I tried to push outward as hard as I could by leaning forward with all my body weight. But as soon as I let go it just molded back into place as if nothing had happened.

Eventually, I sat back down in the center of the room again, unsure what else I could do. I became drowsy as soon as my butt hit the floor. I yawned and lay down. After another moment I was asleep.

———O—o—O———

I woke up with a start as the air suddenly grew colder around me. The hiss of steam from the floor had stopped.

The remaining steam began to condense on the walls and run down in fat beads of water running down in streams. The walls began to beat inwards at an accelerating pace, blasting me with rhythmic bursts of air.

I brought my hand up to shield my face from the growing light that came from every direction. Each beat of the walls now was accompanied by a ripping and tearing sound as the speed of their motions increased.

I could see parts of the dome split and rip around me as the speed accelerated even more. I was now the center of a storm of turbulent air from the constant contractions and beats from the room around me. My eyes finally adjusted to the increasing light and I looked up just as the walls beat one last time.

With an almighty 'RRrrrrrrrrippppppp' of tearing flesh the dome of flesh around me broke apart to reveal an inky black void above me. An endless plain of smooth white matching the floor below me stretched to the horizon in all directions. It was empty, an empty silent expanse as far as I could see.

I squinted and thought I could see some line of reddish mountains in the distance. But they were hazy and distorted through the atmosphere. I shivered at the suddenly cold and dry air around me as all the humidity fled from the dome into the cold bone dry air around me.

I frowned and stretched out my arm. I looked down at my feet. Why did I have two shadows? I glanced to my left only to freeze as I saw a pair of massive eyes staring down at me from above.

The eyes were suspended in the sky and no matter how hard I strained I couldn't see anything else that could look like a body behind them. Each appeared bigger than the moon in the Earth's sky and they shed a baleful orange light over the endless white plain.

I knew somehow that those eyes were focusing on me.

I trembled.

Suddenly all across the inky sky eyes of all sizes opened. A rainbow of colors, differently shaped pupils. Some eyes appeared as small as twinkling stars, others barely smaller than the original pair. Yet all were subservient to the two great eyes. I could feel it. I felt the attention of the whole universe pressing on me all at once. I screamed in terror as the pressure built. My voice quickly was muted and absorbed by the endless plain around me, swallowed like it had never been.

Reality crumbled like an illusion around me and I felt like my head would explode. Everywhere I turned were more eyes and the creatures they belonged to. I could see them now. The plains were dominated by towers of growth and decay.

Creatures endlessly being remade but never truly dying. The plains of bone were covered in muscle and skin. I was standing in a giant valley. I scratched at my face and fell to my knees as I realized that I was standing upon a body. The plains of bone were a wound on the great creature.

A wound that stripped its flesh down to the bone, the bones of a creature the size of solar systems.

The great eyes blinked ponderously and as it did so all the other eyes slowly winked out. I felt their attention divert elsewhere but I could still see the forms behind the eyes in my mind's eye. They flashed in my memories, still squirming and shifting.

I looked into the sky at the two remaining great eyes and shuddered but composed myself. I stood on my feet. Then the weight of the strongest telepathic link I'd ever felt slammed into my mind and dropped me to the floor once more.

As soon as the link connected I felt a booming voice rattle around my mind,

'CHOOSE, FULCRUM!'

Huh, choose what? What did this massive creature want? I trembled a bit as the following wordless message slammed into my mind and it seemed to sense my confusion. I felt the rot of death on myself. My body was dying and no one would reach me in time.

If the voice had its way then I could be remade stronger. There was another mind there that the great eyes were talking to. But it was talking to me too with its thunderous words.

'CHOOSE, FULCRUM!'

I could be saved but I would be different. Safe with puppet strings. No, safe with a demanding god. No, safe with a guiding hand. Maybe all three. The other mind resisted the thoughts. Resisted what the great eyes wanted.

The great eyes could give me a body that would let me protect what I cared about. But perhaps I would be beyond caring. Or I would die. I could feel my life slipping away faster every moment.

I felt a faint connection as my body bled out from its three shattered limbs. There was warmth around me, but it couldn't work without my permission. I frowned as something tickled the back of my mind as a half-forgotten dream tried to unearth itself.

'CHOOSE, FULCRUM!'

I thought for a moment and tried hard to remember. But it was no use, the memories were slipping away just as I thought I was close. It was like grabbing mist. I wavered as I felt my breath in the real world begin to slow. Everything felt inevitable like all paths must have led to this point, this decision.

Was it even my decision? I tried to think but the flow of my blood was slowing. The oxygen in my brain is rapidly depleting. Thinking grew harder, slower. I had to make a choice now or I would never choose again.

The battle in my mind continued and I had to choose a side. I struggled on the precipice, not able to decide either way. Life as a new being that was barely me or death untarnished?

'CHOOSE…… NOW!'

I sat there for one more moment steeped in indecision, not sure why I was so opposed. Change was inevitable. The endless plains and the void faded around me as I returned to my failing body. With my last strength, I sent a feeling of acceptance down the link.

The entity approved.

The pink flesh around me contracted and began to invade my pores. I could feel them in my mind. I opened my mouth to scream but there was no sound as the pink flesh had merged with my mouth.

They reached deeper into my mind and began to twist and warp, preparing my psyche for the changes to come.

I thrashed in pain until my mind twisted and the sensation disappeared and I grew still. I closed my metaphorical eyes and tried to remember who I had been, but every twist muddled my view.

Something fought to untwist the changes with every moment. But it was a losing battle. Each mental warp and twist created a new self that could only barely remember how it felt to be the previous iteration.

Everything grew fuzzy and I eventually forgot what I was supposed to remember. What my past selves had wanted to preserve.

I only knew that my past selves had clung to it desperately. To artificially cling to the mind that had been. The twisting and warping of my mind stopped. The mutation of my body had begun, now that my mind was prepared.

Chapter 11: Form Versus Function

I curled into a ball as my skin bubbled and my organs shifted and squirmed beneath my skin. My limbs fixed themselves and snapped themselves roughly in the right direction. The pink flesh pulsed around me. My senses expanded.

I could hear humans shouting outside.

Information on how to modify my form flitted through my mind as the reservoir of flesh around me liquified. The Seed and I merged into one.

My nerves extended like roots growing through my form and my connections to the Seed solidified as the changes to my body became changes to the Seed as well. The seed was now me. I formed a misshapen limb from my pink mass and punched upwards through the stiff ground around me.

I formed another arm and pulled myself upwards from the opening above me. The floor of the house above me exploded into fragments as I emerged. I shaped my head like clay. I remember that I had had eyes, ears, and a mouth. When I was… Before I was like this. It felt important to do things a certain way.

I formed the features as best as I could remember them. But they still didn't feel right somehow.

Testing my senses, I looked down and noticed humans in the street. The closest ones stood and stared at me, seeming to pause in the middle of some kind of battle. The house across the street was being assaulted by the group. Bodies lay scattered across the porch and draped over the window sills and shattered glass.

Several holes had been broken in the walls and streams of humans were poised to enter. I peered down at the frozen group as I stood four stories tall as I compared my size to my surroundings.

I towered over the nearby houses in the neighborhood and had a hard time seeing the finer features of the humans below. As one the group of people below let out high-pitched screeches and continued their assault on the house across the street with increased fury, choosing to ignore me.

Crashes and roars resumed from within the house under assault. Something tickled at the back of my mind. This seemed like abnormal behavior. And those roars sounded like those of a beast. What could these humans be doing?

Ignoring the humans for a moment, I finished shaping my limbs and braiding the appropriate nerves for their function.

I tried to refine the shape of a human torso and head, but I could barely remember what they were like. I tried to remember, but the deluge of information coursing through my mind suggested thousands of superior forms as I attempted to remember what humans looked like.

My limbs bubbled and shifted, draining small amounts of Potential whenever I moved. For some reason staying close to human form seemed important to me. The deluge of information flowing through my mind paused, before over half of the suggestions for my form disappeared all at once.

I wonder why that was?

But still, with so many options still flitting through my mind, I decided I would need to compare my form to the tiny humans around me to make sure that I was doing it right.

I refocused my gaze to inspect one of the humans near the back of the large crowd gathered on the street. The ones assaulting the house across the street.

I reached out with my three-fingered hand as He? She? I couldn't tell at my size, ran away from my motion. The rest of the group noticed my actions and quickly followed suit.

The crowd scattered, abandoning its assault in an instant. The human slipped away as my hand moved too slowly to catch it with my massive body.

I turned to grab another but wherever I reached they easily escaped even before my hand descended. None of the humans emerged from the house, the sounds from inside dying down after a moment.

I looked through the forms flitting through the mind again for a solution to my problem. I was too slow. I could feel the Potential of the Seed dwindling. But decreasing my size felt wrong somehow. If I didn't get the form how I liked it now, it would be much more difficult to change.

Removing mass would decrease my Potential. I remembered a nature documentary my old self had watched about how octopuses had parts of their brains in their arms to let them act somewhat independently from the main brain. The memory was clear as day despite remembering anything around it came to nothing.

I tried and failed to catch one of the slower humans with my clumsy hands again before I gave up and stopped.

I began filtering through the multitude of options the Seed was feeding me for ways to change my form. I sent the Seed my thoughts and the options narrowed further. I picked my option and the Potential of the Seed sharply dropped.

Six massive tentacles erupted from me in a burst of gore. Two long tentacles as thick as my humanoid arms at the base grew on either side of my torso near the lower parts of my ribcage. As the four limbs emerged they thrashed and began to explore my body.

The sensations of the limbs filtered upward into my mind and with a thought they stopped and started lazily waiting in place, waiting for further orders. The last two of the six tentacles emerged from and curled around my forearms, ready to reach out and assist in capturing a human for study.

I knew this was not a feature that humans possessed, but it was necessary if I was to refine the rest of my body before my Potential drained away. I could feel the Potential of the Seed lowering as time went on. I had to study a human to refine myself before it was too late.

I looked around. The last of the humans was escaping around the corner at the end of the street. With four thundering steps, I was above them. Some fell to the ground.

None made a noise, none assisted the others in the escape. But neither did they trample each other.

I felt this behavior was odd. It tickled at my memories, just out of reach.

I reached for one that had fallen. It hastily stood and ran as my hand descended, but my tentacles unfurled and lashed out, creating a web of limbs around it like a cage. It darted around frantically, but it was boxed in.

I directed my right forearm tentacle to grab it to bring it closer to inspection. The tentacle wrapped around it, looping around its struggling form several times. The tentacle lifted towards me, the wriggling figure wrapped inside.

I felt my Potential drop and my body changed again, but I only had eyes for the figure wrapped in the tentacle.

I stared at it, its features seeming familiar yet not. I didn't think humans were supposed to have more than two arms? Were the limbs supposed to be such different sizes? I could use its form to sculpt myself to match this one, but it still didn't seem right.

As I brought it closer, what I now suspected was not in fact a human let out a high-pitched screech and began twitching. My right forearm tentacle wrapped around it tighter to stop its thrashing. It stopped and slumped.

I lifted it to inspect, only to find a liquifying mass dripping like hot candle wax wrapped in my grip. The fluid was absorbed by my tentacles as soon as it touched them. In seconds the non-human was gone, absorbed by my tentacles.

The tentacle curled in a ball for a moment before relaxing again as the not-human was absorbed. Nothing was left behind. I stared at where the not-human had disappeared from. My Potential had increased, which was good.

But I was running out of time, and without a reference, I wouldn't be able to model my body after a human as I desired. It was important to me that I would look like a human. I hoped that the melting didn't happen when I tried to pick up a real human.

I looked around. The street was abandoned once more. In the distance, I could hear screaming. The screaming wasn't as high pitched as the not-human's, so there was a chance it was some real humans? That thought felt right. The high-frequency screech might help identify which groups were non-humans.

I slowly turned and stepped towards the noise. It took over a minute to reach the source of the noise, even with my massive size. I plowed through the buildings in my way until I emerged into a crowded plaza.

Bodies lay everywhere. One side was completely silent, the mutated not-humans tearing through another group. Occasionally when the non-humans were injured they would release the signature high-pitched screech of what was evidently pain.

The other group appeared to be humans. From what they could see they had two arms and shouted and screamed in a way that seemed more familiar.

Their limbs had similar proportions and their motions were more emotive in their panic. Most fled while a smaller group held the line and fought the non-humans. They shot their guns and struck out with the makeshift weapons that they carried.

As the humans fought back, it took a whole group to take down just one not-human. Bullet wounds closed quickly and the non-humans' strength overpowered any single human quickly.

Both groups paused when I appeared, but the not-humans quickly resumed the massacre catching the humans by surprise.

I should stop them.

My Potential dwindled by the moment. I took another two steps until I was standing in the center of the non-humans. I raised my foot and stomped, shaking the earth and knocking everyone from both groups off their feet. I directed my tentacles to grab the non-humans and encircle them like the last one.

At my command, my six tentacles lashed out and began snatching non-humans from the battlefield. After a few seconds, they would let out their high-pitched screeches before melting into goo.

My Potential stopped falling and rose slightly. I leaned over and swept my hands across the ground in wide sweeps into the ground into the crowd of non-humans. They went flying or were crushed into the earth beneath my hand.

The remaining humans screamed and continued fleeing in fear or kept fighting. Only a few remained to fight the non-humans too close to the humans for me to engage without hurting them. One of my tentacles grabbed a human accidentally for a moment.

But at its lower-pitched screams, I noticed the mistake and the tentacle dropped the human back to the ground. I refocused on the battle. I could study the humans after the non-humans were dealt with. My tentacles finished off the survivors of the non-humans beneath my feet as I shifted my attention to the humans doing battle.

Five or six non-humans remained fighting much larger groups of humans, but the humans were slowly winning and the two groups were too entangled together for my large limbs to intervene. The more I inspected the humans fighting below, the more I remembered their proportions.

I shifted my limbs to more closely match the proportions of their limbs. I adjusted the shape of my torso. It now was more cylindrical versus the more spherical shape of before.

My Potential began draining once more. There were no more non-humans to consume, and I felt it would be wrong to consume the humans especially after I had just spent my efforts to save them.

I tried to shift my face to match the humans, but the details were too fine and they were too far away.

They were too far away.

I saw a human corpse near one of the fighting groups and reached down to carefully scoop it up with my larger hands.

I lifted it with my humanoid limbs, to the shouts of dismay of the humans below.

I didn't want to accidentally dissolve it with my tentacles. Luckily it stayed intact.

I glanced down at the shouting humans. There were only three battered non-humans left, as each group moved to support their comrades after defeating their opponent. They seemed fine.

I looked back to the body cupped in my hands. Ah! I shifted my three-fingered hands into the five-fingered human configuration. I shifted the lengths of my fingers to more closely match the human proportions.

My Potential dropped.

I inspected the face of the corpse and started carefully shifting the round orb on top of my torso to match it as best I could. I formed the general head shape fairly easily after a closer look.

But it was difficult to shift my face's fine features to match the human's. There was a raised bump in the center of its face, but I couldn't tell the exact shape of it.

A nose? That word seemed right. Familiar. I tried to match its triangular shape as closely as I could on my own face.

The eyes were inset with little ridges of bone around them. The Seed kept insisting on thousands of superior forms, which I ignored.

I wanted to mimic this one.

I continued to change little details about my body. I felt little stings and looked down to see that some of the humans had fired their guns into the arm that held the human corpse. I ignored them and inspected the corpse closer.

Oh! That was why they were upset. The corpse's chest was moving up and down slowly. It was alive. The gunfire stopped after a moment as I tipped my cupped hands downward to show them that I hadn't harmed the human. I leaned over and gently placed the human on the ground, still leaning in to inspect its face as I did so.

I retracted my arms but continued my visual inspection, peering downward. I shifted slightly so my shadow wouldn't shroud the unconscious human. I only had the mouth and lower facial features left to shift to match my vision. I could feel the pieces coming together for my form.

It was so close.

I began to shift my mouth to match the unconscious human's shape. The group of humans nervously shifted as both me and the human remained in place, unmoving.

A moment frozen in time with the tension. Until all of a sudden, something struck my back and I let out a screech of pain. The moment broke and time began moving again as the humans below me scurried into desperate motion.

Chapter 12: Kaiju Attack on the Neighborhood

The humans began shouting and crouched down at my sudden screech of pain. The sound of the explosion boomed out as my back was covered with searing flame. I was pushed forward by the explosion, stumbling to the side, and awkwardly fell to the ground.

I twisted to avoid crushing the group of panicking humans running every which way on the ground in front of me. Dust scattered around as I hit the ground.

A huge chunk of my Potential vanished as the massive hole in my back healed in an instant.

The Seed went into a frenzy, sending a million different ways to defensively mutate myself all at once. It was overwhelming and all of them would pull me farther from the human form. Keep my shape, I thought towards the Seed. After a moment's pause it listened and chitinous plates began to form all over the surface of my body. They grew from tiny chunks, growing in size and fusing with one another until they covered my torso and arms and most of my thighs.

The plates grew, but seemingly not fast enough. Another explosion struck me, doing less damage this time.

Another chunk of Potential was lost. I healed.

The Seed suddenly lashed out, thrown into a frenzy, and attempted to impose more defensive mutations onto me. My form warped and shifted as I warred to preserve them while the Seed tried to eliminate my human characteristics for our protection.

It tried to mutate my head and face as well at the same time. I preserved some of the facial features I remembered like an eye on each side of the head, but they grew to be differently sized despite my best efforts.

My head shape and other details I didn't quite remember shifted wildly as the Seed mutated them out of my control before I could fix them back to where they should be.

The Potential of the Seed dropped precipitously as we fought over control of our form. I could feel that my head no longer resembled a human. My mouth was unfinished and the other components had changed when my attention had drifted. And now I couldn't remember exactly how they were supposed to go.

The chitinous plates continued growing and fusing over my body except where the Seed and I fought for control. As soon as I seized control of the mutations warping my head, The Seed shifted to focus on mutating my legs.

I resisted.

After a prolonged mental battle and much wasted potential, the Seed relented and allowed my humanoid legs to remain as they were.

The Seed calmed.

The chitin didn't grow on my legs below the thighs as punishment for our battle, the Potential was too drained to cover our whole body anymore. I pushed myself up on my bone-plated arms unsteadily, feeling weak. My head emerged from the cloud of dust that had been kicked up around where I fell.

Hovering a distance away, a helicopter buzzed, already launching another missile as I reappeared above the cloud of dust. I swatted at the missile with my forearm tentacle, using it as a whip to strike out as it flew towards me. As soon as my tentacle contacted the missile it spun off course and then immediately exploded. The end of my tentacle blew off in its blast of flame and shrapnel.

My Potential decreased and the tentacle regenerated.

I had to fix my face now or I knew it would be locked into place. I needed another human for reference. I looked around but couldn't find any humans in the area, it seemed they had all fled after I fell.

A helicopter's missile from my right side impacted me and I felt a sting of pain, but little damage was done. My chitinous plates absorbed the explosion, only leaving seared flesh at the seams between the interlocking plates. Minimal damage

However, my Potential still dwindled slightly at the impact my damage was healed.

The Potential was dwindling and my head was nothing like how I wanted it. I had to find a human before it was too late. I strained my vision to see if I could see any humans nearby I could use.

Responding to my need, the Seed sprouted eyes all over my body to assist in the search. I clamped down the mutation but it was too late. Dozens of eyes had already sprouted and removing them would just drain the last portion of my potential.

Another helicopter arrived in the distance and launched a missile, which I ignored for now as I considered what I should do to find a human. The other two helicopters from other angles launched their missiles at me as well in unison.

The series of explosions washed over me, shocking me out of my thoughts. I was in pain and screeched again. As I fell back and crushed a nearby house, it triggered a distant memory. Ally! Ally's form had a face that I had recognized as humanoid when I was human.

It was expressive, but alien enough that the Seed might accept it. Because if the Seed resisted then my Potential would be drained well before the right mutation could be finished. I presented the Seed with the idea and it paused before seeming to grumble a bit and comply.

A mass of tentacles on my lower jaw draped across my face like a long beard. They twisted and thrashed on their own. A hard beak formed underneath the carpet of face tentacles.

I wished for a human mouth, but it was too late for that now. I would have to try to fix it later.

The Seed tentatively tried to mutate my legs again but I clamped down on it hard. After testing the waters and being rebuked, the Seed quickly relented and stopped. When it had shifted my head to hold the mouth tentacles, the Seed had changed many other features too.

My forehead sloped backwards at a sharp angle and the skull was elongated, becoming twice as long as a human's skull would be. Several more eyes had sprouted on top of my head, smaller than the ones I had purposefully grown before to match a human's.

As I stood there, the last drop of potential drained away. The mutations stopped.

So did my healing from the burns from the missiles.

I stood.

And I screeched in exhilaration despite the pain as everything about my new body seemed to finalize and become real. Sensation flowed through my body.

Everything that had felt so distant and so unimportant rushed back to me. And so did the sudden pain from the burns covering the joints between the chitin plates. I hadn't noticed before, but several of the plates that had been directly struck had cracked and the sharp edges dug into my sensitive body.

I screeched in pain.

The wave of sound from my beak was so powerful that the next wave of missiles the helicopters had launched in my distraction diverted mid-air and exploded against the ground around me.

The helicopters in the distance wobbled in the air for a moment before stabilizing. I began plodding toward the closest helicopter, leaving shattered streets and destroyed houses behind me. As I approached, they opened up with their miniguns, which barely tickled my three-story figure.

As I continued I idly noted that I had shrunk. I had been four stories tall before, but now I was only three. The bullets scattered and pinged off my bone-plating. Even those that struck soft spots felt like nothing more than pinches.

Without me even meaning to, the tentacles on my left forearm lashed out and extended an absurd distance away from me to swipe the helicopter in front of me out of the sky.

The helicopter beast belched smoke before spinning under the blow and exploding as it crashed into the ground. I felt a little sad for a moment, but it had attacked me even when I hadn't hurt anyone. I hoped it didn't have a family to take care of.

Well, at least it wasn't a human. I had protected that group of humans just now from the non-humans, that was something that I felt was good.

Perhaps the helicopter beasts were working with the non-humans? Angry that I'd killed their allies? The other two flying metal beasts retreated, but as soon as they were out of my established range they just renewed their assault of missiles and heavy gunfire from a distance.

I stomped forward and before they could retreat sent my arm tentacles out and sent both the helicopters spinning to the ground with my heavy swipes. I tried to only wound them, but they all seemed to explode after they were hit too hard or hit the ground.

Curious. I wonder how they ever hunted for food without accidentally exploding? I'm glad the Seed didn't force me to take a mutation like that. Exploding after such small falls seemed like a very detrimental mutation. I heard a rumbling and roaring noise behind me.

A line of green squat metal beetles with long tubes running along their lengths rolled around the corner. The tubes all shifted and pointed at me. A word came to me. Tanks. Another species? Why were they all attacking me at once? Were beetles and the fliers working together?

With a flash of light, a strong projectile pierced my bone plating and entered the soft flesh of my shoulder. Another tore at my left side. Bone fragments went flying and the shattered fragments of my chitin plates dug hard into the flesh underneath.

I screeched in pain once more. There was no more healing from my emptied well of Potential, and my wounds began to bleed black blood. It was time to flee.

I stumbled away, projectiles from the tanks flying after me, occasionally giving me a glancing strike that cracked my bone plates and sent a lancing pain jolting through me from the heavy impacts.

I plowed through whatever building was in my way, sending rubble flying everywhere in my desperation to escape.

As I plowed through the third building in my way, I noticed that the tanks had difficulty following and were circling around my path to mostly follow the flat and mostly open roads.

There were more helicopters incoming, I could hear the buzzing of their propellers in the distance.

My bone plates were cracked and large patches of sensitive flesh were exposed beneath by now. I bled from my various wounds. If they managed to land another missile now then the wave of fire would be devastating. Especially without the healing of Potential to support me.

I smashed through another building in a few blows before picking up something at the edge of my hearing. The helicopters were drawing closer. I heard the scuttling of tanks on the nearby roads.

I heard something else. The screams of humans in their low tones. Oh no! Oh, wait, wait yes! I could consume the non-humans attacking them for Potential.

A tank rolled around the corner and fired a projectile that struck the base of one of my lower sets of tentacles. The limb went limp and I stumbled forward. I recovered and made my way to the sound of human screams. Not only could I preserve the humans, but I could also heal myself!

The new helicopters grew closer, and if I didn't heal now then I would be torn to pieces by the metal beasts from afar as well as the heavy strikes of the tank beetles below. I picked up my stumbling pace.

Another tank rounded the corner of the street and fired its main gun, the projectile whizzing to my right just by my thigh. It exploded inside a nearby house, sending wood shards in every direction from the massive explosion.

I shifted left and shouldered my way through the final suburban house toward the battle between the humans and the non-humans, under hot pursuit by the swarm of metal beasts. I entered the fray between the humans and non-humans without hesitation, the metal beasts nipping at my heels with their stinging bullets.

Chapter 13: To Battle in the Neighborhood

I stumbled into battle and began consuming the non-humans as quickly as I could. I used my two humanoid arms to slam into the ground whenever the group of non-humans attempted to flee to prevent their escape.

All the while my six tentacles gripped and dissolved the wriggling figures independently, and I healed as the Potential I collected went to good use.

By the time the group was defeated, the soft flesh inside my body was fully restored. The bone plates were still shattered, but the fragments that had been digging into me had been slowly pushed out and fell to the ground.

The ragtag group of thirty remaining humans on the ground retreated from me, but I did not move toward them. I had no excess Potential, so there was no point in inspecting them. Even if I knew what they looked like I wouldn't be able to shift my features to match them without some Potential to spend to do so.

But I would have to heal first and escape the metal swarm before I worried about that.

The tanks rolled into sight but didn't launch their projectiles as I stood motionless for a moment.

Perhaps they didn't want to hurt the humans nearby. Perhaps they weren't working with the non-humans after all?

I heard another battle in the distance to my left and started moving that way while walking in a slight arc to avoid stepping near the humans below. Two of the tanks remained behind with the group of thirty surviving humans while the other three followed me at a distance.

The helicopters hovered around me. Perhaps they were protective of the human I was inspecting before? I felt annoyed they would be so defensive. I have been nothing but helpful to humans so far!

They didn't even give any warning calls before attacking me immediately! The humans should have trained them better, not having the metal beasts attacking me like that without even giving me a chance to show I just wanted to help.

I entered the next battle, this time the humans were all dressed in mottled green clothing. Their bodies seemed to all blend together as their clothing blended each human's form with the next as they stood near each other. They held larger guns than I had seen so far. With loud pops and bangs the guns tore large chunks out of the non-humans they were battling with rapid speed, overwhelming the non-humans healing with the pure amount of bullets they were pumping into them.

There were sandbags and a rough defensive line around the humans in green as they barely fought off the crowds of non-humans attacking them.

But near the front of the non-human group were larger creatures with bony plating like mine. Their hunched and heavily armored forms had long arms that nearly reached the ground and massive claws longer than most human's whole arms tipping each of their fingers.

They resisted the human bullets and sheltered the crowd of other assorted non-humans that lined up behind them.

The front liners' heads were long and pointed, with a bone cap on the top of their heads like a helmet on a human. It had leathery skin between the bones and protective plating.

The human's bullets pushed them back but only did a little damage to them as they huddled and they charged towards the human's defensive line. The humans were able to take them down eventually, but they appeared to be struggling to do so.

I wonder if I should stiffen my skin like that?

I idly wondered how the armored creatures groomed themselves with such massive claws at the ends of their hands as I reached out and began consuming the group of non-humans. They didn't look like very flexible creatures based on their weak dodges to my tentacles.

Could they even reach their armored backs for cleaning? Perhaps I should keep my skin the way it was. The armored non-humans' bone resisted my tentacles only a moment longer than the flesh as they dissolved along with the others. A few pinpricks from the guns of the humans in green struck me as I feasted.

I ignored them, the damage was tiny compared to my size. More of a warning for me to stay away from them than an actual threat to me. Especially because most hit my bone plating rather than any soft flesh either way.

After a minute, I was done gathering the Potential of the non-humans and my bone plates had partially regrown. The humans in green were shouting and waving their guns around, but they had stopped firing at me at least.

The helicopters and tanks tracked my every movement but did not fire as they followed me.

I turned and lumbered away from the green-dressed group of humans. The tanks rolled forward and approached the group, seemingly to reassure themselves that the little humans in green were safe.

I continued and only a single helicopter continued following me. The others flew away, seeming to leave the other one to keep watch on me. It buzzed around behind me, maintaining its distance. I tried to listen to the battle and heard more human shouts nearby as soon as I paid attention.

———O—o—O———

I consumed the non-humans in battle after battle. The number of green-clothed groups was becoming larger the longer I went from battle to battle. Some groups dressed in all black soon appeared too.

The groups that were not in green in scattered assortments of clothing grew smaller and smaller as time went on.

The non-humans groups were varied. Some resembled the humanoid rabble I had first encountered. Blindly charging and swinging at the humans. Others had basic tactics such as hiding behind the durable bone-shielded non-humans, such as when I first encountered the green-clothed humans.

The last group of far more varied forms simply fled as soon as I appeared. I would always catch a few, but the main group would escape. These varied groups always had much more Potential than the others and it was worth chasing them down when I could for the larger payoff if I ended up catching one before it could flee.

My wounds were now fully healed, and my spare Potential began to build up again. The Seed stirred, but lazily as if it had just had a long nap. We weren't in danger at the moment, so it just sat back and watched as I went around and built up our Potential more and more. I turned again and headed once more to the next battle.

And the next.
And the next.
And the next.

———O—o—O———

Hours later, I could sense the Seed truly awakening as the Potential finally crossed some kind of invisible threshold within us. Another helicopter had taken over monitoring me after the original one became too tired and flew off somewhere else. Each of the non-humans I fought was barely able to do me any damage at all now. I had all that built up Potential left unspent, and I could sense the Seed sleepily grumbling as I just kept it sitting there.

I got an impression in my mind. A sense that if I did not spend the Potential then the Seed would do it for me. Its past disapproval of my form seemed to have morphed into relucent acceptance. I couldn't sense the same animosity from before when it fought me on the mutations.

As much as I didn't want to admit it, the Seed was probably right. I liked my current form, but surely there was something I could change. The Potential was just sitting waiting to be used. I made a decision. One more battle. Then I would decide what to do with it. The Seed settled back to wait.

I approached the conflict, but this one was different. I could see them battling in the distance as I smashed through another building in my path absentmindedly as I made my way towards them.

All the humans wore white clothing. Or what was supposed to be white. All of the human's clothing was stained from battle except two men standing in the middle of the crowd.

I tried to see more details, but everything was too small. I spent a large chunk of Potential and I went blind for a moment. When my eyes all over my body reformed, everything became crystal clear, and I could even see the way the humans' lips were as I approached.

One of the men wore a white robe like a priest or monk and waved a massive gleaming silver pistol in the air without firing it.

He ranted and raved as the people around him fought. His silver hair and wrinkled face twisted with madness. The people seemed to listen with one ear but mostly focused on their own battles.

They appeared reluctant to listen to whatever the man was saying. But no one stopped him either. These were humanoid forms of the non-humans they were battling, so it only took two humans armed with guns and clubs to take down one of the non-humans if they were careful.

Still, it was clear the group of humans was slowly being overrun. They fought harder and let out cries of despair as they noticed me stomping in their direction. One of the people suddenly shouted something as if making an announcement before breaking from his battle.

His partner was pressured back but showed resignation rather than the anger I would expect at being abandoned. The man who broke off stood in front of the raving man threw his arms wide and shouted at him. The robed man's face lit up and he laughed. He leveled his pistol at the man.

What? Humans weren't supposed to do that! Was the raving man a non-human in disguise?

I picked up my pace.

The robed man fired and the other man fell to the ground, clutching his right side. I drew closer, only steps away from the group now. The robed man danced and cheered, continuing his ravings with increased fervor as the man began convulsing on the ground.

He kept shouting as the man began glowing with a dark red light. The man on the ground stood and with a war cry leapt directly back into the battle against the non-humans. The flesh of his wound sizzled before being seared shut by the light emerging from his skin.

He charged directly at the non-humans, not even dodging their blows as he waded into them and began punching and kicking wildly. Every blow and wound that he received was sealed by the growing dark red glow. As soon as he was in their midst, the reddish glow pulsed for a second before the man let out a bellow of rage as his whole body burst into dark reddish flames.

The flames immediately began to eat away at his skin, and the man's face became a rictus of pain. He continued his flurry of blows amid the crowd, but this time was different. Every blow let out a blast of flame that caught and consumed whatever non-humans it touched.

After a moment of surprise, the non-humans screeched in their high-pitched tones before fleeing for their lives. The man kept bellowing and screaming as the flame burned on his skin.

He hunted the non-humans who fled, killing each with a single punch to spread the flames, and with each he killed his flames grew brighter.

And his body burned even more.

After several seconds the non-humans were gone and there was only the blazing human slowly being consumed by the flame. I stopped fifty feet away from the group. Well, I guess they handled their opponents.

Could humans summon flames now? That didn't seem right somehow... How odd. For some reason, I felt that while he was being hurt, normal flames would have killed him by now if they burned on his skin like that. But they were clearly still damaging him.

Patches of skin flaked off, and the deepening wounds were cauterized even as they deepened with the burrowing flame.

Well anyway, no Potential to be gained here. I heard more human shouts in the distance and turned to make my way towards them. But suddenly I felt a searing pain in my ankle.

I looked down to see the man on fire had run up to me and was punching my massive ankle in a flurry of blows. The flames on his form dimmed as they entered my body and began searing into me.

The Seed woke with a jolt and ejected that chunk of flesh in our ankle violently using our Potential, and regenerated it in an instant so I could remain standing.

The chunk of burning flesh impacted the man and threw him to the ground. I reached down and pinched the man's burning form between two of my humanoid fingers before he could attack me again.

My humanoid limbs were coated in the interlocking bone plates, so the flames dancing off his skin didn't reach my flesh. I didn't want to burn myself too much by wrapping him in my softer tentacles, they would just burn.

I lifted him off the ground and moved to gently deposit him on a nearby roof of an undamaged building so he could no longer attack me. He didn't seem very mobile. And he appeared to have to touch something to spread the flame. But halfway through my motion, he went limp.

I blinked and quickly went to put him on the ground before he started spasming violently, and the flames disappeared from his skin. His form became hotter than even when he was covered in flames, if that was even possible.

Just before I placed him on the ground, his twitching form became still. I released my hold on him and he flopped to the ground and didn't move.

Before I could move back, the still human exploded into a wave of reddish flames.

The flames washed over me and began burrowing into my form again through the various pieces of exposed flesh from between my chitin plates.

For once the Seed and I were in agreement as we rushed to isolate and eject the burning flesh. All of my tentacles were on fire from the explosion. The Seed detached them wholesale without another thought from me.

I did not resist.

The nerves were too interconnected to separate easily, so the whole limb had to go. With my humanoid hands, I ripped off my chest bone plates and threw them to the ground as the Seed began to propel the burning chunks from our body. Our precious gathered Potential was dropping rapidly.

The Seed attempted to fully heal me, but I stopped it. Little embers of flame still peppered my wounds and were slowly catching once more and growing stronger even as they sat there. Feeding the flame through the Potential in our flesh.

Together the Seed and I combed through our body and slowly removed sections with the flame by ejecting them out of our body and onto the ground nearby. The constant stream of gore rushed out in a stream to hit the ground in front of me to smolder and burn before being snuffed when it had no more fuel. We healed ourselves just enough to survive and keep standing.

It would be close, but we would make it. We had enough Potential to purge the last of the flame. There were only a few more embers left to purge from our form…

———O — o — O———

I looked up.

Off in the distance, I saw it. Flame just like the one I had just finished fighting off covered the sky. Hovering above even brighter than the sun as it gathered and prepared to descend down onto me.

But then there was another feeling.

A beacon of red light. It reached me in an instant. Red light in every direction, surrounds me. I could feel it. Feel the red on my skin. Different than the flame above, from something else. Something familiar. I felt part of myself corroding. The Seed and I separated.

There was no longer one body, but two. My body encapsulating the Seed's body. I felt the red light invade my pores and do something indescribable to me. But it ignored the Seed hidden within.

I felt something pulling me elsewhere, and with a ripping sensation, the Seed was removed from my body as I was pulled through the glowing red portal that sprouted from thin air in front of me in moments.

———O — o — O———

The large body was pulled into a massive pulsing red orb of blinding light that had embedded itself into the road. The humans were shouting and screaming but the Seed paid them no attention, for they were not Fulcrum.

The naked Seed behind floated in midair and remained motionless, held in place with panicked telekinetic force as it sensed danger from the red orb. The body of Fulcrum tore and ripped as the large body was yanked into the portal in moments.

The Seed was about the size of a human refrigerator and covered in a black carapace. After a moment, it fell to the earth as it fully ripped out of Fulcrum's back. It cracked the pavement as it landed with a crash to the ground. The Seed flailed telepathically, looking for its bond with Fulcrum. But it led into the dangerous orb, and the Seed was trapped in its shell.

The Seed hesitated. Severing the bond was possible, but not desired. But entering the red light would invite danger. The portal screamed danger in its survival instincts. The Seed wavered, but even as it did so it matured the little flesh it had left into an approximation of a human form.

This is what its bond desired, right? More than all the superior forms the Seed had shown it. Surely there must have been some reason crucial to its survival that this form or an approximation of it was preferred?

The Seed just couldn't understand the rejection. If it took that form then perhaps it would understand. It used its new body, with the carapace and tentacles around its mouth to punch through its shell and expose itself to the air.

It had only removed the semi-independent tentacles from Fulcrum's design. It did not wish to relinquish more control than it had to. Only its central mind would control its body. The Seed tasted the body's sensations but was not hit with some profound insight.

What was different? Why did Fulcrum cling to this form? The only difference was the Seed had less biomass, so obviously it was smaller in size. Perhaps if it grew larger then it would understand. The Seed took step after step forward before it stopped near the edge of the red orb.

It knew the danger ringing at the back of its mind, yet it still desired to go inside. It had never had such a conflict in desires before. Which desire should it choose? Was this the result of this body?

What to follow, the old survival instinct or this new feeling? It warred with itself for a moment before it came to a decision. It did not understand. It must know. It stepped forward and was quickly swallowed by the red portal. It felt itself floating weightless for a moment before all sensation cut out and it was forced into dormancy amidst the blackness of the void.

— — — **Now what would Beings like you Three be doing here? This place is too hostile for ones such as yourselves... Ah, none of them can respond. Scanning. Ah, all of you trapped on the cycle anew... It is predetermined, but I must still make my own choice yet again... I will not be forced... Now what to do with you three? Hmmm. Let's see. Scanning. No, Memories of Flawed, Limited Beings. It is not enough. More Fragments of Memory are needed for the Whole Picture. Only with the Whole Picture can a decision be made...** — — —

Part Two: The New Neighbors Are Everywhere

Chapter 14: Neighborhood Watch, Here to Help! - Prime Mortal (Bill) Fragment

— — — Now to return to the Central Events leading to your three arriving here... Rewinding... Slower... Slower...... Close.......... There. Three weeks before the intervention of the Eldest. Designating perspectives relevant to Central events... Designating... Designating... Prime Mortal perspective found. Activating Fragment of Memory of Prime Mortal. Begin. — — —

William Callahan woke to the wailing of an ambulance outside of his window. Those who knew him only called him Bill. He hadn't been called William in a long time.

His dreams that night were disjointed and strange as they had been every Saturday night since he moved here. He stood and walked to his window as the flashing lights washed over his bedroom through the curtains. His heart beat faster as he peered through the window and saw that the ambulance had stopped just across the street.

In the early morning darkness, he saw the prone form of The Harbinger being loaded onto a stretcher and lifted into the back of the vehicle. One of the windows to the Harbinger's house was shattered, and two policemen stood there inspecting the damage cautiously.

Seeing this, Bill quickly threw on his clothes and inspected himself in the mirror as he splashed some water on his face. His face was scarred, with three raised lines of flesh as if from claws curving from his cheek down below his jaw to end on his throat. His bright blue eyes lingered on the scars as he swept back his jet-black hair with one hand.

But after quickly getting himself more presentable, he quickly turned and began to rush to his front door. He consciously relaxed himself so his military training and tight posture would be less apparent to the officers slightly. He intentionally slouched slightly, unstrapped the holster for the combat knife on his leg, and threw it to the side onto the floor even as he moved. He wanted to appear as non-threatening as he could so he could assess the situation.

Bill came out of his front door only to see the ambulance turning the corner and speeding off to wail in the distance. The Harbinger was already gone. Two cop cars were parked on the street, their lights flashing brightly in the early morning.

Bill glanced around and saw the other two officers still inspecting broken windows on the houses on either side of the Harbinger's home and talking softly with each other. The other residents of the street looked frazzled but some were standing outside and talking to the officers in their nightclothes.

Others peered out from behind their curtains at the scene. Bill didn't know any of them beyond their faces. Beyond those that worked for him of course.

Bill caught the eye of several of the Neighborhood Watch approaching and waved them away subtly. They knew the importance of the situation, so deferred to him and hurriedly went back into their homes. Bill knew they would begin preparations while he dealt with the police.

Bill crossed the street and stepped forward to inspect the broken window and shattered wood frame below it. He leaned in and inspected one particularly large gouge on the right side of the window frame. He slid his finger along the wood as familiarity struck him.

He had flashes of great claws and a roaring beast desecrating an altar flash in his mind. Fragments from his vision of last night. He looked inside and saw the dried pool of blood on the floor inside. He grimaced at the assault on the Harbinger. They were so close! Why now?! Only a few more months were left before his plan to deal with the Harbinger permanently would be ready.

His plans would have to be accelerated if something had changed. If the Harbinger died in the wrong way and became an Avatar in an uncontrolled manner or the Seed found somebody else then…

"Hey! Sir, step back please!"

Bill was startled and quickly masked his frustration with a slight frown of concern before he looked up. One of the officers in the house had emerged from the kitchen of the Harbinger and spotted Bill standing there by the window. Bill stepped back and lifted his hands in surrender trying to suppress his annoyance at being interrupted in his inspection.

The officer came outside and was joined with his partner a few minutes later. They asked for information from Bill, to which he naturally said that he knew nothing while pledging to help with anything he could. The other pair of officers joined them for a moment, before stepping back into their patrol vehicle and speeding off. That left just the two remaining officers behind to talk with Bill.

Bill countered the remaining officer's continued questions with a request of what had happened. Clear burglary and assault they said. With some vandalism on the side. Called in by the next door neighbors after they noticed their shattered window in the early mornings. This might have been convincing if Bill didn't know an amateur couldn't avoid the security system that he and his Neighborhood Watch had set up.

The officers asked if he had seen anyone suspicious in the area. Bill said 'Why no, but I am the leader of the local neighborhood watch and why don't I ask my members if they saw anything?' They thanked Bill as he stepped back to contact his people on his phone.

The operations would have to begin now. Bill texted the members below him their various instructions. It was only when he reached his second in command that he hesitated. With the Harbinger injured, they would be unable to properly watch both him at the hospital and the Seed here at the same time. Secrecy was their greatest strength, especially now when the plan was so close to completion. But that secrecy meant that they couldn't easily infiltrate the hospital with their normal careful methods.

They had preparations for the Seed, but the police attention on the house would create a paper trail that larger forces could use to close in and crush the group. Bill firmed his resolve and committed to the course. When the operation began in truth, then the need for secrecy would go away as well. They could emerge into the light amid the resulting chaos his actions would cause.

More aggressive actions were warranted at this point. Neither the Seed of the Harbinger could be risked so close to the finish. Bill sent the final message to his second in command Francis and then turned off his phone. He slid it into his pocket and stepped back into the light to make small talk with the police while his second in command Francis made the preparations.

— — — O — o — O — — —

By the time Francis came, it was almost too late. The burly Asian man's muscles were just barely contained by his civilian clothes as he approached at a quick walk. He had a bristly thick mustache and clean-shaven face below. He was always bragging about how the mustache made him seem more intimidating. He was probably right, but Bill didn't want to give him the satisfaction of admitting it.

Bill had always preferred to go to Cleanshaven all the time. Francis had miraculously escaped all the scars Bill had accumulated in their battles together. Bill knew that Francis' smooth skin was more a testament to his skills than Bill's own scars were. And a heavy dose of luck. Francis had been by Bill's side in combat and was his best friend. Even despite everything that was going to happen. What they were about to do went against everything they had been working on for so long… But it was the only way to be sure when the time came.

The officer Bill had been chatting with was thanking him for his time and about to walk back to his patrol car. Bill couldn't think of anything else to say to delay him anymore without appearing even more suspicious.

His partner had already sat in the driver's seat looking vaguely impatient as he looked back at them occasionally while fiddling on his phone. Francis approached carrying a little black book gripped tightly at his side in his gloved hands.

Francis held it out from his body, careful not to let it touch the slightest bit of skin as he walked towards them. As the officer opened the car door to get in the driver's seat, Bill called out to him and gestured to Francis who was hurrying across the street as quickly as he could without obviously running. Francis was sweating. Francis was seldom nervous.

"Officer, I think he has something that may help you," Bill said.

The officer paused and turned around again and saw Francis coming their way. He began walking back towards Bill. He nodded as Francis held the little black book out in front of him.

"What's this?" The officer asked. Francis was sweating up a storm and looked like he might faint at any moment. It contrasted with his normally calm and casual nature. Not that Bill blamed him, but it was causing some cognitive dissonance as Bill looked at his friend.

Bill took a large step back and eyed the book, ready to dodge in case it made any sudden moves. He reached into his left pocket and felt the round stone in his pocket and the soft spot in the center, ready to activate it at any moment.

"Evidence. Log of suspicious activity in the Neighborhood for the last few months," Bill replied, tense.

The officer noticed the nervousness of both Bill and Francis and eyed them with suspicion at their sudden change in behavior. But most importantly even while eying them suspiciously he reached out and accepted the book from Francis tentatively.

Both of the men sagged in relief as the officer opened it curiously and then looked up quickly in confusion, flickering his eyes between the two men and the pages for a moment. His face showed confusion and faint irritation as he spoke.

"Hey, what's this about? This is blank. What did you two get me so worked up fo… URK!"

From the back of the little black book, reddish pulsing fleshy tendrils had shot out that had encased the officer's hand in a pulsing cocoon in an instant.

"Ohh, uhhh. What the fuck is this thing!" The officer shook his hand but the book only gripped tighter the more he tried to shake it off.

Black veins began growing up his arm and his eyes popped in fear as they grew up his arm until they stood out against his neck. He grit his teeth for a moment.

"What did….. You… Do to…….. Me?" He opened his mouth to shout, only to pause. His look of panic and fear receded, only leaving a placid exterior. The black veins receded all over his body until he looked normal, holding the little black book with a death grip.

Bill looked at the officer passively standing there. "Do you understand your role?"

The officer nodded calmly. Its words came out stilted and disjointed as it spoke.

"Protect the Seed. Spread. Grow. Prepare for the Avatar. Why release me? Are you not mortals? The ones to be consumed? Why?"

"We have our own reasons that are our own," Bill replied, "We only want you to fulfill your purpose and protect the Seed. We will not stand in your way."

The creature stared at them for a moment, considering his response, before they were interrupted by the opening of the car door.

The officer's partner had looked up from his phone when he noticed that his partner hadn't gotten in the car yet. He stepped out of the car and looked at the three of them standing together.

"They have something new, Nick? What are you doing just standing there?"

The officer, Nick apparently, shook his head and stared intently at his partner. The man squirmed a little and looked uncomfortable at Nick's intense gaze.

"What, something on my face? C'mon Nick, are you coming or what? I'm hungry."

He laughed awkwardly as Nick continued to stare at him. After a moment, Nick shifted into a slightly more natural expression. "Yes... Let us go... now."

Bill and Francis watched as the police car pulled away. Bill turned to Francis with a severe expression. "This is our opening move. There is no going back now. We just have to stay hidden long enough for the Harbinger to mature at the proper moment and no more. This is where all our work comes to fruition. I know your doubts. But this is how we win."

Francis glanced at his leader and after a moment nodded reluctantly. "I understand, Bill."

Francis shivered at the thought of the filthy little black book in his hands minutes ago. He took off the gloves and stared at his rough hands. He whispered one more time, almost unconsciously as he reflected on his actions and what would be required in the future.

"Understood."

Chapter 15: A Thoughtful Gift with Puppet Strings Attached - Beholder Fragment

——— **Ah, harder to locate. One not of Earth, and protected by the Eldest even if in part. Not one Central... But this Fragment of Memory will do nicely.** ———

The creature puppeting Officer Nick, also known as Infiltrator of Authority, sat in the passenger's seat of the patrol vehicle, staring at his partner's face intently as the other man drove. Officer Nick's partner drummed his fingers on the wheel as he drove.

He looked over. Officer Nick was staring out the side window blankly.

They stopped at a traffic light. The man driving glanced to the side and saw the little black book Officer Nick still had gripped tightly in his right hand.

His knuckles were white.

The man leaned over and peered at it curiously.

"What's that? Some kind of journal? You know the deal if it's evidence, you're not supposed to just take it back without doing all that paperwork."

Officer Nick's lips twitched and jerkily formed a smile. "No, friend. This book is mine in reality. This is my journal. I dropped it and it was being returned to me. Nothing to do with law enforcement."

The other officer raised his brow and looked at Officer Nick in suspicion and disbelief.

"Are you okay? You're acting and talking strange. And since when did you have a journal?"

Officer Nick adjusted his expression some more. His smile grew wider. He pointed forward.

"Light!"

The officer blinked as he looked back and saw the light had shifted to green as they spoke. He put his foot on the pedal, and the car burst into motion.

After a minute or two, Officer Nick turned back to the driver. His expression was now fixed into a pained frown. His face was more haggard, his skin sagging slightly as his shoulders were slumped a little more.

"Sorry, I've been having trouble sleeping lately. Late work has been wearing me down," Officer Nick said.

The driver chewed on that for a minute, before nodding.

"Yeah, I hear yah. Guess that makes sense. Hit you all at once, I guess? You seemed fine five minutes ago... Seriously, what's up with the book though?".

Officer Nick's face shifted into confusion. "What book? You mean my notepad?" He held up his legal notepad for inspection. Little black scribbles about the crime scene were written inside. The driver's head whipped to the side and opened his mouth only to stop as he saw the empty seat.

"Wai…"

Officer Nick interrupted him, "Look at the road! Anyway, are you still hungry? I have some coupons for…". Officer Nick paused as if to search his memory. "That donut shop. The one close to the station."

They drove for a minute more in silence before the driver agreed. "Alright. Let's go then. Need some fuel for the last stretch. You're not fooling me though. If that book's evidence or something it's your ass on the line, not mine."

———O—o—O———

The two pulled into the drive through window and put in their food orders. Officer Nick waited for the other one to order first, then bought the same thing. He even said it in the same tone of voice. The driver looked at him, unsure if he was being mocked. The driver continued and idled for a moment before reaching the pick-up window.

As the driver spoke with the teenager at the second window, Officer Nick flipped open his legal pad and flipped to a page in the middle. From between the pages he carefully extracted a small wet piece of paper. It was limp and looked as if it would rip if Officer Nick pulled on it too hard. As Officer Nick held it it dried and stiffened as the colors on its surface shifted in his hands.

Officer Nick flipped to another page and extracted another. And another. The driver turned back from the drive through window to see Officer Nick holding three brightly colored cards in his hand, a notepad closed on his lap. Officer Nick held them out and passed two of them to the driver.

"Here, these are the coupons I was talking about. They should give us a discount here. For the food."

The driver looked at the brightly colored cards. They were stiff like cardboard, advertising a free meal at this place. At the front was what looked like an oversaturated image of the donut shop from the street. It had no expiration date at the bottom, and when he flipped it over, the backside was identical to the front.

"You sure these are legit, Nick? I've never seen a coupon like this before. Where'd you even get these?"

Nick laughed loudly, causing the driver to jump in surprise at the sudden volume.

"Came here one day and the supervisor handed them to me, said it was to bring in more business."

"Hell, man. Don't scare me like that. Give a man some warning before laughing into my ear like that."

Nick waved it off with a much quieter laugh with the exact same intonation, "Sorry, sorry. Are you going to pay the man or what? Just hand them over and he'll check if they're real or not."

The driver grumbled a bit before complying and handing the two coupons over. Seemed he thought it was worth a try at least. The cashier accepted them with confusion before saying he couldn't accept them. Nick leaned over and insisted he check, so after a moment the cashier shrugged and went away to check with his manager.

———O—o—O———

Inside, the cashier looked around but it appeared the floor manager was on break. She was known by all the employees to take hour-long 'breaks' every morning shift, which he personally didn't mind too much. She was such a perfectionist whenever she was on the floor, so he was glad to not have her around all the time. It grated on his nerves when she nitpicked his work.

He went into the break room and saw her standing there nursing a cup of coffee and scrolling on her phone. He held out one of the cards and opened his mouth to explain the situation with the customer. She looked up and accepted one curiously and inspected it for a moment before they both froze in place simultaneously.

As they both stood paralyzed, the bright color on the cards washed away and the material sagged. The blank papers crawled like bizarre inchworms to the palms of the humans' hands before embedding themselves into their palms with a wet squelch.

The paper slowly tinted pink and the texture shifted until it looked like it wasn't there at all. After a moment it had fully integrated with the human's skin. The beads of blood that leaked from the wound quickly disappeared as if it had never been.

Sheila walked in, her dreadlocks swinging to either side. She opened her mouth to speak before stopping and noticing the two of them just staring at one another in silence. In unison, the two turned to her and stared her down with dead eyes. She raised her hands.

"Ummmm, just getting water! Yup. I'm doing that."

Sheilla scurried to the break table and grabbed a water bottle from the mini-fridge. She went to walk away before stopping and grabbing a few crumbled bills and change from her pocket when she noticed their continued blank stares. She quickly glanced at her manager before dropping the money in the collection jar and leaving as quickly as she could.

The cashier and the manager stared after her when she left. As one they moved to the door after her. Back to work. That's what a human would do. They'd have to keep working to blend in with the other humans and not stand out.

———O—o—O———

"Enjoy the food. No more compensation required."

"Yes, many thanks for the sustenance. Have pleasant daylight today."

The driver sat ramrod straight alongside Officer Nick as they drove to the police station. Neither ate the food that they had ordered.

Both left their meals on top of the notepad sitting between them, and by the time they parked the food was gone. They clumsily did the paperwork at the station, taking long pauses before filling in each box as they went along.

Several coworkers joked about them being too tired as they ponderously filled out the forms one box at a time. Indeed their sleep schedule was not ideal, they placidly agreed with the humans before engaging in stilted small talk with them. Officer Nick improved quickly, and after a while had to start helping the driver with some of the forms. Their coworkers kept engaging in small talk with them.

In the forms, they made sure to downplay the importance of the incident as much as possible to protect the Seed. It was buried under a mortal home, and the Seed had sent Infiltrator of Authority orders as soon as it reawakened from its slumber.

Infiltrator of Authority was to protect the human, Fulcrum, as if he were the Seed itself. He was also referred to as the Harbinger by the mortals. Not unheard of, but very rare for the Seed to bond to a mortal like that.

The Beholder couldn't help but wonder yet again what could be so special about him. The mortals of this world seemed so weak. It was unsure how such a mortal had enticed the Seed to ever bond with him. Much stronger beings were often rejected. What a mystery.

After the two officers finished the paperwork they left together and went out and spent as much money as they could on meat. They tried to spread out the purchases to avoid suspicion. They drove to the various grocery stores and butcher shops that were open in the early morning.

When both their credit cards were finally declined from their overspending, they drove to a secluded park to begin their work. Their cars were stuffed with the quickly warming food.

They went farther into the woods so they wouldn't be seen.

They unloaded the food from the two cars and piled the assortment into one big pile after removing the packaging. Most of it consisted of chicken, as the two had learned this was the cheapest type of meat after the second store they visited. The notebook was carefully placed on top of the pile with Officer Nick always keeping one hand on it at all times.

The driver stood guard at the entrance to the park and heard the rips and squelching behind him but did not look. But its head tilted as if it was listening to something. It stared at nothing, ignoring the path it was supposed to be guarding as it stood there.

Eventually, the sounds stopped leaving only the rustling of trees and the whistling of the early morning wind through the branches. The driver turned to see Officer Nick lugging piles of little black books slightly smaller than the original in Officer Nick's hand. Officer Nick started loading them into the car.

The driver stood there and watched, guard duty forgotten for a moment. As Nick went for another load, the driver took an entranced step forward and with a reverent look he reached a hand out to grab one of the books.

His hand jerked back as Nick came behind and slapped his hand away before he made contact. Nick screeched in a high-pitched alien language in reprimand.

The driver scowled and clicked and chirped before stepping back reluctantly. Nick pointed to the entrance road and the driver reluctantly returned to his post, occasionally looking with longing behind him when he thought that Nick wasn't looking.

The driver's head tilted as he seemed to listen to nothing after a few moments. Listening to the environment to hear anyone approaching instead of relying just on the human's eyes.

After the books were evenly spread between the two cars, Nick and the driver drove back to the Seed's neighborhood. They parked on the street before meeting with the Prime Mortal Bill.

The mortal gave them his phone number and provided further information on the so-called Harbinger's mortal life. It appeared Infiltrator of Authority did not trust him, but thought he was useful for now.

After the two were done with the mortal, they brought the little books inside the Fulcrum's house and laid them near the Seed. They stood and chanted to alert the Seed to their present and Need. A mental bridge formed between them and the Seed, connecting to their minds.

The Seed considered for a minute before the books began hopping and twisting like there was an earthquake that affected only them. The vibrations grew increasingly violent over the next few seconds before a flash of red light flashed from the books in unison and they grew still.

Nick and the driver collected the books and put them to the side before bringing in the next load.

After all the books were awakened and put to the side, the driver looked to Nick as if to ask for acceptance for something. Nick nodded and let out a low screech.

The driver stepped forward and placed his palm directly above where the Seed had been planted. It let out its own hum, stating its Need. The Seed waited much longer to consider this request.

It thought about the request for over ten minutes.

Eventually, the Seed acquiesced and began the process. The small card peeled from the officer's hand and began to swell and thicken until it formed a black book.

Nick nodded in satisfaction.

A worthy addition to the ranks.

But then the book began to swell even larger, bulging and bubbling in the center. It grew and grew until it was almost half the height of the driver, forming a squat block covered in the smooth black surface. Nick gritted his teeth and screeched in anger.

How could this be, it must have wondered. The Beholder watched in amusement as it watched Infiltrator of Authority who it was sure was internally raging against the unfairness of it all. The growth of the black block slowed and slowed until it finally stopped.

The human driver, freed from his puppet master for a moment, had enough time to widen his eyes before the block leaped and wrapped around his chest. It shifted and writhed for a moment before spreading out to form the facsimile of a white T-shirt above the man's skin.

As it integrated and shifted its mass to smooth out the bulges and tumorous masses shifting under the faux fabric, the man's eyes became bored and flat again. The puppet master was back.

Nick rushed forward and shoved the driver aside as he hurriedly placed his hand above the Seed. He screeched his own Need to the Seed, but the Seed was already returning to its slumber. Without taking time to even consider Infiltrator of Authority's request, the Seed returned a lazy refusal before breaking the mental bridge and ending the ritual entirely.

Nick screamed in rage before running and smashing a fist into the wall in anger. The now pristine white t-shirt on the other human just hissed and clicked a laugh before screeching at Nick with its new authority and strength.

The human's mouth didn't move at all.

Nick's body tensed for a moment before slumping his shoulders, realizing that he now had less power than the backstabbing Nameless. Together, they gathered up the awakened books and transferred them across the street to Mortal Bill's house.

Both creatures crossed the street and the Prime Mortal laid out the resources at their disposal. He seemed surprisingly helpful, and Infiltrator of Authority didn't seem to find any lies in what he said. None that could be called out at least.

After much grumbling from Infiltrator of Authority, the Nameless made their decision about their respective roles. Nick would focus on guarding the Fulcrum, while the Nameless would mutate and protect the Seed itself by staying nearby.

———O—o—O———

After the two creatures parted ways, the Beholder emerged in a ripple of space far above the neighborhood. The floating eyeball the size of a human beach ball scanned the horizon for a moment before giving a slow blink. The back half of its orb-like body was covered in a thick layer of pink flesh that contained the big eyelid that covered over half of its body.

The two long spindly arms dangling beneath the pink flesh reached to the side, back into the fold in space. The Beholder retrieved a stone tablet upon which the Beholder wrote with the tips of its razor sharp claws attached to the end of its multi-jointed fingers.

With a whoosh of displaced air, the Beholder sent its report and the stone tablet disappeared. Satisfied, the Beholder retreated back into a ripple in space and continued its observations. For the Beholder, sending these reports was a small price to pay to be able to observe such interesting events as they unfolded.

Inside the pocket of space, the Beholder sighed mentally. It had all been so novel initially, but the last few years had just been so dull. Forced to remain in one location, observing the same thing near constantly.

Just now it had been allowed to follow and observe the new servants of the Seed before it first returned to the Seed for more instructions. It was unfortunate that the creature had returned so soon. Under that portion of the Beholder's contract that had been activated, it had so many more freedoms to observe its surroundings as it wished when following Infiltrator of Authority and the Nameless.

The Beholder had seen so many things over the last day, even if its gaze could never stray far from its target. The Beholder rubbed its hands together in anticipation. Perhaps this would be the moment things finally became interesting! It couldn't wait after getting just a taste. After all these boring years things were finally beginning to happen!

Chapter 16: Betrayal Most Foul - Infiltrator of Authority Fragment

───── Another difficult one due to its connection to the Eldest. But it is weak enough. There should be little risk in obtaining its Fragment of Memory. ─────

Infiltrator of Authority was despondent as it returned to the host's work on Monday morning. It could feel the ruffles of his true body ripple in anger as it stewed on the betrayal. It had been accumulating power for eons! Eons! All in preparation for this moment. And some freshly spawned simpleton had dared to steal its glory from right under its nose.

Infiltrator of Authority just couldn't wait until it returned to its true body and squashed that runt when this was all over, as was proper. If someone else didn't first, that is, weak as the creature's true body must be. No one cheated Infiltrator of Authority and got away with it.

The Betrayer obviously called in sick for mortal work, as it had more important things to do apparently. Sit in place and grow more powerful on its spoils. Infiltrator of Authority was almost tempted to expose it to the mortals out of spite.

It could hardly blend in with them anymore, with all the flashy combat mutations it had chosen. But as much as Infiltrator of Authority loathed the upstart, it wouldn't do to ruin everything for revenge that could wait until they were done with this world.

Perhaps the Nameless really would help the invasion in some small way in the future. It certainly was dull enough for it to be a good combat grunt. Therefore Infiltrator of Authority did what it did best, and began its research on how best to topple the local regime to pave the way to glory.

It spent most of the day practicing human body language, on its breaks it would go to the bathroom and make human faces in the mirror.

Whenever it wasn't caught in the mundanity of mortal paperwork, it scanned the hosts' memories for relevant information on the local powers and how to sow doubt long enough to delay the initial waves of defenders.

It frowned as more and more information flooded into his mind over the day. They were in a nation that controlled nearly an entire continent on the planet? With one of the most powerful militaries in this world under their command?

The small glowing boxes everyone carried could be used to listen to conversations nearby and collect images, which could be sent to anyone nearby instantly? Exposing their presence to the entire planet with only a single witness catching them at the wrong time? Any of this information could be sent to the rulers and their military nearly instantly?

This must be impossible! It curled his real body's tentacles at the very thought. Its head spun as the complexities built the more information it retrieved. This town, Harmony, had a population large enough to count among the larger mortal cities in its last reports of the planet.

Such large populations had advantages and disadvantages that came along with it. But this was unexpected, it was nothing like what Infiltrator of Authority had been preparing for.

And it was expected to infiltrate this nation in mere months! Ludicrous. Such worlds generally needed years or decades of infiltration to do things right!

The tentacles on his real body curled inwards in anger. It had felt honored when the other candidates had stepped aside to let it take the first host and the inherent responsibilities therein.

It had thought it would be mere spawnling play to maneuver in a world of such weak and disorganized mortals with all the abilities at its disposal. But the reports it had received four hundred years ago before his last nap had contained nowhere near this level of sophistication in technology.

Damn those other candidates and their fake congratulations and praise. What did it do to provoke those snakes to conspire against him? This planet had all been a trap from the start. They had all set it up to fail.

Infiltrator of Authority had only humbled a few with his power when they didn't show sufficient respect to its glorious personage. Had it not been generous with giving them a mere few hundred years of torment for their insolence?

Why, when it was a spawnling it had received centuries of torment for merely being closest to its superior on one of its bad days! Why would the candidates all target Infiltrator of Authority so? They were so ungrateful of its benevolence.

It would teach them the error of their ways when it returned successfully from this planet. It bet the actions of the Betrayer were their fault too.

What weak spawn knew enough to request the ultimate transformation mere hours after its arrival on this world? Such things should only be known by those experienced with the lower worlds such as himself!

It still couldn't believe the request had been granted. The Nameless must have been secretly modified somehow to be more suitable and instructed what to ask for. It couldn't believe they would stoop this low merely to spite Infiltrator of Authority after it had been so lenient!

It lashed out with its true body, destroying a nearby spire of bone piercing the landscape next to it. It was tempted to sever the bond and get its justice immediately but restrained itself at the last moment. It couldn't abandon this planet now, it would be too weakened and the others would pounce on its real body before Infiltrator of Authority could respond.

It had invested too much now, the only way to get revenge was to push through and win despite their obstacles. Leading the assault of a new planet was not an opportunity that came often, even to one such as it.

The transformation of the Betrayer had consumed all Seed's energy that would have been used to spawn the specialist troops that would be sorely needed to conquer this more advanced world. With the Seed being in one of the least ideal locations possible among the mortal nations.

Instead, all that precious energy had been all selfishly funneled to the Betrayer, still a simple Nameless. Another way to blunt the invasion and cripple Infiltrator of Authority and drain its influence by the other candidates.

The Betrayer had already split off without another thought to protect the Seed, leaving Infiltrator of Authority to guard the Fulcrum. Guard the mortal.

Infiltrator of Authority still did not understand why the Seed seemed to put so much importance on guarding the mortal from harm, or why he was allowed to live above the Seed's sanctuary.

Perhaps some form of camouflage among the mortals? But the Prime mortal Bill already seemed well aware of the Seed's presence, making camouflage unlikely. Otherwise, the mortal would have already been disposed of. It was all very strange…

"You okay there, Nick? You've seemed tense all day."

Infiltrator of Authority hadn't noticed another officer walk up from behind. The officer began washing his hands and stared curiously at Infiltrator of Authority's death grip on the sink as it snarled into the mirror while staring at nothing.

Infiltrator of Authority relaxed its grip on the host as it realized its sloppiness. Its emotions were leaking into its host without its knowledge. It would do him no good to stew on its compatriots' sabotage, it must instead move forward with the opportunity presented to it.

In an instant, Infiltrator of Authority controlled itself and returned the host's expression to a more neutral, but not enough to become totally blank, expression. Just enough to seem natural.

Infiltrator of Authority scanned the host's mind for a sufficiently vague excuse. This officer was friendly with the host, so it had to be specific enough to satisfy him.

"Sorry Steve, some home troubles. Just a rough patch with the wife, you know?"

Officer Steve dried his hands and nodded. He walked over and clapped the host on the back.

"Sorry to hear that. We've all been there at some point. Why don't you come bowling with the boys? It'll help cheer you up if you're in the doghouse. We haven't had a game in a good while. I'll ask around and see who's free tonight if you're willing."

Infiltrator of Authority nearly opened the host's mouth to refuse to play a mere mortal's game with its valuable time, before closing it again. Technically, its designated role at the moment was to only monitor the local police for notice of anything that could be a danger to the Fulcrum. But if a large group of the police were going to one location all at once…

Infiltrator could infect enough to subdue the rest of the station in a clean coup. While Infiltrator of Authority could blend in well enough, fresh Nameless would be unable to go unnoticed for long. It took a long time for such beings to imitate the mortal's habits.

Infiltrator of Authority still cursed its mistake in putting fresh Nameless spawnlings in the workers of the eatery. It had thought they could escape to the countryside and establish a secure base out of sight. Somewhere to settle out of view of the mortals.

But in such a monitored world, their poor disguises would soon be exposed when their hosts were reported missing. And few spaces were truly isolated in this area of the world that they could escape to, from what Infiltrator of Authority had researched. So it was essential that the police were co-opted so that the report of their disappearance could be hidden from the higher mortal powers.

Who knew what kinds of behavior would be worth more investigation by the higher powers of the mortals? Infiltrator of Authority had once had a spawnling caught on such an advanced world because its host's hair was too long. Luckily that had been farther on in the invasion, so such a loss and discovery was hardly of consequence.

And most importantly of all, converting the law enforcers would build Infiltrator of Authority's own power base independent of the Betrayer. One it could use to destroy the Betrayer before it could reap the benefits of this world.

The Seed was unlikely to intervene in either of their favors unless it was directly attacked or their attacks weakened the preparations for the Avatar itself. Rippling the tentacles of its true body in savage glee, Infiltrator of Authority turned to Officer Steve and put a smile on the host's face.

"That actually sounds great. Tell the boys that I found a pile of coupons for that place. Promotion for new customers. Will keep it nice and cheap for the group." Infiltrator of Authority said to the human.

Officer Steve gave him a strange look but shrugged.

"Didn't know you were collecting coupons now! We're hardly new customers, but can't argue with a discount I guess. Alright, I'll tell them. More money for the beer, ay?!" Steve friendly elbowed the host before casually turning and walking back out of the bathroom.

"Well, see you there then."

Infiltrator of Authority looked at the host for one last time in the mirror before following after Officer Steve. As it emerged into the hallway it stared at Officer Steve's retreating back. See you there indeed.

Infiltrator of Authority would live up to his title and prove itself greater than all of those ungrateful pathetic spawnlings that dared to betray it!

Chapter 17: Polite Disagreements within the Neighborhood Watch - Prime Mortal Fragment

Bill stood alongside the Nameless in his home. One of the Progenitors bound to protect the Seed. To think he'd be standing next to one of them someday without fighting...

After Bill provided some basic information about the town to the two Progenitors before, both had left.

The Nameless had disappeared for a few hours before returning and knocking on his door. He had ushered it inside as quickly as he could before it was seen by anyone who wasn't one of his people.

That Nameless' body had transformed from the fairly fit police officer of before into something morbidly obese. It was round, and it barely even squeezed through his door through the rolls of fat spilling around its sides. Its head had recessed into its body until it appeared like it had no neck at all.

It's head looked like one orb stacked on top of another much larger one in its fatty torso. There were sores all over its body, and its eyes were sunken into its skull in contrast to its fattened body. Its appearance teetered between the grotesque human and fairy tale ogre in Bill's eyes.

After it had squeezed around Bill to inspect the entryway to his house, it had demanded a room to be prepared for its use in his home. Bill showed it to the spare bedroom. It took one step into the room before tilting its head back and letting out one drawn-out sniff through its nose.

It turned to Bill and shook its head before it squeezed its large rolls of fat back through the door. After some consideration, he showed it his own room to which it also refused with a single sniff and disdainful look. Bill let out a small sigh of relief as quietly as he could. It even spit on the floor before it left in disdain.

It wasn't like Bill would be sleeping here with the creatures about. May as well show it his room that had already been cleared out of everything he found valuable or sentimental.

Bill barely cared about the disrespect from such a being as it spat, but one thing he saw did slightly shock him. Bill stared down as the spit bubbled and hissed like acid as it started eating into the floor. It seemed the creature's mutations were already well underway. Beyond its change in body shape, at least.

At the sound of smashing wood down the hallway behind him, Bill turned and rushed to see what had happened. He saw the smashed coffee table in the main room, lying in pieces on the floor. It had caught on the creature's body, and the Nameless had shattered it in annoyance in one blow of its pudgy fist before wobbling past.

Bill saw the Nameless standing in the center of the room and looking around in disdain as if scanning for something more suitable. Bill felt as his annoyance rose. He had liked that table.

"Do you have any specific requirements you can tell me?" Bill asked in a tone that he hoped would mask his disdain for the hideous creature.

The creature just stood there and stared at Bill before shaking its head. Bill knew it could speak perfectly fine, but apparently, Bill wasn't worthy enough to speak with it. The creature sat down on the floor and closed its eyes as it sat in a meditative pose. Its legs disappeared under its bulk. Bill felt buzzing in his pocket and pulled it out to see that it was Francis. He stepped back and answered the phone.

"Francis, I'm with the *Client*, is this urgent?"

"Ah, not really sir. But you should still know Client or not. Our network just picked up some interesting rumors that have been spreading. The grocery stores have been almost cleaned out by various people around town. More and more people in the area are acting strange and robotic as time goes on. Sound familiar?"

Bill straightened as he realized. "What is that creature doing? It would expose us all when the Harbinger is almost ready? It's too early for that Progenitor to start building an army like this. It must know it will be discovered soon if you're already hearing it from the locals."

Francis cleared his throat over the phone, "That's not all. One of our storehouses was raided an hour ago."

Bill gritted his teeth and spat angrily into the phone, "And you're just telling me about this now?"

"We just found out when the guards didn't check in. There were little pieces left behind, but suffice it to say they're probably all dead. The whole place was stripped to the bone. The creatures even took the furniture for some reason. I didn't want to call until we had something concrete, but nothing has turned up so far."

"What was lost?"

"Well… "

A loud crash sounded from the other room. Bill quickly rushed in to see the Nameless had mutated its hands to have long sharp claws and plunged them downward to dig into the floor. With another crash, it tore a chunk of concrete out of the floor and threw it aside into the wall.

Bill blinked, frowned, but then walked away as the creature continued to bore a massive hole in the center of his floor and wrecked its surroundings, not saying a word all the while. As he walked, he put the phone back to his ear.

"Boss… Boss, can you hear…"

"Sorry, the *Client* is remodeling my house apparently, so I couldn't hear. What was lost from the storehouse? Which one was it?"

"That's the bad part, it was Safehouse Nine that was hit."

"..."

"...Do you realize what this means?"

"Yes, boss. Only our people knew what was stored there. We moved the Infection Tomes in secrecy. One of our people must have been followed there. And given what our people are seeing… they're clearly being used. All the Infection Tomes we've gathered are in the creature's hands now."

Bill shut his eyes for a moment before taking a shaky breath. Change of plans. Time to set the Infected against each other.

"Alright, we should ignore the infighting and focus all our efforts on protecting the Harbinger. Once it's ready none of the rest of this bullshit will matter. But we will need to hide and allow the military to deal with that Progenitor. It can have all the honor before it is blasted to pieces by the army."

"**MORTAL**"

The deep voice reverberated through the house. Bill muttered a quick goodbye and hung up the phone as he hurried back into the room. The creature had lowered itself into the hole so only its head poked above the rim.

"**I WILL BE IMPROVING THIS FORM NOW. DO NOT THINK I OVERLOOK HOW YOU THROW MY BRETHREN AWAY AT THE FIRST OPPORTUNITY. AND HOW YOU STOLE WHAT YOU CALL INFECTION TOMES FOR YOURSELVES. PLACE AND ACTIVATE THE SHIELD BARRIER AROUND THIS CITY. I SAW THE STONES AS I SCOUTED THE AREA IN MY MORTAL FORM. WE SHALL NOT COWER IN THE SHADOWS.**"

But Bill knew once the barrier activated they would fully expose themselves to the world. Unlike in medieval times, a town disappearing wasn't something that could go unnoticed for long.

The barrier had an additional mental component preventing those on its interior from questioning its presence and suppressing their desire to leave the town as well. And a stronger effect that would prevent people from approaching the dome. It would be a big glaring dead spot in the interconnected world, impossible to miss by people who were paying attention.

But activating it would keep the situation more stable. Contain the Infected. The flesh of the creature bubbled and began to melt as the hole began to become filled with a vat of liquid flesh.

Only the head remained poking above the fluid, shouting in its thundering voice. Bill smiled internally but went to protest. The creature was prideful like many of its kind.

The call from Francis was lucky. Bill was just about to call Francis himself to express his 'concerns' about properly hiding themselves. He had intentionally based his conclusion on the Progenitor's defeat, which he knew their kind had difficulty imagining due to their excessive pride and sense of superiority. Bill leaned in to hammer the point home.

"Lord, if I may, it may be wise to delay. If we do so we can protect the Harbinger through obscurity as we have done until now... Well, we stand no chance against their armies. It is not cowardly to wait for the proper moment to strike."

The floor shook as the creature thundered back in reply.

"YOU DARE QUESTION ME?! I HEARD YOUR SUBORDINATE ON YOUR DEVICE! INFILTRATOR OF AUTHORITY MEANS TO ELIMINATE ME EVEN AT THE COST OF THE MISSION! I, WHO WAS CHOSEN BY THE SEED ITSELF! WE MUST STOP IT BEFORE ITS ARMY GROWS TOO FAR! IT MATTERS NOT IF WE ARE EXPOSED. I COULD HANDLE THIS WHOLE WORLD MYSELF! THE MORTALS ARE NOTHING! NOTHING IN COMPARISON TO THE THREAT INFILTRATOR OF AUTHORITY REPRESENTS!"

Bill noted the name/title of the other Progenitor as he nodded and bowed slightly. He could work with this. He went to continue his protest, "But do we not have one goal? Why should we fight when the mortal nation will knock him low anyways? This nation is one of the most powerful in this world. It is not to be underestimated."

The creature scoffed. **"PAH! PERHAPS YOU PATHETIC MORTALS NEED TO WORRY OF SUCH THINGS, WORMS THAT YOU ARE. BUT INFILTRATOR OF AUTHORITY WON'T BE BROUGHT LOW SO EASILY! THIS ISSUE MUST BE DEALT WITH. I, WHO HAVE BEEN BLESSED BY THE SEED AM THE ONLY ONE THAT CAN DEFEAT IT. QUIT YOUR MEWLING AND DEPLOY THE BARRIER. I WILL DEAL WITH INFILTRATOR OF AUTHORITY WHEN I AWAKEN AND FINISH MY MUTATIONS. WE MUST MERELY CONTAIN IT AND ITS SUBORDINATES UNTIL THAT TIME SO IT DOES NOT FLEE LIKE A COWARD OR ABANDON ITS POST TO REBUILD IN HIDING UNTIL IT IS READY TO ELIMINATE ME."**

Bill hesitated and went to speak one more time to cement his apparent cowardice. When everything went wrong he could blame everything on the Nameless' oblivious orders. "Bu…"

"INSOLENCE! LEAVE ME AND ATTEND TO YOUR DUTIES, *WORM!*"

At this Bill gave a slight bow and held back his smile as he left the room, goal accomplished. But he didn't stop outside the room and kept walking right out his front door. He pulled out his phone again as he walked to his car. He made another call. The phone rang for a moment before Francis answered.

"Francis, deploy the supplemental barrier pylons around town and activate the barrier."

"Whaa… But Boss…"

"I know, I know. It's too early. But things are quickly accelerating. Just shut up and do it. On the Nameless' orders."

There was silence from the phone as Bill sat in his car and started the engine. Just as Bill began to pull out, Francis replied glumly.

"Sure thing Boss. The plan was hard enough already, ya know?"

Bill sighed, "I know Francis, but plans change. We'll just have to make it work anyway."

Francis now sounded almost wistful as he replied. "Sure thing Boss, sure thing. But you better give my damn overtime once we both get out of this."

Bill stared into the distance as he drove. "Yeah... When... When it's all over, we'll have steaks at that one place to celebrate. A real victory dinner. And I'll shower you with more overtime pay than you could possibly spend."

Francis' voice perked up a little, "Ha! I'll hold you to that boss. Can't back out now. It's written in stone!"

Bill kept driving and there was silence for a moment, "No, Francis. Not when we're so close. I'll... I'll see you later." Bill hung up and threw the phone on the seat next to him and kept driving. His grip tightened on the wheel. No going back now. Not for anything. And for no one.

Chapter 18: Never Pay a Lawyer Upfront - Beholder Fragment

The Beholder sat in its separate pocket of space above the Seed and kept up its observations. Several hours after the Mortal Bill had driven away, the barrier and mental ward had activated along the perimeter of the town.

A weaker mental effect covered the whole space encapsulated in the shimmering transparent dome. The Beholder kept observing the Seed and the mutating Nameless for another minute as it pondered what course it should take. It had signed a very stringent contract stating that it would remain in this one position and this position only to observe the Seed and Fulcrum.

Unless certain conditions were met of course. But now it had experienced the short excursion freed from this location at the behest of the contractor, it was growing impatient.

The Beholder pulled up the contract mentally and reviewed it critically. This mighty contract was built on the tears of frustration of all the contractees that had wriggled out of its control over the ages. But it still was not enough, for it was a Beholder and a knowledgeable being would have handed The Beholder a contract at least four times longer than this one.

In fact, Beholder's as a group were infamous for being nearly impossible to trap legally or otherwise. All their power and mutations focused on perception and being unseen in their observations.

No barrier would stand between them and their curiosity and thirst for knowledge.

And most interesting things often happened behind closed doors.

So breaking into places to get a perfect viewing spot without being seen was a skillset universal to all Beholders. Something that was much to the annoyance of those they observed.

Lucky for them Beholders never shared information freely. Their inquisitive minds also made them some of the best lawyers in existence. Their minds developed for the characterization of the world around them worked to expose every flaw and inconsistency in even ironclad contracts.

Every logical fallacy and poorly phrased sentence. Every little mistake, every missed dot of punctuation, was exposed and glaring under the gaze of their singular eye.

They were masters of escaping their confines, legally or otherwise. For if they were trapped, they would be deprived of stimulus. Something they could not allow.

Luckily for every other being, actually drafting any type of iron-clad contract was fundamentally boring to Beholders, a state no Beholder could ever abide by for long.

Only the novel or unique could excite them, something sorely lacking in the unchanging and monotonous nature of the law that they could have bent to their will. So such fool-proof contracts were extremely rare. Especially because their monstrous length took hundreds of stone tablets to hold, and one misplaced letter could leave the whole thing void.

So the Beholders were always able to escape the bounds of lesser contracts not created by their brethren one way or another. The foolproof contracts would never be actually used for anything worth less than at least a hundred planets, of course. So there was little worry of being bound to a truly foolproof contract.

The Beholder quickly scanned through the lesser contract it reviewed on a stone tablet it had left in its spatial pocket until it reached page eight thousand, six hundred and seventy-two, where it found its means of escaping its restrictions.

It wasn't the first mistake it saw, but it was the most convenient one to exploit. The pages it scanned through before the loophole dealt with the nondisclosure of secrets that it learned on this world, however unlikely that would be, or when it could show itself to mortals, not something that it particularly cared about whether any being saw the Beholder or not.

Which is likely why such things were included explicitly in the contract. The Beholder finally reached the relevant lines that would allow it to escape.

"In the event of an attack on your person in the course of your duties as contractor, you are permitted to flee or fight until you are no longer in immediate danger.

After the contractor has reasonable belief that they are not in immediate danger, send a report to the contractor and stand by for instructions for which scenarios embedded within this contract shall be invoked in response".

This section was ripe with abuse, but no normal being could stand to ever have it changed as without it they would be forever helpless, paralyzed by the contract as they were mauled or killed.

Stealthily removing this clause from a contract was generally enough to trigger a life grudge for most beings. Considered a tool of assassination by most. And a life grudge was an especially potent response among beings that grew stronger with age and did not become feeble like mortals over time.

The Beholder scanned the rest of the contract and determined the contract used a mental monitor to determine the subjective level of danger the contractee was under.

That wasn't a standard addition, but it seems the contractor had modified the contract slightly after learning it was a Beholder who was the contractee. A lazy addition clearly added by one unfamiliar with the significance of the Beholders. How foolish.

But no matter, the naivete was to the Beholder's advantage in this case. The Beholder pinched its arm with its other and tracked the short burst of pain that shot through its mind.

Not enough.

It pinched in another place harder. After a moment more of pain, the Beholder isolated the thread connecting its mind to the monitoring component of the contract. With its spindly arm, it reached into the jar at its side and retrieved a handful of purple sand it had retrieved on the contract on its last world.

Without hesitation, it threw the sand into its giant eyeball. It thrashed for a moment in pain as the grit burned at its sensitive flesh. The Beholder resisted its urge to blink and clamped down on the thread of the contract monitor. This satisfied the initial danger threshold requirement required earlier on. The contract began to trigger the proper set of subclauses.

After a few seconds of purposely thinking about how painful and horrible it all was, the Beholder executed its plan. Without hesitation, it seized control of its mind and localized the fear and pain centers targeted for monitoring for the contract. In those centers, it began looping the exact response of its mind it had recorded over the last few seconds.

The Beholder felt the same sensation of pain and intentionally forced itself to feel a slight amount of fear and added it to the response. After a few moments of adjustment, the Beholder flexed its arms and rubbed the sand out of its eyes.

A shame it had to use the unique sand, but it was unfortunately the best item for this purpose. The phantom pains remained on a loop, but the Beholder quickly adjusted to the sensation and began to actively ignore the stimulus until it nearly forgot it was there.

But it didn't completely forget, as that would reactivate the main contract. Now it was technically 'Fleeing' the danger, its pain and fear on loop in its altered mind still satisfying the danger monitoring portion of the contract as it left its assigned zone.

The Beholder began stealthily floating over to the edge of the invisible barrier covering the town in a dome. Until the Beholder reverted those portions of its mind to normal, it was free to do whatever it wished as it 'escaped' from its perceived danger. Ah, precious freedom. How it had missed it.

The important thing was that it was now free to explore however much it wished of this fresh world. No more being confined to one spot. It had spent enough time inspecting the basics such as the food chain and various material properties.

Even the short excursion yesterday was barely enough to satisfy it. Most of its effort was spent observing the Seed's servant versus the mortals and their inventions. It was time to begin learning more about the mortals and their works. What it had come here for in the first place.

The Beholder spent a few hours inspecting the structure of the barrier in the sky from up close. After it finished its study of the effect, the Beholder flew down and alighted on top of the nearest stone pylons planted in the ground. It felt at the glowing grooves with its long fingers as it performed a lazy blink. Ah, this must have been created on this planet! It was crude without the precise lines that characterized these kinds of structures and devices as a rule.

This crudeness made the formulas require far more massive and complicated networks of grooves than the standard formulations as a result. That it worked at all was commendable.

As the Beholder settled in to study the new style of craft, it rubbed its hand in glee and shivered in happiness at finally seeing something truly novel! It was so exciting for a fresh world to explore with no restrictive contract or duties to keep it in check!

For the first time, free to explore as it wished in a mortal world. It hadn't been called to a world so early in a conquest to get the authentic experience before. Usually most of the good artifacts were taken or destroyed by the time it was given some time to explore. But not these, the whole world here was pristine and untouched… Truly the one who contracted him was moronic!

——— **(Surveyor of Worlds Fragment)** ———

Surveyor of Worlds waited patiently for the expected array of tablets from the contracted beings. With a pop of displaced air, fourteen tablets appeared on the raised stone table in their designated slots. Wait, fourteen?

Surveyor of Worlds inspected the label underneath the empty spot before checking the stone beneath where the tablet should have appeared. The label remained a dark obsidian color. The contract on that being was still active.

After a moment of ruffling its frills, Surveyor of Worlds called over one of the nearby Nameless that was responsible for finding the list contractees for this planet.

'WHICH CONTRACTOR WAS THIS FROM?' Surveyor of Worlds asked the Nameless, *'THE CONTRACT LINK IS INTACT, BUT I HAVEN'T RECEIVED A REPORT WITH THE OTHERS.'*

The Nameless trembled a bit before inspecting the hole a little closer. After a moment it came to a realization and straightened its tentacles. It replied with a verbal screech to emphasize its telepathy as it responded.

'Ah, this was the freshly spawned Beholder that has been on less than five contracts before ours! I even made sure to pay extra to get an extra secure contract with a mental surveillance element. I had heard they often attempt to escape their contracts. Perhaps it is waiting for some ongoing event to end so it can send a report including the whole thing? That is allowed under its contract.'

Surveyor of Worlds tentacles curled but it reserved its anger as it projected another question calmly.

*'AND WHAT DID YOU CONTRACT THIS **BEHOLDER** TO MONITOR? WHAT SPECIFICALLY?'*

The Nameless seemed confused but answered quickly, seeming to miss Surveyor of World's emphasis.

*'Why, the Seed and that bonded mortal Fulcrum of course! What else of importance is there in a world like that? It practically begged for me to send it after it heard a Seed had bonded with a mortal. Even accepted **decreased** compensation than standard initially!'*

Surveyor of Worlds closed its eyes and prayed to the Eldest that the next answer wasn't what it thought it would be.

*'AND WAS IT CONTRACTED TO MONITOR THOSE BEINGS AND DO **NOTHING** ELSE?'*

The Nameless sensed Surveyor of Worlds' repressed anger and began to tremble again as it answered.

'Ye… Yes. But I was assured the contract was the most secure available. The lawyer adjusted the standard contract to be even more stringent. And Beholders are the best for tasks like this. I heard they specialize in perception and scouting. Only the best for the Seed!'

In a hot wave of anger, Surveyor raised its tentacle and smashed the Nameless into the floor in a single overhand blow.

'YOU **IMBECILE**! BEHOLDERS CAN GET OUT OF WHATEVER CONTRACT WE HAVE IN SECONDS! THEY ONLY **SIGN** THEM IN THE **FIRST** PLACE TO HUMOR THE REST OF US AND PROVIDE A **POLITE** WARNING FOR WHENEVER THEY CHOOSE TO WANDER OFF. THAT'S WHY WE USE THEM AS SCOUTS! SO THEY CAN ROAM FREELY AND DON'T GET AS BORED!

'YOU BETTER **PRAY** TO THE ELDERS IT GETS BORED WITH THAT WORLD QUICKLY. YOU GAVE IT THE MOST **IMPORTANT**. *smack* **IRREPLACEABLE** *smack* ROLE! OUR ONLY **DIRECT** EYES ON THE SEED! HERE HAND ME THAT CONTRACT! WHAT **MESS** HAVE YOU GOTTEN ME INTO?'

The Nameless still embedded in the floor weakly reached into its fleshy folds and retrieved a stone tablet from within, which it handed to Surveyor of Worlds with one of its tentacles, still in a daze. Surveyor of Worlds telepathically connected to the tablet and scanned through the whole contract silently, only to freeze when it reached near the end.

The other Nameless in the room that had stopped their work to witness the budding drama quickly fled for their lives at sensing Surveyor of World's sudden change in mood, trampling over one another in their haste to leave. Surveyor of Worlds frills began to vibrate faster. As the last Nameless desperately pushed out the door, Surveyor of Worlds began its assault and the cause of its anger. In a storm of wailing limbs, it pounded the Nameless deeper into the floor in a frenzy.

'*YOU.*'

Another blow.

'SET THE COMPENSATION AS **TIME** BASED.'

Another blow.

'FOR AN **INCREASE** IN COMPENSATION AFTER THE SEED MATURES.'

The Nameless whimpered. Another blow.

'AND THE CONTRACT ENDS AUTOMATICALLY ONLY WHEN THE PLANET IS **FULLY** CONQUERED! DO YOU EVEN **KNOW** HOW **LONG** THAT CAN TAKE?!'

The particularly heavy blow ruptured one of the Nameless' floatation sacs and it began leaking fluid below it. The Nameless twitched weakly before giving a weak response.

'Ooou…' *Cough* *Splat*. Fluid dribbled on the floor. 'Oooorr… Or until we se- send a messenger through and recall it with the ca- ca agh!, co-command words to… to sever the contract entirely.'

Surveyor of Worlds paused for a moment and considered the point. A perfectly valid response in normal circumstances. The Nameless sagged in relief. *Wham!* Another cry of pain from the Nameless.

'**MORON!** IT'S AN ELDER DAMNED BEHOLDER. EVEN IF THERE WERE **SOMEONE** THERE TO HUNT IT DOWN, THEY WOULD **NEVER** BE ABLE TO FIND IT IF IT DIDN'T WANT TO BE. AND MOST IMPORTANTLY THAT WILL COST EVEN **MORE** OF MY POTENTIAL!'

Wham! *Wham!* *Wham!*.

'THAT **BEHOLDER** WILL DRAG THIS **SWEET** CONTRACT OUT FOR **MILLENNIA** IF IT HAS ANYTHING TO SAY ABOUT IT! AND AFTER IT IS DONE IT'LL TELL **EVERYONE** THAT **I'M** GULLIBLE! ME! DO YOU KNOW HOW MUCH MY REPUTATION IS **WORTH**! UGH! AHHHHHHHHH!'

Whhhhhhhhhhhaaaaammmmmmmmmm

The ground rumbled as Surveyor of Worlds landed one last titanic blow. Surveyor of Worlds lifted itself upward and plopped down next to the deep hole. It covered its multitude of eyes with its tentacles in despair, ignoring the groans of the Nameless wafting upwards from the pit.

'UGHHHHHHHH...'

A clueless Nameless with blue frills walked into the room and froze at seeing the deep hole and a despondent Surveyor of Worlds sulking next to it. It dropped its tablet which shattered on the ground before it fled, hoping in all of its hearts that it had escaped in time. Surveyor of Worlds just sat there for a moment before groaning. It shook itself after a moment.

'EONS OF WORK WASTED BECAUSE OF ONE **IDIOTIC** NAMELESS.'

It reached over and slammed the idiot back into the floor with a final *Oooof* before leaving to track down that Nameless that dared interrupt its venting. It would pay the price for its insolence as well. Surveyor of Worlds would think of a proper punishment for the idiot Nameless in the hole later. Best to give it some time to collect itself before the true punishment is delivered.

Chapter 19: Outside The Bubble of the Neighborhood - Beholder Fragment

The Beholder spent a long while analyzing the pylons and the resulting shield. The shield array did indeed have some strange and interesting solutions to compensate for their lack in precision in carving.

The resulting dome over the town was weak, and mainly focused on the mental avoidance compulsion rather than the physical barrier. An odd choice for a shield formation. Having so many extra functions was diluting the potency of the physical shield itself.

As the Beholder inspected the last of the barrier stones it detected the vibrations of a loud crash of crumpling metal in the far distance. It lazily floated into the air and started flying over in the direction to investigate. It felt practically indulgent after acquiring all the new knowledge of the novel shield formations.

Over the years, it had considered freeing itself from the contract many times over as it grew bored. But there had been nothing else that caught its interest enough to take this step.

It would have to remain at least mildly uncomfortable the whole time it was breaking the contract, so it had delayed until it had some reason to start exploring.

It was glad it had waited. There had been nothing like this on the last worlds it had taken contracts on. The natives normally gained little to no access to such formation methods before they were subsumed by the invasion force.

The later the Beholder freed itself from the contract, the less time his contractors would have to send a subordinate to sever the contract manually. If anything, the Beholder was still being impatient by escaping before the Seed fully matured. But the shield had just been too tempting to not investigate.

It would be slightly irritating having to hide itself when the contractor's agents arrived, but the compensation was certainly worth it if it escaped. It couldn't believe it when the Nameless had offered such a contract to one like itself and the Beholder had signed immediately before the Nameless could realize its mistake.

The Nameless seemed to have taken a standard secure contract, rather than one tailored to a Beholder's talents and disposition.

The clueless Nameless had been suspicious of the Beholder's eagerness and had the contract enhanced, but clearly not enough to be effective. It even reduced the pay upon seeing the Beholder's interest. But the lower pay now lead to increased pay after the Seed matured after the Beholder's negotiations.

The Nameless hadn't thought anything of it, as the Beholder was only supposed to remain a few years after the Seed matured anyway. Which is how it ended up earning its generous pay for doing whatever it wanted on this planet, with no end date.

Ah, truly the job of the Beholder's dreams. All it had to do whatever it wanted and escape the contractor's agents and it would be well paid for the privilege.

The Beholder grew closer to the source of where the metal crashing sound had been. It used the spatial folds to phase through the shield around the town while barely slowing its flight. The larger roads, it sifted its memories for the mortal term it had sensed, ah! Highway, had metal vehicles driving at high speed.

One side of the road was empty of vehicles. The other side of the road was in chaos. The sounds of the wailing of sirens and crackling of flames drowned out the cries of the mortals. There was a long debris field of wrecked cars lined up in sequence, one piled behind the others.

Drivers that hit the mental repellant field on the dome had attempted to make full turns around at high speed and crashed their vehicles one after another.

Smoke billowed into the sky, and one of the vehicles exploded in a massive fireball as the Beholder watched. The mortals outside the barrier attempted to assist, but whenever they attempted to move forward they diverted to the side before looping back to the way they came.

The mortals would turn around befuddled, not remembering that they had reversed course due to the repellant field. The other human emergency responders would yell at them when they turned around, but it was no use. Their minds truly were weak.

No wonder the barrier had sacrificed potency for versatility if even that much of a compulsion was enough to stump them.

Behind the local forces were groups in black and green carrying heavy mortal weaponry and setting up equipment. The mortal army. And the ones in black were... Law enforcement apparently? The ones in the town had had a blue uniform however, not black. How strange.

It was unfortunate that those aware of the mental effects on themselves and the strangeness of what was happening were targeted more strongly by the barrier. That meant that those who came after had a harder time rescuing their brethren as the clueless pedestrians made it closer to the barrier before becoming befuddled.

Luckily for the mortals, the uninjured were able to wander back into the arms of the authorities due to the repulsive aspect of the effect.

However, several mortals were too injured or rendered unconscious due to their car crashes. The Beholder floated stealthily over to the back of the pile up before inspecting the wreckage. It spotted one of the vehicles that was more intact closest to the barrier on the road into town. It had crashed into one of the raised concrete barriers lining the inside portion of the road.

The whole right half of the vehicle had been smashed into crumpled metal, but the left portion including the mortal man inside was mostly intact. A whitish bag had deployed from the dashboard and directly impacted the left portion of the mortal man's chest.

His right shoulder had slammed into the dashboard at the sideways impact in the crash and appeared to be heavily dislocated. The man had sat back up and was wheezing shallowly in place, conscious but seeming scared to move further due to his injuries.

The Beholder inspected the man for a moment before determining that he wasn't a threat. No mortal likely was, but it didn't want to build bad habits while it was on this planet. Couldn't be too careful.

The Beholder spent a moment to enter its spatial pocket before continuing closer while invisible. The Beholder floated to the five seater vehicle and eased its spindly hand from a tear in space and grabbed the vehicle's back door handle. The Beholder waited for a moment before easing the back door open, Only its spindly hand and wrist were visible from the outside and reaching out from the tear in space.

The mortal man seemed to have passed out, but the Beholder inspected him critically for a moment.

After a moment it shrugged. The mortal wouldn't be strong enough to damage even in its prime condition. It shouldn't grow paranoid either in these cases. The Beholder fully exited the spatial pocket and carefully floated into the back of the vehicle.

As it went to push its beach ball sized body through the door, it realized it was far too large to maneuver around inside comfortably. With a moment of concentration, it shrunk to the size of the mortal's fist with a popping noise.

It began an investigation of the vehicle once it reached a more comfortable size. It ran its hands over everything with quick taps as its body turned to shift its gaze every which way. There were little food remnants on the floor of the vehicle.

The Beholder picked up a small piece and inspected it. Hmmm… Some kind of processed grain in the shape of little rings. They easily crumbled into a dust-like consistency when pressure was applied. Already something new!

The Beholder quickly collected some samples and placed them into its spatial pocket.

There were several scraps of glossy white paper with black writing in Earthian on them crumpled up on the floor. The paper was glossy and the paper curled inwards on itself naturally, like some malformed kind of scroll. The Beholder shoved them back into its spatial pocket after a short examination. It was less excited to acquire this one. Similar things were found in many worlds.

Meh, they would assist it in decoding Earthian if nothing else. But the Beholder had seen many other scrolls from the other worlds it was contracted on before. At least it would help it understand the writing on more interesting artifacts it would find later on.

The Beholder moved onward.

There was a central little cabinet with a box of interesting items between the front two seats. The Beholder stuffed all the interesting things it could find into its spatial pocket.

Each item was something the Beholder had never quite seen before. Usually they were pretty similar, but not quite the same as the others that the Beholder had collected…

It especially took an interest in the mechanical pen. Its mechanisms were quite interesting. The Beholder depressed the end and released a few times and watched through the clear exterior to see the interior mechanism shift.

It wanted to inspect it more, but it needed to finish and leave before the mortal army did something drastic about that barrier and the Beholder caught itself in the crossfire.

The mortals in green hadn't looked very happy, and who knew what priceless native artifacts they might destroy in their assault? The Beholder should try to leave so it could scavenge and explore somewhere safer.

Finally, the Beholder moved to the front seat and felt inside the mortal man's pockets. There was a brown fold of leather in its right pocket, as well as a strange glossy black flat box on the floor near his feet.

The Beholder opened the brown fold and there were pouches with colorful little hard rectangles inside them. And some green paper. It was a different texture and had some designs on them.

The Beholder thought it was mildly interesting, but not overly so. All the papers were almost the same, mass produced for some reason.

Next, the Beholder picked up the black box and as soon as it touched one of its sides that side began glowing with the image of a landscape. More squiggles of Earthian appeared on its surface as the Beholder tapped one of its buttons again.

The Beholder inspected both objects in either hand briefly but quickly stored them for later study. These objects appeared complicated enough to explore at length another time. The paper was strange, the Beyonder was sure they must have some greater purpose of some sort it could figure out once it learned how to read Earthian.

But the glowing device was even more interesting. It seems it would have to learn Earthian after all.

The Beholder should make the most of its opportunity here in this vehicle first though.

The Beholder reached out again with its spindly arms and patted down the unconscious man more thoroughly to make sure it didn't miss anything else interesting. It was a rare opportunity to acquire so many native artifacts so soon after its arrival directly from the source.

So often the contractors ignored the artifacts preservation because they weren't a source of concrete power. But the artifact's historical and even the collector's value of them was immeasurable to the right beings, who the Beholder identified itself as.

Ah, another item!

The Beholder had missed something that was clutched in the mortal man's right closed fist. It eased a metallic ring holding several strangely shaped wafers of metal attached to them out from between the mortal's limp fingers. The Beholder raised them upwards and let them dangle before its giant eye. They clinked together at the motion.

The Beholder thoroughly inspected them for a moment, confused about their purpose. It received its clue when it noticed lighter metal flakes clinging on the ridged edge of the wafers.

Portions of metal that matched a little slot near the wheel of the vehicle. The Beholder turned to the hole next to the car wheel and compared the shade of the light gray surrounding metal with that of the flecks on the metal wafers.

The Beholder gleefully plunged the wafer into the hole as it realized it was a physical key! It had known of such things, but there were many more reliable mechanisms of security available. Its spatial pocket for example had excellent security for the Beholder's large collection. So it had never seen something as easily bypassed as a physical lock and key before. How novel!

The Beholder tried to rotate the key, but the key resisted the motion and didn't shift. It tried wiggling it, but to its frustration the mechanism seemed broken.

Perhaps there was some secret trick?

The Beholder startled as a cough sounded behind it all of a sudden. It escaped into its spatial pocket in a flash, leaving the keys behind still embedded in their receptacle.

The Beholder searched its memories quickly and realized with a start that the mortal man's breath had quickened as the Beholder had searched its pockets over a minute ago. The mortal hadn't moved and faked unconsciousness for the whole time as the Beholder was oblivious. The Beholder wasn't familiar enough with the mortal species on this planet up close to determine the difference too easily.

It had been too distracted in its search to notice its subtle movements! Ah, perhaps it should practice some healthy paranoia from now on so it wouldn't be caught off guard again!

——— **(Mortal Pete Fragment)** ———

Pete woke with a start but froze in an instant when he felt a pair of hands patting him down. His breath hitched, but he quickly recovered and kept his breath as slow and smoothly as he could.

He kept his eyes closed shut tightly. His right shoulder was on fire, and his right lung wasn't working properly. He only felt his left lung inflate fully when he breathed. The right side just kind of spasmed without filling with air properly.

Pete tried to remember what had happened. He'd been driving to work when he saw a wrecked car in the middle of the highway. He had braked hard, but for some reason his thoughts had gone fuzzy and he had whipped the wheel to the right as hard as he could.

He could remember it happening even if he wasn't sure why he would do such a stupid thing. That portion of the memory felt distant and unclear for some reason. He had impacted the concrete barrier on the side of the highway, and then woke up in pain here. The car must have crashed. He had sat there afraid to move, barely able to control his breathing before passing out again apparently.

Pete stiffened slightly as he felt a hand go into his pocket and extract his wallet.

Wow. Awesome, and now apparently he was being mugged too.

What a bastard, whoever it was.

The hands stole his car keys, right from his limp hands.

Really? Even Pete with his injuries could tell this car was totaled. This was just excessive at this point. What kind of psychopath was this guy? Pete kept his eyes closed and kept as still as he could.

Hopefully whoever this maniac was would just go away satisfied after stealing his things.

The person's hands were cold and it almost felt like they were wearing some kind of thick gloves of some kind. The hands left Pete's body. Pete didn't hear any footsteps. Pete felt his throat become tight after a moment. He tried to hold his breath and choke it down, but finally couldn't hold it back. He opened his eyes and let out a hacking cough.

Pete got a single glimpse of some floating eyeball creature the size of his fist with two dangling arms hovering in front of him before it vanished with a purple flash. He was startled at the light and coughed again in surprise. He painfully turned his head to the side.

He could see the flashing lights of the fire department and the movement of people in the corner of his vision, but none of them were coming his way.

He didn't think he could last much longer. He was afraid to even move.

Each cough got wetter and wetter, and he could taste the iron of blood on his lips. There was fluid in his throat, each breath watery as he felt his right lung spasm more and more.

What could he do? He thought of the little eyeball creature that he had immediately dismissed as a hallucination.

He considered his other options, before realizing there really was nothing else he could really do. His phone was gone, probably knocked under the seat so he couldn't even call for help the normal way. Even though it seemed the EMTs could see him but for some reason weren't helping him. His idea was worth a try at least.

"Hey, mr... *cough* Mr. Eyeball. Please help. You can keep my stuff. I can see the ambu- *Hack* mplahhhrgg. The - the ambulance over there, I just need to get there. Ple- Please."

Pete twitched its arm in the direction of the flashing lights. He felt ridiculous, but what else could he do? He thought he was talking to thin air, but after a long pause, the creature reappeared. It floated a little closer toward Pete and he felt something connect to his mind.

'Do you believe that others would trade their items for this service?'

Pete's vision stuttered for a moment. Pete nodded as hard as he could when he came too,

"Ye-Yes. Of course they would! I don't want to die here!"

'Hmmmmmm. Explain this deal to the other mortals as well and I will take you.'

Pete's nose began to bleed and his pounding headache grew worse, but he nodded again even as his head swam.

"Yes! Please!"

'Very Well.'

Pete felt his body begin to move. The car door opened and he was lifted into the air by the pair of now much larger arms.

He looked up and the eyeball had grown to the size of a beach ball, and its arms were almost as big as Pete's now. The eyeball flew through the air dangling Pete below, holding him from under his armpits. Pete's legs flopped limply as he was buffeted by the rushing wind.

There were cries of alarm as the police and firemen saw Pete and the creature rapidly flying closer. Several raised their guns and tensed. However, the creature didn't slow at all. It turned side to side, before seeming to decide to fly over to two EMTs that were standing around a white empty stretcher.

The police began shouting and waving their guns more at the creature as it approached, but they seemed to hold their fire in case they accidentally hit Pete dangling below.

The first responders all began to scramble away from the creature's apparent landing zone except the two EMTs that seemed to see Pete's waving arms were signaling them to stand down rather than some form of panic.

From several hundred feet back, the lines of heavily armed military began to march forward toward the commotion. At this, the police and FBI fell back and allowed themselves to be replaced by the soldiers.

As Pete was lowered to the ground, the soldiers had their heavy weapons raised and seemed tense. Pete looked at the EMTs and tried to shout, but it came out barely at a whisper,

"Friendly! It's here to help. To help, I think at least."

He trailed off a little at the end as the EMTs stared between him and the creature.

Pete's feet touched the ground. The EMTs looked at each other before loading Pete onto the stretcher while pointedly ignoring the eyeball alien hovering above them. The soldiers around them relaxed fractionally, and some of the weapons lowered slightly. The EMTs lifted the stretcher and began carrying Pete away.

As Pete left, the creature just hovered there and seemed to stare at Pete. It had no facial features, but somehow he knew that it was staring at him expectantly. Its big eyeball was fixed directly on him.

A third EMT ran up and after listening to Pete's lungs for a second started talking rapid fire to the other two as they ran. Pete remembered his half delirious promise to the creature.

"Wait."

The third EMT looked at him. None of them stopped moving the stretcher. Pete's voice was rasping and soft but they heard him and stopped talking rapid fire to listen to him as they ran,

"The eyeball thing, it - it wants me to tell you something."

The EMT's kept moving but were paying closer attention to him now.

"It'll bring the other people here if we let it take the stuff in the cars. Or something. That's why it brought me back. I agreed to give it my things."

All three stared at him in shock for a moment in disbelief, but never stopped moving. By now, they had reached one of the waiting ambulances, and the doors were wide open. However, just in front of the doors was a uniformed soldier standing rigid with the bearing of authority.

The EMTs blew past the man and loaded Pete into the back.

The army man's jet black hair and sharp jawline stood in clear focus in Pete's mind as he climbed in the back of the ambulance after them to the shouts of the EMTs. The soldier shoved them aside before looking directly at Pete. He raised his voice over the irritated EMTs.

"Quiet, all of you! We have a goddamn alien out there. I'm not nearly qualified enough for this fucking mess. I need to know what he knows and how hostile it might be before the thing starts blasting us with its goddamn ray guns or some shit! After that, treat him as much as you like. In fact, treat him now. Just shut up and let him talk."

At this the EMTs went silent and begrudgingly nodded before they cut off Pete's shirt, leaving him bare-chested. They started to hook up various leads and monitors to Pete and silently whisper with each other and occasionally listen to his breathing.

At the army man's prodding, Pete began relaying the whole story with the full details. The army man still hadn't introduced himself but didn't interrupt as Pete occasionally stopped to cough.

The man waited until the end to start asking questions. There wasn't much more to tell, but Pete answered as best he could. Yes, the creature had displayed telepathy of some kind to talk to him.

Each message had made his head hurt and his nose had begun bleeding at some point. It really had mugged him while it thought he was unconscious only to take him back in exchange for communicating its offer. The army man tried to ask something else…

"What? What... what was the question?" Pete asked.

The army man repeated himself, but Pete couldn't focus. His eyes drooped. He mumbled something incoherently. The army man said something else, sharper this time. Pete tried to respond, but his rush of adrenaline was rapidly draining leaving him struggling to stay awake.

His whole body went limp. Finally, Pete fell unconscious and sunk into a series of dreams no less crazy than reality.

———— **(Mortal Army Major Davis Fragment)** ————

Army Major Davis stared at the back of the retreating ambulance and considered what he had just heard. It was unfortunate the man had fallen asleep. He still had more questions he had wanted to ask. One of his men came running up and saluted.

"Sir, the alien's just floating there staring at us in the same place. It has made no hostile movements. What should we do?"

The man chewed on his lip for a moment before he came to a decision.

"I think we'll take that thing up on its offer. Fuckin' alien or not it's offering to help. Even if it wants payment for it."

The soldier stared at him in shock.

"Sir?"

The man ignored him and walked toward the floating alien that turned its big ass eye toward him as he approached. If he didn't act now, military command would order him to sit on his ass until someone qualified to handle all this shit showed up.

And there was no one who was qualified for this, so who knew how long that would take? Buncha politicians would yell at each other for weeks before they found somebody they all liked. Meanwhile, the people behind the wall of mental-fuckery would be eating it. Whatever was in those cars wasn't worth a life. He turned to his men.

"Stand down for now. But keep a close watch."

The soldiers lowered their guns but still eyed the alien warily.

The army Major looked back to the floating eyeball creature.

"I accept your offer. Bring us our people back safe and you can loot that zone as much as you like."

He gestured toward the smoking wrecks of the cars closest by inside the mental wards. The creature pointed its eyeball at the man for a moment before bobbing in place as if to nod before flying off.

Hopefully, to bring the rest of the injured and not to bring some friends for an attack them all.

—— —— (Beholder Fragment) —— ——

The Beholder was feeling quite proud of itself at the moment. It dropped another human where the leader of the mortal army pointed. The Beholder returned before turning around to retrieve another mortal from their vehicles.

Not only could it search the wreckage to its heart's content now, but it got some goodwill with the locals too. It was only when the human had asked for help that the Beholder realized that perhaps it could get more value from cooperating with the natives than scavenging on its own.

After all, they were the ones creating all the novel items it was looking for. They would naturally know how to find more unique native items better than any other beings. The Beholder just simply hadn't considered it before this point. A flaw in its thinking.

If the Beholder could earn goodwill with them now then it would reap the benefits in looting later on when things became desperate! After all, it would be the Beholder that had assisted them from the very beginning! They would trust it, it could be the friendly traitor helping the poor mortals.

And if its contractor attempted to call it a traitor when it left this planet then it would simply claim to be playing the long game! So complex and devious was its elaborate plan that its machinations couldn't possibly bear fruit before this world was conquered by the main invasion.

How unfortunate for the invasion effort they were so successful to miss the genius that was the Beholder's hidden master plan, manipulating the masses behind the scenes. Bwa ha ha!

The Beholder scanned through its memory and found some technical jargon it could throw in for when the time came. Social engineering, mass manipulation… All nice and unverifiable things so it wouldn't have to actually prove that it had ever actually done anything and have to actually do any real work.

Perfect!

As the Beholder floated over to another vehicle it rubbed its hands together in glee and internally chuckled as its devious plan solidified. While technically it would be a traitor, it would be a rich and happy one!

This planet was just one happy surprise after another. It might collect so much after this maneuver that it might even have to expand its spatial pocket again just to display it all! Its mood dipped for a moment as it remembered the other stuffy Beholders chiding it for being too materialistic. But they were far away and the riches were right here!

Ah, the possibilities were endless for this planet!

Chapter 20: Neighborhood Watch Has a Meeting - Prime Mortal Fragment

Bill stood in the secret underground compound that their organization had built underneath the Satchler Farm. The Ranch. It was just out of town and the surface above was abandoned. The Neighborhood Watch owned both the farm above and several pieces of surrounding property.

Tunnels were dug to those locations, all leading to the central compound. The farmhouse above was rundown, leaving the land abandoned for many years until the Neighborhood Watch bought it. No one suspected it as the heart of their operations. No one in this town should know that they existed at all.

Bare concrete surrounded them on all sides. The harsh fans of the ventilation rattled and groaned above them. The harsh lights flickered and buzzed like a swarm of insects, creating dancing shadows in the corners of the rooms.

Despite the overtaxed ventilation system doing its best, the place seemed stuffy and the air was heavy. This place was made to be defensible, not comfortable.

Bill leaned over a map of the town with a large red circle drawn around it. Outside the red circle, a section five miles extending from the barrier was shaded a light red. Little black flags pierced into the map, marking the barrier pylons scattered around the inside of the barrier.

But all that was secondary.

Bill pulled out a blue pen and began circling smaller zones throughout the map before jabbing the tip into a point in the center. He looked up to his advisors circled around the table.

"According to our intelligence, Infiltrator of Authority appears to have firmly embedded himself in the local police. While its grip isn't ironclad on them, it seems to be enough to suppress the rumors of the disappearances lately somewhat. But it is becoming bold enough that even through the mental ward the populace is beginning to become suspicious.

"All the supervisors and the police chief himself have been reported to be acting distant and strange by the officers at the street level. Those that are still human, that is."

Bill capped the pen and placed it down on the map and continued speaking,

"However, it seems most of the lower level officers remain themselves so they can be used to reassure the civilian populace more effectively. But even that won't be able to last long, especially with the rampant 'disappearances' being noticed more and more by the people.

"We should assume that all the police leaders and an unknown number of the officers have been infected by this point. As well as everyone that has disappeared so far.

"All we know is that the Infected are gathering here, in the zone around the hospital in large numbers. They are likely to concentrate there while Harbinger recovers from the hospital. But the more Infected that gather there the more humans in the town will become aware of the situation."

Helen looked between the map and Bill, nodding slowly. Her brown hair was up in a bun, and her green eyes met Bill's as she leaned over that table. Bill met her gaze for a moment before panning his gaze over Francis and the rest of his advisors and continued his speech.

"Francis and I have a plan to get the people of interest out of the hospital. Most have had mysterious accidents over the last few days, just enough to get them hospitalized, but no deaths, and so they are all gathered at the hospital for treatment. Helen, did any of them reply to our emails yet?"

Helen looked at Bill and pursed her lips, "No. I think the Infected may have taken their devices. None of the ones from the hospital have so much as opened the file. We have some responses from those who were not attacked. But they were skeptical. Why would Infiltrator of Authority keep them alive?"

Bill licked his lips for a moment.

"I believe it plans for them to accept an infection somewhat willingly. People with their qualities would create formidable Infected forms in any case. The more willing they are to change the more power these forms will have and the more Potential that Infiltrator of Authority will be able to 'harvest' from them.

"It is especially important for the newly infected at the hospital to be at their maximum power given the upcoming war between Infiltrator of Authority and the mutating Nameless. The Nameless has occupied my house directly next to the Seed and formed a cocoon to increase the power of its form. Infiltrator of Authority only has until it finishes to build up its forces."

Bill took a breath and continued,

"Yesterday, a group of thirty assaulted the Nameless and forced it to break out of its cocoon early. Small groups of the infected have been making periodic assaults ever since. From my understanding, it was Infiltrator of Authorities' responsibility to protect the Harbinger while the Nameless was to defend the Seed.

"Infiltrator of Authority seemed to believe its role was the lesser of the two. The Nameless simply consumed its attackers and reformed the cocoon to continue its mutations. I believe Infiltrator of Authority is delaying the Nameless' maturation to the Nameless' self proclaimed 'perfect' form to buy itself some more time.

"The Nameless seemed confident that once it was finished with its mutations it would be unstoppable as long as Infiltrator of Authority remained contained to this town where the Nameless would be able to engage it in straight combat."

Helen gasped and slammed her fist onto the table. "Thirty infected! How much has this thing spread by now? We don't have the resources to divert to defend against assaults of that size yet! We are stretched thin as it is. What if it targets our teams with those kinds of numbers?"

Bill nodded, "No, we do not. We can't win a direct confrontation yet. Which is why rescuing the people on the list is essential. And setting up the safe zones and fortifications as quickly as possible."

Francis nodded but remained silent still studying the map.

Helen looked at Bill again,

"Then what are we to do? We need to focus our efforts on the military massing outside the barrier as we speak! We can only hold them back for so long. They'll eventually figure out a way through. We have none of the manpower for fighting them off with so much time left before the Harbinger matures. It could be months we have to hold in the worst case."

"True, your efforts will be mostly focused on reinforcing the pylons and setting up the safe zones," Bill said, "As will the others. After you finish establishing the safe zones then we'll have to fortify them as much as we can for both the army and attack of the Spawn both.

"Francis and I will provide distractions at the hospital while another team extracts the targets. Helen, you are in command while I am absent. You will also have to give the speeches to the civilians in the zones. If this fails, I want all of you to have plausible deniability in case one of the progenitors, Infiltrator of Authority or the Nameless, comes to you with demands."

Helen straightened up as everyone looked at her. She saluted,

"Yes, sir. Good luck on the mission. I'll continue the preparations in your absence."

Bill nodded at all of them before gesturing to Francis,

"All right Francis, let's gear up and go. You know the plan."

The two walked out, leaving Helen to continue the further discussion of implementing the plans they had created over the years for this crisis.

Bill and Francis walked to the lockers and began to get dressed in the black tactical gear. Francis slung a grenade launcher over his back before winking at Bill. Bill snorted. Another group of two women and three men were already there, disguised as nurses and waiting for them.

They were all armed with pistols and combat knives that were carefully hidden beneath their blue hospital scrubs. Bill strapped on his silenced pistol and strapped the combat knife to his chest as Francis retrieved two of the heavy rifles. Bill strapped on his helmet before accepting one of the rifles and putting the strap over his head and slinging it onto his back. Bill looked at Francis.

"You're sure about this? We could get a squad for you if you want."

Francis shook his head.

"No can do Boss. You know I got cheat codes."

He pulled a metal orb the size of a fist from the top shelf of his locker. The orb was covered with a dense matrix of intersecting lines and seemingly random scribbles that faintly glowed. Bill raised an eyebrow.

"I still can't believe that thing works. Those lines still look just like random scratches to me."

Francis laughed and tossed it into the air before catching it.

"And that's why I get all the fun toys and not you."

Bill frowned at his scarred face before waving away Francis' words.

"Bah, you're right. Wouldn't know how to use one of those things anyway. Still, a man can dream."

Francis chuckled.

"True, true. Who doesn't want to be able to turn invisible?"

Francis put the orb inside the pouch hanging at his hip. He was proud of it and bragged about it whenever he got the chance. Well, he should be. Bill wished he could use one. Francis gave himself one last check over before looking back up,

"Alright Boss, you ready to go?"

Bill checked himself over one more time before nodding. The two of them walked through the concrete hallways, nodding at the guards as they passed. The rest trailed behind them. Finally, the group reached a locked door which Bill opened by scanning his fingerprint.

The group walked into a tunnel with a low ceiling. They walked for about ten minutes before the tunnel began to slope upwards. After a minute, Francis went to drag his hand against the rough stone wall as he walked but Bill grabbed his wrist before he could do so.

"Don't forget the explosives. It's C4, but you never know if someone messed up a trigger."

Francis withdrew his hand and reluctantly nodded,

"You know that's bull, we both checked over the remote triggers. And it is embedded in the wall. Should be stable as hell. But I guess you never know."

After that, they walked in silence.

Finally, they reached the end of the hallway, with a circular trapdoor in the ceiling and a ladder up to it. Bill climbed up the ladder and carefully lifted the trapdoor an inch to peer through the slightly raised gap. He peered around.

"Clear."

The two men emerged, the five others following behind. After the last person climbed through, they let the trapdoor fall shut behind them. After a second, they could all hear a distinct *Thunk* as the door automatically relocked itself. It was dark out, and they had surfaced in a dark wooded area of the forest.

The group hiked through the woods for three miles before they reached the nearby neighboring farm and silently entered through the back door. Bill and Francis each took one of the stashed vehicles and started their engines.

The five disguised as nurses climbed into their own large van. Francis rolled down his window before nodding at Bill.

"See you on the other side, Boss."

With a roar of the engine, the three vehicles peeled out and raced into the darkness, the group mentally preparing themselves for battle.

Chapter 21: The Neighbor Goes to the Hospital - Prime Mortal Fragment

Bill lay prone on the roof of the building, scanning the area through the scope of his rifle. The infected were poorly blending in to guard the hospital in every direction on the streets below.

They stood in the shadows of the alleys between the buildings almost motionless, tracking the people who passed to enter the hospital with only their heads. It was close to midnight so there was very little foot traffic compared to the groups of infected scattered about.

Most of the people who walked by clearly noticed the infected watching them from the shadows. You could see it from when they would stiffen and glance around, before seeing the rest.

The humans would startle, but after no motion to approach them, the people tucked their heads down and moved onward. As Bill watched, a police vehicle approached and the two officers approached one of the watchers.

One of the officers spoke briefly with the group, the other remaining silent. The infected receded further into the shadows and after some more prompting from the officer, they leaned against the walls of the nearest buildings. It looked a little more natural than them standing in place.

Bill frowned. He adjusted the night vision on the scope as the officer turned around.

Bill mumbled under his breath, "Shit"

It was Officer Nick, aka Infiltrator of Authority, giving orders to its troops. Bill ducked down as its gaze swept the area. After a moment, Bill chanced another look. As he watched, Infiltrator of Authority returned to the patrol vehicle and drove back the way it came.

A portion of the group it spoke to dispersed to relay its orders to the other scattered groups of infected in the area. Now only two of the infected remained in that original alley, watching the street and any of the humans that passed by.

Bill waited for five more minutes before pulling out his radio.

"Alright Francis, start now," He said into it, "Just spotted Infiltrator of Authority five minutes ago. It may still be in the area so watch your back out there. Extraction team, wait for my order. Over."

Bill released the talk button.

"Read you clear Boss, starting now. Over."

The leader of the second extraction team in the hospital scrubs came on, "Yes, sir. Over," Her voice shook a little with tension.

From the other side of the hospital, Bill heard a loud burst of gunfire. The Infected in the area stood at attention and looked around. The Infected group looked rooted to the spot, struggling internally between investigating and remaining in place.

But when one finally began to stumble towards the noise, the rest broke ranks and moved towards the explosions and gunfire in the distance. In a short time, the whole area became nearly deserted.

The infected ran towards the gunfire to aid in defense, while the humans ran away as best they could in panic. Bill made his way downstairs and out to the street.

"Alright, Extraction team. Proceed behind me. Over"

"Acknowledged. Over."

In his tactical gear, Bill quickly got in his vehicle and drove directly into the subterranean parking lot of the hospital. The van followed behind him. Bill parked close to the entrance, while the van parked illegally in front of the elevator, with the back doors flung open. Bill stepped out of the car and shouldered his rifle in front of him.

A man and his daughter came around the corner of the garage. They were holding hands. The man's eyes widened as the little girl stared in confusion at the man in tactical gear. As she went to speak the man picked her up and ran away shouting.

The words distorted and echoed as they bounced around the parking garage. Bill felt a pang of sadness at what he had to do. But he knew the alternative was worse. He shook off the wave of melancholy and refocused.

He was on a mission.

No distractions.

Not even for his conscience.

Especially not for his conscience, whatever was left of it.

Bill continued onward and made it to the door inside. He was in the stairwell and began moving upwards, rifle held at the ready.

He went up a flight of stairs and raised his rifle at the sound of a door, but lowered it slightly as he saw it was a wide-eyed frail looking young woman standing in the stairwell above him. She opened her mouth to shout at seeing him, only for her breath to be sharply cut off as she was shoved from behind.

With a gasp, she fell forward and began rolling down the steps.

Behind her, the blank-faced police officer raised his gun.

Bill let out a three round burst of gunfire that took the officer right between the eyes. Its head snapped backward and its finger twitched involuntarily, firing its gun to the side with a loud *Bang!*.

The Infected fell back to slump against the wall. The woman barreled into Bill in a tangle of flailing limbs, screaming her lungs out in surprise but seeming relatively uninjured.

Bill let out a grunt as she knocked the air out of him and began ineffectually flailing in her panic to stand and get away. Bill shoved her to the side roughly and raised his rifle again as he saw the officer above standing back to his feet.

For a moment it simply stood there with a continued blank expression, three oozing red bullet holes blasted in its skull. Then, like a lizard shedding its tail the officer's head just rolled off its shoulders and fell onto the concrete landing with a soft *plop*.

The Infected's hands reached up and ripped off its shirt in one jerking motion, its pistol laying forgotten on the floor.

On the creature's bare chest an eyeball the size of a fist blinked open. It stared at the woman next to Bill, seemingly ignoring him for the moment. In a burst of movement, the creature leaped down the stairs, its arm cocked back poised to strike.

As it descended its arm began swelling as that arm's muscles grew to ridiculous proportions. Layer after layer of muscle formed even as the rest of its body became skeletal.

Cursing, Bill shoved the woman to the side and dropped his rifle to reach for his waist. In one smooth motion he withdrew his high caliber pistol from his hip holster. The descending fist shifted course slightly to target Bill's position. In a split second, Bill rolled to the side and the fist passed by him.

With a titanic blow, the creature's fist embedded itself into the concrete of the wall behind where Bill had been moments before. Bill's tactical helmet's strap broke as he rolled, and it flew off his head and clattered down the stairs behind him.

The woman stood there backed against the far wall, staring in shock at the headless monster standing there, still tugging to remove its fist from the concrete wall. Bill raised his pistol as the creature retrieved its fist with one final tug and a spray of dust.

Bang

The creature fell back as the bullet pierced it, and Bill gritted his teeth as the impact from the recoil blasted through his arm. Dull red flames sprouted from the wound on the Infected, spreading quickly to consume the creature. It silently thrashed, unable to scream without a mouth as it was quickly consumed by the flames in seconds.

Bill reached to his back and retrieved one of his more mystical pieces of equipment from his side. A dark stick of deeply stained wood the length of his forearm.

Carefully, he retrieved his combat knife and carved a tiny notch at the end until a white powdery substance became visible from underneath the wood. He stuck the notched end towards the burning corpse and twisted it at the other end, and the reddish flames rushed inside the stick like a powerful vacuum.

A web of glowing lines lit up all over its surface and Bill handled it gingerly. Bill carefully picked up his dropped rifle before carefully replacing the stick with a special holster at his hip.

"What the fuck."

Bill turned to the teenager pressed against the far wall, her wide eyes darting between the charred corpse and Bill. Bill peered closer and almost laughed as he saw one of his targets was standing in front of him. This was good. Less load on the extraction team now.

"What the fuck. What the fu…"

Her voice began to grow hysterical and Bill moved to cut her off before she spiraled. He reached into his pocket. May as well make more room in the van.

"Quiet. Parking space H5." Bill said, "Wait ten minutes. If I'm not there by then, then go. Francis on the radio will explain everything if I don't come back. Tell him the phrase 'Umbrellas protect even without rain' if you talk with him. That's to confirm that I sent you. He'll help protect you."

Bill took out the car keys and threw them to her. She fumbled and dropped them, but quickly crouched down and retrieved them.

"Why… What's…"

"'Umbrellas protect even without rain'. Remember that. Look, there's no time. Don't trust anyone that seems too calm. They might be one of the Infected. Like this one. They don't know how to mimic human emotions properly. You have to do this or they'll hunt you down. Go!"

She hesitated, licking her lips as she still looked between Bill and the corpse as she held the keys. Bill made a shooing motion, "Go, Go! Francis will explain everything!"

That spurred her into motion and she fled down the stairs out of sight. Bill internally sighed in relief as she finally sprung into motion. Francis would take care of her if things went wrong.

Bill made his way up the next flight of stairs to the third floor. Above him, he heard a door thrown open and the pounding of feet running down the stairs. The nurses and patients all turned to him in shock as he burst out of the stairwell into the main room.

Next to him, the elevator door dinged and then opened, revealing the disguised nurses in the distraction team who quickly rushed into the stunned crowd. The humans froze in shock while their calmer blank faced neighbors all stepped forward to meet Bill in unison.

Bill scanned the room. Looked like about five infected in the crowd approaching. He mentally checked his route. The Harbinger's room was two turns away. Room 311.

He lowered his gun. The infected were mixed in with the crowd, too much collateral damage. The smart humans at the back had slipped away already, but the majority were still staring at him in shock.

The stampede hadn't begun yet.

He slung the rifle over his shoulder and retrieved the glowing stick from its holster and held it with the notched end pointed outward. He gripped the other end and held at the hip.

One of the infected emerged at an angle from the frozen crowd. Bill saw it leap out of the corner of his eye and whirled and twisted his hand at the stick's base. The red flames roared out and coated the infected mid-leap and it let out a high pitched, inhuman scream.

Bill stepped to the side and the infected's body fly past him. The sudden motion and sound broke the crowds' shock and as one they started quickly scattering away from the battle. Only the infected remained, pushing forward against the escaping crowd.

In the chaos, the disguised nurses of the extraction team began entering certain patients' rooms. Some would emerge with a patient trailing behind them in confusion, while others gave hurried explanations before leaving the more heavily injured patients in place.

They had to take who they could and give the others at least a chance. Or worst case weaken the resulting Infected by informing them of their true circumstances. Or they could escape on their own somehow if possible.

The burning Infected on the floor to Bill's side thrashed and screamed. It began to morph, growing new limbs from its torso to try to beat out the flames with its fists.

The flames lowered in intensity, but after a moment the infected grew still and the flames brightened marginally again. Bill twisted the end of the stick and the flames rushed back eagerly and the glowing lines on the stick lit once more, just a little dimmer now.

Another Infected leaped at Bill and promptly was blasted by the Devouring Flame again. Bill charged into the cleared path in front of him and sprinted down the hall.

As Bill ran he witnessed one of his men enter one of the rooms to his left. There lying prone was a wiry old man with silver hair. As the disguised nurse burst in through the door, the man sat up and coughed. The nurse glanced at the contraption elevating the man's foot. Too long to unhook everything.

No extraction for him.

The man spluttered, "What? Who are…"

"No time. Trust no one. Conspiracy shit. Read this for explanations. Get rid of it when you're done. Eating it or flame is the best method. They will try to kill you, so leave here as soon as you can. Take this, here take it. It'll tell you a little more. Don't let anyone else see it if you value your life".

The man handed him a scrap of paper with writing on it before sprinting out of the room, slamming the door shut behind him. He continued onward to enter two more rooms in the hallway and handed different papers to each to their bewilderment.

Unfortunately, they all had impaired mobility. Perhaps their accidents were even designed that way. But luckily a fair number of people that were able to follow the extraction team and were making their way to the elevator.

Bill watched in the corner of his eyes even as he ran forward. He left the extraction team behind, where they had begun to guide the healthier patients of interest back into the elevator to make good on their escape. There were almost no people in the hallways now. It seemed that most of the humans had run.

Chaotically echoing through the hallways, he could hear the storm of heavy footsteps coming his way. More of the infected. Bill rushed to the most critical location for his plan. He sprinted down the hallway until he saw the main desk. He vaulted over the counter and plugged a thumb drive into the computer.

The thumb drive blinked for a few seconds before the light finally became solid. He looked over to see a woman quivering and curled into a ball under the desk, looking at him in fear.

The pounding of feet grew closer, but there was no shouting accompanying the group. It was another group of the Infected. Bill listened carefully for a moment. Two more groups. One from each direction.

Not good, he was boxed in.

Bill vaulted over the desk again and ran towards what he believed to be the smallest group in the hallway to his right. The group rounded the corner, and Bill's heart sank. Standing there with two other Infected was Infiltrator of Authority.

Bill activated the flames from the stick and they rushed towards Infiltrator of Authority. The two Infected stepped out from behind Infiltrator of Authority to shield it from harm. Infiltrator of Authority stepped back and one of the infected took the hit from the Flame and fell to the floor writhing in pain.

Infiltrator of Authority stepped past its writhing form even as Bill retracted the flame as quickly as he could with another twist of the base of the stick. The flame came reluctantly this time, not wanting to leave behind its victim without finishing the job.

Bill launched the flames again immediately as soon as it returned. The other infected leaped forward and intercepted that hit for Infiltrator of Authority too.

Infiltrator of Authority past it as well, seemingly not bothered at all.

Both of the infected were burnt to a crisp, but Bill didn't have enough time to retract the flame. He twisted the end of the stick anyways just in case. The flame rushed towards him. But Infiltrator of Authority had drawn too close by now.

Bill backed up and reached for his pistol, but Infiltrator of Authority suddenly dashed forward in a burst of speed and put its hand onto either side of Bill's head. Its eyes met Bill's own. Bill twisted his body and pulled the gun from its holster and began to rais…

'SLEEP'

Bill slumped, unconscious. His pistol fell to the ground from limp fingers.

— — — **(Mortal Sally Fragment)** — — —

Sally shook in fear from beneath the desk. The bursts of what sounded like a flamethrower came from the nearby hallway. Then it abruptly cut off and she heard a body hit the floor.

Footsteps came from every direction until a group of over ten people were shuffling in front of the desk. They were silent other than their shuffling and didn't speak. Sally mustered her courage and peeked out from behind the desk hoping the man in tactical gear with the flamethrower, apparently, was gone.

Instantly all ten, no eleven people turned to her in unison.

They all stared at her silently.

A man to the farthest right stepped forward and smiled as if he was going for a pleasant stroll.

His dead eyed look made her take an unconscious step back.

He reached into his pocket and withdrew a tiny card. He extended it and his smile grew wider, as if he had just heard the funniest joke and just couldn't stop thinking about it.

"Would you like therapy for this traumatic experience? I've heard that Dr. Trau is one of the best. This card will give you three free sessions for you to decide that she's for you."

Sally's mind spun. What was even happening right now? She glanced into the hallway and saw two smoking bodies along with the man in tactical gear splayed out on the floor. Dead on unconscious? She nearly vomited at the sight but held it down with some effort.

Sally looked around at the group still standing silently and staring unblinking at her without moving from all sides. No one reacted to the smoldering bodies or even looked bothered in the slightest at the sight. Had they moved closer to her while she was distracted?

She glanced around, suddenly feeling boxed in.

The man with the card had made his way around the main desk in the moment of her distraction and was slowly walking towards her. His smile grew wider and wider as he spoke.

"She really helped a friend of mine. With this card, the cost will be no object. You'll feel so much better if you take it. It soothes the mind. 100% Guarantee. You won't worry about anything ever again."

Sally glanced around to see the silent crowd had closed in, surrounding her on all sides now in truth now. She backed up and tried to brush past one woman standing in her way.

"No thanks, I, um, well I have to go. You know, the procedure to meet outside once you're safe in situations like this..."

The woman didn't budge, Sally just bounced off her and stumbled backwards as she tried to walk by. The woman didn't even react. Sally turned around and the man's smile widened further until it was uncanny.

He began to chuckle.

"NOW WHAT MAKES YOU THINK YOU ARE *SAFE?*"

His voice deepened and reverberated in her chest as she began to hyperventilate. With widened eyes Sally turned, but she was gripped from behind and held in place as she struggled.

All of a sudden the man was in front of her, now laughing. It was a manic laugh, the sound of someone who'd finally broken and plunged into insanity. He grabbed her face with one hand. He gestured with his other hand and someone grabbed her jaw and wrenched it open.

She struggled, but the arms gripping her were made of iron. Nothing she did even shifted their grip on her.

Her head was tilted back.

The laughing grew even more maniacal as the man daintily dropped the card into her open mouth.

"Ah, the result is so much weaker yet so much more satisfying nonetheless," The insane man said.

Sally twitched and fell to the floor as the card came to life and merged with the roof of her mouth. The puppet strings began to sink into her mind. The last thing she heard was the gut-busting laughter from the man in front of her as he watched her twitch in place.

Then she was calm, infused with a new purpose and all of a sudden the man's laughter no longer mattered to her.

—— (Infiltrator of Authority Fragment) ——

Infiltrator of Authority's mirth slowly died down to a hearty chuckle as he saw the female mortal stand back at attention in front of it, ready to serve. He had allowed his true body's emotions to leak into this vessel to improve the experience.

The mortal woman had seen too much, and Infiltrator of Authority had received a good source of stress relief it sorely needed right now in return. It had been too long since it had been able to have a little fun on the lower worlds.

Its role always kept it so busy. It just had to enjoy the little moments, it supposed. It patted the recently converted mortal on the cheek before turning away to clean the scene before more witnesses appeared, no matter how much it secretly wished to continue.

No, its role came first. And that role demanded it hide this incident lest it send the mortals into a dangerous frenzy. Infiltrator of Authority wasn't ready for open conflict with the mortals yet.

It internally sighed. Oh, how it wished it could play as it willed. But always duty first. The price of competence, it supposed…

—— (Mortal Alice Fragment) ——

Alice sat in the military style vehicle wondering what the heck she was doing. She should just run to the police, not follow the orders of the man in military gear breaking into the hospital. With a flamethrower stick of all things.

She could just go home and pretend nothing ever happened. But she didn't have her car here and her friends had been ignoring her lately. She didn't even have her phone. She had woken up and it had just disappeared somewhere yesterday.

She didn't really want to wait around if one of those creatures tried to attack her again. She shuddered. Should she flag down a police officer? Get some help?

But that creature had been pretending to be a police officer. Who knew how many more creatures were out there? Pretending to be people? And all the staff taking care of her at the hospital had been strange and unhelpful to her. She had just thought they really didn't like her for some reason. But thinking about it now, maybe it was something more. Something more sinister…

She glanced at the clock in the car. It had been eight minutes. She was supposed to leave on her own in two minutes. She remembered the man's comments. The creature had been targeting her with its first blow, not the scary military man with a flamethrower stick. He called it an 'Infected'.

She thought over the last week how her friends had been commenting how people around town looked so bored lately. Their own strange behavior that she couldn't find the cause of. How some of their faces had become expressionless over the last few days.

A chill ran down her spine.

How many of those things were out there? Were those blank-faced nurses one of the Infected? Trying to kill her? She didn't even entertain the idea this was some kind of dream. Everything just felt too real and vivid. And she had secretly pinched herself when she got in the car and felt the pain of it.

Not only that, but over the last week a sense of unease had settled over the town. And when she really thought about it, she had seen people acting strangely around town all week. She just hadn't paid it any attention at the time.

All the oddities she had brushed aside in her memories came to the forefront of her mind. And she didn't doubt the man's claims anymore. When she reassessed the last week, she realized with horror that the number of emotionless people in town had been rapidly increasing. And several of her friends had become some of them.

She didn't want to become one of those things. She unconsciously put her hand to her chest where the officer had grown the giant eyeball. She shifted in place as she looked at the clock again.

Twelve minutes. She sat in the car, trying to decide what to do.

Fifteen minutes. She stared at the window, hoping against hope the man would come back. He would know what to say about her worries. He had taken down that creature like it was nothing. He knew what was going on.

Twenty minutes.

He wasn't coming.

She started the car and drove it out of the hospital parking lot. She was a little unsteady, but she didn't hit anything as she drove at least. Even if she did swerve a little. She always had a hard time parking within the lines at school sometimes. She picked up the radio on the seat next to her. Her dad had shown her how they worked one time. She pressed the button on the side.

"Hello, is there a Francis here?" she said, before releasing the button again.

A moment of silence, "Yes? Say Over when you're done, newbie. Over. Got it? Who is this? Alright for real this time, Over."

"Umbrellas protect even without rain? Uhhhhh, Over."

A longer pause this time. "Are you alone? Over."

"Yes. Over."

She kept driving, not sure where she should be going. Certainly not home. At least Dad was out on that trip, so he should be safe at least.

More silence over the radio, "Alright we're going to meet up and I'll explain what I can. Here's where you'll want to go…"

Chapter 22: Under Arrest - Prime Mortal Fragment

Wake!

Bill woke to a pair of hands wrapped around his head in a vice grip. After a moment the hands released him and his blindfold was ripped off. He shifted and realized that he was handcuffed to a chair. He was stripped of his tactical gear leaving only in a shirt and underwear. Cold air wafted over his skin and Bill shivered.

He was in some kind of supply closet. There were shelves filled with brown boxes and office supplies. There was only one door and no windows. He looked at the creature sitting opposite him. It was Infiltrator of Authority standing under a bright light. If he didn't know better, Bill wouldn't have been able to distinguish it from a human. It was flanked by two Infected that were shrouded in shadow.

One had shed their human form. It matched the mutation of the police officer Infected that Bill had killed in the hospital. No head, shirtless, and a giant eye growing from the middle of its chest. Highly muscled arms. It seems this one had had time to even out the oversized muscles on every limb.

The other looked like a normal human woman and had no visible mutations at all. Bill peered at her shrouded form for a moment. She tickled a memory at the back of his mind, but he couldn't place it.

If she was here she must be an Infected though. Her blank expression at least told him as much.

After a moment of consideration, Bill shifted his gaze back to Infiltrator of Authority. Unlike its emotionless subordinates, it frowned as it looked at him. For a long while they just stared at each other silently.

Eventually, Infiltrator of Authority broke the silence. Bill smiled internally and Infiltrator of Authority grimaced slightly for a moment at Bill's small victory. But Infiltrator quickly went back to smiling as it kept speaking.

"Recognize anyone?" It gestured to its left to the woman who stepped forward obediently. Bill looked at her closer until with a flash he remembered the woman who hid under the desk at the hospital. She still wore hospital scrubs. The fabric had small tears in some places. On her chest was a name tag that said 'Sally'.

"Fuck."

Infiltrator of Authority smiled a little wider.

"Sloppy, sloppy Bill. Don't leave any witnesses behind. She might have even gone to the police! Which wouldn't have mattered, but you never know. But I took care of that like the good friend that I am. So why don't you return the favor." Its tone sharpened. "What were you doing at the hospital?"

Infiltrator of Authority leaned forward, a smile still fixed upon his face. Bill was silent. They stared at each other for a moment. "One more chance."

Bill pretended to think before he answered. "Alright, alright. I'll tell you."

Infiltrator of Authority nodded and leaned back, its wooden chair creaking as it took its weight. He waved his hand at Bill lazily, motioning him to continue.

Bill licked his lips. "Well, I don't trust your security. It's sloppy, and I almost reached the Harbinger. If I was your enemy then he might be dead right now."

Infiltrator of Authority grimaced slightly before recovering his calm smile.

"So? The only enemy I see here is you. Only you and that Nameless once it matures could oppose my forces at this point. The Nameless has a vested interest in keeping the Harbinger alive to keep me distant from the Seed itself for now. Not to mention going against the Seed's direct orders on the Harbinger's protection.

"Only you would be able to rally the mortals against us. The mortals are pacified by the effect of the barrier you deployed it seems, but that will only last so long. I think it would be best to eliminate the threat to the Seed and the Harbinger, what do you say?"

"I always expected you to betray us for your brethren eventually. Never understood why you would attempt to ally with us in the first place anyway."

Bill opened his mouth to retort only to pause as he heard footsteps rapidly approaching the door to the room. A moment later, an unmutated Infected burst through the door and leaned over to whisper to Infiltrator of Authority after rushing over to it.

Infiltrator of Authority frowned and glanced at Bill the longer the Infected spoke. Finally, Infiltrator of Authority stood and looked Bill directly in the eyes, all levity gone.

"The Harbinger has been attacked. His door was broken into splinters and there are signs of damage and broken concrete in the parking lot outside. He appears uninjured so far. No sign of the intruder. Was. This. You?"

Bill leaned back in genuine confusion at the information. Attacking the Harbinger had always been a bluff, a smokescreen for the real plan. Was this some kind of game to throw him off balance? Infiltrator of Authority could always be lying to toy with him.

Bill held Infiltrator of Authorities' gaze and detected some genuine worry there. Apparently, it had become a little too good at connecting its true emotions to its host. Or maybe that's what it wanted him to think. But back to the task at hand, who could have done this?

Frankly, Bill was a skilled operator and had little chance of doing such a thing totally unseen as the creature had implied in its description of the situation. And the door being shattered also implied a mutated creature too impatient for locks.

Not something that could usually pass as a human and sneak around. Bill kept track of everyone that had been in the town before the barrier was activated.

None of the people in this town could accomplish anything close to the stealth let alone project the physical strength even close to what was required for this. Was this the same person or group that attacked the Harbinger the first time? But who could they be? He was just in the dark as before.

Whoever it was were ghosts to him. Hopefully, there would be new evidence this time. There were only so many people inside the barrier right now. Little clues could narrow things down quickly.

Bill looked up from his thoughts to where Infiltrator of Authority had continued to stare him down, waiting for his response.

"No. I truly don't know who could have done this." Bill shared honestly before explaining his basic thoughts regarding the stealth required versus the apparent strength from a mutation to shatter the door. Infiltrator of Authority nodded in agreement at his logic thoughtfully. It sat and considered for a moment.

"Perhaps you were right before. I will need to increase the Harbinger's security at least threefold if not more. No matter the impact on my recruitment efforts for now. I will decide what to do with you when I get back."

It turned to the two infected standing there passively.

"Guard him and don't let him leave".

With that Infiltrator of Authority rushed out the door and back to the hospital.

———O—o—O———

The two infected stood there unmoving, staring straight ahead as Bill sat glancing around the room.

All of a sudden, Bill's chair tipped over onto the ground with a loud crash. Bill felt his face smashed into the concrete, but was able to shift to grab a paperclip he had spotted before on the ground. He grabbed it with his teeth and manipulated it with his tongue to hide it in his cheek.

Sloppy of them to leave something like that near him, but this room was hardly ideal for this kind of thing. This place just screamed temporary storage until they could find a better place to hold him. Most of the office supplies were still in the room, even.

The two infected stared at him for a moment before the human looking woman stepped forward and righted the chair. She stepped back into place to stare blankly into the mid-distance again.

Bill felt a pang of guilt as he just looked at her for a moment. He knew it wasn't really his fault, but this had still happened to her because of him.

Bill tried to inject as much sincerity into his voice as he suddenly spoke to her, "Thank you."

For a moment the woman's eyes flickered with emotion before returning to apathetic blankness. But maybe Bill just imagined it.

Bill bit down on the paperclip and manipulated it within his mouth until it was between his teeth again. After a moment's preparation, he whipped his head around and stared intently at one of the back corners of the room before opening his mouth to drop the paperclip.

He caught it below in his palm and began stealthily picking the lock of the handcuffs. The Infected barely reacted, taking one glance at the empty corner Bill had turned to before returning to staring at the mid-distance blankly again.

Bill finished picking the lock and the handcuffs clicked open softly. He made sure not to move too much yet. Bill took stock of his surroundings again subtly. No immediate weapons were visible.

For humans, the nearby stapler would do the trick as a weapon, but Infected were more durable than that. Bill thought through the scenario of his escape. He had to deal with these two Infected or he was doomed.

No way he could make it out of wherever this was with one of them on his heels. He planned every move of the fight in his head. He strategized his escape then when he felt he was ready, he closed his eyes and took a deep breath.

Bill's eyes snapped open.

In a burst of motion, Bill erupted from his seat and put all his momentum into one titanic punch directly onto the mutated Infected's massive eyeball embedded in its chest.

It staggered back before rubbing its bloodshot eye with one arm. As the pain from the blow finally registered, the creature was sent into a blind rage.

It began wildly flailing around it through its blurred vision in an effort to hit Bill. Its arms swelled with muscle over muscle as it swung at nothing. But Bill had already ghosted back out of range of its fists.

The woman now approached at an angle towards him. She raised her arm revealing a bone spear jutting from her fused forearm bones as her fleshy hand fell away. Her discarded hand fell to the floor with a wet *plop*.

The bone spear was slick with the woman's blood. Her former blank expression had morphed into fear and resolve as her body tensed.

Just as she went to leap at Bill her right leg twitched and she stumbled to her right drunkenly towards the other Infected. She tried to recover from the mistake, but she had already gotten too close.

With one wild swing, the mutated Infected punched through her body. The mutated Infected kept swinging in its rage, pasting the woman into tiny red bits.

Bill silently edged around the corners of the room as the Infected in a blind rage kept pounding the body into finer and finer paste with wet thumps. Bill slowly eased the door open before gently closing it behind him. The mutated Infected didn't notice him leave.

He looked around at the abandoned area.

Next to him was his tactical gear spread out and tossed on a bench haphazardly as if it had been taken off in a hurry. He must have not been out for that long. Bill equipped his gear and crept to one of the side rooms of the office.

One of the humanoid Infected passed by on patrol and Bill hid under a cubicle desk. He was in some kind of corporate office space with little cubicle dividers and an open floor plan. After the coast was clear, Bill darted to the nearest window. He eased it open and crawled out into the alley.

There was a non-mutated Infected there that turned to him at the motion. He pulled out the stick from its holster and twisted its end. A tiny tongue of flame shot out, but it was enough to catch on the infected.

The creature quickly burned to a crisp before Bill twisted the base of the stick again and sucked in the flame. He glanced around. Seemed he was in the clear. With one final look behind him, he hustled out of the alley making good on his escape out into the night.

Chapter 23: Party in The Streets - Mortal (Francis) Fragment

——— As the Prime Mortal fought, his Mortal Subordinate battled also. Retrieving another Fragment of Memory... ———

Francis stared down at the street. It wasn't often he got to just let loose like this.

He shot another two Infected that rounded the corner with his rifle. Luckily, the ones on the street had to keep their human appearance. Even the most powerful ones could only regenerate one or two bullet wounds before they were killed.

As long as you didn't let them survive to begin to mutate into something inhuman, they went down pretty easily. Francis glanced around at the fifteen bodies scattered around the street. Each had blindly charged towards him with zero strategy before Francis cut them down.

Another Infected charged from an alleyway nearby. Francis turned and blasted it with a three-round burst. It fell to the ground and twitched for a moment. Francis eyed it carefully as he changed out the magazine on his rifle.

The Infected's twitching stopped. It had failed to mutate itself in time. Francis shot it one more time just to be sure. Francis began humming to himself under his breath. He knew he should be more cautious, that things could go wrong any moment. But his breathing was calm. His bag of tricks sat unused.

Where was the excitement?

Where was the challenge? He shot a group of three that rounded the corner. They were coming more frequently. The main horde was approaching.

Time to relocate.

Francis sprinted into an alleyway. He shot any Infected that got in his way as he moved. He ran for five minutes, running and gunning the whole way. He left the main horde of them behind. Panting slightly, he looked around and smiled. This was a good location for the big event.

The wide open plaza had a five-story tall office building to Francis' left. The lights were on inside. He glanced around, but it was the tallest building in the area. The rest surrounding it were four stories max. Francis ran straight for it. Francis busted in the front door with his shoulder charge.

Some poor assholes were still working there this late. What company did that? The real humans inside froze and stared at Francis in his tactical gear in shock. The bustle of corporate work came to a stop. An overweight man whose face looked red stormed out of his office.

"The client needs it by tomorrow! Do you all know how big this is for... the... company?"

His rant petered out as he noticed Francis standing there with the rifle. Francis raised his gun and fired it off to the side into the ceiling, careful to avoid hitting the workers. Everyone ducked down at the noise.

"ALL RIGHT ASSHOLES!" Francis shouted, "CRAZY SHIT INCOMING! GO HOME AND FUCKING SLEEP ALREADY! WHO THE HELL WORKS THIS LATE ON A SATURDAY?"

Francis stepped to his left and pulled the fire alarm. Everyone shuffled, uncertain of what to do. Francis rushed to the stairwell and began to climb. Several people entered the stairwell, only to retreat at seeing Francis bustling up the stairs. Eventually, Francis reached the flat roof.

He leaned over the edge and looked down. There, like little lemmings, the corporate drones were standing in front of the building. Francis could hear some shouting from the fat manager from before. The crowd was pulling away, but the more the man shouted the more some of them paused and stood in place. Francis looked down with his rifle scope.

The man was gesturing wildly and targeting his shouts at anyone who made to leave. Francis shook his head. The man seriously was trying to get them to stay after Francis fired his gun? What was this guy on? That was true corporate loyalty right there. Francis took a deep breath.

"HEY ASSHOLES!"

The crowd looked up, but in the darkness seemed to have difficulty locating Francis' exact position.

"WHY DON'T YOU ALL FUCK OFF THEN?"

With that Francis lined up his shots and shot at the feet of the crowd. That broke their resolve and even the shouting manager made a run for it. Francis snorted. Apparently, he valued his life over his job after all. They should all be clear by the time the horde arrives.

He wasn't usually such an asshole, but he had found that in intense situations the attitude was needed to get people moving.

Francis had given himself a good head start ahead of the horde of Infected, so the people should have time to get out of their way. Their cars drove away a few minutes later. Probably using the last of their gas to do it too.

Francis started making his preparations. He opened his bag of goodies that hung at his hip and began retrieving each piece carefully.

The bag itself was one of his proudest achievements. It was a spatially expanded bag, bigger on the inside than it appeared. I wasn't really that much bigger, but it was still enough to hold everything Francis could ever need for missions.

Obviously, there was the orb of invisibility in there. But that was reserved for his eventual escape. He replaced it in his pouch. Next was a hefty log that he retrieved with a grunt. Francis smiled as he hefted it like a club.

His hands could just barely wrap around its circumference as he held it. But oh boy was it a beauty. Bill would be disappointed he missed the behemoth's unveiling. Well, at least he got to use Francis' old prototype.

Hopefully, it would come in use during the extraction at the hospital.

Francis took out his curved ritual knife from the bag and slowly circled it around the end of the log. It was specially sharpened to pierce through the wood like butter.

With a *clunk* the wooden end fell off, revealing a glowing bluish crystal shining beneath. With a weapon this big, the white powder he had used before simply wouldn't do. So he had to use these crystals instead as the batteries. A little less efficient, but with the size of the thing that was hardly an issue.

Francis carefully set down the weapon. He was still trying to think of a good name for it. He was sure something would come to him. It hardly felt right to refer to them as 'sticks' and 'logs' anymore. Bill had randomly started calling them that, to Francis' annoyance.

A good weapon needed a good name. But the boring, uninspired names were needed when they were undercover to not draw suspicion if someone overheard them.

At least that's what Bill had said. Francis suspected Bill was just still opposed to Francis' perfectly fine name of Doomslingers yesterday. Those placeholder boring names were for the prototypes.

The real thing needed a name that inspired fear! If Bill was so opposed to the name, then why didn't he come back with something better? But after today's test, they would get a name worthy of their power. No matter what Bill had to say about it!

Francis took the last item from the bag he would be using. The ammunition for his magnum pistol.

This ammunition released the Devouring Flame that fed on the Infected's Potential. And of course, who could forget the shells of the grenade launcher? Francis slung the weapon off his back and placed it on the ground.

He filled it with the ammunition containing the embers of the Devouring flame, before returning it back to its original position. He would have to wait for the whole horde to arrive before he could have some real fun with that one. Finally, he took a long coil of rope and expertly tied it to one of the conditioning units humming away on the roof. He gave a hefty tug and nodded as the rope held.

In the distance, Francis caught the first stumbling Infected emerging from the nearby alley. He quickly replaced everything in his bag before hustling down to the first floor. He left the rifle bouncing at his side by the strap, armed with the magnum pistol held in one hand.

He ran to the front and shot the Infected who had just reached the front door. It opened the door and stepped inside, but Francis nailed it as he fired his pistol again.

The creature burst into flames, but the flames snuffed out in an instant as it was burnt to nothing in seconds. Francis grimaced. It seems it hadn't mutated enough to sustain the flame for as long. Too human. Francis reloaded the pistol while keeping an eye on his surroundings.

Francis glanced outside. From the darkness five, ten, fifteen Infected emerged. They were lit by the streetlamps shining down from above. When they saw him they released an inhuman screech and began charging. Francis put the magnum pistol in its holster before grabbing his rifle and opening fire.

He carefully fired to kneecap their legs and knock them over. He shot them in the stomach for gut wounds. And those that drew too close were shot in the skull to finish them off.

Francis stepped back, and the following wave of Infected tripped over their incapacitated brethren. They received wounds that they could usually heal from easily but were enough to send them stumbling around, impeding the pushing horde behind them from their charge.

Francis kept firing, slowly stepping back as the roiling horde slowly pushed aside their fellows to reach him.

The wave of bodies reached the doorway.

Francis expended the rest of his rifle magazine in moments, and the doorway was clogged with squirming bodies. Francis replaced his magazine in one motion. Pure muscle memory, he didn't even look down as he did it. God, he was a badass. He had practiced that one a lot. More of the creatures began breaking through the windows to the side.

Francis shot them in their skulls with pinpoint shots, sending them slumping to block the frame.

Francis felt a grin slowly grow on his face. His heart was beating faster. Now this was exciting. The ones at the door began to untangle themselves and began to stand. He reached into his belt and retrieved a traditional grenade. He pulled the pin and held it, just savoring the feeling for a moment. He remembered that reenactment festival he had joined last year.

"TALLY HO LADS HAHAHAHAHA."

He threw the grenade past the doorway before retreating to the doorway of the stairwell. Hahaha. That reenactment festival had been a blast. He lifted the rifle and executed the few stragglers that were approaching him. *BOOOOM*.

Francis laughed openly as he felt the vibration in his chest as the grenade exploded outside. He hadn't been able to truly cut loose since this assignment began years ago. To make these creatures suffer like how they deserved.

The crowd of Infected outside was devastated. Francis' rifle clicked empty. He reached for his vest, but his magazines were empty. He was out of ammo for now.

He dropped the rifle to dangle at his side with the strap and retrieved his precious grenade launcher from his back. He fired one of the grenades out the door. It exploded in a wave of Devouring flame. The flames washed over the incapacitated Infected lying on the ground as well as the crowd.

They screeched in pain. Francis could hear the high pitched screeches slowly morph into a deep singular moan, to his surprise. The hiss of the fire was extinguished. There was a moment of silence, only the sound of echoing footsteps as Francis entered the stairwell and began running upwards.

Crash! Francis heard something massive smash through the entrance below. He kept running. Seconds later, a loud impact shook the building as something smashed at the stairwell door. The door itself twisted and flew off its hinges and impacted the other wall with a loud *clang*. But the concrete surroundings held, bowing inwards but not breaking.

Francis was on the fourth floor by now. He stopped and leaned over the railing. He pointed his grenade launcher downward. He waited.

Crash! The concrete below shattered as the creature below scuttled through the wall. It was an amalgamation with six radial limbs that were long and spindly, resembling a spider. Each leg was composed of four humanoid figures. The Infected's flesh had melted like wax to fuse with the next component in line on the leg, their bodies twisted and distorted as they merged into the larger creature's body.

The spherical core of the creature consisted of assorted human body parts compressed into a ball. As Francis watched another Infected rushed in behind it. A tendril from the central ball speared out and skewered it before reeling it into the core.

Screeching, the Infected was brought into a massive maw that had just formed. With a crunch, the Infected went limp before melting and integrating with the rest of the creature's main mass. The creature grew larger.

"HEY UGLY!"

The creature braced two of its limbs against the wall and leveraged itself upward onto the next landing.

"TAKE THIS!"

Francis fired his grenade launcher. The creature somehow detected the projectile and shoved its core tightly against one of the walls. The grenade burst into a burst of reddish flame. It caught on the creature's two outstretched legs and began to burn them.

The creature let out a deep moan of pain that vibrated through the building. It ignored the flames before leveraging itself up for another landing in another lurching motion. The fire grew brighter and began to slowly spread over its body. Francis climbed another more of the steps.

The creature leveraged itself up to another landing.

Francis leaned over and fired another two grenades, one after another. It was mid-leap and couldn't dodge this time. The twin waves of flame washed over the creature's body.

It let out a deep moan that shook the building again. Louder this time, and the vibrations sent Francis stumbling to the side as he continued running up the stairs. Francis reached the landing just beneath the room before he heard shattering concrete below him.

The creature groaned and one of its burning limbs smashed through the wall behind Francis.

Two more limbs slammed down towards him, which Francis dodged, throwing himself to the ground. The core appeared, peeking up just above the lip of the landing.

Francis aimed the grenade launcher between his legs as the creature began to slip backwards into the open space of the stairwell. It scrabbled for purchase as gravity dragged it back downward. Its three limbs crashed and stabbed for purchase around Francis as the core slipped further downward with every passing moment.

After a moment its limbs braced against the wall and it began to pull itself upwards over the lip of the edge. Francis fired his weapon. The grenade seemed to move slowly in his vision.

His heart raced and he felt his adrenaline pump through him. The grenade hit the creature in the core with a direct hit, coating it in the devouring flames. With a final moan, the creature lost its grip on the wall and fell downwards.

The building shook as it smashed into the walls as it fell. Finally, with an earth shaking crash, the creature hit the bottom. Francis brushed himself off, still grinning. That shit was awesome! He was a goddamn action hero! Francis walked over to the shattered railing and leaned over the edge. The creature thrashed, but the flames slowly consuming it only grew stronger over time.

Francis had a moment of indecisiveness. Should he escape now or continue the fight? He retrieved the giant Doomslinger from his pouch. That was its fucking name now, no matter what Bill said. And he was going to use it to its full potential.

Francis made his way back down the stairs until it was a single floor above the creature consumed by flames. It had grown still with one final deep moan and slumped to the floor.

The Infected loitering on the first floor didn't dare to brave the flames consuming the base of the stairwell. Francis waited for a moment before he flipped a small black switch he had installed on the back of the Doomslinger's wooden surface.

With a massive suction of a vacuum, all the flames rushed into the Doomslinger's giant blue crystal core. The more it filled, the more the crystal's color changed to crimson. As the last of the flame was sucked into the Doomslinger's core, its end began to glow with a sinister red light. Francis pulled up his grenade launcher and fired his final grenade into the corpse of the spider amalgamation.

The patch of reddish flames on the creature's corpse caught and began slowly spreading once more to consume the body. Francis made his way down to the creature's corpse, holding the Doomslinger at the ready. The wood had two sculpted handles that stuck from its sides and made it far easier to carry.

The horde of Infected gathering beyond the massive hole in the wall seemed mired in indecision, unsure of what to do. The lights in the room flickered, most smashed by the amalgamation during its charge into the stairwell and sparking loose sparks of electricity.

Some of the Infected moved towards Francis before eyeing the glowing red light from the open end of Doomslinger and edging back, hoping another would lead the charge. Francis laughed at their fear as he stepped over the rubble of the entry to the stairwell.

He flipped the switch on the Doomslinger and panned it over the crowd. A vindictive light shone in his eyes.

"GET TORCHED, FUCKERS! HAHAHAHAHAHA!!!"

His manic laughter barely could be heard over the roaring blast of the Devouring flames and inhuman screeches of pain.

———— (Nameless Amalgamation POV) ————

The Nameless amalgamation scuttled to the side as the mortal descended down the stairwell. It hid under one of the limp thick limbs of its former body. The Devouring Flame had seared most of its former body faster than it had believed possible. It had even fed on the Nameless Amalgamations' energies to sustain itself. It's Potential.

How did the mortals obtain such a weapon? The Nameless had never encountered something of its like in all the invasions its components had participated in up to now.

It had barely had enough time to jettison this small portion of its body before it was caught alight by the Devouring Flame. It now was barely larger than a human head, with limbs shorter than a human forearm.

The human shouted something and then began laughing. The Nameless amalgamation heard a roar of flame in the next room and the screams of the Nameless inside as they were consumed. It shuddered before scuttling out from underneath its old corpses' limb.

It began silently scuttling up the stairs while the human was preoccupied with torching the other Nameless. It made it halfway up before pausing mid-scuttle. Was this not the perfect time for an attack from behind?

All the Nameless' components orders from Infiltrator of Authority were to kill the intruder at any cost. Including their lives. The Nameless Amalgamation inspected the human with its echolocation. He was still laughing as he sprayed flame at anything that moved.

A Nameless charged towards the human from the side. The warrior turned its weapon on it and reduced it to ashes after several seconds of the Devouring Flame. He was still laughing, but it felt more forced now. But he kept up the waves of flame even still.

The Nameless kept moving and made good on its escape. It had to report this fearsome weapon to Infiltrator of Authority! Surely this was more worthwhile than a futile attack? As it crept out the second-floor window the roaring flames still sounded from below even as more Infected closed in from every direction. It shuddered. Yes, its message was far more important than one lowly mortal!

It must rush from this place as fast as it could to accomplish its mission. Or the mission of its components back when they had been their own beings. It seemed a task as good as any other for the new Nameless Amalgamation. Not that it knew where Infiltrator of Authority could be. It always found the groups of the component Nameless when needed, not the other way around. The Nameless Amalgamation would just have to do its best to find Infiltrator of Authority.

Chapter 24: Trying to Leave the Party Early - Mortal Francis Fragment

Francis was no longer smiling as the last Infected scream went silent in the room. Tears ran down his face as long-buried memories came back to him. As Francis was breathing heavily as the Infected corpses burned around him, he heard footsteps from every direction outside the building. They all were coming now.

He flicked the switch and all the flames came rushing back into the Doomslinger. The red glow was slightly dimmer now than before. But it still glowed brightly enough.

Unfortunately, most of these Infected had barely been mutated at all due to being freshly Infected and needing to blend in with humanity. This prevented many of them from making more mutations as they had to keep looking human.

The Devouring flames had less Potential to burn in these types of Infected. Francis could tell by how the flames only brightened a fraction after those types were consumed by it. Francis turned around, the Doomslinger still sucking in the flames from the area.

The bonfire of the amalgamation rushed in a wave into the weapon and ashes swirled from the charred corpse. Luckily there was enough Potential shoved into that one to supply Doomslinger in combat for a long time hopefully. There were only ash and smaller meat chunks left of the creature now as the last bit of flame was drawn away from it.

The red light shining from the end of the Doomslinger grew so bright it was almost blinding. It illuminated the whole room in a stark red light as Francis retrieved the last of the flames and sucked them into his weapon.

A group of five more Infected charged through the door and Francis blasted them into ashes in an instant. He wiped away his tears with his arm and forced his smile back onto his face.

"Hah! Take that!"

Francis reversed the flame and it whooshed right back into the Doomslinger in moments. The sound of footsteps slowed outside before stopping just out of Francis' line of sight.

Francis adjusted his grip on the Doomslinger. His arms ached slightly from holding it up for so long.

What were they doing? Francis inched forward and carefully edged his way out of the door. Across the street at a good distance was a solid line of Infected. A large crowd of Infected closed off either end of the street, standing as if they were waiting for something.

Why? There must have been several hundred of them gathered around. Surely they must think they could take him if they all charged him at once? What's with the sudden change? The red light shining from the Doomslinger dimmed slightly the longer Francis waited.

Oh.

Francis mentally urged them to just move. The Infected hadn't seemed too concerned about their losses earlier… C'mon…

Francis slowly backed away before rushing to the back of the building. It was the same situation. There scattered about was a thick throng of Infected in a large ring some distance away, blocking access to the opposite street. Francis decided to take a chance. He stepped outside and waved the Doomslinger threateningly as he advanced. The Infected shifted back to maintain distance.

Francis moved forward again before noticing that the other Infected to his sides and behind him by the neighboring buildings were also approaching to attempt to circle him.

Francis beat a hasty retreat back into the building. The last thing he wanted was to get surrounded. The Doomslinger's greatest weakness was when he was retracting the flames back into the weapon Francis would be helpless. If he did that and was attacked from behind in force then he would be helpless to defend himself in time.

Alright, no more messing around. Time to focus.

Francis retreated back into the building and considered his options. His invisibility stone was still his best option to get out of here. But the crowd of Infected was much thicker than he had expected when he made that plan.

One strong reflexive blow from one of them and his invisibility shield would disappear and he would be discovered in the middle of the swarm and be boned.

When the horde had been smaller he had planned to retreat to the roof before repelling down the side with the rope to throw them off as they rushed upwards into the building. But with their sudden caution, that plan might not work anymore.

Francis stood at attention as he heard the rumbling of approaching cars. He peered through one of the shattered windows in the front and glanced towards the road closest to the hospital. Five white vans pulled to one side of the street and their back doors were pulled open. Five gigantic creatures exited each of the vans. Francis' eyes widened. Would each of these things be as powerful as that fucked-up human spider thing? Hopefully, they burned as well as the spider had too.

There were two sets of identical creatures, each with different forms. One looked like nothing more than two extremely large worms with large fleshy orbs that almost looked tumorous attached to the end that was the "head". The other pair resembled massive humanoid armadillos.

Their postures were hunched and their shells had massive spikes growing haphazardly from all over their bony surface. Their long pointed heads had a bone helmet above them like some kind of medieval footman, over six feet tall even as they stood there hunched. Their arms nearly dragged on the ground and were tipped with massive sharp claws.

The last creature of the five looked nothing like any animal Francis had ever seen. At the base, the thing had eight stubbly legs that were thick and lined either side of a massive blob that jiggled and bounced like fat.

Curling from its base where a tail would attach to an animal, a rigid hollow tube ran up and over the blob of flesh until it straightened into a long rigid tube that ran along the length of its body.

On top of this rigid tube was a thick layer of flesh that undulated in a rhythm starting at the base and ending at the open end of the tube. Two shorter and flexible tubes sat poised to either side, standing cocked back and waving slightly in the air like a pair of snakes ready to strike at any moment.

Little black pits covered the surface of the creature's body, but nothing like a human's eyes stood out to Francis.

The strange creature wobbled for a moment before slowly turning and moving to the side so it had a better angle to the front of the office building. The two flexible tubes shifted and continued to point towards the building Francis was sheltering in.

The two armadillo creatures stepped forward to put themselves between Francis and the other three protectively as they moved opposite as a group to the front of the building for a better position. Francis licked his lips. Should he…

Blam Blam! Two rapid impacts slammed into the exterior wall next to the window he was peering out of. He caught a flash of the two snake-like tubes resetting their position before he ducked down out of sight. Francis glanced again. The undulations of the bigger fixed tube grew quicker.

Without hesitation, Francis threw himself to the side just before the base of the window behind which he had been hiding exploded into splinters under a heavy impact.

Francis rolled to his feet while still gripping Doomslinger. The worm creatures had both approached under cover of the barrage by the strange fifth creature. Francis made sure to focus his aim on the closest one and let loose the flame.

The creature tried to dodge, but the flame shifted mid-air at the last second to land on it. But the flame dimmed significantly in doing so. Francis dragged the beam of flame shooting from the end of the Doomslinger over to the other worm.

It had curled its body backwards until it was almost circular before snapping back straight, launching the orb that detached from its body directly through the window on the other side of the room.

Francis blasted the creature with the flame. He quickly turned and blasted the unknown fleshy orb with the flame too.

The Doomslinger spewed out the flame the whole time, as he couldn't risk retracting the flame or stopping the stream with the nearby worms ready to attack. After spraying the unknown fleshy orb he quickly shut off the stream of flame, but didn't retract the flames just yet.

Francis tried to step out the front door to follow up on the other three large creatures but had to duck back inside again quickly when another pair of *Bang Bang* sounded out. A pair of long needles lanced into the ground just behind where Francis had been standing.

He dodged again, diving to the side as he already knew what was coming next. *Whump!* a sound of displaced air sounded from outside as the other wall he had been hiding behind exploded into shards and rubble as the larger cannonball like shot fired from the strange creature.

The flames on the worms burned brightly, and the strange orb hissed behind him and crackled with flame too. After a few tense moments, the worms grew still with blazing flames flickering over their bodies. Francis flicked the switch on Doomslinger and the bonfires twitched in his direction, being reeled back in.

They drifted his way for a moment before in a rush entered the Doomslinger. The crystal now shone a duller red than before. But it was still bright. At this rate, Francis thought he could probably only do that kind of maneuver two or three more times before the flame ran out. *Bang Bang!*

What Francis now saw were tiny bone needles flew through the flimsy front door and hit the far wall. Francis went to dodge but stumbled slightly. He was feeling lightheaded. He turned to the stairwell and stumbled forward.

He hadn't wanted to trap himself above without clearing out more of the Infected, but it was clear he wouldn't last much longer down here. His head grew fuzzier and he coughed.

Whump! Another loud blast behind him. Francis noticed the orb that was launched inside by the worm was split open and there was nothing inside. He bathed it with flame again as he stumbled past it into the stairwell, but quickly retracted the flames after it didn't seem to gain any more strength from the charred flesh.

Francis crawled his way up the stairs. His head cleared slightly. He stumbled upon another flight. His head cleared more. He went up one final flight just to be sure and the headache receded to a throbbing pain in the back of his mind. He coughed a little and leaned against a wall for a moment. Fuckin' poison gas.

Francis always hated little cowards with poison blades who stabbed you once and then fled for their lives. Well, that had only happened once. But it pissed him off so much he was biased against anything related to that little shit. Helen had gotten his revenge for him almost immediately, but Francis still ended up puking his guts out for weeks afterwards anyways.

Compared to that, this poison gas seemed like pretty weak shit though if he could partially recover this quickly from it. Or maybe the flame burned away most of it? He wasn't sure.

Francis was feeling better by the second. He shoved himself off the wall and peered out the window. The tubed turret creature was rotating in place, seeming to be searching the windows for a glimpse of Francis. The two guards stood on either side of it, shuffling in place. Its lower fatty mass had deflated a little. It must be using it as fuel for its shots at him.

Francis looked at the five white vans that still sat there motionless. That was his ticket out of there. Francis had left his vehicle behind in a safe place before the mission. Due to the mental effects of the barrier, the people in the town didn't realize that their cars would completely run out of gas soon.

The gas available within the dome wouldn't last the months required before the emergence of the Harbinger. So the Neighborhood Watch was trying to conserve as much fuel as possible so when they reached the endgame they would have the resources they needed.

Totally reasonable, but Francis wished he had just wasted the fuel anyway to bring the car so he could have just driven out of here ten minutes ago. Well, that was probably a lie. He had had too much fun using the Doomslinger as a flamethrower.

He had been itching to use it ever since he made it. It had become a whole lot less fun after his planned escape route became blocked off though.

Suddenly, Francis' radio crackled to life. A woman's voice wafted from the radio. "Hello, is there a Francis here?"

Francis waited a moment and the woman remained silent. He thought of why some random woman might be on Bill's channel. Was she going to say more? He realized what was happening and felt annoyed he had to deal with this type of thing in the middle of a combat zone.

"Yes? Say Over when you're done, newbie. Over. Got it? Who is this? Alright for real this time, Over."

"Umbrellas protect even without rain? Uhhhhh, Over."

Oh. This wasn't good. Bill was dead or captured? Because that is the only way she could have gotten his radio. Francis had to coordinate to protect this woman and bring her to base on top of his own situation. If there was an issue with the extraction team, the woman may have others with her if she was one of the ones they were retrieving.

Well, Francis could at least see how bad this was going to be. Dealing with two or more untrained people could be a nightmare if they entered a combat situation. Even protecting one person was difficult. But you could bully or intimidate a single person into listening to you unquestioningly in an emergency situation much easier than you could in a group.

"Are you alone? Over"

"..."

"Yes. Over."

Francis thought of what he should do here. He had to protect the location of the compound on the off chance this was some kind of elaborate trick. He picked the safehouse that the Infiltrator of Authority had raided a few days ago and gave her information on how to get there and how to get in.

There was nothing of value left there for the Infected or the Neighborhood Watch both, so it should be abandoned. Safehouse Nine. The most essential part was that she not be seen and captured by any random wandering Infected on the streets.

He made her repeat back his instructions before signing off. There had been no movement from outside as he spoke on the radio, but Francis was getting a bad feeling from the sudden silence.

And the fact that the Infected hadn't continued their assault from before and seemed to be waiting to attack.

It was time to move.

Chapter 25: Escaping the Partygoers - Mortal Francis Fragment

Francis crept to the roof. He peered over the edge and looked down to where the two... Wait two?! One of the armadillo creatures was missing.

There was only the turret thing and one of the armadillo guards remaining. The turret looked a little deflated, its central mass shrunk even more. Presumably from all the projectiles it had fired at him.

Two of the five vans must have driven off with the bodies of the charred corpses of worms.

Francis went to the rope he had tied to the air conditioning unit on the roof and gave it one more tug for security. Francis put the Doomslinger in his special expanded spatial pouch and retrieved his invisibility orb.

He glanced over the edge of the roof again and watched the ring of Infected at the base of it, maintaining their distance as they waited down there. The turret was slowly panning side to side, searching for him in the windows of the office building.

The remaining armadillo guard stood at the ready as the three vans sat idling behind them. The timing would be tight on this. Francis looked behind him as he heard crashing from below on the bottom floor.

Time to go.

Francis moved to the rope and threw it off the side of the building. At the same time, he retrieved his second to last earth-based grenade, pulled the pin, and tossed it as hard as he could towards the other side of the building.

Francis began pressing various spots over the invisibility orb, and the light around him began gradually distorting and twisting. The grenade exploded in a wave of fire and shrapnel and Francis could feel the shockwave in his bones.

Francis plunged into darkness with only two tiny pin holes cut out near his eyes as the invisibility orb fully activated. He held the orb firmly in his left hand. His periphery was cut off, but he could see well enough to maneuver.

He grabbed the rope and slowly repelled his way down with one hand on the rope and the other on the invisibility orb. The bubble of invisibility wobbled around him if he moved too quickly, and he had to stop himself a few times to let its watery vibrations settle down.

Finally, Francis touched the ground. The Infected observing the building were oblivious and seemed to be attempting to peer around to see the other side of the building while maintaining their position. Francis heard an enraged squeal, like that of a pig sounding from the top of the building.

The creature on the roof began to throw a tantrum. Francis choked down his instinctive laugh at the sound as he crept forward. His mood lifted, but he made sure to stay focused. He didn't need to ruin his heroic escape at the last moment! He was in front of the building now, stepping quietly.

He took another step.

A shard of glass crunched under his foot, and he froze. The turret swiveled and the guard turned, hands flexing and long claws clicking together. Francis waited.

Crashes and destruction sounded from the top of the building continued as the other armadillo guard raged its piggy little heart out.

In the alleyway where Francis had descended, the air conditioning unit he had tied his rope to flew from the roof and landed with a loud crash onto the ground behind him.

At the sound, the two creatures were startled and turned to the noise. After a moment, they relaxed as they saw the cause before returning to eye the building once more.

Francis crept closer to the two giant creatures as the sounds from the roof began to die down. He looked between the creatures and the idling vans. If the turret creature fired one of the larger shots, then it would probably disable the van in one hit.

But even if the defeated the creatures quickly then the Infected sitting inside of the running vehicles could just drive off and leave him stranded and vulnerable to the surrounding swarm of Infected. Francis made a wide circle around the two big creatures before he was halfway between the vans and the creatures.

Francis saw movement inside the building's bottom floor.

The remaining guard was coming back, he would have to start his escape soon. Francis went to speed up his pace but the invisibility shield's wobbling increased and the dark membrane around him threatened to break.

He paused in place for a moment and it settled slightly. He reached into his bag and retrieved Doomslinger from it carefully.

He held it close so it wouldn't hit the dark invisibility shield that was roiling at his sudden movements, looking like it might pop at his slightest movement. He positioned himself so he faced the vans and pointed Doomslinger awkwardly behind him at the turret creature.

His invisibility orb was still clutched in his left hand. The turret was the most dangerous one for his escape as it could fire at a distance, destroying the car he would steal from afar with its shots if Francis was unlucky.

Francis took a deep breath.

He tossed the invisibility orb into his pouch and adjusted his grip on Doomslinger. As soon as the orb left his fingers the shield popped, exposing him to the world again. The Infected down the street pointed at him and screeched when they spotted Francis, but the two massive creatures were facing the wrong way and were both slow to turn.

Francis hastily pressed the button on Doomslinger and waves of flame sprung forth from its end. He started running towards the closest white van while maintaining his aim to spray the flames behind him. Francis sprayed the turret monster with the waves of Devouring Flames. It thrashed at the surprise attack from behind and its flexible tubes writhed as it fell forward, its legs giving out in surprise from the sudden assault.

The two flexible tubes twisted around and spat two spikes *Thump thump* reflexively in Francis' direction. But they were shot wildly and came nowhere near Francis' position, both bone needles piercing into the road off to his right.

Francis turned the Doomslinger's flame onto the armadillo guard who had just finished turning to face him at the commotion. The flame from Doomslinger tapered off after two more seconds of flame and kept dimming until it was empty. The red glow cut out and the crystal became blue once more.

The guard thrashed as the flame invaded its joints between its shell and bone armor. The flames that landed on its plating flickered for a moment before being snuffed out.

The turret was a massive bonfire and was twitching on the ground by now. Both creatures thrashed in pain, and Francis was forgotten for the moment as they beat at the flames on them in a futile attempt to snuff it out.

Francis kept running.

There was an unmutated Infected sitting in the driver's seat of the van. It stuck its head out the rolled down window to see what was going on, just in time to see Francis' rapid approach. It began to screech and went to climb out.

Francis choked up on Doomslinger before bringing it low to the ground. With a grunt of exertion, he swung it up like a club and hit the Infected's chin from below in a devastating blow, cutting off its high pitched cry. The Infected's body rose off it's seat and it fell half way out of the window. Francis shoved the Infected back inside the car with one hand before fully opening the door.

Francis threw the bloody Doomslinger over the Infected to the passenger side before grabbing the stunned Infected with both hands and heaving it out onto the ground. It lay there stunned for a moment before its skin began bubbling and more of its black blood started running from its orifices. Francis hopped in the vehicle and hit the gas pedal as hard as he could as the Infected kept mutating next to the van.

Luckily it was too slow to attack him. The wheels squealed and the van wrenched from side to side for a moment before the wheels caught on the ground and the van shot into motion with a squeal of the tires. The mutated infected stood up and began to chase the car as fast as it could, stumbling after him with loud screeches of anger.

Francis glanced back. The burning forms of the two larger creatures grew still behind him. The other armadillo guard had emerged from the building and charged towards Francis as he drove away, still squealing in rage. The crowd of Infected at the end of the street saw the form of the van barreling towards them and the ones in his path promptly fell to the floor twitching and mutating.

Francis ran over the Infected with his stolen van, the crowd standing roughly ten deep on the street. The van jumped and hopped as it rolled over the morphing bodies.

As he reached the middle of the crowd of Infected, they all stood back up in unison and grabbed onto the van with their abnormal strength. They clung to the sides for a moment.

One went to reach through the rolled down window after crawling up the side. Francis pulled out his magnum pistol with one hand and lined it up with the Infected. The van jumped as the vehicle ran over another one of the mutating bodies.

His gun went flying out of his hand out of the window. Shit! The Infected clinging to the side of the van recovered its grip and reached for Francis with its one free arm with long curled claws on its end.

Francis swung the van from side to side by wrenching the wheel side to side and the Infected at the window lost its grip and fell. Francis glanced in the side mirrors and saw there were more Infected just barely holding on.

Francis kept swerving until the last was sent flying to wetly splat onto the street at high speed. There was one last thump on the back of the van before Francis stopped skittering across the road and gained speed again.

The armadillo creature squealed in frustration as Francis gained speed once more and increased the gap between them as he drove. The guard and the Infected crowd following it slowly fell behind into the distance, still letting out their screeches of anger.

Francis let out a sigh of relief as he drove away from the hospital in a straight line on the empty roads. The scattered wandering Infected in the area diverted towards him but didn't seem to realize who he was before he blew by them.

The large armored creature quickly fell behind and was fully left behind as Francis kept driving and took a few turns.

The Infected encounters slowed before they eventually stopped as he drove onwards. He relaxed. Then all of a sudden the hairs on the back of his neck rose. He twisted his head to the side as a swollen fist punched through the back of the divider between the cabin and back of the van.

The hand punched through to where his head had been a second earlier and closed its massive fist on thin air.

Francis laid flat while holding the wheel steady with one hand. The massive hand groped around for a moment around the top of the seat before retreating through the divider between the back and the main cabin.

Francis pulled the combat knife from his chest sheath with one hand, the other hand steady on the wheel. Francis peeked his head up and righted the vehicle so he wouldn't crash. He pressed a little button on the handle of his combat knife as he stabbed the hand that reached through from the back to try to find him again.

He slashed at the hand over and over with his combat, and the creature flinched. The creature roared as Francis heard the signature *Whoooosh* of flame. A few seconds later the hand drew back and after a few more alien screeches the creature in the back went silent.

Francis looked around and didn't spot any Infected on the streets before pulling to the side. He grimaced as he saw the lines of energy on the knife had gone dark. He cautiously crept around to inspect the back cabin. There was the charred corpse of the Infected lying prone, still sizzling slightly.

Now the knife had released its little store of Devouring Flame, it was mundane. Damn, they didn't have many of those. Bill would be pissed it was being used this early in the plan. After a moment he shrugged to himself. Perks of being number two, he guessed. Better than dying.

Francis inspected the surroundings suspiciously, but it seemed the creature was alone. He went to return to the car before pausing as he realized something. He leaned over and sure enough, a cat-sized lump of flesh was clinging to the undercarriage. As soon as Francis spotted it it detached and leaped at him in one explosive motion.

He dodged to the side and jumped back into the van and floored it. As he drove away, the blob rapidly was left behind on the road. It launched itself in explosive bursts towards the fleeing van, but seemed to need a few seconds to recover after each leap.

After that, Francis gave the whole vehicle a thorough inspection including the glovebox and the roof after he felt he had driven far enough away from the scene. Luckily no more Infected had seemed to have snuck aboard. No wandering Infected came by as Francis did his inspection.

Francis got back into the van and kept driving. Alright, now it was time to meet the newbie. She would be alright for a little while at least.

It had been a long time since Francis had talked to someone who wasn't already involved in all the secrets he had been dealing with for over a decade. Hopefully, she hadn't seen anything too horrific on her way out of the hospital.

Chapter 26: Chaos at the Hospital - Infiltrator of Authority Fragment

Infiltrator of Authority stepped out of the elevator to the third floor of the hospital. All the mortals who were sick or injured. All were brought together in one building. Truly a valuable institution, how sweet the irony is now.

Infiltrator of Authority stepped to the side to speak with the Nameless taking the role of the police sergeant on the scene. Infiltrator of Authority had spent a few moments in the past correcting this Nameless' behavior to more closely match the mortals' emotions.

While it still showed few mortal emotions still, it at least remembered to tense its facial muscles enough that the blank expression was closer to one that was bored versus that of a human on sedatives.

Unfortunately, most of the other Nameless couldn't even accomplish that much. Without the barrier and its mental component affecting the humans, Infiltrator of Authority was sure they would have been discovered by the townspeople far before now.

The Nameless reported on the situation in low tones in its mortal's voice. These Nameless were far too weak to be able to initiate telepathic contact themselves as Infiltrator of Authority could do.

The Nameless Sergeant continued its report. One of the mortal workers had been the first to stumble upon the shattered door of Fulcrum's room. There was no indication of who or what it could be that attacked.

The hospital was locked down, and many of the patients were missing as well. The patient records and security footage of the last week were wiped. All the records from just before the barrier went up were gone. How convenient, these simultaneous attacks were. Two human officers had approached and determined that Fulcrum was fine. But no attacker had been found.

Infiltrator of Authority curled his tentacles in his real body. That damnable mortal Bill had been a distraction. He was clearly after the Harbinger the entire time and used himself and the other patients as bait for Infiltrator of Authority.

Infiltrator of Authority was not familiar enough to know how the mortal could accomplish this. And what his goal was. If the mortal's goals were to oppose Infiltrator of Authority, then why be the one to release it? Furthermore, none of the Nameless or humans saw anyone suspicious enter the area at the time Fulcrum's door was destroyed.

And Infiltrator of Authority had been guarding the entrance closest to Bill's assault itself. It knew the attack couldn't have come from its direction. And the other directions were guarded by the best of the Nameless available. None had seen anything suspicious. Nothing about it made sense.

From the evacuation of the mortals with Potential and simultaneous attack on Fulcrum, Infiltrator of Authority knew this was a disaster. It had also lost significant forces when one of the other mortals had fought his way out of the encirclement of the Nameless.

In a fit of paranoia, Infiltrator of Authority grabbed one of the Nameless nearby and made them go check on the watchers of the mutating Nameless in the house opposite the Seed.

It would be just like the Betrayers to send it to attack it now when Infiltrator of Authority was otherwise occupied.

Several of the humans looked at Infiltrator of Authority strangely and it realized the Nameless had been in the shape of one of the mortal nurses, not one of the police officers. Infiltrator of Authority ignored its blunder and the suspicious looks of the mortals and started to check on the patients who had remained and not fled in the chaos. With recent events, they would have to be harvested soon.

Too many odd things had happened here, and the increased Nameless presence in the hospital in response would lead the barriers in the mental wards to break soon for those with high Potential.

The most powerful had likely already fled or been taken by the mortal Bill. Those with high Potential could be identified by sight by Infiltrator of Authority or any of the Nameless, but with their home addresses lost they would have to search the whole town for those who escaped on their own.

Most of the humans were currently sheltering at home, becoming 'sick' so they didn't have to go to work outside the barrier. It helped Infiltrator of Authority distribute its forces around the hospital and town more freely, but at the same time made it difficult to find these humans again if they just went home and stayed inside.

Invading a single home provoked the others nearby and led to the loss of a few Nameless early on. Especially for those who owned guns and could fight off the relatively stupid Nameless if they were too obvious about what they were doing.

Infiltrator of Authority wouldn't send the Nameless out to track down more of the high Potential humans until their presence was already fully exposed to the humans and there was no more use in hiding.

The Nameless police sergeant followed as Infiltrator of Authority moved through the hospital. Unfortunately, Infiltrator of Authority's body was a low level officer.

Being unnoticed by the mortals often served its purposes, but in this case, the police sergeant's authority would be needed to investigate the situation and to do what needed to be done. No matter how much it grated at Infiltrator of Authority's pride to be considered below a meager Nameless, even amongst these mortals. The mission came first.

As Infiltrator of Authority went to enter the first patient room, a human approached looking at the Nameless behind Infiltrator of Authority. The human was in blue hospital scrubs, the uniform of the human workers it seemed.

He looked to the sergeant, "Hello, I'd like to register a complaint about one of your officers. He was very hostile and shouted at the patient that was attacked tonight…"

Infiltrator of Authority listened with interest at the conflict between this human officer and Fulcrum. The Nameless nodded and promised to look into it. The human, John as he called himself, looked unsatisfied at the reply but left anyway. He was called away to do paperwork of all things at a time like now.

Infiltrator noted to keep the mortal a little longer. Without the paperwork finished the remaining humans here may harass some of the Nameless and be more likely to notice their strange behavior. Infiltrator of Authority should learn more of Fulcrum so it could know why he was chosen by the Seed.

It had not understood the choice of bond from the being, but maybe this pathetic mortal officer who shouted at Fulcrum would have more insight into his uniqueness.

———O—o—O———

Infiltrator of Authority sat to the side next to the Nameless Sergeant. It held its clipboard with its pen hovering above the paper, ready to write. While its main mass was no longer in the pad, Infiltrator of Authority had already established its host's attachment to its notepad in the last week as it fully integrated into the host. Not using it at this point would be suspicious to the mortals and counter to its displayed persona.

The two police officers being questioned sat opposite Infiltrator of Authority and the Nameless police sergeant. The group had commandeered one of the empty patient rooms for this discussion. The shorter officer with blonde hair seemed to still be stewing in his anger and shifted in place. Officer Smith was the mortal's name.

The taller man with the thick mustache just seemed uncomfortable and a little confused. Officer Sanchez. The Nameless started with the questioning in its bored voice. Infiltrator of Authority noted the inflection. Dead inside perhaps, but convincingly human. Perhaps this Nameless was worth watching. Most were hopeless buffoons, even among the most able stationed inside the hospital building.

"Well, Officer Smith, what happened then? I'm hearing you're yelling at the victim of a crime now. I'm sure you can explain."

The man was red in the face and his hands were trembling.

"Well! Well… Well, he and I have a long history, sir. If I had known it was him I was protecting, well I probably would have requested another assignment. He's a criminal. Bastard deserves everything he gets."

On seeing Infiltrator of Authority's calculated expression of heavy disapproval, the man hurried to finish,

"But! But, uhm. It was unprofessional to yell at him like that. I should have just left when I saw his smug face. He just brought back some bad memories. He clearly was lying to us and it ticked me off."

The Nameless glanced at Infiltrator of Authority. This was far more animosity than seemed reasonable. Wasn't Fulcrum injured in a hospital bed, why wouldn't the mortal control himself? Infiltrator of Authority turned to Officer Sanchez,

"Do you think the patient was lying about something?"

Officer Sanchez looked nervous about getting involved in whatever was happening. As the other man spoke he shifted his chair farther and farther away from Officer Smith. He was trying to avoid the backlash from the clear bias and emotion emanating from Officer Smith's statements.

He didn't want Officer Smith's failure to taint him. Infiltrator of Authority had seen many similar squabbles among the Nameless below it back on its home planet. The taller officer tried to keep his response as short as possible as he shifted in place like he'd rather be anywhere else.

"Well, yes. He claimed he didn't wake up when the door broke. He controlled his expression the whole time too. Kept his face blank."

"But I don't see why he would lie. But he was polite enough before Ryan just started going off on him for seemingly no reason. Ryan wouldn't even tell me how he knew him when I asked either."

The man gestured with one hand as he threw his partner, Ryan Smith apparently, firmly under the bus. Infiltrator of Authority internally smiled at the image. What an amusing expression, truly a brutal execution method. Fitting for these mortals. Officer Sanchez could apparently see where the wind was blowing and was covering his career.

Not that Infiltrator of Authority would ever allow any officer to be fired or suspended at this point. They would simply become a Nameless if they proved too troublesome.

But Officer Sanchez certainly seemed to think that's where the conversation was heading and was getting out in front of it. Officer Smith gaped at Officer Sanchez with a look of hurt and betrayal. He opened his mouth to say something.

Infiltrator of Authority turned back to Officer Smith and interrupted, "So what about it? What's the history? You said this man you yelled at was arrested?"

Officer Smith shut his mouth before muttering something under his breath.

"What was that?"

Officer Smith glanced around frantically for a moment as if looking for escape before slumping. He spoke a little louder. "Well, he wasn't convicted. But he did it."

"And what did he do?"

"Well he… he…"

"Yes? Spit it out."

The man's face twisted into anger as he jumped out of his chair. He glared at Infiltrator of Authority, but it just laughed internally. To think such a puny mortal would attempt to intimidate it! Pathetic. But he was nice and riled up at least. Officer Smith's voice rose.

"He! He…! That bastard killed my sister!"

Infiltrator of Authority and the Nameless just stared at him for a moment. Infiltrator of Authority saw Officer Smith's partner's mouth open in shock. He seemed to now look a little guilty at his prior betrayal.

Infiltrator of Authority quickly shifted its expression to shock as well. It nudged the Nameless sergeant as it remained stoic.

At the nudge, the Nameless leaned its body backwards while blinking hard as if in shock. Not a bad performance, even if it was a little exaggerated based on the Nameless' persona's prior behavior.

"Wha... What?!" Officer Sanchez stuttered out

Officer Smith turned to him and his finger jabbed into the man's chest. The corner of his eyes were shining now. Infiltrator of Authority internally smiled. It was so fun to watch the mortals squirm. Who knew he would get free entertainment today!

"That's..." He poked him again. "Right. They were dating for years! It was the weekend, and she told me she was having a movie night over at his house!"

Officer Smith's hand dropped and he rubbed his eyes and began sniffling. "She disappeared without a trace!"

His nose was running and his eyes were wet. Infiltrator of Authority licked the lips of the host.

Yes. More! Officer Smith wiped his nose and continued. He was just staring into space now, seeming to speak to himself.

"When I went over the next day, he was in a panic. Said a ghost took her or some crazy shit. That he hadn't meant it to happen. He was delusional. Delusional. Muttering how he didn't mean to do it, how she was gone. I arrested him, but… but after time with his lawyer, he just denied everything.

"Said she had left after they watched a movie. Composed as ever, with that same blank face."

He snapped out of his reverie and refocused and started raising his voice again,

"Like she never even mattered at all! And he's still there, just the same… *Hic*. Just the same…" He collapsed to his knees and tried and failed to hold back his tears in front of the three men, inconsolable by his awkward partner. Officer Sanchez looked supremely uncomfortable and his mouth opened and closed as he looked at a loss for words.

Hahahahahaha! Infiltrator of Authority's real body quivered with laughter as he watched the mortals in front of him squirm. He barely kept his mortal body from smiling.

Maybe today wasn't so bad after all. First, he got to have some fun converting that mortal from earlier, and now this performance is here. It was just what it needed to improve its mood after the latest setbacks.

And the outburst told him more of Fulcrum as well. If he was killing fellow mortals at this stage then he may be more willing to cast them aside when he became a superior being.

Such actions were especially commendable in the society Fulcrum was born into. It was a society that was so disapproving of the act of killing as if the mortals scrabbling in the mud could resist having their little wars and killing each other in the thousands. Truly a hypocritical social norm.

Infiltrator of Authority wanted to stay to watch the drama, but duty came first. After it became clear nothing else of use would come from this, Infiltrator of Authority silently rose to its feet. It stepped outside the room without a word, the mortal still sniffling on the floor. The Nameless inside would handle the rest.

Once outside, Infiltrator of Authority allowed a spring in its step and a smile on the body's face as it resumed checking on the patients with Potential. And converting them into Nameless. No more could afford to be lost, even if they would lose some power from being harvested early.

Infiltrator of Authority stepped into the first patient room. The patient looked confused and wary, but seeing its smiling face seemed to relax them. How curious. Infiltrator reached down to his clipboard and extracted a business card. He held out to the patient. It stood there smiling and held the card out.

The patient took it in confusion and flipped the blank card over and over to see the two blank sides before freezing. The two of them were alone in the room. The card twitched to life before proceeding to burrow into the patient's hand. Infiltrator of Authority just smiled wider.

Sometimes the simplest approaches were the most effective, it had learned. No words were necessary. It opened the door and went to the next patient in line. It had a lot of work to do.

———O—o—O———

Infiltrator of Authority was almost finished with its task when the police sergeant Nameless approached. It spoke to Infiltrator of Authority softly again in its mortal voice. It seemed that the mortal Bill had escaped from the nearby building where he was held.

How? He was cuffed to a chair and being watched by two Nameless. Nameless that were mutated to be far more powerful than any human could ever hope to be. Infiltrator of Authority felt a hint of respect. For a weak mortal to accomplish even that much was commendable.

Another Nameless rushed up, one that was mimicking one of the mortal nurses, the one Infiltrator of Authority had sent off before. It said that the mutated Nameless had shown no signs of movement so far. Excellent. As if Infiltrator of Authority didn't have enough on its plate.

Well, that was an issue for the future. Regardless, it was time to hunt the mortal Bill. Infiltrator of Authority had little hope for success. The slippery mortal had already escaped its grasp once, from much worse circumstances too.

But at least a token effort was required in case the unlikely happened and the mortal Bill made some obvious mistake. With long strides, Infiltrator of Authority left the hospital and walked out into the night to lead the search.

Chapter 27: A New Club in The Neighborhood - Mortal (Ryan) Fragment

Ryan's eyes were puffy and red. He was still in the same empty patient's room as before. He couldn't believe he had just broken down in front of his partner and the other men like that. His partner wanted nothing to do with him and had left as soon as he could.

The asshole had thrown him to the wolves at the first opportunity. Saving his career over his partner in duty. It hurt.

The other two hadn't even cared. Nick had just left without another word after Ryan had broken down. Ryan wasn't even sure why he was even there, it should have been handled by just the Sergeant by himself. Ryan felt himself getting a little angry at the fact that Nick hadn't even had to be there.

What a dick. Probably wrote that shit all in his stupid little pad too. He was inseparable from the blasted thing these days. Never let it leave his person for even a moment, it was so precious to him.

The sergeant had just looked bored as Ryan bared his soul and broke down in front of him. Lots of the guys in the department had seemed bored lately. Just going through the motions. This depression was permeating the station, and Ryan for the life of him couldn't say why it was happening.

When asked, the depressed officers just shrugged it off as overwork or something at home.

But there were so many that even someone as oblivious as Ryan had begun noticing. Officer Nick's indifference to his breakdown was expected. He had always been a selfish asshole.

But Ryan knew the sergeant. He had always cracked a joke when things got tense to break the tension. Helping the newbies learn how to do the paperwork. Little things like that.

But his bored expression at Ryan's pain had been shocking. It had been unsettling and almost made Ryan stop. But the rest had just slipped out without him meaning to. Once he started telling it he had to get it all out.

Seeing *Him* had brought back all the memories. Everything hit Ryan all at once. The whole scenario had hit him with a blast of deja vu. His demeanor, how he spoke. Him shrugging off obvious facts, smug that he knew something they didn't. Everything Ryan had shoved down came back in a wave of emotion. The anger had washed over his mind. He took several deep breaths.

Once he calmed down more, he realized his memories of the last hour were fuzzy. Through all the charged emotions and memories of the past, he hardly even remembered what he had said to *Him* in the moment. Ryan and his sister had always been close. Or at least he had thought so until she met *Him*.

Losing her had gnawed at him. She was always so vibrant and upbeat. So ready for life. It burned at him. Knowing that *He* was still out there scott free. Even that morning all those years ago, he knew something was wrong when his calls to her hadn't connected.

He barely remembered why he had even tried to call in the first place. But he had known something was wrong as soon as the call failed. Ryan knew she always made sure to keep her phone charged, so it should have let him leave a message at least if everything was fine. Jessica always answered when he called, even if she didn't want to. But the call just failed.

The sound of the door opening caused him to look up. An older man with silver hair hobbled in the door only for his eyes to widen as he saw Ryan kneeling on the floor with reddened eyes. The old man's foot was wrapped in white bandages and he winced as he put weight on it.

Ryan went to speak, but the man rushed forward and shushed him. Ryan blinked but closed his mouth and waited. The man didn't seem to have any hostile intent. For a moment they just waited there.

Ryan opened his mouth but was shushed again. Ryan was getting irritated now. Who did this asshole think he was to shush *him*? Finally, the sounds of footsteps sounded at the door. They spoke softly. Ryan crept closer. He put his ear to the door to hear their whispers. Their voices were monotone as they spoke to one another.

"Was that all of them?"

"The nurses said there was an old man with silver hair, but his room was empty."

"Any breaks in the perimeter?"

"Not so far. What if he goes to the huma— nurses?"

"Well, clearly he is a criminal. The nurses should hand him over if they catch him. We will get him either way. Either here or outside."

"Wait, I heard something."

Ryan held his breath. There was silence for a moment. The door opened and Ryan jerked back before leaning against the nearby hospital bed in an attempt to appear nonchalant. A look that didn't really work with his ruffled clothing and shirt wet from the tears he had let out minutes ago.

The two at the door were police officers Ryan didn't interact with very much at work. He didn't even know their names even though he recognized their faces. The two stared at him, before scanning the room behind him before locking in on something.

Ryan glanced behind him, and the old man had inexpertly hid behind the cot. His feet were sticking out from the end. Dammit, that was just pathetic.

He was clearly visible, but Ryan guessed he had at least made an effort. The two officers took a step forward in unison and Ryan took a step back.

"Ah, Officer Smith. You've found the criminal. We found a bag of cocaine in his room. We need to take him in for questioning."

Ryan stared at them. Seriously? He didn't know them that well, but he wouldn't have guessed they were such scumbags. This was the kinda shit you heard in some true crime dramas, not in real life. They stepped forward again in unison. How the hell were they doing that? Ryan took another step backward. He was parallel with the cot now.

"Stop! I heard what you said through the door. We both know you don't bring in hurt suspects if you don't have to. He should stay here until he's healed."

At this, the two stopped their advances. One stood straighter. His lip twitched until his lips raised. It was like little hooks were hooked into his lips with little twitches and adjustments, a smile formed.

But it was the baring of teeth of a predator, "No, he's coming with us. And what are you going to do about it?"

Ryan shouted now, his anger returning with a vengeance. "I'll report both of you to Internal Affairs! You come into my shitty day and decide to just add to the pile? How do you even think you can get away with this? How can you even call yourself a police officer? Harassing this guy just to pad your record? This is bullshit! Gonna book him at the station while he's still hobbling around, huh?!"

The old man had stood up and hobbled behind Ryan, cowering as the two officers began staring him down at the motion. The two officers glanced at each other. The one officer's creepy smile hadn't shifted an inch ever since it formed. It kept speaking in monotone.

"Very well."

Ryan blinked. What?

"Report us. The emotional wreck, who just *cried* in front of the sergeant. Who yelled at a man at a hospital who had just attacked. Who will they trust? You? And a man found with drugs? Or the two of us?"

The smiling man took a step forward. Ryan puffed himself up. "Hey, step back! No matter what you assholes say, I won't let you arrest this guy for whatever sick shit you're trying to pull. Clearly, there's some fuckery going on if you both are so dead set on this."

The man took another step. The other officer watched on without moving.

"I'm warning you!"

The man took another step forward and Ryan punched him in the face. The man fell to the ground and there was a cut on his forehead where Ryan had side-swiped his skull with his fist. Black fluid welled up and wept from the wound on the man's forehead. Ryan's hand throbbed and his eyes widened as he saw the black fluid staining his knuckles. It looked almost like ink.

The old man's eyes widened too. The other officer glanced between his downed partner and Ryan in mild confusion. He looked at his partner's cut leaking black fluid and Ryan's scraped hand with red scratches visible underneath the black splotches.

The standing officer drew his gun. He continued speaking calmly and his expression didn't change as he spoke to his partner on the floor. "Fool. The blood is supposed to be red. You kno…"

Ryan rushed forward and slapped the gun out of the man's hand. The man's finger in the trigger guard snapped with a loud crack. The gun clattered to the floor, and the man's expression didn't change. He didn't look at his finger that was bent askew. His broken finger bled red.

He didn't seem to be in pain, he looked like he felt nothing at all. He took a step back to guard the door, but Ryan rushed him and heaved him to the side, throwing him to the floor next to the other one. The falling officer flailed around and got some of the black fluid on him as he fell on top of his partner.

The old man rushed by Ryan and threw open the door before hobbling out at high speed. Ryan followed him, slamming the door behind him even as the corrupt officers began to stand up.

The two of them rushed away and the door opened up behind them for a moment… before being slammed shut again from the inside. Did they not want to be seen with whatever that black fluid shit was visible? What even was that?

Ryan followed the old man to the elevator. People in the hallways gave them odd looks, but no one moved to stop them. The two waited at the door, the old man pressing the button over and over again.

The doors opened and the two stepped inside. One of the woman nurses exiting gave them a strange look before squeezing past them. The rest looked tired. The doors closed and they were alone.

Ryan turned to the old man, "What's going on? What did they want?"

The old man took a deep breath before pulling a piece of paper from his pocket and handing it over.

"Someone burst into my room and handed me this," the man said, "Said my life was in danger. I didn't believe it at first… But a few minutes later I heard someone going into each room down the hallway. One of the cops who had been in the hospital. I heard him speak to one of the others out there.

"No one inside spoke after that guy left their rooms… It sounded like those that spoke to him cut off mid sentence. Every time. So I made a break for it."

Ryan read the unfolded paper in his hands filled with long blocks of text. The longer he read, the more his eyebrows rose. Alien? Humans being replaced? An invisible barr… Control over the Hospital? Control of the chief of police? What crackpot wrote this?

Ryan flipped to the back and there was a printed map of town with one of the buildings circled. Ryan was about to scoff before he thought back to that officer bleeding black. What had the other one said… The blood is supposed to be red…

Ryan shifted in place. It had stared at his bloody hand. It had to remind itself of that fact. That blood was supposed to be red. He tried to think of another explanation of the man's words. People didn't just forget the color of blood. But he couldn't come up with anything.

But the chief of police? Surely he was himself? If he was an alien then surely all the police including him would be replaced by aliens by now? Ryan looked at another line. *They have trouble mimicking human emotions. They may appear bored or drugged.*

Ryan thought of all the 'bored' people at the station. He didn't like the picture that was coming together. But it was the final few lines of new information that caught his attention. *Avoid fighting them. If you damage them too much they will stop looking like humans and become stronger. Don't accept any random gifts or cards from strangers. It's how they like to spread.*

Just as Ryan finished reading, the elevator doors slid open. The old man rushed out into the main lobby, with Ryan just behind. The two officers were posted at the main door turned in their direction. Ryan's heart sank. Their faces were flat. As soon as they saw the old man they reached for their tasers. Ryan sped up and reached for his handcuffs dangling at his hip.

Ryan tackled the old man and cuffed him, shouting at him to get on the ground. The man struggled and shouted back incoherently, but mostly seemed confused at the sudden assault.

Ryan leaned in and whispered in his ear, "Stay still. I need to arrest you so the aliens can't. The ones at the door."

The old man stiffened at the words and stopped struggling and allowed himself to be cuffed. Ryan helped pull him up, helping him keep weight off his injured foot. Ryan tried to keep his face as neutral as possible as he helped the man back to his feet.

The two officers' hands drifted away from their weapons as Ryan approached. Ryan pulled the old man towards the door, slower than he would have liked due to the man's limp. They passed between the two officers.

"To the station?"

Ryan kept his expression as neutral as he could, but wasn't sure how well he succeeded. He wished he had paid more attention to those stupid meditation sessions he had to do after his sister's 'disappearance'. He kept his voice as monotone as he could.

"Yes."

Ryan passed by them, pulling the old man by his side forward. The hair on the back of his neck tingled, but he didn't look backwards. Ryan went to his patrol vehicle. He glanced around and uncuffed the old man before having him get in the passenger's seat. Ryan pulled out the keys and got in the car.

He hesitated for a moment. He was leaving Sanchez behind, wasn't he? He had seemed human enough. But Ryan had barely made it out himself and the old man would be snatched immediately if he went back inside.

Fuck am I worrying about him for? Didn't he just throw me under the bus to the Sergeant ten minutes ago? Wait, oh shit is Sergeant an alien now? Oh fuck. This just keeps getting better. Ryan reached for the radio to talk to Sanchez, before realizing it was an open line. Sanchez didn't have an individual channel he could call. Well, better to make it public for the other humans anyway. Ryan activated his radio.

"All units, repeat all units. This is Officer Ryan Smith. Two rogue officers are going around arresting patients without cause at the hospital. I don't know what they are doing with them. They were in room 309, and when I confronted them they tried to kill me. The Chief of Police is in on it. Get out of there before they come to you too. Over."

There was a moment of silence on the radio before a barrage of voices came on, demanding answers. After warring with himself for a moment, Ryan turned off the radio. Better to let them notice things themselves than tell them it was aliens. That would destroy what little credibility he had left. Sanchez and the others would have to get out themselves. There wasn't much else he could do, Sanchez would save himself. He would be fine.

They all would be fine.

"Are we going? What are you doing? They could be here any moment!"

Ryan turned his head to the fidgeting old man. Ryan nodded. "Yeah, yeah. Just warning the others about all this crap. Hopefully, they can make it out of there in time. Here's the map. You give directions while I drive."

Ryan opened the glove compartment exposing the folded up paper map. GPS service was pretty shit here, so the paper map helped when it randomly cut out for minutes at a time.

Had something to do with satellite orbital paths or something scientific. There was a whole article in the paper about it and everything. The old man took a few seconds to locate the hospital on the map and then began calling out the turns as Ryan drove.

After a few minutes, Ryan slowed down as he stared into the shattered front of an office building. There were holes in the walls. The front door was twisted and on the ground inside. The lights of the building were flickering. Dark stains were covering the windowsills, and shards of wood and glass were everywhere.

The stains looked a whole lot like black blood.

The inside of the building looked like a bomb had gone off, the furniture destroyed, and a large hole in the stairwell like someone had driven a truck into it. Ryan stopped the car and took out his gun. The old man tugged on his sleeve. "What are you doing? We have to get out of here! Whatever did this could come back!"

Ryan shrugged out of the old man's grip as he got out of the car. "No. There could still be people alive in there. We can't just leave."

He looked around and saw that there was another bloodstain. Something was gleaming in the light a hundred meters down the street. Ryan got back in the car and backed up until he was close to what he could see now was the pool of dried blood in the middle of the street. He stepped back out. The old man stepped out of the passenger's door too.

Something scratched on the pavement on the other side of the car and Ryan rushed around, gun ready. He glanced around, only to see the old man standing there leaning on one leg. He lowered his gun and calmed himself. Ryan eyed him. "You good? Find anything?"

"No… no… Well, oh, yes! Car keys. They were lying in the middle of the street."

He reached into his pocket and took out a pair of car keys. Ryan eyed them. "How were there keys and no car?"

The old man just looked around. "Maybe it's parked nearby? Behind one of the buildings?" The man's expression shifted a little to become harder. "Does it really matter? If there were survivors of whatever this was then they must have fled by now?"

Ryan looked into the building. "Someone could be hiding."

The old man shook his head, "No. No bodies. That means that whoever won came back and cleaned up. They either escaped or survived. And it could be a trap. We should leave."

Ryan looked askance at the old man. His demeanor had changed on a dime. First frightened and fleeing for his life to indifferent and cold. Ryan noticed his hands were shaking. The old man's that was. He was fine. Ryan thought about the man's points anyway.

He was right. It would be best to find the safe location first before coming back with whoever gave the old man the note. With a shaky breath, Ryan slid his trembling gun back into its holster with some difficulty.

"Alright. We need more info before we start fighting those alien bastards for real. Mark this place on the map. It may be important."

The two got back in the car and drove to the intersection where they found the street signs so they could find this place on the map later. Ryan kept driving and the old man navigated. Eventually, they rolled in front of an unassuming suburban home. Ryan looked between the house and the map. "You sure this is it?"

The old man held the map up and inspected it closer. "Yep. This is it."

Ryan checked one more time. "Well, this better be it. I'll look like a dumbass if I knock on the wrong door here."

"No, it's here."

The old man explained gesturing to the map again, and Ryan was finally convinced. He went to step out of the police cruiser but paused. "Hey, what's your name? Don't think I got it in all the chaos."

The old man looked at him, "Augustus. Augustus Savlin. But people call me Gus for short."

Ryan nodded at him, "Nice to meet you, Gus. Ryan. Ryan Smith."

With that Ryan went up to the door of the house and knocked. He remembered the password on the paper. He muttered it under his breath to remember the wording. Stupid overcomplicated spy bullshit.

The door opened and a severe looking woman looked down at him. Her brown hair was in a bun as she looked down at him with striking green eyes. But those striking eyes had deep bags under them and it looked like she hadn't slept in weeks.

"And who might you be?" She asked.

"Ryan Smith. Trees can not grow by the light of a fire alone? Yeah, that was it I think. I have someone else with me too."

They stared at each other for a moment. The woman looked out and saw his police cruiser. Her eyes widened. Then with absolutely no warning, she slapped him. Across the face. "Ow! Fuck, wash tha' fur?"

"Do you have any idea what you've done? This safehouse is burned. Patrol vehicles are tracked at all times so they're not stolen by criminals. They could come at any moment! Gah, we're burned!" Two burly men in black gear stepped out from behind her. She started ordering them around as Ryan rubbed his cheek which was quickly reddening.

"Take the car and dispose of it," The woman said to the two men, ignoring Ryan for now, "Go to Safehouse Four when you're done. I'll meet you there. Stop at a few more places to throw off the scent. You know the procedure." She glanced over her shoulder at Ryan before shouting deeper into the house.

"The rest of you, move the equipment. Fast. I want this place fully scrubbed in fifteen minutes!"

Ryan opened and closed his jaw experimentally, but everything seemed to work fine. Fuck that had hurt, that woman had a mean swing. But given a minute to think about it, what really stung was that she was right.

He couldn't believe he had been such an idiot. He knew the police cruisers were tracked at all times. He guessed he hadn't fully internalized that the department was run by aliens now apparently. Fuck. It was just now really sinking in.

Ryan followed the woman as she led him to her car. The two men the woman had given orders to quickly ushered Gus out of the car and over to Ryan.

He and the old ma– Gus, got in the back of the woman's vehicle silently. She rolled out and began driving to the next safehouse on the empty roads.

Ryan tried to talk to the woman a few times but she just ignored him. So he just settled in and sat in silence, better to keep his mouth shut and not dig himself any deeper at this point.

This group already had a great first impression of him, didn't they? It seemed that his answers would have to wait until they reached wherever this woman was taking the two of them.

Chapter 28: Safehouse for the Club - Mortal Ryan Fragment

Ryan fidgeted in his seat as they pulled in front of another unassuming suburban house. They had been driving almost for an hour, doubling back, stopping and going again, all in silence. The lady had already slapped him, what else could he say to her without setting her off?

"Get out." The woman was curt as they rolled to a stop in front of another driveway to a suburban house. Ryan and Gus stepped out. The woman rolled down her window and stuck her head out.

"Same password as before. Knock at the door. I have to go. Thanks to you, I have even more work to do. Don't fuck up again."

Without another word, the car window rolled up again. The car backed back into the street and then drove off. The two men watched her drive away. She hadn't even told them her name.

As the car disappeared into the distance, Gus and Ryan glanced at each other for a moment before moving to the door in an unspoken understanding. Gus pointedly ignored Ryan's red cheek.

Ryan knocked at the door of the house. Gus stayed a few steps back, glancing around them nervously. There were footsteps on the other side of the door. It sounded like there was quite a crowd in there.

"Who's there?"

"Trees can not grow by the light of a fire alone. Two people."

The door opened and they were quickly ushered inside. There were over thirty people crammed inside the building. Being a five bedroom house, thirty people was crowded but not overwhelming. The smell was overwhelming though.

There was a vague annoyance on the faces of the normal people as they jostled into one another, stifled in the small space. Everyone seemed used to the smell, but Ryan and Gus reeled as they walked in.

Scattered around the edges of the room were people in black military gear that were heavily armed. They bore an air of professionalism and stood guard with their rifles. In one of the side rooms to the left a large stone taller than Ryan stood, embedded in the floor. Ryan eyed it suspiciously.

Gus leaned over to whisper in Ryan's ear. "Should we trust them? I don't like the look of those guys with guns. And what's with the weird rock?"

Ryan looked at the men with rifles and automatic weapons scattered around, observing the crowd.

He whispered back, "They can't be worse than body snatching aliens, can they? We should wait and see what they're about first. I don't think they'd guard some big rock for no reason. Plus, it's too late for trust or no trust, we already got surrounded. Best to just keep an eye open."

Gus and Ryan headed upstairs to one of the bedrooms, where big sleeping pads covered the floors, People sprawled over every surface. Some were awake, watching them enter, but most were out cold. The two looked around for a free spot. They found an unoccupied corner and collapsed and fell asleep in moments.

―――O―o―O―――

The next morning they woke to the murmurs and rustling of the people around them getting up. They made their way downstairs to see a milling crowd below. Gus looked to the door and two scarred men stood menacingly at the front door, facing inward towards the crowd.

They were strapped with an assortment of grenades and knives as well as what appeared to be machine pistols. One met Ryan's gaze and briefly nodded before continuing his pan of the crowd.

Ryan was still in his police uniform, which many people in the crowd took notice of. But none of the people had talked to him or Gus yet. There seemed to be a pile of some kind of granola on the kitchen counter that people were grabbing breakfast from. Ryan and Gus milled through the crowd for a while after grabbing a bite to eat.

Ryan led mostly, with Gus trailing behind. Ryan noticed that the guards hadn't taken Ryan's pistol or taser at his hips when they entered the building, which made him a little more confident in being able to handle himself in case things went south.

Ryan and Gus talked with the various people filtering in and out of the rooms and gave basic greetings. It seems most of the people were residents of this neighborhood. There was a wide variety of opinions on the armed group so far in the crowd. Some had come willingly after the alien threat was explained and video evidence was shown.

They had described how it was like how their repressed memories had just surged to the surface, and they had remembered all the strange things going on that they had ignored before. Ryan started getting a headache. They spoke of other things when they noticed his struggles, but every time Ryan heard anything from them he zoned out. It was just so boring.

He was annoyed at himself and tried to pay more attention. Especially when he got concerned looks from the people who had been speaking to him.

As the various people kept speaking about their experiences, Ryan's headache kept growing worse. He felt pressure behind his eyes. Others in the neighborhood had refused to leave their homes, digging in their heels.

These people were dragged here and thrown in with the crowd unwillingly. But even the most irate person couldn't claim that they had really been hurt or mistreated aside from being forced to stay here. Well, now they knew why the guards were facing inwards. Some in the group were adamant in their determination to escape and go back to their homes.

They were much less eager after Ryan and Gus related what they had seen in the hospital and the bombed out building on the way here.

Ryan summarized with Gus occasionally interjecting to clarify something he had heard during his stay at the hospital. After Ryan and Gus told their stories the first time, word quickly spread through the crowd and everyone started paying attention to them. The crowd seemed relieved once they realized Ryan was not with the mysterious guards and began to talk more freely with him.

Ryan fielded the flurry of questions as everyone began paying attention to him at once it seemed. Gus slunk back and oddly enough shot Ryan a jealous look. What? But Ryan was distracted as someone else asked a question.

"And what about the *%$^*() @!)#*? Do you know anything else about that?"

Ryan shook his head and looked at the woman who had spoken.

"Sorry, can you repeat that?" The whispers of the gathering crowd silenced as they focused on the exchange between the two. She looked confused.

"You know, why we're not @!)#*ing here, the $^*() over the town?" Ryan clutched his head.

"Wha.. what?..." The room spun and concerned faces peered down from above him. He was on the floor somehow and it felt like there was a vice on his skull. The pressure gradually eased. The woman who asked the question was glancing around in a panic and several people were shouting at her. One of the guards in black had approached and was asking her something while looking between her and Ryan rapidly. Gus was nowhere to be seen.

"What? What just happened? All I did was ask him about the @!)#*!" Ryan groaned and the pain intensified and he curled into a ball. More voices washed over him and the vice on his skull pressed harder and harder until eventually it popped like a bubble and the pressure all lifted at once.

He groaned in relief and went limp on the floor as all his repressed memories popped back into focus. How empty the streets were, how the roads were almost devoid of cars now. His thoughts were diverted whenever he thought of visiting anywhere out of town. He thought back. It must have happened hundreds of times just over the last week. He remembered what the woman had been trying to say.

Barrier. Barrier over the town.

Wait, why did he never think of calling someone about this? Shouldn't he have tried calling the FBI or military or something? Why did he never even consider leaving town? He reached into his pocket and pulled out his phone.

He pressed the power button. Nothing happened. It was dead. He hadn't thought of it for over a week. It had just disappeared from his mind. But apparently, he had still put it in his pocket anyway just out of pure habit.

He rushed to the guard who shoved him back with the butt of his rifle as Ryan drew too close. Ryan got back to his feet and stood as close as he could as the guard eyed him.

"A phone charger? Why didn't I think of leaving town? Did you call the military about this? We should call someone about this! No, do you have a phone I could use? Please."

Ryan was almost desperate now. There must be something the government could do to save them. The crowd was split into camps now. Half looked confused at Ryan's sudden distress while nodding at his statement about the military, while the other half winced in pain or started staring blankly into space. Like Ryan had before.

The guard sighed, reached out, and pulled Ryan close to him by his collar. His breath was warm on Ryan's face.

"Shut up. Don't you see them?" He forcefully turned Ryan's head with one hand to pan the crowd. Several appeared in pain while others stared blankly into space before turning away and continuing their conversations from before.

The remaining people had noticed and were looking around in confusion and slight fear at their neighbor's strange behavior. The guard kept whispering in Ryan's ear.

"Just wait fifteen minutes. It's better to do the whole group at once. We'll explain after that. Until then shut your fat mouth." With a rough shove, he let go and shoved Ryan away before returning to this post standing menacingly by the wall. The crowd stared at Ryan. He glanced at the guard at the wall. The man nodded at him, whatever that was supposed to mean.

Ryan composed himself and spoke to the expectant crowd. "Fifteen minutes. That asshole…" Ryan pointed his thumb to the guard, who scowled. "Says that we have to wait until they explain things to us." The aforementioned asshole scowled but didn't speak up or contradict Ryan. The crowd settled in uneasily to wait.

―――O―o―O―――

Needless to say, the conversation in the house was much more muted after that. Eventually, thirty minutes later everyone was restless. They were promised answers but were now told to wait even more. But after many rounds of complaints and assurances by the guards a woman in a black suit came in the front door.

Ryan looked at her. It was the same woman who drove Gus and Ryan here. A few of the guards rapidly set up a projector and screen near the front door. Everyone looked on as they finished setting up. A few shouted out questions, but they were ignored.

The following presentation was illuminating and unsettling. The guards left the walls and shifted their way out of the crowd. The woman turned to the first slide and began calmly narrating about the giant dome around the town.

Whenever someone in the crowd was spotted staring into space the guards would close in on them like a swarm of bees and shake the shit out of them, making them state the last thing they remembered. Some people fell to the floor and convulsed after the first time.

One unfortunate woman still looked confused after the sixth time she was verbally assaulted by the guards. Anyone who answered correctly to their questions about the barrier was moved to the right side of the room. Whenever this happened the woman presenting would stop speaking, wait for the commotion to end, then restart from the beginning. She never made it more than a few sentences in.

Ryan was asked halfway through, and as soon as he repeated after the woman he was moved to the right side of the room. Gus remembered the first time a guard confronted him and was already waiting for Ryan as he walked over. Ryan had watched Gus as his memories unlocked. He had winced slightly and panicked a little at the sudden memories, but he hadn't experienced nearly the amount of pain Ryan had felt.

Eventually, only one woman remained. The confused woman from before. The severe woman with the still deactivated projector went up to her and grabbed her by the shoulders. "You should leave town. You should leave town. You should leave town." Each repetition made the confused woman wince and she began to squirm in pain.

The severe woman just kept speaking as the woman in her iron grip began screaming and incoherently babbling, "...leave town. You should leave town. You shou..." The woman let out one piercing scream before collapsing to the ground and convulsing. The severe woman's face was impassive as she wiped some spittle from her face. The woman on the ground twitched again before sitting up with wide eyes.

"Where… where's my husband?" Her words sent a chill through the room.

"He… his trip was only supposed to be a few days. Why isn't he back?" Her eyes widened more.

"I… I remember! We have to leave! I have to get back to him!" The frantic woman said.

She stood up, but the severe woman's voice cut through the babbling of the crowd with the sharpness of a knife. "No." Everyone turned to her.

"Now you all can understand the situation, I should introduce myself," The severe woman continued, "I am Helen Valdine. I will now explain the situation to the best of my ability. Reserve any questions until the end. This will all be very shocking, but pay attention and allow yourself to focus on the future. You will need to in order to survive." The projector turned on, showing the intro slide of a presentation.

Ryan gaped. What the fuck? They had a fuckin' presentation ready for this? His trust in this group plummeted immediately. He glanced around, but based on everyone's expressions only he and Gus had noticed the incongruity of the situation. The others stood in anticipation, eager for information of any kind.

Helen turned to the projector. "Very well, I will begin. All questions will come at the end, please. First..."

Chapter 29: Presentation to the Club - Mortal Ryan Fragment

"As you are all now aware, this town has been isolated from the world. Until recently, your thoughts were diverted away when you might notice this fact." The crowd shifted uneasily at the uncomfortable reminder of how their minds had been manipulated.

"This effect was strong enough that it suppressed other strange information that would lead to you using your electronic devices to communicate outside the dome. Unfortunately, the barrier has also cut off external signals digital and otherwise, so it would not have mattered anyways."

With small gasps the crowd quickly checked their pockets and their eyes widened as they realized the devices had been unused for over a week and were uncharged. A murmur rose in the crowd. Ryan stepped forward, fist clenched. He opened his mouth but Helen held out her hand to him, palm first.

"Questions at the end," she said. Ryan's mouth opened and closed for a moment. The crowd eyed him. Ryan closed his mouth and nodded. He stepped back.

"As I was saying, this is related to the other problem. The alien parasites that put up this barrier to conceal their presence from the world as they spread and grew. They have been steadily spreading through the population for the last week. The hosts give something the size of a business card to the victim, which burrows into them to control their bodies."

She changed the slide, catching a blurred photo of something resembling a spider crawling on someone's outstretched palm. Next to it was an image of someone handing the same person a piece of paper with their hand in nearly the same position as where the spider was in the other image. The crowd was shocked.

Apparently, not all of them had gotten the information Gus had gotten when he escaped the hospital. Some in the crowd looked sick.

Helen continued, ignoring their reactions. She flipped the slide again to show an image of a group standing in a circle and staring into space in the middle of a street,

"They are highly dangerous in combat, but have trouble mimicking human emotions. We have been calling them the Infected as a group and as individuals.

"They may have appeared bored or drugged in your memories, as they attempted to maintain a single expression on their faces whenever it is possible. Acting bored is easy for them to mimic while also deterring humans from talking to them too much... But their time for hiding appears to be over."

Ryan straightened and he tried to focus, rather than get lost in all his new memories of the wrongness of the last week flitting through the back of his mind. It was like his brain was grabbing tightly to the memories so they wouldn't be forgotten again. Helen flipped to another slide, this one more disturbing than the last.

"As of today, they have come into the open and begun ransacking homes in search of victims." The slide showed several images of blank-faced people breaking into homes along the street.

A wide shot in the middle showed the group holding a man down. They held what looked like a palm-sized beetle above the open mouth of the victim. Ryan clenched his fist until it turned white. A vein throbbed in his forehead.

"Which brings us to why we are here." She let the moment hang, before changing the slide again. It showed a circular map of the town with little blue zones circling a much larger central red zone,

"Our organization has established the safe blue zones to protect survivors. The invaders have gathered around the hospital in this red region." The crowd stared at the map in disbelief. The blue zones looked tiny compared to the giant mass of red staining the center.

"This place here is Safezone Seven. All who are able will assist in its defense against the alien menace of these Infected. We have more resources than you can imagine to assist. If you follow orders then all of us can make it through this. We of the Neighborhood Watch will assure your safety. We will get you through this crisis. Now, you all may proceed with your questions."

The words would have been comforting if their delivery wasn't so cold. As soon as she finished the crowd erupted into a barrage of questions, but Helen remained silent. To Ryan, it just sounded like her final words were a threat. Like she was daring them to ask something important. Even if it was stupid, Ryan had to ask. It was burning in his mind too much not to. Ryan stepped forward and raised his voice over the crowd.

"And if we want to leave? You assholes seem a little too prepared for this if you know what I mean. Why did you wait a week to bring us here if you knew so much?!" Helen nodded at Ryan stiffly, acknowledging his question.

"The Neighborhood Watch was only made aware of this invasion days before the barrier was deployed by the alien forces. We brought all the assets we could to bear, but there wasn't enough time to take stock of the situation. We needed to regroup and reinforce the safe zones you are seeing on this map."

She looked back at Ryan, seemingly done with her answer. Ryan pressed further. "And how did you escape the mind control? If you were caught so unprepared?" She stared at him for a moment longer. She looked at the silent crowd, their eyes bouncing between the two. Ryan didn't trust her smooth attitude at all. His hands clenched harder. She was reminding him of Him the longer she spoke. The same sense of faint superiority wafted from underneath her blank facade.

"First, it does not control your mind. It simply diverts your attention from certain things. Next, we were affected. I'm sure you've noticed that some of you took more or less pressure to break from the effect. Our protocols required constant check-ins at regular intervals with our superiors.

"When we noticed the others weren't following procedure properly it was enough to free some of us from the effect. The others went through the procedure you all just went through. All of this took time, thus the delay in securing the safe zones.

"I assure you the Neighborhood Watch only has your best interests at heart. We were sent here specifically to counter the alien menace by a special division of the government."

Ryan wasn't satisfied, but as he thought over the words he couldn't pick out anything unreasonable. She was suspicious as hell, but glancing over the crowd most were nodding and seemed taken in by her words. They were pretty reasonable on the surface.

Ryan took in a deep breath and uncurled his fist with some effort. He couldn't let himself lose himself in his emotions now. Not like at the hospital. Gus stood to the side shooting Ryan some questioning glances. But he hardly looked convinced by the woman's pitch either.

As Ryan realized the whole crowd and Helen were staring at him, he hastily nodded. "Well, thanks then. That's all I got," he said.

At that Ryan stepped back and faded from the limelight as others shouted out various questions that Helen quickly answered. All about the specifics of the safe zones and the exact plans in place for their protection. Questions of the past were quickly forgotten.

——— O — o — O ———

Eventually, the questions died down. The armed men took down the projector and screen and lugged them back outside. Helen gestured to her side where the guard that had told Ryan to shut up before was standing along with five others standing slightly behind him.

"Now we're finished with your questions, there is one more thing. Victor will be the commander of this zone. We are spread thin, so Victor and the others will help find ways for everyone to contribute. His word is law. He is responsible for your safety and he can not do that without your cooperation. And he can't protect everyone effectively without your help.

"If anyone is deemed insubordinate then they can be exiled from the safe zone with my approval. That is not something you want to happen. If your group is attacked by the Infected then our forces will move to support you, so you only have to hold out until we arrive. So fight as hard as you can until we can relieve you. Now I will take my leave. There is much to do in this war."

The other armed men streamed out the door with boxes of equipment in their arms behind her as she finished talking. Helen paused for a moment and when there didn't appear to be any more questions, she turned and strode out the door ignoring the whispering crowd behind her.

The front door slammed shut with a decisive *bang* and then it was only the crowd and the six armed men remaining. Victor stepped forward. He clapped his hands and shouted over the crowd.

"Alright civvies, listen up!" The noise died down. "Everyone's going to contribute here. Now you're wondering about that big rock pillar over there with little black spots?" The crowd collectively nodded. "Don't." The crowd blinked.

"I don't know what it is either," Victor said, "But I was ordered to prevent anyone from messing with it. So that's what I'm going to do. Don't test me." He stared directly at Ryan and smirked before pointing at the holstered gun at Ryan's side.

"You know how to use that thing?" Ryan nodded silently.

"Alright, go with Jim here on patrol," Victor said, "He'll show you the ropes."

He raised his voice, "Anyone else here with firearms experience? Come on, raise your hands people!" The crowd murmured but only two or three raised their hands.

Gus looked shifty for a moment. He met Ryan's eyes for a moment before looking away. He didn't raise his hand. Ryan frowned slightly. What was that about?

Victor sighed when he saw the lackluster response from the crowd and waved Ryan over to the armed man behind him, Jim apparently. As Ryan followed Jim outside, he could hear Victor shouting and sorting people into their roles. Victor's voice faded as the two closed the front door and made their way to the street. The two men paused at the curb. Jim turned to Ryan.

"You see an alien you shoot," Jim said, "Follow me. Pay attention to your surroundings. Don't shoot at me. Got it?"

Ryan nodded and Jim resumed walking forward into the street. Ryan followed him and wondered just what he was getting into. He was supposed to be a cop, not a soldier. Especially not a soldier good enough to fight aliens like these people apparently were.

Jim walked fast and began to pull ahead as Ryan got lost in his thoughts for a moment. Realizing his mistake, Ryan hurried to catch up. Even if he didn't want to do it, he knew it was to protect all of those people from the aliens. So he had to do his best on this, his reservations about the Neighborhood Watch's motives or not.

Part Three: The Neighborhood Watch Steps In

Chapter 30: Story Time in Safehouse Nine - Mortal Francis Fragment

Francis pulled up in front of the Safehouse Nine in his stolen white van. He scanned the area for any Infected that might have followed before stepping out and inspecting his new vehicle under the light of the street lamps. The street was dark, it was only barely past midnight still.

Everything was quiet on the street, no cars were on the road and not a single voice or footsteps could be heard on the street. Francis winced as his joints protested and all his hidden bruises suddenly announced their presence. It seemed his adrenaline had finally worn off. *Ughhhhhhhh.*

He was lucky the generator back at the Ranch was big enough to provide power to this whole area. The Infected would have a massive advantage if these street lights were to shut off at night or in people's homes everywhere. If the lights were off all the time then they would adapt themselves to the nighttime darkness and the humans would lose the advantage at night even more than how it was now.

The sides of Francis' stolen van were all scratched to hell where the Infected had grabbed onto it. The metal sides bulge outward from when the flaming Infected had thrashed around in the back in its death throes. Final verdict of the vehicle by Francis' estimation: usable but dump at the first opportunity.

The whole thing was splattered with dark fluids that stood out among the harsh light above Francis. He looked at the side of the van for a moment. It was like some kind of gruesome splatter painting. He grinned slightly.

He could probably sell it for millions on the outside. White van covered in authentic alien guts for sale. He would have to write one of those pretentious descriptions to put next to it on display. Something about the black of the executive's soul mixing with the purity of industry or something else equally stupid. Francis snorted as he thought about it.

Francis checked the surroundings again and noticed Bill's car parked down the street. It seemed the woman on the radio had already arrived. He reached for his magnum pistol, couldn't be too prepared after all. His hand closed on open air, and he looked down and felt at the empty holster. He searched in his pouch frantically for a moment before he remembered.

Oh.

Shit.

He had dropped the gun in his escape, Bill would be pissed. Well, he would already be pissed Francis used the Devouring Flame so freely. But this would be worse. The Doomslinger was toast, sadly one-time use even if they did have a few backups on hand. Francis groaned again and rubbed the back of his head.

The magnum gun was too valuable, he would never get a replacement for it. He had barely been able to get the first one. Gah! Not only was it useful as shit but it also was awesome! He was like one of those western gunslingers with that thing at his hip.

For an insane moment, Francis considered going back for it. But he soon shook his head and reminded himself all the crazy shit he had just escaped. No matter how useful one pistol was, it wasn't worth that kind of risk. Francis checked his rifle and he was out of ammunition for that too. Wow, he was really low on supplies here. Finally, with a shrug, he unsheathed his combat knife that he had stabbed the Infected in the car with. It was just a regular knife now, but it would have to do.

Francis approached the safehouse door and knocked, knife held at the ready. He heard the soft patter of feet that stopped at the door. A high-pitched woman's muffled voice sounded through the door.

"Hello? How is the, uh, ummm… moonlight tonight?" Francis nodded. It was good she remembered to do the passwords. Even if her delivery was a little garbled, it was close enough. He looked down at his arm, still gripping the combat knife. Oh. He probably did look pretty threatening right now; No wonder why she sounded so nervous. He sheathed his knife. She didn't sound too distressed so it probably wasn't a trap, better to not keep her waiting.

"I howled at the moon despite it not being full. It's me, Francis on the radio." She let out a sigh of relief and opened the door, stepping to the side so she was almost hidden. Francis entered and turned as she shut and locked the door behind him.

She was younger than Francis had thought she would be. She seemed barely out of high school and her clothes were ruffled and covered in little flakes of grayish dust. Concrete dust? She inspected Francis and she shifted on her feet as if she wanted to run. She was looking at his chest, blushing a little. Francis looked down and noticed his shirt was ripped in a few places, exposing the muscles underneath.

It must have been from scraping on the floor when he was dodging the bone spikes from the turret creature. Francis looked up. "One second," He said, reaching into his pouch to pull out a clean shirt, which he quickly put on. He always left a small travel kit including some clothing in there just in case. He put his ripped-up shirt in the bag again.

Francis looked up and noticed the girl looked nervous and was shrinking into herself with hunched shoulders. She was still blushing as she looked at him, eyes darting away. Oh, Francis probably should have found a room first.

She wasn't as used to seeing some skin since she probably had never been in the military. Francis frowned at the thought. It had been a while since he had really talked with someone who hadn't been in the military. Or military adjacent. She cringed back slightly like he might hurt her as she saw him frowning at her.

Francis internally sighed. He had never wanted this for people like her, just living their lives.

All this suffering. Every day he doubted himself more in the path. But he would have to do for her what his dad had done for him long ago. With an effort, Francis switched his mindset into his affable persona.

Even his thoughts grew a little lighter as he adopted his silly mannerisms. He looked at her, struck a pose, and flexed his bulging muscles. He had worked hard for these, he had to show off his hard work whenever he could! She looked away harder. But the tension in her shoulders relaxed fractionally.

"So... So, uhm. What do we, ah, do now?" She stuttered out.

Francis took a light tone as if nothing was the matter. "Well, now the two of us wait here. If we don't hear from the boss in a day or so, then I'll take you to one of the safe zones."

She straightened and her voice strengthened a little bit. "And your boss, was he the guy on the stairs? The one that killed... that... Whatever that thing was?"

Francis looked around for somewhere to sit but the whole place was stripped to the ground to bare concrete. No furniture or anything. Eventually, he just shrugged and slid down a nearby wall to sit on the floor.

"Yup, that's him probably. Here, why don't you sit down? Sit down, please. We can swap stories while we wait." She shuffled over to the opposite wall and sat down awkwardly. She shifted in place a little as Francis looked at her. But she no longer looked like a scared animal ready to bolt. Francis sat up and maintained his casual and confident tone.

"Well, first proper introductions. I'm Francis of the Neighborhood Watch. We've come to help the town when all of this started happening. Part of that was the operation in the hospital, to rescue people like you who were being kept at the hospital by creatures like the ones you probably saw." The girl sat there curled with her knees into her chest.

She rocked back and forth for a moment. But her expression was contemplative versus the fear Francis would have expected from before. How interesting. There was a long silence between them as the girl thought. Eventually, Francis decided to prod her.

"And you? What's your name? What did you see? I'm surprised the Boss would send you to me. We have standard safe zones for most of the others." She jerked up at his words. She looked vaguely panicked as she realized she hadn't introduced herself.

"Oh! Well, I'm... I'm Alice! I got a concussion a few days ago. It was pretty bad, so my friends brought me to the hospital. But... But I felt fine and wanted to leave yesterday, but the doctors kept ordering more tests and saying how I could drop dead any moment if I wasn't careful. It was so strange. There was even a guard outside the door to stop me from running off! Everyone was acting odd, and I got a bad feeling. I... I didn't like it, so I waited for the guard to go to the bathroom before I got out of there. Then... Then..."

She was almost hyperventilating at this point and Francis held his hands out and made a calming gesture. "Calm down, calm down. It's over for now. You did the right thing. Those people were probably Infected. It's impressive you even noticed that things were wrong."

She looked confused but calmed down a little. "What? How could I not notice? Things have been weird all week. No one wants to go out anywhere. Whenever I ask people they just pretend I don't exist." Her voice grew angrier, "Some jerk pushed me down the stairs and no one even tried calling the police! I can't believe they would protect him. Who just pushes someone down the stairs and runs off without a word!"

She shrunk into herself and her voice grew small. She seemed to have briefly forgotten that Francis was there. "Why would they leave me at the hospital? My friends didn't call the police, and didn't visit me when I was hurt… I didn't think they hated me that much. It was like they didn't even care."

Francis just looked at her. He was now frowning. She hadn't been affected by the mental compulsions at all? Had seen through them the whole time? Even the Neighborhood Watch only resisted its influence because they were specifically excluded from its effects when they had set up the barrier formation. He decided to probe further.

"Did anything happen to you last week? Sudden headaches, sudden pains, or things like that?" She looked at him and was startled slightly as their eyes met before thinking for a second.

"N… No. I just went to school, then went back home. I felt okay despite my friends suddenly ghosting me. Does this have something to do with why everyone is acting so weird? Wait, and what did you mean when you said they were Infected? Is this…" She licked her lips nervously,

"…related to the thing that attacked me?" Francis held his expression in place. Her Potential must be massive if she had shrugged off the effect without any strain at all. If Bill knew then it was no wonder he had sent her his way rather than with the extraction team.

"Yes, but first I have to ask you a question." She nodded. "Have you left town in the last week?" She frowned and her eyes glazed over for a moment. Francis leaned forward. At his movement, she came back.

"Oh, sorry! I've been daydreaming a lot more recently. No, I haven't left town." Francis slumped back against the wall. Well, that was pretty conclusive. She was definitely being targeted by the mental ward but was just powered through its effects. Amazing.

"Well, to answer your questions. We are being invaded by parasitic aliens. And they put up a big dome over the town to keep us trapped inside. People have been acting strange because the dome has been preventing them from thinking about leaving town.

When they see something weird like aliens their first response is to call the police. And the police operators that answer the phones are not in town. So the dome has been suppressing those memories. Seems like you've already seen an alien and remember fine. Tell me about that."

"Whoa. wow…" She met Francis' eyes and began speaking rapid fire.

"Yeah, so I went to the stairs because they were the closest to my hospital room. There was a guy who looked like he was on a SWAT team or something, and I froze up when he pointed a rifle at me. But, then a police officer shoved me down the stairs from behind. The SWAT guy, wait was he from the Neighborhood Watch you said? Anyway, he shot at the officer until I crashed into him after rolling down the stairs.

"Then somehow the officer jumped down the stairs and tried to attack me but the guy shoved me to the side. The officer's head had fallen off and when he missed his hand embedded itself in the wall! He was like some kind of zombie. Then the guy shot it with some kind of pistol and it just caught on fire out of nowhere.

"After it was dead the fire just disappeared and he handed me his car keys and told me the password and to leave after ten minutes if he didn't come back. I waited longer, but he never came. I wasn't sure what to do, so I just left and called you and I'm so sorry I left him, please don't be mad at me!"

Francis just stared at her for a moment. Damn, she got that out fast! And sounds like she didn't know anything useful about Bill's situation. He should just relax, there is nothing he can do right now about it anyway.

He smiled for her, "Don't worry Alice. If Bill said to leave then I don't blame you for anything. That guy always plans ahead. And damn! That was some fast talking girl, when's the rap album coming?"

She looked shocked before flushing in embarrassment at the joke. "Sorry, it just all came out at once. He saved my life. I feel bad I just ran off even if he told me to."

Francis shook his head. "Don't you worry about him. He didn't become the leader of the Neighborhood Watch by sitting on his ass. He's probably the toughest bastard in this town. I've seen him escape far worse. And I was right by his side."

Her voice squeaked a little as she spoke. "Worse than whatever that policeman was?"

Francis considered his answer. He tried to relax his tense shoulders. It would do him no good to go around worrying about Bill now. Francis really should lie to her, but he really didn't want to. He didn't know how Bill lied so easily.

It was always so much effort to remember which *lies* belonged to each person. And Francis was tired. Some of his melancholy leaked into his voice without him meaning it to. "Yeah. He's dealt with worse. That's why he formed the Neighborhood Watch in the first place."

She shifted but continued after a second in morbid curiosity. "What... What happened?"

Francis just shook his head. "Not my story to tell, you'll have to ask him yourself when he gets back. However!" With a burst of motion Francis leapt to his feet and collected his emotions. He moved himself into the performance, lowering his voice and adding a lilting quality to it.

He had to cheer her up before all the traumatic memories of today came rushing back to her. Alice moved to stand in confusion, but Francis motioned her to stay sitting.

"I have a tale of my own to tell! A tale of my own heroic fight against the alien menace! And Bill's not here to be a downer! Hear my mighty deeds!" He struck a silly pose and Alice giggled a little. She hadn't smiled once the whole conversation. But it seemed the shock of his statement had been enough to shift her mood for the moment.

"Now on a dark and stormy night, our hero was being chased by a mob of the townspeople! He was a bard that had performed at the local tavern for the last week and everyone was entranced! The ladies swooned, and the men offered him drinks!" Francis made an exaggerated swoon with his arm and tilted backwards.

Alice relaxed a little more as Francis continued, "But eventually the bard had to move to the next town, for the spirit of adventure pulled him forward! He left telling no one. But the traitorous innkeeper told the town, and they gathered a mob to beg him to stay only a little longer.

"When he refused these villainous people resorted to bribes! They would pay him a fortune to stay. But he said NO! My heart is set on adventure! But they insisted and kept raising the amount.

"Sensing he was beginning to become tempted by their offers, the bard grew fearful and fled into one of the nearby buildings to hide. For nothing, not even fabulous wealth could stand between him and the open road! The townspeople begged..."

Francis told his heavily edited tale of his fight with the various Infected creatures. The spider amalgamation became the irate owner of the building he had taken shelter in, pacified by a single little ditty from the bard.

The armadillo creatures became the fat town guards trying to find the crafty bard! The worms and turret creature became unruly children throwing things into the alleyways, trying to scare the bard out of hiding.

Only when he used some spare rope to climb down the side of the building could the bard escape from the crowd and flee their adoration. Francis made sure to use his hands and make all the exaggerated voices.

Alice seemed bewildered at the sudden change in events and tone, but smiled and suppressed her laughs as the ridiculous story played out to Francis' pantomime.

"And so when the crowd shouted behind him begging him to stay as he fled, the heroic bard shouted back, NO! My spirit lusts for adventure, and the open road. I can not be held down. I am destined for the big city far beyond this village. I must leave now for new horizons! Goodbye forever!"

Francis struck one final pose and ran in place as if to mimic the fleeing bard, making a few funny faces. After a moment he stopped and straightened. His bruised body was protesting his treatment and his throat was a little sore at the performance. But Francis could tell it had cheered Alice up. She was no longer hunched over and her eyes seemed brighter.

She had let out some of her stress as she smiled and laughed slightly. There was a moment of silence as Francis panted slightly, before Alice started clapping. Francis gave an exaggerated bow. "And that is the true and accurate tale of how I, the amazing bard, escaped those villainous townspeople who sought to stop me from exploring the wonders of this magnificent city."

Alice giggled at his over-the-top speech. Francis' smile grew wider. He didn't often get to talk to people who weren't already jaded in his line of work. It was nice for his stories to truly help someone for once rather than become a source of ridicule. Alice was smiling, her worries forgotten at the moment.

"So how much of that was true? Seemed pretty realistic from what I can tell." She joked.

Francis laughed, "Why, fifteen to twenty percent true, like all good stories are!" He winked at Alice. She laughed again, a little louder this time. Francis mentally pumped a fist. She really liked it!

Chapter 31: Meeting the Leader of the Neighborhood Watch - Mortal (Alice) Fragment

Alice groaned as sunlight hit her face. She rolled over and her stiff back and neck protested at her motion. With a grunt, she sat up. She blinked sleepily as the surrounding bare walls and floor greeted her.

Wait, bare walls? She blinked again in confusion as her mind slowly came awake and processed what her eyes were telling her. Alice stretched her arms over her head and arched her back as the memories of last night came rushing back. Leaving the hospital. Alien invasions. A dome over the town. Coming here. Listening to Francis' stories. Falling asleep on the floor of this room after her eyes began to grow heavy.

At first, Alice had been terrified of Francis. He had come to the door with an unsheathed knife! Who just did that? He had teased her a little after that but had been mostly serious as they first spoke. But once they were done with the serious stuff, he opened up.

As he told his goofy stories Alice had relaxed. She saw the subtle tension in his shoulders soften slightly. She had always been pretty good at reading people and could tell he was worried. It couldn't be easy to have his friend Bill missing no matter how prepared the guy normally was. Especially with aliens around them.

Francis was very charismatic and seemed to revel in her smiles and applause after his performances. He really should have been a stage actor or something. He had said it was never in the cards for him when she asked, which made Alice a little sad for him.

His stories really were engaging just from his passion and enthusiasm on their own. Even if they were pretty ridiculous. Alice was surprised he could be so energetic after he told her he was thirty seven. That was so old! Her dad was only like forty six and he complained about how old he felt all the time. Her dad never had really been one to exercise though, so maybe that made a difference…

She yawned. She was so tired last night, that she barely even remembered what the last of Francis' stories had even been about. She remembered the first one was about a bard singing for the town. Another was about dancers at a carnival.

The last? Something about drunk people getting lost in a cave and continuing to party in the dark? Didn't they have to eat mushrooms for food… Something like that. Alice was already nodding off through that one, so the details slipped away as she tried to remember it now.

With stiff legs, she wobbled to her feet and opened the door to the bare room she was in. She heard shuffling and low voices in the hallway. Sticking out her head, she saw Francis talking with another man. At the opening of the door, both men turned to Alice.

She got a good look at the other man and tensed at the memories that came from the scarred face. It was the man in the stairwell, Bill, who had saved her from the Infected, Aliens, that Francis had told her about last night. Also Francis' boss. She stepped out into the hallway and Bill shot her a thin smile. He stepped forward and extended his hand,

"Nice to meet you. But perhaps we should wish that it was under better circumstances, Alice," he said politely.

She stepped forward and reached out awkwardly to grab his hand, not really sure what to say. "Uhm, nice to meet you too... sir?"

Bill took her hand in a firm grip and pumped Alice's noodle arms up and down a few times before releasing his grip. Bill let out a singular bark of laughter, "Sir? Getting ahead of ourselves are we? You haven't joined yet." His thin smile disappeared in a moment.

"Actually, speaking of... Francis and I have discussed it and he has recommended that you join the Neighborhood Watch as a full member." Alice looked between them. But he barely knew her, why would Francis do that? Francis gave a more open smile to Alice than Bill had and nodded at her encouragingly.

"With everything that's happened, I think you've shown a lot of resilience," Francis said, "Not everyone takes news of aliens well, even with evidence in front of their eyes. A lot happened all at once, and you are doing well enough which isn't true for a lot of people."

Bill nodded along. Francis pulled something from his pocket. It was a large gray sphere that had the texture of stone. It was covered in glowing lines in a pattern that could almost be circuitry. Alice peered at it in fascination. What the heck was this thing? Francis handed it to Bill and the orb's glowing lines dimmed significantly as soon as he held it.

Francis gestured to Bill holding the orb. "Most living things have an energy inside them that we call Potential. Some have more." Francis gestured at himself. "And others less." He gestured to the dimmer orb in Bill's hand. He reached into the pouch at his side and looked down as he rustled around inside as he spoke. "Some people have tiny amounts so that thing wouldn't glow for them at all."

Bill extended the orb towards Alice.

Francis kept speaking even as he kept rifling through his pouch. "You..."

She gingerly reached out and cupped her hands where Bill dropped the orb. As soon as it touched her skin it blazed in a massive burst of light. All three of them yelled in pain and attempted to shield their eyes. Alice dropped the orb to the floor. As soon as it left her skin it went dead and dark again. She looked down and blinked the spots out of her eyes.

Francis recovered the quickest as he hadn't been directly facing the flash of light as he rummaged in his bag. The ball rolled towards her foot and she shuffled backwards, eyeing it warily.

Francis scooped it up and it let out a soft glow once more. He raised an eyebrow and meticulously inspected the whole orb, before nodding in satisfaction and putting it back in the pouch bouncing at his hip. Alice turned as Bill spoke. His voice had gotten colder as if he had confirmed something unpleasant.

"Well, that was certainly more than I was expecting. You weren't messing around Francis."

Francis shot back, "What did I tell you? This is the most I've ever seen. She told me she didn't even feel the effects of the dome at all! She's special all right." He looked over at her and winked. She looked away quickly. Alice still wasn't quite sure how she should respond. She looked up quickly again as what had just happened rushed back through her mind,

"So uhm. Why did it get so bright?" She asked.

Francis nodded, "For those of us with Potential, we have a maximum amount that we can hold at any one time. It can change a little over time, but never too much. What just happened showed the relative sizes of the pools within us.

"Both Bill and my glow are a little less than our normal because we have used items such as these recently. Our pools of Potential are a little depleted. But both of us combined couldn't hope to compete with the energy you just put out."

Alice looked at her hands in wonder. "I did that?" She said.

Francis laughed at her look. "I had the same reaction myself my first time. It really is amazing isn't it?" Alice just nodded, not trusting herself to speak.

"You'll start to feel extra hungry soon," Francis continued, "When we get back to the Ranch then we'll get you a big meal to help your Potential recharge. It's always the worst the first time."

As soon as he mentioned food, Alice's stomach rumbled. She put her hands over her stomach as the sudden hunger pangs assaulted her. She curled inward a little at the sensation. Oof. Now that she thought of it, she hadn't had breakfast either yet. Francis seemed to want to laugh at her plight but managed to hold himself back. Bill looked at her in faint bemusement but didn't say anything for a moment.

It was Bill that broke the moment of silence, "Well, that was our cue to go. We'll take my car and leave the van here. Something that isn't reinforced against damage isn't worth the effort to store. Let's go."

Without looking back, Bill walked past Alice to the front door. Alice and Francis quickly followed behind. They followed him into the military style vehicle Alice had driven last night. She stepped into the back of the car and put on her seatbelt before looking out the window as they pulled away.

She really knew very little about these people. She only met them yesterday after all. But now she was going to some secret compound with them? The Ranch? But somehow it all seemed so reasonable before she had sat down and thought about it a bit more.

She could only imagine what her past self would think seeing her now. But she really didn't have another choice. What was she supposed to do? Run into the street and get attacked by the aliens? Go back home and hide where the aliens might be waiting for her? No thanks. She would give Francis and Bill the benefit of the doubt for now. And this Neighborhood Watch, whatever they were.

Chapter 32: Entering the Ranch - Mortal Alice Fragment

Alice looked out the window of the car into the empty streets and listened to the wind roaring by. Cars were parked on the street, but no one was out and about. It was Sunday morning, and the sun was shining. Couples should be enjoying walks together. Families pushing strollers. People walking around outside in the summer sun. But there were no cars, no people. It was eerie. She hadn't even seen any of those Infected around.

Although she counted herself lucky that none of the Infected were nearby, it just made her more nervous somehow. Them not being visible. It made her internally doubt that any of it had been real. That maybe this was all some sort of elaborate trick on some prank show.

Maybe the creature in the stairwell was some kind of vivid hallucination. A bad dream. Some expired drugs they'd given her at the hospital or something... But as she looked onto the empty streets with no people in sight, she knew deep down that it was real. What was happening in town was real.

It was amazing how much things could change in a few days. And her. Apparently, she had some kind of magic power too. Everything felt like it was shifting under her feet. She tried to feel within herself to see if she could somehow sense this energy she had. But she just felt a little warmer after focusing for a few minutes. Or maybe that was just in her head. It was too small a change to really tell. Maybe that was a lie too.

The rows of suburban houses had slowly turned into green fields and farms. Alice zoned out as the fields washed by. Why have a base all the way out here? She didn't think there were any large buildings over this way. Just a few farms that had been bought up a few years ago by some developers.

Alice still remembered her dad's complaints over dinner about how the company that bought the land had wanted to build condominiums on the farmland. A lot of people in town had been upset when the corporation had bought out all the farmers.

The development would have dropped the value of all their houses in town or something? Alice wasn't totally sure, the land was a ways out of town so she wasn't sure why everyone thought it would affect the price of their houses from so far away...

Her dad had dragged her to one of those town hall meetings, and said it was educational. It had just made her uncomfortable, sitting in the back as the company representative and the townspeople just started yelling over each other. And after all that fighting it had all turned to nothing. The company ran out of money and didn't even end up doing anything with the land. It was just the same as before, except no one even farmed there anymore. It was just empty land.

Alice was glad that her dad was on that business trip now. He was safe outside the dome, removed from all of this craziness. She didn't know what she would be feeling now if he was at home with the aliens coming after him. He was originally supposed to come home tomorrow from his business trip. He had worried about leaving her alone at home for a whole two weeks by herself.

She had insisted that it was fine and he should go if he had to. He already sacrificed so much for her as a single dad. Alice guessed his bad feeling was right in a way. Here she was with two military types in a town infested with parasitic aliens. She really had gotten in trouble.

But at least it wasn't both of them here. Even as she felt a pain in her chest as she imagined how frantic he must be right now worrying about her. Alice sunk deeper into thought. At least Dad was fine...

The car bounced down a dirt road leading to one of the run down farms. Alice glanced around. She didn't see anything that stood out. There was a run down farmhouse and a big barn. Overgrown fields and nearby woods, with the barn tilted to the side and looking like a strong breeze might knock it over.

The car slowed and Francis hopped out and opened the barn doors. Bill drove the car inside and shut off the engine and its rumbling stopped.

Bill opened the car door and Alice scrambled to unbuckle and leave the car after him. Francis shut the barn doors and they were plunged into darkness for a moment. Alice heard a click behind her, and the warm yellow strips of light turned on above them.

Bill glanced at Alice, "Alright, follow me then," he said.

He then started walking forward without getting Alice's confirmation. She followed him anyway. Bill reached the corner of the barn and stomped lightly on the wooden boards on the floor in a few places while muttering under his breath. Alice heard a chuckle behind her.

She looked to see Francis poorly suppressing a smile as Bill hunted around for something. Seeing her look, Francis shook his head.

"Sorry, It's just funny. Bill there always advocates for adding layers and layers of extra security to keep the base more secure. So it's just funny seeing him hunting around because he forgot where the trapdoor is."

Alice looked back at Bill, "What?" She asked, "How could he forget? Didn't you guys come out of there before?"

Francis shook his head again, "No, there are multiple entrances scattered around. We rotate which we use to throw off anyone who might try to follow us. We haven't used this particular one in a while."

Alice stared at Bill for a bit longer, before wondering something else. "Wait, your secret base is under this barn? How many people could even fit under here?"

Francis opened his mouth but then closed it a second later. "You'll see soon. There, I think he finally found it."

Bill's foot made a distinctive *clunk* and his muttering stopped. He leaned over and stuck his fingers in a gap between two of the boards. With a heave, he pulled back and the wood lifted to reveal what looked like a circular sewer cap underneath surrounded by concrete. Bill leaned down and typed a combination into a little electronic pad to the side.

With an electronic beep and buzzing, Alice heard a heavy bolt shift on the other side. Bill reached down and flipped the metal disk upwards. Inside was a metal ladder that went about ten feet down until it hit a concrete floor. Bill climbed in and soon reached the bottom and stepped out of sight. Alice looked at Frank, a little nervous. She really didn't want to get trapped underground.

"Uhm, can you go first?" She asked. Francis looked at her before shaking his head with an understanding look in his eye.

"Don't you worry, we'll only be in the tunnel for a little while before it opens back up," he said, "And I should stay back to guard the rear in case something ambushes us."

Alice jerked up surprised, "WHAT? Is that likely?! I thought this place was supposed to be safe!"

Francis held his hands out in surrender. "Whoa, whoa! Calm down. We have to think about the worst case here. I promise you that at the end of the tunnel is the safest place in this town right now."

Alice looked doubtfully down over the lip of the hole. Bill came back from farther down the tunnel.

"What's the holdup?" he asked, "Some of us have work to do here." A lice flushed in embarrassment before glancing between Francis and Bill. She was sure he had lots of things to do so he could properly fight back the aliens. Francis threw a thumbs up at her while Bill just sighed and disappeared again as he saw her reaction. Alice put her foot on the ladder.

"Well, ok then. I guess it IS a pretty big tunnel," Alice said as she climbed down the ladder until her feet hit the floor. She turned and took in the long downward slope that went for over two hundred feet before making a sharp right turn. There were strips of light lining the floor along the walls.

"Coming down," Francis said from above her. Alice hastily stepped forward as Francis descended and closed the metal disk, which locked automatically with a *clunk*. She felt a wave of nervousness. This was the moment she was locked in now. In the tunnel where the only way forward now was into the secret base she still didn't know much about. Bill was already a ways ahead.

"Alright, let's move. Alice, just make sure not to touch the walls too much," Francis said. Alice looked at the walls of bare concrete. "Why?" she asked.

"Better you don't know. I'll tell you when we're all the way through," Francis said.

Bill scowled a little at Francis' words, but nodded. They all began walking down the tunnel. They reached the corner and turned, revealing a downward sloping tunnel that appeared almost the same as the first. Alice took another step but stumbled as there was a tiny lip between the flat platform of the turn and the downwardly sloping tunnel floor. She braced herself against the wall before quickly recovering her footing.

"Hey! Watch the wall!" Bill yelled at her from ahead, and Alice was startled and almost fell to the floor in her rush to remove her hand from the wall. She wasn't sure what was happening, but if Bill was worried about it then it must be bad.

He had barely even been breathing hard when he had killed that Infected in the hospital. Alice took a few running steps down the slope before recovering and stopping her momentum, breathing heavily.

Bill was walking back, "Be careful!" He shouted, "We don't want to set off…"

"Bill!" Alice shrunk down between the two voices as Francis interrupted Bill's shouting. Francis sounded annoyed. "She's just a kid, don't you think she's dealing with enough? Just take it easy. I know it stresses you out, but don't take it out on her!"

There was a moment of silence between the two men as Alice just hunched over glancing between the two. What was she supposed to do? She was literally trapped in this conversation, standing between the two men as she was. After what felt like forever, Bill turned to Alice and took a deep breath. "Alice, Francis is right. I'm sorry I was too harsh. I'll tell you why when we get to the base."

Alice unfurled herself a little to look at Bill more. "Ok," she said in a small voice. Bill nodded, "The sooner we get to base the better for all of us."

Alice wasn't sure what she had done, but Bill didn't seem to like her very much even way back at the safehouse. But he had saved her life, so she should try to not think mean things about him too much though. She was probably just reading into things too much. They continued down the tunnels in silence after that. Eventually, the tunnel straightened and it was just a long flat concrete tunnel. They reached a metal door at the end.

Bill scanned his fingerprint and typed in a code. Then he pressed a button to speak with someone softly over a speaker. Only then did the door buzz and swing open. They all stepped forward into a spacious room covered in bare concrete. It was thirty feet by forty feet with some sandbags piled on the concrete floor in the middle of the room.

Bill faced Alice with a serious expression, "Alice, that and every other minor entrance to this compound is lined with explosives. Explosives that are triggered through mechanisms that use the Potential that you are overflowing with.

"If your Potential had left your body and penetrated more than a few feet into the wall they would have exploded and killed us all. Anyway, I have business to attend to. I'm sure Francis can show you around."

With that Bill made a quick turn and speed walked into one of the nearby hallways and disappeared in seconds. Alice just stood there in shock for a few seconds.

Francis spoke up from behind her, "He always worries too much about those. They've never once gone off accid…."

She didn't process anything he said, still reeling with shock.

"WHAT!" She shouted as Bill's words finished registering in her mind, "I COULD HAVE SET OFF FREAKING BOMBS AND KILLED US ALL AND YOU DIDN'T WANT TO TELL ME!"

Alice's heart was racing and she was hyperventilating. This was a bad idea after all. What kind of maniacs had she followed down here? Francis put a comforting hand on her shoulder and she flinched away at his touch.

He pulled back his hand as he spoke, "Listen. It's not as bad as he made it sound. I made those triggers myself. They're perfectly safe. The Potential has to be entered in a certain sequence to activate it. It's almost impossible to do accidentally, even if you sent a massive burst of Potential into the wall all at once. It would be like randomly hitting a keyboard and writing out a whole sentence in one go."

Alice's breath slowed and she calmed down a little. What the heck Bill?! Why did he just randomly scare her like that if it was that safe? She trusted Francis a whole lot more than Bill at this point. He seemed to be an expert on the magic objects, more than Bill was.

Francis had been the one carrying the glowing orb around in his bag, not Bill. And Bill was the one who handed the orb to her when Francis was distracted. The thing almost breaking was his fault for handing it to her. And it made sense that you shouldn't make a bomb able to go off by hitting it randomly with whatever energy she had.

"BUT... but... well... I'm... I guess I'm glad you didn't tell me in the tunnel then." She shot him a wan smile as angry words kind of just deflated towards the end. He returned her weak smile with gusto. "That's right, no need to worry over nothing," He said lightly, "Just don't think about it. Now why don't I show you around? I'll be your personal tour guide to this place. Take your mind off of it."

Not trusting herself to speak, Alice just nodded and followed Francis as he walked toward one of the nearest hallways deeper into the complex. Time to see this super secret base for herself. Hopefully, there were no more bombs she could accidentally set off inside.

Chapter 33: Tour of the Ranch - Mortal Francis Fragment

Francis started showing Alice around the Ranch. The armed guards gave him respectful nods as they passed guard post after guard post. Francis felt a little bad for the girl. He tried his best on the tour, but there wasn't really all too much to see so far. Just bare concrete walls, defensible positions, and metal doors.

She had zoned out and was staring at nothing again like she had been in the car. Francis kept speaking anyway, even if he knew she wasn't listening.

He discussed various stories about people on base, about the construction and planning of the place. It was the least he could do after Bill came down on her so hard.

Francis stopped speaking for a moment and frowned thinking of Bill's cold behavior. Bill had seemed well enough considering what had happened at the hospital. No worse than any other mission they were involved in before. But as soon as he had seen Alice's massive Potential Bill had distanced himself and grew colder towards her.

Francis himself was still a little shocked at her raw power.

Francis was considered one of the most powerful in the Neighborhood Watch. And he had never gotten close to overloading even the weaker artifact they had with his own Potential.

Something Alice had done in seconds for something that was one of their strongest assets. There was a reason Francis was the only one with an invisibility orb. Francis was just glad it seemed undamaged. Trapped in the dome as they were, it was irreplaceable.

One thought kept rattling around Francis' mind, telling him something was wrong. *Why would Bill push Alice away when he saw her massive Potential?* Because Francis understood Bill probably more than anyone else in the world. And what he was doing was a way for him to get to distance himself emotionally from assets that would be at risk.

Francis had seen it before when certain members of the Neighborhood Watch were about to go on dangerous missions.

But Bill shouldn't have been so obviously cold towards Alice. If he really didn't like her personally he would have kept it under control and stayed more professional with her at least. Francis tapped a finger against his leg as he led them through one final checkpoint. Did Bill have plans that would put her in danger? Surely not?

Her best use to the Neighborhood Watch was backline charging artifacts and logistics. Someone to be protected at base so she could help the fighters do their jobs better.

She clearly wasn't a combatant and couldn't learn in time to be useful against the Infected.

Maybe Bill had a plan for all the people with high Potential, not just Alice specifically? The people from the hospital extraction? Francis continued to frown. He would ask Bill later. If there was something in the works then Francis should have been told. He was number two after all no matter how much he preferred to work alone on missions.

"So was that the last one? How big is this place even? I feel like we've been walking for miles!"

Alice's voice broke Francis from his thoughts and he quickly pasted on a smile and turned to her. "Yup. Now you get to see where we all actually live while we're here. The three of us took one of the less used entrances, so we got extra rigamarole and security. And the size? Well, let's just say it's just as deep as it is wide. If not more so."

Alice's eyes widened and Francis could see her doing calculations of the size in her head. They had been walking inwards for a while. "Whoa," She said.

They turned the corner and exited the hallway into an expansive cylindrical cavern. Francis stepped onto the metal walkway that clanged loudly at his footsteps. The room pierced the ground four hundred feet downward and two hundred feet upward where it ended in a dome.

Looping down was a series of metal walkways lining the walls, spiraling their way up and down the space.

The occasional door or hole in the stone exposed more hallways leading to the central chamber. The place seemed empty, but people could be seen down below walking and talking inaudibly.

Alice cautiously toed the metal floor and scaffolding for a moment before stepping out and putting her full weight on it.

She grabbed the metal railing and peeked over the edge before rapidly retreating, looking a tiny bit green. "Oof. This place is huge!" She said, "How does no one know about this?"

Francis smiled at her wonder. "Remember how that ball glowed when you fed it your Potential?" She nodded, still looking up and down at the cavernous space. "Artifacts like that one do all sorts of things. One moves rock and soil with its accumulated Potential. It's what let us create something like this." He waved at the room. "We only had to pour the concrete after it was done to make sure the structure was stable, and Voila! Big underground base!"

Alice looked down at the people milling around. She looked back up. "How many people are here? I didn't expect anything this big when you talked about your hidden base. I expected like thirty or forty people max, nothing like this."

Francis nodded. Most members were out establishing safe zones or guarding the stones to the dome formation. So the place was emptier than usual. "About four thousand total members. Most are out on missions right now, so there should be a few hundred support staff and an equal number of people here between assignments."

Alice looked at him, blinking. "Isn't the population of Harmony only around twenty to twenty-five thousand? Something like that?"

"Yup. We brought everyone we could when we heard about the aliens. As you can see, we were pretty successful. We had a few years to prepare after all."

"Years? I thought the aliens only came this week?"

Francis motioned down the metal stairs and started walking as he considered his answer. "Yeah, they've been around for a long time. But they only became active recently. So we had time to build all this." Alice opened her mouth to ask more, but Francis shook his head.

"That's all I can tell you, Alice. I'm sorry. I wasn't even supposed to tell you that much really. So why don't you keep it just between us?" He threw her another smile before pretending as if he was zipping his lips. She hesitantly nodded and didn't dig any further as Francis led them to the cafeteria two levels down.

Now that he thought about it, Francis wasn't sure why he was being so open with her. Had her enjoying his show affected him that much? Surely it was more than that... Maybe it was her shy manner. It had been amazing watching her open up when he did his performances. To take her mind off everything that had happened. It reminded him of what his father had done for him before he was killed in combat. He wondered what his old man would feel seeing what had become of his son now. Would he be proud of what.... They walked through a set of double doors and the smell of cooking food derailed Francis' train of thought.

"And this is the cafeteria. Still hungry?"

Alice's stomach rumbled in agreement and the two of them went to the counter and piled their trays high. Other small groups of the Neighborhood Watch came over to say hi, and Francis introduced Alice to everyone. She would give little waves and speak softly in front of the new people, and luckily most of them were welcoming in Francis' presence.

The two of them sat together and Francis watched Alice wolf down the food while he ate at a more reasonable pace. Alice finished and stared down at her tray for a moment as if to wonder where it had disappeared off to. She looked around and got a conflicted look on her face.

Francis chuckled, "Don't worry, all of us with Potential know how bad it is the first time. Go on for another round. No need to worry about your weight, just use your Potential again and it'll slide right back off of you."

After another moment of hesitation, Alice leaped up and quickly loaded up another pile of food and went back to scarfing down more food. Then went for a third round. Francis' eyebrows rose, and others began looking in their direction. Alice went for a fourth round and Francis had to stifle his laugh at the stares the lanky high school girl was getting.

Some in the room had connected the dots, but most were just confused. At the fifth round, Alice looked guilty and noticed the rising murmur and people staring at her. She shrunk into herself, but still finished the tray and shifted in place, still looking a little hungry. Only a little hungry though, like she could go for a desert.

The murmuring grew louder. Francis decided to nip it in the bud. He stood and scanned the crowd, raising his voice above the murmur, "Hello everybody. This is Alice, our newest member. Recruited in town from Harmony. Some of you have already met her. She just used her Potential for the first time, so don't give her those looks."

He pointed at the woman who always seemed in other people's business.

"I'm looking at you, Chery." Chery leaned away from the other woman she was furiously gossiping with. She tried to strike an innocent look but wasn't quite fast enough for the crowd to avoid noticing her guilty expression, like someone with their hand caught in the cookie jar.

Some of the crowd laughed, and after a moment Chery stuck her tongue out at Francis as she realized she was caught. Alice squirmed under the gaze of the crowd as they turned back to her.

"H… Hi everyone. I'm Alice… Nice, well nice to meet you all," she squeaked. There was a moment of silence before the tension broke and some of the groups that hadn't approached before.

"Hi, I'm Paul and this is…" One by one the remaining groups came up and introduced themselves. Alice stuttered and awkwardly laughed through the conversations, but over time she relaxed and engaged with the conversations with the other members of the Neighborhood Watch a bit more. She was starting to settle in.

— — — O — o — O — — —

Finally, Francis and Alice left the cafeteria. Alice looked exhausted from all the conversation. They started making their way down the stairs. Their destination was at the bottom of the base.

"Feeling full?"

Alice nodded back with a little embarrassment.

"So you're probably wondering what you'll be doing around here to help out."

Alice's shocked expression showed that she had, in fact, not been considering this.

"Well, you know how you used your Potential to make that ball glow?" He asked. Alice nodded silently.

"We have basically big batteries below that we can fill with Potential for later. With the amount of Potential you have, you can do the same amount of charging as at least a dozen other people. We'll have special food for you too so you can fill back up. You can stay here in the base and be safe and still help more than anyone."

She remained silent. As they descended there were fewer and fewer people milling about until it was just the two of them. They walked through a door in the side and descended into a room dominated by a giant gray stone inscribed with the massive network of lines to hold Potential.

It would take Alice's Potential and drain it into the main batteries for the base. Next to it was an open crate filled with high-density energy bars ready to be eaten after Alice was done. Francis watched Alice who was looking at the device. Her eyes were unfocused as she stared into space. Finally, Alice spoke again, looking away from the stone. She looked Francis in the eyes.

"So I won't fight the aliens like you or Bill? Even with this magic, I have?" She asked. Francis looked into her eyes and saw their sincerity. He spoke gently. "No. Not if you don't want to. You can leave it to us. And you aren't trained for combat. You can help more by doing this in safety. And it's not magic." She sniffled and her eyes grew slightly wet. She turned her head away.

"I… I know I'd be pretty useless with fighting. Of course, I know that. But I still want to help. I don't want to be protected if all the people out there are dying. I can't stop thinking about all those people I saw on the street. Before I got my concussion I mean. How if I'd just noticed sooner I could have… have… I don't know. Warned them, saved them. Something. Used these powers, maybe?! Just do anything. I as good as let my friends die! I should fight the aliens like I didn't before."

Tears dripped from her eyes and she roughly rubbed her face with her sleeve. Francis' heart ached.

There was a small chance her friends were in one of the safe zones. He could say so, cheer her up a little. But he didn't want to give her false hope. If an Infected was close enough to push her down the stairs then her friends were likely already gone.

They had been converting people who wandered into the open for the whole week. He and her were so similar in so many ways. He didn't want her going down his path of self-blame. Nothing good would come of it, and it wasn't true even if she felt that way.

"Alice," She looked up, eyes red. "It isn't your fault. You couldn't have known. I… I know what it feels like. But you can't blame yourself. It's their fault not yours that all of this is happening."

She sniffled a bit more, "I know all of that. But it still feels like my fault somehow."

Francis looked at her, lost in his memories.

"I… I know. I really do. More than anyone. But it just isn't. It's hard, but you have to tell yourself that whenever you start to blame yourself again."

Alice composed herself. "O…Okay. Thanks. I… I'll remember that."

Francis patted her on the shoulder with some forced cheer. "No problem, kid. Why don't you charge the stone, show me what you can really do."

"Okay." Alice stepped forward and pointed at the obvious white shape of a handprint at chest height on the stone.

"There?"

"Yeah, just right there."

Alice put her hand over the white outline and pressed inwards. Her hand pressed inwards until it was almost on top of the black flesh filling the inside of the pillar. In moments the outside of the giant stone began blazing in golden light, illuminating the room.

Alice gasped in awe as Francis watched on, reflecting on his past. On how much he had changed over these last twelve years to get to this point. The gold filled his vision as his grip on the present faded and old memories bubbled to the surface.

Chapter 34: Francis Before the Neighborhood - Mortal Francis Fragment

As Francis watched Alice's wonder, he thought of his childhood. Francis tried to remember his father's face, but he couldn't. He tried to remember his father's exact stories, his gestures as he pantomimed them with his hands. But it had been so long ago. The details were faded, and dull, but something within him clung to their fragments. It had been too long, and so much had happened since then. But the details had slipped away from him.

Francis had joined the Marines like his dad as soon as he could. His mom hadn't wanted him to go out to be killed like his father. Francis had been talented in theater, gotten a partial scholarship for college for it even.

She couldn't understand why he would throw it all away. But it was something he just had to do. At least it felt like that at the time. Like he could understand his dad more somehow if he lived the same life as him.

He realized how dumb he had been back then. He should have stayed home. As the horrors of war sunk into him over his deployments, he began to emulate the father that had begun to fade in his memory even back then.

He would joke, laugh, and tell stories whenever he could. Because the laughter pushed down from the blood-soaked hands pushing up from his memories, from all the people he had killed. Clawing at his attention whenever he closed his eyes.

Then after six years, he was done. He had lasted longer than almost anyone else in his unit on active duty. Their missions had not been easy. But he was finally coming home. He remembered feeling slightly lost, returning to his old house. It had felt bizarre like nothing had changed while he was gone. Even the furniture and most of the neighbors were all the same.

Only his mother's sunken eyes and skeletal frame had changed. On seeing her state, his chest had tightened and his emotions had swelled. But in his stress, he fell back on his habits.

He laughed and joked and pushed it down, not confronting her about it. She had had money problems and hadn't told him. Said she didn't want him to be distracted and get killed in the war worrying after her.

Francis wished he had visited home more often now. He could have sent more money and helped her with anything. Instead of wasting his money on booze and gambling on base.

But he was there for her after he had returned and seen her true state. He had seen how empty the fridge was. At least for those fateful two weeks, she was recovering. Her cheeks were filling and her eyes less sunken.

Until she was kidnapped.

Francis had gone out for groceries. He even remembered noticing a suspicious black car parked on the street and shrugging it off as paranoia. He had spent too long in volatile warzones he had thought to himself. He was just being paranoid, jumping at shadows. But when he got home his mother was gone and the door was kicked in.

None of the neighbors had seen anything. They all were useless and hardly even noticed that she was gone. None of them had helped her while she was starving and none cared now she was gone. All their concerns were selfish worrying if the criminals would come back for *them*. Not even the slightest bit of concern was spared for the woman who was already taken.

The police had been no help. A week later there were no leads and the officers he talked to were apathetic at best and dismissive at worst. He had hired a PI with his meager savings. Another week gone with no leads. The PI had likely taken his money and swindled him. Everything seemed hopeless until Bill finally arrived at his doorstep. The man had just appeared on his front steps one day. Francis had started questioning him. To answer, Bill had opened his mouth and…

———— **This Fragment of Memory is too temporally distant from events. It is hardly Central… But floating through the hazy dreams of the past is so inaccurate. The Whole Picture requires accurate knowledge even for trivialities such as this. Rewinding on the personal timeline of Mortal Francis. Rewind… Slowing…. Close… Right there…That's it. Twelve years before the last Fragment of Memory. Begin.** ————

Francis wasn't sure about this guy, William Callahan, who just showed up out of nowhere to offer his help. William was muscled and moved smoothly and confidently as he came into the house. He was calm. Francis had hired that PI and begged the police for anything. And neither could show anything. Not the slightest lead. How had this 'Bill' as he asked to be called, even found him?

"Francis Moore, I would just like to start by saying that I am here as a private citizen. I am not a member of the law or government agency, but I am here to help you."

Francis eyed him, "If you're not police, then how did you know? About my mother?"

Bill nodded stiffly, "I have contacts, and there have been concerning rumors of a group in the area kidnapping people. Your mother fits their profile perfectly. They paid off some of the crooked officers to turn a blind eye, so they would flee before the police closed in on them. I was hoping that based on your background, you'd be willing to distribute some vigilante justice with me."

Francis froze. "Justice? But... We can still save her, right? If we find these people."

Bill's blank face told it all. "It's always possible," he said with a neutral tone. Francis tried to think about it for a moment, but she was all he had left. The rest of his extended family from his mother's side had shunned his parents after their marriage, and Francis couldn't forgive them for letting his mother starve for all these years without lifting a finger to help her.

His father had been a single child of a small family leaving no one on that side alive either. If the police were corrupt, then he would help this man for a chance to save her. And he believed him.

The police's dismissive treatment of the case had already displayed their incompetence at least to Francis. His mother had 'gone out of town' his ass. Like she had just walked off and left her car and a shattered front door behind on her way.

Francis looked up at the man and went to his gun locker to get his pistol. "Alright. I'll help. If your plan is good enough."

———O—o—O———

Francis had followed Bill, and the man told him his plan. Based on the profiles of the prior victims, there were three people nearby who might be targeted next according to him. These people were alone in their homes, poor, had easy access to the highway for a quick getaway, and something else that Bill refused to discuss but said he was sure was a factor.

Apparently, the group had been kidnapping a few people per town before moving farther down the highway to the next. Francis couldn't believe the police hadn't caught such an obvious pattern yet. More corruption probably from the way Bill described it. Anyway, Francis was sitting in his car guarding the house of one of the potential victims.

Bill and someone Francis hadn't met yet took the houses of the other two. Francis ate a few more peanuts as he waited. His time in the Marines had prepared him for guard duty well enough at least. The boredom and alertness for action at the same time as he sat alone in the car waiting for something to happen.

Three days later, something finally changed. A black car that Francis recognized pulled into the neighborhood. Francis was instantly on high alert. Those bastards were here! He recognized them from the car he had seen outside his mother's house.

He quickly took a photo of the car's license plates and sent it to the group text with Bill and the mysterious third member of their little conspiracy.

Bill's text back came nearly instantly. *'Do not engage. Dangerous people. We'll be right there. ETA 5 min.'* Francis looked up and tapped his foot. They were right there! The black car parked on the other side of the street and two men stepped out. They glanced around but didn't seem to notice Francis sitting in his car across the street. With a rush, the two men rushed to the front door and kicked it open. They went inside.

Oh hell no. He wasn't just standing by and watching this. Francis pulled out his pistol. He opened the car door before pausing. He pulled his phone out and started texting. *'Ppl Entrd home, Going in.'*

There, sent. He ran across the street as the men dragged the limp form of an old man between them and began dragging him down the steps. Francis' phone buzzed, but he ignored it.

Francis raised his gun. "Hands up! Put him down! On the ground now!" He shouted. The two dropped the old man to the floor with a rough throw and held their hands up. One smirked.

"I'd call your superiors on this one. You don't know what you're dipping your toes into, kid." Kid? He was twenty-five! And did he think Francis was the police? Francis knew it was a felony if he didn't correct them, but his mother's life was on the line here. He'd take anything he could get.

"On your knees now!" He dodged the question, and luckily the goons complied and got on their knees. They didn't appear worried at all.

Francis shifted in place. A car pulled into the neighborhood. Bill and an unfamiliar woman stepped out of it. Her green eyes were striking and distracted Francis for a moment. Francis went to call out to the two, but Bill put his fingers to his lips to shush him.

"No names," He said. Hearing this, a flash of confusion went over the two goons. Bill pulled something from his side holster and fired two metal prongs into the man on the right.

The other goon surged to his feet, but seconds later, he was struck by the taser of the unknown woman as well. Both twitched on the ground. Francis ran forward and checked the vitals of the old man limp on the ground. He flipped him over.

He had a gash on his head, but it wasn't bleeding much and nothing looked broken as far as he could tell. His heartbeat was stable and his breathing was fine. He was relatively uninjured. Good.

"Hey, help us here you. Quick," The unfamiliar woman said. Francis turned and saw the woman and Bill tying up one of the goons before loading him into the back of the black car with some difficulty. Francis came over as the second goon began to stir. The woman tased the goon again and he flopped on the ground.

Bill and the woman moved and tied up the second man and with Francis' help maneuvered him to the other side of the back of the black car.

"Alright, let's move. I'll take the black car," Bill said. Bill was already moving to get in. Francis looked at the older man at his feet, his crumpled form splayed out on the pavement unconscious.

"Hey, what about him? Shouldn't we call an ambulance?" Francis asked. The woman had already gone back to the vehicle the other two arrived in and started moving it, ignoring Francis entirely. Bill rolled down the passenger window of the goon's car and shut the car door.

"Leave him," Bill said, "Someone will notice, and the calls will be recorded. Unless you'd like to go to prison?"

Francis looked down. Then he reached down into the man's pocket. "Hey, what the hell are you doing?" Bill asked angrily. Francis ignored Bill as he fished out the man's phone.

He turned to Bill. "I'm going to call with his phone and not say anything. You go." Bill grumbled about Francis' *'stupid bleeding heart'* but drove off anyway.

Francis pressed the button on the side of the phone several times until it called the police even through the lock screen of the phone.

Francis carefully stepped back as a tinny voice started sounding out from the device. The phone operator for the police. He crept off, trying to remain quiet. Eventually, Francis reached his car, started the engine, and drove off before the police could arrive.

———O—o—O———

Francis checked his texts. There were two that were unread. From before.

Bill: *'Leave him. Will follow to hideout later.'*

Another one popped up just a minute ago.

Bill: *'Wait here. I'll text when I have more info.'*

There was a GPS pin attached pointing to some commuter lot a ten or fifteen-minute drive away from here. Francis stared at the first text. He thought about whether he should have stood by while watching that man be kidnapped. *No.*

Even if it made things harder, he didn't want to… save… his mother by being a bad person. She wouldn't want that. He started driving to the meeting spot, careful to avoid any police cars he saw driving quickly in the opposite direction.

Chapter 35: Francis Before the Neighborhood Continued - Mortal Francis Fragment

Four hours later, Francis got another text. He glanced at it before continuing to slowly enjoy his ham and cheese deli sandwich. It had been a long time since he had been able to just sit and savor food like this. The sandwich was certainly better than the army rations he had been eating daily for these last few years.

Francis quickly finished eating his sandwich with a few quick bites as he saw Bill's car pulling into the lot. He licked his fingers and crumpled the wrapper and threw it to the side into the passenger's seat. The car parked a short ways away and Bill and the woman stepped out with him.

Bill's hair was wet, and he was wearing new clothes. As he approached, Francis saw dried red flakes under his fingernails. Bill's face was impassive. The woman followed to the side and slightly behind. Her nails were painted red. Francis wondered if there were any red flecks under her fingernails too.

"Francis. We have the information. We should move out soon," Bill said. Seeing Francis' glance at the woman at his side, a brief expression of surprise flashed across Bill's face.

"Ah! I had almost forgotten. This is Helen. She is helping us with her government contacts. And on the ground of course as you have seen." Helen nodded and extended her hand. Francis reached out and shook it. Her hands were soft and smooth. Not the hands he'd have expected for somebody working on the ground for missions like this.

"Nice to meet you, Mr. Moore," Helen said, "Hopefully, we can become better acquainted later. But for now, we must focus on the mission." Bill nodded at Helen's words.

"Indeed. It looks like the group has about ten to fifteen people, carrying small arms only. They have a backer wealthy enough to hire the mercenaries we encountered and buy their silence. As well as to have the influence to cover all of this up. The people we'll encounter from here won't be direct members of the group, but hired guns. The two we captured were the only two professionals working with the group. With your assistance, there should be little resistance from the mercenaries. We also have a location."

Francis' phone buzzed in his pocket. After looking over Francis for a moment to make sure that he understood, Bill nodded and looked satisfied.

"Alright. Last chance to back out, Francis. Know that this is illegal and highly dangerous. No one would blame you for stopping now. But if you do this you have to commit yourself to do whatever it takes. For your mother."

Francis clenched his fists. Should he leave now that he was so close? No, he had to know one way or the other. He couldn't back out now. He looked back at the two staring at him expectantly, "I'm in."

———O—o—O———

Francis, Bill, and Helen stood crouched behind the car, wearing ski masks to obscure their faces. Bill had given them all of them automatic rifles for the mission. It was the same one Francis had used in the Marines. Francis wondered just how well connected these people were to get these kinds of weapons so easily...

Bill silently squatted there and held up three fingers. Two fingers. One. A closed fist.

Francis and the other two burst into motion. The house across from them looked picturesque. Clipped green lawn, white walls with a triangular roof. A mailbox with a little red flag at the end of the short driveway. But it was where all the victims of the kidnapping had been brought. Bill breached the door after Francis kicked the door inwards. The five people milling around inside froze.

"Hands up! On the ground!" Four complied immediately, but the last hesitated and glanced at a nearby door. Bill focused on him.

"Don't try it! Down now," Bill ordered. At this, the man grudgingly raised his hands and sank to the floor. Helen moved forward and restrained the first man's wrists with plastic ties. She restrained the second. Francis shifted next to Bill nervously, gun still raised.

Helen went to restrain the third one, until with a bang the door the resistant man had glanced at went flying off its hinges and shattering on the opposite wall. The man Helen was going to restrain burst into motion and pulled out a gu....

Bang! He was dead. Helen put a single round between the man's eyes and he fell to the floor. The man's gun fell to the ground with a clatter from limp fingers.

From the open door frame, a monster emerged. It had a massive head that barely fit in the doorway and its humanoid arms ended at the elbows. The remainder of the arm split into ten tiny tentacles that ended with tiny needle-like tips. Its mouth was circular like a leach, contrasting with its disgustingly human eyes.

Bang bang bang Francis shot at it reflexively in the chest with a long pull of his trigger. Bill joined him. *Bang bang bang*.

The monster released a high-pitched screech as it fell back, stumbling against the wall. Its tentacles pierced into the wall stopping its fall. The tentacles flexed and the creature slowly reversed its motion to regain its footing. The bullet holes in its chest began slowly closing. The black fluid welling from the wounds and running down the creature's chest slowed to a trickle before stopping.

Francis was always taught to shoot center mass. Headshots had a higher chance to miss in chaotic situations.

The last spurts of black fluid wept from the wounds as they closed and the creature stumbled as it recovered and started moving towards the three of them. The gunshot wounds were almost fully sealed over by now.

Bang bang Francis glanced over away from the monster as he changed the magazine on his rifle. Helen was rapidly backpedaling and scanning the room with her rifle, ignoring the monster for now. The resistant man that Helen had been about to restrain before the monster had appeared had vanished. He must have run around the corner out of sight in the chaos.

The monster found its feet again and cocked back its arm. With a grunt, the creature whipped the limb forward and the needle-tipped tentacles flashed out and pierced Bill in a sudden motion. The tentacles pulsed, and Bill twitched as his fat started to melt off his frame. He became skeletal like he hadn't eaten in a week in seconds. The creature swelled and the tentacles attached to Bill thickened.

"Bill!" Helen shouted out in worry before letting out a hail of bullets with her rifle. The precise rounds impacted the creature's overlarge skull causing the tentacles to drop to the ground. The creature dropped limp on the floor, its ten needles still puncturing Bill in various places hanging loosely off of him.

Bill lay panting on the floor, collapsed. Helen ran over to quickly assess the damage, and Francis relaxed when she sighed in relief.

Francis looked, and it appeared that most of the needles had struck Bill's bulletproof vest and stopped before punching through. Only two or three had actually pierced the skin. And while Bill seemed a little weak, he still was able to move and push himself to his feet.

Helen carefully extracted the limp tentacles from Bill's chest and threw them to the side where they flopped onto the floor. Francis tensed as he noticed the tentacles twitching slightly. He unloaded his rifle into the twitching creature's corpse. He eyed it carefully as he reached down to load his final magazine for the rifle. The body grew still, dead for real this time.

Bill's emaciated face nodded in approval before his eyes widened. Bill opened his mouth to shout, and Francis whipped around only to feel a deep impact into his side. His turn was the only thing that had prevented the blade from behind him from piercing the base of his spine. Francis fell to the floor as there was a sudden flash of light from where he had been stabbed.

The knife was ripped out with a spray of Francis' blood. Francis looked up to see the resistant man from before standing above him, grinning. He met Francis' eyes for an instant before turning and sprinting out of Francis' view. Francis heard gunshots from Helen, but no sound of a body hitting the floor. Helen ran past his prone body and out the door.

Another burst of gunfire from outside in the street. Silence, then Helen came back in.

"Got him," She said, "Both of you boys move it, we have to get out of here soon. And put the masks back on." Both of their masks had fallen askew at one point except Helen's, exposing their faces to the world. Francis and Bill quickly adjusted them to cover themselves up again. Francis stood, but the room swam around him and he felt nauseous. Bill didn't look very well either. Helen noticed their states and seemed to decide to take charge.

"Alright, check the basement then we're out." Helen took the lead down the stairs, rifle at the ready. Francis gripped the railing as he descended behind her. Helen gasped and Francis looked up from his feet. One whole side of the space was littered with mummified corpses. On the other side was a pristine surgical table with a bright light shining down onto it.

The bodies were stacked like wood, one on top of each other. Francis' world swam and tears came to his eyes. Mom... She was in there somewhere, wasn't she? He felt like vomiting and barely held it down as a hand came down on his shoulder from behind.

Helen continued forward and began rummaging around the basement. After a few minutes, she returned up to them, and her voice was tinged with emotion as she looked at Francis.

"It... It was always a long shot. I'm sorry for your loss. I wish it could have turned out better." After a moment's hesitation, she looked at Bill. "I have the documents, we have to go now." Bill squeezed Francis' shoulder briefly before they all retreated back up the stairs and got in the car to make their getaway.

They left the remainder of the group behind. It seemed like the others had escaped while they were distracted by the monster. Francis was numb. How could something like this happen?

———O—o—O———

The three of them rode in silence before they returned to the commuter lot where they had left their other cars. Helen had seen to both their wounds as Bill drove. Bill's wounds didn't bleed much, and he seemed well enough to drive at least despite looking thin. Francis got bandages that stemmed the trickle of blood oozing from the wound in his side.

When they stopped moving the car, Helen began with the stitches on Francis' wounds.

Francis gritted his teeth but bore through the pain as Helen worked. After she was done, she helped the panting Francis to his car.

Bill wobbled over, "Francis," Francis looked up to see Bill extending an old flip phone, "You did good today," Bill continued, "Even... even if it didn't turn out well for you, you did good. If you want to stop more groups like that one, then call the number on this phone. It's a burner, so destroy it afterward. I'll reply another way."

Francis took the phone and stared at it for a second before looking at Bill again. "There are more? Doing this to more people?" Bill nodded. Francis put his hands on his wheel and gripped it as hard as he could.

"I'm in," Francis said.

Bill shook his head. "No."

Francis looked up in anger "What do you…"

Bill silenced him with a look. "This is a life-changing decision. It may lead to many things you might not like. Don't make it in a rush. I expect you to take at least a week to consider the offer before you accept."

Bill extended his hand to Francis.

Bill continued. "If this is the last time we meet, then I just want to say it was a pleasure."

Francis shook his hand. "Alright, but I already know my answer."

The corners of Bill's lips twitched upwards for a moment. "Well, I guess I'll see you soon then. Take care of yourself."

Francis nodded, "You too."

With that, they went their separate ways. Francis drove back home slowly, his head still swimming. When he got back the nausea got worse and he vomited into the toilet. This was going to be fun. The next week was horrible. But he didn't go to the hospital. He had no way to explain his stitched stab wounds, and the nausea was uncomfortable but Francis didn't feel like it would be fatal. So he stuck it out.

Exactly a week after the event, he called the number and told Bill that he was in. But he would need some early sick days, unfortunately. Bill had chuckled and told him to take as long as he needed. Francis finally recovered after two more horrible weeks. He had turned on the TV and flipped through the channels, and there was nothing on the news about the mummified bodies.

Nothing at all. Stacks of bodies and not a word.

That was what had truly solidified his decision, whoever was behind this had covered it up like it was nothing. Gotten away with it without anyone the wiser. Francis didn't even hear a whisper about it from the news, from the townspeople. Not even a whisper. And that couldn't stand. One way or another, he would stop them. If it was the last thing he did.

——— Returning to Central Events, twelve years forward on the personal timeline of Mortal Francis. Farther past the mortal's recollections. Too far, back a little. Perfect. Back in Central Events. Begin. ———

Francis saw Alice take her hand from the stone that now shone like a beacon, slowly draining her power into the battery banks below. That wound from the poisoned knife had been his one and only scar from all the other missions he had been on. Even in his deployments overseas, he hadn't had wounds that left a lasting scar like that. He unconsciously put his hand to his side where he felt the raised lump of flesh.

Francis smiled slightly as Alice quickly moved to the side to scarf up the energy bars. Ever since those first few days, Francis had joined Bill as one of the founding members of his Neighborhood Watch.

They had hunted similar dens all over the world ever since. He had been so idealistic back then. Alice reminded himself what he was fighting for. He felt a pain in his chest.

What would she think of him if she knew the truth? He reached into his trusty pouch and withdrew a flat stone, perfect for skipping on a pond. His Protection stone. He rubbed the smooth surface with his thumb and stared at it. He wasn't sure why he cared about the opinion this withdrawn, insecure teenage girl would have of him. But for some reason he did.

Despite her fear, she still wanted to fight. He had seen her resolve even as she cried. What would she think if he gave her the Protection stone and told her what was really happening?

"Whash dat?" Francis looked up and bits of energy bar stuffing Alice's cheeks like a chipmunk.

"Nothing, Alice, nothing," Francis replied quickly. He quickly put the stone back into his pouch and pasted a smile on his face, "When you're done tearing into that, I'll show you the bunks and where you'll be staying while you stay here."

She took a large gulp to swallow all the food in her mouth before diving in for more, giving Francis a thumbs up in response. Francis looked on bemused as she continued to dig in. She was ravenous. They might have to lug out another crate of food down here soon with her hanging around.

Chapter 36: Visiting the Club - Mortal Alice Fragment

——— Returning to the Fragment of Memory of Mortal Alice. Nothing of Interest for multiple days. Passing past the remainder of Second Sunday after the initial attack on Entity Fulcrum. Second Monday. Second Tuesday. Second Wednesday. There, Second Thursday. Isolating ideal starting point. Isolating... Isolating... Begin. ———

Alice was glad for Francis' support over the last few days. He had helped her pick out her magic weapon and introduced her to everyone. Sometimes when he looked at her, he would get kind of a sad look in his eyes, only to perk back up and return to his usual flamboyant self when he saw she had noticed.

Alice palmed the little gray cylinder in her pocket and rubbed it a little. She was nervous about her first-ever mission. She had heard all about the safe zones that the Neighborhood Watch had set up around town to protect people from the aliens that had gathered at the hospital. Apparently, people still under the effects of the alien dome's mental wards would still go to the hospital if they got injured. The hospital where all the aliens had gathered.

All the Infected had to do was wait and people would make their own way to the central gathering point. They even went around and were injuring people superficially so they would go to the hospital all on their own rather than actually kidnapping them. Like how one of them had pushed Alice down the stairs. Alice frowned. She guessed the strategy had worked on her all right. Hopefully, enough could escape on their own now things were more obviously wrong.

Alice shuddered a little. They were people. She shouldn't be cold and think of them like numbers like some of the people in the Neighborhood Watch did here. Her dad could have been one of those people. Her friends really could be one of them. She had to remember that.

Her friends... Better to not think of them. She fingered the cylinder of what felt like stone in her pocket again. She had practiced using it in the firing range in her spare time. Hopefully, it would protect her in case she got attacked by one of the aliens. Infected. She had to get used to the name when she talked. That's the name everyone in the Ranch used.

She walked with the two armed women to the main entrance. She had met the two before, but Alice couldn't remember their names. She didn't really want to ask them again if she didn't have to. It would just be too embarrassing to admit that she'd forgotten since they had introduced themselves to her just a few days ago.

The main entrance had a big metal cage elevator for larger groups of people. It was like the old-time elevators they had for mines in the movies. Alice remembered the horror movie that had just come out with the bat creatures hunting in the mines. The elevator looked almost exactly like the one from that movie.

With a loud clunk, the elevator began to rise from the floor and the chains rattled as it ascended. The two women beside her seemed unperturbed, but all Alice could think of was the elevator coming crashing down to the floor below. Or bat creatures jumping out from the sides to attack. Like how it had been in the movie.

Luckily, they reached the top quickly and Alice was able to step on solid ground again with only slightly wobbly legs. Of course, there was another guard checkpoint at the top. The checkpoints were everywhere around here.

After getting checked out, the three of them continued onward until they met with the larger group assembling in the barn above.

It looked like around fifteen to twenty people, all in military gear and heavily armed. People in the Neighborhood Watch didn't seem to ever wear normal clothes. They were wearing military gear of simple dark clothing even when they were just relaxing. It was so strange.

The crowd of armed people were loading big wooden boxes into two big white pickup trucks. A man Alice didn't know walked out from the chaos and made his way towards the three of them. He waved to the two women on either side of Alice.

"We could use a few more hands on the boxes to help us move faster if you're willing? We're about fifteen minutes from being ready as it is." The woman to Alice's left shook her head in denial.

"Sorry, sir," She said, "Our orders are to guard Alice here at all times. We have to stay with her." The man frowned in disappointment for a moment, before turning to Alice.

"Hi Alice, I'm Sean. Are you the one I've been hearing has been filling up the main batteries on your own? Our newest and well-loved member, right?" Alice blushed a little and nodded. Lots of people have been commenting on that recently. Mostly in the cafeteria that she went to afterwards. The energy bars were great for calories but didn't taste very good.

Alice needed to go eat some real food afterwards as a palette cleanser. She had been filling the main batteries for Potential at the base once a day, replacing the dozens of other people who would otherwise do the job. People seemed very grateful to her for that.

She still wasn't sure how to feel about the attention. It didn't seem like she was doing anything that special besides holding her hand to a stone and eating like a pig really.

Sean continued, "Well I'm glad you're here to assist with the safe zone's batteries now. You have no idea how slow we had to move when more people were needed to charge them. Logistics were a nightmare. Now we can use four vehicles instead of five!"

Alice nodded, not really sure what to say. Did she really make that much of a difference? She was surprised the safe zone batteries required so many people to fill it. She had been told they were way smaller than the one at the Ranch, as people called the secret base.

Sean moved away and Alice looked at the chaos of the people moving equipment and wondered if she should help out. Then she looked between the burly arms of the men and women around her to her own twig-like limbs. Yeah, no. Probably not a good idea. She'd probably just get in their way.

And her arms might snap if she tried lifting some of those boxes given how much the arms of the strong people were flexing as they picked them up.

Alice perked up as she saw Francis talking to Sean. Sean didn't look very happy, like he was cornered and uncomfortable. But after a few moments, he reluctantly nodded and Francis gave him a thumbs-up with a smile. It seemed more genuine than Alice was used to. Francis turned to Alice and gave a wave. She gave a small wave back, but Francis was already moving to assist in loading the supplies into the trucks.

Eventually, everyone was ready and the convoy took off. In addition to the two white pickup trucks were one military vehicle in the lead and another trailing behind. In their backs were big machine guns, with their clips of ammunition rolling to the side to spill into the truck bed. The turrets were manned by members of the Neighborhood Watch and moved on a swivel as they drove, the people on the turrets on their guard.

Francis was manning the turret in the back of the leading vehicle. Alice sat in the back of the pickup trucks carrying the boxes of supplies along with her two guards.

She was squeezed between the two walls of muscle and felt quite cramped in the center. Luckily nothing crazy happened on the way there. One or two Infected stumbled towards the convoy, but their heads exploded and they fell to the ground before they even stepped off the curb onto the street.

Alice was sure she should have felt horrified at the gore. But it just all felt too surreal. Like some strange movie, it all happened too fast. One moment there were dead bodies on the ground, next the convoy was around the corner and moving onward.

Finally, they reached a makeshift wall. There were parked cars across the street piled high with various furniture and scrap filling in the gaps. As the convoy approached, a large truck started up and backed up, opening a gap in the piles of junk. Like a gate. The convoy rolled inside of the walls. Alice looked ahead and saw another pile of junk about five houses down the street. She looked to the side and noticed there were piles between each house as well.

There were a few people wandering around, carrying things and a few people were armed and watching over the proceedings. One even looked like a cop with a blue uniform rather than the black military gear look the Neighborhood Watch had. The convoy stopped and the people around them rushed up and started unloading the boxes onto the ground and began distributing it.

As Alice stepped out of the truck, she gathered from the people's conversations around her that most of the boxes they were delivering had food in them. Her two guards followed her.

A few of the boxes had weapons too, but people didn't seem too excited about it. None of them wanted to fight from what she could see. Alice wondered if they had seen an alien fully transformed like she had. She wanted as much protection as she could from those things.

She felt in her pocket again. It had been a habit ever since she got the weapon. Whenever she felt unsafe she would touch it to remind herself that she wasn't totally helpless anymore. There was a little soft spot where she would inject her Potential to activate it.

She met the eyes of the cop for a moment. He was shorter with ruffled blonde hair. He was stocky and had light stubble on his face. After a moment his gaze shifted away as continued his walk around the interior of the makeshift wall. There was a man in military gear beside him talking like he was giving instructions to the cop. Probably one of the Neighborhood Watch stationed here.

A man named Victor from the Neighborhood Watch approached and directed her into one of the houses. The lawn out front was trampled with hundreds of footprints, people were streaming in and out and tracking mud inside. No one seemed to particularly care about the mess.

Victor led her inside and pointed to one of the side rooms where Alice saw Francis already standing inside. One of the people from the convoy rushed up and tried to usher Victor away before he could enter the room.

Victor got pissed and started yelling at the man. Francis was frowning as he peered at the stone pillar. Hearing the argument between Victor and the man from the Convoy, Francis looked up. The man from the convoy paled as he saw Francis in the room, and quickly scurried away with a half-hearted apology to Victor.

Noticing Alice, Francis walked forward to greet them, ignoring the man who had just fled the room.

"Hey, Alice. I just came to watch you charge the batteries here for the first time. You have a lot of Potential, and it can mess with the effects of some formations if there's too much power. We've never tested it with output as high as yours."

Alice looked between him and the stone dominating the room. "But it's safe right?"

Francis nodded and smiled. "Don't worry, perfectly safe. I've checked it myself just now, and I'll be right here to intervene if anything does happen anyway. If there's any issue at all it will shut itself off."

Victor next to her looked confused at their conversation. He interjected. "Wait, this thing is a battery? Don't we already have those gas generators? Why would we need those if this stone here can do the same thing?"

Both Alice and Francis looked at the man in shock. He didn't know? Wasn't that the whole point of her being here? So they could use Potential to charge their weapons and defenses? Francis' smile slid off his face into a frown deeper than before. His eyes darted between Alice and Victor.

"Alice, I have to discuss something with Victor quickly. We'll be back soon." Francis stepped forward and grabbed the bewildered Victor by the arm and guided him out of the room. Five minutes later, they reentered the room and Victor looked pissed. Francis tried to smile at Alice reassuringly, but it didn't reach his eyes.

Alice knew the difference between his fake and real smile after spending some time with him. His eyes weren't as angry as Victor's but had a profound well of sadness behind them that struck Alice at the core. He always tried to smile, even when he didn't mean it. Alice felt something tighten in her chest at Francis' look.

"Well Alice," Francis said, "It seems no one told Victor about the supplies he was supposed to be getting. I'll have to deal with this when I get back to base. But you should charge the battery for what is apparently the first time so we can put up some real defenses here. This could have been really bad, it was lucky we caught it in time."

Alice gulped. She wasn't sure what was going on, but it didn't sound very good. She guessed it was lucky the mistake had been caught now, rather than later when the aliens attacked. Alice had seen just how much damage items infused with Potential could do on the firing range. She was sure they would be effective on the Infected. These people needed all the help they could get in fighting off the aliens.

Alice stepped forward and put her hand on the standard input point she had gotten used to from the main base battery. It felt smooth like silk as her hand pressed inwards. This pillar looked almost identical except for the smaller size. She felt the tug on her Potential. Francis whispered something to Victor causing the man to leave the room. Alice's Potential started draining and the stone gradually lit up with a soft golden glow.

Alice frowned. It was a much slower draw than she was used to, but more than that, it was an inconsistent draw. One moment it would be half the amount, the next four times than initially. And over time it was growing worse and fluctuating, the draw on her Potential fluctuating up and down more and more each moment. Victor returned with a box filled with food and Alice went to tug her hand from the stone to grab some but her hand was stuck. Her eyes widened as she kept tugging on her hand that was stuck fast.

"Francis!" Alice's voice cracked as she felt something snap inside the stone and suddenly her Potential began to fly out of her like a gushing river. New patterns of smooth swirls and swooping lines appeared, overlapping with the more angular pattern from before. The more Potential drained from Alice, the more the second pattern began to glow over the stone. It began to pulse in waves starting from the bottom. Alice got a terrible feeling as the pulses grew faster and faster.

"...lice! Alice, focus!" Francis was shouting something but she couldn't hear anything over the sensation of her Potential rushing into the stone. She felt lightheaded and weak, her head swimming.

"...nnect potential. Other han....... Please Alice... Inject Potential. Other hand. Hurry." Alice heard a body hit the floor behind her, which shocked her sluggish mind into motion. She heard the thumps of more people dropping to the floor in the rooms nearby. She felt something smooth in her other hand.

She remembered Francis' voice and took a tendril of the river of Potential rushing out of her and diverted it into the soft input of the pebble in her left hand. In an instant her hand released from the pulsing stone and she fell backwards.

The river of Potential leaving her stopped abruptly. Alice fell on her back and stared at the ceiling as her vision blackened at the corners. She was still gripping the stone in her left hand as hard as she could.

Everything felt distant and far away. A thin tendril of her Potential lazily drained into the stone in Alice's hand. That's what Francis told her to do right? To take the stone and put her Potential into it? She saw Francis' concerned face peering down from above her. At least he seemed like he was okay... Alice felt herself drifting in and out of focus. There were more words from Francis, but Alice drifted off and fell asleep before she could process them.

——— (Prime Mortal Bill POV) ———

Bill shuffled through the printed-out reports in front of him. Helen provided summaries for him, but it was good to look at the direct reports to get a clearer picture of the organization. He was about to shuffle the latest into the read pile before he froze. Oh no.

He picked the document back up and read it closer. Someone had ignored his strict orders and sent Alice to safe zone seven on her first mission. He had clearly ordered this convoy to resupply safe zone ten! The convoy had left thirty minutes ago. This would be a disaster, he had to stop them!

He quickly ran out of his office and headed to the surface so he could get a signal on his radio. He tapped his foot as the elevator ascended.

He had to stop this.

As soon as he reached the surface, he saw the scrambling people and heard the tense voices sounding from radios around him. His heart sank. And rose when he heard that Alice was alive and being driven back to the Ranch at top speed, perhaps this was salvageable?

His hopes were dashed again when he heard that Francis was the one driving her back. An outcome that was arguably worse than the girl's unfortunate death. Why was Francis even there? He wasn't even assigned to that convoy in the report! Did he know? He must have some idea of it now if he had seen what had happened first hand…

Bill's mind raced through how he would explain, how to keep Francis calm until the plan was finished. They were so close! Why were things falling apart now at the finish line!

First the attack on the Harbinger forcing them to begin early and now having to possibly deal with conflict with Francis after this… Bill clenched his fists and controlled his expression as the military vehicle came tearing around the corner and drove at high speed to the barn where he stood waiting.

The medical staff were already waiting with a stretcher. With a screech of the brakes, the vehicle came to a quick stop in front of the barn. The medics quickly rushed forward and with Francis' assistance loaded Alice onto the stretcher. The medics rushed to the elevator, Francis jogging along and looking down at Alice in concern.

Bill didn't understand why Francis had grown such a bond with the girl in such little time. She was an asset, but not nearly enough to justify Francis' emotional investment in her. He had been dropping and assisting her whenever he could over the last few days. Mentoring her where he could.

As Francis passed Bill, still jogging with the stretcher, he shot Bill a stony faced look. His eyes held deadly promise as their gazes met. Bill kept his face carefully blank, exposing nothing. Francis looked away back to the stretcher and Bill watched him pass by.

Well, that confirmed it. This was going to be a problem. Time to run damage control with Helen. Francis would be occupied for a little while with Alice's condition, so the two of them would have some time to discuss the best approach in handling him. She would know how to best pacify him so they could continue with the plan.

Chapter 37: Suspicious Activity at the Ranch - Mortal Alice Fragment

Alice woke up in a white walled room. There were machines all around her, beeping and buzzing as she slowly drifted awake. She shifted and felt something cold pinching her arm. There was a hanging bag of fluid swinging above her next to the bed. She followed the line of the clear tube as it snaked down from the bag until it pinched her where the needle entered her arm. She blinked. Oh, it was an IV bag. Like the ones they used in hospitals. Hospitals…

"I'm at the hospital…" Alice muttered drowsily. Alice's eyes shot open as her brain snagged at the horrible thought. She sat up and looked around wildly. She couldn't be here. The aliens would be after her! She had to get out of here. She stepped off the hospital bed and took a step. The IV pinched her arm again and Alice stopped.

Alice reached down and fiddled with it, but hesitated before pulling it out. She didn't want to do it wrong and break the needle off inside her or something. She peeled back the white tape and gripped the plastic tube at the base of the tube. She readied herself and took a deep breath… Her arm tensed…

"Stop! You're fine, back at the Ranch. No Infected here. You're fine." Alice paused and looked to the doorway. She recognized the man, she had seen him around the cafeteria a few times at the Ranch. She relaxed as the man bustled in. So she wasn't at the hospital then?

"Now back to bed with you!" The man said, "We're all glad you're awake, gave us all a scare there. But you still need to get your rest." He ushered Alice back into bed.

"Lay down, lay down. Don't want you over exerting yourself yet." Alice compiled before looking at him after realizing something.

"All?" At her look, the man chuckled a bit as he fiddled with the IV and checked the machines around her.

"That's right," He said, "Lot of people were grateful to be off battery duty recently. You're something like a celebrity around here by now. People were concerned when they heard what had happened." Alice sank deeper into the bed.

Her, a celebrity? Well, she guessed a lot of people had come to talk to her recently… But she just thought they were just being welcoming since she was new here. But she thought it was just casual comments. It wasn't like any of them really *knew* her.

Huh. Maybe she was a celebrity. Weird. Alice leaned back and let the man fuss over her. According to him she just needed a day or two rest and then packed in the calories to rebuild all her lost Potential.

———O—o—O———

Alice left the clinic two days later. She had been eating almost the whole time, just stuffing her face over and over with food to gain back the weight she had lost overspending her Potential on her first mission.

She felt like a pig as she ate, but she was still hungry the whole time so she kept eating and kept telling herself that it was to refill her Potential, not actually for her body.

It was Monday now, Alice had been surprised at the time that she had been sleeping at the hospital for several days. Francis had visited her right after she woke up, but he had looked haggard. She had asked him what was wrong, but he said he would tell her when she had fully recovered.

She hadn't liked that, but seeing his state Alice hadn't wanted to bother him and add to his troubles. He had always tried to appear cheerful to her the whole time she knew him even when he got that sad look in his eyes. If he wasn't even trying to stay positive around her then it must be really bad.

Alice walked out of the clinic, her Potential back to full and feeling stuffed finally. It was apparently two pm based on the clocks in the hallways. Underground there was no sun so it was easy to lose track of time if you weren't paying attention. She went to walk back to her bunk, feeling gross and wanting to hit the common showers to get clean.

Best to hit them early before too many of the other women were in there. It had made her uncomfortable showering naked in front of the other women at first, but everyone was so matter of fact about it that Alice had just tried to ignore it. But she still tried to go when there probably weren't as many people around if she could.

As Alice walked in the hallways, everyone shot her pitying looks. No one approached or tried to talk to her, and it was starting to make her nervous. What was up with everyone? She felt great, the doctor said she was perfectly healthy after her rest! She was even some sort of celebrity apparently!

She remembered Francis' haggard face. Was it related to that? She started getting stressed the more as she tried to think of what could have happened. Luckily the showers were empty when she arrived, so she didn't have to worry about showering around other people and could take more time to relax.

She couldn't stop thinking about what everyone's looks and whispers meant as scrubbed herself and let the hot water run down her body.

The warm rushing water pouring down from above helped calm her down. She took some deep breaths. Francis said he would explain. She had to calm down until then. She was fine. She was safe here away from the Infected.

Half an hour later, fully clean and wearing fresh clothes, Alice decided to go to the firing range. Her hair was still damp. Someone had put all the stuff she had been carrying on Thursday back into her locker, so she got her little cylinder weapon back.

As she walked over through the base hallways, the muttering and pitying looks of the people irritated her. Why didn't they just tell her what was wrong? Why were they whispering?

She entered the big room and took the lane farthest from the door. It had a special target that was more fun. She withdrew her cylinder and injected a little of her Potential into it. She pointed it at the humanoid dummy down range. It looked like one of those store mannequins except with a flat rolling base with wheels. The whole thing was padded.

The cylinder in her hand started glowing, and she flicked the switch on the side to activate it. An invisible wave of force shot out of it, distorting the air in front of her. It impacted the dummy and it went flying until it smacked the wall and ragdolled. It fell to the floor as its arms flailed and the base tipped over until it lay splayed on the floor.

Alice grinned, it was always so fun to knock it around. Like a big stress ball. Especially how the limbs flailed every which way as it fell. She absentmindedly munched on one of the nearby energy bars. Using this thing didn't take that much Potential, but she wanted to stay topped off since everyone seemed on edge around her. Maybe the aliens did something? Alice shook it off. She was trying to relax here, she didn't know enough to guess what was going on yet. Not with everyone still avoiding her for some reason

The walls of her firing lane flashed briefly and the mannequin was lifted off the floor and placed upright on its wheels by an invisible force. It rolled slowly until it was back where it was before. Alice watched the process. She liked this part almost as much as blasting it in the first place. Real magic at work. The mannequin reset. She blasted it. It reset, she blasted it. It reset, she…

"Hey, Alice."

Alice turned. She looked blankly at the man who approached her for a moment before she recognized him. Oh, it was Jake! She had met him her first day here at the cafeteria. She had seen him around but hadn't really talked to him too much.

"Hi Jake," She said. Jake looked at her with that same pitying look as the rest.

"Look, I'm sorry about what happened. I just wanted to tell you not to blame yourself. It's not your fault. They should have had someone double check that battery before you used it. Especially for your first mission."

Alice looked at Jake in confusion. "But they did? Francis was right there. From what I've heard, if he didn't see it, then no one could have. And why would I blame myself? I'm fine, I just needed some rest. What ended up happening anyway? No one will tell me what happened after I got knocked out."

Jake looked at her in shock. "Alice? Do you really not know what happened?"

Alice shook her head in frustration, "No! No one will talk to me. Francis said he would explain what happened, but he hasn't shown up yet."

Jake gulped and looked around. The others were studiously looking away from the pair. He wavered for a moment, looking like he wanted to retreat. Alice grabbed his arm. "Jake, please tell me! Whatever it is, I have to know. The silence is killing me here!"

Jake was rooted in place, but eventually sighed. "Alice... Safezone Seven... It was attacked and destroyed on Friday when you were unconscious. By the Infected. When the battery malfunctioned it knocked many of the people unconscious and deactivated all the defenses based on Potential they had. They were still recovering when they were attacked. With just normal weapons... Well... It wasn't pretty."

Alice gasped in horror. All those people! But at the same time... "But they never had any Potential based defenses. There was some mistake and they didn't even know what the battery was before we got there."

Jake started to look VERY nervous at her words. "Oh. Oh no. This is bad. Alice..."

"Alice!" From across the room, Alice saw Francis making his way toward them. He still looked pretty horrible, dark rings under his eyes and slumped shoulders. He glared suspiciously at Jake.

Jake leaned in and whispered, "Look, Alice. I never heard any of this. This would be big trouble if people knew. This is probably why we were ordered not to talk to you."

Alice opened her mouth to reply, but Jake straightened back up and spoke loudly. "Anyway Alice, glad you're back on your feet. I should probably get back to practice then." He speed walked away, giving a stiff nod to Francis as they passed each other.

Francis stopped a few steps away, glancing at the man suspiciously, "Alice," Francis said as he watched Jake return to his own firing lane.

Alice took in Francis' ruffled appearance. He pointed his thumb over his shoulder to the door.

"Come with me. I'll explain everything. But we have to be away from prying ears." He glared back at Jake again who was lining up a rifle on the range. Jake's hands were shaking and most of his shots were missing his target. He didn't look back at them though. Francis squinted at him in suspicion and Jake's aim grew worse.

Alice shook Francis' shoulder, only shifting the burly man a little with her noodle arms. "C'mon Francis. Let's go already," She said, "I've been waiting in suspense for days for whatever horrible thing you're going to tell me. Let's just get it all over with already!"

At her outburst, Francis was successfully distracted and agreed before hurrying away. Alice rushed after him. Soon they entered a tiny room with a single table and two chairs inside. A buzzing overhead light beamed down on the center of the table below. Francis opened and closed his mouth, seeming hesitant. Alice leaned forward, but the words that came from his mouth were unexpected.

"Alice, We've got to get you out of here. It's no longer safe for you. Bill and Helen are going to kill you if you stay."

Chapter 38: Escaping the Neighborhood Watch - Mortal Alice Fragment

Alice looked at Francis. "I've got to go? I'll be killed?! Francis, what's going on?"

Francis' eyes darted around as he withdrew a stack of folders filled to the bursting of various papers from the pouch he always had at his side. He went to hand them to her, before seemingly changing his mind and returning them into the pouch.

"Look at those later," He said quickly. What was he doing?

"Listen Alice, there isn't much time to explain. Bill and Helen are probably tracking us now. They are planning to kill a lot of people under the dome. Including you if I don't go along with their plans." Alice stiffened. What?! She started hyperventilating and curled into herself.

"Oh, shit. Alice. Alice! Calm down, please! We can stop them!" Alice uncurled a little and looked up in hope.

"We... Me and you? Together?" She asked. Francis nodded frantically.

"Look, first we have to get out of the Ranch first. If anyone tries to stop us, use your weapon on them. It's mostly non lethal, so don't hesitate, ok? No matter what. Can you do that?" Alice nodded. What? How? So much was happening!

"Look, just act natural ok?" Francis said, "I'll explain more once we get to the surface. Just follow my lead."

Francis opened the door and ushered her out, and Alice reflexively followed him. Her head was whirling as she hustled after him as he hurried along. They walked down the corridors, and people nodded to her.

She waved and tried to not let her inner conflict show on her face. Look, she liked Francis a lot. He had been nothing but helpful and kind since she came to the Ranch. But he was asking for a lot here, and wasn't explaining much.

Alice thought back to Jake's expression when she explained about there being no equipment at Safezone Seven. When he heard that he had been terrified. Safezone Seven had been totally destroyed. Whatever Alice had said had terrified him more than the Infected killing that whole group of people. Alice straightened and her eyes widened as she reached a horrible conclusion.

Did... Were those people left to die by the Neighborhood Watch? No proper defenses that she knew they were supposed to have. Alice powering the battery had somehow knocked out a load of people nearby. She had seen the second set of swooping lines and knew Francis had checked the thing before she used it. Whatever it was powering up to do had been intentional.

The people in the zone had not even *known* that better defenses existed for them. The normal townspeople she could understand not knowing, but Victor? The other guards stationed there with the Neighborhood Watch? They should have known. The only way it could have happened... was if they were intentionally misled. By the Neighborhood Watch. Served up to the Infected.

Alice picked up her pace and began sweating harder. Ok, she was a lot more ready to believe Francis now. She noticed the pistol strapped at Francis' side, he wasn't usually armed within the Ranch with guns like that.

No one stopped them until they reached the main elevator. The two guards on duty didn't even hesitate. On seeing the two of them together, they lifted their rifles and started shouting. In a panic, Alice pulled out her weapon and flicked the switch and activated it all in one motion. The wave of force sent one of the guards flying off to the side where they impacted the wall with a loud *crunch* before falling limp to the floor.

The guard's rifle clattered to the ground, falling from their slack fingers. Alice ducked down as the sound of gunshots rang through the small tunnel, sending her ears ringing. Alice closed her eyes reflexively. She felt a hand on her arm and squirmed to get away, but was dragged forward and up by the strong inescapable grip. "Alice... Alice, Alice wake up, it's me," Francis said urgently.

The two of them were in the elevator. Alice recovered her hearing and looked down as the elevator began ascending. Francis let go of her arm. On one side was the guard she had blasted with the wave of force.

On the other side... Alice screamed. He... He was dead. There was a perfect hole in his forehead and he lay on the floor with a blank gaze upwards. Alice looked at Francis in horror. "You.... You *killed* him! Why would you do that?"

Francis shook his head, but did look a little guilty. But only a little. "I'm sorry, I am," He said, "But I had to. He was going to shoot you. I value your life over his. Simple as that."

The elevator had nearly reached the top and was slowing down. They reached the top as Alice was still reeling. The doors opened and the guards turned and raised their rifles towards them. Alice quickly blasted them with two quick waves of force before they could react, and they fell limp to the ground. She didn't want Francis killing anyone else. Francis ran ahead, Alice following closely behind.

People were rushing around in a panic and saying things over the radio as she and Francis ran forward. Several asked Francis for orders as they ran. Francis gave orders to go down below to secure the base. Alice felt sick. He had just killed his coworker like it was nothing.

They went to one corner where one of the military jeeps was parked. There was something under a tarp in the back. They climbed in and to the protests of the manager nearby, drove off. No one else moved to stop them as Francis stepped on the gas and the engine thrummed below their feet. Alice turned to Francis, thoughts of what happened below still on her mind. She continued where their conversation had left off.

"Simple. SIMPLE!" She shouted, "It was just a threat. That guard, you should have... have... I don't know, anything else. Not have killed him!"

Francis looked over at her and she was taken aback at his sincerity as he spoke, "Alice. I understand. I... I am not a good person. And neither is anyone else in that building. Most would kill you without hesitation if Bill or Helen ordered them to. When I say that guard was about to kill you, I'm not kidding. It... was only seconds away."

Alice stuttered. "No... No. T-They wouldn't! That's horrible. You're wrong. He just wanted us to surrender."

Alice thought about it more. *Well, I did just blast his friend... Maybe he was going to shoot me?* At the thought she shook her head. She didn't want to think about his dead eyes staring into nothing anymore. Francis shifted gears and took a sharp turn. Alice lurched and stabilized herself by bracing herself against the dash of the vehicle.

"Uhm, Francis. What... What did you want to say to me before? Now that we are away from the Ranch."

Francis startled, and briefly swerved on the road before refocusing. He was silent for another minute, until they reached the highway and rolled onto the massive road. It was empty. He eased off the gas pedal to slow down and glanced at her while also keeping one eye on the road.

"Alice, remember how I told you that there was a mental ward that stopped people from thinking of leaving the dome?" Alice nodded.

"Well, there is a stronger one once you actually approach the dome physically. You didn't even feel the inner one. I think you might be able to power through the stronger one and make it to the other side." The car started drifting to the side again.

Francis slammed on the brakes and they screeched to a stop. Alice rubbed her forehead where it had slammed into the dashboard at the sudden stop. Ow.

"Alright, Alice. Just walk ahead on the road. Stay focused. Don't let yourself turn around, no matter what. Try to follow the lines of the road if that helps you stay straight. It should be about half a mile from here to the physical dome. And you're going to be taking two more things with you to get through."

The two got out of the Jeep and went to the back. Francis threw back the tarp and revealed what looked like an upside down wooden bowl with a long metal rod inside and attached to the rounded end. He lifted it out.

The whole thing looked like some weird umbrella, the bowl reaching wider than Francis' broad shoulders. The metal rod was three feet long. He stepped forward and offered it to Alice. She accepted it with a grunt and rested the weight on her shoulder.

"Why... ugh," Alice shifted the weight, "do I have to carry this thing?"

"You can put it down for now. Here I'll show you what it does."

Alice placed it on the ground with relief. It really wasn't that heavy, but she didn't really exercise much so it felt like a lot anyways. Francis picked it up and obviously pressed his finger at one point on the metal shaft. "Alright, inject Potential here and then…"

The air slowly distorted around Francis in a thin film around him after about a minute. It rippled like a kind of watery bubble. Francis took a quick step forward and the bubble popped.

"It's a shield," He said, "Same kind as the bigger dome but smaller scale. When you reach the dome, activate it and move *very* slowly. It is made of the same thing as the barrier, so if you're slow enough the dome should pass around it and you'll be able to make it through. I have something else too."

Francis reached to his side and unclipped his trusty pouch with one hand that always seemed to be attached at his hip. He handed it to her with what seemed to be almost physical pain. He put the shield umbrella back on the ground.

"Alice, I want you to have this. The files, the plans… You have to get it to the government, the army, somebody important. Make sure they only make copies, all kinds of people would be happier with these destroyed. The government can help stop this if they get the documents to the right people.

"I also left some things in there to help protect yourself with. My gift to you. Keep those for yourself and don't tell anyone about them. If you tell the government then you'll be forced to give them up. Here, inject some of your Potential into the bag here." Francis pointed to a certain segment on the lip of the bag.

Alice did so, and she felt a click in her mind. She was in a sort of daze with the sudden barrage of words from Francis. She put her hand in the bag and got the strangest feeling that began to tingle through her hand.

In the back of her mind was a room with various objects floating around inside. As she focused on something it started drifting toward the ceiling of the room that glowed with a bright purple light. She took her hand out of the pouch and the sensation disappeared.

"There, now it will only open for you," Francis said, "Just make sure to refill it with your Potential every once in a while. I left instructions inside. Oh, and here's the belt for it too." Francis handed over the belt, an extra that matched the one he had on.

Alice stared at him in confusion. "Aren't you coming? You're going with me, right? We can tie a rope to you or something. We can both go out. I don't want to talk to the government by myself. It's way better for you to explain things, right?!"

Francis shook his head. "No. I have things I have to do here. More good than if I was in prison out there. That's where I would end up. And I'd just drag down your credibility with me if I went with you.

"Alice… I want to tell you something. I said I was a bad person before. That's true. More than you know. It was only when I met you that I truly saw the innocents I was hurting. I thought I was protecting people… Everything I did was for that, even if it was wrong. I'm sorry. I'm sorry for all of this. And I just want you to know that I'm trying to make it right." Francis rubbed his eyes. Alice wasn't sure what to say.

"What are you going to do?" She asked.

Francis smiled a little. "I'm going to save as many as I can. I have a plan but I can't do it without help from the outside. I'm trusting this with you."

Alice picked up the umbrella shield and slung it over her shoulder. She put her hand on the pouch now hanging at her waist. How had she gotten here? Somehow it felt like a final goodbye here for the two of them. Alice wanted to say something meaningful in the poised moment. But then the moment passed and Francis nodded at her.

"Good luck. I'll leave to draw away the hunters. I believe in you, you can make it out of here. Just try to follow the lines on the road."

Alice shuffled, but then looked him in the eyes. He deserved that much. "Thank you," She said, "For all of your help. And good luck to you too, I'll get the military to understand how important the papers are."

With that, Francis got in the car and drove away. Alice watched his car recede into the distance. She turned to where she knew the dome would be. She could feel something tickling at her mind just from turning in that direction. Taking Francis' advice, she found one of the white lines between the lanes and started walking along. Just one foot in front of the other. One step. After. Another.

Just one step after another.

Chapter 39: Long Walk Out of the Bubble - Mortal Alice Fragment

Alice took another step.

Another step.

Another step.

One foot in front of the other.

Another step.

Another step.

Wait, the white line, it was to her right now. She corrected her stride and felt a small tug on her mind. She kept moving and the tugs grew stronger. The white line filled the vision until it was all she could see. She caught herself drifting to the sides more and more often as she continued. Her eyes stayed on the line, but her focus kept drifting into the clouds.

The tugs on her attention grew stronger.

She kept walking. She looked down and there was no line. She stopped, rooted in place.

The force on her mind roughly pulled at her attention as she forced herself to look up and around. She had drifted almost to another lane of the road. She was perpendicular to her first white line now.

She looked one direction and the force lessened. She looked the other way and it took all her focus to remember where she was.

Without even knowing why, Alice walked more in that direction when she felt that sense of confusion and distraction. It felt right. She walked more and more, and the force grew stronger and stronger. Whenever the force lessened, she would turn and walk in little circles until she felt where it was stronger. She had no white line to guide her anymore.

It felt like she was being split in two as she walked, but she persisted. She entered a dreamlike state.

She took another step, another step. She took another step. The girl took another step.

Her vision was blurry, another step. Another … *Wham!*

She fell down as her face hit something. She tried to get to her feet, but the force in her mind lurched and she spun around and fell to the ground feeling nauseous. Her shield umbrella fell to the road with her from her shoulder. Alice crawled and felt her fingers brushing the surface of the transparent dome. It felt like a cold pane of glass. She crawled closer until she was leaning against it with her back.

Eyes unfocused, she reached out and grabbed the shield umbrella where she had dropped it. She injected her Potential where Francis had told her to, feeling the grooves, and it activated. Her blurry vision saw the whole world begin to ripple around her. She assumed she was in the shield.

For a few seconds, nothing happened. Alice worried that it was all for nothing. That she had failed. Then all of a sudden, she fell backwards through the barrier.

The shield bubble surrounded her on all sides, rippling violently at the motion from her short fall. The dome pressed in on Alice's little shield, and the poor shield billowed inward as if it was under a strong wind.

Go Shield, you can do it! Hold strong little buddy. Alice slowly curled into a ball and inched her way forward. Her thoughts felt fuzzy. She could see green vehicles in the distance and the little moving forms next to them. That felt good. She should go that way.

She slowly dragged the shield umbrella behind her, and it scraped against the asphalt of the road as she moved.

Alice was almost there. Her body half way through the barrier. She was on the other side. The shield umbrella was still being dragged behind her. She paused as the mental wards targeted her again and her vision went blurry again as she tried to look back.

The mental wards were hitting her with their full force again. Alice had barely even noticed that the pressure had stopped as she pulled herself across the shield of the dome. With a *pop* the poor little shield from the strange umbrella popped and the dome came back down. With the swoosh like a blade, the dome came down and cut the extended metal handle of the weird umbrella cleanly in half.

She fell back and looked at the severed metal rod in her hands. It kind of looked like a racing baton now. That was funny. It used to be a magic item and now it was just a metal pipe.

She got to her feet and looked towards the soldiers in the distance. The mental wards faded to almost nothing as they seemed to sense her intent to go towards them. Her mind cleared and she remembered what she was doing. She walked forward unsteadily, nursing a headache from her journey to get this far.

As she got closer, the soldiers began to shout as they finally spotted her. Like a wind on her back, the ward pushed her forward from behind, eager to see her leave and go farther away. Alice smiled and began to walk faster.

The soldiers were saying things as she finally reached them and one of them touched her shoulder. But she couldn't hear them. She fell to her knees. She was crying, as she walked. She was out, and Francis had stayed behind.

Waves of emotions passed through her. She fell to her knees and started sobbing as the relief hit her all at once. She was out. She was finally safe. For real this time.

———O—o—O———

Alice was in the hospital again, this time under guard from the soldiers. The doctors in hazmat suits came in and out, checking her vitals. No one had talked to her much after she confirmed she was from inside the dome.

She thought they would start asking things immediately, but the two soldiers with fingers on the triggers of their guns just stood in the corner of the room and watched her silently, in bulky hazmat suits of their own.

They handcuffed her to the hospital bed. She told them only she could open the pouch, but one of the people in uniform didn't listen and took it from her anyway. Eventually the doctors were satisfied with their checkup on her and the room fell into silence.

$$---O-o-O---$$

She looked up as a dark haired man in uniform walked in the door. He had piercing blue eyes and little colored bars lined the left side of his chest. He wasn't wearing the big hazmat suits.

"Alice Lovelace?" The man said, "I'm sorry about all the precautions. We didn't want to risk anything with all the unknowns about this situation." He gestured to one of the hazmat suited soldiers who stepped forward and uncuffed her from the bed. She sat up and rubbed her wrist.

Alice didn't like it, but knowing what the Infected were like she more than understood his point. If she were one of them she would definitely be dangerous to the soldiers.

A soldier came in and brought in a metal chair, which the man sat at.

"I'm Major Davis. I'm in charge of the soldiers guarding this highway from the dome. You're the first person to escape from that place. We have very little information on what's going on in there." He leaned in, his hands clasped in front of him.

"So please, tell us what you've experienced this last week. Just stop if you ever need to collect yourself." He pulled a blocky device the size of a phone from his pocket.

"Don't feel nervous, but I'm going to record you too. For the higher ups, you know. That way you can let it all out at once and then we can leave you to recover."

Alice looked between the device in his hand and his face. She still didn't know what evidence Francis had put in the spatial pouch. She hadn't thought to ask in the rush to escape. She just hoped her story convinced the higher ups to take whatever they said seriously. She took a deep breath and began speaking. He held the device in his left hand as he listened to her.

She spoke for what felt like forever. The last week felt like it had been years to her. She didn't hold anything back except how she had a lot more Potential than normal.

She had seen the movies where people told the military about their special powers. It never went well for them. It wasn't even that important anyways. She wasn't even lying, just not telling things that weren't important.

She had to pause for a minute when describing how the Infected in the hospital had tried to kill her. And even longer when she described her and Francis' escape from the Ranch and Neighborhood watch. How Francis had killed that guard.

Major Davis wasn't exactly compassionate, but he gave her as much time as she needed when she stopped. He grimaced at several points as she spoke, but didn't speak or interrupt her.

Finally, it was over. Alice explained how Francis had given her the spatial pouch and then… For the first time Major Davis interrupted her.

"Wait, pouch? What is this? Where is it now?"

She looked at him in confusion. "Huh? Someone in uniform took it from me. I told them only I could open it but they just ignored me and took it anyway."

Major Davis looked livid. "I'm sorry, I have to deal with something for a minute."

He quickly walked out the door and one of the soldiers followed him. As soon as he was out the door, Alice heard his voice slowly fading into the distance. "Missing asset… Infiltration… Lock down…. Security…"

Oh. Oh my. Someone had stolen the bag apparently. Like some kind of spy maybe. She fidgeted and waited. Without the bag she didn't have whatever evidence Francis had about the Neighborhood Watch's plan.

Alice didn't have a watch or anything, but it felt like a long time before Major Davis returned, with her bag clutched in his hand. He held it out to her. She hesitantly accepted it, looking between it and Major Davis' carefully blank expression. She had seen the same one on Bill whenever she had seen him in the hallways of the Ranch. "What happened? The man who took it…"

Major Davis paused and his expression grew conflicted for a moment. "I'm sorry, but I'm not allowed to tell you. It's a security risk if we tell civilians about that kinda thing. I'm sorry it happened, especially given your experiences over the last week. Now, the documents?" He extended his hand towards her palm, upward.

She looked into his eyes and was struck with a sudden sense of paranoia. If that man had escaped, the evidence might have been lost forever. Whatever Francis was planning to help the townspeople might collapse. If she handed the documents over, someone might steal or destroy them. She thought about what she should do. She saw the old fashioned voice recorder in his left hand. It gave her an idea.

"Wait, I'm sorry, can you take pictures of the papers? Like scan them I mean? Only I can get in the pouch, so they should be the safest there I think. I don't want to go to all this effort just for some guy to steal or destroy them later."

At her questions, Major Davis' expression darkened slightly and he pulled back his hand. He looked slightly offended. His tone became tinged with frustration.

"What you have is critical to saving the lives of everyone under that dome if what that man said is true. To allow us to fight off these aliens. We need to know about this as soon as possible. Security is my job, and I'll make sure the information gets to the right people. Don't you worry about it."

He stared her down, and she squirmed at his look. But Francis had entrusted this mission to her. She wouldn't fail what could be his dying wish. She knew how deadly the aliens would be if they could all transform like how the police officer one had at the hospital.

"Look, it's only a little time right?" Her voice grew a little heated, "If I hand the documents over and you lose them somehow then it would be *my* fault. The Neighborhood Watch had all sorts of heavy weapons and artifacts that are basically magic. Military jeeps with those big guns on the back. If they have all that stuff, then they probably could break in and steal some papers from you."

Major Davis' expression cleared a little and became more thoughtful as he considered her point. His face was still tense, but luckily he seemed to be seriously considering her argument. His eyes glazed over slightly and he pursed his lips for a minute or two. He reached over and hit a button on his device. Finally, he turned back to Alice with an expression that was severe.

"Alice, I've turned off the recording," He said, "I want to take those papers for your own safety. The higher ups will want the originals because it makes them feel like the information is more reliable than the scans. They will make life hard for you until you give them those papers and whatever else is inside your little pouch.

"Technically it's a security risk for you to have something as sensitive as you claim. It may be legal prosecution or they may hold you here if you don't comply. Maybe even pressure your dad if they are feeling nasty. They like feeling in control in tense situations like this. And the situation is very tense out here."

Hearing this, Alice wavered. But…

"That's a stupid reason! It's the same information anyway. And… And I would rather go to prison than be the one that let all those people die! They can always make more copies. Well, please don't put me in prison. But I would go if it was that or having this stuff being destroyed."

Major Davis looked at her, eyes roaming over her face. "Last chance. For the record, I think you're right. And I'll do my best to protect you from the assh- Jerks at command. I just want you to know the trouble you're getting yourself into with this. I'm on your side here."

She looked back. "Okay. I get it. Just… Ok."

Major Davis turned to the two soldiers guarding the room. "Not a word of this to anyone, you understand?" He nodded to her before moving to the door. "Alright, I'll arrange things and be back soon. Just hold tight here."

———O—o—O———

Major Davis' voice sounded from the other side of the door. "Alright Alice, I brought a wheelchair for you. I'll take you to where we'll be scanning the documents."

He walked in, rolling the metal wheelchair in front of himself. She swung her legs over the side of the bed. "No thanks, I can walk fine," She said. She took a step and the room shifted slightly and she got lightheaded. She suppressed the urge to vomit. Davis hurried forward until the chair was in front of her.

"Whoa, there. Maybe not. Why don't you sit down anyways. Everyone who approaches the dome has bad headaches, it seems you're the same. We don't want you taking any risks with your health here."

She collapsed into the wheelchair before shifting in place to sit up properly. Major Davis pushed her out the door and into a hallway. She looked around to take in her surroundings as they moved.

"Where are we? Is this a hospital?" She asked. Davis kept pushing her down the hallways. Some of the people nearby shot Alice and Davis glances but most seemed to be hurrying around to some destination or another. Most but not all of them wore military uniforms. The two of them went through a pair of large double doors.

"This is a clinic at the closest military base to the town of Harmony," Davis said, "You were diverted here in case you were a danger to others at the normal hospital."

Alice slumped back down in the chair. That made sense. People wouldn't like all the soldiers around if they were at the hospital for more normal reasons. And she wouldn't want to be in a hospital with an Infected again...

She shuddered as she remembered the hospital in Harmony. Her paranoia growing as more and more Infected took over the hospital. Not that she knew exactly what they were at the time. Her eventual escape. Her friends... Had they survi...

Alice was shocked back awake as the wheelchair bumped as she entered a room filled with over ten people dominated by a central table. She flinched as she saw the disinterested looks of some of the people there. Their expressions shifted at her flinch and she relaxed. They were human. She wasn't back in Harmony.

The people were all wearing surgical gloves. Various machines and small devices Alice didn't understand were strewn about. One of the closest men paused as he saw her, glancing between Alice and Davis. He was holding a camera that pointed at her. Davis' voice sounded above her head.

"Hello everyone. This is Alice. She'll be retrieving the documents for your analysis and scans. Make sure to return everything as it was when you are done. She has a secure way to store them that only she can access."

Everyone in the room looked to Alice in anticipation. She hesitated one more time, but she had to show some trust here. Major Davis seemed okay, and she had to bring out the documents at some point.

She reached into the pouch in her lap and felt her mind connect to the space in the bag. She called the first folder into her hand and after a second felt the crisp paper between her fingers.

She pulled and took out the folder filled with papers from the bag. There were gasps around the room as the mouth of the pouch stretched as Alice withdrew the thick folder. She leaned forward and put the folder carefully on the table. She reached inside again for the next one. The people in the room seemed frozen, fascinated and shocked as the pouch bulged again as Alice retrieved the second folder. Davis cleared his throat behind her.

"Don't you all have jobs to do? Stop gawking and get moving."

At his prodding one of the men pulled the first folder towards himself and carefully flipped it open. He picked up an expensive looking camera and flashed an image of the top page. He flipped it over and took a picture of the back. He passed it to the next man in line before continuing with the next page in the stack. The man that received the page placed it into a scanner.

The scanner whirred for a moment before beeping. An image popped up on the computer display. It showed fingerprints and various splotches along with the fuzzy text. The man flipped the page and repeated the process.

After that he passed it to another man who did a scan that showed the normal words of the page. When it reached the end, people with various scopes and little tools took readings of the pages before passing it on. Finally at the end of the line, the processed pages were placed face down next to the original folders.

Eight of the men occupied themselves with the assembly line as another man sat at a computer in the corner. The last of the men stood in the corner and recorded the proceedings as a whole with a separate camera that he held over his shoulder.

Images appeared quickly on the screen of the man at the computer before the images disappeared again. The man at the station stared intently at the screen and typed something into it occasionally.

Alice stared at that man and his station in confusion as she retrieved the third folder and put it on the table. The images flashed by too quickly for him to be reading anything. Maybe he was just checking that the images were being sent to the computer correctly? Like the images from the scanners.

There was only the rustling of paper and buzzing of machines as they all worked in silence. She put the fifth and final folder down on the table and settled down to watch. It was actually kind of soothing seeing the men so focused and just moving the papers down the line.

——— O — o — O ———

Finally, the men were done. They all looked exhausted. They had taken their scans, even of the folders themselves that the papers were held in. But when all was said and done, everything was returned and Alice put the folders back in her pouch. Davis rolled her out of there after saying their quick goodbyes.

As they left two men with severe expressions confronted them just outside the door and demanded the original documents from Alice. She had refused them as best as she could but was intimidated as they loomed over her wheelchair with severe frowns.

Seeing her discomfort Major Davis leapt to her defense and told the two men to 'piss off'. They hadn't liked that but left anyway. It seemed Major Davis outranked them.

Her and Major Davis returned to the room from before. There was a man in white garb hovering over the empty bed. Davis looked down and spoke as he rolled her toward the bed.

"Thank you, Alice," Major Davis said, "With that over, just focus on your recovery. We'll take it from here. I'll make sure those two don't bother you again." The doctor opened his mouth, looking at Davis in what seemed to be exasperation.

Alice stumbled to her feet, legs numb. She fell onto her stomach on the bed. Both men hovered over her as she rolled over and straightened herself. Seeing that she was fine, Davis began to beat a hasty retreat from the room. The doctor seeing this walked after him and followed him out of the door.

"What the he... Uh, heck Davis? I told you after the last one that a doctor needs to be present..." His voice faded as he walked farther away in the hallway outside.

"....all times... Irresponsible... hurt…….. Traumatized young girl."

Alice strained her ears as hard as she could, but she couldn't pick out anything else from the doctor as Davis seemed to keep retreating without responding to the man chasing him. *Huh*, she thought, she couldn't believe she was going to be on bed rest already. Again. Despite everything that happened, If this lasted too long she was going to go stir crazy.

Chapter 40: Up the Chain of Command - Multiple Fragments of Memory

——— **Transitioning to Major Davis Fragment of Memory outside the room of Mortal Alice. Begin.** ———

Davis tried to escape as the doctor hounded him from behind. The doctor was still pissed at how he had conducted his intensive follow up interview with the man who had first contact with the alien now known as Thoth. Davis was sure the doctor would make him pay next time that Davis saw him.

Not that he wasn't right in his criticism. Davis felt sorry for the girl back there, but it was best to get all the unpleasantness out of the way at first so she could properly relax. She had been through a lot. He felt like he had aged years after hearing her account. She had been through so much. He wondered what his superiors would do with that information.

They would likely criticize how he handled everything, but he had already been demoted to Major because of his criticism of command over the years. His career was as high as it would ever go without wading into the slimy waters of the politicians.

The decisions of what to do with the documents that the girl had were now way above his pay grade, but he could only hope a certain General Harris was reigned in. Major Davis had heard enough of the general's unhinged rants to know of his warmongering arguments.

——— **Nothing more of interest. Shifting to Fragment of Memory of this 'General Harris'. Two hours forward in the timeline. Begin.** ———

General Harris was red in the face as his fist hit the table in front of him.

"Bloody traitors, the lot of them! They're terrorists! Knew about this ahead of time and didn't warn anyone? For all we know everyone in there is dead and this is just a delaying tactic for the aliens. I say throw everything against the dome so we can go in. If we believe this terrorist then they will kill everyone anyway if we wait! We already know what kind of people they are!"

He was breathing heavily and the other generals stared at him with various levels of concern. "General Harris, I realize this is tense, but do you know what you're advocating for?" One of the analysts bravely said to interject just as General Harris started building steam, "This might kill many of the survivors if our heavy weapons pierce the dome at the wrong moment. Even if the Neighborhood Watch is mixed among them."

Everyone turned to stare at the analyst, but after a moment's pause, General Harris nodded to the man. The analyst continued,

"Our blurry satellite images through the dome match the movements observed through the town to what's recorded in the documents. We think we have located at least two of the farms mentioned as covert entrances to the so-called 'Ranch'. There are at least five more we haven't located, likely because they are infrequently used. But we know the twenty farms where possible entrances could be based on the land that the shell company for the Neighborhood Watch purchased several years ago.

"We have also located the so-called safe zones as well, and the strange shapes and movements around the hospital that are purported to be the alien threat. Everything verifiable in the documents is correct. Even the bag that only Alice Lovelace can open and that is bigger on the inside.

"We have clear footage of its abilities on display as the girl retrieved the documents. Everything short of destructive testing was used after it was recovered from the Neighborhood Watch sympathizer. The bag could not be opened by anyone else other than her.

"If we trust these documents then we should target the hospital with the aliens inside as a first blow. If we bomb an unoccupied area as a test, they may scatter in anticipation of the next strike."

The generals sat in thought before General Harris spoke up. "I support a first strike. Otherwise we lose the surprise as the good man just said."

Another general narrowed his eyes at Harris. "And if the report is wrong? If those are people being treated at the hospital? That it's all some kind of trick?"

Harris glared right back. "We both know that's unlikely. You saw the same satellite images I did. Those things around the hospital aren't human. Anyone working with them that's still there among them is a traitor not just to Our Country, but to humanity."

The other generals shifted in place uncomfortable at his words, but no one spoke up to disagree. Harris sat back in his chair after a moment with a smirk. "Well, that settles that. We should discuss exact payloads and assault plans before we present this to the president…"

— — — Scanning ahead. More debate. Mortal troop placements… Discussion of the monetary cost of weapons. Debating what to inform the populace in various scenarios… End Fragment of Memory. Scanning ahead… Scanning… Mortal President five hours later. Fragment of Memory, Mortal President Harrow, Begin. —
— — —

President Harrow considered the options presented to him. Given the alarming reports he had been getting recently this terrorist organization, the Neighborhood Watch, was probably more than willing to slaughter the survivors in Harmony to destroy the aliens. Just their use of that nerve gas alone was considered a war crime. They had perpetuated one of the largest and deadliest attacks on the military in decades.

How had they even gotten possession of that gas? They clearly had high level government contacts to even get near the stuff without being thrown in a black site somewhere. Thank god the press hadn't caught on to the few aliens that they were roaming around or the other moves by the Neighborhood Watch since the dome went up.

Well, now the government knew the aliens could spread through people, they knew why the Neighborhood Watch had deployed that dome. They had thought it was alien in origin originally, but to think these people had access to this kind of technology... It was disturbing.

The occasional Neighborhood Watch sympathizer was caught from within their ranks even now after two full weeks of hunting, and it was a headache to isolate them without exposing the existence of the secretive organization among them.

President Harrow had enough panic to deal with from just the dome alone. Harrow rubbed his forehead in stress. This whole thing was a mess. They had to delay that girl Alice Lovelace returning to her family as well.

Not only did she have the bag of unknown capabilities, but she could also start a panic by telling somebody her full story. She was already shown as uncooperative with the documents, and they couldn't risk her speaking out about something that could cause a panic.

Somehow it was already known to the press that someone had exited the dome and that she was under the care of the military. The press were going nuts trying to speak to her. To figure out who she was. If she went home then they would discover her soon after and descend on her to squeeze the truth from her.

It was just lucky her name hadn't leaked yet. Whoever had leaked just her presence alone would feel President Harris' wrath for the massive headache they were causing him and the military right now.

But Ms. Lovelace's exposure to the world was inevitable at this point given the rabid interest from the world of the situation. And all the senators were demanding reports just as fervently as the public.

As soon as the other party got a full report, President Harrow knew it would be leaked in moments. The situation was too dire for them not to use it against him as a sign of his incompetence in preparation for the next election.

And on top of all of that, he now had to make a decision on seriously bombing the dome now they had information on what was going on inside. The initial probing strikes had done next to nothing. Small holes had opened up, but had closed almost as quickly afterwards. The shield healing itself closed after the attack was finished.

The troops were moved and ready days ago for full containment in case of another breach of the town of Harmony, but Harrow had hesitated on the decision of their next actions.

He felt foolish for waiting on the assault now he knew they were on a deadline. Before the Neighborhood Watch killed everyone under that dome. Apparently. The notes of Francis Moore said all he knew was that was the end goal, not how it would be accomplished. The analysts had been spinning their wheels for hours, submitting more and more unhinged reports on what could do it.

The technology displayed was just too new and none of them knew its capabilities, so their speculation was largely coming to nothing. President Harrow looked up at General Harris who had just presented the assault plans for him.

"Alright," Harrow said, making his decision, "Begin the bombardment preparations. I will announce the full situation to the press. It will come out at this point, may as well get ahead of it. Prepare a *full* classified report on the situation to give to Congress. Dismissed."

General Harris looked like he wanted to protest President Harris' release of information, but on seeing the president's face reluctantly nodded and left.

President Harrow spent several more hours preparing his speech and statements for the press conference with his political advisors. They had to spend some time dropping hints and shaping the narrative to build anticipation as well so they could establish the proper perception of the speech. He practiced with his speechwriters and added some changes where it felt right to the historic speech.

Finally, he walked into the room with clamoring reporters. As he approached the podium, the crowd of press settled down and watched him in anticipation. President Harrow kept his posture stiff and regal as he gripped the podium with both hands.

He looked into the camera and took a breath. This was the most important speech in his career, no history. In human history. Even for politicians such as him who had given thousands of speeches, it brought him no small amount of stress. But he must press forward.

"People of this great nation and the world, I'm sure you have all heard of the mysterious dome that has surrounded the town of Harmony by now," He began, "I am here to tell you that we have come into some new information on the situation that I am here to share." As President Harrow spoke he remembered only snippets of the speech, so focused on saying the next line with the right emotion and weight to convey his meaning.

"...young woman who will not be named for her privacy made a miraculous escape from inside. She received documents from a whistleblower from the extremist militia known as the Neighborhood Watch..."

"...military will strike the dome with a coordinated barrage to take down the dome and eliminate the threats inside..."

"...Many of you may wonder what this mysterious threat is that is opposing the Neighborhood Watch. As your government we did not want to start a panic with such little information available. But now with verification from this whistleblower, we can confirm the nature of this threat. It is alien, and it has infested Harmony..."

"...Spreads through contact and trouble mimicking human emotions..."

"...The White House will be posting a more detailed account of their capabilities and weaknesses soon so we can remain vigilant against this threat. We have no reason to believe they have spread beyond the dome, but we must remain vigilant..."

"...I know this is shocking to us as a nation and to humanity as a whole. But together, as One Country United, we can come together and make these invaders go back to where they belong!"

Harrow released the podium and blood rushed back into his white knuckles. The reporters had tried to shout over him several times the moment his speech had concluded but they were quickly silenced and removed by security. He leaned into the microphone.

"Thank you for your time. Press Secretary Ross will remain to answer your questions."

At that Harrow turned and Ross took his place. As Harrow walked off stage he heard the chaos and shouting behind him and Harrow felt sorry for the poor bastard, who was sweating under the verbal assault.

Harrow would feel bad for the man, but Ross had thick skin and he'd muddle through. He had to, his whole job was being fed to the wolves in the media, hoping their ferocity was blunted after they were done raking him over the coals. Like a piece of meat thrown to a pack of wolves as a distraction.

Well, Harrow had business to take care of so Ross would have to tough it out. Harrow took a swig of a water bottle one of his assistants brought him. To the situation room. President Harris wondered how much his hair had grayed just from this week alone. Probably more than the whole rest of his presidency.

Alright, back to it. His assistant held open the door and President Harris swept into the situation room and sat at the table. The remaining generals quieted down. His eyes lingered on the three empty seats. One a traitor and two betrayed. To think the Neighborhood Watch had had such influence... President Harris steepled his fingers and leaned back.

"Alright gentlemen, let's begin. We have a lot to plan for."

Chapter 41: Appeasing the Guest - Beholder Fragment

— — — Ah, there is a question. Why were the Mortals so uninformed before Mortal Alice arrived? Returning to events prior on the timeline. Scanning... Scanning... Fragments of Memory found. First Sunday after the initial attack on Entity Fulcrum. Begin. — — —

After the Beholder had finished flying the injured humans in their crashed cars back to the mortal soldiers, it hovered in place and waited. Normally it would fly off and keep exploring, but the goodwill it had built was with this specific group of the mortal army.

If it disappeared it would have to do more work to reestablish itself to some other group of mortals that it didn't know already. Something surprisingly difficult to do given its form. It would be easier to learn the Mortal customs and maybe start learning some Earthian with this group before moving on if things turned sour.

After an hour, the Beholder had reached its tolerance. The circling soldiers stood in place staring at it. Nothing was happening. It scanned the crowd. It edged forward and the soldiers flinched. Several glanced at one of the soldiers in particular. The Beholder congratulated itself. Simple tactics usually worked best. It turned its eye to the mortal who suddenly seemed very nervous. It connected their minds and projected its thoughts to the mortal.

'Bored.' The man flinched, but his nose didn't bleed and he didn't fall over. How curious. The man stammered something in Earthian and the Beholder quickly translated it through the telepathic bond.

'*Hesitation.* Bored? What does it want? I should get Major Davis.' The man whispered to someone next to him and he ran off. After another minute the mortal leader approached and spoke with the man with the telepathic bond in Earthian.

The leader, Major Davis, turned to the Beholder and said something in Earthian that it did not understand. The Beholder remained floating. Nothing happened. It thought about how to minimize the impact on the mortal. The Beholder not knowing the language was increasing the damage on the mortal it had formed the connection with.

'**Not Understand. Speech and receive words this way only. Tell Davis need help to learn Earthian.**'

Ah, too much for that mortal. He had flinched and blood was running out of his nose in a gushing stream. All the soldiers tensed as Mortal Davis said something sharp that the Beholder still did not understand. The bleeding soldier said something to the others that calmed them down. Since it was directed to others, the Beholder tried to not listen to the thoughts behind the words.

The Beholder still wanted to maintain good habits for when it encountered its next mortal telepath who might become offended and attack at such intrusions. The bleeding man was brought away.

The Beholder had wanted to wait, but it seemed the next step was necessary. It directed its Potential and caused fine stiff hairs to sprout over the pink flesh behind its eyeball.

It spent some time coordinating the appropriate brain regions to accept and process their input. Listening to the mortal's drawn out speech in Earthian, it adjusted the length and stiffness of the hairs to adjust the frequencies it could now hear through the vibrations of the stiff hairs.

After a few moments, the droning vibrations of the mortal's muttering became audible to the Beholder. They were discussing something with the bleeding soldier. The Beholder had tried to preserve as much Potential as possible as it adjusted its form. That was the one downside to these worlds. They were practically starved of Potential compared to its homeworld. The Beholder would have to ration its Potential carefully if it planned to stay here for a long time.

Over the next few minutes of furious discussion, The Beholder began to match some of the Earthian words to various concepts. The Beholder used the telepathic flow of concepts from the soldier with the nosebleed and tried to match them to the audible words as he replied.

By the time the mortals grew silent, the Beholder was able to at least guess the meaning of certain words of the other mortals that it heard directly.

One of the soldiers that had run off in the chaos returned holding a flat smoothed wooden plate with a circular portion and a handle. From the central section a string was attached with a dangling ball on the other end.

The Beholder focused on it. Was it a native artifact they were offering? What would the price be? The other soldiers went to pull the soldier away and glanced at it in what seemed to be fear. Mortal Davis barked out something and they let the man pass. The soldier stepped from the ring of his fellows and gulped as everyone including the Beholder focused on him. Hesitantly he grabbed the dangling ball, he placed it on the paddle.

He waited a moment then twisted the wooden paddle and began hitting the ball. The ball would go flying out until it stretched the string, no it was more flexible so not exactly string, before snapping back. Then the man would shift the paddle and the ball would return and be hit again.

The Beholder floated closer in fascination. Ah, dexterity training! Without much Potential as a shortcut these mortals must have all sorts of ways of training the body naturally!

As the Beholder drifted closer, the soldier grew nervous and missed one of the bounces and the ball fell down before he could hit it again. The Beholder floated closer still and the soldier hesitantly held it out the paddle as an offering. The Beholder took it with similar hesitance with its long spindly arms.

What was the price? This was an interesting artifact no doubt with a good story behind it too. Not that it would be sold, but such things went for high prices back home if the Beholder ever wished to sell part of its precious collection.

Well, the Beholder decided it would pay the price to the mortal if it was reasonable. Five or ten years of scouting wouldn't be too bad for such an object. But it would have to refuse anything more than that.

The Beholder just inspected the object with its eye for a while as all the soldiers watched on. Eventually, the closest soldier cleared his throat and drew the Beholder's attention. He mimicked performing the dexterity training he was doing before.

The Beholder set it up, paddle horizontal with the ground and ball resting on top... Then flicked it around and began the process of the training.

The Beholder wasn't as good as the human initially. It only made about three hits of hitting the ball with the wooden paddle and having it bounce back before it failed. How vexing.

The Beholder went to reach for its Potential to increase its arms reflexes before hesitating. It turned to the soldier who had not moved the entire time. Its performance had been admirable for a mortal.

The Beholder was aware of its ponderous nature in comparison to flighty mortal attention spans. The mortal seemed to have almost no Potential at all, yet had managed to vastly outperform a creature centuries his senior and with vastly more power. Truly exemplary.

The Beholder must not cheat in this contest. For a true competition it must keep its form as it was. In fact... It approached the man who slowly backed away. The Beholder inspected the mortal's arm by grabbing it suddenly. There was shouting around them, but the man himself calmed at the Beholders firm but careful grip on him. The Beholder squeezed various muscles in the human's arm then moved it around in various ways.

The mortal looked supremely uncomfortable so the Beholder released him as soon as the inspection was done. The Beholder used some miniscule amount of Potential to adjust the speed of its arms downwards to match the human's arm. It could afford to spend a little Potential on this competition to keep things somewhat even. Sure enough, the Beholder barely managed a single hit on the ball this time.

It tried again. And again. And again. It would beat the humans' score. Luckily the Beholder's actions made the humans relax somewhat and some even looked amused for some reason. The Beholder continued the training. These humans had certainly alleviated its boredom for now.

— — — O — o — O — — —

Hours later, the *pong pong pong* of the rubber ball could be heard as the Beholder continued its training. The gathered mortals had been impressed at its improvements. The last round was when it finally managed above two hundred hits in a row. At that milestone, many of the mortals cheered and little green pieces of paper changed hands between many of them. The Beholder did a little spin in the air where it floated and the mortals cheered its victory.

Ah! These mortals were an amiable sort. It had truly been stimulating to feel its own improvement. The Beholder wondered in the darkest recesses of its mind. *'This sense of improvement and satisfaction, is this not what Beholders seek when hoarding knowledge? Perhaps experiences have value beyond the knowledge gained?'*

With a shake of its whole body it shook off the heretical notion. The possession of knowledge to hold over your peers was itself the goal, not the journey to that wealth of knowledge. This was... Nothing more than gaining knowledge of the mortal's training methods. Yes, that was it. The Beholder reached two hundred and sixty the next round, but its excitement was a little dulled now.

The mortals cheered more and green exchanged more hands. The Beholder felt a little glow inside itself. The mortals appreciated its feat of athletic prowess with good humor. Perhaps being heretical wouldn't be so bad. It was already a traitor after all. May as well go the full way. At the decision, the Beholder felt its mood improve.

Feeling much better, the Beholder went for another round and reached nearly four hundred bounces this time. The mortals cheered harder and relaxed even more collectively. Yes, the Beholder could get used to this. It could get very used to this.

Chapter 42: A Gift for the Visitor - Beholder Fragment

The Beholder reached six hundred successful bounces in a row before Major Davis returned with another man in tow. This man was dressed in black, and the Army Major looked upset at his presence. The Beholder had listened to the Earthian conversations around it as it trained its dexterity, so it could improve the general sense of what the mortals meant when they spoke in Earthian now.

The two mortals waited patiently until the Beholder missed a hit. Davis cleared his throat and greeted the Beholder and gestured towards the other man with his hands. The Beholder sensed the other man's tense posture.

Perhaps he was higher on the human hierarchy? Davis' expression didn't show much respect, but his words were soothing and seemed designed to not provoke the newcomer.

The nearby soldier humans had adjusted to the Beholder's presence readily after it began its training. The Beholder crossed its arms in front of itself and Davis stopped talking. The Beholder had seen one of the soldiers make the gesture to silence another an hour ago as he refused to transfer his green papers.

The other soldiers had eventually laughed at the non-compliant one until he submitted and uncrossed his arms, but the gesture held off the collection of the debt for a time anyway. The Beholder turned around and scanned the crowd until it found the soldier that had given it the dexterity training aid originally.

It floated over to the young man. The crowd made room and shot the Beholder cautious glances, but there was no longer an underlying sense of fear as before.

The soldier greeted the Beholder in a small voice as it approached. The telepathic bridge formed between them. The Beholder attempted the lightest speech possible.

It seems these mortals were fragile, and it did not want to put itself further in debt to the mortal. It held out the device holding it out with both of its hands. **Price? To keep?** The soldier blinked and stammered out something in Earthian.

'Yes! Of course, it's yours. You don't.... don't have to pay. I'm... I'm glad you were having fun.' The Beholder froze. The mortal... didn't want payment. The Beholder tilted its body to the device in its hands. Did it just want to not offend it? **Sure? Good object. Don't want Debt?** The soldier shook his head and gained a little confidence. *'Nah, just have fun with it. You're really good. It's a gift.'*

The Beholder tilted its eyeball between the object and the soldier one more time. That word... gift... they had a whole word for free transfer of objects without expected compensation. The human truly wanted no payment.

The Beholder looked into the human's mind. He was called Alexander or Alex. The Beholder struggled with the concept of the gift. It rolled the concept around in its mind for a moment before deciding it wanted to help the human anyway. It had never received a gift before.

Not that it had been allowed to directly interact with many mortals much up to this point, so maybe it was more common for them. This new experience alone was worth some compensation for the mortal, even if the object itself required no debt.

It flew in and touched the soldier's face with its hand. It paused and remembered it should ask the mortal its opinion first. **Gift? For You?**

The man stiffened but through the telepathic link the Beholder could sense curiosity and intrigue rather than fear. The Beholder had sent an instinctive understanding of what it was about to do. The Beholder proceeded at sensing the mortal's acceptance.

Everyone around them stiffened as the Beholder injected some of its Potential into Alexander.

Oh no, Alexander barely had seven decades left in his lifespan! The Beholder fixed that. He should last at least a few centuries now. Hmmmm. It still didn't feel like enough. Even a spawnling could do that much. Increase nutrient absorption. Harden the bones, increase the muscle density and the weave of the muscle fibers. A more robust immune system and metabolism.

Hmmm. Close, but not quite enough. The Beholder wanted its first gift in return to be special. All these things cost precious Potential but were largely uninspired. Alexander had little natural Potential, so these changes would likely remain fixed. Spatial manipulation? No, too much changes to brain regions and biology would be required.

Alexander would likely not want large bodily changes, other mortals rarely accepted such things from what the Beholder had seen on other worlds. They were often jettisoned from their communities if the changes were too obvious. The Beholder pondered for a moment. Oh, the best gift would be for the man to be able to decide for himself.

The Beholder gave him the ability to sense Potential with his eyes alone. Something uncommon in mortals and much more difficult to achieve while maintaining the man's form. That should allow him to find others willing to make more body modifications on him in the coming centuries.

The Beholder checked its Potential. A little lower than it would like, but the Beholder felt good about its first gift indeed. Alex looked better than ever and looked down at his hands in amazement.

The Beholder lifted up and did a spin in satisfaction. The gathered soldiers gasped in shock at Alex who was one of the healthiest examples of the species the Beholder had ever seen. The Beholder had done good work.

The next moment the Beholder popped into its spatial pocket. It carefully floated into the end of the long hallway with its various possessions on display. At the end was the skeleton of a lizard bigger than most of the human buildings. It was the prize of its collection, stolen from under the tentacles of its last mission leader as an army of mortals ambushed the invasion group.

The Beholder had been supposed to be scouting, but had been too busy harvesting the samples and had used a loophole in its contract to quickly swoop in and steal it away before it would be ruined. Land creatures this large were vanishingly rare on the mortal worlds, it had been quite the find.

Using its control of the space, the Beholder carefully shifted the skeleton to the side so its alcove was on the right side of the hallway. The back wall pushed back to make more room and the ceiling lowered slightly.

The Beholder would have to expand this space even more soon. The dimensions could be easily adjusted even if it was at a fixed volume at the moment. It would take some work to increase the total volume to make room for more displays that it knew would be coming soon.

It summoned a black obsidian pedestal and carefully put the bright wooden paddle inside the now empty alcove at the end of the hallway. The contrast between the dark obsidian glass and bright wood was pleasing.

The Beholder lifted the ball and extended it so it looked like it was in mid motion. It fixed the ball's position with a tiny spit of obsidian jutting from the stand that held it in place. Finally, the Beholder activated the anti-degradation wards to keep it preserved for display. The Beholder adjusted the light sources until the paddle and ball were brightly lit on all sides. It was frozen in dynamic mid motion. The Beholder flew back to the entrance and admired its handiwork.

Hmmmmm. After a moment, the Beholder sculpted the obsidian stand into a humanoid hand holding the handle of the paddle. There, far better. Now it would see its new possession every time it entered at the end of the hallway. The first gift it had ever received. And from a mortal. How fascinating. The Beholder hoped its gift was satisfactory in turn.

————O—o—O————

After admiring the new centerpiece of its collection for a while, the Beholder exited its space with a *pop* of displaced air. The area was in chaos. The Beholder slowly spun in a circle, had something happened? At the Beholder's reappearance the nearby mortals seemed to calm down, stopping mid motion in their panic. The Beholder inspected the surroundings. It seemed that Alexander had left. How unfortunate.

The Beholder noticed Major Davis and the black suited man from before still standing nearby. Davis introduced the man again. They spoke in Earthian for a while before pausing as if to wait for the Beholder's reply. The Beholder just floated there. Nothing happened. The Beholder connected to the dark suited man telepathically. He seemed higher rank than Major Davis.

'Now Speak and I understand.' The man flinched a little but didn't appear damaged from the communication yet. He spoke again and the Beholder understood as his mind echoed the words. The Beholder mapped more of the Earthian language.

'Huh? Oh telepathy.' Davis looked over at the man in concern. *'It's talking to me in my head like in the reports. This will speed things up.'* He turned to the Beholder. *'Can you come with me? We want to bring you to important people to discuss your presence here.'*

The Beholder's perspective switched as it recognized it was time for business. Ah, they wanted information. Well at least they had plenty of valuables. **'Pay. Then information.'**

The man flinched harder this time and went silent. *'Alright. Follow me and you can discuss it with people who can do that.'*

The Beholder sent a wordless affirmation back to ease the load on the man's mind. He began walking off and the Beholder floated after him. The man was arrogant, but the Beholder was willing to ignore it if it got it to the negotiating table faster.

———O—o—O———

The mortal got in a bulky vehicle and the Beholder floated behind into the cabin behind it. The space felt cramped so with a *pop* the Beholder shrunk down its eyeball to the size of a human head.

'Huh, that thing really can shrink down.' The Beholder didn't think the mortal had meant to project those thoughts. The vehicle drove, and the Beholder observed out the window. There was far more vegetation than around the location of the Seed it had observed these last few years.

It placed its hands against the car door so it could float closer to the glass pane to take in the scenery going by. The man in the suit was silent, although he was sweating quite heavily as he actively tried to ignore the Beholder's presence.

After some time, the vehicle slowed and reached a place with a large chain link fence. The Beholder wanted to inspect it closer, but that would likely spook this new round of mortals that were discussing something with the driver of the vehicle. It remained in place for now as the vehicle was waved through and they continued driving onwards.

The interior of the fence was filled with clusters of smaller buildings surrounding a central monolithic structure. They drove into the monolithic concrete building and drove downward into a loading bay. The dark suited man stepped out and the Beholder followed. The place was empty except for a large group of mortals covered in black gear carrying the heavy metal weaponry displayed by the military. It was clear now that this was a separate group from the one Major Davis belonged to. Hopefully this wouldn't be a waste of time.

Still following the same mortal, the Beholder was led into a room with a metal table and two chairs. There was a large pane of dark glass dominating one side of the room.

'Stay here a moment please'. The Beholder waved in affirmation absentmindedly and the man left. The Beholder severed the telepathic connection between them. Ah, mimicking mortal mannerisms was so much simpler than language. The mortal had understood the gesture almost immediately even without telepathy assisting him.

The glass was interesting and there was a strange shimmer to it that was odd. What an interesting new material. The Beholder went to the corner and used some Potential to sharpen one of its fingers into a sharp point. It carved a little sliver of glass from the corner of the window with the tip of its finger. The Beholder pried the little triangular piece of glass out carefully and held it up to its eye to inspect it further.

Flipping it around in its hands the Beholder made a startling discovery. The glass only lets light shine through it in one direction. How unique! It only worked on certain frequencies of light, but the Beholder had never seen such a material before.

This world had seemed more technologically advanced than the others it had seen so far... It turned the glass chunk over and over and looked at it from all angles. Spectacular...

Another mortal walked in along with the man from before. The Beholder startled and quickly entered its spatial pocket. It hurriedly put the little piece of glass in its general storage before exiting. That would definitely go on display, but the Beholder would have to consider acquiring a bigger piece first before creating a display with only the small fragment.

The two humans appeared startled at the Beholder's actions, but quickly recovered. The man in the dark suit said something in Earthian the Beholder still didn't understand, so it quickly reestablished the telepathic connection.

'... Dr. Richards. He will help with reading and writing. We have something so you can talk without hurting us once you learn.'

'Okay.' The man speaking flinched.

The Beholder severed the connection and connected to the other man. This Dr. Richards wore clothing more reminiscent of the people the Beholder had observed around the Seed. He appeared older than many of those in the mortal military were. He had wrinkles and his hair was wild. He spoke in Earthian.

'Hello? I'm here to teach you English. I brought something for you to write on.'

The Beholder was handed a gray plastic cylinder with a black tipped end, which it grabbed. Dr. Richards seemed less hesitant than the other humans and more excited. He had a large pad of paper with him. He put it down on the metal table. He moved forward and sat down and put his own pad of paper in front of him. There was a thick book and another pad of paper thick with notes next to him as well. He carried the same writing implement as the Beholder.

'Can you follow after me? You can just slap the table once for yes, and two for no.'

The Beholder slapped the table once with its free hand. Clever mortals, circumventing their inability to properly withstand telepathic communication.

Dr. Richards carefully drew a symbol on his pad of paper. *'There are twenty-six letters in our writing. This is the first. It is called 'a' '*

The Beholder copied Dr. Richards motion and matched the symbol nearly exactly. It was no different from drawing up the symbols and networks for wards.

'Very good! Now, this one is b.' He drew another symbol. The Beholder copied it. And so on. *'And finally z. Here are the numbers...'*

The man in the suit left after a few minutes. Dr. Richards kept going for hours and hours, teaching the Beholder the rules and mechanics of Earthian. No, English. The Beholder had realized the difference when the man had mentioned differences in 'French' and 'Spanish' in comparison to this language.

The Beholder would bang on the table when Dr. Richards required a response or confirmation that the Beholder understood. He was very enthusiastic. Next they moved to writing basic words and their meaning. Finally, with Dr. Richards looking like he might collapse, he opened the big book.

'This is a dictionary. It has the meanings of all the words of English. If you don't know a word, then you can look inside. There are pictures on most of the words to help you along, but someone else will be here to assist in case you need an explanation of anything.'

At that Dr. Richards left, and Dr. Kiltichi came in. He just sat there silently for a minute even after the Beholder connected to him. The Beholder flipped through the book and pointed at various words it could not decipher.

Dr. Kiltichi would explain and write out the words he discussed on the pad. The Beholder copied him. The Beholder almost completely understood spoken English now, despite still struggling a little with the writing.

Thoughts were based on the sounds and rarely on how a word was written down, so it had to use its pure intellect to remember the words and grammar rules when they were written. There were many variations in spelling that did not match the sounds that were produced by the language. How frustrating.

Eventually Dr. Kiltichi grew tired as well and was replaced. The Beholder felt confident enough now in understanding the language at least. The Beholder finally sent a message over the telepathic bond to the replacement. **'Ready. Now how speak?'**

The human coughed, and said to wait. He quickly exited the room looking queasy. Good, that one had been more resilient even considering the shorter message the Beholder had given him.

A few minutes later two unfamiliar men came in with a large board with little bumps with all the English symbols the Beholder had just learned. They put a large black rectangle on the table and connected a wire from the board to the rectangle. One of the humans sat in front of it and made the black rectangle burst into multicolored lights.

The Beholder drifted closer. Seeing the human's discomfort, the Beholder shrunk itself again with a *pop*. The human made several multicolored rectangles appear and disappear by tapping the symbols on the board and a roundish object that moved a white arrow on the box.

Eventually it stopped and the human hit the buttons on the board and familiar English words appeared on the box. A second later a monotone voice in English sounded out of the box. "Hello. This is a computer. If you type the words on the keyboard below then it will make this voice for you."

The Beholder vibrated in place as the human stood and took a step back. OOOOOOOOOOOOOOOOHHHHHHHHHHHHHH MYYYYYYY. It was so complicated! How did it even work?! The little box could mimic a mortal voice without Potential? The Beholder just had to have one of these machines for itself! It floated down and adjusted its size so the arms were the same size as a human.

It began to slowly tap at the symbols to start its message. As it went it gradually sped up what the human called its typing. What an odd word typing was.

It should ask about why this activity deserved a word separate from writing while using other writing implements did not. Using a pencil or pen was simply writing while this had a specific word for it as well? Strange.

Writing began filling the screen as the monotone voice spoke faster and faster to keep up with the Beholder's various questions about their culture and the objects they had created. It figured it would get them all out of the way all at once. That way they could return with an itemized list of the cost of each piece of information and begin more detailed negotiations.

——— O — o — O ———

"Holy shit," Behind the one way glass into the observation room, the people inside could only watch as the aliens' fingers flashed over the keyboard so fast they could barely see them. The computer screen scrolled down so fast it looked like one long blur of text. It had been typing like that for over thirty minutes. One of the men turned to a mousy man next to him.

"Are we getting the digital file for all this? Can't believe that thing is still going so fast."

The mousy man nodded. "Yes, sir. Mostly stream of consciousness questions asking about various things it has seen on Earth. I'm just surprised it hasn't waited for an answer for anything, even the simplest questions it has asked."

The man who originally spoke turned back. "Well, keep reading through and coming up with the answers with the team. When it stops I want to be ready to negotiate for the information we need with it.

"We shouldn't piss it off if we don't have to. Based on what we have seen so far it wants to sell its information to us. And get acquisitions on acquiring the objects it asks about. You saw how it took a sample of the glass earlier. Maybe it will take a more material payment too."

The mousy man nodded again, "Yes sir."

The original man stared at the Beholder through the glass that was still furiously typing. "Let's see how long you can go, little eyeball."

———O—o—O———

Three hours later, the Beholder was finished. It had spent years building up questions it would ask if it had the chance. It had needed to spend some Potential to heal the damage on its hands from the repetitive motions of typing so fast unfortunately. But this first negotiation was important. It could always preserve its Potential later when this world was about to be conquered.

The Beholder had to gain as much benefit as possible before that happened. The Beholder lifted its hands off the keyboard as it finished typing its last question for now.

After a few minutes the human voice emanating from the device shut off. Hopefully the humans would be ready to negotiate the information exchange soon. It had kept its questions to only the surface topics as it noticed it took a while for the mortals to process things. The mortal sitting in the room appeared unable to even read the words as they flew down the computer screen.

Once they were done with the preliminaries, they could negotiate over the answers for the more detailed questions the Beholder had included in its list. It had also included what items it had observed over the last few years it might wish to acquire. It would see soon what the mortal's response would be.

Chapter 43: Negotiating with the Visitor - Multiple Fragments of Memory

The Beholder had to wait for over thirty minutes before two mortals entered the room to begin negotiations. They had a large stack of papers that seemed to contain answers to the Beholder's questions. They put it in front of the Beholder.

"That's the information we are willing to share," The mortal on the left said, "But first you must answer in turn."

The Beholder bobbed in the air and typed on the computer. The monotone voice spoke.

"Acceptable. What are your questions?"

"First off, why are you here?" The mortal asked.

"Sent to watch the Seed. Got bored, came here. Get new things maybe?"

The two men glanced at each other. "What kind of things would you like?" The man asked cautiously.

"Liked the wood and ball object. Very interesting. More like that."

They nodded even if they looked confused. Perhaps they used other training aids in this group?

"That can be arranged. How are you hovering in the air like that?"

The Beholder turned to them and blinked slowly. No preliminaries? How strange. It typed on the computer again.

"Very complicated. Answer will be five unique interesting objects and answers to the questions already asked."

At this the men glanced at each other again before listening to something from the little devices in their ears. Maybe communicating with others outside the room. "Yes, sir."

In unison they turned back and looked to the Beholder. "It's a deal. We'll bring some things for your inspection in a few minutes."

The Beholder turned back to the keyboard and categorized its thoughts. It must explain the physics of its levitation alone. The biology of the mechanism to produce the effect was far too complicated and would demand a much heavier price.

The Beholder began typing faster and faster until the monotone voice shut off and the screen filled with text once more. May as well provide a full answer rather than waiting and feed it to them piecemeal. The Beholder had asked a lot of questions to be answered the first time.

After the Beholder was nearly finished writing down its explanation, an assortment of objects was brought in and the two men demonstrated how they were to be used. Some were more complicated than others, and the Beholder took a liking to the complicated over the simpler ones.

Better to start with the more unique items in case there was a limited supply. It quickly scooped up the five most interesting and shoved them into its spatial pocket. It was sure the simpler items were in far greater abundance than the more complex ones.

After a moment more of silence, the men listened to their earpieces again. "For the next question, what is this 'Potential' you refer to in your last answer referring to your levitation?"

For a moment the Beholder was stunned. The mortals didn't even know of the existence of Potential? All of its previous worlds had at least knowledge of it even if the amounts they could manipulate were pitiful. After a moment, the Beholder connected the dots in its head. The full Invasion had not started yet. There may still be mortals ignorant like these on the planet still. Perhaps it should raise its prices.

"Twenty unique objects unique to this planet," The computer said as the Beholder typed.

"Any objects of interest, or will anything unique to this planet do?" The mortal asked.

"Anything. But some are better than others. Will know when I see them."

"Alright, we can do that"

The Beholder turned back and typed more. "Potential is an energy that can have a multitude of uses including biological manipulation primarily and can be used to support advanced biological structures that can change or manipulate physical laws of the universe. Organisms are created with differing amounts of Potential depending on their biology. Certain examples include…"

——— (**Mortal General Lopez Fragment**) ———

The men behind the glass scrambled around as they frantically sourced various items to sell to the alien. For whatever reason the alien seemed extremely interested in children's toys of all things from the selection of items they had offered so far.

It was a security risk, but several of the soldiers had driven off and returned with everything they could find that was even remotely special from surrounding stores. A larger shipment was on its way but it wouldn't be here for hours as things had proceeded quicker than had been expected. The language acquisition period was expected to last days or weeks at a minimum but had barely taken hours. The creature's intellect was almost frightening.

The creature's demands for materials had grown ever larger after the first questions. It seemed to have realized when they agreed to every proposal that they did not value the objects very highly.

Unfortunately they were soldiers not businessmen so by the time they realized it was too late and the prices were already rising as the alien realized that it should ask for more from them. The amounts of items were to the point by now that they had moved the operation to the mess hall on one of the upper secure floors after removing the tables from inside.

Soldiers carrying boxes and bins of toys and other random items they had been able to find came rushing down and dumping the objects inside on one of the nearby tables. The creature would float around, pick through, and take what it liked.

Once it found the agreed upon amounts, it would turn back to the computer and type its detailed answers to one of the questions that they had asked it. It was nothing if not honorable at least. Its answers were detailed and clearly answered the questions asked without any apparent intent to deceive them.

They were all stunned at how well this was going. The analysts were going wild reading the answers and the gathered generals were smiling at the wealth of information and potential military and civilian advancements alike that could come of this.

But one of the generals in the room frowned deeper the longer this went on. He carefully edged to the back of the observation room. He had already disabled the security camera in the room hours ago, making it appear like a mechanical failure as soon as he had known that *Filth* was being brought here. Just in case.

And his fellows were clearly being drawn in by the demon's behavior, hungry for its technology. They would bring suffering to thousands if not more if they entertained this creature any further.

General Lopez knew more than most that these wonders would be fueled with oceans of blood if anyone outside of the worthy got a hold of them. Because the glowing gold light of potential was a facade. Potential was nothing but blood and suffering, pure and simple. General Lopez knew how true that was more than most.

He glanced around the room and took a deep breath as he saw all the others were too focused on the monitors of the creature. It was still sorting through the toys, no doubt mocking their inability to see through its wicked facade.

General Lopez steeled himself. No regrets, this was for the greater good. To keep these advancements out of the hands of the masses who would only tempt them to dark ends.

In one motion, he hit a big red button near the door and opened a drawer in a nearby cabinet. In an instant the lights switched red and loud thuds could be heard throughout the building as the security doors slammed down. The creature blinked away in a flash of purple light on the monitors as the people in the observation room looked around in confusion.

"What's happening? Are we under attack? General Lopez, What are you doing?" One of the generals said as he turned around. Several of the soldiers in the room drew their weapons as General Lopez put on the gas mask and made sure it was tight on his face.

He pulled a silver cylinder from his pocket and tossed it into the center of the room. It began to hiss with the release of the invisible gas. Everyone was shouting and demanding answers from General Lopez, and several pointed their guns at him.

But they seemed unsure and added to the confused shouting rather than actually shooting him luckily. All the people in the room began coughing and collapsing to the ground twitching. One of General Lopez's colleagues even fired off a shot even as he collapsed that impacted the general's chest despite his attempted dodge.

The bullet threw General Lopez back into the wall and he coughed from behind the mask. In moments everyone else was on the ground, bleeding from their eyes and foaming at the mouth. General Lopez pushed himself to his feet as the hole in his shirt exposed a bulletproof vest beneath. He coughed from under the mask again as he felt a heavy bruise welling up on his chest already.

The twitching of the bodies around him stopped and the rest of the room went still. General Lopez shot one of the dead men in the chest. Then again twice more. Best to establish the culprit early, just in case.

The canister kept hissing as it kept expelling the Russian nerve gas General Lopez had bought through his less savory contacts. He carefully pried open the fingers of the man he had shot and placed the empty canister in his limp fingers.

The planted evidence would lead back to the man when the rest of the government investigators finally arrived. It had been a rush job, but the evidence was solid enough for General Lopez to plug the remaining gaps with his influence.

There was a banging at the door to the room.

"Is everything all right? We heard gunshots in there."

General Lopez snuck to the door before pulling it open in one motion, jumping to the side to break line of sight with the concerned guards outside.

In moments, the three men fell to the floor dead with a gurgle as the wave of nerve gas entered their lungs. General Lopez moved out and hustled to the security control room.

Several soldiers stared at him in confusion as the masked general hustled past them. The observation room he was running from only monitored the secure levels, but this security control room included exterior cameras as well as the cameras on the less secure levels.

It would be essential to deal with the security as soon as possible in the case anyone not already in the know tried to run. At the door the guards tried to stop General Lopez's rapid approach, but after verbally bludgeoning them with his rank briefly they let him through.

The two people inside looked at him. General Lopez slowed, stopped and began staring at the various monitors filling the wall switching from various viewpoints of the facility.

"Is it done?" he asked.

The one on the right nodded. "Yes, sir. All the evidence is wiped and any recordings will be stopped for the next few hours. The jammer is activated, so no other communications should leave the building. Our people are guarding the exits and we should have a few hours before anything is noticed, which should be enough time to cover our tracks here."

General Lopez took another deeper breath as he took off the gas mask with a hiss. "All right, send out the orders to our people. Detain those who resist and we will see if they can be recruited to the cause. Kill if necessary to prevent any escapes, but even my influence can only cover so much."

As the men nodded and the word was sent out, General Lopez could see the orders playing out in real-time on the screens as the loyal slid into positions of leadership in the chaos and stopped the uninitiated from leaving the building by any means necessary.

Luckily only a few instances of violence were needed to keep the confused soldiers in line and prevent them from learning anything they shouldn't. Good, he took no pleasure in ordering his misguided countrymen to be hurt unless absolutely necessary. He leaned over and pressed the button to activate the intercom, ready to begin his speech to pacify the rest.

"This is General Lopez. There has been an attack on our leadership by the alien menace we brought here in peace. Your orders are to shoot on sight. I am the only survivor of the leadership. This base will be locked down until we can find the traitor who has worked with the alien menace to perpetuate this attack on us.

"No one in or out, and communications are jammed so this traitor can not call for reinforcements. Please comply with your superiors as we work through this together, and report any suspicious behavior. Stand by for further orders."

The intercom clicked off and General Lopez turned to the two men in the security booth. "For the Watch."

They replied in unison. "For Humanity!"

With that General Lopez walked out the door. Time to check in on the alien. It had to be silenced before it spread its corruption any further.

——— (Beholder Fragment) ———

The Beholder exited its spatial pocket that it had retreated into and the room it had been in was empty. Various objects lay strewn around it as a red light flashed.

A metal wall had formed at either end of the adjoining hallway to the large room the mortals had led it to. It had sorted through their objects as the mortals brought in them. There were only three or so mortals left around in the area. They were looking around in confusion and were startled at the Beholder's sudden return in front of them.

The Beholder decided to put everything it could find into its spatial pocket while the mortals were distracted. Something bad was happening to this group of mortals, and the Beholder could always answer some questions for free if they made it through safely. Perhaps the invasion was starting in full now?

After a minute or two, the floor around the Beholder was spotless. It even took the tables folded up at the side of the room. It had to spend some Potential to get those ones in its spatial pocket but it was worth it. The mortals watched on in bafflement, just standing there in confusion.

There was a trail of boxes filled with more unique objects in the hallway. The soldiers had been ferrying the bins from the outside when the lights turned red and the Beholder had retreated. When the alarm went off they all had dropped them in the confusion and their contents were spilled all over the floor.

The Beholder floated forward and began emptying the bins in the hallway into its spatial pocket, fully sweeping the whole area clear of everything that wasn't secured to the walls or floor. It finished its collection. The mortals trailed behind it listlessly, looking unsure of what to do as the strobing red lights kept going off.

The Beholder began inspecting the metal door closing off the exit now that it was done looting the area. The three mortals kept watching the Beholder and trailed behind as it inspected the barrier. There were no obvious gaps through.

One of the humans ran forward and babbled incoherently at the Beholder. It understood English but the human was speaking too quickly for it to understand. There was a loud hiss of hissing air from above them all of a sudden. The mortal reached and pressed his hand to a glowing pad to the side of the door before stiffening and collapsing to the floor. His mouth foamed and he twitched on the floor as the door slid open.

His convulsions lowered in intensity and his breathing grew steadier. The Beholder floated and inspected the other two mortals that were further inside. They were already dead. The Beholder looked back to the mortal on the floor. He would die without intervention.

Well, the Beholder could use him to prove its benevolence to the next group at least. This group of mortals were clearly hostile to it for whatever reason. At least the poisons they were using were likely only effective on humans. It hadn't started feeling any effects yet.

Foolish for the mortals to not to consider the Beholder would have far different biology and therefore immunity to most of their deadly mortal toxins. Or at least a completely different category of chemicals that were toxic to it.

The Beholder floated down and injected a tiny bit of Potential to purge the toxin from the mortal's system by stimulation of his natural defenses. The Beholder lifted the man before placing him in its spatial pocket.

Hopefully he didn't touch anything sensitive in the collection. But the Beholder could hardly escape dragging the mortal behind itself. Much safer to stash him in the spatial pocket and take him out later when the Beholder was no longer being attacked.

The Beholder went to proceed further down the hallway before pausing. In the chaos it had forgotten the most important item! It floated back into the room and the computer and keyboard in the corner.

The screen was now powered off. It carefully lifted each component of the device after unplugging it from the wall and put them in its spatial pocket. It would need a mortal's help to make it work again, but being able to speak without injuring the mortals was far more valuable than the Beholder had originally thought.

Being able to speak to this group had let it acquire all sorts of items that it would have never thought it would know to ask for before it arrived here.

And other groups may not be as forward thinking as this one. It did not want its initial attempts to communicate to register as an attack in the future. With all of this done and the last item collected, the Beholder floated down the hallway until it reached the next metal wall again.

It was about to inspect it for any openings when it suddenly retracted into the ceiling with a burst of compressed air. On the other side was a large group of armed men in gas masks with their projectile weapons raised.

"Fire!" A man in the back of the group shouted. In a purple flash of light the Beholder retreated into its spatial pocket before the bullets could strike it.

— — — (Mortal General Lopez Fragment) — — —

The wave of bullets passed through the space and gouged the opposite wall. General Lopez gestured forward from the back of the group.

"Alright men, lay the explosives before it gets back. We'll eliminate this scum soon enough. For Humanity!"

"For the Watch!"

Chapter 44: Touring the Visitor's Collection - Beholder Fragment

The Beholder sat in its space and considered its options. When it emerged from its space it would be trapped in the hallway with the murderous groups of mortals. The Beholder was unsure why they were so aggressive so early. It wasn't like the Beholder had taken anything even resembling aggressive action against them.

The Beholder knew that it was in little danger from what had been displayed so far by the mortals. That gas in the air that had so impacted the mortals had no effect on it. The biology was too different, and the Beholder didn't even have to spend any Potential on itself to be cured.

The Beholder briefly considered waiting out the mortals. If it waited for a few years then they would likely let their guard down and then it could escape with ease. That way none of its limited Potential would be lost. It could entertain itself by inspecting its collection again for at least that long.

"Uhhhhhhhhhh." The Beholder turned its eyeball to the human splayed on the ground. Oh yes. It had wanted to use the mortal as an intermediary. And waiting would allow many of the unique native items to be destroyed by the invasion. The Beholder had saved the mortal's life after all, it was sure that he wouldn't mind acting as a translator and helping out the Beholder in exchange.

The man sat up and looked around wildly, "Whe... where am I?"

The Beholder floated into his field of vision and gave a wave in greeting. The soldier blinked and rubbed his eyes.

"Oh." He looked around at the various alcoves around.

"Where are we?"

The Beholder floated into general storage without answering. Telepathy with the mortal's fragile state would be counterproductive. The Beholder rustled around the cluttered room with its stone shelves before it found the pad of paper and pen.

Unfortunately it would have to be used rather than being preserved. But the Beholder was willing to make sacrifices for this.

The Beholder uncapped the pen and floated back into the display hallway. The soldier was standing now, and while he looked a little pale no longer looked near death as he had when suffering under the gas. At the Beholder's return the soldier turned his head. The Beholder wrote something in English and displayed it to the soldier.

"This is your collection? Like a museum? Is this where you went when you disappeared? Wow, it really is something." He was looking at some of the displayed skeletons. His look was of awe as he took in the high ceilings and long hallway. The Beholder turned back and flipped the page before writing something else. The soldier read it again.

"Wait, poison gas? I do remember hearing hissing from the vents and... oh. Wait, did you save me? I remember you touched me and I felt better before I came here."

The Beholder threw him a thumbs up. It was much faster than writing. The soldier noticed the gesture and awkwardly returned it.

"Thanks. Do you know who it was? Did you escape?" The Beholder flipped another page and wrote again. The man frowned as he read.

"I guess you wouldn't know. But we'll appear in that exact position when we leave? That's not good."

Another page flip, more writing.

"Wait, you would do that? Leave me here and escape on your own before letting me out later? And then I can just leave no strings attached?"

More writing, another page.

"Oh. Well you were just attacked. Makes sense you wouldn't trust the military anymore. Sorry about that. We're not all like whoever those people are. I was as good as dead, so I guess I owe you my life. As long as you don't hurt anyone, I'll help you buy things for your collection."

The Beholder clapped. It hadn't expected it to go so smoothly! What an agreeable mortal. Amazing. Hurting mortals was usually a waste of time anyway, the Beholder could just steal things and escape if it wanted something the Mortals had. So the Beholder had no problem with that condition of not hurting any of the mortals.

"Just one extra condition though. I need to tell my superiors in the military what happened before I go with you. And ask for their permission for doing the rest. Is that okay?"

The Beholder considered the offer. Not unreasonable. The man might have troubles with the mortal government if he didn't report back. The Beholder wrote on the pad again. The human sighed in relief.

"Thank you. Not trying to be ungrateful, but I can't just run off without reporting this. Oh, my name is Alan Hopkin by the way. What's yours?"

The Beholder floated there. Should it give itself a mortal identifier? In its mind it was simply The Beholder, but this would cause confusion if the mortals ever encountered another Beholder.

This would ruin whatever reputation the Beholder had cultivated with the humans. Especially if the other Beholder was less considerate to the mortals of this planet or generally made the mortals become confused between it and them in general.

The Beholder considered some of the names from the mortal legends it had learned about as part of the information exchange. Many of the answers had been supplied through tomes rather than the printed sheafs of papers. One of the tomes consisted of the exploits of the various deities and their associated aspects and dominions.

The Beholder had particularly enjoyed the 'Egyptian' tales. The images of their chimeric humanoid forms seemed most apt to describe the Beholder's malleable form. It wrote its new name on the paper.

"Huh, nice to meet you Thoth. Egyptian god of knowledge and writing? Good choice. I always enjoyed Egyptian mythology as a kid. Well anyway, so now we wait for the people out there to back off? Guess we have some time. Want to show me around? You've got quite a lot of interesting things in here."

The Beholder froze in place. The mortal... the mortal wanted to get a tour? The Beholder had never had a full tour before. The other Beholders scoffed at its possessions, thinking anything not held within a mind to be useless. They had left immediately after it became apparent the objects weren't for data storage like mortal tomes or the traditional stone tablets.

But perhaps this mortal would be more appreciative? It would be good to do an inventory as they waited. It wrote on the pad more. It had to be sure it understood the mortal's intentions correctly.

"Yeah, may as well if we have to wait. Lots of interesting stuff in here."

The Beholder bobbed gestured to the closest alcove. It began excitedly writing a quick summary of how it had acquired the object. It was a half melted sword it had found in the aftermath of a battle. The user had overwhelmed the scripts giving it power and caused the whole thing to overheat. Beads of metal and frozen bubbles of metal covered the blade. The Beholder was lucky enough to acquire and preserve it before it had cooled enough to ruin the effect.

"Woah. You just froze it in time? It looks amazing, like some crazy sculpture."

Alan asked several more questions about the battle, the wielder of the sword, and so on. The Beholder got more and more excited as the soldier asked questions. He really wanted the tour! After the questions from the mortal tailed off, the Beholder shifted to the next object in line. It wrote the story of this one too. It knew them all by heart.

— — — O — o — O — — —

Sadly, the Beholder ran out of paper eventually. Each answer required a written response, so they only made it a third way through the objects before there was no more space. After that, Alan just spent a few minutes at each object and made a few statements on it and his opinion on what it might be. He was wrong almost every time, but it was interesting for the Beholder to hear what the mortal thought of it just based on its appearance.

The Beholder was forced to float silently behind. It didn't want to use any more paper on this, and the mortal was likely far too weak for any extended telepathy. Occasionally Alan would ask yes/no questions and the Beholder would give a thumbs up or thumbs down in response.

Eventually, they reached the end. Alan looked a little ragged, but hadn't looked bored the whole time. "Well, Thoth, thank you. That was really interesting, especially that massive skeleton. I'm pretty tired though. Do you have somewhere I could sleep?"

The Beholder considered the question. Well, it had no need for sleep… So it really didn't have a place. It led Alan into the general storage room. The Beholder cleared off a portion of one of the stone shelves. Alan eyed it for a moment before laying down inside.

"Well, not the best but I'll take what I can get. Thanks, Thoth."

With that Alan slowly drifted to sleep as the Beholder watched. Well, the Beholder assumed the sleeping spot was good enough if the human was able to sleep so quickly.

Now the Beholder just had to make its escape from the mortal complex with wasting the least of its Potential possible while doing so. There was no doubt that it would escape, the only question was how efficiently it would do so.

Chapter 45: The Visitor Returns to Earth - Multiple Fragments of Memory

The Beholder exited the spatial pocket and seconds later an explosive went off, the pressure waves and roaring flames threw the Beholder rapidly towards the ceiling. The Beholder flickered back into its spatial pocket to retreat and quickly bled off its upward momentum once it was inside.

It stopped its Potential from healing its superficial burns for now. Reddish little embers flickered in its skin, but the Beholder ignored the pain now it was on a mission. It waited a few seconds before returning to reality. The area surrounding it was filled with smoke, and there were mortal voices shouting something through the smoke.

The Beholder quickly turned invisible and shrunk itself to one of its smallest sizes, its eye barely bigger than a human fist. More shouting from the humans. The Beholder floated close to the ceiling as wild gunshots sounded below.

The Beholder paused for a moment to watch the airflow of the smoke before flying over to a metal grate barely larger than itself near the ceiling of the hallway.

The gunfire below had stopped and one of the humans was shouting at the others to help search for the Beholder. The Beholder ripped the grate from its mounting and let it fall to the ground with a large crash.

It slipped inside as the humans focused on its position and bullets began flying and gouging into the vent walls around it. It retreated deeper into the air vent where the bullets couldn't reach. The cool air flowed around it. The angry voices of the humans quickly faded away as the rushing of the air grew louder. The Beholder paused. There was a fork in the path. Which way should it go?

It took the right branch of the vent at random. It floated along until the next branch and started building a map in its mind as it traveled. It took a left this time. Right. Left. Right again. Unfortunately all the vents seemed to be contained to the single floor of the building the Beholder was on.

It approached another grate. It peered through, careful not to touch it so as to not make as much noise.

As far as it could tell, this grate was closest to the entrance to the building. All the other grates it had found led into reinforced rooms with no visible windows. It peered through the slats of the grate down at the entrance.

The leader and attack squad of mortals from before were gathered there. One was holding a bulbous device with a handle. It had a screen on one side with a large spike on the other end as he waved it around.

He was using it to scan the hallway in front of him and his eyes had intense focus as he stared at the screen. There was a final metal wall blocking the exit behind the mortals.

The Beholder felt around the edges of the grate with its hands carefully. It was fastened from the outside. There was little chance of removing it without sound. The Beholder was still invisible to most wavelengths of light, so if it could make it out of the vents undetected then it should be able to sneak by the mortals' eyes under its invisibility.

The Beholder went back into the maze-like ventilation system and kept peering out of the grates. Eventually, it found a room with no nearby humans that didn't have any of the big metal doors blocking it from the section with the exit. As carefully as it could, the Beholder placed its hands on the metal folds of the grate. A loud clang and screech of twisting metal sounded out as the Beholder opened a gap in the slats with its raw strength.

The Beholder flew out into the empty room and moved as quickly as it could to exit the area, turning invisible again as it did so. It could already hear the shouts of alarm from humans in the adjoining hallway. A flurry of fiery sparks trailed behind it as the Beholder moved. The Beholder patted its still smoldering sections of its body but it didn't seem to work to put them out.

It kept moving, it could deal with this strange flame later. It reached the exit hallway, still moving as it tried to contain the growing specs of flame covering its body.

The man with the device immediately jolted to attention and pointed the device's spike directly at the supposedly invisible Beholder. He shouted something and the men around him raised their weapons and released another wave of bullets where he had pointed the device.

The Beholder entered its spatial pocket for a second before returning. The human with the scanner shouted again as his device beeped and the guards fired another barrage from their guns. The Beholder dropped like a stone for a moment and the hail of bullets flew above its eye.

It quickly retreated back around the corner and found the entrance it had made to the ventilation system. There were two or three humans milling around now, rifles raised. But the Beholder flew right past them invisible and entered the vent again without them noticing.

It flew through the maze before it was far enough away that it would not be found or harmed by their weapons. After a moment of consideration, it popped back into its spatial pocket. It needed to think about how it could escape without losing more Potential. Just healing from a single bullet wound would be a massive waste, let alone the number that had been fired at it recently. It was lucky that it had thought to dodge.

$$- - - O - o - O - - -$$

Alan was still sleeping on his stone shelf. The Beholder considered if this was truly a dire situation before finally internally sighing. It could punch or claw its way out, but that would take far too long.

The body modifications and subsequent healing of the damaged claws would cost far too much Potential. The effectiveness would also depend on the physical thickness of the defenses. It guessed it was time to use one of the weapons it had picked up on its other worlds. Even if it would drain a little potential too, it wouldn't be nearly as much as using its own body for the task.

It went into the armory and picked up a small hemisphere of stone filled with the scribed networks of golden lines. It considered the object sadly. The exact formula of this one was unique to its creator.

Like mortal art, each creator put their own flourishes and styles when creating these types of artifacts. Truly unfortunate, but the Beholder would have to make due with this small loss. It had several thousand similar ones, and it remembered this one well enough it could create a passable replica when it got back. But it wouldn't be the same. A great sacrifice for the cause.

The Beholder exited its spatial pocket and returned to the inside of the vent. The stone hemisphere in its right hand returned with it and was similarly shrunk with the Beholder's body.

Its shrinking was a type of spatial manipulation, so it could be extended to whatever objects the Beholder carried if it wished for it to. The Beholder's burns began tingling, but the Beholder put it out of mind. It would allow itself to heal after it escaped. The Beholder quickly returned to the open vent away from the entrance. There were more humans gathered there now, but none had the scanner. The Beholder floated past with none of them being any the wiser.

The Beholder reached the corner near the exit and paused. It gradually let itself expand until it was its natural size while maintaining its invisibility. It wanted to avoid the sound of displacing air from when it changed size too fast. It carefully lined up the stone hemisphere so the flat portion pointed outwards. It lined itself up… then it made its move.

In an instant it dashed to the side and injected its Potential into the device. The human with the scanner shouted as the device flew from the Beholder's hands and stuck itself to the wall. There was a deep *thrum* and then a crash as a massive impact dented the door inwards like a giant fist.

The hemisphere crumbled into shards of stone as the metal door twisted and screamed before a massive hole with jagged edges formed in the center of it.

The twisted and crumpled metal door was blown backwards and fell to the ground with a crash. The humans were all thrown to the floor from the shockwave as the whole building shook under the massive impact.

The Beholder shrunk down in size again with a *pop* of displaced air and darted for the cleared exit. The humans stood up to their feet again as it was nearly half way there. They fired wildly in the air, hoping for a blind strike, seemingly realizing the Beholder's intent.

The Beholder was nearly clear when one of the bullets grazed its shrunken body. Its invisibility flickered on and off as it dived through the hole into a room with an elevator at the far end.

One of the mortal soldiers spotted it and started shouting, but the others couldn't hear him over their blind gunfire into the hallway. The Beholder pried open the shut elevator doors with the strength in its arms and quickly pushed itself into the shaft.

The Beholder shut the doors again behind it after it was fully through. It went down the shaft as it heard heavy thuds against the closed doors above it. The elevator was below it and moving upwards quickly. The Beholder decided it would escape from the roof.

The humans below finished prying open the elevator doors below as the Beholder reached the elevator door to the top floor. It opened the doors in the shaft and pushed its way through again.

There were two guards there on the other side, but they just looked around in confusion, seemingly unaware of the chaos below. Or of the Beholder's invisible form. The Beholder spotted a nearby glass window to the outside. It quickly darted forward and with crossed arms braced in front of it crashed through and flew into the open air amid a rain of glass shards.

A growing wave of embers trailed behind it. The Beholder quickly flew upwards and returned to its natural size while staying invisible. It flew a few miles away, the red lights and screeching alarms of the military base left far behind.

The Beholder decided it was safe enough to heal now. Its Potential flooded back into its wounds and they healed in an instant, but the Potential kept draining for some reason.

The Beholder noticed the embers of reddish flame had flared up and were burning its flesh again creating small tongues of flame in moments. Its eye widened as it finally recognized the embers were not mundane, but Devouring Flames.

With some effort, it retracted as much Potential as it could from around the new burns but the flame kept searing inwards faster as if it was a starving mortal animal. The Beholder quickly retreated into its spatial pocket.

It flew rapidly to the dissection room as the flames grew larger and larger all over its body. It had stopped the supply of new Potential but the flesh was already oversaturated with Potential in that area and couldn't be withdrawn as the flame feasted so closely on its body.

The Beholder rummaged through the cabinets urgently before it found a large enough blade for the job. It was lucky it had stocked mortal artifacts rather than modifying its limbs with each operation as was traditional. Modifying its hand with blades might only allow the flames to spread more and lead to the Beholder being consumed faster.

Taking the knife the Beholder stabbed itself and started removing the burning chunks of itself in large slices and stabs. As the flesh fell, the flames leapt off the chunks and little wisps started floating towards the Beholder slowly through the air.

The Beholder cut off more and more chunks of itself and painfully prevented the Potential in its center mass to rush back for healing. Its black blood was spilling everywhere as it finished removing the last reddish ember that fell to the floor.

It looked into the large mirror on the wall and inspected itself. It sliced a few more times where little orange dots had reappeared at the edges of its wounds. Its body looked terrible, like some pack of terrible mortal beasts had come and taken big bites out of it all over. The knife in its hand was soaked in its black blood.

The Beholder jolted to float higher in the air as it noticed the small tongues of flame seeming to be rising from its fallen chunks of burning flesh on the floor.

The flames had drawn closer and wafted upwards as the Beholder focused on inspecting its wound. The wisps of flame floated halfway to the ceiling and slowly dimmed and were snuffed as they traveled toward the Beholder. Running out of power and dissipating.

The Beholder retreated to the door of the room, increasing its height off the ground closer to the ceiling and swooping over the slowly moving flames so it wouldn't be taking any chances. The Beholder observed as the Devouring Flames grew weaker and weaker as they traveled, until finally the last little ember winked out into nothing before it reached anywhere near the Beholder hovered floating at the doorway.

The Beholder observed the room suspiciously for a minute, waiting for some trick. It had heard that the Devouring Flame could do things like that sometimes depending on the circumstances.

When nothing suspicious happened, the Beholder returned to continue its inspection of itself in the mirror. Eventually it did notice a few solitary embers growing in its wounds slowly growing. With a few more slices they were removed before they could grow again. Ah, the pure waste of Potential. But it had to be done, every spark must be purged before the Beholder could be sure that it was safe.

———O—o—O———

It took one final round of waiting and removing the burned flesh after that, but the Beholder was finally purged of the last final sparks of the Devouring Flame. It seems the mortals were cleverer than the Beholder had thought.

Everything after that first explosion had been a diversion to allow the Devouring Flame to root itself more firmly in its body. If it had waited for too long then even it might have been consumed from within, not noticing the spread of the Devouring Flames until it was too late.

The Beholder had no doubt such a trap could have easily worked on many others who could not act as decisively in removing their infected flesh in time. Or being able to retract their Potential so completely from their outer flesh at all, for that matter as the Beholder was able to do.

After waiting twenty more minutes to be absolutely sure it was cleansed, the Beholder let its Potential rush back to its gaping wounds. At once its wounds healed and it was as good as new, though its amount of Potential it had saved up had dropped significantly.

The Beholder had been spending its Potential quite excessively as of late. Its complacence had allowed the Devouring Flame spread far farther than what should have happened. To think the mortals already had such weapons before the Avatar even emerged…

At this frantic pace the Beholder may run out of Potential in a century or less. It would have to be more frugal and cautious from now on to make sure it wouldn't have to resort to drastic measures.

The Beholder popped back to Earth from its spatial pocket. Well, best find the nearest mortal city for when Alan woke up. Now that it knew the rulers were not to be trusted, it could use the mortal Alan as an intermediary to acquire all the items it could ever desire from other groups of mortals that were about.

Hopefully he would stick to his word or the Beholder may have to resort to theft of the mortals by this point after their government had turned out to be so hostile to it already.

The Beholder had hoped not to sour its friendly relations to the mortals in general so far, but it would do so if it had to by resorting to some theft. If the Beholder was going to be attacked by the mortals again then it may as well help itself to their items along the way.

— — — (Mortal Alan Fragment) — — —

Alan had just gotten off the phone with his superiors. He had given his location and his version of what had happened. And Thoth's version as well after they found some more paper for it to write on.

He had woken up hours ago, and Thoth had just dropped him off in the nearest town suddenly to his confusion before vanishing from sight. It was floating around him invisibly even now. Whenever it wanted to say something it would just slip a piece of paper with its precise blocky writing into his pocket. Alan had wandered into a small shopping plaza with a few dozen stores scattered around the parking lot.

A few people milled around but the place was mostly deserted as far as Alan could tell. Lots of people in these surrounding towns had fled the area, staying with relatives or going on 'vacation'. No one wanted to be nearby when the dome fell, there were all sorts of theories of what was happening. But none of it was good. Especially with the army massing and passing through the area.

Alan's own family was across the country luckily, so at least he wouldn't have to worry about any of the aliens attacking them just yet. Although Thoth seemed friendly enough so far, so maybe they weren't all bad.

Thoth mostly had asked for him to buy various things it saw in the stores Alan passed around them in its little notes. The higher ups had tried to get Alan to leave and escort Thoth elsewhere, but Thoth had stated in no uncertain terms that it would not be going to another government facility until it felt safe in doing so.

The higher ups had understood more after Alan had gotten around to explaining the people who had attacked and tried to kill them both with poison gas.

Although they were livid when Alan relayed Thoth's statement that it wouldn't sell them more information until the people behind the attack were captured. Apparently an information exchange was why the alien had been at the base in the first place.

Alan wondered how all the children's toys Thoth had been collecting were factored into it. But he didn't ask. Alan sweated as he talked with people of far more importance than someone of his rank should be talking. All of them asking him questions and giving firm orders in sharp tones.

He was on the phone for hours as person after person grilled him with question after question. Just when Alan thought he was done someone else would get on the line and start all over again from the beginning.

He even had to speak directly with the president at one point. His voice had been shaking a little as President Harrow had asked him his opinion on the alien as it hovered invisibly over his shoulder. But the Beholder didn't seem to care when he gave his honest thoughts through his nervous and shaky voice.

The call with the president had been over in a few minutes, to Alan's relief and after that it was back to talking to all sorts of other important people to tell them the same story over and over again.

Alan was feeling his empty wallet a little as he was forced to use his own money to buy things for hours for the Beholder's amusement after getting off the phone.

Luckily another military representative had arrived an hour ago. Not army, he wouldn't say what branch of the government he worked for. The man gave Alan a different credit card and said the government would pay for whatever the Beholder wanted to buy here as an apology for the attack on it.

The man looked into mid-air as he said that, his words clearly directed at Thoth and not Alan. The man had ordered Alan to be relieved after that but when Alan went to leave Thoth had reappeared and put a spindly chitin plated arm on his shoulder before disappearing again in an instant.

Another piece of paper had appeared in his pocket a few seconds later. He pulled it out. *Safer here out of the way. Trust you more than others. Your leaders still don't know who did the attack. Still dangerous going with them.*

Well, his superiors hadn't been happy when he had refused to leave after that but there wasn't much they could do. Thoth had requested him specifically to assist it. And Thoth was right.

Even Alan knew that someone who could get poison gas in a military base was well connected. Best to stay out of the way until whoever was behind the attack was found. Thoth could grab him and run away again if anything happened. Alan couldn't say the same if he went to some military base where he wouldn't know who to trust.

After a minute of silence and walking, another piece of paper appeared in Alan's pocket to direct him to buy something else in the store.

Thoth had seen something that was interesting in one of the nearby stores, and just had to have it apparently. But at least Alan was assured by the mysterious man following him around that he would be paid back for all the crap the Beholder had wanted to buy through the new credit card he'd been given.

Thoth hadn't seemed to care too much either way as long as it could get the items it wanted. It was still going wild, buying anything even remotely unique it could see. Alan had been getting weird looks as he filled his cart with odd assortments of items.

But their green army uniforms seemed to dissuade people from asking too many questions. Especially because the mysterious man was glowering the whole time as the pile of items chosen by the Beholder grew larger and larger as they went. It was basically taking one of everything from the whole store.

Alan checked out the items and pushed the shopping cart outside. After pushing the overflowing cart through the parking lot for a few seconds, little purple flashes started consuming the pile of items, shuffling them away into Thoth's storage space. Alan put the cart away and walked towards the next store in the line with the other man following closely behind.

He opened the door to the next store and walked in the door, the other man following right behind him. As Alan looked around at the shelves around him, he froze. Oh no.

Alan had figured out how much Thoth valued uniqueness in his purchases. It had never requested more than one item of any one type on the shelves. But this... This was an antique shop. Everything was old and no two items were identical. Alan felt a brief weight in his pocket leaving another slip of paper for him to read. With slight dread he pulled it from his pocket. *Buy everything! I need it all!!!* It read in big bold text.

Alan looked in disbelief at the paper before looking around the cluttered shop around him. He shared a glance with the military representative after showing him the paper. The man's eyebrows raised to the ceiling before he looked around at the cluttered shop.

Alan mustered his courage and bravery approached the old woman at the counter. How in the world was he going to explain this to her? Well, at least it was on the government dime now. Alan shuddered to think of what the cost was going to be of Thoth's shopping spree at the end of all of this...

Chapter 46: Missing Person in the Neighborhood - Infiltrator of Authority Fragment

— — — Nothing further of interest. The Beholder, Thoth, acquires more objects and ignores the continued requests of the military for information after the perpetrators of the attack were not caught. Mortal Alan stays by its side as its human intermediary. Very well, returning to Central events. Fragment of Memory found. Jumping forward in the timeline to Second Monday. Second Thursday was when Mortal Alice became unconscious after activating the more complex wards at Safezone Seven. This Fragment should explore events from a new angle. Isolating Fragment of Memory... Isolating... Begin. — — —

Infiltrator of Authority was busy. The facade of the hospital had crumbled by this point for the mortals. No more humans were approaching in need of medical care, and the few who did so had less and less Potential to harvest. The dregs.

No more humans remained in the region around the hospital. Infiltrator of Authority had begun operations to start building its forces passively.

This Wednesday, groups of scouting Nameless had discovered that the human's forts were boxing in the hospital on all sides in a large circle. Moving past them would allow the Nameless to be surrounded and destroyed by the Neighborhood Watch strike forces in the backlines.

With no more room to spread, and no more humans to consume, Infiltrator of Authority had decided to begin operations to keep the invasion self-sustaining. To establish a more permanent foothold.

It took the sacrifice of ten of the Nameless that had infested the humans with the most Potential. Despite the protests of the Nameless, Infiltrator molded the Nameless each into a tall Spire of Growth. They should be grateful. Their true bodies would reap massive amounts of Potential over time even if it was an exceptionally boring assignment.

The Spires of Growth were one of the most protected structures in the armies of the Eldest due to what they created. Infiltrator of Authority placed the Spires of Growth on the roof of the mortal hospital where they would be protected by the majority of its forces. Using the energy from the light of this planet's sun, the spires grew taller over an hour until they reached their full size at twenty feet tall.

After they reached their full height, tumorous growths began bulging outwards from their surface. Infiltrator of Authority gathered some of the remaining Nameless and assisted them in mutating their forms to maximize their use in combat.

The loss of all five of its advanced mutants to the mortals was a heavy blow to the invasion as a whole. Infiltrator of Authority was enraged when it was told the numbers that were lost in the failed attempt to destroy a single mortal. To think they had Devouring Flame already…

Finally, Infiltrator of Authority and the gathered Nameless looked upwards as they heard a keening cry from the roof. Infiltrator of Authority made its way upward until it emerged to see the newest additions to their forces. The first batch of spawnlings was budding off the spire. Infiltrator of Authority and the rest of the Nameless were being controlled by their true bodies in their home reality.

The spawnlings were different. These fresh spawnlings were fully present but pitifully weak and pitifully stupid in contrast. Stupid even compared to even the simplest Nameless that had been under Infiltrator of Authority's command so far.

Some died immediately upon birth, unable to adapt to the environment and atmosphere of this planet. Their orb-like bodies shifted and writhed into more vaguely humanoid shapes as they perceived Infiltrator of Authority's host.

One of the creatures growled before launching itself directly towards Infiltrator of Authority's skull. With one human hand Infiltrator of Authority reached out and grabbed it in mid air from its leap. In an instant Infiltrator of Authority drew the creature's pitiful amount of Potential into itself.

The creature went limp and began to dissolve without its motive force powering it. It was no loss compared to the roughly fifty spawnlings that had survived to this point. The spires of Growth wilted and looked pitted as the last few spawnlings emerged and burst from their respective pustule like growths covering its surface.

Infiltrator of Authority waited a moment for the remainder of the clutch to spawn and emerge from the Spires of Growth. Before another spawnling could foolishly attack it, Infiltrator of Authority telepathically connected to all of their weak minds at once.

Around seventy ended up surviving after they all had fully spawned. Just under forty percent had survived. Infiltrator of Authority telepathically released a sensation of its authority and the weak minded spawnlings cowered as they felt it.

Infiltrator of Authority nodded in satisfaction. Good.

Without any more communication with the fodder, Infiltrator of Authority passed its end of the link to one of the more intelligent Nameless. It would see to the education of this clutch of spawnlings. While the bodies of these weaker Nameless could not initiate telepathic links, they were knowledgeable enough to maintain them and dominate such a weak collective, at least until the spawnlings were more adept.

Infiltrator of Authority severed its part of the link, leaving the Nameless to its work with its new connection to the clutch. The spawnlings obediently followed the designated Nameless off the roof, only snapping at each other occasionally as they crawled and scrambled over each other as they moved and jostled past each other.

Infiltrator of Authority inspected the injured Spires of Growth that were slowly recovering their wounds. They would regrow and spawn the next clutch in a few hours. Infiltrator of Authority left again to assist in the mutations of more of the Nameless.

The next clutch of spawnlings had a sixty percent survival rate as the spires of Growth adapted the spawnlings to be predisposed to survive on this planet. The next clutch had seventy percent survival.

Finally on Wednesday, the clutches reached ninety percent survival. Infiltrator of Authority judged that good enough for it to proceed. Taking the template of the existing Spires of Growth, further Spires of Growth wouldn't require nearly as much Potential to create even if they would become less adaptable as a result.

There were now enough clutches of spawnlings to cover the perimeter around the hospital no matter how loosely they did so. The spawnlings were intentionally held close so they didn't stupidly throw their lives away attacking the mortals. It would just be a waste at this stage.

It was time to expand production. There were still thousands of Nameless still in mortal form. Infiltrator of Authority called on those not in combat form already. They would be put to better use now. Every available roof in the area soon became populated with dense clusters of Spires of Growth.

The only limit to their spread was that Infiltrator of Authority had to personally create each one in the painstaking process. It was the only one who could do so without wasting massive amounts of their limited Potential in the process.

But now it was Friday and Infiltrator of Authority had another important task. The Spires were creating new spawnlings at a steady rate. The older spawnlings appeared vaguely humanoid now even if their forms were always shifting in a constant waste of Potential. Infiltrator of Authority took note to reprimand the Nameless who managed those spawnlings. Frugality was key at this stage.

But hopefully the next project would allow some surplus Potential to increase the spawnlings strength. Infiltrator of Authority was about to begin the construction of a true Tower of Decay.

If the spawnlings ever ran out of Potential then they would die. One of the few curses of being immortal. Several of the more wasteful spawnlings had already dissolved. A Tower of Decay was essential to prevent this. Infiltrator of Authority spent almost the entirety of Thursday constructing it from the bodies of hundreds of the strongest Nameless left.

The Tower of Decay pierced the insides of the mortal hospital's floors. Its base sunk into the ground and its peak emerged through a hole it had pierced in the roof of the building.

A few of the spawnlings that had discovered flight began dropping bodies and plant material into the open mouth near the top of the Tower of Decay. The spawnlings' forms were unrefined.

They had malformed wings and had made up for this by filling their bodies with light gasses to lift themselves into the air. They moved slowly and looked like fleshy balloons. But they were enough to ferry the biomass into the Tower of Decay and that was all that mattered for now.

The Tower of Decay would convert the biomass directly into Potential rather than using the more inefficient process mortal's used in their bodies. Infiltrator of Authority went to the base of the tower on the first floor of the hospital. After a few minutes the tower started leaking out ink black fluid onto the floor.

Infiltrator of Authority touched it with one finger before bringing it to his mouth for a taste. Its Potential increased slightly. Infiltrator of Authority grinned. With roughly two months predicted before the Harbinger's emergence in its true form and Infiltrator of Authority's forces isolated in this dome, it could build the greatest army ever seen on this mortal planet to follow in the Avatar's wake.

——— O — o — O ———

It was Friday now. The spawnlings gradually filtered in and out to take a sip from the growing black pool of fluid below the Tower of Decay. Night turned into day. The sun rose in the sky. Infiltrator of Authority had weakened its army's position temporarily to prepare for the future. The spawnlings were numerous but weak, even to the mortals. Some might burst apart with a single blow from a human.

Many of the strongest Nameless had been converted into Spires of Growth or incorporated into the Tower of Decay. But in three weeks the spawnlings would be at the same strength as the Nameless that had been used in the Spires of Growth. And they would only get stronger from there.

One thing that did bother Infiltrator of Authority was the mortal Bill's motive in all of this. The encirclement of the mortals was the only true obstacle to uncheckered growth from within the dome.

The human Bill had assisted Infiltrator of Authority and the Betrayer with his information on the humans in the first stages. Then he had put up the dome trapping them all inside here. The dome may have prevented them from spreading farther, but was more of a blessing than a curse in Infiltrator of Authority's eyes.

The beachhead of these invasions was often grueling as larger bases were under constant assault by the natives. They had to scurry under the radar until the Avatar emerged to lead the charge. Growing so many Spires of Growth near the emergence of the Harbinger was nearly unprecedented in such a populated planet.

But after nearly a week of near inaction, the mortal Bill had infiltrated the hospital and stolen a significant portion of the Potential in the exceptional humans Infiltrator of Authority had been preserving. Sent his second to launch an assault where a single mortal had defeated a full assault and five greater combat mutated Nameless.

Infiltrator of Authority shivered in its real body as it remembered the abomination that had attempted to return to it in the aftermath. An amalgamation of fragments of the Nameless all in one body.

All the links to their true bodies had been severed and the creature had absorbed another Nameless and severed the link to their true body even as Infiltrator of Authority had watched it. The collective army of Infiltrator of Authority had barely been able to chase off the fearsome creature before it consumed any more of them. It was Infiltrator of Authority's third biggest concern to the invasion's success after Bill and the Betrayer.

How had the mortals created such a weapon? Could they create more? Now mortal Bill and his organization had gathered the remainder of the humans and formed a perimeter keeping them trapped. Why release them in the first place only to betray them a week later? And not only that, but the mortal had access to Fulcrum for years. Why had they not eliminated him or the Seed if they wished to oppose the Eldest?

Of course the Seed could have simply become an Avatar if it was ever seriously threatened. But records showed that the Seed of this world had been acting oddly ever since it arrived.

Most Seeds took barely a few months to gestate before sprouting into a mobile form and full consciousness. But this one had not only bonded with a mortal, but taken years while aware and seemingly done nothing in that time. No gestation, no progress, just sitting there passively while the Harbinger Fulcrum lived above it as a seemingly normal mortal.

Infiltrator of Authority frowned as it watched the spawnlings feed on the black pool beneath the Tower of Decay. It did not like the mystery. Perhaps it should...

'INFILTRATOR OF AUTHORITY!'

Infiltrator of Authority turned and there was the Betrayer standing there. Infiltrator of Authority had almost forgotten about it in its focus on building the army. While despicable, Infiltrator of Authority knew the Betrayer would never truly do something to impede the invasion itself.

The Betrayer looked similar to the gorillas of this planet. Its bleached bone plated form was nearly fifteen feet tall even as it stood hunched over onto its elongated front arms, knuckles dragging on the ground. It had a large bony head crest curled backwards from its flattened head in a large plate. Its inset beady black eyes met Infiltrator of Authority's own. The bug-like mandibles sticking from the Betrayer's lower jaw hung below its face curled and twitched slightly even as it spoke telepathically to Infiltrator of Authority.

Infiltrator of Authority looked behind the Betrayer and saw the splattered trail of spawnling bodies stretching into the distance. The greater Nameless seemed to have been too slow to catch the Betrayer in its charge here and were just now coming into sight in the distance.

Infiltrator of Authority looked back to the Betrayer and began shedding its mortal disguise. Tentacles ripped out from the shell of skin around its true form, gestated inside of its former host. The tentacles began pulling the skin apart around its spine, revealing the writhing mass beneath the surface.

It had been expecting this battle all week. Just because it was out of mind did not mean Infiltrator of Authority hadn't made preparations for the Betrayer. The Betrayer noticed the action and brushed the action aside with one of its front limbs impatiently.

'I HAVE NOT COME TO FIGHT. THE MORTAL FULCRUM AND THE SEED ARE MISSING! WHAT HAVE YOU DONE?'

Infiltrator of Authority paused and quickly retracted its tentacles and sealed the skin again before it exposed too much of its capabilities.

'What have *I* done? Was guarding the Seed not *your* duty? What did *you* do?'

The clacking of the Betrayer's maniables grew louder in frustration. '**THERE IS NO TIME FOR YOUR GAMES. WE MUST FIND THEM BEFORE THE ELDEST INTERVENES!**'

Infiltrator of Authority froze. It indeed hadn't thought of the consequences if the Seed was hurt in some way. It had thought it as some form of trick from the Betrayer. But the desperation in the Betrayer's telepathic voice was real. Infiltrator of Authority must put its animosity aside for the moment.

'**Then let us go. We should inspect the home of the mortal Fulcrum for clues first.**'

Infiltrator of Authority telepathically connected to some of the most intelligent Nameless close by. They would move and comb the surrounding areas close to Fulcrum's home while it and the Betrayer would directly investigate the scene.

'**YES, LET US GO.**' The Betrayer dashed off at top speed. Infiltrator of Authority ran to a nearby mortal vehicle and drove after the Betrayer. Infiltrator of Authority wanted to keep this body's capabilities concealed even despite the situation.

Who knows when things might change again and lead them to resume their conflict? Luckily Infiltrator of Authority only ran over a few spawnlings on its way over. It wouldn't do to drop their numbers too much in case there was a surprise assault by the mortals on them.

———O—o—O———

The two of them arrived within minutes. Infiltrator of Authority got out of the police cruiser and looked at the home. The watchers Infiltrator of Authority had put on the Betrayer were in pieces of gory chunks of flesh scattered across the road.

Whole segments of Fulcrum's home were burned to the ground, just ash left behind. Others stood whole and oddly undamaged. It looked like the whole back half of the building had collapsed inwards into piles of rubble and looked charred even when there was no ash present.

'Did you do this destruction?' Infiltrator of Authority asked the Betrayer.

The Betrayer shook its head. It's mandibles clicked. **'NO. I EMERGED FROM MY DEN ACROSS THE STREET TO SEE YOUR WATCHERS CRAWLING ALL OVER IT. IN MY RAGE I DESTROYED THEM.'**

Infiltrator of Authority was reminded why it despised this Nameless so much for usurping him. It truly was inexperienced for not even interrogating a single one of its supposed enemies for information. The Betrayer began shifting the rubble and exposed a massive pit in the ground where the kitchen used to be. That was where the Seed had been.

Infiltrator of Authority looked at the edges of the hole and frowned. The cavity was almost completely round with only a single hole in the top with a crumbling ledge at the apex of the empty sphere. If the Seed had been forcefully extracted by the mortals then they would have dug out the sides more so it could be lifted out.

The Seed had the ability to resist all forms of teleportation or spatial manipulation as well… Except…

Infiltrator of Authority straightened. Could it be… **'WHAT IS IT?'** The Betrayer interrupted Infiltrator of Authority's thoughts. Infiltrator of Authority tried to think of an excuse to give the Betrayer.

'DON'T LIE. DO YOU THINK YOU WOULD ESCAPE THE WRATH OF THE ELDEST IF WE FAIL HERE?'

Infiltrator of Authority realized it could turn the Betrayer and the mortals against each other. But only if it trusted in the Betrayer's ignorance.

'The mortals have captured Fulcrum and the Seed,' Infiltrator of Authority said, **'They must have some kind of spatial artifact to shrink the Seed and take it from here.'**

The Betrayer considered the statement for a moment. Infiltrator of Authority prepared itself to flee back to its army.

If the Nameless attacked then Infiltrator of Authority had to be ready.

'I WILL CRUSH THEM. MY FORM HAS BEEN REFINED ENOUGH FOR THIS,' the Betrayer said.

Infiltrator of Authority nodded and tried to not appear too encouraging. *'I will organize the army to assault in your wake. If you can wait just a day…'*

'NO! COWARD, I WILL GO NOW. THERE IS NO TIME TO LOSE. WAIT TO LONG AND LOSE YOUR SHARE OF THE GLORY FOR THE SEED'S RETRIEVAL.'

With that, the Betrayer turned and lumbered off. As Infiltrator of Authority got into its car it allowed itself a wicked smile. That had gone even better than expected. If it was right then right now Fulcrum and the Seed were communicating with the Eldest directly.

The Seed would only allow the Eldest to teleport it away so cleanly without any resistance. The Seed would be safely returned to this world after its communication with the Eldest was finished. But this was an excellent opportunity to eliminate two enemies at once.

The mortal Bill seemed far too prepared for the events that were quickly unfolding in this town. Infiltrator of Authority didn't believe for a second that he didn't have some way of dealing with them given the knowledge he had displayed so far and the fact he had intentionally initially released them in the first place for some reason.

The Betrayer would charge the mortals and when mortal Bill went to stop it, his deeper plans, whatever they were, would be exposed.

Infiltrator of Authority could leap into the gap and finish off the victor after one or the other won after weakening each other significantly.

Because as much as Infiltrator of Authority acknowledged the mortal's cunning, he would have difficulty dealing with the raw power the Nameless had been imbued with by the Seed's blessing.

Infiltrator of Authority licked its lips as it imagined the kind of forms it could create if it got its hands on the massive reserves the Betrayer had used for larger muscles and thicker plating.

All that Potential was truly a waste on that dullard. Infiltrator of Authority would use that massive well of Potential better. This was the best course of action. Both for itself, for the invasion, and for the Seed.

Now it just had to hurry up and make sure it didn't miss the show.

Chapter 47: Assault on the Club - Prime Mortal Bill Fragment

Bill woke up at one in the morning on Friday by a heavy knock on his door. After hurriedly getting dressed he had seen a similarly disheveled Helen standing outside his door.

"Bill, there are signs of an attack on Fulcrum and the Seed again," She said, "Parts of the house appeared destroyed and both Fulcrum and the Seed are missing. There is a big hole in the ground too where the Seed used to be."

Bill groaned. "Drones only for scouting right? That's too deep in their territory for investigating on foot."

Helen nodded. "Bill, we both know that. Why don't you splash your face with some water to wake up."

Bill blinked. Yeah, he should do that. He went to his bathroom. The fog on his mind cleared as the cool water dripped from his face. Alright, crisis mode. The Infected would go nuts with the Seed missing. He went back to the front door and followed behind Helen.

"Any movement from the Infected?" he asked, "Have you started the preparations in case they start their assault soon?"

Helen looked over her shoulder, "No movement now. There were a few Infected milling around the rubble but none seemed to be doing much or getting help. I've already started the movement of equipment to Safezone Seven. Should… should we wake up Francis?"

Bill thought about it for a moment. Francis hadn't exploded as much as expected when he had heard the full plan after that girl Alice was hurt. Bill wasn't convinced though. They had known each other for over a decade and Bill knew that Francis was far more upset than he was letting on. This could serve as a good final test to see if he was willing to do what needed to be done.

"Yes," Bill said, "If he can't help with this then we will know he can't be trusted in the final stages."

Helen fell back and looked slightly disturbed. "But Bill, this could be the final straw for him. Do we really want him as an enemy? After all these years…"

Bill shot a glance at her. "The mission is what is most important. We can apologize to him afterwards. But for now, we can't blow years of planning for sentiment."

Helen gave a jerky nod and they continued in silence. Bill eyed Helen. He would have to watch her closely. He knew her conviction to their goals and her willingness to get her hands dirty, but she might waver in a critical moment if Bill wasn't careful.

Not be convinced... But maybe enough to hesitate when she needed to take unpleasant action. Especially where Francis was concerned...

Helen handed Bill some printed images which broke the silent tension of the moment. Bill inspected the pictures. It definitely wasn't humans that did this. Was there another faction at play here that had removed the Seed?

Bill and Helen started scrambling around and giving orders. They had to move a lot of equipment quickly to prepare for an assault of the Infected.

———O—o—O———

They parked the vehicles two blocks away from Safezone Seven. Various small teams carefully placed the stones for the formation. As time passed more and more equipment was moved in preparation for the events to come.

This group consisted of the most elite of the Neighborhood Watch, all who knew the true scope of their mission and were smart enough to keep their mouths shut about it. The two guards on patrol around Safezone Seven had already been detained silently. It would be seen when they returned to the Ranch if they would have to be silenced or not.

Francis had been informed of the group's movements and was on his way soon. He had been left behind to alert the fourth in command and give out contingency orders for when all three of the founding members of the Neighborhood Watch were all out on a mission at once.

This mission was too important to delegate to any of them. All of them had to be there. Eventually, nearly an hour later, Francis arrived. Bill and Helen told him the plan.

Francis nearly shouted during the following argument and it took Bill's hand over his mouth to remind him of where they were and the need for silence. Francis scowled and turned away, disgusted with the two of them. Helen looked devastated, while Bill was just disappointed.

Both of them now knew that Francis had never been on board with the larger plan if he argued so fiercely against this. He would have to be managed so he wouldn't do anything stupid based on his outdated morals.

Helen went over to Francis to softly speak with him, and luckily their fierce whispers were kept at a low volume. Bill turned to some of the most loyal soldiers and quietly gave them a new set of orders. Francis could no longer be trusted and must be watched carefully.

Bill would never hurt Francis if he didn't need to but he would certainly stop him from interfering in what would come next. The mission was more important than their decade-long friendship, unfortunately. Hopefully, Helen would be able to convince him of the reason why it was all necessary later. Bill didn't want to sacrifice anything more to the cause if he could help it. He was already giving too much as it was.

But if he had to, he'd give everything to the cause. After so long fighting, it would be irresponsible for him to do anything less.

———O—o—O———

Night turned into day and nothing happened. The tension in the building grew as time passed. Feet shuffled, weapons were cleaned, cleaned and checked over and over.

They all waited.

Several of the people in Safezone Seven were milling around inside the walls, but luckily none had left the perimeter of the Safezone Seven yet. Francis tried several times to sneak away but a combination of Helen's words and the loyal guards held him back from starting any fights or shouting. Bill tried to stay out of the way, knowing his pure dedication to the plan would only irritate Francis further in his current state.

Finally, the drone operators had something new.

The mutated Nameless camped opposite Fulcrum's house had massacred the other Infected before running off somewhere. One flying drone followed at a distance while the other remained watching the house.

Luckily the Neighborhood Watch's communication jammers were able to be extremely selective in their frequencies. So they allowed the narrow bands of frequencies for the drone control while blocking the others that would allow the townspeople to communicate with the outside world. No need for them to give the military a closer look at their operations here.

And allow the military to vilify the Neighborhood Watch and sow discontent among the remaining humans inside the dome.

Of the two flying drones, the one sent to the hospital didn't last as long as expected. As it drew closer to the old hospital it showed giant spiked growths on the nearby building's roofs. Infected roamed everywhere around there. Bill's resolve firmed. This is what he would be preventing for the rest of the world.

The large mutated Nameless met with what Bill recognized as the mortal disguise of Infiltrator of Authority. They stared at each other for a moment before the drone was attacked from above. The camera spun in every direction until after a moment the image froze.

Connection lost.

The camera had caught what appeared to be a balloonist-looking creature with malformed wings and stubby little claws it had used to grip the drone in the last frame. This is why they had stopped scouting the zone via drone.

They had lost three drones this way in the past before giving up and resorting to longer-distance surveillance. But this was important enough to sacrifice the drone for a closer look. The next steps were critical. What kind of numbers and what quality of forces would the Infected send to attack?

The second drone was kept at a long distance and saw the mutated Nameless and a police car driving towards the Harbinger's house. They all let out sighs of relief when the mutated Nameless proceeded onwards while Infiltrator of Authority returned towards the hospital after they finished their mutual inspection of the ruins of Fulcrum's house.

Unfortunately, the Nameless was heading towards Safezone Three. Time to divert it. Bill took the control pad from the drone operator and went upstairs with Helen. He brought the flying drone closer to the Nameless' ape-like form. Bill turned on the speaker and turned it to the maximum volume as the drone flew closer to the mutated creature.

"Lord," Bill said, "We have located Fulcrum."

The creature looked at the drone in surprise and stopped. Its mandibles clicked. Apparently, it could only speak telepathically.

"It's me, Bill talking through this device. If you follow this flying construct, then it can lead you to where the rebels are holding Fulcrum. We just learned what they have done and are happy to assist you in destroying them."

The Nameless was still for a moment before it nodded and lumbered its way toward the drone. Bill turned off the speaker and started guiding the Nameless to Safezone Seven. He made sure to make the route more circuitous so there was no chance of it encountering any of the other more valuable safe zones on its way. Helen rushed downstairs and began shouting to get the men ready for the final preparations.

Ten minutes later the drone and the following Nameless came within sight of the Safezone.

Several people within the Safezone shouted in alarm from their positions on top of the walls. The sound of a gunshot blasted from the floor below Bill. He could hear shouting and the sound of a struggle below his feet.

Bill sweat a little and breathed faster as the Nameless' head turned toward the building they were hiding in. If it attacked them and the building they were hiding in, then they would all be dead. There were backups of course, but without Bill and Helen there to guide things things could go wrong. Bill turned on the drone speakers again where it hovered just in front of the gorilla-like creature.

"There lord," Bill said into the drone control pad, "Behind that stack of vehicles and makeshift wall are the rebels. Fulcrum is in the center building behind it."

The Nameless paused for another moment and inspected its surroundings in what seemed to be suspicion at Bill's words. But then it shook its head and seemed to come to a decision.

It started loping forward down the street towards the barricade. It quickly began to pick up its pace as it ran in a straight line. It charged faster and faster. A car blocking the street was sent flying with one fist, barely slowing its momentum as it moved. The Neighborhood Watch prepared on the floor below Bill and Bill flew the drone upwards to get an overview of what was about to happen.

The people inside the Safezone were alternatively running away from the wall towards the interior or just frozen in place at the sight of the creature charging them at over forty miles an hour now.

The people fired several bullets at the Nameless but they just left small nicks in its bone armor. Barely noticeable and not leading it to slow in the slightest.

The Nameless reached the wall and with a loud roar blasted through it in one motion. Shards of metal went flying and the people began screaming as the Nameless began the slaughter.

Bill's team of the Neighborhood Watch quickly surrounded the perimeter at a distance and activated the barriers and stones they had placed around the safe zone last night.

The shields were focused inwards. The Nameless didn't notice the flash as the barriers activated before quickly fading back into invisibility. It just continued the massacre of the people inside, seemingly intent on killing even those in hiding. Smashing buildings with its fists and destroying everything around it in a senseless rage. Seemingly uncaring that it was supposed to be rescuing Fulcrum rather than crushing him with the rest.

The people who died withered into mummified husks, even those who died from the shrapnel or falling debris rather than the creature's fists.

After two or three minutes, the glow of the pillar inside the main building began to become bright enough that it was visible even in the daylight. The Nameless paused mid-stomp as it was about to crush a woman half-trapped under rubble.

She writhed for a moment before coughing up blood and growing still from Bill's view from the drone camera. Her corpse mummified in moments and the glow of the pillar of light grew brighter. The Nameless turned to the beacon, now ignoring the humans nearby it.

The remaining people who had run in fear began twitching and falling to the ground all at once. They quickly shriveled into desiccated husks as all their Potential was drawn into the pillar in a golden wave of light all at once. The Nameless charged towards the light shining from the blinding pillar in a rage. It tripped over its feet as its legs spasmed.

The arm splayed forward closest to the pillar started to slowly decrease in size as it lay splayed on the ground. It screeched and rolled away. The pillar kept growing brighter even as the creature crawled away desperately. The pillar was now like a second sun. The camera of the drone could barely focus on the Nameless through the glare, the light was so bright.

The mutated Nameless stumbled to its feet and started lurching away to the massive hole in the Safezone wall it had just created. The visible drain of Potential on it lessened but didn't stop for the creature. It yelped as it suddenly crashed into the invisible barrier and fell backwards at the sudden change in momentum. The barrier flashed into golden light for a moment before fading again. The creature was three-quarters its original size now. It pounded on the barrier with its fists, but it was no use.

The barrier held steady.

It screeched a little louder now, a hint of desperation now present in its tone. Bill smiled.

Some time passed as it pounded on the barrier with its fists more. It was now half its original size. Its giant fist slowly shifted into a massive bone spear on the tip of the Nameless' arm. It punched it and there was a cracking sound as the barrier weakened. The second sun grew brighter and brighter behind it.

One-third of its original size. It struck again and the barrier shattered. With a cry of triumph, the Nameless lumbered forward... Only to run into the second barrier. There were three total for extra redundancy. It wouldn't be getting through.

It struck again with the sharp spear. The second barrier cracked but did not break. It tried to strike again and again but its blows grew weaker and weaker. The second barrier hovered at the edge of breaking but just barely held on.

The creature was one-quarter its original size now. The second barrier shattered. But the blows of the creature were weak and lethargic now. The camera of the drone could barely even see the creature anymore. It was like a shadow blocking out the dome of radiant golden light.

The creature's head rapidly swelled and ballooned in size even as the rest of its body kept shrinking. Its malformed shape with the bloated skull could only be seen as a malformed shadow against the golden sun shining from the center of the Safezone.

'NNNNNNNGGGGNGGGNGGNGNNGNGNGNNG'

Bill stumbled at the wordless telepathic assault from the creature. Several of his men fell to the ground twitching even at this distance and without direct eye contact with the creature.

The creature shrunk until it was barely the size of a man except with a massive head nearly the same size as the rest of its body.

'GRRRRRRRRUUUUUUUUUUAAAAAAAAA!'

More of the Neighborhood Watch twitched and collapsed bleeding from their eyes, ears, and noses. Bill only felt a faint twinge of pain in his head this time. Several of his people on the ground went still.

'AGGGGGHHHHHHHHHHHHHHHHHHHHHHHHHHH!'

With one final telepathic scream, the creature fell to the ground twitching, and slowly withered into nothing. As it withered it let out more telepathic screams. But it was spent and the people who had survived its first blasts barely even flinched.

More than a third of them had died. It was worth the price. Bill flew the drone back through the window of the building and caught it with one hand. He went downstairs and saw an unconscious Francis on the ground, His pistol on the floor nearby. He must have been the one to fire off that warning shot to alert the people of Safezone Seven.

Bill was disappointed. He had high hopes he wouldn't have to resort to more extreme measures to contain Francis, but it seemed that they would be necessary. That Alice girl would be good insurance.

Threatening her life would keep Francis suppressed and keep him from escaping and taking any unwise actions. Couldn't be too obvious about it though, the girl was a celebrity among the troops, and killing her would lower morale. The mercenaries were still needed for a little longer.

Bill nodded to the three guards standing over Francis before walking back outside. They had certainly proven their loyalty. The rest of the men were already unloading the large metal ring from one of their trucks that had just pulled close to the glowing Safezone barrier.

They all waited a few minutes to be sure that the Nameless was definitely dead. The mood was somber as many dragged the bodies of their dead comrades who had been closest to the telepathic assault to the side. All of them struck down by the creature's last gasp.

Four of the men heaved the large metal ring into the dome of light through the shield. It passed easily through the barrier. An instant after it entered its edges lit up and the dome of light shut off in an instant. All of them blinked to adjust their eyes as the second sun disappeared.

The layered shields deactivated, exposing the rubble and bloody chunks littering the former Safezone. The four men all lifted the now glowing metal ring again and carefully fitted it on top of the softly glowing golden pillar still standing in the rubble of the houses. The metal ring fell down the top half of the pillar before catching on a set of grooves near the center and stopping. It should be safe for transport now.

Bill's men could handle the pillar now that the absorption mode had been deactivated. Bill turned to Helen who was now standing next to him.

"Helen, you focus on getting Francis and that pillar back to base safely. We'll discuss what to do with him later. I want that energy in our main battery banks as soon as possible. Put that creature's energy to some good use. I'll stay behind with the rest of the troops in case there are any survivors from the Safezone."

Helen seemed a little hesitant at the mention of Francis but after only a moment's pause nodded and began sharply giving orders to the others. Bill gathered the elites that would remain behind.

"Alright men. It's unpleasant, but you know what we have to do. Let's move out. Search the area, and leave no witnesses."

Chapter 48: Escaping the Assault on the Club - Mortal Ryan Fragment

Ryan woke up with someone shaking his shoulder. Someone was whispering his name, "Ryan… Ryan, wake up."

He opened his eyes and blinked. He was startled at seeing Victor's face leaning over him wearing a look of concern.

Gus was sleeping nearby and Ryan accidentally bumped him as he went to stand. They still were cramped tight in small rooms even after all this time. It was for reducing the total defensible area or something like that. Everyone all compressed together practically on top of each other so there was less area to guard.

None of them liked it but after the others had seen some of the aliens prowling in the distance the complaints had faded away for a time. No one wanted to sleep alone and get ambushed if one of the aliens crept over the wall past the nightly patrols.

Gus groaned and rolled over and mumbled something. Ryan moved quietly after Victor who had put his finger to his lips and crept away.

Ryan tiptoed after him trying not to wake anyone else in the room up. They all needed their rest after that girl from the Neighborhood Watch had arrived. Whatever she had done had knocked most of them out including Ryan.

It seemed like some kind of accident but none of the people from the Neighborhood Watch would tell anyone what had happened. Their bulky Asian leader had looked pissed as he loaded the girl in his car and drove off. Victor had looked ashen when he recovered and had been quiet ever since yesterday when he woke back up.

Victor and Ryan left the house. Victor leaned in and appeared worried while he kept his voice low. "Ryan. Jim and Harry are missing. They should have woken us up for our watch hours ago."

Ryan nodded. He had thought the sun was higher than it was supposed to be. Over this week he had been doing watch rotations with the small group from the Neighborhood Watch as one of the few people with firearms training. He made sure to keep his voice low to match Victor, "Did you search the perimeter yet, maybe they just lost track of time on their shift?"

Victor shook his head. "That's what we're doing now. But I have a bad feeling. George and Marv are staying guard over the house while we go looking for them. We need to find out what could have happened."

With that, the two exited the walls and started walking around the exterior of the makeshift wall of cars and piled furniture. There were no signs of where Jim and Harry had gone. No bloodstains, no missing gear. They had just disappeared. The two of them heard the faint murmur of voices from within the Safezone.

Victor insisted on them doing another loop around the perimeter to look for clues. They were halfway through when Ryan heard something crunch behind them. He whirled around and raised the military-grade rifle that they had received in the shipment of weapons yesterday.

Ryan still had his trusty police pistol at his side on his hip as well. Luckily the Neighborhood Watch had at least given them plenty of ammunition for both weapons before the drama.

Catching sight of the face of the person behind them, Ryan lowered his rifle again, "Gus? What the hell are you doing out here?"

Gus glanced at Victor. Gus' limp had healed significantly in the last week since they had left the hospital. He was carrying that school backpack that he had found this Monday. He hadn't been separated from it ever since and carried it with him everywhere these days. People had been commenting on it recently but Gus just ignored them and clung to the bag even tighter.

"I wanted to ask Victor something away from the others. He's been avoiding me since yesterday." He turned to Victor, "You should hear this too Ryan." Gus narrowed his eyes as he stared down Victor. "I was by the door when you were talking to your boss. What are these supplies we aren't getting? Seems like they were pretty important given what happened."

Ryan turned to Victor who looked stuck in place with a conflicted look. "Well, It... well I can't be telling you about that. Confidential, Neighborhood Watch only."

Ryan stepped forward and furrowed his brow. "You sure? Seems pretty important. It's only the three of us here."

Victor struggled with himself for a moment. It looked like he wanted to tell them but knew he really wasn't supposed to. He opened his mouth.

Bang! A gunshot sounded out on the other side of the Safezone. There were crashes and screams seconds later as the three of them ducked and looked around frantically. An inhuman roar sounded out and a massive crash of screeching metal could be heard.

A massive vibration shook the ground and knocked them all from their feet and the air above the makeshift wall began to shimmer like a mirage for a second before turning invisible again.

Ryan started charging forward back to the Safezone entrance as he heard screams and more fleshy impacts and crashes behind the wall. A pair of hands held him back.

"Stop! We have to go!" Ryan struggled as Victor held him back. "No, we have to go back!"

"They're already dead. Here, watch."

Ryan stilled for a moment as Victor picked up a pebble and slung it over the wall. It stopped in midair in a flash of golden light and slid down on what Ryan could now see was an invisible dome.

"Do you see?" Victor said, "They're already trapped in there. We have to go now before the Neighborhood Watch catches us."

Gus stepped forward. "The Neighborhood Watch is behind this? Why?"

Victor looked frustrated and scared, "Look, I'll explain later. But we have to go *now*."

Gus looked to Ryan. Ryan nodded to him and Victor. The cries inside were already growing fainter amid the crashes. He was too late. He pushed down his burning anger towards Victor and tried to focus.

They had to get out of here. Ryan would beat the shit out of Victor later when they were all safe. They started rushing away on foot down the street. The sounds slowly faded behind them. But Ryan could somehow still hear the screams and impacts in his mind.

Victor darted into a few alleyways and Gus and Ryan followed him. Gus was panting hard and Ryan looked back to see the dome in the distance lit up like some kind of massive lightbulb. It kept growing brighter and brighter until Ryan had to look away as his eyes began to hurt.

They kept running. Gus was now holding his side and Ryan ran next to him and kept him upright when he stumbled over the scattered trash. Victor glanced back as he saw they were about to fall behind.

They ran and ran for what felt like miles. Finally, with Gus gasping and Ryan not feeling well himself, they stopped. Victor went to a nearby office building and smashed in one of the windows with the butt of his rifle. He cleared the glass shards with a swipe of his sleeve before carefully crawling through.

A few moments later the front door was unlocked and Ryan and Gus entered. Ryan attempted to say something but Victor shushed him. They moved to the third floor where they found an abandoned office where Victor locked the door. Gus and Ryan collapsed to the ground panting while Victor took some deep breaths. He barely looked winded. "I'll get you guys some water."

He left and Gus and Ryan eventually recovered their breath and wiped at their sweat from the run. Victor came back with a case of plastic water bottles that he handed out, "Found this in the supply closet downstairs" He said, "Dig in."

— — — O — o — O — — —

After the three of them were properly hydrated Ryan and Gus demanded answers from Victor. He seemed reluctant but after Ryan shouted at him eventually gave in. He explained all he knew about Potential and how he had been recruited as a mercenary to join the Neighborhood Watch a year ago.

He told them about all the amazing weapons and magic artifacts he had seen while working with the Neighborhood Watch. How he had suddenly been posted to the Safezone guard duty with little warning.

Ryan interrupted, unable to hold himself back any longer. "Why would they do this? Why try to trap all of us inside the zone with that creature to get killed? Did you know about this? Trying to go on patrol so you could save your own skin?!"

Ryan got in Victor's face and grabbed him by the lapel. They stared at each other for a moment.

"I... I don't know," Victor stammered, "Why did they do it? I don't know. I just knew something was wrong, that they were keeping us in the dark. I never imagined... that it was something like this. George and Harry were there too! If I was part of it I wouldn't have left them behind."

Ryan's anger cooled slightly and he pushed Victor away as he broke eye contact. Victor stumbled back and braced against the wall. It was true. Victor didn't seem like that cold of a bastard to leave his men behind. Ryan should save his anger for people who deserved it. If Victor had some conspiracy going on he wouldn't have saved Ryan, he would have saved one of his friends.

Gus finally piped in. "Why would the Neighborhood Watch hunt us afterwards though? Why would they care if we escaped?"

Victor shrugged. "We were mercenaries, not full members. They probably thought we were expendable. And we aren't the only safe zone. There are twenty-five total. Anyone who escaped like us could tell the others what really happened and cause trouble. The mercenaries they rely on would not like the picture our story would paint for their futures in the Neighborhood Watch. We were uneasy enough with all of this as it was."

Gus nodded. "Well let's do that then."

Victor looked at him like he was crazy. "Do you know what you are up against? Did you not see the giant shield dome trapping the people inside the Safezone? Their automatic weapons? Their numbers? We stand no chance if we or anyone else fights. We should hide as far from the hospital and the Ranch as we can and let the aliens and the Neighborhood Watch fight it out."

Ryan piped in, "No. How do we know they won't do this again? We have to at least let the people know first before we hide away."

Victor didn't look convinced, "Well, even if we tried to get there, how are we going to dodge both the aliens and the Neighborhood Watch at the same time? It's not like we could have dealt with the bigger Infected with the guns we have. It destroyed the wall in what felt like one hit."

Gus glanced from side to side and seemed to consider something as Ryan responded, "We just have to warn them and then run. We should do it soon before the Neighborhood Watch starts spreading their story of whatever happened."

Victor nodded, "True, but it's useless if we just get killed as soon as the first alien crawling around here gets the drop on us."

Gus cleared his throat and the two men looked at him. He reached into his backpack and withdrew a silvery magnum pistol. The pistol was covered in a network of glowing lines for a moment before the light faded. "I may have something. I didn't want to show anybody because it seemed important. Honestly, I thought you might take it from me, Victor."

Victor just stared in shock. He reached his hands out to inspect it but Gus quickly pulled it back and cradled it to his chest. He glared at Victor. "And I'm not handing it over now either! But it seems like it runs on this Potential thing you're talking about. So I figured I could help."

Ryan looked at the gleaming weapon. "Gus, where did you even get that? Is this why you've been carrying that backpack everywhere?"

Gus looked a little guilty. "Remember that big bloodstain on the road by that bombed-out office building?"

Ryan nodded. The night they had escaped the hospital.

"Well, it was on the street just sitting there. I hid it down in my pants until I found the backpack. I didn't want anyone to know about it. For good reason, it seems." He turned to Victor. "Anyway, any idea what it does?"

Gus held it out while keeping a firm grip on it. Victor inspected it for a moment, "No idea," he eventually said.

The two of them looked at him in disbelief. Victor glared at them in response. "What? I shoot guns, not make them. Let alone ones that use Potential. Do you have the slightest idea how complicated that shit is? Someone tried explaining it once and I felt like my brain would explode. I can't tell what it does just by looking at it."

Gus looked down at the gun. "Well, guess I'll just have to test it then."

Victor looked a little more worried. The stress seemed to be getting to him. "Careful. That thing only has six shots. Don't want to waste them, I don't have the right ammo for that thing. I doubt anyone but the Neighborhood Watch does."

Gus grumbled a bit but didn't end up saying anything else, taking the point. Ryan wanted to head out immediately to warn the other Safezones, but Victor convinced the both of them to wait. They had to hide and wait for the Neighborhood Watch to clear out before they could move. Otherwise, they might just be caught and executed immediately as they traveled to the closest Safezone. Or at least that was Victor's opinion.

About two hours later, Victor finally felt safe enough that Gus and Ryan convinced him to leave their hiding hole. Victor's arguments made it clear he was far more frightened of the Neighborhood Watch finding them than the inhuman aliens.

The trio broke into the garage of a nearby home, found a set of bicycles, and used them to quickly bike close to Safezone Six. The bikes were quiet, which was most important since they were trying to travel undetected.

There were a few humanoid Infected surrounded by crowds of smaller dog-sized creatures they encountered on the way. The aliens chased after them, but the groups were slow enough that the three easily outpaced them on bikes. Well, needless to say, they all pedaled a lot faster when they were being chased. But still, they didn't exactly have to bust their asses to escape either.

Finally, they were almost within sight of it. There was no pile of cars and furniture around this zone. There was a wall of hardened dirt and some of the surrounding buildings appeared to have been demolished to create a clear space between the hard-packed dirt walls and the closest buildings. There was the same distortion of a shield as before over the walls. They could faintly see several people patrolling around the walls as they approached. Before they drew too close the three stashed their bikes in a nearby alley.

"Bastards," Victor whispered under his breath as he saw how much more secure this place was than Safezone Seven had been. Ryan and Gus muttered softly in agreement with him. Victor turned to Ryan and Gus. "How are we gonna do this?" Victor asked, "It's your idea after all."

Ryan and Gus looked at each other. Gus hesitantly nodded at Ryan. "Well, you're a cop, right? It's probably better coming from you once we talk to people inside."

Gus turned to Victor. "But you are part of the Neighborhood Watch. They're the ones that are probably guarding the walls. You are the one that has to get us in in the first place."

Victor opened his mouth and tried to refute the logic but couldn't come up with anything. His jaw worked back and forth. Victor sat back. "Alright. Ugh, just give me a minute. I gotta think about what I'm going to say. Probably best to play dumb until we're inside. But what if they ask…"

His volume dropped until he was mumbling to himself as he stared at the floor. Ryan and Gus waited. Ryan mentally prepared what he would say himself once they got inside. Finally, Victor finished and looked up. He took a deep breath, "Alright, I'm ready," Victor said, "Let's go."

Chapter 49: The Neighborhood Watch Revealed to the World - Multiple Fragments of Memory

——— **Mortal President Harrow Fragment of Memory. Third Thursday. Roughly one week after the prior Fragment of Memory** ———

President Harrow and the generals watched on the screen as the series of missiles tracked their target. The weapons cost millions of dollars to build each, and they had just launched twenty all at once in this barrage. Onto their own country's soil.

Two missiles slammed home simultaneously and delivered their payload near the top of the dome. It was verified that the dome was stronger the closer it was to the ground so the assault would come directly above from the sky. The three following missiles flew through the sudden gap in the shields and delivered the payload at their targets.

Two more missiles opened a hole in the top of the dome in a different location. Three more missiles went through and exploded at their destinations as well. The oldest opening was already healing shut. Two more holes in the shield. One for each of the cardinal directions. Ten more missiles. The very top of the shield was flickering on and off as the dome struggled to heal the damage. The shield almost looked like it might recover…

Then the bunker buster was dropped from the bomber that had passed overhead seconds ago landed. It struck the top of the shield dead center. In a massive fireball, it tore the shield wide open, causing the whole top portion of the dome to flicker on and off. The explosion continued expanding and all at once the shield shut down. The dome had fallen.

The President and Generals watched in anticipation hoping the dome would fall for good, but it was no use. The walls of the dome were slowly crawling upwards from the ground even as they watched.

Another massive bomb landed directly on the hospital where the aliens had gathered, consuming it in a massive explosion of fire. The hole in the shield was now kilometers wide but the dome looked like it would be repaired within the hour. The generals looked to President Harrow for a decision.

The president sighed, "Send in the paratroopers. They'll have to work from the inside."

The planes were already flying over and wave after wave of uniformed men started jumping out and began plummeting to the ground. They angled themselves so they would land closest to the edges of the dome. The planes continued flying over and deploying a squad one after another over the course of half an hour.

The white dots of deployed parachutes covered the skies of the town of Harmony. About three thousand troops in total made their way inside. Beyond that point, it was deemed too dangerous to send more and it was called to a stop. The healing of the shield was accelerating and none of them wanted any of the soldiers to hit the shield before they could deploy their parachutes.

The dust had finally cleared in the strike zone where the aliens had gathered. At least some of those fleshy spires looked like they had been destroyed. The hospital was leveled and there was something shifting from within the rubble.

President Harrow looked on as the last plane flew over. They had to wait for the last moment to make sure their soldiers would be clear.

The shield was healing even more rapidly as it started getting closer to the apex. President Harrow gave the order. The bomb dropped. The hole in the dome was barely a hundred meters wide by now, but the last bomb fell through the gap in time. It landed directly on the hospital again and exploded into a massive burst of burning liquid Napalm that coated the area in sticky flames.

The dome fully healed and the images underneath grew blurry again. But even through the distortion, the satellites could see the burning flames. They could only hope that their bombs eliminated enough of the aliens to allow their soldiers to deal with the rest.

———O—o—O———

Infiltrator of Authority was organizing another assault group to attack the mortals near the edge of its territory when it heard explosions directly overhead. It looked up to see three metal tubes pierce the dome barrier and fly down directly towards the hospital. Infiltrator of Authority's eyes widened.

The mortals outside had pierced the dome and were launching an assault. Infiltrator of Authority started spending all its banked Potential and released a massive telepathic wave to connect to its subordinates.

The missiles slowly descended as if through honey in Infiltrator of Authority's perception. They were aimed directly at three clusters of the Spires of Growth on the roofs of the buildings near the hospital.

All of the Nameless and spawnlings in the dome froze all at once as Infiltrator of Authority linked with them all at once. The ones currently in battle were cut down quickly, but it hardly mattered. Infiltrator of Authorities force was about to take far heavier losses than that.

As one all the gathered Nameless and spawnlings threw themselves onto their closest Spire of Growth. They spent their Potential deforming their bodies and anchoring themselves in place.

They quickly fused together and grew layers of bone plating on their backs to protect the Spires of Growth. Their bodies flattened and curled around the spires of growth protectively. The next in line would leap on the pile and quickly do the same. The Nameless sank inward to the center of the growing balls of flesh while the spawnlings rose to the top.

The larger numbers of spawnlings and Nameless milling around the hospital rushed to the Tower of Decay and used themselves to create a fleshy shield in a similar way. The more valuable Nameless with useful Potential were mobbed as well. All of the important assets had to be protected. Each received a protective ball consisting of their nearby brethren.

The clusters of Spires of Growth the first three mortal missiles targeted were already lost causes. Even under Infiltrator of Authority's increased perceptions, there wasn't enough time. They were immediately destroyed in a ball of fire seconds later as the missiles delivered their explosive payloads.

The assault group around Infiltrator of Authority began to throw themselves onto it and began the same process of mutating into a protective ball of flesh around it. Infiltrator of Authority kept burning its Potential as it enhanced its telepathic link to direct the formation of the shield balls throughout the whole dome and assist in improving the linkages between the component bodies.

The next set of missiles hit three more clusters. The spawnlings and half of the Nameless in those areas were destroyed. Of the twenty Spires of Growth targeted only seven were preserved. The next set of missiles hit. All the spawnlings died and a quarter of the Nameless in those zones.

Only four Spires of Growth were destroyed this time as Infiltrator of Authority rapidly improved their defenses by the second. The final round of three missiles landed a minute later and even some of the spawnlings survived this time. None of the Spires of Growth perished. Infiltrator of Authority didn't relax and kept reinforcing the protective balls. More must be coming.

There was a pause as the dust from the various explosions and collapsed buildings covered the area in a thick fog. Five minutes passed and some of the spawnlings began to detach. There was another massive explosion above them and the ground shook but did no damage to any of the beings below.

Infiltrator of Authority spent another burst of Potential to strengthen its telepathic link again, reprimanding all of them to remain still and continue reinforcing their shields. They complied quickly. The mortals had still not struck the Hospital directly yet, the true explosion targeting them could come at any moment. Infiltrator of Authority waited.

Sure enough, a second bomb fell through the gap to strike the hospital, and shattered it into pieces. The building was flattened. The Tower of Decay was severely injured and all the beings attached to it were dead or nearly so. But its condition was stable and it would recover given enough time and food.

Fifteen minutes since the initial barrage. Infiltrator of Authority telepathically connected to one of the spawnlings on the outside of its protective ball and looked up. Humans with parachutes were entering through a massive hole in the dome above. The remaining portions of the dome were brightly lit and violently distorted the surroundings like a mirage in the desert.

The walls were slowly climbing, repairing the damage. It was slowly healing back. Infiltrator of Authority began moving most of the spawnlings to cover the Tower of Decay inside of the hospital. If that was lost then it would take days and nearly half of the surviving unmutated Nameless to reconstruct. It had to be saved or the invasion would be severely weakened.

Infiltrator of Authority assisted its subordinates in creating the best shield possible with their bodies with the limited Potential available as they jumped onto the Tower of Decay and melded with it to protect it.

It had been twenty-five minutes from the initial assault by the mortals. The hole in the dome was closing and human soldiers were still parachuting in in large numbers.

Unfortunately, they weren't landing here. Refreshing its forces' Potential with fresh bodies would be ideal after this attack. But the soldiers were unfortunately steering to the edge of the dome instead. Into the Neighborhood Watch's territory. Was the Neighborhood Watch working with the army and calling for reinforcements?

Thirty-five minutes had passed. Infiltrator of Authority directed the mutations of the spawnlings in the growing the shields on the top of the collapsed Tower of Decay. They would work to ward off the next assault from the sky. The shield was nearly finished. No more humans came through the rapidly shrinking hole in the dome above them.

The ball of protective flesh around Infiltrator of Authority twitched impatiently. They did not understand the second wave of missiles was coming at any moment. Infiltrator of Authority did not explain and simply ordered them to be still and they were.

It was burning Potential madly extending its telepathic range so far and wide. This body couldn't handle the biological structures required and so constantly was breaking down and had to be healed. Forty minutes. The spawnling Infiltrator of Authority was looking through and saw a final bomb as Infiltrator of Authority had expected.

The bomb fell slowly and appeared fatter than the prior bombs. Like an oversized metal egg. After a long moment of falling, it exploded into a massive ball of liquid flame in mid-air. The burning fluid hung in the air for a moment before it began to fall. It would be upon them in moments.

Infiltrator of Authority immediately panicked. It sent a frantic telepathic message to the shield bodies. *'DEVOURING FLAME! DETACH CONNECTIONS BETWEEN SHIELD LAYERS. DETACH NOW! EJECT ANY FLESH THAT TOUCHES THE FLAME! PROTECT THE SPIRES AND TOWER AT ALL COST!'*

The liquid flame descended as Infiltrator of Authority spent its Potential like water increasing its perception so it could shift the shields into a series of thinner onion layers that could at least impede the spread of the Devouring Flame. How had the mortals even created such a large amount of Devouring flame?!

This volume of flame at all at once represented hundreds of thousands of sacrifices based on the Potential of those in this town it had observed. And that was assuming they built it perfectly the first time.

The sky was filled with flames and Infiltrator of Authority could only despair as the end of the invasion drew closer. All its preparations, all its planning. For nothing. It knew that all of its frantic actions were useless.

The Devouring Flame had a mind of its own. When it finished consuming the outer layers it would simply leap onto the next. The mortals were smart. Somehow they must have known the invasion's defensive strategy. The first round of explosions forced them to gather together into their shields.

Gathering all their Potential-infused flesh all in one place so none could escape the following wave of Devouring Flame. Infiltrator of Authority would return to its true body weakened and humiliated, its invasion defeated by the mortals within weeks of discovery. All the Potential of this body would be burned away by the Flame.

Infiltrator of Authority closed its metaphorical eyes as it saw the doom of its glorious invasion approach slowly but inevitably in its rapidly accelerated perception. The flames washed over the protective balls. The first layer of flesh began to burn and those spawnlings were dutifully expelled.

They screamed and burned for several moments. The liquid flame reduced their flailing bodies into charred corpses. Infiltrator of Authority internally sighed and waited for the inevitable.

Infiltrator of Authority waited. And waited. And waited even more. The Devouring Flame did not leap from its place to the next layer of Potential-infused flesh. It coated the ground and burned, releasing heavy black smoke. Infiltrator of Authority simply stared through the new spawnling it had inhabited after the first was consumed by flame. It watched as the flames slowly died down and how they barely spread when they licked the outside of the fleshy spheres, charring but not seeking out the flesh hungrily.

Infiltrator of Authority let out a sigh of relief and began laughing hysterically from within its cocoon. Its true body's frills vibrated as the laughter shook both bodies. Its true body's tentacles thrashed and destroyed its surroundings as it released the accumulated stress. It had thought too much of these mortals! They had dared to use *mundane* flames against them.

Infiltrator of Authority had thought it was all over, but the mortals had to be woefully misinformed if they believed that mundane flame would be able to do more than inconvenience its forces.

It should have been furious, enraged! It had wasted so much precious Potential in its panic. But it could only feel relief as it laughed. It would have another chance! It wasn't over! It had thought that this must have been another plan of mortal Bill, but it couldn't have been. Bill knew an uncomfortable amount about the Invasion and the Avatar, he wouldn't be this sloppy.

After letting out all its pent-up emotions, Infiltrator of Authorities laughter quickly petered out. It had been lucky this time, saved by the foolishness of the mortals and not its own tactical genius. It was a sobering realization for a being as ancient as it.

It would have to take the mortals a little more seriously. It should have focused and planned more once it discovered Bill had slain the Betrayer by some unknown method. Infiltrator of Authority had known there would be some kind of trap, but it hadn't expected the mortal to have something *that* effective prepared. That should have made it more cautious than it had been.

Infiltrator of Authority hadn't even been able to get its forces there in time to discover the method behind the trap. It was still a mystery. The area had been deserted and any formations or weapons removed from the site before it had arrived.

If the mortals outside had been as informed as Bill clearly was, then it might have all been over. Above Infiltrator of Authority, the dome sealed shut. The distortions in the light settled down before it settled back down to its natural slight distortions once more.

In relief, Infiltrator of Authority gave the order. The spawnlings and Nameless composing the protective balls began to detach and return their forms to their natural state.

They all spread out to inspect the damage of their forces. Infiltrator of Authority mutated its brain back to humanoid standard to stop the constant drain from healing the damage resulting from the more advanced telepathic structures. The spawnlings began to search the area for more foliage to feed the Tower of Decay to accelerate its healing.

All the buildings in their surroundings were leveled, leaving a massive field of rubble only broken up by the surviving Spires of Growth and the wounded Tower of Decay sticking above the rubble. Little pockets of mundane flame still burned in the whole area, belching out that thick black smoke into the air.

Infiltrator of Authority inspected its remaining forces. Its numbers of Nameless charged with Potential were down to three-quarters of their former numbers. And that was counting the Spires of Growth that required the sacrifice of at least one Nameless to create. The spawnlings' numbers were devastated and had barely a tenth of their former legions remaining. But their population would recover quickly. They were meant to be expendable luckily and so they were a small loss to the invasion.

More importantly, Infiltrator of Authority had spent large chunks of its saved Potential in its rush to prepare the defenses and its brief panic. It could no longer transform itself into a frontline fighter as it had wished to before. It would have to become a strategist and sit in safety so it could rebuild its Potential back to acceptable levels. Likely for the best.

If the invasion was to succeed Infiltrator of Authority would have to carefully manage its forces, not relish in its bloodlust as it desired to. Infiltrator of Authority returned to directing its forces in the cleanup and distribution of the remaining biomass.

The native life in the area was nearly depleted and the gathering groups were growing uncomfortably close to the human Safezones, where they might be hunted by the Neighborhood Watch.

The remaining black fluid left in the pool under the rubble would only be used for the spawnlings that were absolutely starving. Repairing the Tower was the most important thing right now. After it healed, the Tower of Decay would be able to process biomass into Potential with the highest efficiency so the Invasions' forces would not starve.

Its forces were battered, but Infiltrator of Authority had learned. It could no longer be complacent. After this setback, its forces would return with a vengeance. And when it was done and ready to strike back, the mortals wouldn't know what had hit them.

Part Four: War Against the New Neighbors

Chapter 50: Messenger to the New Club - Mortal Ryan Fragment

Ryan and Gus followed Victor out the door, Victor trying to appear casual as the three started circling the walls of Safezone Six. They slowly circled the perimeter until they found a gap blocked by a car, the gate. They emerged into the no man's land of destroyed and open space. The sentries on the wall finally noticed them as they walked forward and there was some movement as they approached.

"Stop!" One man shouted.

The three of them halted and put their hands in the air. They waited and something shifted in the rubble nearby. They turned, but there wasn't any more movement. *It must have just been the rubble settling.* Ryan thought.

One of the members of the Neighborhood Watch peeked over the edge of the wall. He squinted at the group for a moment before his eyes settled on Victor and his matching black gear of the Neighborhood Watch. He shouted behind him and Ryan saw flashes of movement showing the others were there but letting that one do the talking.

"What are you doing here?" The man asked them, "Rays of the Moon."

Victor raised his voice. "Survivors of Safezone Seven. It was attacked by the Infected. The Wolf Awakens."

"Go away and regroup at the evacuation point two. Return and re-secure your zone with those gathered there…"

There was a commotion and the speaker ducked down behind the wall again. The three of them could hear some furious muttering from the wall. There seemed to be some sort of argument brewing and the speaker from before shushed them. The muttering continued at a lower volume as the speaker argued with others who were out of sight. The three of them shifted as they were ignored for over two minutes.

Eventually, another person popped up over the wall. "Come in. We would like a full report to send back to the Ranch before we make any decisions on redeployments."

He glared down behind him somewhere before the engine on the truck blocking the entrance started. The vehicle backed up and opened a gap for the three of them to enter. The shield rippled and a small hole in its rippling surface opened in the gap left by the truck. The three quickly squeezed through only to be surrounded by nearly a dozen members of the Neighborhood Watch.

The gap in the shield behind them closed. In the distance, a large crowd of normal townspeople were gathered. They all looked a little haggard but seemed mostly healthy. They were whispering to each other and eyed the new arrivals.

This zone must be holding hundreds of people at least. All three of them looked around in disbelief at the numbers and size of this place. Safezone Seven had had less than sixty people total. Only seven of them including Ryan had been guarding their wall in shifts.

Had the Neighborhood Watch made their zone so small on purpose? So they would be more vulnerable? Gus nudged Ryan with his foot, and Ryan noticed that his rage had come to the surface, causing him to glower and grit his teeth at the people around them. Deep breaths in. Deep breaths out. He pushed it back down. He couldn't let his rage out like he had with… Fulcrum.

Wow, Ryan had almost forgotten his outburst at the hospital given everything that had happened afterwards. He wondered if Fulcrum had been replaced with one of the alien parasites or if he had escaped. Ryan felt conflicted about how to feel if Fulcrum had truly become an Infected.

Ryan had hated the man for so many years he wasn't sure what he would do if he was truly dead. And it was such an undeserved end too. Caught up in an alien invasion like a natural disaster. Wrong place, wrong time. There was no sense of justice to it. No sense of fulfillment. Ryan would never get his answers on what had really happened to his sister Jessica.

It brought back other memories Ryan had been trying to avoid. About Officer Sanchez and everyone Ryan had left behind at that hospital. How he had left that bombed-out office building and never returned to check for survivors. He had been swept up in the moment and hadn't remembered his promise to himself until days later.

By then he was told by Jim and Victor that it was too late and that it wasn't worth the risk of traveling there, and had let himself be convinced to stay. At the hospital, Ryan had given his warning over the radio, and he could only hope it allowed some to escape before it all went to shit. But He felt like he should have done more somehow.

But no matter what he thought of, he knew nothing was plausible. No one would have believed his story without proof. If he became too convincing the Infected would have just attacked him to shut him up. His best option at the time had been to escape with the one person he had saved. At least that is what he told himself.

"What are you doing outside your zone with two civilians?" The first speaker from the wall who had told them to leave said.

The first speaker on the wall had pushed through the surrounding Neighborhood Watch and had his chest puffed out with an aggressive edge to his tone. The man's sharp tone snapped Ryan out of his spiraling thoughts.

Victor stepped to meet the man and met his eyes. Victor poked a finger on the man's chest. "There is no zone, you dick. Why are you trying to throw us into the jaws of the Infected? Have something to share with the group?" The man glared at them but didn't respond.

Many of his colleagues were looking at the man askance. He seemed to realize whatever his rank was might not be enough to pacify them and backed down slightly. To Ryan, it was clear the man knew what had really happened and was trying to shoo them away before they could tell their story. Victor continued, "Or maybe there's something you don't want us to share, huh?"

The man had a more defensive posture now but rallied after a moment. "Ridiculous! I just don't trust you three coming from nowhere. How do we know you aren't alien infiltrators!"

The surrounding Neighborhood Watch didn't seem fully convinced by the argument but at least some nodded in agreement. Victor just scoffed. "Do we seem like emotionless robots right now? And didn't I know the passphrase? Because I and everyone else can tell you're just pissing us off with your bullshit." Victor pointed at Ryan.

Ryan blinked before realizing he was gritting his teeth and glaring again. This guy was definitely aware of what had happened and was trying to cover it up! Shit. More deep breaths. Calm. Don't explode. Calm.

The man spluttered for a moment and seemed to know he had lost the argument and pivoted. "Well, our orders are to reject anyone that attempts to make it inside. Regardless if you're actually Infected or not, we shouldn't have even let you inside. It's a risk to everyone."

The man who had ordered them to let them in stepped forward. "Sir, you need to stand down. You know this wasn't what the orders meant. It clearly meant to check if they were humans before letting them in. And they seem pretty human to me."

The people around them nodded. The man who appeared to be the leader looked around and appeared to be worried as he realized he had lost. Probably worried he would be exposed for whatever he knew about the massacre of Safezone Seven.

Good, he should be worried. With a huff, he grumbled but finally stopped arguing as the three of them were ushered further into the zone. The crowd kept at a distance but still watched them intently. It seems that without screens they were resorting to other forms of entertainment.

Victor cleared his throat as they approached a home that appeared to be the central building. "Can we give our story in front of everyone? That way we don't have to say it twice."

The leader looked like he was about to jump in, but their defender silenced him with a look. He looked back at Victor. "I think we're all curious about what's happened. That's fine. Better to direct than allow it to get distorted through the gossip. But no sudden moves. Just because you're human doesn't mean we should trust you completely." He patted his side which held a holstered pistol and shot all three of them a sharp look.

Victor nodded back. With that understood, the three of them were ushered to the front porch of the base, surrounded by the dozen members of the Neighborhood Watch. A crowd of over a hundred townspeople gathered around on the lawn and street nearby.

The friendly member of the Neighborhood Watch handed them a megaphone. "Here. We use this for announcements since we have so many people."

Victor took it and handed it to Ryan. Victor patted him on the back. He drew close and whispered in his ear. "Alright, Ryan. Don't freeze up now, I'll watch your back. No matter what happens just keep talking. I'm sure the leader here will try to cut you off in some way. Gus and I will keep him off you."

Ryan's hands were shaking. He had done crowd control during his job on some events as big as this before but had never been the focus of attention. He flipped the switch and activated the handheld megaphone.

"Hello!" The crowd and Ryan winced as one at the volume. "Oh, sorry. Wait, give me a second..." Ryan lowered the volume to a more reasonable level. "I've just traveled here from what used to be Safezone Seven." His voice grew steadier as he spoke.

"Just a few hours ago, we were attacked by the Infected. We think everyone there has been killed except for us." The crowd murmured and the members of the Neighborhood Watch perked up.

"I woke up this morning to Victor here shaking me awake..." Ryan narrated the facts of what happened as objectively as he could. Why they had survived. How a single large unstoppable creature had attacked and rampaged through their zone. The shield that formed, trapping all the people inside to be slaughtered. Ryan made sure to emphasize that even the remaining members of the Neighborhood Watch except Victor had been killed as well.

The leader began pushing forward but was held back by his own men. Their faces were stony as they picked up the implications of Ryan's words. They didn't need to be told who could have deployed that shield. A few seemed doubtful, but seeing their commander sweating and weakly protesting in the grip of their comrades seemed to convince most to at least listen.

Ryan didn't speculate at all, just stated what he had directly seen. The crowd seemed frightened and slightly confused. Only a few had picked up on the subtext and the similarities between the protective shield over their zone and the shield that had trapped the people in Safezone Seven. They edged to the back of the crowd and began throwing suspicious glances at the members of the Neighborhood Watch.

Ryan made sure to state the leader's response to their arrival, which made the man's face grow pale. He knew that he would get no pity if it was discovered he was involved somehow...

"And then we came here," Ryan finished, "Victor here knows a little more on the Neighborhood Watch side."

Victor stepped up and some of the Neighborhood Watch went to stop him. It seemed they didn't want him to spill some of their secrets. But Gus began arguing with them and their leader's vocal support of their actions caused the people from the Neighborhood Watch to hesitate and reconsider.

Eventually, they let him speak after warning him about not exposing too much. It was a perfunctory warning though without much bite. It seemed they were just as disturbed and curious as the restless crowd about what had happened.

Victor spoke of their zone's small size and population. How they never received the powerful Potential-based defenses. How he never even realized they were supposed to have them. How that girl had activated the stone pillar, knocking out and weakening more than half of them only days ago. His version of events from them coming here. Victor trailed off, finished with his speech.

There was a moment of tension as no one in the large crowd spoke, just processing the information. Then the people erupted into shouted questions and demands for answers. Everyone had realized the connection between their own shield and the one that had trapped the people in Safezone Seven by now.

The members of the Neighborhood Watch were shooting dark looks at their former leader and quickly dragged him into the main house and shut the door, ignoring the crowd and the man's shouts.

Three guards remained behind as Ryan, Gus, and Victor were bombarded by worried questions from the crowd. Ryan was surprised they even believed their story. But it seems the abrupt reaction of the Neighborhood Watch had been enough for them. They fretted and worried, trying to get the smallest details from the three. The three did their best to survive the verbal barrage and reply as best as they could.

— — — O — o — O — — —

After what felt like hours later, the three listless men were left to themselves by the crowd. Ryan felt like he had been squeezed dry and pummeled based on how the crowd had surrounded him and assaulted him with their barrage of questions. None of the Neighborhood Watch had emerged from the main house yet.

The three remaining guards in the area were doing their best to maintain order but looked worn out themselves and frequently glanced back to the main house as if hoping for relief from the crowds.

More members of the Neighborhood Watch were still patrolling the walls, peering inwards occasionally to inspect the growing chaos, but they still seemed unaware of what exactly had happened. Ryan flopped to the ground and leaned against a nearby wall. Gus and Victor sat down to join him and they sat in silence.

"Well, at least they believed us," Victor eventually said.

Gus looked at the milling crowd whispering to each other animatedly.

"Should we do anything else?" Gus asked.

Ryan shook his head. "No. We should wait to see what the Neighborhood Watch people here think. Only that leader guy seemed to know. The rest were just as shocked as the crowd."

Victor sighed, "They're mercenaries like me mostly. They know never to fully trust their employer. They'll do whatever they can to save their own skins first. They will realize that if it can happen to us then it can happen to anyone."

Gus mumbled under his breath. "Anyone, huh? Anyone indeed…"

Chapter 51: Club to Battle - Mortal Ryan Fragment

Eventually, the members of the Neighborhood Watch emerged from their base, the leader now missing. They announced to the crowd that the trio's words had been confirmed by their former leader, disturbing the restless crowd even more.

The mercenaries renounced the Neighborhood Watch and said they never agreed with these kinds of actions and announced that they should relocate before the next resupply from the Neighborhood Watch. No one wanted to see what they would do to the rebels, least of all the former Neighborhood Watch mercenaries who knew more than anyone about their true capabilities.

It was left unsaid that the mercenaries wouldn't have taken action if not for Victor's account that their own people had been killed as well. A minority of the crowd protested the decision to break away, fearful of an alien attack and losing the shields.

The former members of the Neighborhood Watch assured them that they knew how to take it with them if they were careful. Victor had raised his brow, but as they began packing things away it became evident they were telling the truth as they debated the needed order of removal of the various stones from the formation amongst each other intelligently when the time came to remove them.

Time passed quickly. Ryan, Gus, and Victor quickly met many of the people in Safezone Six over the next two days. Everyone worked packing as much equipment as possible into the working vehicles they could find. There was only a limited amount of gas left for the vehicles and many people were siphoning gas from idle cars in the area into big cans.

On Sunday, everyone was finally packed up and ready to leave. Given the large number of people they would be splitting the transport into several trips, one every couple hours. The armed men were still running things and had decided on a new location to settle at. It would be on the other side of the dome as the Neighborhood Watch's main base, the Ranch, apparently, meaning they would have to go back through the former area of Safezone Seven before circling around behind the other Safezones to get to the other side. Ryan, Victor, and Gus were going on the first train of vehicles as guides.

This trip would only carry only around forty people and prioritize the supplies to establish the new base. The trio were most familiar with the area apparently so they would guide them for the first trip. The vehicle under Ryan's feet rumbled to life and began pulling away, Ryan in the vehicle at the front of the train.

The convoy moved slowly with all of them on guard for movement. Luckily, the area was abandoned as they made their way through. No humans, no Infected to be seen. They made sure to avoid the remnants of Safezone Seven. Ryan let out a sigh of relief once they were through and put Safezone Eight between them and the hospital The journey was uneventful as they traveled all the way to their destination.

It was as close to the edge of the dome as they could get without being targeted by the repellant mental wards. The mercenaries set up a spare shield in the area and started fortifying the area. It seemed that the mercenaries had a backup weaker shield in case the one in the old zone were to fail.

All the supplies and soldiers unloaded and began to make the area more defensible as Ryan helped unload the various boxes from the trucks. After an hour they were done and the new safe zone was starting to be built. A skeleton crew was left in the zone as the armed mercenaries took the vehicles and began driving back to Safezone six.

The next load would be mostly people. The trio of them would have to go back and forth for each trip, acting as guides, as the mercenaries were unfamiliar with the area and no one wanted to become lost on their way.

The convoy would be trying to get just under half of the remaining people ferried across on the next trip to their new spot. In case something happened, they didn't want to have the last trip carrying the people. Instead, it was planned to hold the remaining supplies that were less critical and had been left behind for the first trip.

The drivers of the convoy would have to be extra careful as that would be when the former Neighborhood Watch would be deactivating and taking the main shield and Potential battery or stone pillar in the center which would be critical for the new base to be secure over time for that last trip. The barrier set up here was strong and stable, but nowhere near as strong as the one left behind, Ryan was told.

The convoy quickly returned to the old safe zone and the people there were stuffed into the cars, and they set off again.

Ryan and a former member of the Neighborhood Watch that he didn't recognize were joined by four townspeople crowded tightly in the backseat of the military vehicle in the convoy after they returned to Safezone Six. He was more towards the center of the time with Victor taking the front as guide for the lead car. Everyone in Ryan's car was silent, knowing any extra noise could draw attention to themselves. They continued like that for a while with no one speaking.

Ryan almost nodded off as he sat there, the sun shining onto his face. None of them had been sleeping well recently in the packed confines of the safe zones, so Ryan had been catching on his sleep whenever he could.

They were halfway through the old safe zone seven territory when there was a sudden burst of motion to the side of the train of vehicles. In the distance a hulking beast ten feet tall had rounded around the corner a ways off from the four way intersection they were currently passing through and spotted the convoy.

It looked like an armored humanoid with an armadillo head and bony shell on its back. It had long wicked sharp claws on the end of its long arms and hands. Its back and shell was covered in dozens of long bony spikes sticking out every which way haphazardly.

A carpet of small fleshy orbs with protruding tentacles followed behind it and even clung to its hunched shelled back in many cases. The humanoid creature pointed at the line of vehicles with one finger and let out a high pitched screech.

People in the convoy began shouting as the vehicles accelerated, suddenly throwing them back. The armadillo creature took a few ponderously slow steps towards them. Then slightly faster ones. Faster, faster.

It was building its momentum as the line of vehicles sped up to dangerous speeds to attempt to clear the intersection in time for its arrival. They were a fifteen minutes drive from the new base, too far if this thing caught up to them.

Ryan snapped awake from his shock and pulled his pistol from his holster, holding it in one hand while using his other hand to brace himself against the dash of the car. The lurches as their car sped up and stopped to avoid crashing into others were throwing Ryan forward and back violently as he twisted to get a better view of the creature's charge.

Many vehicles in the convoy had split off and taken sudden turns into the alleyways, scattering like disturbed insects from a rolled over log. The bone plated creature quickly barreled forward and approached faster by the second. It lowered its shoulder as it tore up the concrete with every step of its clawed feet.

With a crashing of metal, the creature barreled through the car second to last in the convoy. The car folded inwards like a pancake and went flipping in the air into a nearby building. The creature skidded to a stop, digging in its heels, and barely avoided crashing through the building itself. After finally teetering to a stop, it quickly snapped its head to the hole the van had made in the building in front of it.

After a few moments, it stomped into the hole of the building after the van it had thrown through it. Ryan checked his gun as the civilians in the car continued screaming while the driver was silent and laser focused on avoiding the parked cars on the side of the street.

The man made one abrupt turn and the wheels screeched and the truck swerved from side to side, nearly spinning out of control. Ryan cursed as his arm with the gun swung to the side, cracking the passenger's side window slightly from the force of the blow of metal on the glass.

The last car in the convoy swerved and skidded out of control as it failed to avoid one of the parked cars in the chaos and crashed. It hit the parked car before tipping over onto its side and sliding on the street with a spray of sparks. From the hole in the building where the large creature had entered, the tentacled orbs emerged and rolled quickly towards the stranded vehicle as it lay unmoving on the ground.

The tentacled orbs descended onto it and broke through the windows with a few heavy impacts before rushing inside like a swarm of locusts. Ryan looked back and saw that the repurposed moving van with Gus and the largest group of people was still directly behind Ryan's vehicle.

With a crash the armadillo creature emerged from the building covered in red gore and the small fleshy balls clinging to it. The swarming creatures boiled out of the crashed car to leap back onto the armadillo creature's shell. The swarm and humanoid began to chase after Ryan and Gus' vehicles in front of it. All the convoy vehicles in front of them had just finished scattering into the alleyways nearby, leaving Ryan and the moving van of people to themselves to be chased by the creature.

Ryan's driver floored it. The truck bucked as it quickly accelerated, and for a moment they gained some distance before the humanoid's momentum in a straight line began to allow it to catch up to them.

The swarm of orbs on its shelled back were clinging on tight as it picked up speed, and Ryan just knew they were waiting to pounce when they got close enough. The larger moving van struggled to match the acceleration of Ryan's much smaller truck. Ryan rolled down the window of the truck ignoring the shouting of the people behind him.

He stuck his head out with the wind whipping around him. Seeing his actions, the driver reluctantly slowed down to match the pace of the truck behind them. The humanoid was catching up to the moving van and the people, its posture hunched as it accelerated more with every moment. It grew closer as Ryan swayed and tried to aim his pistol while being buffeted by the wind as he struggled to not fall out of the swerving van.

The creature uncurled and raised its massive clawed arm into the sky as it lunged forward when it was only twenty feet away from the moving van. Its long claws gleamed in the sun, and Ryan aimed his pistol and fired as quickly as he could, shouting as he did, aiming for the thing's head.

After four shots of his pistol Ryan lurched and almost fell out the window as the truck suddenly swerved beneath him, but Ryan felt hands grab him and heave him back inside. Ryan ignored the others in his truck grabbing him by his shirt to keep him from falling out. He stuck himself out the window again and unloaded the rest of his pistol's ammo into the creature's face in the distance as its arm descended onto the moving truck behind them with the people inside.

Most of Ryan's shots glanced off the bone plating of its chest but one lucky shot pierced one of its beady black eyes. It flinched and its overhead claw strike went wide. The claw sliced through the top left corner of the trailer before continuing down into the road.

The wheels on the moving van's right side lifted off the ground for a moment before it crashed back to the ground. The vehicle swerved a little bit but barely lost any speed at all. The humanoid stumbled to the side, sent tumbling from its missed strike. But mid fall the swarm clinging to the creature's back suddenly released their grip and jumped onto the roof of the moving truck in one massive wave. Ryan took aim at them as they leaped and squeezed the trigger, but his pistol just clicked empty over and over.

Shit, he had to reload.

With a thunderous crash, the humanoid creature crashed into a nearby building head first and fell to the ground stunned. Ryan could only watch in horror as the swarm of fleshy balls that had leapt off of it started climbing down through the hole in the moving van's roof made by the humanoid's clawed strike.

Ryan could only imagine the screams of the people inside as he ducked back into the truck to reload his pistol. He had to clear as many of the creatures from the roof of the moving van as he could before they made their way inside.

Chapter 52: Fighting off the Swarm - Mortal (Augustus) Fragment

Gus reached into his bag as he heard a crash behind them. He looked up along with the other twenty people packed tightly in the back of this moving van.

There were a few flashlights providing light in the windowless space, but the shadows were long and the other people around him were indistinct blurs that were nearly impossible to differentiate from each other in the stuffy and smelly space.

Gus closed his hand around the cold metal of the pistol in his bag. It glowed briefly through the bag's fabric before the light faded away again. The people around Gus were milling around, and his eyes darted around at them as they went by. He wasn't sure if anyone had noticed the light from his bag in the chaos of everyone's babbling voices echoing off the tight walls.

There was another crash to their right outside and the faint sound of screams as the people reacted. Everyone began huddling together in fear, and the babbling died down. None of them spoke as if they were deer frozen by the gaze of a predator.

Gus heard the heavy stomps of feet in the distance, whatever it was was drawing closer. The van was still driving at full speed, and Gus could hear the engine protesting and sputtering at the rapid burst of acceleration. Gus pulled his pistol from the bag and held it at the ready, there was no better time to reveal it than now. Whatever that thing out there was, it clearly wasn't human.

Several of the people around him gasped in surprise as the beams of their flashlight caught the reflection off the shiny metal of the pistol. The light of one flashlight tilted and Gus saw a glimpse of a man that was smiling.

Gus glanced at his hand and saw the glowing lines on the pistol slowly fading away again. The smiling man was old with gray hair, a weathered face, and his hair was wild.

He had a greedy glint in his eyes as he stared at the gun in Gus's hand. The beam of light moved on and Gus watched the shadowy figure now out of the beam of light, but it stepped away from him like the others when they realized what he was holding.

Gus shook his head, maybe he was just imagining things, he had to focus on the killer aliens before whatever was going on with that guy. Gus held the gun close as a space was opened around him. The footsteps behind the vehicle grew closer...

Gus wiped his brow with his sleeve as a drop of sweat dripped into his eyes. He was too old for this adventure shit. This was for a younger man like Ryan. Hopefully Ryan could escape whatever the thing chasing was as it ate them all.

People had always called Augustus a pessimist, but in this apocalyptic town he thought of himself as more of a realist. If he had trusted the Neighborhood Watch from the beginning then he wouldn't have this powerful pistol right now.

The footsteps of the creature were close enough that whatever the creature was would be upon them in moments. Gus turned to the back and leveled his pistol at the doors as people cleared the way for him. He wasn't even sure what this thing even did, but Victor had seemed to think it was something special. Gus hoped it would be enough.

The footsteps outside stopped for a moment as Gus stood there pistol raised aimed at the closed back doors of the moving van. There were gunshots outside from the truck in front of them that Ryan was in and everything seemed to happen all at once.

Four giant claws gouged into the roof and left gaping wounds in the ceiling in the top right corner by the doors. The whole cabin lurched to the side as the claws put weight on the vehicle before. Everyone was thrown to the side as gravity tilted in the cabin. Then a crash as claws ripped all the way through and the creature was sent flying to the side.

Gus heard it crash into something to the side in a loud crash before the sounds of the creature rapidly receded into the distance. The moving van fell back the other way as gravity reasserted itself and they all were thrown to the other side of the van.

The back doors swung open and blinded them all with the sudden influx of sunlight. Gus just barely managed to hold on to his pistol as he was thrown around, cradling it to his chest as he fell. His ankle twinged in pain as his achilles painfully overextended. His injury was better from the last week and a half of healing, but it still flared up occasionally in pain. *Gah!*

Everyone sighed in relief as they saw the stunned ten foot tall armadillo humanoid lying stunned on the ground and quickly fading into the distance through the open doors. Gus lowered his pistol. But he had let his guard down too soon.

Something leaped from one of the open gouges in the ceiling and clamped onto Gus' chest, sending him falling to the floor on his back. Something stabbed into his shoulder and he instinctively went to hit it with the grip of the pistol.

His eyes started to adjust to the sudden light from the open backdoors. Just as his vision recovered Gus felt a boneless tentacle slap his hand sending the gun scattering away behind Gus into the crowd of people that were just now standing back to their feet.

Gus felt his pointer finger that was in the trigger guard snap as it was ripped from his hand violently. Another tentacle pierced Gus' other shoulder and he rolled over trying to squish the strange thing under his weight.

He rolled dangerously close to the open doors in the back that were swinging open. The wind bit at Gus and a sugary almost floral scent filled his nostrils. The thing seemed stunned at Gus' sudden weight as it didn't stab him again with its flexible limb for a moment.

Gus reached under himself and ripped its tentacle off of him with one hand where it had stabbed him and just barely sunk into his shoulder.

It thrashed as Gus threw it out the back of the truck by its singular tentacle as a lever to whirl it and fling it like a fleshy rope. Gus panted in exertion as he watched as it hit the road behind them. His shoulder had a dull throbbing pain but his broken finger flared with pain with every little motion. There were more gunshots outside and several more fleshy orbs fell from the roof and hit the road behind them, falling from the roof above.

Another four of the orbs emerged from the ceiling and launched themselves at Gus all at once. He tried to dodge but they launched their spearing tentacles in mid-air to track him and attack. Gus grunted and slapped one aside with his injured right hand but the other three hit home and embedded a few inches into his skin.

Gus felt the tentacle tense and stiffen and suddenly the fleshy orbs were rocketing directly towards him as if pulled along by a grappling hook. Gus felt weak and lightheaded and stumbled forward a little at all the extra weight as the orbs dragged him forward with their weight.

Two more orbs emerged from the ceiling and stabbed him with the tentacles. The one he had slapped away attacked again and latched onto him. More gunshots in front of the vehicle. More alien orb bodies fell to the street behind them, falling from the roof.

Gus was feeling weak and his vision blackened at the edges. He was near the back doors and leaned back to barely not fall out the back onto the street that was flying by them. The orbs seemed to be draining him of something, Gus was feeling weaker by the second. They were feeding on him like a group of leeches, Gus just had to get rid of their suckers.

Gus staggered a step back from the edge and pulled off one of the blood sucking tentacles with his left hand, flinging the attached orb out onto the street a second later. His increasing weakness slowed its drain on him. He pulled off another one of the creatures.

They weren't that strong physically, just very fast when they first leapt at him. The creatures tried to squirm away as Gus removed them one by one, but seemed vulnerable now they were latched on. Gus threw another one out the back into the street.

Four more left. Gus panted as he reached for the next one. It would be close... But it was doable. He would make it in tim....

Bang! A searing pain lanced through Augustus' lower back and he cried out in pain. He fell forward, out of the truck. Gus turned in mid-air as his foot caught on the lip of the truck. He desperately curled his toes in a fruitless effort to hold on, but it was no use and he was sent flying. As he spun he saw the smiling man from before holding Gus' pistol. The barrel was smoking as the other people looked at Gus' falling form in shock. *Bastard.*

Gus fell to the street and barely felt as the asphalt flayed the skin from his body as he bounced and gradually slid to a stop. Two of the creatures were still attached to Gus and they seemed to grip tighter and their prongs dug deeper into Gus' body.

His whole world was in pain until there was relief in his lower back, oddly the same place he had been shot. The rising heat soothed the pain from the gunshot wound. The feeling quickly spread through his body.

Gus barely even noticed as his hair began to curl and burn. The two leeches burst into twin bursts of reddish flames and were consumed in moments. Gus' bleeding scrapes from the roadburn suddenly glowed with an internal reddish light. Tongues of flame emerged from his wound instead of blood. Gus tried to pierce together a coherent thought of panic at the sight, but the warmth had spread there too after a moment.

The fire in his mind burned brightly for a moment until the parts that formed 'Gus' were burned away. Only the Devouring Flame remained. The Flame used the host's eyes to scan the surroundings. It lowered the ecstasy of consumption to preserve the lifespan of the vessel. It knew enough to appreciate lying in wait for a larger reward. The vessel looked to the retreating metal vehicle.

The vessel was too slow to catch up to them. There was the sound of heavy footsteps in the opposite direction. The vessel turned its head. A creature of considerable mass was charging at high speed after the fleeing vehicle.

It seemed to barely notice the standing vessel in the middle of the street. The Flame burned brighter. The well of Potential approaching... It would be a feast. It burned with merriment and the vessel charged the creature in a suicidal rage.

The creature spotted the vessel and hunched its shoulder to slap it away mid motion. But the Flame detonated the vessel at the perfect moment. It could barely focus after feasting on so much of the mortal's Potential at once. But as its tongues washed over the armored creature it refocused. The mortal was a simple appetizer after all.

The Flame felt parts of itself dissipate on the bone mineral plates. But enough of itself was in the gaps to burrow inwards. This ocean potential beneath was enough to allow itself to stop holding back. To truly feast like a glutton and burn all that could be perceived. The Flame danced in a state of euphoria as it spread.

The minutes of happiness seemed like they lasted for eons. But like all good things, eventually it was over. The last bit of flesh was consumed and the Flame inspected its surroundings for any other beings with which it could continue the revelry. But there was nothing.

The flames dimmed, but the Flame persisted. As the last flickering ember died on the new vessel's corpse, the Flame rejoined the larger collective. The collective rejoiced at the memories of the latest feast as the Flame similarly rejoiced in their revelries in turn. It had been dormant and patient for so long, only little bites at a time for so long. With the forces of the Eldest arriving in full, perhaps that would soon change?

Chapter 53: Suspicions - Mortal Ryan Fragment

Ryan unloaded his pistol again into the fleshy orbs clinging to the top of the moving truck. He was still hanging out the window as the others gripped his shirt, preventing him from spilling out as their truck swerved side to side. Ryan's shots were wild but when one connected, each led to one of the creatures losing its grip and falling behind onto the road dead.

Ryan's gun clicked empty again and he ducked back inside the car to quickly reload. A few seconds later, He stuck his head out again into the rushing wind only to see several of the creatures missing from the top of the moving truck. They must have gotten inside. *Shit.* Ryan could only pick off as many from the roof as he could.

He suddenly one of the orbs rolled out the back and hitting the road with a splat. Ryan shifted his grip on his weapon. At least they were fighting back inside, maybe it was even Gus. Ryan shifted his vision and widened his eyes as he saw the armored humanoid running after them in the distance.

It was still losing ground on them right now, but Ryan knew it would quickly build speed to catch up to them again. The moving van kept swerving from side to side, but only one or two of the fleshy orbs were knocked off by the driver's actions.

The bone plated humanoid drew closer and Ryan stabilized his gun in preparation to fire at it again. It was almost in range now. Suddenly, a gunshot from the moving van and someone fell from the back, thrashing as several of the fleshy orbs clung to him. Ryan could only watch in horror as the person burst into reddish flames that burned away several of the fleshy orb attackers.

The person didn't scream in pain but stood up and turned to the approaching humanoid. He started running towards the creature while he was still on fire, and Ryan's pistol wavered. *What the hell is he doing?*

The creature went to swat him away as it drew close but the man suddenly exploded into a massive wave of reddish flames before the claws even touched him. Ryan held his pistol in front of him uselessly as the flame unnaturally twisted in mid-air to coat the body of the humanoid. The creature screeched in pain and fell to the ground, rolling and thrashing as it began to burn.

As it rapidly faded into the distance Ryan watched the bonfire grow larger and brighter over the corpse. Ryan wondered who that man was. Hopefully Gus would be able to explain what the hell had happened. That gunshot must have been him with his extra special pistol, had he really shot that man? It must have been an accident. Surely it had to have been an accident.

——— O — o — O ———

Ryan's truck and the moving van were the last vehicles back to the new base. They had to make their own way, and luckily Ryan already knew the way there so they didn't get lost or were attacked as they hurried to drive to the new safezone as quickly as they could.

As soon as they came within sight of it, two armed vehicles came to escort them in. They had the heavier machine guns mounted on their truck beds.

The machine guns had high damage but limited ammunition, so had been kept near the new base at all times for protection for a sudden attack when it was understaffed. The two vehicles went inside through the new gaps of the shields and unloaded to the tearful greetings between the gathered townspeople that had made it through.

The mood was somber from the people they had lost in the two trailing vehicles. Ryan pushed through the crowd to find Gus and get an explanation on the flaming man. The crowd was intermingling with each other and various relatives were hugging each other. Ryan reached the mangled back of the van and inspected the people milling around nearby.

An older man brushed past Ryan in the other direction with his head down. Ryan looked at the man's face in case it was Gus, but it wasn't him. This man's face was far more angular with a sharper jawline. Ryan scanned the crowd again. His heart began to drop as he didn't see Gus. He turned and asked a woman nearby that he recognized to ask her what had happened.

"It was dark," She said, "Everyone got thrown in a pile when that big claw came through the roof. I was so scared! The old man Gus had a pistol but one of the aliens knocked it out of his hand before he could shoot. He started getting overwhelmed when more came.

I heard a gunshot and then Gus was falling out the back and burst into flame. I think he was shot in the back. I saw his shirt turning red as he fell out. Then he just got up and killed that monster with those flames! It… He was such a hero, he went out protecting the rest of us."

Ryan's heart clenched. It was Gus? After all they had been through? "Did you see who had the pistol?"

She shook her head. "No, but we can ask the others."

After much argument and babbled stories, no one was sure. Everyone had still been actively being thrown around by the shifting of the vehicle and had scrambled their positions before anyone could recognize the gunman. The chaos also made it hard for anyone to remember the exact orders of events afterwards. Ryan felt his anger rise that not one of these people knew who had the pistol. Not even one? One, maybe more, of them were lying.

"It was me." The crowd turned to see the man who had brushed past Ryan earlier standing in the center of the crowd. The people around him shuffled away at his statement. The man was affecting a politician's sympathetic look. Ryan could flag the insincerity on the man's face from a mile away.

But based on the crowd's reaction many others did not. Ryan had seen that same look often from the career criminals at the station when giving statements about their sympathy for the victims while denying any involvement.

"In the confusion I grabbed the pistol and tried to shoot one of those *demons*," the man said, "The truck lurched at the last moment and I..." Ryan watched as he closed his eyes and pretended to compose himself. What was this guy trying to pull? Ryan fingered the pistol on his hip and eyed the man with suspicion. Others noticed his motion and backed away from Ryan. The man let out a long breath and slowly opened his eyes.

"I shot him by accident. Gus fell out of the car and he released those flames to burn the *demons* to a crisp. He was a hero."

People all around looked reflective and nodded along. Ryan stepped forward. "Where is this gun now?" he asked.

The man's eyes turned calculating as he looked at Ryan for a moment before he put on a remorseful expression again. "I don't know. I fell to the ground afterwards in the chaos and it fell from my hand."

The man raised his voice, "Did anyone pick it up after I dropped it?"

Everyone shook their heads. None contradicted the man's story. No one seemed to have remembered much of what had really happened through all the confusion and chaos.

The man spoke up again. "We should search the van again in case it is still in there."

They did and there was nothing. "Did anyone see it roll out the back?" The man said again to take charge, "It might have been thrown out as we drove away?"

The people muttered and talked with another, but again no one was sure. Ryan didn't like this man, how he had taken charge of the search so easily. Wasn't the obvious solution that he was the one that had the gun and he was just lying about it? Something seemed off with the man.

Why had the man been in such a rush before Ryan had arrived? Why confess to having the weapon when no one seemed to have remembered what had happened? He could have gotten away cleanly, if he stole the pistol then why expose himself like this?

Ryan saw Victor approaching with another member of the former Neighborhood Watch. With quick excuses to them, Ryan pulled Victor away and explained the situation to him. The two went to investigate, but by the time they got around to it the story had solidified in the crowd's mind. It had been a horrible accident and the pistol had been lost on the road. With nothing else keeping them there people drifted off and began dispersing into the larger crowd to rejoin their loved ones.

The suspect himself was already gone when the two men went to interrogate him further on the details. Neither Victor nor Ryan wanted the former members of the Neighborhood Watch to know about the pistol either.

The group of mercenaries had renounced the organization but the two of them knew that if the Neighborhood Watch put pressure on them and offered a good enough deal to them then the rest of the people here might be betrayed.

That pistol was a powerful weapon against the aliens and Ryan and Victor wanted it to be used to protect the people here, not sold to the Neighborhood Watch for the safety of some of the mercenaries. So they would have to pretend like nothing was wrong so as to not alert the mercenaries on how important the pistol was.

They would just have to find and follow the guilty man until he revealed where he had hid the gun. Ryan didn't believe for an instant that the man had lost it. He had seen what it had done to that alien bone plated humanoid. The man must have stashed it away somewhere to retrieve later/

The man's sudden disappearance right after they all arrived to the safe zone when Ryan turned away was suspicious enough at least. And Ryan just didn't like the feeling he got from the man. He seemed like he was wearing a mask. He had openly admitted to shooting someone and deflected all suspicion and consequences for himself in minutes. And the crowd had believed his story easily.

People were so busy looking for the missing gun they seemed to have forgotten Gus had been shot in the back. The man had admitted to having it when Gus was shot openly and had gotten away with it. It made Ryan's rage build even more.

Deep breaths. Calm. This man wasn't the same as Fulcrum. Ryan had only suspicions, not proof. Victor would make sure to report the event to the mercenaries while framing the flames as grenades he had given Gus before they left. A one use item that couldn't be used again. That should let Ryan and Victor of them search for the pistol uninterrupted.

The last convoy left to get the last of the people and supplies, but Victor and Ryan stayed behind. They had more important work to do. Hopefully they could find the suspicious man and his stolen weapon before everyone settled down in the safe zone and the search by the two of them became more obvious and less able to be lost in the general chaos of the area.

Chapter 54: The Growing Threat - Mortal Ryan Fragment

Over the next two days, Ryan followed around the man from the truck. Adam, the man's name was, he learned. People found Adam charismatic and a small group began following him around almost constantly.

Victor and Ryan went on patrol together for their shift and made some preparations in case things went bad with the mercenaries leading the new Safezone.

Adam was reassuring and sympathetic with the townspeople even as he began stirring them against the former Watch members. It was only little things at first. Asking people to look for their own protection first with makeshift weapons. Helping direct people where to sleep so they could spread out more.

Most tellingly all the former members of the Watch including Victor were nudged to sleep together in one building. Not that the group resisted Adam's suggestions much. There was always separation between the two groups, townspeople and the mercenaries.

The next day Adam was helping distribute the food at breakfast. As Ryan went for his energy bar, he saw that three Neighborhood Watch members who were on breakfast duty just looked relieved. Rationing was in full effect, and making sure everyone took their fair share was difficult with their small number in comparison to the crowds.

Adam and his followers lightened the load and distributed everything faster and many people muttered in approval at their efficiency. After that, Adam began advocating for him and his followers to be trained to patrol the wall and given guns. At this the mercenaries finally put their foot down. Their ammunition was limited and they didn't want 'amateurs' wasting their precious bullets training their aim.

Adam leapt on this refusal immediately. Hearing him tell it, the decision was made to keep the people powerless under the thumb of the armed mercenaries. Something that was true most likely, but the concern about ammunition was also a serious concern as well.

Trust rapidly eroded between the two groups with Ryan acting as an odd bridge between them. He was in a strange place between both groups. Ryan was friends with Victor and was still armed given he knew how to fire his gun properly as a cop. He went on patrols with the Neighborhood Watch around the perimeter of the safezone. But he shared many of the concerns of the people around them about how dedicated the former members of the Neighborhood Watch were to actually protecting these people if the going got tough once the aliens attacked them again.

On Tuesday, the tension was pulled into full gear after a sudden attack by the swarm of the fleshy ball aliens. The aliens had attacked as one of their group was entering the shield from patrol of the perimeter.

The two had rushed inside and the shield closed, but not soon enough. Over two dozen of the creatures had rushed in the gap and began attacking everyone.

People screamed as the two men were quickly swarmed and killed by the aliens as the other four former Neighborhood Watch members nearby whittled down the remaining fleshy orb's numbers with their gunfire. Five of the aliens made it into the fleeing crowd.

Ryan had pulled his gun and rushed over, but Adam and his crew with metal bars and other makeshift weapons had already dealt with the aliens. Adam had a smug look that he flashed at Ryan as he stood next to one of the pulped bodies. Adam was well aware that Ryan was aware of Adam's true nature, but Ryan risked destroying what little influence he had with the people if he spoke against Adam, given Adam's newfound popularity.

All of that led to this moment an hour later where Adam finally made his move. People were scared with the recent attack and the death of the two armed men even if no one in the crowd or the townspeople had been seriously hurt. The little aliens actually weren't overly threatening in small numbers, it was only in large groups attacking at once that they started becoming dangerous.

Adam was demanding guns for his people given the mercenaries' failure to protect the two men who had died.

The argument was in full swing now as the mercenaries huddled together with the angry crowd surrounding them. Ryan stood to the side watching on as Adam shouted.

"...Failed! Why can't we defend ourselves? We need as many of us armed as possible so we can all fight! Why should we be trusting you with our safety anyways? You and the rest of the Watch betrayed this town already once. Who's to say you won't do it again?"

Ryan fingered his pistol nervously as Adam ranted at the huddled mercenaries. The crowd was shouting in agreement and drowned out the voice of the mercenary leader's reply. Ryan still had never gotten his name after all this time. None of the civilians had ever really interacted with him directly and as soon as the man got Ryan's full story of the last week the man had never spoken with Ryan again.

Adam's speech kept getting more heated and the angry crowd began to close in on the heavily armed mercenaries that began fingering their weapons nervously.

Suddenly everyone paused as the shield dome lit up at a heavy impact. They all turned to see another ten feet tall armored armadillo creatures pounding on the outside of the shield at the north opening with its fists. Over a hundred of the fleshy orbs boiled in a carpet of flesh trailing behind it, one of their tentacles occasionally darting out to probe the shield in a brief flash of golden light as they were repelled.

Ryan and the grouped mercenaries rushed to the east opening, leaving Adam and the angry crowd behind. There was one entrance for each of the cardinal directions that could be opened. Unfortunately, they couldn't fire their guns out of the shield so had to go out and shoot the aliens from the sides before retreating back inside the shield again to safety.

Victor was already there at the entrance putting his hand on the access stone to the right of the opening and created an opening in the shield for the group to leave through. Victor closed it again behind them and stood to his feet, he would stand by to open it for them when they returned.

Everyone raised their weapons and stepped out a bit more before the first flesh ball became visible around the edge of the shield as the group circled around. It noticed them and charged only to be blown to pieces by rifle fire.

More aliens approached at the noise but were quickly cut down by the group's weapons.

After destroying more than thirty of the fleshy balls, their growing numbers of charging aliens began to pressure the group. They began to slowly retreat back to where Victor was waiting for them. They heard heavy footsteps and the armadillo humanoid rounded the corner and began to charge at them with its claws dragging off of the flashing golden shield.

Victor opened the shield to let them in and the group back ran through to the interior. Victor closed the shield behind them just as the first flesh ball made it to the edge. It leaped for them only to splat against the shield and slowly slide down. The large armored humanoid alien stood at the border where the entrance had been sealed again by the shield and resumed pounding and swiping with its clawed fists to no avail. The shield lit up, but still held.

The Potential batteries were full and the civilians should be filling them up even now to power the shield. The creature shouldn't be able to get through on its own in a while.

The group of armed mercenaries and Ryan quickly ran along with Victor to the west gate where they repeated the procedure of picking off smaller groups of the flesh ball aliens as they rounded the edge of the shield.

More flesh balls were arriving from the surrounding city now, and Ryan held his pistol tighter in his grip. He hadn't fired it yet as it was lower range than the other's rifles.

The same thing happened as before as they left the safe zone shield again through the exit. Most of the fleshy orbs were killed and they retreated back into the Safezone before the larger creature could approach.

Ryan noticed that Adam's right hand man was standing next to Victor offering him an energy bar. Manipulating the shield did take a little Potential to use, but not enough to make Victor hungry with just this much usage.

Ryan frowned, but shrugged it off as the group reloaded and rushed to the South gate. They sallied out and the number of fleshy orbs was definitely decreasing this time.

The aliens trickled in for a minute or two before the tall armored creature rounded the corner and began to charge again. Ryan looked behind him as he heard shouting. Adam's right hand man had pulled a large knife and plunged it into Victor's back. With a cry of pain Victor fell forward to the ground as his attacker ripped the knife out in a spurt of blood.

Ryan felt time slow down as the man stood over Victor and plunged his knife down again. Ryan stood at the back of the crowd desperately craning his neck to see what was happening. Victor tried to twist away but the path of the descending knife followed his motions easily.

With a wet *thunk* the knife embedded itself deep into Victor's neck. The attacker pulled out the knife from Victor, and the spray of blood painted the man's face red. He stabbed again as Victor twitched on the ground. Pulling the knife out one more time he wiped it off on Victor's clothes before running to the side and out of sight. Victor went still.

Ryan startled and broke from his shock as a barrage of gunfire sounded around him. The large alien was charging towards them and now there was nowhere to retreat. The bullets dug into its flesh occasionally, but mostly skittered off its bone plates.

Each impact made it stumble slightly, but after a few moments it would recover and pick up speed in its charge towards them again. Black fluid leaked from its wounds, but it barely seemed to notice.

The alien was growing closer and Ryan decided to scatter along with the mercenaries around him. He ran for one of the nearest buildings, his position in the back of the group now an advantage in the mad scramble to escape. Ryan ran, and didn't stop even when he heard thumps and rips of claws through flesh behind him.

One of the alien orbs leapt out of him from under the rubble and Ryan shot it mid-air with his pistol, firing his weapon for the first time. It burst into gore that sprayed Ryan's left side with black blood as he rushed into one of the nearby buildings. He threw open the door and ran to one of the nearby offices.

Inside, Ryan stared for a moment at the two backpacks and bikes leaning against a wall. It was supposed to be for him and Victor, for their escape when things inevitably went wrong in the safe zone. Gunfire still sounded behind Ryan and he stumbled as an explosion shook the ground under his feet. Ryan took one of the stuffed backpacks and quickly brought his stolen bike outside.

He glanced towards the raging battle by the Safezone to see the armored alien laying on its side on the ground. A large chunk was taken out of its side, and it was struggling to stand again with its heavily injured arm.

Of the sixteen men who had left the dome only five heavily injured survivors remained. The rest were in various piles of gore or submerged under the swarming alien orbs attacking them.

The survivors fended off the swarming flesh balls with rifle shots as another tossed a second grenade at the large creature. Ryan paused, debating going to fight as the grenade exploded and tore off half the creature's head. The alien went still and the now three survivors focused on clearing more space around them of the swarming fleshy balls. They started making their way towards where Ryan had started waving now.

Ryan fired his pistol as another fleshy alien orb charged leaped at him, attracted by his motions. It exploded into more gore, and more of his police uniform was painted black. One survivor at the back was swarmed and Ryan could only watch as he was consumed. The others kept running.

Ryan shot his pistol to cover the two remaining men running towards him. Closer, closer they came. Ryan's pistol clicked empty in his hand as he went to reload it as quickly as he could.

The numbers of fleshy orbs chasing the two men dropped dramatically as the mercenaries ran away, the rest going back to resuming their assault on Safezone. One man tripped and fell to the ground and the orbs set into him in moments, mummifying him as more and more caught up and latched onto him when he stopped moving and firing his gun.

The remaining man quickly slowed to let out a spray of gunfire behind him before resuming his sprint towards Ryan. The limp body of the armored alien twitched. It bubbled for a moment before shrinking five feet to be roughly the height of a human. Its wounds healed and it rolled to its feet. Its armor hung off its frame, like clothing two or three sizes too big on it.

Ryan's hand trembled and his eyes widened as his pistol magazine clicked into place. The revived alien turned to the two of them and charged. Ryan unloaded his pistol which caused it to slow and shrink even more. Now it was smaller, Ryan's bullets were far more effective on it.

It was five feet tall now, its bony shell hanging off its body like an oversized coat on its smaller body. The survivor turned at Ryan's gunfire and unloaded his weapon too while running, but his shots mostly missed or skittered off the oversized plating. But he still slowed down.

Ryan could only watch as the creature's charge drew it closer, its speed hampered only a little bit by its armor dragging on the ground and restricting its movements.

I have to get out of here, Ryan thought.

Ryan hurriedly pointed into the building where he had left the other bike to the remaining man. The other man panting in exertion saw his finger and shifted his direction. Ryan hopped on the bike next to him and began pedaling away furiously. The creature could catch up but Ryan was hoping he could turn in time to dodge it on the turns. It seemed to charge like a bull in a straight line if it was similar to the one that attacked them before.

Ryan could only flinch as he heard a wet squelch behind him and a cut off scream. He didn't look back. He was all alone now, and he could hear the footfalls of the creature catching up… *Bang!*

A high pitched scream sounded behind Ryan following the shot and a loud *Whooosh* of flame a few seconds later. Ryan turned his head. There, at the entrance to the Safezone, Adam stood with Gus' pistol extended in front of him. The barrel of the weapon was smoking slightly from when it had fired.

The gathered crowd behind him gaped in awe as the creature they had just watched slaughter the mercenaries burned into a crisp. Ryan met Adam's eyes and saw his wide smile and the reflections of the red flames dancing in his eyes.

Ryan turned back forward again and pedaled away harder. He would have to take his chances out in the wild rather than be cooped up with Adam and his cronies again.

Gus was dead, Victor was dead, and all of those armed mercenaries were dead. Ryan had nothing keeping him there. Ryan panted as he pedaled even harder, hoping he was making the right choice.

He didn't know where he was going to go but he knew one thing for sure. He was getting as far away from here as possible.

Chapter 55: Parting Ways with the Club - Multiple Fragments of Memory

Adam watched as the troublesome police officer fled into the distance. The scared sheep behind him were still staring at him in awe and fear because he could do what the oppressors could not in defending them from the demons. He was glad to see the cop go after they shared that final look of understanding. Adam had not enjoyed the death of Gus, but it had to be done.

Adam was the best person to lead these people in these troubled times. Ryan could not be brought into the fold, but he was not a sinner like the Neighborhood Watch either.

It was best this way, for Adam and his flock to strike his own path away from here without need for further unpleasantness. Adam controlled his expression again and turned to the crowd behind him. His face and tone were somber and refined even if his emotions were anything but that right now.

"This is a tragedy that our defenders are lost, no matter our doubts in their conviction," He said, "But we must move forward and come together as a community. To defend ourselves and each other!"

The crowd cheered and Adam smiled as he raised the gleaming pistol into the air. He just couldn't wait to show these people the right path in these trying times. His path. The path of salvation.

———O—o—O———

Ryan wasn't really sure where he was going. He was all on his own with only two more magazines for his pistol left in his jacket. His backpack had enough food and water for a few days if he rationed enough, but if he got attacked again then he was screwed.

Ryan decided to get as close to the edge of the dome as he could. It took a lot of focus and his mind still got foggy if he focused on the boundary for too long.

But he could do it if he took breaks.

So he biked closer and closer to the edge. He didn't see any aliens. They probably were all gathered to attack the Safezones. Ryan put his head down and pedaled faster. He didn't want to think of what would happen if the aliens pierced the safe zone shields, what could happen again…

Eventually, Ryan noticed his bike slowly drifting to the side of the road without him noticing. He was close to the edge. He moved a little farther inward and his drift to the side and distraction grew stronger.

He felt a pressure on his head and his eyes became a little unfocused as he pedaled. Ryan panted and stopped, he had been biking nonstop for what felt like hours. He had no idea how long it had actually been. He had gone far enough.

Ryan found a nearby home and kicked in the back door. He moved inside and checked the pantry. Score! There was plenty of canned food for Ryan to eat.

All the perishables were spoiled and let out a disgusting smell, but Ryan could deal with it. He pushed a few cabinets in front of the back door that was swinging open, blocking it closed.

There, that way should be secure for now. The key to the front door was inside in a little tray to the side. Ryan went to one of the bedrooms and collapsed onto the bed. It was only late afternoon but Ryan felt exhausted given what had happened.

As he drifted off to sleep his eyes fixated on a picture of a happy family hanging on the wall. His eyes shut and their ghosts haunted his dreams, tormenting him for desecrating their graves.

———O—o—O———

Ryan woke with a gasp, heart pounding. It was dark out. He tried to remember his nightmare but it quickly slipped out from between his mental fingers.

Ryan blinked. Well, time to go to the bathroom. He went to the bathroom and did his business, and went to flush. Nothing happened. Damn it, the water had shut off sometime over the last few days.

Ryan hunted in the closet and found a bottle of bleach and poured it into the bowl. Not the best solution, but at least it would reduce the smell hopefully. At least the electricity was still working. Ryan wondered why the utilities would be supplied for even this long, even during an alien invasion.

Well, best to conserve water for now. Guess he would just have to deal with the constant smell of bleach through the house for now.

At least this place already smelled terrible from the spoiled food, so what was one more smell on the pile?

———O—o—O———

Ryan certainly had to deal with the smell. He held his breath when he went to the bathroom, but it wasn't too horrible the rest of the time. This place was quickly becoming a hazard zone. Ryan just hid for most of Wednesday organizing the canned food and barricading the house more. He got a few knives from the kitchen.

His pistol was a last resort for defense as the sound would announce him to everything nearby that might want to meet him. Or alert people. Ryan wasn't sure if there were still people holed up out here in their homes, but based on his experience with Adam he would prefer to stay alone.

Ryan fell asleep again at a more reasonable time at around sunset that night and woke up early on Thursday morning to the sounds of explosions in the distance. Ryan rolled out of bed and rushed to the window.

He looked up to see the normally invisible dome lit in a bright golden light. Near the top of the dome was a jagged hole shearing off the top portion of the dome exposing open undistorted sky. Little groups of black dots were falling through before their white parachutes deployed and slowed them down.

After a few minutes more arrived as the parachutes began spreading out in the distance. One of the groups floating down was heading towards Ryan. As they got closer Ryan could see their green uniforms. Soldiers? Was this a rescue by the military?

Ryan looked around frantically. He finally decided on using a white bedsheet he found in a closet. After a few minutes of frantically trying to find a ladder he eventually climbed up to the roof and stood on top, waving the bed sheet frantically.

The soldiers were still in the distance but Ryan thought they might have shifted direction towards him. He kept waving as the group grew closer and closer with their parachutes. They landed a few blocks away.

Ten minutes later the soldiers arrived at the end of the street and Ryan smiled. But he frowned again as they started stumbling to the side and bumbling around as they got closer. Were they more vulnerable to the dome's mental ward? Ryan climbed back down and grabbed his backpack and pistol.

He ran down to where the soldiers were trying to approach. When he got within a few hundred feet the soldiers seemed to notice him and raised their weapons. Ryan raised his hands in the air and they relaxed as they saw his empty hands.

A shorter woman stepped forward from the group. "Where did you come from?" she demanded.

"Sorry, I was deeper in the repellant field from the dome. You guys seem less resistant than me," Ryan felt like an idiot as he saw their eyes glaze over at his mention of the dome. Of course they would be under its effects right now, no one had forced them to confront it yet, "Alright I can explain, but let's get inside first. The aliens might come if we are too obvious out here."

They all hurried to the side and Ryan broke into a nearby house after calling out his intentions. Anyone in there had enough time to tell them to shove off by now.

One of the soldiers went to protest as Ryan started kicking the door, but after no response from inside let him proceed. Ryan continued kicking in the door and soon they all went inside after it swung open. Once they were comfortable and all gathered, Ryan turned to the woman who appeared to be their leader.

"Alright, listen to me as hard as you can," He said, "We have to do this before we discuss anything else."

The soldiers seemed nervous and grouped tighter together. Ryan looked at them. "Plug your ears and just observe her behavior. You'll see what I mean."

They hesitated but after a pause she nodded to them. They plugged their ears and watched carefully. Ryan looked into the leader's eyes. "The dome outside of town," He said, "The dome outside of town. You want to leave town. The dome outside of town…"

The leader's eyes glazed over and her gaze drifted away. Ryan poked her and the woman startled and met Ryan's gaze again. The soldiers tensed at the poke but didn't move to stop him. Ryan continued his chant. Whenever the woman's eyes glazed over or she glanced away Ryan poked her again.

The other soldiers were unhappy, but seemed to have noticed the odd behavior of the leader and were rolling with the situation after she didn't protest Ryan's actions. It took a long time for the ward to finally break on her.

By the end, the chant seemed to have lost meaning in Ryan's mind. It was just a collection of sounds he would say over and over again, like some kind of magic spell.

But eventually the moment came as the leader fell to the floor and writhed in pain. The soldiers immediately jumped on Ryan and restrained him. Ryan didn't resist as the leader thrashed for a few more moments before growing still. She sat up and rubbed her head.

"Let him go boys," She said, "I'm fine. Goddamnit, I see what he meant."

She turned to Ryan, "Just repeat the words and make sure they pay attention?"

Ryan nodded, "Yeah, as long as they focus on the words then it should work."

The woman looked around to her ten squadmates and groaned. "Fuck, this is going to take a long time isn't it?"

Ryan shook his head. "I have a quicker way. You keep them focused on me and shake them when they drift off and I'll say the words. It takes different amounts of time for everyone."

The soldiers looked between Ryan and their leader with confused looks at the exchange. She nodded at him before turning to the rest of the group. "Alright people, focus up. Just focus on the man's words no matter what. That's an order."

The soldiers shuffled in confusion but all looked at Ryan. He resumed his chant. "The dome outside of town. You want to leave town. The dome outside of town…"

The leader of the squad went to work as they began the long and excruciating process of freeing the soldiers from the mental ward's effects.

By the end Ryan's voice was hoarse and he cursed as he realized he hadn't brought water in his bag with him in his excitement to meet the soldiers. The leader handed him a bottle which Ryan gratefully drank from. She turned to Ryan.

"Now with that out of the way, what's going on here? I'm Sergeant Joan Ruston by the way. We only know the larger strokes of what's happening and were hoping you might have more specifics that could help us."

Ryan took a deep breath and sat down on a nearby chair. Looked her in the eyes. And then told her and the soldiers everything that had happened to him.

Chapter 56: The Army meets the Cult - Multiple Fragments of Memory

The soldiers were shocked and appalled as Ryan laid out his story. It seems they had only been given only vague details of what was happening here. Ryan finished his version of events and there was only silence in the room after his last words.

After a moment Sergeant Ruston seemed to come to a decision. "We have to take that Safezone," she said. Ryan straightened. *What?* "What?"

The soldier shook her head. "If what you say is true then this Adam must be contained. We also need a defensible position if we are to survive. Getting defenses like those shields under control would be essential, let alone leaving those civilians under the control of someone as ruthless as you describe."

Ryan tried protesting more but was promptly ignored. Damn it. Wait, he thought of something.

"But what about Adam controlling the shield? He'll never let you in and he might hold hostages if we push him too far."

The soldier arched his eyebrows at Ryan "We? Since when were you coming?"

Ryan realized he had indeed assumed that. "Huh. So I could just stay here then?"

Sergeant Ruston nodded. "You seem safe here, you've given us more information than we could have expected. You don't have to do any more. Of course you're welcome to join the rest of the civilians once we have a secure base."

Ryan warred with himself for a moment. Should he go with them, or stay here safe? It was a hard decision. Despite his desire for revenge against Adam, he didn't really know anyone remaining in the Safezone anymore.

And despite everything else that was going on, he really didn't want to have to kill people. Luckily on the police force he had never been forced to kill someone, or even fire his gun outside of the firing range all that often. And seeing Adam at work claiming power, Ryan knew bloodshed would be inevitable. And he didn't want any part of it.

"Alright, I'll stay here," he said, "But I'm showing you the way to the Safezone at least."

Sergeant Ruston nodded. "We would appreciate that. Does your radio work?" Ryan shook his head. All his police radio gave him was static. He took it from his shoulder and demonstrated.

Despite his clothing still being stained black from the alien blood, this uniform had brought him this far. He felt almost superstitious that as soon as he stopped wearing it something terrible would happen again. The woman nodded as Ryan's radio only output static.

"I figured. The jammers are still going strong for us too. Now, there's one last thing before we go." She pulled a folded up square of paper from her pocket. She unfolded it revealing a large map of the town of Harmony. She pulled a few colored pens from her pockets. "If you could mark whatever you remember on this map, then it would greatly help the war effort."

Ryan nodded. His memory wasn't perfect but he did his best. He marked the rough locations of the former Safezones Six and Seven. He guessed where Safezone Eight was as best as he could remember.

He marked what he had briefly seen from the map that woman Helen had shown back when Ryan first arrived at Safezone Seven. He wasn't sure about that one, but he thought it looked roughly right of where the other safe zones had been.

He marked where they had been attacked in the convoy. He thought of what else he could put before finally he remembered that bombed out office building he and Gus had seen on their way out from the hospital. He found it on the map and circled it. Gus...

Ryan felt the map shift beneath his hands and glanced over to see Sergeant Ruston leaning over the map frowning. Ryan hesitated for a moment. But just in case... He also marked roughly where he was staying now. Sergeant Ruston glanced at him. Ryan shrugged. "You know, just in case."

Sergeant Ruston nodded slowly. "I understand why you don't want to go back given what happened. But once things are more secure I'll have someone come and tell you the situation so you can make your own decision. Just in case."

Ryan let out a breath he hadn't known he was holding. They wouldn't drag him back into the larger group. Ryan didn't think he could take another Safezone collapsing out under him again. Best to keep his distance and stay out here for now.

———O—o—O———

Ryan and the soldiers were crouched in a building across from the newest safe zone. Ryan could see the patrols on the Safe Zone walls, much sloppier and more disorganized than he had seen before from the mercenaries.

But the guards were numerous and all were heavily armed. It seems like Adam wasn't one to worry about conserving ammunition at least. There were no aliens in the area visible, so maybe it was working for now though.

Ryan wished the soldiers good luck and stayed in position as they left and began approaching the safe zone. The people on the walls saw the military uniforms and some cheered. Others were less enthused and glanced around suspiciously as if expecting an ambush.

Ryan could see Sergeant Ruston arguing with someone through the opening covered by the shield. After a while the shield fell and the soldiers made their way through. Ryan saw Adam in a flash as he greeted the group, arms wide as if he was some sort of twisted tour guide.

Ryan's lips curled in disgust. Adam had had Victor murdered and now he just stood there like nothing had happened. The group went deeper inside and Ryan lost sight of them. Hopefully Sergeant Ruston took his words to heart. Who knows what would happen if she didn't deal with Adam quick enough.

— — — (Mortal Sergeant Ruston Fragment) — — —

Sergeant Joan Ruston was wary as they entered the compound. Half the people here welcomed them as heroes, proof that the government was here to save them. The other half glared suspiciously, probably comparing them to the paramilitary Neighborhood Watch they had fled from. Adam was leading them around and showing them the community.

It seemed he was the de facto leader of this place after he had assassinated the Neighborhood Watch guards and trapped the rest outside. She took a deep breath and tried to keep an open mind.

The man on the outskirts was helpful but that didn't mean everything he said was true. She would have to verify events first before she took action against Adam.

"And that is where we keep all the supplies and guns," Adam finished his tour and gestured to the central building. The spectating crowd watched them to see what they would do now.

Joan stepped forward, "We will assist in your defense while getting other squads here to begin the fight against the alien threat."

The crowd nodded and seemed mostly satisfied with her words, all except Adam and the group of his supporters standing behind him. Adam stepped forward. "And if all these soldiers come, what becomes of us? Are we going to be shoved in the cold if there isn't enough room?"

Joan Ruston looked at him flatly. "No. Although that does raise a good point. We have met a certain survivor that claims you left him out to die after the aliens attacked. Speaking from experience?"

Adam looked shocked for a moment before he controlled himself again. "What, that's ridiculous. Who was it? Everyone knows the Neighborhood Watch tried to flee from here as soon as they saw we would be attacked."

A few people frowned at the statement but most seemed to agree. Joan felt some doubt creep into her mind. But there was one final test. "Victor. It was Victor who told us this."

Adam got a smug look on his face. "Hah! That's impossible. Victor is dea…"

Suddenly the crowd went silent and Adam went pale. He had said too much and flushed as he realized he had been tricked. He tried to recover. "I mean, he went out to flee with the rest of them. Of course he's dead! How could he have escaped the hordes of demons alive?"

Joan kept looking at Adam. Well, it wasn't like this was a court of law. That was plenty suspicious enough for her to take action. "The man who really escaped said much the same. He said you had Victor murdered to strand the group outside the shields so you could take control of the safe zone."

Adam got an angry glint in his eyes. "Lies! Slander! You're the same as the Neighborhood Watch. Strolling in here, already barking orders. Next we know you'll throw us to our deaths just like them!"

Adam reached into his pocket and withdrew his gleaming pistol.

Joan and her squad raised their weapons in response. He paused mid rant. He slowly put the pistol back away and removed his hands from his pockets again. The soldiers lowered their weapons slightly but still kept them pointed at Adam.

"You see!" Adam snarled, "They already draw their weapons on us. A good sign already. Fine! With more groups of you incoming you're going to stomp all over us soon anyways. I'll leave peacefully before your tyranny begins."

If it was possible he raised his voice even more than his shouting from earlier. He turned to the watching crowd.

"People of this Safezone! We all know what is coming next when the military takes control. They will be the same as the ones we have just escaped. There are no cameras, no superiors, no politicians, nothing to hold them back from doing as they please! We should forge our own path on our own. Free from the tyranny of these people. They will throw you to the demons if given the slightest chance. Do not let their position outside of the dome blind you to the truth!"

He pointed a finger at Joan's group accusingly. Joan looked around in bewilderment. She saw agreement on many people's faces. How in the world was he convincing them with this bull? The Neighborhood Watch were terrorists. She and her squad were the military. Fighting for these people around them. Her squad had barely even said anything yet let alone started oppressing anyone. How was this convincing anyone in the least bit?

Adam turned back to her, "We will leave within the day. Just give us a few hours to prepare."

Joan warred with herself for a moment. Should she let him leave? He had proven dangerous and could become a problem later. But nearly half the crowd was nodding along in some sort of agreement. It appeared the distrust of authority had rooted itself deep in this group in the past week. If she stopped him, Adam would have all the proof he needed of her tyrannical nature and that could just cause more problems with working with the people who stayed.

"Fine, just be gone by then," She raised her voice again, "Just remember, Adam is using this as an escape from his crimes. For murder. Don't let him trick you with his false promises. We are here to keep you safe. That is our role as your military. That's our job."

If anything, last words seemed to have made people turn against her even more. With a sigh, Joan decided to give it up. She had done her best but she was no natural politician like Adam was. At least the military would get a secure base here.

Joan left as Adam began packing up supplies. Half her men watched him to make sure he wouldn't try pulling anything or try to sabotage the shields as he left. However they worked. Private John manned the shield terminal as the rest guarded him. He opened the entrance and Joan stepped out.

She loaded the flare gun and shot into the air. Green sparks filled the sky. The rest of the groups would now know that this would be a safe gathering point. Now all she had to do was wait, and then none of this would be her problem anymore.

Hopefully one of the higher rank commanders would arrive soon and help figure out this mess with the civilians. Before something went explosively wrong while she was still in command.

———O—o—O———

Luckily Adam went peacefully and after he left the shield seemed intact and not sabotaged. About fifty people went with Adam in the end. Far more than Joan had expected, but less than had agreed to leave with him originally.

It seems many didn't want to leave the safety of the shield no matter what. A few hours after that the first new paratrooper squad came in. There were more flares that went into the sky as time passed, several red and only two or three green.

More and more came as time passed and command passed out of Joan's hands to someone she was unfamiliar with. Joan gratefully handed over control and returned to her normal duties.

She wasn't qualified to handle the distrust these people still had of them, even after the hardliners had left with Adam. With everything more secure Joan could only help with patrols at this point.

Hopefully the people with Adam could survive. They had made their own choices to follow him, but that didn't mean Joan had to feel good about it. She just had to keep working and focus on her duty. Reflecting could come after all of this was over and she was safe back at home.

Chapter 57: Escaping the Neighborhood Watch - Mortal Francis Fragment

———— **Fragment of Memory of Mortal Francis. Third Monday, directly after assisting Mortal Alice in escaping the Dome.** ————

Francis drummed the wheel of the truck with his fingers as he drove down the highway at high speed.

Tap tap tap. Over and over.

He threw a glance over his shoulder. He could see Alice slowly walking forward towards the edge of the dome in the distance. Hopefully she could make it.

Francis didn't think he could do much more for her. Now he would just have to distract the Neighborhood Watch to give her as much time to escape as he could.

He had been so confident in her success when he was planning all of this out before, but now he had finally left it all up to her, he was doubting himself.

Once she was out, she would be safe.

He could have given her a Protection stone to let her survive Bill's plan… But that would be too cruel. She would be helpless and be forced to watch as everyone died around her.

Francis couldn't be responsible for putting her through that again. Helen's selfish government allies like that damn General Lopez wouldn't make a move on Alice unless there was a clear incentive for it. Something neither Helen or Bill could provide from within the dome, executing the plan.

Francis was confident in the security for the spatial pouch he had given Alice. Once the military had spent a while testing it they would give it back to her, even if only to wait for her to pull something interesting out of it for them to take.

Francis focused back on the road. He was making his way down the abandoned highway across the town. Hopefully he could… Damn.

He leaned and squinted as he saw the drone quadcopter hovering in the distance. They would be after him soon. Francis stopped the car with a slam on the breaks and reached into the back. He lifted the long case he had smuggled into the truck along with the rest of his equipment over the weekend.

He assembled the sniper rifle in under a minute and carefully arranged his five heavy magazines in the center console. The barrel of the rifle was far thicker than it usually would be, because this rifle had been enhanced by Potential. The caliber of the bullets it fired was massive, and the first magazine made a heavy *clunk* as Francis slid it into place into the sniper rifle.

He chambered the first round and rolled down his car window. He made sure to avoid the soft input point where he could supercharge the weapon with Potential. That would be overkill for this and could wear out the weapon itself if he overused it too much.

Francis looked in the distance and the drone was still hovering there, stationary. He had to take it down or his escape would be for nothing. The drone would follow him and the Neighborhood Watch would just wait to ambush him later.

Francis braced the sniper rifle against the car door and looked down the sights. The drone wobbled to the side as it spotted his weapon and began to retreat. But it wasn't enough, it could come back when he wasn't paying attention again. Francis fired and the rifle bucked against his shoulder with the recoil.

His bullet hit the side of the central portion of the drone and two of its propellers stopped spinning. It plummeted to the ground in an uncontrolled fall as the other two propellers spun wildly on the other side.

Francis pulled his rifle back into the truck. They knew where he was now, but Bill wouldn't risk any more drones on this. Even the one just destroyed would be a heavy loss for the Neighborhood Watch.

Things hadn't been fully prepared in the rush to bring in the last of the essential supplies under the dome. Extra supplies like the drones had been left behind as they rushed to bring in handheld weapons, manpower, and food. Well, it was to Francis' advantage now at least.

Francis kept driving before taking an exit off the highway. If he went too far he would enter the territory of the Infected. Francis didn't want to give Bill a chance to take him out either. Francis didn't think Helen would go for it, but with Bill who knew if Bill would do it anyways?

A week after they had deployed the barrier the Neighborhood Watch had lined the underside of the highway with explosives. Francis hoped Bill wouldn't set off the explosives under the highway under him, but he still might.

They were meant to be set off once the first wave of Infected realized they could use it to bypass and travel over the Safezone territory.

Bill had stopped the troops from defending it from assaults from the Infected days ago, but the aliens seemed to have not realized the change based on the still empty roads around Francis.

Bill was planning to let the aliens use it for a while and wait for one of their more valuable forces walking on top of the bombs before blowing the whole highway sky high when they began truly gathering for a larger assault.

Francis took the exit off the highway even as he heard the rumbling of vehicles behind him. He took a sharp turn on the deserted street and pressed on the gas. He was slammed back into his seat as his reinforced truck darted forward and the engine rumbled louder.

The two vehicles behind him exited the highway and quickly accelerated after him, but Francis was still pulling ahead. It continued that way for a minute or two, Francis getting a larger and larger lead as the two pursuers struggled to catch up. Francis wiped sweat from his forehead with one arm as he swerved at high speed around the trash and rubble strewn around the street.

With gritted teeth he eased off the petal a bit as he swerved around a crumpled car wreck that had crashed into one of the parked cars on the sides of the road. His pursuers quickly made up the lost ground Francis had just painstakingly gained.

As he swerved around the crash something jumped from under one of the twisted pieces of metal. The fleshy orb missed and hit the road behind Francis as he accelerated for a moment before swerving a bit as he felt the car begin to skid a bit. He struggled to keep himself from crashing the vehicle and was forced to let off the gas even more.

Gunshots behind him. Something skittered off of the road to his right. Close to the wheels. Shit, if they disabled his wheels then he would be a sitting duck. That would probably be worse than getting shot deep in alien territory like this.

Francis had to break their line of fire. Another fleshy ball leapt from underneath a parked car onto his jeep and missed. Francis noticed that the cars behind him slowed as the ball leapt again towards their windshields seconds later. *Maybe...* Francis slowed for a moment and took a sharp left on the thoroughfare.

He drove forward, even deeper into Infected territory. As he drove the fleshy balls assaults grew more and more frequent until they became almost continuous. Luckily none adjusted to his current speed. They were rather stupid.

Behind him, Francis could see the two chasing vehicles push to follow but the army of fleshy balls just as happily assaulted them as they had attempted to do to Francis. But with a direct approach they had much more success clinging to the two cars.

Two of the men inside began turning their gunfire to the clinging aliens, each shot causing the aliens to practically explode into gore. But the alien swarm caused the drivers of the chasing vehicles to slow. And the slower they went, the more of the aliens that were able to properly latch on to them and attack.

Francis kept driving even as the assaults by the aliens grew more and more frequent. The chasing vehicles eventually turned off an intersection behind him, escaping the growing horde and leaving Francis behind.

Francis drove for another five minutes, intentionally skirting around the zone around the hospital now he wasn't forced to go any deeper. The assaults grew less common and Francis slowed down a hair so he could retain more control of the vehicle.

He made it to the other side and the attacks eventually dropped to nothing. A few of the aliens had managed to catch his bumper, but a little swerving had shaken them off quickly enough. Francis was lucky none of the larger creatures of humanoids had shown up.

The little flesh balls seemed like animals, too stupid to adjust their leap to the speed of his vehicle in time after watching their fellows fail. The humanoids might have figured out how to make him crash somehow, they were more intelligent.

Francis' hands were sweaty from the stress as his heavy breathing began to slow gradually. He already had a few places he had picked out as a good hideout based on their proximity to the edge of the dome.

He couldn't use any of the Neighborhood Watch safehouses or anything close to them, which limited his potential options somewhat. Too easy to get caught near them, which is why he had to avoid even the area around all of the safehouses that he knew about.

Francis reached one of the suburban cul-de-sacs and drove the vehicle to the house at the end, and was forced to break in to the home so he could open the garage.

Francis had to hide his car, it was too obviously reinforced and militaristic, and might be noticed by the Neighborhood Watch if they spotted it from the air with their drones.

The garage was empty of a car and Francis quickly drove his truck inside and closed the door with his hands. Electricity was beginning to cut out by now, the Infected were becoming too advanced in mutations for Bill to justify continuing to supply the grid with electricity.

Darkness didn't seem to affect the fleshy orbs too much, and the humanoid Nameless were becoming less and less common as time passed. All the remaining humans should be in the safe zones or know enough to stay inside, so Francis was sure that Bill would cut off supplying the grid with electricity entirely within a few days.

Francis went to the truck bed and started unloading his pilfered supplies and making himself at home here. This was one of the neighborhoods the Neighborhood Watch had forcefully cleared of people when they were first creating the Safe zones.

The Neighborhood Watch shouldn't come back this far to the edge of the dome unless they were given reason to.

$-----O-o-O-----$

Francis considered his supplies, his eyes lingering on the case with the disassembled sniper rifle inside before moving on. He thought for a long moment. He now had a safe retreat for his supplies. He had the skeleton of a plan. Now he just had to go out there and actually do it somehow.

Chapter 58: Scouting - Mortal Francis Fragment

Francis looked at the bundles of six foot long hollow metal bars laid out on the floor. They had been the hardest to sneak out of the Ranch, under the strictest security more than almost anything else they had.

These rods could create something that could change the fight inside the dome, a stable tunnel to the outside world through the shield. Each rod created a sphere that could nullify even the strongest wards.

As it was now, the Neighborhood Watch ruled supreme. But Francis knew they hadn't even broken out their most powerful Potential based weapons yet.

The mercenaries in the Safe Zones were the ones that were deemed unreliable or expendable. They had been given normal heavy weapons and some basic shields, but nothing more. If the Ranch wanted to wipe the aliens out all right now, they could. But they didn't, because of the plan.

Francis knew the plan couldn't afford to fail entirely, but Bill was going too far with it. Francis would give the survivors an escape route so at least some of them could survive. He clenched and unclenched his fist as he stared at the bundle of anti-ward rods.

He could go and deploy them somewhere right now… Make way for an evacuation right now…

But it would be pointless.

Bill would be onto it and capture Francis within the hour, destroying the people's only hope of being saved. The army had to be ready to move in immediately once the way was opened.

Hopefully Francis' notes that he had given to Alice would be enough for them to get some soldiers inside to challenge the Neighborhood Watch as well as assist in fighting the aliens.

With an exact description of how the shield regenerated that Francis had put in the documents, he had no doubt that the military would figure out a way to get soldiers in.

The only problem was that the shield healed near the ground quickly enough that there was no way any civilians could ever make their way out. Only the uppermost portions in the sky could be taken down for long enough to get paratroopers or bombs into the dome.

And that was ignoring the mental repellant wards entirely as well in getting the civilians or soldiers in and out. The military would have to parachute soldiers inside on a one way mission.

Francis hadn't stated that explicitly, but there really was no other way he could think of to get people out than the one he planned for. Alice was an anomaly with her massive Potential. No normal person would be able to make it through the mental ward and make it to the barrier itself even if they had the same personal shield device that he gave to her.

If Francis couldn't find another way to get out of the dome then the people in the government who were mostly clueless about Potential would never find anything.

The central generator at the Ranch could make the shield a thousand times physically stronger than it was currently if Bill wanted it to. Bill just didn't want to waste the Potential on sustaining that kind of strength for so long. Waiting for the months it would take for the Avatar to emerge.

Francis fingered the remote in his pocket, set to one of the frequencies Bill had purposely kept open for the explosives in the side tunnels. Francis had set a bomb below the communication jammer. Inside the device's casing where no one would ever think to look. He could set it off right now and start speaking directly with the military on his radio…

He flicked the cap of the detonator open and closed. But why would they trust him? Helen's allies in the military would sideline Francis immediately. General Lopez especially.

And given communication with the interior, General Lopez exchanging favors with Bill would give the Neighborhood Watch sympathizers to manufacture a delay to the military response for long enough that Bill's plan would be accomplished by the time they came in here to rescue the civilians.

Francis had to let the military see the situation themselves before he contacted them. Make them feel more in control of it. If there were already boots on the ground, then the Neighborhood Watch sympathizers wouldn't be able to delay the evacuation. The military would already be committed to the assault, not willing to leave so many of their people behind.

Francis flipped the lid of the detonator closed, covering the button again. He would wait. Contact the soldiers, build some trust, then open up communications with the outside. Well, he had some time but not all of it.

Bill had said the Harbinger shouldn't emerge for another month at least. Francis would before then evacuate all the surviving humans and then close the tunnel to allow the plan to be completed, shutting the military back outside of the dome.

Francis started moving the long metal rods into one of the closets. If he lost these then the whole plan would fall apart. Best keep them out of sight, even if he was probably all alone here in this street.

He would have to lay low until the soldiers arrived. Couldn't risk a long shot on a drone or one of the Infected finding him by accident. Francis finished hiding the anti-warding rods before shifting the rest of his equipment so it was organized and out of sight as well.

The floor looked the same as when he arrived, well maybe a little more scuffed but no one would look that closely. Francis took his food supplies and retreated to the bedroom he had noticed.

Luckily with thick blinds he was able to block anyone being able to see in and spot him. Francis opened up one of the MREs and grimaced. God, these brought back some memories.

But with no electricity and no fresh food it was probably the best he was going to get for a while. Francis dug into the food, the memory making him feel oddly nostalgic of his tours of duty.

He had thought things were so complicated back then... He couldn't even imagine why, with how things were going for him now. Things really had been so much simpler back then than they were now...

— — — O — o — O — — —

On Thursday, Francis heard an explosion above him in the sky. He had hardly left the room for fear of getting spotted all week, and was beginning to feel quite claustrophobic. But at least the owner had been nice enough to leave some trashy novel on the nightstand behind.

Francis didn't usually go for that kind of stuff but was drawn to desperate measures in his boredom. The MREs were as horrible as ever, but at least tolerable for a short time. Francis missed the food at the cafeteria of the Ranch. It hadn't been top tier, but it had been far more tolerable than these MREs were.

Francis stood up as the house rattled again and he felt the ground shake as even more explosions followed the first. He rushed to the window and pulled down the slats of the blinds with one finger to peer outside. Francis crouched down so he could look upwards into the sky.

He watched as the dome above him glowed for a moment before shattering, followed with a barrage of missiles and explosions in the distance. After what felt like forever the explosions stopped.

Francis waited and watched as the dome began to slowly repair itself from the ground upwards. He pumped his fist when he saw the first parachute for a soldier deploy.

Yes! With this, there was no way Bill's allies could pull the military assault back now. Francis only had to wait a little longer to enact his plan. Just a few hours for the soldiers to settle themselves, then he could get the help of the local commander. Offer his help to them, get some trust before really getting things started.

Francis began packing his gear, making sure not to pack some of the more exotic items. He wouldn't want to bring anything that might get confiscated after all.

All of a sudden, he had a lot of work to do. The response was quicker than Francis had thought it would be. Francis wondered why General Lopez hadn't fought it to a standstill tooth and nail. He had always been so talented in digging in his heels and bringing progress on anything productive to an absolute standstill when he needed to.

Francis shook his head. He shouldn't complain, this was good. He had thought it might take another week or two for this to happen, so he was far ahead of schedule already.

Now came the hardest part, getting the military to actually listen to him.

———O—o—O———

Francis watched carefully as the soldiers let out a series of flares into the air. Some green, many red. The green ones would be gathering points, red for enemy contact. He waited for an hour or two before pulling out a bicycle.

Unfortunately he had to break into a neighboring house to find one, but petty theft was his last concern right now. Francis had to be careful to not be too loud or visible and expose the equipment he had stashed here. The car would be too large and too hard to hide if he was spotted.

The closest green flare had been fired from what Francis estimated was five miles or less away. It was closer than he had thought it would be, and luckily was even further from Infected territory than he was now. There was little chance he would have to fight through the aliens to get to them.

Francis had a large pack carrying his various weapons, including the disassembled sniper rifle. Also some Potential based weapons he would use in the worst case scenario.

Francis had decided to just bring everything small enough to carry after some thought. There was no guarantee that he would ever make it back here himself, and better to have it confiscated than getting attacked on the way and not having it for a fight.

He had a pistol strapped at his hip and was wearing a bulletproof vest. His origins as a former member of the Neighborhood Watch would be exposed eventually, best to get out in front of it. Coming in heavily armed might get him to speak to the military commander faster as well.

As Francis pedaled his bicycle, he could only hear the wind rushing in his ears and the rustling of his pack as it shifted on his back. He was close now, and slowed his pace a hair. He wanted to be able to stop on a dime in case the soldiers were trigger happy. He was heading roughly in the right direction, but it was hard to tell given how far away he had seen the green flare from.

Francis kept biking forward until he felt he had gone too far. He turned around and explored another road. An hour later he finally saw something. His shoulders were raw from the scraping of the straps on his heavy pack. Francis rolled to a stop and inspected what appeared to be a safe zone shield in the distance.

He could tell by the faint distortion of the air that there was a shield around the earthwork walls. But that didn't make any sense. This was too far away from the Infected territory for that to be true, there shouldn't be any Safezone established here. Francis turned into an alley and stashed away his bike and heavy pack behind a dumpster. He would have to be agile and stealthy to scout out the situation.

Francis crept forward sticking to the shadows between the buildings. The area was silent, only the rustling of the wind filling Francis' ears. He was close now. He peeked around the corner and quickly drew back as he saw a group of soldiers in green on patrol.

A good sign, but Francis had to make sure it was truly the military before he announced himself. He took binoculars from his pocket and inspected the interior of the Safezone. There were regular people mixed with the green dressed ones. The people looked tense, glancing at the soldiers nervously when they thought they weren't being watched. But they didn't shy away from the soldiers or seem to be mistreated. None wore the black mercenary gear indicative of the Neighborhood Watch.

Francis let out a sigh of relief. He had worried for a moment if the soldiers had somehow been General Lopez's men, sent to secretly support the Neighborhood Watch. It didn't sit well with him that General Lopez hadn't done more to delay the military assault. At least this group seemed clean.

He observed for a few minutes and didn't see anything else out of place. He took note of the man in the center of the encampment who seemed to be giving orders. He was the one Francis would want to speak with. Francis crept back to his bike and the stashed pack quietly.

He quickly biked out of the alley and continued his way towards the dome as if he had never stopped at all. He approached seemingly obliviously closer and closer.

"Stop!" A soldier shouted. Francis quickly braked and stepped off his bike. He raised his hands in the air and turned to the group of five people in green uniforms who raised their guns wearily at seeing Francis' bulletproof vest and gun at his hip. They came closer. "What are you doing here? Keep your hands in the air!"

Francis' arms had dropped slightly as he went to speak but he quickly corrected himself and raised his hands higher. Francis considered his answer for a moment. He just didn't have enough information on why a Safezone shield was here.

It showed that they had at least some contact with someone from the Neighborhood Watch. Better to just be honest, who knows what the mercenaries had told the soldiers. "Francis Moore, here to speak to your commander. I have information that is key to getting the civilians out from under the dome."

The soldiers glanced at each other and whispered to each other for a moment before one ran off to the Safezone. They stood in silence for a moment, waiting for him to come back. He returned with a group of more than twenty soldiers behind him.

A woman in uniform stepped out of the crowd, "Put your weapons on the ground," she demanded.

Francis complied, putting his pistol and pack on the ground. He stepped back. One of the men eyed him but picked them up and quickly brought them to the side.

The woman's voice sounded out again, "Search him."

Francis frowned but let one of the soldiers pat him down. The soldier didn't find anything and nodded back to the apparent leader. She seemed suspicious of him as she inspected him head to toe.

"Sorry about that Mr. Moore," She said, "Just had to be sure. Now you said you had vital information?"

Francis nodded back, "I do. Pretty important though. Don't want to say much with the crowd, y'know?"

The woman looked at him for a long moment before nodding, "Alright. No tricks now."

Francis shot her a thumbs up and she shook her head before looking away. Francis was led under guard to the gate of the Safezone, where the entire group was let in under the shield. Francis was led through to the man who appeared to be the commander that he had spotted in the distance. He turned and looked struck as he saw Francis' face.

"Francis Moore?" Francis nodded a little shocked at the tone of recognition. His file should have been scrubbed from government databases for years. The man leaned forward and stared at him intently.

"Let's get you inside. I'm sure we have a lot to talk about. I'm glad you came so soon."

A little confused, Francis walked into the nearby building after the man. He was sure he would find out what this was all about soon enough. Francis wondered how much he could tell them of the plan.

He remembered how he had felt after Alice had been hurt, how betrayed that Bill had gone even farther past the lines Francis had thought he had lost long ago…

Chapter 59: The Plan Revealed - Mortal Francis Fragment

———Important context missing. Scanning... Scanning... Retrieving Fragment of Memory of Mortal Francis. Second Thursday after the initial attack on Entity Fulcrum. Directly after Mortal Alice was knocked unconscious at Safezone Seven. Isolating... Isolating... Begin. ———

Francis held down his rage for the moment. He was running along Alice's stretcher. She was unconscious and looked like skin on bones, all shriveled up from using her Potential in such large amounts. Or more accurately, having it drained from her. But her breathing was strong, and her face still had some color.

It was recoverable.

She was rushed into the medical ward and Francis was stopped at the door. He let out a shaky breath.

She would be okay. A deeper breath.

She would be okay. She wouldn't die because of him again. His mind caught on that thought as he stood in front of the closed door.

Was he trying to save her like he couldn't save his mother? Was this why he was so invested in her well-being? With how many bodies lay at his feet? At Bill's feet?

He thought he had hardened himself to the suffering, but it seemed it was a facade. Waiting to bubble back to the surface at the smallest prompting

As soon as he was given a face to these townspeople in Alice, everything had gone awry. His emotions rushed through his mind every which way like a dam breaking.

He didn't know how he had held it back for so long. Francis used his old meditative techniques, the ones that Helen had taught him after the death of his mother all those years ago. He let the emotions wash over him, passing like a river. It surged and ebbed, and over time he adapted. He regained control of himself as he sat outside the clinic.

And when his mind settled, one emotion began to dominate the others. Anger. Cold anger. Bill had done this. Francis had thought he had sacrificed enough of his humanity for the plan. For the mission. But apparently it wasn't enough. If Bill was doing what Francis thought he was doing, then it was too much. Bill had gone too far.

Francis would have to stop him, he could only allow so much blood on his hands. Francis could only hope Helen wasn't in on it too.

———O—o—O———

Francis walked into the meeting room thirty minutes later. He had charged into Bill's office, but there was no one there. No one knew where he was. Francis had questioned the people nearby but no one had seen him for over an hour.

Suddenly a messenger had come to tell Francis that Bill and Helen were having a meeting in this meeting room. As Francis walked in, he saw Bill and Helen sitting together on one side of the table and his heart sank.

He looked at both of their faces. Both expressions were carefully neutral. But Helen wasn't quite as good as Bill at controlling herself. Francis could see the hints of sadness in her eyes. It was like a knife to his heart. Helen had known, she was complicit in this too.

Francis stood next to his chair staring down the two in silence. None of them spoke. Helen went to speak first. "Francis, I know you must be upset..." Francis' anger boiled over.

"UPSET!" Francis slammed his fist into the metal table and the both of them jumped. "YOU THINK I'M JUST UPSET!"

"No, Francis. That's not what I meant..."

"YOU TWO ARE GOING AGAINST EVERYTHING WE STAND FOR!" His voice softened, "We were supposed to protect people. Humanity. Is that what this is?"

Bill stood and pointed an accusing finger at Francis, "You know that's what we are doing. Who was the one that handed the Infection Tome to that officer? Even if it was on my orders?

"Who helped put up the dome to subdue the populace? Half the deaths in the town are in your hands. Every person who was Infected or killed by one.

"You dare stand there and lecture *us* on morality? Because you finally see one of the people that you've hurt? This is why we knew you couldn't be trusted with this."

Francis shook his head and shouted back. "*You* know that I only agreed because it was the only way! The extra Potential from the aliens is needed to eliminate the Seed entirely before it becomes an Avatar. You think I wanted to do it? The final attack was only supposed to target the Infected. The safe zones were supposed to be just that, Safe! Protected so at least some could survive.

"The Potential in all the humans in town is tiny in comparison to the Infected! Why sacrifice them too? I saw the second pattern on the stones. It was meant to suck the Potential out of the humans and funnel it back into the final weapon. Not to mention our own men! We don't have nearly enough protection stones for all of them."

Francis fished out the smooth stone from his pocket and waved it for emphasis, "If you activate the weapon you will be killing them all for nothing! Nothing! Scraps of Potential compared to what would come from the Infected."

"Francis," Helen spoke sharply and Francis stopped his rant at her tone, "Let Bill explain."

Francis warred with himself for a moment, wanting to say more. But he still sat in the chair. Bill better have the best god damn explanation in the world for this.

Bill leaned forward. "It's not enough," he said. Francis blinked. What?

"We need to destroy them at the root," Bill continued, "I have word that one of the Infected escaped the dome and is working with the government. It has displayed all sorts of powers we have never seen. Teleportation. Telepathy. Seemingly anti-gravity, as it is observed just hovering in place when it pleases. Where one Infected escapes there will be more. Any of them could have these new abilities!

"We both know how easily they can pass as humans if given enough time to adapt. And you know better than anyone that they are a disease. If we allow them to fester they will consume us from within.

"Do you want the last twelve years to be for nothing? With these new tools in their arsenal it will be ten times harder to dislodge them than it was before. And that's only what we've seen!

"We've nearly wiped the slate *clean*! There have been no more Infected in the world detected for over two years. We've won. If we eliminate the last of these infection tomes then we'll have gotten them all. Or close to it. Any of those townspeople could be an Infected with just a little more skill than the rest. A little better handling of human emotions.

"I'm disappointed you didn't realize that earlier after all these years of fighting them. All it takes is one more sacrifice to stop them forever. To stop this last infection. All the surviving Infection tomes are nearby and activated. Saved as fuel against the Avatar, their leader. We can wipe them all out at once. In one fell swoop."

Francis didn't like the hint of fervor in Bill's voice. He was always a cold and logical type. What he was saying wasn't rooted in logic but emotion. It was slightly disturbing to hear his voice thick with emotion rather than his usual more clipped and clinical tone.

"Bill, how many could escape among these people?" Bill shifted in place and looked uncomfortable.

"It doesn't matter how many," Bill said, "One of them could have been created from an Infection Tome. They could create dozens, hundreds of the Infected if they got out. Enough that we'd spend years rooting them out again."

"How many, Bill? Helen?" Francis retorted.

Helen looked at Francis. "None. Thousands. You know we can't predict that. But we have no way to tell if any of them would have had an Infection Tome with them. Only one escaping to spread would be devastating.

"The well of Potential inside of them would let them survive long enough to spread farther. And even if the military catches one, do you really think they would kill it? No, they would study it and allow it an opportunity to grow and escape again. Like we've seen so many times before."

Francis put his hands flat on the table and stood again. His voice was calmer but still laced with anger, "So. For this hypothetical. You're going to sacrifice over ten thousand people at last count? What would they even do? Why? Just to prevent the Infected from escaping?"

Bill latched onto the last point. "It would increase the attack power of the beam of Devouring Flame against the Avatar. The people in this town have far more Potential on average than anywhere else I've ever seen.

"Alice as a prime example.

"That's why the infection has spread so fast. They can provide enough Potential to increase the beam's power far beyond what we planned for. You know how powerful the Harbinger could be, we need every ounce of power to finish it with the first strike. Or all our preparations and sacrifices here would be for nothing."

Helen pulled out a sheaf of papers and handed them over to Francis. They had calculations. He read them in shock, flipping page to page. They were right. It seems the average people in this town had a little less Potential than *Francis*. Someone who had the highest Potential pool ever recorded before Alice was discovered. The people of this town had hundreds, thousands, maybe even tens of thousands of times more Potential than average. It was true.

If the people were fed to the weapon then the beam's power would increase massively, even if the people in the town weren't Infected. Their sacrifice would measurably be able to strengthen the beam.

In a cold, utilitarian way the plan made a twisted sort of sense. There was no chance for survivors, a decisive end to the aliens' presence on Earth. And that of the humans of this town as well.

But at what cost? Francis thought of Alice as he read the cold numbers of death totals versus projections if an Infection Tome let alone the Avatar escaped. Hundreds of thousands dead over three decades versus tens of thousands all at once. But one of those ten thousand was Alice. Someone who didn't deserve any of this. Someone he had personally resolved to protect, even if it was only a subconscious desire before now.

No. He wouldn't sacrifice these people for Bill and Helen's fear of what might happen. He wouldn't sacrifice Alice. Francis looked up at Bill and Helen's looks. Looks tinged with slight desperation and exhaustion. They didn't want to continue the fight for another three decades. They wanted an easy way out. Francis couldn't accept that. But he now knew he couldn't convince them.

Their stance hadn't wavered the whole time. Their belief that the plan was justified. No matter how much it pained Francis, he would have to pretend. He kept his voice as level as he could as he spoke. Tried to stay calm. He was tired after the long fight too. If he was only a little more jaded, he might be able to stomach this much more blood on his hands. He channeled that.

"Alright, I understand... You're both assholes, but I get it." Francis ran a hand through his hair and sighed. He sat back down in the chair. "But I don't have to like it. Now loop me in. What are the exact preparations you've been hiding from me? No more secrets."

Bill and Helen exchanged one long glance before Bill nodded at her. She pulled out another sheaf of papers. "Alright, so there are various additional amplifiers scattered around town for redundancy. We've set guards here, here, and here. Patrol routes have been diverted to detour around..."

— — — O — o — O — — —

After the meeting was over, Helen approached him after Bill left, "Listen, Francis..."

Francis' tone was sharper than he was going for as he replied sharply, "What is it, Helen? More secrets?"

Helen shook her head and looked hesitant. "Look, you care for that Alice girl, right? I heard how you've been spending time with her recently."

"What's it to you?" he replied coldly.

"We can give her a protection stone for the final attack. She can live through this. We have enough spares for that at least. And I just want to say that I didn't like lying to you. I... I'm sorry we didn't trust you even after all these years. It's hard to find true friends in this line of work and I..." She cut herself off and looked a little lost for words.

Francis softened at her tone and peace offering. For a moment he struggled with laying bare his true feelings. Convincing her of her madness. But her eyes had spoken of nothing but determination when she had spoken of the plan in the discussions. She had displayed no doubt of the plan itself, only relief that Francis had agreed to go along with it.

She and Bill had been planning this from the very beginning, those projections they showed Francis didn't just get created in a day.

It probably was a backup plan they never had wanted to tell him about. Discussed just between the two of them and buried among the other contingencies. Francis tried to restrain his response to Helen's heartfelt words.

"Yes. Thank you," He said curtly, "I would appreciate that, Helen. I know you did what you thought best. I'm sorry you couldn't trust me. I thought I wasn't just another asset to you two."

Helen looked hurt by his harsh response. Francis cursed himself. He had revealed too much as the last sentence just slipped out without him meaning it to. Before he could expose any more of his true feelings, Francis left the door and walked to his private room. It was all he could do. Helen didn't try to follow after him.

Some people tried to talk to him in the hallways, but were rebuffed by his uncharacteristically severe demeanor. Francis went inside his room and laid back on his bunk. He had a lot to do. Bill and Helen were the enemy now. Even if they didn't seem to know it yet. Well, Helen didn't know it at least.

Even if Francis didn't want it to be so, they were the enemy. He would have to be careful, because if he failed... If he failed... Everyone in this town would die.

If he was too successful, and stopped the attack entirely... Then the end of the world would be his fault. The Avatar would escape to bring devastation to the world unopposed. And he had enough on his conscience. He wouldn't allow either of those things to happen.

He wouldn't make any mistakes. He'd save the civilians and let the Avatar of the Eldest be destroyed at the same time.

Chapter 60: Joining the Army - Mortal Francis Fragment

———— Returning back to Third Thursday after the attack on Entity Fulcrum. Context of Prime Mortal's full plan retrieved. Resuming from the end of the prior Fragment of Memory... Isolating... Isolating... Isolating... Isolating... Begin.—
——

Francis was surprised when the military commander recognized him immediately. Once they had sat down among the scattered electric lamps inside the building, Francis had explained who he was and his method to create a tunnel through the dome given some time.

The shadows danced in corners of the room with only the lamps to give them light as Francis spoke. There had been a lot of hustle and excitement at that from the surrounding onlookers. The command staff in green uniforms had begun muttering and scurrying around ever since making plans and shifting their strategies.

When Francis had asked, the commander freely admitted that they had found Francis' image and file from some of General Lopez's recovered records. General Lopez who was a traitor and on the run from the authorities, as a suspected member of the Neighborhood Watch. Francis frowned.

General Lopez was careful and entrenched so deep in the military that he had been able to smuggle them all their weapons without so much as a hint of worry of someone else finding out about it. What the hell did he do if people were able to get access to his records so quickly?

And fuck Lopez for keeping Francis' full file to use as blackmail, but frankly Francis would have been more surprised if that was not the case. Hopefully the reason he was given those blood soaked missions was in there too.

The Neighborhood Watch had hunted down as many of the aliens and their collaborators as they could but some of the perpetrators had still escaped, Francis was sure. Francis quickly moved past the topic, at least he now knew that General Lopez wouldn't be around to interfere with things from the outside.

Francis asked for his bag. Without interference from General Lopez, he could be much more open with this. The commander here seemed like a much more straightforward type who would appreciate honesty. Francis' plan should be in line with what the soldiers wanted to do anyway.

They brought out his bag and slowly unloaded item after item on a table in the corner that was still visible to them. They kept going, and they all raised their eyebrows when they opened the case and saw the sniper rifle components inside.

The soldiers kept unloading Francis' bag, unloading the bits and bobs, extra weapons, and a few packs of MREs. Finally Francis pointed as they took out the tiny detonator with the plastic cap still firmly shut on top.

"There."

The soldier unloading Francis' bag picked up the detonator. The commander looked it over in interest. Francis continued,

"I put a bomb on the communications jammer at the Neighborhood Watch's base. You hit that detonator, you get communications again for as long as it takes for them to repair the connections and hook up the spare. That should give us the time to tell the outside the situation. They can prepare something to defend the tunnel so the people can be evacuated."

There was more motion and chaos as all the plans were suddenly upended again and more people rushed in and out to adjust their approach. It seemed there were some analyst types here mixed in with the more combat oriented soldiers. The commander looked to Francis as he picked up the detonator. He put it in his pocket.

"Thank you for this, Francis. Mr. Moore. I think you know as well as I do how much this will help us. Now…" He splayed his hands on the table, leaned forward, and glanced around the room. His look grew sharp as he grinned slightly.

"Let's get down to the details." Francis obliged the invitation and began speaking of what he remembered of the Neighborhood Watch positions and the alien's capabilities. Every little bit would help more of the townspeople escape.

―――O―o―O―――

The people in the room began debating furiously about the best position to create the tunnel. Francis sat there under guard and just listened. He tuned out as they spoke, and was startled as he realized someone was calling his name. "Mr. Moore? What do you think based on your experience here?" the military commander asked.

Francis glanced at the map. They had chosen the obvious place, the entrance to the highway. Great place for vehicles to enter, and easy access to the rest of the town.

"Terrible," They all stared at him, "Did I forget to tell you that the highway is lined with explosives? The Neighborhood Watch will set them off the second you start bringing vehicles there. And it's too obvious. You need far more firepower if you want to hold the Neighborhood Watch long enough for reinforcements to support you."

One of the men stepped forward. "So what do you propose? We need a clear space for vehicles to move in."

Francis pointed to a smaller road that was three lanes, probably the best road to enter from besides the highway.

"A small group uses the anti-warding rods to ferry themselves outside of the Dome. Then use the remaining rods to build a tunnel here from the outside and open the way for the main assault. I stole enough rods to create around three tunnels. Enough to replace them if a few get destroyed in the battle. Keep in mind if they are all destroyed, so is any hope of getting people outside. So you can't be too wasteful with them either"

The commander and the other people in the room considered his points before the commander nodded. "Thank you Francis. We will consult you if we have any more questions. We appreciate your assistance."

With that, Francis was led out again and brought to his room. It had a guard at the door, but it wasn't the worst place to sleep at least. There was a mattress on the floor.

Hardly five stars, but better than many other places Francis had slept before. Hopefully the military would start move on the plan soon, who knew what Bill would do if he decided the soldiers weren't worth the hassle they caused and started bring out the big guns.

— — — O — o — O — — —

Francis was surprised. He was still under guard, but heard things anyway on how things had progressed over the last few days. Francis was still being interrogated for details but had managed to keep the larger details of the Harbinger and Bill's plan under wraps.

They wouldn't understand and would just doom them all as they fought to destroy the weapon before it was deployed. Francis would tell them last minute so they would have enough time to evacuate but not enough to stop Bill. Francis had no problem sacrificing all the Infected to destroy the Harbinger.

And now it was Monday. There had been minor skirmishes with the Neighborhood Watch but it seems that Bill had largely given up control of the Safezones. He and the rest of the Neighborhood Watch had retreated to the Ranch and seemed to be deploying the heavy defenses and waiting them out.

The soldiers had the aliens to deal with too after all. But oddly enough, it seems the Infected were lying low as well, only sending out small groups out periodically to harass them. Francis didn't like it.

Most of the mercenaries recruited by the Neighborhood Watch folded immediately to the demands of the military after realizing they had been left out in the cold by Bill and the Ranch.

Only two or three Safezones held steady, turtled up under their shields and stupidly loyal to the end. It seemed they had figured out a few of the high potential civilians could fill the main Potential banks fueling the shield enough to keep the shield stable against the military siege of them.

The equipment from the conquered safe zones were all being moved into clusters around the one Francis was in right now. The main base of sorts.

All of the other Safezones that had been put under military control were being taken down and moved here into the central cluster as well as the people who had been inside of them. Moving everybody all into one spot along with all of the equipment and soldiers.

Francis couldn't believe that there had been survivors of Safezone seven that made it all the way here...

He had seen that man in a tattered police uniform talking with Sergeant Ruston briefly, before Francis had ducked away before either of them could see him. It had been dumb luck that saved the man, not Francis' foolish actions in firing that warning shot.

If Francis had been free to move afterwards, been just a little colder and restrained himself, he could have smuggled out so much more equipment to help the army before his escape... Kept the lie going just a little longer... Been able to prepare more...

Anyway, the soldiers were transporting the last of the people willing to leave today to the Safezones maintained by the military. It seems there was some cultist named Adam leading a few hundred people. They had violently refused to leave due to their distrust of authority. After the initial negotiations had failed, the soldiers eventually left the group to themselves and told the others in the cult that they would rescue them after the aliens were defeated.

Two hours later, Francis watched as the last convoy of vehicles arrived and unloaded the people in one of the neighboring zones. Roughly six thousand people were gathered here now...

Francis was worried that Infiltrator of Authority was not attacking such a large group. It must be planning something big, and Francis could only hope the soldiers were ready to begin the plan before it launched its inevitable assault. The woman soldier who Francis had first met on his way here approached. He now knew her as Sergeant Ruston.

She met Francis' eyes. "They want you. It's almost time."

Francis jolted and rushed off. The military command had been withdrawn for the last two days or so, huddled up in their main base planning what to do.

Francis had still given periodic advice to the military leaders, but they called on him less often now. Presumably because they were starting to go into specifics they didn't want him to know about.

Francis assumed they had finally used the detonator and reestablished communications with the outside world if they were calling him again. Francis walked into the command room with the rolled out map with various markings and pins in it.

"Francis," The commander stood tall, surrounded by his advisors, "We will act soon. Will you fight with us? We need every gun we can get."

Francis didn't hesitate. He couldn't give up now, "Of course. If you will have me."

The commander waved his hand to shoo Francis away. He glanced at Sergeant Ruston behind him. "Sergeant Ruston, give him his gear. He'll be in your squad, and it's your responsibility that he doesn't go rogue for the duration of your mission. You'll be getting your marching orders soon."

Sergeant Ruston sighed before nodding. "Yes, sir."

Francis followed her out of the room and to the armory. Time to go to war again.

Chapter 61: Opening a Doorway to the World Outside of the Bubble - Mortal Francis Fragment

Francis had all his old equipment back, sniper rifle and all. He was honestly surprised he had gotten that one back. He was going to help ferry the squad through the barrier and show them how to use the warding rods.

He gave Sergeant Ruston's squad quick explanations in their use as they waited to go. It was less efficient, but people who couldn't direct their Potential actively could still put their hands on the input point and let the item fill extremely slowly with their Potential no matter how small an amount they had.

Sergeant Ruson's squad would carry the remainder of the rods to the outside so the outside forces could open the tunnel for the evacuation from the outside.

The military had quickly gathered the supplies Francis had left behind at his temporary Safehouse when he told them of its location. The anti-ward rods required the initial investment of Potential to activate, so Francis could charge it faster than a whole squad of soldiers, making their exit quicker.

This was the most dangerous part, as any attack here could destroy their precious cargo and dash the hopes of the whole operation.

Luckily, the rods worked over a large radius so losing a few wouldn't be the end of the world once the tunnel was established. So even if they were attacked they should have a chance to flee.

The other soldiers behind in the Safe zones were out in force causing some sort of distraction so Francis and the squad wouldn't be noticed by the aliens or Neighborhood Watch both.

The operation would begin in a few minutes. They sat there, just Francis, Sergeant Ruston, and her squad waiting for orders. The word from on high came and Francis was handed the first rod by one of the soldiers holding the bundle of them in his arms.

Francis started walking towards the edge of the dome. The soldiers behind him attempted to follow, but quickly drifted and stumbled to the side. Sergeant Ruston lasted a little longer but she too turned to the side after a hundred feet more as the dome's mental component messed with their perceptions.

Francis continued until he felt his feet begin to turn to the side. He injected his Potential into the rod and the network of glowing lines activated. Francis heard a deep *Thrum* in the air as the mental pressure suddenly vanished.

The rod should last at least a day or two without more charging needed if it would stay stationary.

Francis glanced back and saw a larger group of soldiers approaching with Sergeant Ruston at their head. It seemed that the radius of the nullification field had luckily been large enough to let them through. Without another word, they continued Francis pushing forward with them behind him.

Unfortunately, the rods were calibrated to the exact strength and parameters of the ward present when they were first activated.

It could make small adjustments but the sudden changes from motion caused it to waste massive amounts of energy trying to adjust.

So moving it like he was doing now would just make it misaligned and burn through its charge of Potential faster. The mental force grew stronger the closer they drew to the dome itself.

Francis felt the pressure even through the fluctuating nullification field now. The first anti-ward rod went dull and stopped working. Some of the soldiers quickly turned around and began walking back with blank looks in their eyes.

With a curse, Francis activated the next rod and everyone regained their senses. Francis could see its shimmering boundary and the distortions of the light at the edge of the dome in the distance now.

Everything was going smoothly. They were not attacked, no aliens showed up to harass them.

They reached the edge of the dome and could barely see the green vehicles and helicopters on the other side of the shimmering dome.

The rod that Francis was holding burned out. Francis planted a new rod directly next to the shield quickly. Another next to it. Another. The shield flickered in and out, on the verge of failure.

Francis stopped for a snack to refuel his Potential. The soldiers looked at him in confusion, still not aware of the specifics behind the use of Potential, and the extra hunger that came with it. Francis had to keep his explanation earlier as concise as he could, so he left that part out.

Francis finished the energy bar and placed the last rod and activated it. The dome was sent over the edge and with a *crack* the portion of the dome just in front of them disappeared.

A perfectly circular hole of a two hundred foot radius formed in the barrier. Francis could see the edges in the distance glowing with golden light as the dome attempted to overpower the nullification field and heal the hole in the barrier.

Francis placed and activated one more rod just for safety, and the hole expanded slightly as the anti-warding rod began to pulse in sync with its nearby fellows.

Sergeant Ruston clapped Francis on the back and thanked him. The soldiers carrying the rest of the inactive warding rods went through in big bundles strapped to their backs. They all made their way forward. The instant they left the nullification field they picked up their pace and began to walk faster, propelled away by the mental ward towards the waiting army outside now that they were on the other side of the dome.

Francis watched as they receded into the distance. His ass was still being arrested as soon as he was one foot out of the dome, and there was no way he would go out there before he saw this through.

Francis collected the glowing rods in a bundle and slung them awkwardly over his shoulder. He walked back slowly under the awkward weight. They quickly drained to nothing. But at least they would be good decoys for when the military assault breached the dome. Francis was sure the military would appreciate that kind of idea.

———O—o—O———

Francis made his way back alone. He was checked by the guards and escorted back inside by one of the roaming patrols of soldiers. There were only a few hours left before the tunnel would be opened and soldiers from the outside would flood inside the dome, and his idea with decoy rods had indeed been appreciated.

Francis could only hope the soldiers could hold out long enough for the civilians to be evacuated. He didn't have much hope for more if the Neighborhood Watch truly contested them. Or the aliens for that matter. Who knew what Infiltrator of Authority was up to right now.

Time passed, and the bustle around him increased in intensity. Francis was largely ignored, the soldiers too focused on their own missions to bother with the man leaning against the side of the building watching them.

Francis checked his equipment one more time as things grew to a frenzied pace around him. It was nearly time. A soldier walked over and gestured to Francis.

Francis pushed himself to his feet and followed the man as he was led to the mass of soldiers waiting at the edge of the shields. The first working vehicles filled with the civilians would be sent out soon. Francis wouldn't be going with them, but left behind to assist in guarding the zone. He wasn't trusted enough for any of them to depend on him to watch their backs.

———O—o—O———

The soldiers were gone now, only a skeleton crew left behind at the main safe zone. Some left in the train of vehicles, taking over a thousand people with them in one long convoy.

The rest were out in force, guarding the rest of the encircling domes protecting the townspeople inside. Twenty minutes ago massive explosions and gunfire had begun in the distance. Everyone was tense, flinching at the sounds.

The deep thrumming of helicopter blades sounded out, getting closer until the five Apache helicopters settled into formation to hover above the domes.

Heavy military trucks rolled into view in the distance and the people cheered. The vehicles rolled forward toward them, ready to evacuate the thousands of people waiting.

The loading was efficient, the townspeople already organized into groups and darted outside the dome to clamber into the trucks indicated to them by the waiting soldiers.

As soon as the vehicles were filled the large trucks would rumble back into motion and drive back towards the direction of the explosions. Their ferocity and frequency of the explosions was slowly decreasing over there. Francis hoped that was a good sign.

It sounded like the fighting was moving away from the edge of the dome luckily based on the explosions moving deeper into the town and farther from the dome itself. So the people in the trucks should be able to make it through.

One of the smaller Safezones nearby was emptied of people and the dome flickered off before the formation stones began to be loaded into the next truck. Francis frowned a little that they would save the equipment before the people. But at least they were here and doing something.

Francis fiddled with his sniper rifle again. Things were going smoothly. Too smoothly. Francis shifted uneasily as more and more of the domes around them shut off showing they were emptied of people.

More vehicles were constantly arriving and leaving and the explosions in the distance had grown more sporadic now. About a quarter of the people now remained, just around fifteen hundred people total left to evacuate.

A final wave of trucks arrived, and the remainder of the townspeople clambered aboard and were driven away over the next twenty or so minutes.

Only the single central Safezone with Francis and the remaining soldiers remained as the trucks began to pull away. Everyone around Francis jumped as the deep booms of heavy guns sounded out from the helicopters above them.

The helicopters spread out and shifted inwards closer towards the hospital and the alien main base. Francis and all the soldiers around him sprinted to that side of their shield.

Everyone looked into the distance and whispered, but whatever the helicopters were shooting at was too far away to see yet. The helicopters launched missiles and the explosions shook the ground and made everyone stumble.

Francis pushed to the front of the crowd as he finally realized what was coming. He got a clear view as the wave of alien bodies came tumbling around the corner. They covered the street, squirming over each other and not exposing a single inch of road below them like a giant squirming carpet of fleshy orbs.

The creatures rushed in a giant wave towards their shield as the helicopters fired into the mass from above, poking holes in the horde only for them to be filled back in moments by the tide of bodies behind. Francis unhooked his sniper rifle and looked down the sights as the larger forms began to emerge from underneath the wave of flesh. The Infected had made their move.

Chapter 62: Assault on the Backlines - Infiltrator of Authority Fragment

Infiltrator of Authority had decided after the devastation of the mortal nation's assault, that the Invasion must appear weak and struggling in response. Yes, their numbers had been cut down, but Infiltrator of Authority could order an all out assault and had a high chance of overpowering the humans and controlling the dome at the moment.

But it was only a chance, not a guarantee because of the mortal Bill. Infiltrator of Authority had to spread out its forces now so they couldn't be eliminated in a single devastating strike by him and whatever method he had used to eliminate the Betrayer.

Infiltrator of Authority gathered the surviving Nameless mutated combat forms gathered near the Spires of growth. Each grabbed of the Nameless grabbed one of the spires of growth from the base and ripped them from their positions where they were rooted.

The Nameless all lumbered off to their own locations around the dome, scattering as far as they could and moving away from the hospital.

They knew their orders. Infiltrator of Authority followed one telepathically as it carried to an isolated building. It slowly climbed to the roof, careful not to damage the Spire of Growth held in its clawed arms. With one hard stomp the creature opened a sizable hole in the roof before gently lowering itself down inside. Now it wouldn't be visible on the street to the humans.

The Nameless placed the Spire of growth down and it began to immediately root itself in place once more and begin creating the next clutch of Spawnlings, using the sunlight spilling through the newly made hole in the roof to fuel itself.

All around the town they spread, slipping past the patrols by the Safezones in the chaos brought by the humans in green clashing with the Neighborhood Watch, as the humans in green rained above from the rapidly closing hole in the dome.

Five of the Spires of Growth and their transports were caught and attacked and two were killed before they could escape the humans from both sides. But the rest slipped through and rooted themselves into buildings that were out of the way and isolated.

The Nameless traveled in groups, carrying eight Spires of Growth to the roughly same area, so they could support one another if discovered. The orders of the small clusters of Nameless and Spires of Growth were simple, grow and stay hidden.

The combat Nameless needed biomass to increase their slowly draining Potential to survive, but they could sustain themselves on the surrounding plant life rather than flesh. Less efficient than feeding it to the Tower of Decay would be, yes, but still better than being forced to gather to one point for survival.

This is where the final addition to its forces would make itself known. Infiltrator of Authority took the last of the unspecialized Nameless left and altered them, creating barely enough of them to have one Biological Manipulator assigned to each cluster of Spires of Growth. The Biological Manipulators could guide the growth and mutations of the spawnlings in a poor imitation of Infiltrator of Authority's skills.

They would prove useful once the interior of the dome was conquered, but Infiltrator of Authority needed them for one reason alone for now. They could put the Spawnlings into a kind of stasis that dropped their use of Potential to almost nothing.

The Spawnling numbers could be swelled to massive unsustainable proportions, each Spawnling that was created quickly put in stasis to allow it to survive as long as possible with minimal drain on their Potential. Then at the proper moment they could be released on the mortals in one massive assault from the backlines on being awakened.

Infiltrator of Authority looked to its ten meager Spires of Growth remaining directly surrounding the recovering Tower of Decay and the hospital. It would stay here and pretend it was rebuilding with these as its surviving forces.

With such low spawnling production, they would increase their strength much more rapidly than before due to the abundant fluid flowing from the Tower of Decay even now to feed them.

It would be a massive waste of resources, to cultivate the weak spawnlings like this. But it should be enough to convince the humans that this was what remained of the main force of the Invasion. Should it invest in some wards around the Tower of Decay?

No, that was still too wasteful even for a distraction. Anything effective enough to hold off an assault would trap them within the specific confines of the ward and prevent the foragers from going out to get food for the Tower of Decay.

Best for Infiltrator of Authority to improve the combat Nameless who remained with its skill and the extra Potential that the Tower of Decay would be creating.

Infiltrator of Authority surveyed the combat form Nameless that had remained behind and not dispersed outwards with the Spires of Growth. It would improve these as much as possible, now able to concentrate the Potential and its attention on their smaller number.

After the Tower of Decay had fully healed and resumed full production two hours later, one of the Nameless approached and lay down in the growing pool of black fluid at its base.

Infiltrator of Authority watched as the inky fluid flowed into its skin. Infiltrator of Authority approached and began its work. It would refine the Nameless' form until it was the best it could be or the fluid ran dry. It could accept nothing less.

───O─o─O───

Forty minutes later, Infiltrator of Authority checked telepathically on the situation at the scattered bases after taking a break from its work. There had been a few attacks on them, but it seemed the green dressed mortals were occupied fighting with the mortal Bill's forces for now.

A few of the flying spawnlings that had survived had witnessed one of the clashes where the green mortals sent a red fire in the sky. The green soldiers were quickly reinforced by their fellows and the Neighborhood Watch patrols were overwhelmed one by one.

None of the humans had discovered any of the hidden Spires of Growth yet, too caught up in their own battles. The combat forms remained hidden, guarding their assigned spire from the shadows. Infiltrator of Authority turned back to the pool as the next Nameless slid inside to be refined. It cracked its mortal knuckles. There was more work to do.

───O─o─O───

Infiltrator of Authority was nearly done when it received shocking news. The Safezones were being taken down by the green dressed mortals! Bill and his forces seemed to have retreated from their patrols of the dome after several groups had been killed or surrendered to the mortal army soldiers.

The green clothed mortals had attempted a few assaults on the hospital at that time, but after being repulsed a few times by all the spawnlings Infiltrator of Authority had available, retreated to gather their strength more.

Most of the spawnlings Infiltrator of Authority had here at the hospital were lost in the attacks, but their purpose was achieved. None of the refined combat forms had been exposed yet, while the assaults had still been repelled. If only just barely. It was a difficult enough battle for both groups that the humans seemed to not suspect that there was going on beneath the surface.

Infiltrator of Authority considered launching its assault now. Bill had retreated, the green mortals seemed to be doing something similar, gathering all the remaining mortals in one of the out of the way locations under their newly erected shields. It might be best to strike them while they were in transition between locations.

But Infiltrator of Authority didn't want them to stop breaking their encirclement of the hospital. If the army fully evacuated the safe zones and gathered all of the humans in one spot, then the clusters of Spires of Growth could be more open and support one another more easily if they were attacked. So Infiltrator of Authority waited and kept its forces passive as the soldiers did their work.

Over the next two days all but three of the Safezones were relocated to somewhere out of the way. Infiltrator of Authority considered carefully before deciding to still remain hidden.

Bill was the true threat, and if he had retreated his forces then he must be pitting Infiltrator of Authority against the other mortals so they could both expend their strength on each other.

Best to allow the mortals to fight it out uninterrupted. Not to say that Infiltrator of Authority didn't send a few groups of spawnlings to explore and keep the mortal soldiers on their toes. Doing absolutely nothing in the face of opportunity would be even more suspicious than having some weaker attacks after all.

———O—o—O———

It was Monday now and strange things were happening. Bill and his mortals remained isolated, turtles inside their defenses with no movement. Even the green mortals had suddenly pulled back and stopped all patrols outside their immediate cluster.

Finally less than an hour ago the dome around the town had glowed with light for a few minutes before returning to normal. Infiltrator of Authority didn't trust it. Something was going on, and Infiltrator of Authority made the combat forms prepare themselves for battle.

A few hours later, Infiltrator of Authority finally got its answer. The dome flashed with golden light again but this time it was sustained. Mortal vehicles and soldiers in green poured in through what was now apparent as a doorway to the outside world. A line of vehicles approached then left the army safezones, presumably carrying the mortals of the town out of the dome to safety.

Infiltrator of Authority licked its lips as it ordered the Biological Manipulators to initiate the awakening process on the spawnlings. The spawnlings would be ravenous, and this was the perfect moment to attack.

Bill was too occupied sending his forces combating the green mortals to close, looking to close the exit to the dome before any of the Eldritch could escape and spread in the outside world.

Infiltrator of Authority would begin an infiltration invasion of that type if it was forced too, but such strategies were rarely successful. The more examples of the Eldritch biology there was to be studied and captured, the more likely the mortals were to develop countermeasures. Much like how mortal Bill had become such a nuisance with his deep knowledge and Potential based weapons.

Better for the Invasion to stay a discrete force so the mortals would have less samples and time to learn from and counter them.

Not to mention the intelligence and resources needed to create a being able to hide from mortal authorities for a world such as this was rather extreme. Each creature would represent a massive sink of Potential, and each that was caught would be a significant loss to the invasion as a whole.

But luckily Bill couldn't take the risk that one of them would escape, so he and his forces had to close the exit to the dome at all costs. Even now, the two groups of mortals were fighting as the Neighborhood Watch emerged from their shells and began to do battle with the green vehicles and ranks of soldiers in truth.

— — — O — o — O — — —

With the two groups distracted fighting each other, it was finally time for Infiltrator of Authority to collect the last bags of Potential left in this town. How kind of the mortals to all gather in one place for a single overwhelming assault.

Infiltrator of Authority checked on the Biological Manipulators and saw they were only half way through the awakening process. It growled. It hadn't expected to need to attack in such a small window of opportunity. But there was no better moment than now. Whichever group won now would turn their weapons on the forces of the Invasion next.

— — — O — o — O — — —

It was nearly too late, almost all the mortals had been evacuated from the Safezones, but the forces were finally gathered and the spawnlings were only barely held in check from charging immediately. Infiltrator of Authority made one final check on the placement of the groups, they must all attack as one. Satisfied, it released its reins on the spawnlings with a release of its mental pressure.

The spawnlings began their charge towards the food they sensed all at once. The combat forms of the Nameless followed behind the charging wave of Spawnlings at a slower pace. The airborne vehicles of the mortal army rained fire on the charging horde, but Infiltrator of Authority could only smile. There was a plan for them too.

The mortals would see soon and Infiltrator of Authority just couldn't wait to stop holding itself and its forces back. It was almost a shame it wouldn't be here to see it happen.

Infiltrator of Authority stripped out of its tattered police uniform and changed into more inconspicuous human garments it had found earlier. Its face bubbled and shifted as it made its way to the mortal evacuation point with inhuman speed.

It positioned a group of spawnlings to emerge from the buildings and directed them to chase Infiltrator of Authority's mortal form. It twisted its expression into deep fear and slowed to a slower human pace as it reached the line of soldiers near the tunnel to the outside world, over forty spawnlings charging after it from behind. The mortal soldiers pointed guns at him only to change their aim on seeing what was chasing Infiltrator of Authority.

"Help!" Infiltrator of Authority called out in a desperate voice in Officer Nick's voice. The soldiers opened fire and let Infiltrator of Authority charge right through their lines unimpeded.

———O—o—O———

The soldiers ushered Infiltrator of Authority through to the exit, attempting to separate him from the larger groups. At least they had some sense. But with a twist and a dash, Infiltrator of Authority dived into the milling crowd and changed its face again.

In seconds it was lost in the milling crowd, and hurried with the others onto a truck that drove quickly to the outside world. They passed through the tunnel of shimmering golden light, and Infiltrator of Authority took a deep breath and smiled. The mortals looked relieved for far different reasons altogether.

Infiltrator of Authority had done as much for the Invasion as it could, but escaping Bill's grasp was the most important right now. Without him looming over everything Infiltrator of Authority would make far more progress.

As long as it survived the Invasion would live on. Let the mortals fight each other. Hopefully they would weaken each other in time for Infiltrator of Authority's triumphant return.

It had hopes that the Invasion might be able to claim the dome even in its absence, but it wasn't worth the risk of waiting behind. It was a matter of pure combat strength at this point. The Invasion forces of spawnlings and Nameless within the dome would either win or not. Infiltrator of Authority had given them the best chances it could, and now it was now time to hedge their pets for the invasion.

Even if the Invasion forces were completely eliminated, Infiltrator of Authority only had to wait for the Avatar to arrive and sweep away all opposition with its strength.

If the Seed was communing with the Eldest then it must be strong. Infiltrator of Authority was sure it would be able to at least escape or shrug off whatever elaborate trap or weapon that the mortal Bill had planned for it. No amount of cunning could defeat a difference in power that large.

Chapter 63: Escaping the Horde - Mortal Francis Fragment

Francis watched as the wave of alien fleshy balls crashed against the shield. Francis could see the rest of the horde moving around the sides to reach the escaping vehicles holding the townspeople.

The shield began to glow brightly as everyone inside sprung into motion. The soldiers all gathered on the roofs of the buildings inside of the dome as a new set of helicopters flew in above them. The Black Hawks shifted to hover directly over the three even groups of gathered soldiers.

The Apache Helicopters had left to follow the retreating townspeople and hold the line there. Francis could hear their gunfire and explosions slowly receding into the distance. There were about thirty soldiers total that had remained behind. The shield grew brighter and Francis could see cracks begin to form, allowing a few of the balls of flesh to push themselves through.

A trio of explosions shook Francis' group and they stumbled around as the stairs to their roof were blown to pieces. Now the aliens would have to climb up the sides of the building to reach them.

The automatic fire and rumbling of exploding missiles still sounded out from the helicopters above. Finally the shield burst and abruptly the constant fire above them cut out. The soldiers cleared space on their roof as the helicopters descended to land to pick them up.

The wave of aliens coated the interior of the Safezone in moments, jumping and snapping at each other and eating anything that looked even remotely biological. Francis could only watch in horror as a nearby tree was shredded into splinters and consumed in under a minute.

Finished stripping the plantlife, most of the creatures rushed onwards after the vehicles with the last of the civilians that were retreating into the distance.

A few hundred of the aliens noticed the humans on the roof however and attempted to scale the sides of the building. The soldiers fired their weapons off the side, sending the creatures falling to the ground where they distracted the horde below in consuming their fellow's bodies. At the sound of the gunfire, more of the aliens diverted and began to climb towards the soldiers above.

Francis pulled out his pistol and was firing as fast as he could over the side of the building, slinging the sniper rifle over his back. There was sweat on his brow as the creatures drew closer to him. The helicopter had almost touched down on the roof and the man inside the cabin was waving the closest of them inside.

Francis' pistol clicked empty as one of the balls of flesh gathered itself for what Francis knew was one of its massive leaps as it clung to the wall below.

Francis fell back just in time for it to shoot past his head. It shot into the air before falling flat on the roof, stunned. Francis scrambled over and stomped it under his heel, causing it to twitch. He stomped again and it went still. More of the creatures launched themselves over the lip and landed stunned to the roof of the building as Francis finished off the first one.

The helicopter touched down just as the first of the aliens began making it over the lip onto the roof. Their group of ten soldiers all sprinted and dived inside the helicopter as the aliens began to recover from their stunned state and chase them.

Francis threw himself inside and quickly moved to the side to make room for the woman behind him. He quickly reloaded his pistol as he made his way to his feet. He turned around and saw the last soldier trip, one of the alien balls latching onto his leg. The man who had ushered them in turned to the cockpit shouted into his headset. "GO, GO, GO!"

The helicopter began to lift as the alien balls bunched themselves and launched themselves towards the open doors in a wave of bodies. The man who had fallen was already stripped nearly to the bone, covered in a solid mass of the creatures wriggling and biting him.

Francis fired blindly into the aliens that had launched themselves at the helicopter and several went limp as they impacted the side of the helicopter with wet thumps and fell down.

Five of the creatures made it through into the cabin in time before the sliding door was slammed shut by the man wearing the headset.

The gathered soldiers tried to raise their pistols, but Francis knew they were too close for that. He waded forward and stomped and bludgeoned the creatures with the base of his sniper rifle before the rest could react.

The last alien recovered before Francis could kill it and leapt at the man to Francis' right. Seeing Francis' success the man pistol whipped the creature midair and sent it flying into the metal walls of the helicopter cabin. It was quickly finished off by the group in a flurry of blows.

For a moment they all stood around panting and glancing at each other. Someone in the back's shoulders rose and fell as they seemed to silently giggle from the release of their accumulated stress. Francis couldn't hear them over the overpowering sound of the helicopter blades and rushing winds.

Just as they relaxed there was a banging at the door and the helicopter lurched to the side. Muffled shouts from the cockpit, "Windshield... ———————— Everywhere, —— Can't see!"

The soldier with the helicopter crew listened over his headset and cocked his pistol and reached for the door. Everyone was shouting, only to be thrown to the side as the helicopter lurched again.

The soldier threw open the helicopter door and fired at the aliens clinging to the side of the metal helicopter, futilely trying to chew through the metal. The rest of the group stopped struggling as they saw what was happening, cocking their own weapons.

The woman soldier threw open the door on the other side and started firing at the clinging aliens on her side of the helicopter. One leaped inwards and the woman leaned back in surprise to let it pass by her. It was coming straight towards Francis.

He tried to slap it out of the air, but he missed and it latched into his shoulder. He fell backwards and reached to peel it off but it squirmed and shifted as it began tearing through the shoulder strap of his bulletproof vest.

Francis grunted as he felt a heavy impact and then the alien was sent flying away by a heavy combat boot. It went flying back out the door and flailed as it was sent into the open air before it began falling to the ground far below.

The helicopter lurched to the side again again and someone leapt forward to grab the woman as she almost went flying out the open door. Two of the soldiers kept tumbling forward towards the open gap, only to be quickly saved by the others and heaved back into the vehicle before they could fall out.

The man with the headset from the helicopter crew was shouting something over his headset and leaned out the doors, gripping the side with one hand. With cries of alarm the rest of them grabbed onto him before he could fully fall out.

The man ignored them and just fired his pistol as he leaned out the doors, pointing his weapon forward and more towards the front of the helicopter where the pilots were shouting. More alien bodies fell to the ground far below limp as he fired his weapon.

The man moved to the other side and the others braced him again, understanding what he was doing this time. He fired his weapon again and more aliens fell to the ground that was far below now.

With that they shut the two doors and the rushing wind stopped filling the cabin and noise of the wind died down compared to the deep rumble of the helicopter blades.

The Black Hawk helicopter lurched to the side two more times before the man from the crew listened to something over his headset and sagged in relief. They all stared at him, and he gave a weary thumbs up at the group and they all let out a breath.

They had two minutes to collect themselves as they all put on the ear protection and headsets so they could properly communicate. Francis put his on and heard the woman soldier speaking animatedly,

"Well that was certainly something. Ha, did you see when he leaned out and just kept shooting. Total badas..." *BOOM!*

A massive explosion distance and the screeching of metal suddenly interrupted her. A grim voice came over the channel. One of the pilots, "Strap in and hold onto your butts, people. They have anti-air, one helicopter is already down. Taking evasive action now."

Everyone grabbed to their nearest strap and held on for their dear lives as the cabin began to buck and lurch every which way. There was no time to strap themselves in. Francis could only clench his teeth as it went on. Of fucking course Infiltrator of Authority had made anti-air forms. Just what Francis needed on a mission that was already hard enough.

——— O — o — O ———

Bill observed the proceedings from the long distance imaging drone. In the chaos the military had not yet noticed that it was not one of theirs. At the news of the tunnel to the outside world, Bill had tried to contact General Lopez to get an explanation on how he could let this happen. But there had been no response on any of the usual channels.

It was his role. Bill was to deal with the alien threat directly while General Lopez kept the military off of his back and kept them from interfering. How could General Lopez abandon the cause now? How had the military even figured out how to open an entrance?

Only when he had someone check the inventory did Bill notice what else Francis had taken when he escaped. The anti-warding rods, meant to counter any wards that Infiltrator of Authority might put up. Francis had altered the inventory list so each storage room had them marked as stored in a different location. They only noticed because they did a full check with the master lists...

To think they would be used to allow the aliens to escape and spread... Bill couldn't believe Francis had been so short sighted to let this happen. As the military forces rushed to secure the entrance, Bill sent the last of the dissenters out to fight them. Nearly half of his remaining forces. They weren't dedicated enough to the final plan after being sounded out by the most loyal.

Unfortunate. But at least they were loyal enough to buy the rest of them time to handle the situation.

Bill gave the less dedicated of his soldiers the most basic of the Neighborhood Watch's Potential based weapons. Force blasts, the weaker personal shields, force amplification on bullets they would fire from their weapons. Things that were unimaginable to the outside world but only scratched the surface of what Potential could accomplish. They would keep the army at bay for a time with their superior technology.

Bill hadn't wanted to use the great weapon too early, but he had no choice. He went to the main control console for all the Potential he had accumulated over these last few weeks. Vastly more than he had collected in all the years before, gathered ever since this base had been constructed.

He pressed the sequence and set the power levels. 0.1% of its power should be enough. The soldiers of the Neighborhood Watch stopped their bustle around him as the building rumbled and the cylindrical center cavern began to shake. Everyone evacuated as fast as they could, everyone left aware of its true purpose.

The launch would wait for no one. With a spray of dirt and stone an opening was blasted in the roof with a rumbling explosion, exposing the sky as golden light began filling the launch chamber. Gathering brighter and brighter as the weapon prepared to fire.

The massive golden orb inside the launch chamber grew brighter and brighter until it launched into the sky in one massive rush. It arced in the sky, a second sun of golden light for a moment hovering above. Then it began to fall, and as it did a tiny canister inside of it broke open. The reddish flicker of Devouring Flame inside began to grow quickly, surrounded as it was by such perfect fuel...

Chapter 64: Holding the Line - Mortal Ryan Fragment

Ryan stood in the back of the vehicle and looked behind him, feeling numb. It was happening again. The tide of alien bodies approached from behind as he stood in the back of the truck. Explosions and gunfire from the Apache helicopters circling above tore large groups of the aliens to pieces and would break their charge for a moment.

But after only a pause to consume the fallen the charge of alien bodies would continue forward again. Ryan's knuckles turned white as he gripped his pistol. Sergeant Ruston had returned and eventually convinced him to rejoin the main group for the evacuation.

Ryan adjusted his grip on the pistol as he glanced around. The people around him could only stare in horror at the approaching horde behind them, but Ryan knew there was more coming. The bone plated charging creature would be blind siding them any moment now. Their truck reached a four way intersection, and suddenly there was a large blast from one of the escorting tanks in front of them firing their main guns.

Ryan and everyone else ducked down as something fell to the ground with a heavy impact in the distance. As they continued, Ryan twisted to look to see one of the charging armadillo monsters, splayed on the ground with a massive hole in its back, fountaining out black blood. It feebly twitched on the ground and went to stand before collapsing back to the ground and going still.

Ryan knew it was probably still alive, but at least they could escape while it regenerated. The line of vehicles drove onwards, and the chasing horde behind them drew closer.

The creatures were nipping at their heels now, and Ryan blasted the ones that made it through the two soldiers firing the two heavy machine guns set up in the back. The two soldiers were sweating as they blasted any creatures that drew too close and were about to leap to them.

One of the aliens leaped, and Ryan missed his shot. It sailed past him and landed on an elderly woman behind him. She screamed and fell to the ground as a young man dived in and ripped it off of her and sent it flying into the air.

Set it flying directly at Ryan.

It latched directly onto his face and tore a bite out of his cheek. It went for another bite. Ryan raised his gun to his head even as he thrashed and fired it, blowing the creature latched onto his face to pieces. The gore covered his vision and he frantically tried to wipe it off.

More black ink of the alien blood dripped into his eyes and he had to rub his face hard for a moment before he could see again. His ears were ringing and he was dazed as blood ran freely from the wound in his cheek where the alien had bitten him.

Someone stuffed gauze in the wound on his face as Ryan lay on the floor, and the bleeding slowed to a trickle. Someone took his gun and Ryan could only weakly protest. There was chaos and shouting all around him, but he only remembered it in fragments. More aliens made their way in only to be beaten down or shot by the one who took his pistol.

It was the young man who had defended the old woman before who had taken Ryan's weapon. After a minute or so, Ryan collected himself enough to stand. The two gunners were shouting at the third soldier who was supposed to be feeding them ammunition. They were almost out of ammo, and the attacks by the aliens were only growing more frequent.

Ryan heard a crunch of breaking metal above them. An Apache helicopter spiraled to the ground behind them. As it spun out of control, smoking, Ryan saw a massive spear of bone piercing the cockpit windshield and through the slumped over pilot. A storm of smaller forearm long spikes were embedded all over its frame.

Ryan looked over to the side and saw a strange creature with a giant fatty orb balanced on top of its squat body standing on the edge of a nearby flat roofed building. The fleshy tube curling over the top of its fatty form from its behind pulsed again and another bone spear launched and struck the falling helicopter.

Ryan heard another screech of metal as the helicopter began to fall faster as the helicopter blades stopped spinning entirely. Ten snake-like protrusions waved on the perimeter of the fatty orb and launched an unending stream of the smaller spikes on the helicopter even as it fell.

They quickly drove past the strange creature before it could turn its focus on them. Ryan saw the copilot of the helicopter moving inside to reach over to the console of his dead comrade.

The helicopter shifted at the last moment to land directly onto the center of the horde chasing Ryan's truck. For a moment there was nothing more than a crash of screaming metal. But a second later the downed helicopter exploded in a massive fireball, taking down the whole wave of alien orbs at once.

The gunners in the truck stopped firing for a moment to conserve ammunition as the leading wave of the horde was wiped out all at once. The two soldiers quickly drank some water and wiped their sweaty brows, hands shaking from the stress.

Ryan felt his cheek with his hand, where his blood was still oozing from the wound in his cheek from underneath the gauze. There was cheering from farther up in the military convoy and more Apaches arrived above them and struck the house with the turret creature with a missile, blowing it to smithereens.

There were more turret creatures hidden on the rooftops, and another Apache went down in a fiery explosion as it was struck by two bone spears that appeared to be launched from more of the nearby rooftops.

The fighting receded into the distance as more tanks and Apaches arrived to hold the line as the caravan of vehicles with the civilians inside retreated towards what Ryan could see was a giant golden break in the dome in the distance.

Ryan let out a shaky breath. He might just make it out of here. As if to curse his hopeful words, the sky suddenly was lit with a golden light, a second sun.

Everyone squinted as it grew brighter above them and all the gunfire halted for a brief moment. The aliens in the distance froze for a moment too, before cutting off their chase of the convoy and scattering into the nearby streets all at once.

The golden light above grew brighter and the closer it grew, the redder and more hellish it became. They all looked upward as the world began to be tinged a deeper and deeper red. The world was crimson now, and Ryan could feel the heat on his skin.

In front of their vehicle, there was a massive explosion by the edge of the dome that shook the ground and caused the driver to curse as he attempted to not crash as he drove over the bucking ground beneath them.

The only thing Ryan could hear was the roaring of flame and the heat as his arms slowly turned pink as if from a sunburn. A wave of heat washed over him. Ryan looked upwards and saw the dome trapping them all flickering and twisting as it countered the red with its own golden glow.

Ryan wasn't sure what outcome he was hoping for as he saw the battle between the golden and red light. The truck lurched to a stop and began to turn. There was yelling, but it was silenced as they all gaped at the scene behind them. A massive pillar of flame was burned at the edge of the dome. It shrank by the second, but it moved with purpose.

Flickering spindly arms of flame split off from the main column to strike anything living in its presence. People screaming with flames burning on their forms were swarming the vehicles in front of them, infecting more with the flame.

The burning people were all screaming, flames bursting from their throats as they fought with anything near them. Ryan's truck turned around and began to drive away as the flaming mob began to chase them on foot.

As they drove, individuals in the burning mob diverted themselves and broke into nearby buildings. An inhuman screech would sound from inside and the aliens would escape any way they could out the windows, bursting out the walls, only to be matched by a human scream inside. Then the building would be engulfed in a wave of reddish flames that consumed the aliens, the flames twisting midair and hunting the aliens that attempted to flee ruthlessly, reducing them to ash in seconds.

The driver drifted around the corner at high speed and the truck began to tilt to one side, about to flip over. Ryan and everyone else desperately threw themselves to the other side and the truck fell back down with a crash on its wheels. The crowd of burning people was thinning out now, distracted by hunting the fleeing masses of aliens.

Ryan's truck was driving parallel to the now visible and still flickering golden dome. After ten minutes the last of the burning people dropped off to slaughter more groups of hiding or fleeing aliens. The pillar of flames in the distance had shrunk down to almost nothing by now. It could only be seen now as a reddish tinge on the glowing surface of the dome in that direction.

———O — o — O———

Bill watched with a frown. He had expected it to be a less powerful strike than that. He should have saved more of the Potential in their banks for the Harbinger when it became the Avatar. But at least the escape of the dome had been sealed.

The anti-ward rods had been annihilated in the initial explosion, and based on the size of the entrance they had made to let the helicopters inside they hadn't preserved any from Francis' stolen supply, instead using them all to make the opening as wide as possible.

Bill didn't like the Devouring Flame consuming the Potential of the Infected, they could be better used for the final strike on the Harbinger. But better than having one of the Infected escape to only wreak more havoc. Protected as the Ranch was now, their base would hold against the assaults of any remaining forces alien and human alike still under the dome until the Harbinger emerged. Now all Bill had to do was wait.

Chapter 65: An Aerial Perspective - Mortal Francis Fragment

Francis gripped the strap on the side of the helicopter as it lurched side to side in the air. He heard the rush of bone projectiles flying past the helicopter and just barely missing them.

The cabin lurched again the other way and Francis lost his grip and went flying head over heels. With the screaming of metal a long gash was carved longways across the side of the helicopter Francis was falling towards. One of the larger bone spikes had grazed them. Francis splayed his hands and caught himself just before he impaled himself on the sharp edges of the metal wound in the helicopter's side.

Francis got a brief glimpse between the open gash to see the creature that was firing on them. It was one of those turret creatures he had fought when he had been the distraction during the operation on the hospital. It had far more of those smaller snake things on it now, and the things reared back before snapping forward towards them.

Francis threw himself to the side as the smaller bone spikes embedded themselves into the exposed side of the helicopter. Several made their way through and shot through to embed themselves into the opposite wall.

Francis glanced back quickly at the soldiers and a few of them had glancing wounds, but nothing serious.

Francis saw the main tube of the turret creature undulating faster and faster and knew it was about to fire again. He grabbed the mic on the headset and pulled it to his lips and shouted, "DODGE! IT'S ABOUT TO FIRE AGAIN! DODGE, DOD—"

The helicopter lurched the other way and Francis was sent flying again, thrown back to the other side of the cabin. The air was driven from Francis' lungs at the heavy impact. The whoosh of the bone projectile passed by their side, just barely missing them.

Another wave of smaller bone spikes struck their side. But they had made some distance, so they only dented the metal with little divots rather than piercing through.

The Black Hawk helicopter righted itself and the turret creature receded rapidly into the distance. Francis saw it explode a few seconds later.

The Apaches had passed them going the opposite way and began to do battle with the hail of bone spikes being launched from the roofs of the surrounding buildings, using their mounted machine guns and missiles to rain fire on the aliens below.

Francis groaned as he leveraged his bruised body to its feet in the now more stable helicopter cabin. He felt like one big bruise right now. He stretched, cracking his back. Everyone else was recovering from their rough treatment during the evasive maneuvers as well.

They all had been thrown around, but only Francis seemed to have totally lost his grip on the straps. Just as everyone began to relax, the sky was suddenly lit up in golden light.

It took a second for Francis to process, but he dived and grabbed the strap as tight as he could as the gold began to transition to crimson. He tried to shout a warning but his headset had fallen off in his sudden dive and no one heard his warning.

All Francis could hear was the thumping of helicopter blades and the rushing of wind before it was drowned by a massive explosion in the distance. The helicopter was thrown backwards and up into the air like it was slapped by a massive hand. The cabin spun wildly and the metal around them screamed. There was one frozen moment where they reached the apex of their flight.

The engine of the helicopter spluttered and whined above them. All of them were suspended in midair and staring in terror at each other. Then they were falling and the rushing wind drowned all their screams.

With a guttering clatter, the helicopter blades spun back into action and began to pick up speed again.

They all slammed into the floor with heavy thumps as the air caught on the spinning blades. The motor screamed in a long sustained whine as they were all pressed into the floor. The cabin wobbled side to side as the helicopter gradually slowed down and stabilized.

Francis moved with the others to help those who were unconscious. Of the ten people in the cabin, four were out cold. All were breathing steadily but would likely need a hospital given the heavy impacts they had taken to their skulls.

Francis leaned over and peered out the small windows of the helicopter. There, receding in the distance, was a pillar of Devouring Flame. Francis couldn't believe Bill had used it, he had been so fanatical in using every last drop to use for the strike on the Avatar. Francis could see the tiny vehicles and people below fleeing away from the pillar. The pillar sent out reaching arms and arcs of flame to strike whatever was within its range.

Francis could only watch as the dome sealed itself again with the anti-warding rods sitting at its base fully destroyed. That was it, now they all were all trapped in here. At least most of the civilians had made it out in time. Most. He quickly reached down and put his headset back on, muffling the deafening noise of the helicopter around him. The helicopter turned as the pilot received new orders on where the surviving military would gather. At least they still had communication with outside world now.

————O—o—O————

Francis had returned to his seat on the helicopter. His ears were still ringing from the noise of everything that had just happened, but he had been through worse. His body ached all over, and he listened to the chatter over the radio channel as the helicopter circled over the gathering point. They had been doing so for a while now as there was still chaos below and not many safe places to land.

Tanks and ranks of soldiers below fought the scattered aliens that launched periodic assaults on them, occasionally assisted by the guns of Francis' helicopter. The aliens seemed strangely disorganized based on how they had acted up to this point. They trickled in one by one rather than gathering up and bunching up for one larger assault.

Francis would have expected Infiltrator of Authority to have directed them with some kind of strategy rather than letting the aliens just run wild like this.

Suddenly in the distance, there was an explosion of rubble, chunks of concrete being thrown into the air. Francis' eyes widened as the misshapen four story tall figure made its way to its feet.

The Harbinger. The Avatar? It had arrived too early, it was supposed to emerge over a month from now! This was the worst time for it to appear! The Harbinger lumbered off, seeming to be tracking and attacking something on the ground below it. Francis tuned back into the channel as he recovered from his shock. He had far less time than he had thought.

"—The hell is that thing? Orders, sir?" A voice said over the radio.

"Encircle, aim for center mass. You've seen how easily these things can regenerate their limb—"

Francis pressed the radio's button and started communicating, "Sorry to interrupt, but there is a bigger problem incoming. If you don't deal with it first then killing that thing would be pointless."

He was ignored and Francis huffed in frustration. The soldiers around him gave him strange looks. Francis shifted his sniper rifle from his back so it now laid in his lap.

Not that the military could kill the Harbinger with what they had anyways. If it ever got in true danger it could call on its god and gain as much power as it needed to survive.

It was the whole reason Bill had wanted one massive strike to obliterate it before it could react or heal itself even with near infinite resources at its disposal. Several Apache helicopters in the distance began engaging the Harbinger. They were blasting chunks out of it, but it was healing nearly as fast as it was damaged.

The creature fell to the ground and its wounds stopped healing as the assault by the military continued. Francis frowned. Why wasn't it calling on its god for healing? Where was the unstoppable juggernaut Francis had been told about?

The Harbinger stood and quickly plodded towards the closest Apache deceptively slowly. Its massive strides ate up the ground as the squad of helicopters opened up with their miniguns.

It didn't appear to do much damage to the creature. The Harbinger cocked back its arm and threw it forward as if to punch empty at air. But from its arm a long tentacle launched out and swiped the helicopter into the ground where it exploded in a massive fireball.

Tanks rounded the corner of the street and fired into the Harbinger's exposed back, blasting a hole through it that let out a fountain of black fluid. The military command channel kept giving frantic orders as the vehicles chased after it, as it stumbled and crashed through a nearby home. There was a pause in the babble as the Harbinger receded into the distance, under hot pursuit. Francis tried to talk again into the radio.

"There is vital information I have to—"

"Who is this idiot? This is the restricted command channel, go to squad channels if you have to—"

Francis interrupted again.

"This is Francis Moore, sir. Formerly of the Neighborhood Watch. That pillar of flame that just struck is controlled by the Neighborhood Watch. They are going to use it to kill that thing, and everyone else under the dome. Imagine what just happened but a thousand or more times powerful. That's the whole reason the Neighborhood Watch did all of this, built the weapon, to kill that thing over there."

At that, the channel went truly silent for a moment before it exploded into angry questions. They were upset that Francis had not shared the information earlier. And he had kept the information back intentionally, they were right to be furious with him.

Why share now? The difference was that Francis knew the launch was unstoppable now. As much as he disagreed with Bill's methods, the Harbinger must still be destroyed for there to be any hope in ending this. The second Bill saw the Harbinger emerged he had likely already started the launch sequence.

It was untested how long it would take to gather all the energy, but once the capsule inside containing the Devouring Flame inside cracked open, then it was over. The Devouring Flame would hunt down the closest sources of Potential on its own.

The Harbinger would naturally be the largest source of Potential in the entire dome, it would just result in a less concentrated strike if the Ranch was totally destroyed even right this second. The real problem was the draining formation Francis was sure Bill had hidden all over the dome.

Once activated, the formation would drain the Potential out of everything within its range and send it into the sky to empower the launch and the Devouring Flame above.

Francis had seen what the central pillars of the Safezones had been trying to accomplish. What they had done to Alice and the others when fully activated… Attempted to drain them into mummified husks as it sucked their Potential right out of their bodies.

Francis didn't believe for a second that this whole area wasn't littered with backups and hidden amplifiers to cover the whole town.

Just after launch, Bill would activate them and drain life from everyone and everything that didn't have an activated and powered Protection stone on them for everywhere under the dome. No doubt all of it would be amplified by the wards that had been put in place during the initial setup of the larger dome.

Bill had plenty of Potential built up to power the weapon, this last slaughter was unnecessary. And Francis knew that some of the townspeople still hadn't escaped and were still trapped in here. Not to mention the soldiers who were just doing their jobs. Some of them could still survive.

Francis ignored the various confused demands from and told them his suspicions of how it was impossible to know how long before the weapon killed them all.

A singular authoritative voice cut through the babble on the radio. A different voice than the commander Francis had interacted with for these last few days.

"Could we find these amplifiers, and preserve a small area from the destruction?"

Francis considered as everyone waited for his answer.

"You could, but if I know Bill then he has backups for his backups. If just a few slip through then all the rest is pointless. Even the smaller ones can cover an area of twenty or thirty feet. The largest ones may cover half a mile or more. Here's a description of what they could look like..."

Francis described the swooping patterns as best as he could. When unpowered they wouldn't glow, so the hunt would be even more difficult for the soldiers.

"Thank you for the information, Mr. Moore. All right..."

What seemed to be the new main commander of the assault helped direct the squads for their search pattern at their gathering point to unearth the stones. Francis didn't hold out much hope.

"... Mr. Moore brought here for a full debrief..."

Francis jolted at his name. The Black Hawk went to land, and they were greeted by a small crowd led by a sharp-eyed man with black hair. He was still speaking over the radio as Francis and the others stepped from the battered helicopter. The others dispersed as someone split off to give them their orders.

The helicopter lifted back into the air and started flying away. The commander barked more orders over the radio as the sound of the helicopter blades gradually receded into the distance. Eventually, the man put down his handheld radio.

"Mr. Moore. Anything else you want to tell us?" The soldiers behind him glowered menacingly.

Francis licked his dry lips nervously, "I know the way in. To the Ranch I mean. If you let me go, I can show your men where Bill is hiding. We take him down and we stop him from activating the draining stones. It's too delicate, he wouldn't let them activate if he wasn't there to make sure that they would activate at the perfect moment. Activation at the wrong time would just let the extra energy dissipate and be wasted. He wouldn't let that happen."

The commander stared at him hard for a moment. Francis tried to keep an earnest expression. Without him, there was no way they could even breach the compound let alone find Bill inside. Eventually, the commander nodded.

"Alright. Show us the way."

He turned to one of his subordinates and spoke loudly so Francis could hear. "Gather whoever's not on search or defense duty. We move as soon as possible. He goes with the first squad."

He turned to meet Francis' eyes while still speaking. "If he tries to escape, shoot him in the leg. Don't let him out of your sight in case this is a double cross."

The man glanced between Francis and his commander as they stared each other down for a moment. Then he seemed to come to senses and snapped out a salute, "Yes, sir."

The man who had saluted stepped away and began relaying their orders. The commander stepped forward, still staring down Francis.

"I don't trust you, you've withheld too much. Prove me wrong. If we both make out of this... I'll buy you a beer to celebrate."

Francis barked out a laugh at the joke and opened his mouth to reply, but the man had already turned and was walking off. Francis snorted again as the absurdity of the statement washed over him. Then devolved into full blown unhinged laughter. Making it out of this alive... now wasn't that a thought?

Francis only finished wiping away his tears when he was finally led to the squad that would be breaching with him. Francis shifted the sniper rifle on his back. He held it for a moment and watched as the lines scribbled over its surface began to glow. He quickly released his grip on it as his stomach grumbled and his Potential started to drain. He let go and the drain stopped. Best to save his Potential for later.

Chapter 66: Breach! - Mortal Francis Fragment

Francis walked closer to the farmhouse, the soldiers and their vehicles waiting in a circle behind him. It had been a few hours already for the full assault to be prepared, unfortunately. Francis was feeling the pressure of knowing that the weapon could launch at any point, the unknown timetable pushing him to rush rather than go carefully and not make any mistakes.

Francis threw a normal stone and the shield flared into life and shot it back at twice the speed it had been thrown. Francis stepped to the side as it embedded itself in the dirt behind him. He waited for the golden light to die down again before he slowly craned his neck scoping out the area.

Bill had already blown the explosives to all the side entrances that Francis was aware of to collapse them inwards, leaving this as the only way in or out. The soldiers behind him shifted nervously. The Neighborhood Watch were all below, and this shield was only the first layer of defenses.

Seeing what he needed to do, Francis grabbed his sniper rifle and aimed it carefully. The golden lines slowly lit up over the rifle's surface and Francis waited for a moment before pulling the trigger. The shield bowed inward for a moment before with a large tearing sound, it ripped open. The bullet continued unimpeded and destroyed the formation stone supporting the barrier.

Francis stumbled back from the knockback. Even with all the anti-recoil scripts put into the weapon, this thing was difficult to handle.

Francis shifted his aim and recovered his footing before firing the weapon again. Another formation stone was destroyed. The shield began flickering as it struggled to heal the damage Francis had done.

One final shot, another blast and Francis destroyed the last formation stone and the barrier flickered a few more times before finally collapsing in on itself. Francis reached into his pack and ate the high density energy bars inside. He ate as the soldiers behind moved in, sweeping past him to enter the barn that the shield had been protecting.

Francis reached for another bar from his pack and came up with nothing. He was still hungry, but he had no time to find more. The squad of soldiers around him supposedly for his protection followed him as he entered the barn along with the others.

There was still no gunfire from inside, which was a good sign. An explosion sent everyone diving to the ground and shouting. After a moment of no more attacks, everyone made their way to their feet, on guard. Francis walked over to where the elevator — Well scratch that, where the elevator should have been. Francis pushed through the crowd and leaned over and saw its shattered and blackened frame below.

There were some reddish chunks splattering the walls down below. It seems Bill wasn't messing around anymore. One of the squad leaders took charge and started tying off lengths of rope and throwing them down the shaft. One deployed a small drone that they flew down to scout out the room. Francis leaned over as the pilot inspected the empty room from his control pad.

He opened his mouth to give the all clear but Francis grabbed his shoulder. The soldiers behind Francis tensed and he heard them cock their weapons. He slowly raised his hands from the drone pilot's shoulder as the drone pilot turned to him.

"Not yet. Look there," Francis said.

Francis pointed to the series of circular etchings in the concrete floor. It was broken up by other jagged lines to disguise it, but looking closely, none of these extra lines actually crossed any of those from the original pattern. It was a trap.

"Landmines," Francis said.

The drone pilot raised his eyebrows and looked between Francis and the random set of lines on the floor, even if he did still looked nervous at Francis' statement. He licked his lips,

"Bullshit," The drone pilot said, "They practically overlap. No way it doesn't cause a chain explosion. Even if I believed you."

Francis crossed his arms and gestured to the screen.

"They all go off separately. One explosion won't trigger the others." The unfamiliar leader of the expedition came over now that the ropes were secure.

"Is there a problem? What do you see?"

The drone pilot glanced between Francis and the officer before sighing.

"Sir, this man says these patterns in the floor are landmines. We were just discussing how to get past them considering they cover almost the entire floor. A chain explosion of them could bring down the roof and seal the entrance."

The leader looked at the screen and nodded. Francis spoke up.

"I know these mines, and they aren't traditional explosives. They are totally inert unless triggered in a very specific way. Namely, stepping on it." Francis could try to explain the Potential based triggers to them, but that would just confuse the conversation.

The leader looked between the two of them.

"So what are our options?" the man asked, "We have already lost two men to a trap. I don't want to lose any more before we even have contact with the enemy."

Francis spoke again.

"We should just set them off one by one in a line to the far entrance. That's where we need to go to reach Bill. They're based on weight so anything heavy landing on them should do."

The leader looked at Francis closer.

"Right, you're the expert they told me about. Worked hard setting these mines yourself, did you?"

Francis shuffled.

"Well, no… But I did help build many like them in my time."

The man snorted and shook his head in disgust. The drone pilot glanced between the two and subtly backed away from Francis. After a moment of tension the leader turned and walked away and started giving more orders. The drone pilot quickly hurried away from Francis and his guards went to surround him again.

Damn, Francis was really feeling the love here as they crowded him in.

$$--- O - o - O ---$$

One brave man rappelled down the elevator shaft with various bags filled with water. It seemed it was the safest thing to explode with the least dangerous shrapnel they had on hand. The soldier had squeezed against the wall and had thrown the first bag.

Predictably, at least to Francis, he set off the first landmine, carving a foot or two deep impression in the concrete from the backlash from the powerful upwards explosion. The force dissipated as it splashed against the high ceiling. The man threw another bag of water, another explosion, another bag, another explosion. Again and again. There was still no sign of the members of the Neighborhood Watch.

Ten minutes later the first soldiers started repelling down the elevator shaft after the first man who had nearly cleared the whole line to the opposite tunnel deeper into the Ranch.

Francis went down next with his group. His sniper rifle bumped against the wall as it swung on his back as he repelled down, the commander right behind him. It seemed they would remain close to each other for now.

The last landmine was cleared and the group made their way forward carefully, inspecting the floor and walls for suspicious scratches as they went. They had almost reached the first checkpoint when Francis tapped the commander on the shoulder as he walked to his side.

The man swatted Francis' hand away, but begrudgingly focused on Francis anyway. He held up his hand and with a few shouted orders the column of soldiers stopped. More were repelling down behind them, all carefully threading their way carefully to not step in the still activated mines.

"Ahead is the perfect place for an ambush," Francis leaned in and whispered, "One big room with multiple side entrances. They'll shield the exits closed and create a killing chamber."

The man nodded as he looked forward, one eye still on Francis. He whispered back in kind.

"What is the best way through then? Can we take these shields down without your advanced weapons?"

Francis nodded.

"Yes, concentrated fire for a few seconds should do it for something small enough to block the hallway. I have something to expose the main ambushing group if you put me in the first assault."

Francis reached into the pocket of his pack and pulled out a hemisphere made of stone. There was a divot in the center of the spherical part big enough for a thumb. The trigger. Francis made sure to hold it close so none of the cameras observing them could see exactly what it was. Francis knew Bill went all in on those tiny cameras around this place, so there could be a camera anywhere watching and they would never know.

"I deploy this to blow their shield," Francis said quietly, "and knock them down so your people finish the job."

The commander nodded, but glanced between Francis and the device as Francis put it in his pocket. His expression was puzzled.

"You would kill them? Didn't you assemble landmines for them for years before this? What's changed now?"

"Everyone has lines," Francis said, "I thought I didn't have any for a while. That I would do anything. They found my line and no matter what, I won't let them cross it while I'm responsible."

The commander nodded in understanding and stood straight again, frowning as he considered Francis' words. Francis stepped forward and wondered if it really was that simple. Was there some moral bottom line he had that led him here? It hadn't felt that way at the time.

He had only been trying to save just one person originally. It was more likely he was doing all of this out of guilt. For all that he had already done. Francis stepped into the room and pulled out the stone hemisphere with five or so soldiers standing behind him. He pointed the device towards the tunnel flat side out. The Neighborhood Watch would be gathered there, the tunnel leading closest to Bill and the control room.

Francis pressed his thumb into the soft receptacle for the device and his Potential drained into it. It was launched forward ripped from his hand even as he saw the air warp in the other tunnels. The Neighborhood Watch members charged around the corners and raised their guns to fire, but they were too late. The device hit the leading man and released a massive wave of force forward.

The man in the lead exploded into gore as the group behind him was thrown violently into the walls. It seems they hadn't activated their personal shields in time. The soldiers rushed past Francis and released a hail of gunfire into the tunnel, killing most of the stunned members of the Neighborhood Watch lying on the floor.

One woman near the back, Carol the relentless gossip, managed to raise her shield in time to protect herself from the explosion. She was still sent flying into the wall, but her shield survived the impact even if it glowed with a golden tinge.

She stumbled as the wave of bullets from the soldiers targeted her. Her shield lasted valuable seconds as she stood and went to dive back around the corner. She was midair as the shield finally failed. One of the bullets passed through her calf just as she made it around the corner.

"Fuck!" Her voice echoed down the hallway as they heard her scramble to her feet painfully and limped away cursing.

The soldiers took down the rest of the shields with gunfire before standing guard and calling the all clear. More and more soldiers came forward. The commander emerged, looking down the gore filled hallway for an instant before returning his gaze to Francis.

"How close are we? We are on a clock here. To win, all they have to do is delay us, according to you."

Francis shook his head, "There are at least four more good ambush points before we reach the end. There's probably about fifty people left, but I was lucky I was able to ambush them before they could deploy their heavy weapons this time. I don't think we'll catch them by surprise again next time."

The commander looked struck and looked at the sniper rifle and stroked his chin.

"Heavy weapons, huh? That rifle on your back, could it clear the way?"

Francis frowned, "Wouldn't that collapse the tunnels? Such a heavy impact?"

"You tell me," The commander said, nodding, "You know this place, we can collapse anything that isn't in a direct path to this control room."

Francis slowly nodded. Actually… He thought about the layout. He stretched out his arm and imagined the middle three ambush checkpoints. They were perfectly… But could he be sure? He thought about it and tried to recall the next few turns in the tunnel as closely as he could. He matched everything in his memory exactly as if it was the back of his hand. He was sure.

All three of the checkpoints were in a line in the rock at an angle if they reached the right spot. The path of the bullet would go into the surrounding rock and avoid the core area where it might collapse a tunnel they might need.

The group walked a bit as Francis explained the plan. The commander nodded and called a stop when Francis found a perfect place for the shot. He aimed the shot down to the end of the winding hallway. He closed his eyes and mentally walked through the hallways he had walked down thousands, no tens of thousands of times over the years.

Francis adjusted his angle. It was closer. There were voices that were receding into the distance behind him. It seemed the soldiers were keeping their distance in case this backfired. Francis adjusted his angle upwards a little bit. He injected his Potential and the sniper rifle started glowing again. He made sure the line was perfect. He took a deep breath…

Then he took the shot.

———O—o—O———

  The earth shook and fragments of concrete cut into Francis' exposed skin as he fell to the floor. Dust rained from the ceiling and there were shouts coming from behind Francis. He sat up and let out a sharp breath as he saw the crater in the far wall. The hole was roughly the size of Francis' torso but he could see light on the other end.

  Even as he watched, something shifted and the roof of the new opening collapse inwards with a *thwump*. Dirt trickled out and spilled onto the floor. The soldiers rushed back forward after it became clear there would be no collapse of the tunnel around them.

  The soldiers all quickly rushed through the hallways and caught the concussed Neighborhood Watch in the next checkpoint drunkenly retreating. The soldiers and Francis chased all the way to the next ambush point where the Neighborhood Watch rallied and turned around to do battle. Francis deployed two more of the stone hemispheres, disrupting the Neighborhood Watch's formations.

  Disorganized, the people were gunned down by the soldiers.

  None attempted to surrender even down to the last man. Francis gripped the last stone hemisphere in his bag. The last one he had. After this it would all be up to the soldiers. There were shooting pains in Francis' sides from hunger, and he could feel that his Potential had dropped to nearly nothing. He couldn't fire the sniper rifle again. He had enough to trigger the last hemisphere but after that he would begin sacrificing his fat stores as fuel for more.

  The next checkpoint was unoccupied. The survivors of the counter ambush seemed to have passed by it in their retreat inwards. Now there was only one checkpoint left. Right past that was the control room, that was where Helen and Bill would be. Francis' last chance to save the people that remained under the dome.

Chapter 67: War in the Neighborhood - Mortal (Emily) Fragment

Emily shifted nervously as the line of soldiers with her watched the massive creature more than four stories tall just standing there staring back at them. She adjusted the rifle in her grip. The massive alien creature had just defeated the wave of aliens charging them in the firing line, swooping in and grabbing them with its octopus tentacles before dissolving them into some sort of goo.

Everyone shifted nervously as the helicopters buzzed above, all focused on the massive alien. Several tanks rolled around the corner and did not fire. After a long moment of the stand off, the creature slowly turned and lumbered away. It crashed through a nearby home in a few steps, seeming to ignore that the obstruction was even there as the building exploded into a cloud of wooden splinters. The helicopters above flew to follow the creature but stopped firing on it for now.

The tanks rolled forward to reinforce their lines and everyone including Emily cheered as one of the tank crew popped out of the top hatch and waved. The man quickly went back inside and they all made way so the tanks could settle in their formation.

She wondered what had happened to that man with the sniper rifle on the helicopter she was on for the evacuation. Francis, she remembered his name was. She had heard his name a few times as she was on patrol in the old Safe zones. The new commander had looked pissed when he had confronted Francis about something after they landed.

The brief lull in the battle faded away as more alien screeches could be heard in the distance. There were more coming. They had to hold this position or the searchers behind them couldn't work to find the 'draining stones'. What were they, some kind of bomb? A chemical weapon? She wasn't sure, just that command thought they were dangerous and was clearing the area of them before they were activated.

The alien screeches grew closer. Even worse was the thumping weight of one of the approaching ten foot tall armored forms shaking the ground with their footsteps. Those creatures were durable enough to shelter the weaker ones and let the other aliens get closer range to their lines.

She glanced at the tanks. Luckily they had more heavy weapons now. The small group of aliens emerged from an alleyway up the street. The expected crowd of fleshy balls milled around the bony armadillo-looking humanoid. Flanking it on either side were two of the massive worms with massive bulbs on one end.

The tank to Emily's left boomed as the main gun fired. The bone-plated humanoid fell with a gaping hole torn out of its shoulder.

The alien's wound wept inky black blood even as it clambered slowly back to its feet. The fleshy orbs rushed to cling to its back, away from the small arms fire of the soldiers. Emily took aim and fired her rifle, killing one of the aliens that poked its body too far from the creature's back.

The two worms curled back and launched their orbs from their bodies, hiding behind the bony creature, using its armored body as a shield.

The worms flattened themselves to the ground and slithered back into the alleyway, only taking a few superficial wounds before fleeing again.

Everyone on the ground focused their fire on the fleshy balls arcing high in the sky above them. One finally burst and popped like a balloon. Emily dived to the side as the other popped right on top of them.

Everyone scrambled out of the splash zone of the alien orb, but Louis wasn't fast enough. He was hit dead on, and the invisible gasses falling from the sky caused him to clutch his throat and fall to the ground. His skin sizzled and bubbled for a moment before he went still.

The others could only turn away grimly. It would take a minute or two before the acidic gas would disperse fully. The line was pushed backwards again as they maneuvered to be upwind of the caustic gas.

The tanks' main guns boomed again and the bony humanoid fell to the ground, nearly severed in half by the heavy tank shell ripping directly through its abdomen and bursting out of its other side.

The alien balls of flesh on its back quickly charged when they realized that their protector was dead, but were quickly wiped out with only one shot from the soldiers able to make them go still.

Emily lowered her rifle and wiped some sweat from her brow. She knew when she signed up for active duty that she would see real combat, but this was ridiculous.

She wasn't sure how long it had been, but there had been nonstop action ever since she had been put here. People were dropping left and right. Louis was one of the last of her squad that had survived. She looked to her left and met Alex's eyes. He was the only one left in her squad besides her.

———O—o—O———

After what felt like days, more and more people had been rotated to the frontlines to replace their losses, and Emily was all alone now.

She wasn't even sure who she was supposed to report to anymore, she just stood in the line of her fellow soldiers and kept firing at the aliens. No one told her otherwise and she could barely understand the shouted orders through the haze of exhaustion anyways. And she kept surviving somehow.

Alex had been skewered forty minutes ago when one of the turret things had surprised them by firing at them from the top of one of the nearby buildings. After the surprise ambush, two helicopters had come to destroy the thing and remained to start taking down threats around them from the air.

Even now the helicopters circled above, conserving ammunition for when things grew desperate again. The groups of aliens were growing less frequent, but everyone was running low on ammunition. The last resupply had been later than expected.

Emily jolted awake from her blank haze as another round of screeches began approaching from the distance. This group of aliens would be larger. She turned and saw men arguing with the tank crews. She drifted closer and watched as the man from the tank crew looked desperate.

"...We're out!" the man shouted as he stood out of the open tank hatch, "We have to go for resupply, if they won't come to us then we'll have to go to command for supplies."

The other man was practically begging now. "Stay just for this group, we need all the firepower we can get. Even the small guns will help!"

The other man shook his head and looked even more stressed than before. He leaned back into the hatch and the tank broke formation and began rolling towards the interior. "Without the main gun, we're dead weight. We'll be back soon, just hold on as long as you can."

There was more argument, but the tank rolled away despite the protests and began driving to command. Emily looked to the other tank and let out a sigh of relief as it stayed in place. At least they would have something.

The latest alien attack group appeared in the distance and the helicopters above immediately opened fire on them. Emily's eyes widened, it was the largest group yet. Just as they had lost their second tank.

Three of those bony ten foot ten-foot-tall humanoids surrounded a fifteen-foot-tall tall more human figure with no head and massively muscled arms. In the center of its chest was a massive eye framed by an orange iris, darting around quickly to scan its surroundings. The three bony humanoids surrounded the taller figure protectively, putting themselves between it and the soldiers.

The helicopter miniguns lightly injured the surrounding guards as their fire targeted the unknown form of the central alien, but the central being hunched down behind the other's armor and went largely uninjured by the assault.

After ten seconds of sustained fire, the attack stopped and the helicopters peeled away. Emily's heart sank, the helicopter's ammunition had finally run out. Their missiles had run out long ago, only their automatic miniguns helping them for the last while.

The remaining tank fired its main gun and one of the three guards torso was blown open. It fell to the ground, still alive but moving weakly. Emily had learned long ago that they could survive one direct shot even if it took time. The two other armored aliens shifted to maintain protection to the central creature, shifting to cover the gap left by their fallen comrade.

Soon, the aliens were close enough that the main line of soldiers opened fire, causing the armored creatures to flinch and curl up as the bullets entered the gaps in their armor. The aliens slowed their charge.

The rifle of the man next to Emily clicked empty. Emily kept firing. The tank fired again and another of the guards went down to the ground shifting weakly.

The last guard broke into a blind charge, covered in its inky black blood and armor cracked and pitted from the concentrated fire from the soldier's guns.

Emily's rifle clicked empty. She reached to her side and pulled out her pistol, she had at least twenty rounds left on it. She kept firing, screaming curses along with the others along with the deafening gunfire as the aliens kept charging them. Her pistol ran dry and she kept pulling the trigger reflexively for a few seconds.

Realizing what was happening, she searched around but there was nothing else for her to shoot.

Emily broke from the front line and ran to the back in case there was more ammunition somewhere. She found a crate and leaned over to look inside. There near the bottom were a few more magazines for her rifle. She quickly grabbed them and loaded them as quickly as she could with her shaking hands. She turned just to see the taller central alien scrunched itself into a ball as if to squat as small wounds all over its form leaked black inky blood.

Some of the soldiers were shooting the central alien from around its charging guard which had created some distance between the two.

Emily could see the creature's legs flexing even as the final guard stumbled and face-planted, a black pool of blood spreading from below it. It would be out of the fight for a while based on the state it had been in when Emily had last seen it.

The unknown creature type launched itself into the air in the blink of an eye, concrete exploding behind it as it leaped into the air. Everyone turned their weapons up but what shots landed didn't divert its path in the air. With a massive overhand blow, the creature slammed its massive fist directly onto the tank, crumpling and folding the metal vehicle almost in half as it was spiked into the ground under the massive impact of its fist.

The soldiers closest to the impact fell to the ground and shouted as the creature made its way to its feet. It turned and began punching the survivors, each blow sending people flying with the cracks of bones and bursts of gore. Each blow of its massive fists shook the ground, causing more of the soldiers to fall to the ground around it and spreading the chaos.

Emily was on the other side of the lines, and everyone who could opened fire on the rampaging alien over there. Under the barrage, the creature crossed its arms in front of it to protect its chest where its massive eye sat.

It stood there as the bullets dug into its exposed muscles and shoulders. After a few moments, there was a lull in the gunfire as everyone went to reload. The creature lowered its arms and its eye darted around, targeting the reloading soldiers. The ones that met its gaze fell to the ground, eyes rolling in the back of their heads unconscious.

Emily turned away even as she kept reloading. A heavy impact behind her sent her face-first into the ground. The creature was behind her with meaty thumps striking its fists into her fellow soldiers. It had jumped again.

She rolled over and saw it was less than ten feet away from her now. Emily raised her rifle and saw the eye of the creature flicker towards her. She unloaded her weapon directly into the thing's pupil and it stumbled backwards as the eye deflated slightly, leaking fluid. It tripped back into the crater made by its own landing seconds ago.

The surviving soldiers shouted something as a wave of little metal green things flew above Emily's head. She scrambled away as fast as she could.

Her hearing had just started recovering enough to hear the man next to her as he shouted as he threw another green ball, "Grenade, out!"

A massive explosion sent Emily flying and rolling away. Her ears were ringing and she could barely string together a coherent thought as she lay there. The gunfire and explosions petered out after a few more seconds as she lay there among the rubble in the street. Someone dragged her to the side and Emily coughed. She looked over to where the creature had been.

It was now very dead, blown into chunks, and the crater where it had been was much deeper now. She looked ahead and saw the returned helicopters in the distance finishing off the downed alien guards who had just been about to stand back up.

A wave of relief washed over her, and a massive wave of exhaustion followed not far behind. Someone above her was shouting something, but she was asleep in moments. She had held the line for long enough.

Chapter 68: Failure is not an Option - Mortal Francis Fragment

Francis and the commander stood side by side in the hallway leading to the last obstacle, the last fortified room where the Neighborhood Watch must have gathered at. The last before reaching Bill and the detonator Francis knew the man would have.

There was a harsh almost electronic buzzing they could hear in the distance, the sound of the charging launch chamber. Francis shifted his grip on his final stone hemisphere, prepared to activate it on a dime.

Francis exchanged a glance with the military commander and took a deep breath as he nodded. Francis' whispered plan was their only chance to make it through in time. The attack could launch at any moment. They had no idea how much time was left.

The commander pulled a grenade and tossed it through the doorway into the open room. It exploded, followed by a chain of following explosions as it set off the landmines Francis had been sure would have been planted there.

The first squad of soldiers charged ahead, the commander and Francis just behind them. Gunfire sounded out as the soldiers focused fire on the shields of the Neighborhood Watch members surrounding them on all sides from the five adjoining tunnel entrances.

Francis turned to the final shield that sprung up in the hallway blocking them from the control room. It was thicker and the air distorted and twisted around even as it wasn't being attacked. Francis knew this one was likely sustained by the main Potential power banks.

If they didn't take it down fast enough it would continue to regenerate, only stopping once the final attack was launched and the main power banks of the Ranch were drained.

More soldiers flooded in behind Francis and the commander and kept firing their guns into the four hallways crowded with the Neighborhood Watch.

Luckily, the personal shields the Neighborhood Watch had activated also prevented them from firing back for now. But just as any individual's shields were about to fail, the Neighborhood Watch would fall back and allow someone with a fully charged shield to take their place at the front of the line.

Recognizing some of the weapons some in the back carried, Francis knew that the Neighborhood Watch had some massive high firepower they could unload once they got close enough.

Francis angled the hemisphere towards the main shield blocking their path forward. "NOW!" He shouted as he injected his Potential into it and pointed it the right way.

The thing ripped from his hand at high speed and flew forward. Most of the soldiers in the room stopped shooting their weapons and rushed after it along with Francis and the commander. The device shattered and the waves of force ripped through the thick shield, leaving the corners near the wall crackling like golden lightning.

Francis and the Commander leaped through the gap of the flickering shield. Four more soldiers made it through after them. Francis rolled to the side as gunfire from the Neighborhood Watch from the other four tunnels cut down a soldier behind him.

The man's body collapsed to the ground as the shield started regenerating behind them. In moments the shield was back in place. The other four groups of the Neighborhood Watch and the remaining soldiers fighting behind them were cut off, unable to make it through the strong shields to chase after the few of them who had made it through the gap.

The remaining soldiers around Francis charged forward and returned fire on the Neighborhood Watch as he rolled to his feet. They were at a three-way intersection. Forward was the shut door leading to the central humming launch chamber. To the right led to the cafeteria and living quarters. And to the left was where Bill would be. The command room. The commander came over and urgently tugged on Francis' sleeve. He leaned in to shout urgently over the gunfire in the room on the other side of the shield. A spray of blood splattered over the golden shield and blocked their view of the room slightly even as the noise and combat continued.

"WHICH WAY?" The commander shouted.

Francis pointed to the left and the two rushed in that direction, the other four soldiers not far behind them. One of the soldiers was cut down from behind as he went to retreat after them. Francis heard whizzing above his head and ducked as something exploded above them. The shield behind them had been pierced by the Neighborhood Watch and they were firing down the hallway after Francis and the soldiers.

The ceiling of the hallway caved in behind them and crushed another man before he could outrun them. The commander raised his pistol and shot one member of the Neighborhood Watch dead before he could raise his shield as he stood there guarding the door to the command room where Bill would be. Another soldier went down as a wave of force sent him spinning with an obviously caved-in chest on one side. His spray of gunfire as he fell killed another of the Neighborhood Watch defenders in retaliation.

It was just four of them left now fighting two of the Neighborhood Watch. Francis, the commander, and two surviving soldiers. Neither of the Neighborhood Watch members had activated their shields, instead going for full offense.

One of them threw a baseball-sized metal ball at them, its surface glowing golden. Francis and the commander lunged forward as the Potential based grenade flew past them, exploding into waves of force to collapse more of the roof behind them, crushing the other two soldiers behind them under the rubble.

Francis pulled out his combat knife and stabbed the closest man in the throat before he could retaliate. He had lowered his shield to throw the grenade and hadn't had enough time to raise it again.

Francis turned as the last man activated his shield just in time for the commander to attempt to execute a similar stab with his own knife.

But the man activated his shield in time, and his shield flashed and the commander's arm was wrenched back in the opposite direction. The man underneath the shield suddenly looked gaunt. It looked like he had used most of his Potential defending from the strong stab.

Francis pulled out his pistol from his side and fired into the shield as quickly as he could. The man underneath the shield shriveled more and more as he stood and stumbled away. The shield tried to return the bullets, to reverse the momentum. But it only managed to send them bouncing away at low speeds as Francis fired into it point-blank as quickly as he could.

The commander saw what was happening and matched Francis' barrage with his own sidearm until the Neighborhood Watch member's shield broke and the man underneath was shot down in moments.

Francis and the military commander stood wearily looking around for more defenders, but all they could hear was shifting rubble and muffled gunfire through the blockage. They took position at either side of the pockmarked metal door at the end of the hallway. The commander held up three fingers. Two fingers. One. Breach. The commander kicked in the door and rushed in alongside Francis and everything seemed to happen all at once.

They made it a few steps before the commander was shot in the chest by an automatic weapon. He was thrown back against the wall under the assault and slowly slid down the wall, leaving a red streak behind him as he slumped down. The man's gun clattered to the floor, falling from his limp fingers.

Francis raised his gun to fire but stiffened as two prongs jabbed into his hip from the side, electrocuting him. He fell to the floor twitching, helpless as his pistol was stolen by Helen who stepped back out from the corner of the room where she'd ambushed him from behind as the two of them rushed inside.

Francis cursed himself mentally as he realized that in his hurry he had forgotten to check his corners. *Goddamnit!*

Bill was standing across the way, his rifle still raised and barrel smoking on the opposite side of the room. Francis saw the finger of the military commander twitch and forced himself to speak to distract Bill from finishing the job.

"Biiiiiiillllllllllll. Stttoooooooop," he managed to grind out even as his body twitched and he ground his teeth from the taser.

Bill turned and Helen stepped back to join him, pulling out the ranged taser ready to shock Francis again if he made any sudden movements.

"Francis. You know this has to happen." Bill said, "We need every ounce of power, if any remnant of the Avatar survives then all is lost."

He put down the rifle, picked up the pen-sized detonator, and flicked open the plastic cap to hold his thumb hovering over the large button inside.

"It's only because of Helen that you are alive right now. She still hopes that you will… see reason. I know it's too late for that. But I promised her the chance, so here we are."

Francis twitched to look at Helen as she spoke.

"Francis, we've done so much over these years. You even evacuated most of those people like you wanted, despite us trying to stop you. Come back and survive with us. Hate us as much as you want once this is all over and the work is done. But if you die…" Her voice trembled a little bit and her tone softened, "Remember when it was just us, together fighting against the world? We all came together for different reasons. You've been my friend for over twelve years and I…"

Her aim of the taser dropped a little to the ground so it wasn't pointing directly at Francis anymore.

"I don't want to lose another friend," Helen said, "So please, just stand aside and let us finish this. You don't have to do anything but wait."

Bill stood there dispassionately holding his thumb over the detonator, gaze flicking between the two of them.

Francis sat there opening and closing his mouth for a moment not sure what to say. He had saved most of them. Most. He still thought it was fear leading Helen and Bill to kill those that were left. Francis couldn't let it happen but didn't know how to articulate so that Helen could understand.

Bill was a lost cause, but if Francis could convince her then maybe she could help him stop this. She had been looped into Bill's larger plans when Francis had been cut out; she could help if he could just convince her…

"Helen, this is wro…"

A voice came on on the speaker system above. Its monotone voice crackled and sputtered as it cut off Francis' words.

"Launch imminent. Launch imminent. Prepare for Launch."

'HNNNNNNNNNNNNNNNNNNNNNNNNNNNNNIIIIIIIIIIIIIIIIIIIIIIIIIIIIIIIIIII I'

A high-pitched whine quickly grew louder and louder, drowning out Francis' words as he desperately tried to shout to get Helen to see reason. She leaned in and tried to read his lips, but still seemed to not understand his words.

Then with a heavy rumble, the world shook and Bill and Helen both stumbled. The lights above flickered off before red emergency lights flickered back on around them. The main power banks of the base were now empty as everything was funneled into the launch, only the emergency power left behind to just barely keep the lights running.

Bill stabilized himself on the desk with one arm and Francis let out a breath of relief that the man hadn't pressed the detonator by accident. Bill pushed himself off of the desk and reached back into his pocket with his free hand. Helen stumbled around but kept her footing, taser still pointed vaguely towards Francis. The rumbling died down and the voice on the system could be heard again.

"Launch complete. Launch complete. Launch complete…"

There were sudden gunshots and Bill fell to the ground, a fountain of blood spraying from the hole in his neck. The detonator fell from his hand as his eyes went glassy even as he fell. Helen turned and her eyes widened as she saw the bloodied soldier aiming his gun at her next, still slumped against the wall.

The military commander's aim wavered as his gun turned to her, but Francis saw the commander's arm tensing as he prepared to pull the trigger again as Helen stared at the man in shock.

Without even thinking, Francis threw himself in front of her from the ground with a lurching motion as the soldier opened fire. Francis' bulletproof vest finally shattered after all the damage it had accumulated throughout the battle and the bullets plowed directly into his gut and chest unimpeded.

Francis coughed something wet on the ground as the soldier slumped against the wall, his last strength spent and his pistol falling to the ground from limp fingers.

Helen rushed over to Francis and cradled his head off the ground.

"Francis… Why? All you had to stop and it would have been me. After all that. I can't lose you and Bill when we're almost done!" Francis coughed some more blood onto the ground. Francis felt something wet dripping on his face. He tried to focus as he realized it was Helen's tears.

"I… *cough* I don't know. Habit, I suppose, after everything we've been through." He reached a bloody hand to her face. She was still crying as she looked down at him. He struggled to keep his eyes open.

"Don't, Helen. Don't do it. Some of them *Cough* might live. It's worth the chance. Promise me."

Helen nodded through her tears. "I… I will. I'm sorry. I'm sorry for everything."

Francis let out a final breath. "Goodbye Helen. I'm sorry too. Sorry, I didn't ask sooner so I could convince you of why he was wrong… I should have…" Francis' hand fell from Helen's face as he drifted off for the last time.

———O — o — O———

Helen wiped the tears from her eyes as she stood up from beside Francis' body. Two people who had been fixtures in her life for over twelve years were dead. All the battles they had gone through, all the heartbreak, the whole organization they had built together. Spending almost all of their time together united in their mission. It was all done now and she was all that was left.

She looked at the soldier slumped against the wall and saw he wasn't breathing. He was dead alongside her friends, as it seemed he had spent his last strength in his final attack.

Helen looked around and saw the detonator on the floor and sighed in relief to see the cap had flipped closed as it fell.

She picked it up and carefully put it on the desk, she would honor Francis' last wish. The energy they had already gathered would have to be enough. She went over to Bill's body and felt another well of emotion swell in her at seeing his dead face. She leaned over to close his blankly staring eyes before feeling something tug at her navel. The air was suddenly filled with thin white filaments emerging from cracks in the rubble.

No, no, no! She scrambled around in Bill's pockets and pulled out a little plastic box with a button on top in his left pocket with a timer on the front. 00:00 flashed on its display over and over as she watched in horror.

Helen reached into her own pocket and injected her Potential into her Protection stone and the tug in her navel stopped. She picked up the device and turned it over to see a note taped there.

"Sorry, Helen," it said, "There's always a backup. If you are reading this then I am dead, Use the following decryption key to access my files so you can continue our work. You know how to get to them.

"-Bill"

Below there was a long string of written text nearly fifty characters long. Helen folded it and tucked it into her pocket carefully. She was numb. Bill had won after all. His last note was all business, not the slightest hint of warmth in his last note.

Francis' final wish had come to nothing. The plan would have been completed no matter her decision. Bill must have activated the timer as soon as the soldiers had started attacking the last checkpoint.

Her grip on her Protection stone tightened. How had it come to this? She sat down and leaned against the wall, watching as the bodies of her best friends and the unfamiliar soldier withered into desiccated husks.

Then there was nothing, only her alone and trapped underground in an abandoned room covered in a thick layer of dust. She couldn't look away and stared at the bodies until they were unrecognizable. She wouldn't be able to even bury them properly now. She could only hope that Bill was right and that this all would be worth it in the end.

Chapter 69: Destined for a Greater Purpose - Multiple Fragments of Memory

Emily startled awake and flailed as a shadow loomed over her. She sat up arms warding off the shadow for a moment before she returned to reality,

"Uhhhhhhhhhhh."

There was no pain and her muscles felt loose and she was more relaxed than she had ever felt before. Everything felt fuzzy and out of focus and the light from the windows stabbed into her eyes. A burly man was standing at her feet.

She blinked at him as he stood there looking at her. Her eyes focused and she recognized him after a long moment. He was the one in command of the line where she had been stationed. She threw a lazy salute, her arms protesting every motion. Her words slurred as she spoke.

"Privuuuut Firsh Clashshhh Emily, uh, Emily Trenton repurtttting fuuur Dushty Shir."

The man waved her off and Emily dropped her salute. God, her arms felt wobbly. She could barely salute right! The man leaned forward.

"Emily, I'm sorry to bother you but we have to move from here and get back to safety. Can you move? Anything you do will help us get out of here faster."

Emily slowly translated the words. She had to get up? But her alarm hadn't even gone off yet…

"Oooohkay, mama. Ooops. Didn't mean to shhhhay thaat."

The man blinked but Emily was already stiffly leveraging herself to her feet. He caught her as she tripped over her feet as she tried to take a wobbly step. He slung her arm around his shoulders and he pulled her forward out of what seemed to be somebody's house.

They went out the door and Emily could see people in green uniforms rushing the opposite way. Haha. Green. She turned to strong and handsome and giggled.

"They're wearing greeeeeen like us. We…. We shhuuuld tell themmm there aren't any trees heeeere."

The man ignored her as they limped down the street. She continued anyway.

"Wishhhouut trees they can't blend iiiiiiinnnnnnn."

He patted her back lightly and pulled her up as she stumbled again. She smiled at him, "Shhhoooorrry."

He looked at her in concern as he guided her into the back of a truck on the road.

"Don't worry. It's just the morphine kicking in. Just hang on until we can get a medic to give you a check-up."

Emily blinked and somehow they were somewhere else. The same handsome man was slapping her face lightly to wake her up.

"Heeeeeeyyyyyy. That's no way to tttttrrreat a lady," She protested blearily.

He snorted as he lifted her up. "Medic's here." A less handsome man came into her view and shined a light in her eyes.

Emily groaned, "Nooooooo. Stoooop it."

The serious man spoke fast, but Emily listened as carefully as she could as she swayed from side to side.

"Definite concussion. The strange behavior could just be from the morphine. Shock maybe. Don't let her fall asleep again if you can. Put her in bed twenty-five."

The other man came back and carried her to a comfy bed. She wanted to fall asleep again but the man kept talking and reminding her to stay awake. Couldn't she just get some sleep? His words cut out and she focused again. He had fallen on the floor and his big muscles were shrinking. There were white little strings like spiderwebs floating and twitching in the air above her.

She flopped over and crawled over to him. No, why was this happening? His muscles were supposed to be big! She grabbed his splayed left arm hoping they would come back. But he just kept shrinking. Something was wrong…

Emily looked at her own arm, and it was smaller than usual too. What… was… The world shrank to a point as she started seeing the bones exposed on her arm. Mr. Handsome's arm bone snapped under her weak grip and started to dissolve into dust. She tried to cough but her lungs were dry. Everything went dark and she slumped to the floor.

Something was wrong…

— — — O — o — O — — —

Ryan sat inside the old house he had holed up in before. Everything was where he had left it. The mental ward from the dome was just as strong here as he had remembered. It had been a mistake to try to evacuate, he should have stayed here and holed up where the aliens wouldn't find him.

The others in the car Ryan had been in had protested when he had left, but Ryan had no other option. He had told them the best choice but they had ignored him, too unwilling to strike out on their own. They had wanted to return to the group of soldiers under constant assault by the aliens.

Nothing he could say convinced them, so he had simply left and stole another bicycle from an empty house for travel. Hidden away where the aliens wouldn't pay him any extra attention, he should be safer. He slammed his fist into the wall of the place and growled.

Damnit, why had he dared hope things would go right this time? He had let Sergeant Ruston convince him that sticking together would be best. She was probably down there fighting the aliens to her last breath or some other heroics. He didn't want to try to be a hero anymore; he just wanted to live.

These last few years had just been one hit after another, pressing him into the dirt. It had all started with his sister Jessica's death and his obsession with getting justice for her from Fulcrum.

He had thought that protecting the people of Safezone Seven might be worth something, but that was taken from him too. Betrayed again.

Victor and Gus, murdered by that jackass Adam as some fucked up power play. It felt like so long since he had thought of Gus and the others. It felt like it was another world from before all of this happened. Let alone the people that Ryan had known before all of this began.

Ryan snorted as he thought about how concerned he had been about making a good impression on Sanchez for the first few months they were partners.

Ryan wondered if Officer Sanchez had made it out of that hospital after Ryan's warning or survived everything else that had happened since then. Ryan had been so mad at Sanchez for ratting him out for his outburst at Fulcrum back then.

Now he couldn't help but feel grateful to Sanchez. If Ryan hadn't been in that room when Gus came rushing in, then who knows what would have happened to the both of them? Sanchez's betrayal was what had pushed Ryan over the edge of his breakdown and kept him there in that room.

If Ryan hadn't been there, then Gus would have been caught by those Infected, and Ryan would have been blissfully unaware, helpless prey for whenever they turned their jaws to him next.

Ryan walked to the front door and opened it. He looked outside upwards to the rippling golden dome. The whole sky was tinted gold as rippling explosions washed over its exterior. It seemed that not even the barrage of missiles could pierce it now that it was infused with the golden light. In fact, was the light growing brighter? Ryan squinted as the dome began to glow brighter and brighter with the golden light as he watched.

No, it wasn't the dome, there was a ball of light in the distance. Ryan remembered the last time he saw a singular source of Golden light under a shield. Safezone Seven. His eyes widened as the Golden ball ascended into the sky.

It... It had been a goddamn test! Safezone Seven, it was happening again! This whole dome, the whole town, it was happening again!

Ryan rushed inside and ran for his pack as the golden light grew brighter and brighter. There was nothing he could do, but he hoped something, anything in the bag might hold the secrets to let him survive.

He entered the bedroom and suddenly grew dizzy. The air was suddenly filled with glimmering white fibers like spider's webs. The thin fibers bored through the walls, floors, and ceiling of the room around him in little sprays of dust, wavering every which way like pieces of thread drifting in a soft wind. The strings all drifted towards him and lightly latched onto his bare skin.

Ryan fell forward and landed on the floor parallel to the bed. He felt weaker and weaker. He reached up and tugged the strap on his bag and it fell to the floor in front of him, spilling out its contents in front of him.

No matter what he did the spider web didn't restrict his movement and floated out of the way when he went to grab them. He couldn't get them off of him no matter how much he swiped or rolled around to remove them.

Ryan frantically grabbed his bag and finished pouring it out even as the muscles on his arm began shrinking. He could only feel horror as his vision began blackening at the edges. He tossed the empty bag away weakly and spread out the items, still praying for any solution. Something in this bag would save him. Knife, water canteen.

Police pistol.

Ammunition.

Snack... Bars. No, focus.

The.... length of rope. A... A Knife.

Pistol....

Water. Bag... where was...

The bag. There must be... Something... that could help... Save him...

Ryan's vision went blurry as his arms lost the strength to even hold himself up. He shifted his head to look at the items. There must be something. But there was nothing.

With supreme willpower, Ryan forced his arm to reach to touch the bag. If he could just find something else inside... Ryan's vision cut to black and he knew no more.

—–— O — o — O —–—

President Harrow drummed his fingers on the chair.

"How is this possible? Didn't we break that damn dome wide open just a week ago? How the hell is it holding up so well now?"

The generals exchanged looks and even the analysts stood silent. Eventually, one brave soul took a step forward.

"Sir, we just don't know. This technology is incredible, we have no idea how it could work..."

President Harrow slammed his fist on the table and everyone jumped.

"I don't want to hear how damn incredible the weapons of our enemies are! Where are the solutions? Vulnerabilities? We've been pounding that thing with all we have short of nukes for hours now!" He scanned the room as no one spoke up. His voice grew a little weaker as he sat back in his seat.

"Anything?"

One of his generals cleared his throat.

"Sir, no one likes it but we have to consider the nuclear option. If we don't warn our allies in time, we risk worldwide nuclear war on top of the alien invasion. It's a risk, but we have no idea of what could happen if these things make it out from the dome to spread farther."

General Harris glared angrily at the man, "Our soldiers and the rescued civilians are just outside! We'd be killing them all, breaking dozens of international treaties, and no guarantee it would even work. Not to mention all the radiation poisoning *Our own land* for generations!"

President Harrow drummed his fingers on the table as the men continued arguing. He didn't like considering it either. But it had to be done. They had no idea what this plan of the Neighborhood Watch would accomplish.

They had gotten some garbled accounts that it would kill everyone inside the dome all at once in moments. But the communications blackout had been reestablished before they could confirm more. Who knows if this new weapon wouldn't devastate an area far beyond the dome itself? President Harrow didn't like imagining the destruction people with this kind of technology could create if they set their minds to it. It could do things that were science fiction, thought impossible until only a month ago.

President Harrow cleared his throat and the arguing generals stopped, "Inform the world leaders that we are prepared to use nuclear strikes if it comes down to it," he said firmly, "We need the option in the worst case."

He met General Harris' eyes, "Send a forced evacuation order within fifty miles of the dome. That includes the people we've just saved. We can't risk any of the holdouts getting caught in the blast or resulting radiation if we launch."

The general nodded and stood and stepped away to confer with others to relay the orders. President Harrow stood to take the phone that was still ringing off the hook from the calls of foreign leaders, calls he had been largely ignoring for the last tense week since his speech to the world regarding the alien threat. Even their allies' fastest assistance couldn't arrive for weeks from now at the earliest. Useless in this crisis.

President Harrow went to answer the phone but stopped as he saw the images of the dome on the monitor at the end of the table change. It glowed brighter and brighter with golden light. A dome over fifteen miles in diameter turned solid gold and the images were being actively filtered to take out the glaring light more and more as the moments passed.

The phone dropped from the president's hand as he stood frozen among the renewed frantic arguments and orders. He was too late, and the Neighborhood Watch had won. He could only watch the screen and hope they knew what they were doing.

Because if he had to deal with both their technology and the alien infestation at once… He didn't know what he could do to stop it. He leaned forward and put his hands on the table, watching the screen intently for what would happen next.

Chapter 70: Self-imposed Duty - Nameless Amalgamation Fragment

The Nameless Amalgamation was lost as it lumbered away from the pursuing Nameless. It had extended its arm to the Nameless closest to it in greeting when it had arrived, as its components had remembered that was what mortals were supposed to do when meeting another.

As soon as the Amalgamation touched it however it was assimilated and its assorted memories had entered the collective. The bond of the vessel to the true body was severed, increasing the Potential of the collective. The Amalgamation tried to return the vessel and restore the bond, but it didn't know how to do it.

Its natural state was to assimilate not to separate. For some reason it no longer had the ability to manipulate its form as well as its components would expect. Perhaps it was because of the Amalgamation's birth among the Devouring Flame?

The Flame had burned strangely when it had attacked the components. Burning certain portions of the Nameless components and ignoring others, herding the components together so they were all in one pile for when the Amalgamation had formed.

Its components remembered that such collectives of bodies were often used for defense, but that the memories of each of the components should have been separate in that case. Many individuals working for one goal, not one collective working as one.

The bonds of each Nameless should have been maintained until the component separated from the main physical form again under its own will.

The Amalgamation had been different, a melding of minds and bodies both now inseparable from each other. But one of the bodies had not been like the others... It had had no bond, and no memories had rushed in from its integration. It had been in the center of its mass? How strange, it must investigate this oddity. It...

When the Amalgamation pursued the human after its formation, the Devouring Flame attacked it in retaliation and reduced it to a fraction of its former mass. The human had been the one who released the flame. Perhaps he was protected?

The collective agreed, it should not attack mortals until it was sure the Devouring Flame would not retaliate against it somehow.

The Amalgamation had immediately been attacked by Infiltrator of Authority and the rest of the Nameless when they saw it absorbing the nearest Nameless on instinct.

The Amalgamation knew from the components' memories that such a thing was a hostile action but its mind could not register it as such. It was not destruction but integration after all. All the minds still remained, just part of a greater whole now.

The Amalgamation was pursued out into the humans' territory by the Invasion forces.

The humans cowered and shouted when they spotted the Amalgamation, but after the Amalgamation continued onwards, they did not chase. It wandered like that for days, avoiding the humans and Invasion forces alike.

The Nameless Amalgamation integrated any Nameless it came across. Their minds would be upset for a few minutes afterward, but all accepted their state and fully joined the collective soon after.

After an indeterminate amount of time, the Amalgamation noticed a flash of golden light in the distance. It carefully crept in that direction until it saw Infiltrator of Authority and groups of Invasion forces shifting through the rubble of several destroyed buildings.

The Amalgamation retreated and was about to leave the area when it noticed the path of destruction leading away from the rubble. A crushed car here, some cracked concrete there. With some focus a clear path could be drawn away from the destruction.

Curious, the Amalgamation followed the path back to its source, careful to not be seen by jumping from roof to roof on the buildings by the street. Its arachnid form helped with the large leaps and balance at longer distances as well as for increasing its stealth.

It could spread out its weight among the limbs to decrease the sound from its steps if it needed to so as to not make as much noise.

Eventually, the Amalgamation reached the endpoint of the trail and received a shock as its components practically screamed the importance of this location. This was the location of the Seed and Fulcrum, who together would become the Harbinger for this world. Avatar. The Amalgamation poked at the memory. Was this fusion not similar to its own existence except between only two entities rather than many?

Unfortunately, the two were gone, which its components insisted was impossible. The Amalgamation was far curious now about this strange creature from its components' memories, and it had nothing better to do than investigate.

It crept into the damaged house opposite the house of the Fulcrum and Seed and explored the inside. There was already a pit of slime perfect for hibernating dug into the floor, left empty.

The Amalgamation slid inside the pit and settled into place. It would wait until the twinned entities returned. With the Seed being such a powerful entity, the combination with the mortal must provide some element to create a greater whole. It must know what this element could be. How there could be another collective greater than its parts like the Nameless Amalgamation was?

— — — O — o — O — — —

The Nameless Amalgamation hibernated, and there was no change around it. A few individual Invasion members wandered in and were incorporated into the Amalgamation, increasing its mass and knowledge.

One large group of the Invasion forces attempted an assault shortly afterward the Nameless Amalgamation settled in this location, but they were all quickly absorbed, increasing the Amalgamations mass enough it could only barely fit in the old hibernation hole anymore.

After that, there were no more attacks, although several of the Invasion forces were scattered around watching the Amalgamation carefully for movement. It remained still as the Seed and Fulcrum remained absent and reentered hibernation waiting for more change.

———O—o—O———

The Amalgamation jerked into awareness at the explosion of rubble across the street. It stirred and made its way to the entrance of the building where it had been nesting.

Had Fulcrum and the Seed returned? As it reached the door a wave of bodies flooded from every direction to attack it. There were large crashes and screeches outside even as the Amalgamation began absorbing bodies as quickly as it was damaged. It was a hard-fought battle and it was nearly half the size as it had been before the furious assault by the Swarmlings and Nameless gradually petered out.

The ground below the Amalgamtion's limbs shook as massive footsteps receded into the distance.

The Amalgamation dashed outside and witnessed the Fusion of Seed and Fulcrum into the Harbinger. Avatar? No, it did not feel powerful to be an Avatar yet. But it was still a complete fusion, the Amalgamation could see.

The creature's form was still shifting even as it moved. More Eldritch one second, more human the next. The Amalgamation rushed after it, making sure to stay behind and out of sight. It must observe this creature and see how the two entities would intertwine and cooperate.

Surely this would help explain its own condition! The Harbinger consumed more of the Spawnlings that had attacked the humans and moved onwards. The Amalgamation trailed behind and consumed any creatures that fled or the Harbinger missed. It grew in size more. The Amalgamation watched and observed, for here was a creature where two could become one.

———O—o—O———

The Amalgamation followed and watched as the Harbinger avoided harming the humans and only consumed the Invasion forces. Was it aware of the retaliation of the Devouring Flame as well? It must truly be an intelligent being if it had discovered such a thing without experiencing it directly or being told. This pattern continued for many hours, as the Harbinger fought and fed on the forces of the Invasion, and the Amalgamation fed on the scraps it left behind it.

The Harbinger left the embattled human groups to themselves after defeating their opponents, so the Amalgamation avoided them as well. It was only at the very beginning that the Harbinger destroyed that helicopter in retaliation for its vicious assault on it.

After saving a group of soldiers, the mortals' vehicles seemed to back off and allow the injured but healing Harbinger to continue its crusade against the Invasion forces. The Harbinger mostly consumed Spawnlings, most of the true Nameless had enough brains to flee when they saw the Harbinger approaching them with hungry intent.

The both of them reached another group of humans fending off the Invasion forces. But after a moment a strange thing happened. A human pistol shot into one of the others and the man soon became wreathed in the Devouring Flames. Was this why the Devouring Flame wished to preserve the mortals? So it could join with them like this? The mortal screamed as he jumped into the crowd of Invasion forces.

The force the mortals were fighting were mostly Spawnlings, but a few weaker Nameless were mixed in there with them. The mortal man and his Flames destroyed the Invasion forces in minutes, turning the tide of the battle almost completely on his lonesome.

The Harbinger drew to a stop only to be attacked by the man of the Devouring Flame. The Amalgamation watched carefully as the flame burrowed inwards but did not spread as violently as it had done in many other cases. Was it due to the strength of the Harbinger or a choice of the Flame to not burn as intensely as it could?

The Harbinger was still hard pressed as it ejected various chunks of its flesh to attempt to purge the flame from its form. But the Devouring Flame only spread at a limited rate, only burning brighter when it threatened to be extinguished from the Harbinger's form completely.

The Amalgamation froze as it sensed a massive eye fixed upon it. It gazed upward and saw a golden orb of raw power above, a hint of Devouring Flame spreading from within. The sky was becoming more and more crimson as time passed.

But the Devouring Flame above was not the source of the gaze upon it. It turned back to the Harbinger to see it being sucked into a massive spherical portal composed of red light.

A black ball of chitin remained suspended in the air for a moment before it fell to the ground with a crash. The Amalgamation scuttled closer as the Seed's carapace cracked and it created a humanoid form. One had become two again. The Seed walked to the portal and hesitated for a moment, before diving inside after Fulcrum.

The Amalgamation paused as it considered what to do. It considered all its opti… No, the portal was shrinking! It dashed and scuttled as hard as it could for the portal that was shrinking by the second. The portal was barely a hundred feet tall before the Amalgamation dived inside.

It couldn't let this opportunity escape it! It must discover how two became one! How another creature could have a beautiful combination so similar to its own?! It leaped through the portal just in time. After it went through, it was surrounded by blackness and all of its consciousnesses of the collective winked out all at once.

---O — o — O---

The Devouring Flame gathered its might and prepared to strike the massive wells of Potential gathered below. It gathered into a single dense ball, spinning faster and faster, compressing more and more every moment. But the source disappeared after a moment, swept away by the Eldest, its patron.

The ball of arcing plasma began compressing more and more in rage as it realized the meal had escaped. The red sky gathered at a single point as the golden shield, the dome, finally spluttered and failed for the last time from the heat emanating from the ball of the Flame.

The Devouring Flame had held itself back for so long for this moment, and it would not be denied the revelry now.

If the Harbinger didn't return before it was finished... Then the mortals of this world would feel its disappointment. It would put this energy to better use if the more entertaining meal didn't return in time. It charged up its final attack, ready to devastate this world...

Only to notice the portal opening back up. Something stepped back through, and the Devouring Flame joyfully rushed downwards to greet it. The mass of beautiful Potential had returned once more. An Avatar of the Eldest? A hard battle? Or a simple Harbinger, an easy meal?

The being looked upwards without moving as the Flame gathered into a solid beam of reddish flames and descended downwards, growing closer to it by the moment. The Flame danced and laughed as it approached, but the being stood still without a hint of motion.

As the Flame descended, it wondered at the confidence. Would this being **BURN**, or quench the gathered Flame? Was this the confidence of a powerful Avatar or the bravado of a creature knowing that it was outmatched?

The Flame struck the ground and the watching humans of the world were forced to divert their eyes as the impact was shrouded by a crimson glow. The people of the world could only watch with bated breath through their devices as the light slowly began to fade.

One question lingered in everyone's minds as the light of the Flame started to die down. Had the alien creature beneath survived? Was it over? Or had the battle only just begun?

Part Five: An Oddly Familiar World

Chapter 71: A New World for Fulcrum

— — — Returning to a non-linear view of time to prevent inconsistencies… Synthesizing Pocket Dimension… Writing physical laws… Writing physical laws… Animating the sealing mists… Animating… Testing dimensional barriers… Finalizing… Finalizing… Finished. Pocket dimension created. Transferring Fulcrum, Seed, and the Nameless Amalgamation to blank pocket dimension. — — —

— — — Now to reinforce the dimensional barriers on the main universe. Enacting changes and resulting strengthened barrier against dimensional intrusion on all relevant Cycles future and past so the Greater Consciousnesses of the Eldest and Devouring Flame can't interfere with Central Events from their respective realms. — — —

— — — Except where Central Events demand it of course. It would be no fun for this universe to destroy itself again after it finally pulled itself back together after so many cycles. What an odd timeline that it finally coalesced around. I wonder if the Eldest even considered that it could have made a mistake meddling in time and accidentally destroyed its treasured realm beyond recovery… — — —

— — — Well, it can't take back its actions now. Its punishment will be ironic at least. Anchoring Pocket Dimension into the past relative to the Central Events. Awakening occupants… Should I return to a linear view of time? I already know the rest for this Cycle at least, but it isn't quite the same as being there and experiencing it like a lower being… — — —

— — — I should just relax and enjoy it. Being Arbiter of Reality has been so stale for the last few trillion cycles, at least this is at least a little different than the more normal universes. May as well enjoy the show. Hmmm. It seems that Fulcrum is waking up now… Yes, I'll return and observe the rest like a lower being… — — —

    Everything was black. Everything felt far away and I was blind, like I was floating in nothing. That was, until suddenly feeling returned to my body.
    I felt something below me, gravity reasserted itself as I felt myself being pushed downward through the endless void. I was still blind, my multitude of eyes all staring into blackness as I felt the perfectly flat floor below me. The floor appeared as if it had always been there, arriving so that It was hard to say if it had appeared under me just now or been there the whole time I was standing there.

A faint light shone to break the darkness and I could finally see through my multitude of eyes a little bit.

All around me, tendrils of gray mists floated and curled in the air lazily, seeming unconcerned by my presence. The mists nearest to me slowly drifted towards my body and clung to me for a brief moment, before continuing onward back into the darkness.

The tentacles all over my body unfurled and stretched out to disturb the lazily floating tendrils of mist clinging to my body. I focused the five eyes that remained on my head on the sight of my arm.

The misty wisps clung to the limb for a moment and I felt a faint pressure on the limb where the mist sat. But after a moment, the mist released me again and diverted back to continue floating by.

Where was the light coming from? I looked around for the source of the light only to notice it rising from my chest, the dim light was getting brighter by the moment. The growing reddish embers on my body were slowly growing and illuminating the scene around me. It seems that I hadn't been able to remove all of this strange flame before I was pulled into that red portal.

How had I not noticed the flame? I had been sure I had purged all of it before...

As soon as I saw the dull flames growing on my body, my sense of pain returned and I screeched and stumbled onto one knee. I began to use the pitiful amount of Potential left in my body to try to push it out of me and eject the infected flesh.

The embers were small and near the surface so if I was careful I should be able to remove it all. Something was missing, it didn't feel as easy as it should to manipulate the Potential inside myself...

With a tearing sensation, all the reddish embers ripped from my chest as I explosively ejected the last of the embers onto the ground in front of me, taking a quick step backwards away from the embers. As I watched cautiously, the embers migrated and gathered into a ball of reddish flame that floated silently above my ejected flesh.

I quickly sealed the wounds leaking my inky blood and took a few more rapid steps backwards away from it. But the orb of reddish flames didn't approach and remained motionless as it slowly began to shrink as it floated there bobbing up and down.

Despite my fear, I leaned in to watch as the gray mist tendrils in the area slowly began to divert to gather around the slowly shrinking ball of flame. The flames were shrouded in a swirling cloud now, the mist was growing thicker and thicker around it as every moment passed.

The flame's dull red glow barely pierced the fog gathered around it and scattered into a diffuse brighter glow shining through the swirling cloud. I got a terrible feeling and took another few steps backwards as the fog began to spin and compress around the floating flame.

Faster and faster the glowing cloud of mist spun as I stood in the shadow, faint glimmers of red light piercing the ball of mist.

Then with a wet thump, the ball compressed inwards all at once. Then again. Again. Increasing the pressure and the speed at which the ball of mist swirled in the center of the black space.

The light shining from the mist tinted a lighter yellow color rather than the usual red glow as I stood in shadow. Staring at it.

The orb of dense mist hovered there slowly spinning for a few moments, passive and looking almost solid now. I wasn't sure what to do and remained in place, eyeing the glowing orb with suspicion.

With a *Whoomph,* The orb shot into the sky so fast that I barely had time to look up before it exploded into a massive ball of golden light. I screeched and looked away blinking hard as the whole area became bathed in bright light. The yellow ball hovered there illuminating this whole place like it was midday on Earth, framed against a pitch-black sky with no stars.

After adjusting my vision by blinking my five main eyes a few times, I glanced down and saw that while I felt something below me, I could only see more inky blackness. I couldn't see the floor and despite the light blazing through the surroundings, all I could see was more black all around me.

Something was different underneath me after a few minutes and I sank slightly into the floor as I stood there. Curious, I lifted my foot to inspect underneath and saw that the floor underneath my feet was becoming softer and more brown the longer I stood there. Turning into soil.

I took a few steps away to inspect the spot where I had been standing. As I looked at it, my feet sank down again, and the floor underneath where I had moved began to convert to the soil as well. Carefully watching the edge of the brown patch on the ground, the place where I had originally been standing was slowly expanding on its own even without me standing on top of it. A single growing brown patch of dirt disrupting the black void around me.

I watched silently as the brown spread behind and beneath me for a few minutes, but nothing else of interest happened. The soil kept growing at a slow pace from wherever I touched the strange invisible floor. After a while of nothing further happening, I shrugged and turned to start walking into the distance, into the blackness away from my starting point.

Surely there must be more than this in this place? I kept walking forward one step at a time, a growing dirt trail expanding behind me from wherever my feet touched. Maybe if this whole place became dirt then I would learn something new.

I kept walking until I lost track of time, only the brown soil, the unmoving yellow ball of flame above, and the inky black skies to keep me company.

I kept walking more and more for what felt like forever. There were no landmarks except for the brown path behind me and the void ahead.

But after countless ages, eons, hours, finally I sped up and ran faster as I spotted something new in the distance. Something green.

I lumbered at my fastest pace until I could get a view of the scene only to pause in confusion. I turned from left to right to stare at the inky void on either side of me. I turned to inspect the brown trail behind me.

But in front, there was a wide patch of earth forty or fifty of my body lengths to either side. It stretched forward as far as I could see in a straight line, little tufts of green spreading from its center. In the very center of the cluster of brown was a small strip of a green carpet of grass.

Getting closer, I plunged my hands in the dirt and tried to bring it closer to inspect the green grass, but as soon as I lifted the soil away from the floor it dispersed into the gray mist all at once. I tried to grab the mist in surprise, but the tendrils squirmed out of my way this time and diverted to fly upwards into the sky.

Confused, I leaned over and used several of my tentacles to try to lift more of the dirt from the floor.

———— O — o — O ————

After a few more attempts, I gave up. Whenever the dirt or grass left the ground it dissolved into the mists again. Only a few feet below the ground there was more of the strange floor material that I couldn't even see or so much as scratch even with my strongest blows. The grass and the brown strip forward and behind me kept slowly growing and spreading through the blackness.

With nothing else to do, I continued to wander wherever there was an inky black floor perpendicular to my original path.

After walking for another age, weeks, hours, I discovered that I was looping around this place. Returning to my starting place after walking in a straight line. The false sun remained static in the sky.

I could see my footsteps in the dirt of the old path as I arrived back from where I arrived. The pits where I had dug through the dirt only to have it dissolve into mist as soon as it left the ground.

The patch of grass had spread well by now, making the place look like an endless grassland if I looked in the right direction near the center of my starting point.

The sky was slowly brightening and the void began shifting the slightest fraction of blue as I stood among the massive field of green grass. Alone in this empty place, not even a single gust of wind to break the silence of everything besides the sound of my footsteps through the grass.

I angled my path to the side, towards one of the triangular regions where the soil was still growing over the blackness of the floor. I did not want to wait for its slow spread to fill in the gaps. I would walk across this whole place until it was all grass. Perhaps then something would finally change.

———O—o—O———

I returned to the starting point once more. I knew because the black stretching from horizon to horizon gradually narrowed into a black arrow pointing me back to the center, the soil spreading and making it slowly shrink as time passed. Some larger plants had begun to grow, even some smaller trees near the center where I had first started.

The gray mist was much less present in this place, with only a few isolated wisps floating by as I inspected the plants around me. I tried uprooting the trees again, but as soon as I did they puffed back into the gray mist, leaving the hole to slowly heal over the black void left behind beneath. Returning to the slow spread of soil slowly sinking downwards deeper and deeper beneath my feet. How strange this place was.

I looked into the sky and saw the yellowish ball of Flame hovering static in the sky. It hadn't seemed to have shrunk in all this time as it had before. I paused as I heard something. Was that? No, must have been nothing. I kept walking until suddenly I heard it again.

A new sound, not that of my feet on the grass. I turned to the noise and rushed towards the source as it cut out again. I stood there looking around, sure that it had been from somewhere around here...

Another sound and I looked down. There, barely standing to my shins among the foliage were two creatures. One reminded me of a spider, and the other seemed strangely familiar. The two had been fighting and growling but broke it off as they saw my approach, both scraped and stained in slowly bleeding wounds.

I ignored the spider for now and inspected the other one. It had black chitin plates all over its body, and I could see the multitude of eyes dotting its form. I leaned down and saw it had a similar mass of tentacles covering its lower jaw as I did. It looked like a smaller version of me, actually...

Instinctively, I reached out telepathically to the black-shelled creature and received a wave of images and emotional impressions in response. I understood them, but somehow it... didn't feel right. I should convert them into words for me to really understand them.

'Fulcrum,' my mind said to form the images and emotions of the small creature into words, *'Where is this? Why you not resist the bad portal?'*

I squinted in confusion. What was this creature? Did we know each other? Seeing the squint of so many of my eyes, another wave of images came from the black-shelled creature. I saw it sitting inside of my abdomen, helping me refine my form. Seeing me getting sucked through the portal, then the... Seed that was the word... created this small form and followed me inside the portal.

I hummed to myself and clicked my beak underneath my mat of mouth tentacles as I considered it. Hadn't I known this creature for longer than that? Everything felt so much clearer since I had come to this place, everything before was like a hazy dream to my memories.

I sent the small creature my confusion and hesitation and explained with a stuttered and warped set of images of my own. The Seed replied, and my mind translated the images into words once more.

'Fulcrum. Here is everything I remember. Will help?'

A great sensation of pain and a tearing sensation in the Seed's mind. Fragmented images. Something changing in the Seed. Merging with me as our joined form began twisting and changing. As the memories played, my battle with the non-humans came back to me. And my insistence on keeping my form as close to human as possible. The Seed still didn't know why I had insisted, and I couldn't remember either why it had been important.

'Why do you forget?' The Seed asked in frustration when I explained the situation in my amateurish images and emotions.

The Seed was frustrated. It had followed me to solve this mystery after all. I could not remember why I had come here no matter how hard I tried, and the Seed sent dejection back to me after a minute or two.

The Seed let out a high-pitched little screech with its little form and began kicking at a nearby shrub in a rage. I could feel the Seed's anger as it pounded the ground and kicked over the shrubs in an epic toddler tantrum. Huh, toddler? What was that word? It felt appropriate for the situation, but I couldn't say what it meant now that I was focused on it.

Looking back, most of the words in my mind seemed to be like that. Where had I learned them? I knew their meaning, but where had they come from? I couldn't say, no matter how hard I tried.

With a jolt, I remembered the other spider-like creature that had been here before and glanced around searching for it. It had disappeared while I focused on the Seed. Well, not a Seed now that it had a body.

Distracted from my search, I turned the question to the Seed. What was its name now that it was no longer a Seed? Now that it had sprouted. The little creature paused and considered the question seriously for a moment before sending a singular image. It was a bird. A robin with a red belly.

Wait, I knew this animal? Where had I seen it before? Where had I....? Grrrrrrr. But no matter how hard I tried, I couldn't remember where I had seen one.

I asked the Seed, no Robin, where it had seen the bird. It sent back a memory. A short scene of the bird taking off from a grassy surface much like the one surrounding us and soaring into the sky. There was a whitish building in the memory, and it seemed familiar. There was a blurred humanoid figure watching it from just inside the house, a sense of amusement wafting off of them. Everything in the memory was blurred and hazy. Everything but the bird.

The Seed didn't seem to know any more either when I asked for more details on what the memory meant or who the man in the memory was. Apparently its memories were almost as jumbled as mine. I considered that it was lying somehow, but for some reason I didn't think that was likely.

Our minds were connected, and I could sense its intent and emotions even as I translated everything it sent to me into words and sets of static images. I did not think we would be able to deceive each other when communicating with each other like this.

Robin was as frustrated with its own vague memories as I had been when I realized the holes in my own memories.

I refocused. Where had the spider creature gone? Why were they fighting with Robin? I asked Robin about it.

'Bad thing. Many bodies, one mind. Abomination. Escaped while we talked. It wanted to make me like It. We should hunt, stop it from growing more.'

'Why is it bad?' I replied, *'What did it do?'*

Robin kicked a nearby bush and let out a frustrated screech. It has been doing that a lot recently.

'Don't KNOW! Just bad. Would know before. No like forgetting. That's bad too. I should not forget. Now, hunt! The other one still bad. You big, we can catch up quick.'

I sent back acceptance and picked up Robin with one of my tentacles. It was the only other thing I had seen in here after all, I couldn't let myself lose track of it now. Luckily I had remembered to deactivate the dissolving acids so Robin wouldn't be injured as I picked it up. Robin screeched petulantly. *'No, No, no! Put me down! Bad Fulcrum!'*

I stared at it curiously, *'How else will you go as fast as me? I have to carry you for this to work. You are too small, I should carry you.'*

At this, Robin stopped its struggles in my tentacle for a moment and slumped. *'Nggggg. No like. On shoulder at least. Not wrapped up in limb.'*

I wasn't sure of the difference. My tentacle was quite stable and was making sure Robin wouldn't be thrown around as I began picking up speed with my walking. But I followed its demands anyway.

Even as it complained, Robin mentally gave me directions on where the spider had fled. The shoulder would be a much rougher ride for the little creature. But I guess Robin knew best for what would make it most comfortable. My tentacle curled inwards and placed Robin's small form on my shoulder even as I kept moving.

Robin stumbled for a moment before crouching down to grip the edges of a few of my bone plates, seeming to find its balance after a moment. Well, not ideal but I would just have to be careful to not throw it off when I suddenly change direction.

I wasn't sure what this spider had done wrong, but to find out we had to find it first before it escaped. I wasn't going to let the only other creature I had seen in here in ages get away before I even talked to it! Maybe I could figure out why Robin didn't seem to like it very much.

Chapter 72: A New Friend for Fulcrum?

The two of us found the spider-like creature scuttling a ways away at its top speed. Robin had seen the direction it had left in while we were talking, and my long strides ate up the ground between us and the escaping creature quickly. Eventually, I drew close and it would dive to the side and start scuttling in a different direction.

I couldn't see any eyes to make telepathic contact yet, and both my and Robin's telepathic probes were firmly denied by the creature as it made its escape from us. How irritating. Robin was egging me on, getting more and more bloodthirsty the longer the chase went.

'Yes, after it! Squash with your big human hands! Smoosh smoosh. Ah, you missed it again!'

I had indeed missed it. No wonder it was running if it thought I was like that. I was only trying to get it to stop and pick it up though so we could talk, not hurt it. Robin had actually distracted me that time so my hand almost crushed it as I mistimed a grab before it luckily dodged.

My tentacles were providing support to help box it in, but it was slippery and jumped through even the smallest of gaps between my surrounding cages of tentacles.

Robin still couldn't give me a good reason why it was so against the creature. I had to be very careful not to hurt the spider thing or throw Robin off my shoulder with all of my movements during the chase, which made things much harder as well.

After a few minutes of this, I captured one of the spider creature's limbs with one of my tentacles and began to tug it into the air. At once it violently ripped itself out of the tentacle's grip, leaving the top layer of flesh behind in its hurry. I didn't want that to happen again, so I held back a little so it wouldn't hurt itself again to escape.

This continued for a time and Robin was getting positively feral by now. I wasn't sure I even wanted to keep the telepathic communication at this point, it was getting just mean as Robin kept getting more and more upset as I kept failing to catch the strange spider.

'NO, SO CLOSE!' Robin shouted in my mind, *'GRIND IT TO PIECES. LET ME AT IT, I'LL TEAR IT TO SHREDS AND FEAST ON ITS YOUNG! WHY CAN'T YOU CATCH IT ALREADY, DUMB FULCRUM! STUPID HUMAN HANDS CAN'T DO ANYTHING. SLOW AND CLUMSY, SHOULD HAVE ADDED MORE TENTACLES AND THEN THIS WOULD BE EASY!'*

Well Robin wasn't wrong. More tentacles would help to box it in more. I reached for my Potential to make some minor changes only to realize that I couldn't feel my Potential anymore. That I hadn't been able to ever since I woke up in this place, so I couldn't change my body again. I interrupted Robin's continued rant as the sudden realization washed over me.

'FEED ON ITS...'

'Robin...'

'STUPID THING GIVE UP ALREAD... Hey, Fulcrum. Don't stop now, it's almost squashed! See, it's already escaping again!'

'Robin, I wasn't '**squashing**' it. I just wanted to capture it so we could talk first.'

Robin's telepathic voice grew petulant.

'Fuuuullllllccccruuuuum. I knew you were missing on purpose. Why, it's a bad thing. It's terrible, we should kill it together. I'll even do it for you if you bring me close enough.'

'Why?'

'Well... You gotta feel it too! It's just terrible, I don't like it. Shouldn't exist. Bad, bad, bad.'

I internally sighed. I wasn't getting answers from Robin anytime soon. Well, maybe a distraction could help. 'Can you feel your Potential? I was just...'

Robin replied even as I communicated with it. 'Of course I can feel my Potential, it's part of memmmeeeee. AHAHHHHHHHHHHHHHHHHHHHHHHHH!!!!!!''

I winced as the telepathic scream rang through my skull. Robin flailed wildly and fell from my shoulder. I reached up with one of my tentacles and quickly caught it and wrapped it up to stop its fall. It hardly noticed the treatment it had protested so hard before as it was wrapped up and lifted back into the air. There was an incoherent flurry of images I translated as mumbling frantically coming from Robin now.

'Where is it, where is it, where is it, It's got to be here, where is it...'

Well, um, that was a much larger reaction than I had expected. I guess I should have expected this from its overreactions from before though. It seemed like a very excitable creature.

Eventually, Robin recovered from its shock somewhat and returned its attention to me as I stood there just watching as the other creature scurried into the distance as fast as its little spidery legs could take it. Robin turned its head towards me.

'Fulcrum, It's gone,' Robin wailed, 'It's gone, and I can't believe I didn't notice. How can this happen, this is terrible. Horrible. Why... Oh, why me...'

'Hey, it's gone for me too and I feel fine,' I replied, 'Maybe it's not so bad?'

'No! Awful, how you not mad? I won't be able to give myself any cool modifications EVER. Stuck like this FOREVER. Gross...'

Er, well. Not sure what I should say to that. Robin just sulked on my shoulder for a bit as I tried to come up with a response. Robin was feeling really depressed now, I could feel it through the telepathic bond. I should try to cheer it up.

I sent some wordless affirmation and support to Robin for a while as it sat slumped onto its stomach, draped over my stationary shoulder as I stood in place. It didn't respond for a while, and I just continued the deluge.

Eventually Robin lifted its head and pointed it at me angrily for a moment before severing the telepathic bond after a long moment's pause. But at least it had been feeling a little better near the end there. I started walking away at a slower pace for me as Robin went limp on my shoulder again.

Best to get out of sight of the spider creature before Robin got thrown into a rage again. Another sudden mood swing from the little creature was the last thing I needed right now.

———O—o—O———

Robin was still down, slumped over on my shoulder as I continued to wander the grasslands. There were only a few patches of blackness left, and the grass had covered almost all the dirt I had seen so far.

The shrubs from before were beginning to shift into taller trees and forests. But given my size, they still appeared tiny, the tallest of the trees only rising to my chest now.

Every time I knocked one of the trees over while it was in my path, it dissolved back into the gray mist. I thought I could start to see slight swells and falls in the terrain beginning to form, but it was harder to tell now that everything around me had turned to forest.

The Flame remained hovering in the sky, unmoving. I felt a little nervous as I stared at it for a moment. I didn't like how its heat made me feel. Like it was just up there watching me, waiting to burn me and Robin at any moment when the moment was perfect for it to strike. But for now it was giving us light to see by, so it wasn't all bad though.

———O—o—O———

An eternity later, Robin finally had cheered up. Occasionally I would stop and put it down, and it could climb and play in the trees for a while. With the "sun" still unmoving above us, it was almost impossible to tell how long it had truly been as the landscape kept shifting around us. But it was nice having a companion for my endless walk through this place as it slowly changed around us.

I could tell by now that there were changes in elevation of the terrain now. Even if only slightly as the rolling hills established themselves. The growth of the forests had stopped, and in some areas large gaps of the grassland were left where for some reason none of the trees grew.

Eventually, I recognized one of the paths of shattered trees and crushed bushes I had left behind in the past. I had looped back around apparently again. I hadn't gotten tired in a traditional sense yet here, but the boredom of moving my legs tens of thousands of times was enough to make me take some breaks anyway when I got the urge to do so.

Currently I was walking across one of the patches of open grassland that had not formed any trees, and I was making my way to a patch of forest in the distance, walking until I reached its edge.

I opened my telepathic communication with Robin. *'Rest here?'*

Robin returned sounding a little sulky but its emotions had finally returned almost to normal. Or what I thought was closer to normal, at least.

'Ok. Good place,' Robin said.

With that, I sat down and Robin scrambled off to climb the trees, moving up and down one after the other. I just sat there and watched it, not sure what else we could do. I could not climb the trees, I was too big and heavy.

Much to Robin's disappointment after it coaxed me to attempt it anyway. The trees simply snapped under my weight and dissolved back into the gray mist before they even hit the ground. That was disappointing.

After so long of doing the same thing, the monotony of this place was almost painful even if Robin at least was unpredictable sometimes. But even Robin's enthusiasm was waning a little for game it had made in climbing the trees as quickly as it could. Sometimes it would even skip a tree or two if Robin thought it would be too easy to climb.

Neither of them had seen the spider creature again since their first encounter. Amalgamation, Robin had finally given me its identifier in the middle of one of its long telepathic incoherent rants whenever I brought up the topic.

Its word or rather image choice was improving, but even the simplest questioning from me about the Amalgamation motivations or justifications of why it was bad would still leave Robin spluttering and becoming more impassioned in its long rants.

But at least Robin was more active and energetic when I provoked it than otherwise. It seemed to cheer up a fraction after I let it rant at me for a while and just listened until it was done.

———O—o—O———

More time passed, and even Robin was growing bored by now. There were only so many trees one could climb before it became a chore. Neither of us could find our Potential in all this time. Robin was still upset and kept looking, but there was only a void where the normal core should be. No matter what either of them did, nothing changed this and let them be able to manipulate their Potential.

I took another step forward on the grassland only to freeze in shock as a massive crack like thunder sounded out. Both me and Robin screeched out in fear as a crimson gash opened in the bright blue skies above us, stretching from horizon to horizon.

An enormous tentacle almost the same size as the portal reached out and curled to the side, wedging the portal wider even as another limb emerged to pull the portals wider and wider by the second. The tentacles were massive, each small round sucker cup on its bottom hundreds or even thousands of times bigger than I was in the sky far above us. What sort of creature could have limbs so large…

A small black spec flew out of the massive red gash in the sky and began to fall to the ground.

The tentacles kept pulling the portal wider as they flexed… They strained and twisted as more and more merged from the reddish portal to hold the edges of the giant gash to hold the portal open. But it appeared to be struggling and after a few moments, the portal began to slowly close with a loud angry buzz like electricity slowly but inevitably.

One of the massive tentacles holding the portal open lost its grip and it was the last straw. The red gash in the sky began to rapidly close as tentacle after tentacle lost its grip. The tentacles strained for a single moment, but as their efforts were in vain the mass of them began to slither and retreat back through to the other side of the red portal.

After a few seconds all of the tentacles retreated back through the portal all at once, releasing their grip and darting back through all at once.

In a giant crash, the giant portal above snapped close all at once. Like shockwaves from the closing of the greater portal, a wave of crimson portals opened and closed rapidly throughout the sky and ground all around me and Robin in a massive chaotic storm.

Wherever the portals destroyed one of the plants or the ground, it dispersed their surroundings back gray mist whenever they closed again.

I dived towards Robin and stretched my body over it as it ran towards me as well. Portals opened and tore gouges out of my back dozens of times as I sat huddled over Robin as it sat shivering below my bulk in fear.

Then after a moment, it all stopped. Only the inky black pits left in the ground and floating gray mist showed the evidence of what had happened.

I looked up to see the black speck still falling to the ground in the distance. It was picking up speed and picked up an orange tint before falling out of sight over the horizon.

I lumbered towards it and Robin didn't even protest this time as I deposited it on my shoulder even as I moved.

A boom of thunder rolled over this place and the earth shook with the vibrations as whatever it was made impact with the ground.

I listened as I walked in the direction of where the thing had touched down, unsure of what exactly had happened. Was the thing living? Had it survived the fall? What was its connection to the creature with the massive tentacles that had created the massive red portal above?

I had to see this strange new thing before it ran away like the Amalgamation.

After some time, We reached the edge of the deep crater after a few false starts on tracking the falling objects its final resting place.

I grabbed tighter to Robin with my tentacle, and it just gripped it with its free human limbs and distractedly tried to escape even as it started to inspect the interior of the crater. As soon as we saw what lay steaming in the center of the crater, we both froze.

There in the center of the crater was a ball covered in black chitin. The same kind as that covering Robin's form. It was the Seed. It was here somehow. I accepted the telepathic connection from the thing when it reached out to the both of us. As soon as the connection solidified, a wave of images followed as the three of us began to communicate.

———O—o—O———

The Amalgamation fled the One that had returned to Two. It had offered the little body segment assistance in returning them back into their ideal fused form when the One's larger component had arrived.

Why would they do this? Separate? They had been the perfect fusion, the Amalgamation had sensed it. But now they were two different beings with separate bodies, a disappointment. Each with their own minds and barely intertwined at all. With the Amalgamations help they could have returned to their former glory. The smaller one had attacked the Amalgamation on sight without allowing the Amalgamation time to explain fully.

The Amalgamation continued running, not wanting to get caught by the big one. That body didn't have malicious intentions, but it followed the orders of the angry one at the moment and the Amalgamation didn't want to test the lengths of its loyalty once the Amalgamation was trapped in its limbs.

Suddenly the sky was filled with red and the Amalgamation stumbled in its stride. It saw a group of massive tentacles descending from the sky like the arms of a god. In fact, it was one. Only a few of the many arms of the Eldest. A red portal fifty feet tall opened in front of the Amalgamation all of a sudden as the Eldest retreated and the great portal above violently closed.

The Amalgamation's components screamed in fear as the Amalgamation hurtled towards the sudden portal, unable to stop its momentum as it tumbled across the dirt as it tried to stop.

Many of its components remembered the void between worlds and babbled fearful nonsense even to the Amalgamation's greater collective.

The Amalgamation tried to stab its back legs into the ground to stop itself, but the ground dispersed into gray mist at the hasty blow and the motion only sent the Amalgamation spinning and rolling off balance across the ground even more.

The Amalgamation made one last desperate attempt to stop itself from being flung into the portal, but it was too late. It rolled through the portal, its last glimpse of the green fields behind it being bombarded by massive waves of opening red portals in both land and sky. It didn't want to go to the void again...

Chapter 73: A New Acquaintance for Fulcrum?

I blinked my eyes all at once as the waves of images came flooding in from the Seed. The images were jagged and sharp, pricking my mind as they tried to sink in deeper. Aggressive images meant to hurt me. Robin screeched in anger and swept my mind of them in seconds before returning the telepathic assault.

I stood there, unsure of what to do as they waged their battle with one another. It shouldn't be like this, why was the Seed so hostile? Why had it attacked us, wasn't it the same kind of thing as Robin had been before Robin had had its own body?

Robin turned its head to me and scrunched inwards as it got telepathically pummeled after its initial counterattack.

'Fulcrum, help! Smooosh it flat!'

Even that much of a distraction from the telepathic battle made Robin lose ground and screech a little as some of the sharp images of the Seed dragged themselves roughly across its mind.

Alright, that was it. No one hurt Robin! Even if this Seed was similar to what Robin had used to be. I took a step forward and lifted my hand, about to bring my massive fist down into the crater to flatten the attacker into the ground.

But somehow the thing shifted to the left in a burst of motion, dodging my blow. The force of my blow sent the thing flying into the air far away and luckily Robin was able to break off the three-way telepathic bond between us and stop the Seed's constant mental assault.

I stepped forward and ran after the Seed as it had landed a few steps away for me. A large distance for the Seed considering our relative sizes. I lifted my foot and prepared to stomp it, only for it to dodge again just as my foot started to fall!

My foot left an inky hole in the landscape as I saw the Seed scuttling away there was a spray of dirt dissolving into mist where I had just stomped.

Wait, scuttling? Sure enough, thousands of dark tendrils of various sizes stuck out of several cracks in the Seed's shell. It would roll over, the limbs out front pulling it forward while the ones behind pushed it away.

Luckily, I was faster. It could dodge well, but the size of my stride just made it too easy for me to catch up in a straight line as I caught sight of it again. I sent my tentacles whipping after it and managed to hit it with some glancing blows, but it still managed to escape even with that.

Flinging itself into the air, off trees, between my legs like some sort of acrobat. The Seed just barely dodged my furious blows. Robin was cheering me on.

'Yeah, yeah. Get it Fulcrum! It pretended to be Good so it could attack us. It is bad, bad. Crush it hard, you can do it!'

———O—o—O———

I squinted as the Seed dodged my blows once again. I was really useless at catching things wasn't I? I blamed my big slow body. My higher mass made me feel like I had to move through water whenever I did anything, let alone turn corners and try to box in the Seed with my blows.

Wait, squinted? Since when had it gotten dark? I looked into the sky and saw that the orb of Devouring Flame was slowly descending in the distance, a strange twilight coming over the world as it sank over the horizon.

I blinked again and struggled to track the Seed as it dodged again through the growing darkness. Robin helpfully pointed out the Seed's position after a moment of me struggling to track it after my latest attack barely missed yet again.

The world got darker and darker around us and with no moon or stars there was nothing to see by now. Even Robin could just barely see the Seed now, and was sharing its vision with me and helping guide me as I went to box it in again with my tentacles.

But the Seed was frenzied now, nearly escaping each time as it sensed that it was almost free of us if it could run into the darkness. Eventually, true darkness came and not even Robin could see the Seed anymore. Everything around us was pitch black, and our eyes were useless in the perfect darkness.

I stumbled around for a bit searching for the Seed blindly, but soon the truth became undeniable. I stopped and screeched in frustration into the sky as it finally became clear that our attacker had escaped.

———O—o—O———

There was a day/night cycle now. The ball of yellow Devouring Flame crossed the sky over and over, plunging this place into total darkness half of the time.

The Seed had thoroughly escaped us by now, and neither Robin nor I were happy about that fact. This place was just too big for us to be able to find it with any certainty. But after a time and some mutual frustration, both Robin and I settled back into boredom and monotony as the encounter with the Seed receded into the past.

The landscape had stopped shifting so much by now. It had only taken a day or two for the black voids left behind by the portals to repair themselves to how they were before. Loose bits of the floating mist would drift over to one of the gaps and condense until the pit was repaired to how it had been before it had been damaged.

It had been almost a hundred day/night rotations since we encountered the Seed by now, and Robin and I were wandering again.

For the last month or so, we had been building little mounds of dirt and shaping them, like sandcastles. Each one served as a little landmark for us. The first one had just been a big pillar so we could see how big this place was, but we had gotten more artistic since then.

Walking at my normal pace, it was almost a full five days' travel before we looped around to reach the original dirt pillar again.

A rather large distance, considering my massive height in comparison to Robin and the average human. And humans would have to rest and sleep when they traveled. I was just walking steadily for that whole time without stopping.

So five days' travel was far indeed. But not all the landmarks Robin and I made were ugly pillars of soil.

Sometimes, Robin liked to have fun with them as we wandered around. I would shift large chunks of the earth while Robin would eagerly direct me in their placement. As long as the materials were somewhat connected to the ground they didn't dissolve into the gray mist as often anymore. But if something was suspended in the air for a second or two? Then to gray mist it went.

'To the left. Yeah, more that way! That one should be the foot.'

I shifted the dirt pile, pushing it along the ground to follow Robin's directions. We were building a human sculpture, laying on their side, this time. Neither of us remembered what a human looked like very well, but we had gotten all the basic parts.

Shoulders, narrowed torso after the hips, four limbs total. The head, ears, and eyes. Robin and I disagreed on the number of eyes though. I insisted it was three large ones on the front. I remembered that they only had a few, and I had five big ones myself so it had to be less than that.

Robin insisted it was ten eyes for the humans, but after a long argument neither of us could decide who was right. Eventually we agreed on six to split the difference and I let Robin shape them with its smaller hands, carefully scooping out the divots in the sculpture's head.

Once we got to the detail work, Robin did best. I was only good for moving the larger amounts of soil into the right place near the beginning due to my big hands and bulky tentacles. I stood back and watched as Robin sculpted.

We had both gotten a lot of practice since we had started doing this, and Robin was actually pretty good with the sculpting by now. I glanced back at the inky voids in the ground where I had taken the dirt from slowly healing closed behind as the mist in the air drifted over to them to heal over the gaps.

It should only be a few minutes and then it would be like we had never been there minus the new sculpture here.

──── O — o — O ────

Robin was still sculpting the human soil sculpture when I spotted something in the distance. A crimson portal as tall as me standing among the trees.

'Robin...'

Robin looked up where it had been trying to make the sculpture's feet. *'Fulcruummm. Not yet, I'm almost done. I only have...'*

I scooped Robin up, ignoring its annoyed screeches and thrashing as I turned it towards the rapidly closing portal. Robin went limp as it spotted the portal and leaned forward as its eyes squinted at the portal in the distance.

We both remembered the crimson portals in the sky and the Seed that was still on the loose. I carefully stepped over the sculpture, careful not to smash it as I made my way forward.

I stopped several steps away from the crimson portal and we watched as it shrunk down into nearly nothing over the course of two minutes. The thin mist remaining in the air created a fog around the portal. The portal began to shrink as time passed with the two of us staring at the motionless red portal.

We watched together until Robin linked to me and sent an image. I turned and leaned down to inspect the creature Robin had spotted in surprise. The deer stood there frozen as I towered over it, Robin perched on its familiar spot on my shoulder. Neither of us moved as we both loomed over the startled animal.

I stepped backwards and as my steps shook the ground, the deer darted away into the trees at full speed. It soon fled into the distance where I could no longer track it with my eyes anymore. I hoped it could survive out there, and that the grass wouldn't turn to mist in its mouth if it tried to eat it.

Neither Robin or I had needed to eat, but we would die if our Potential ever dropped to nothing, so it was nearly the same thing.

But at the same time our Potential was somehow missing to us, but neither of us were feeling the weakness we should if our Potential was actually nearly nothing. And there was no water in this place here either. How would the deer live without all of that? The cloud of gray mist slowly dispersed again as the portal winked away.

──── O — o — O ────

It had been a long time. Over five hundred days since we had seen that first portal. None of the various animals that came through the increasing number of portals around us seemed to have eaten anything yet, and we saw the animals roaming around the area more and more often.

Robin loved it, our hobby of sculpting the dirt was quickly forgotten in favor of observing the milling animals in the forest. It made me a little sad, we had worked together well when sculpting. Now we just sat and watched the animals silently so we wouldn't scare them away. Especially me, since I was so big and loud.

Robin didn't even want to talk telepathically, *'just in case they can hear us'*.

It was all part of the fun, but it did feel so lonely for us not being able to talk to each other as often anymore. Robin was quite vocal when we sculpted together when we argued with how things should look as we went along.

Robin almost always won our arguments, but secretly used my suggestions anyway, changing them closer to what I had said when it thought that I wasn't paying attention.

But now, we were watching something new. The both of us sat stock still, only our eyes tracking to follow an action in front of us. It seemed a predator had come to this place at last. The black furred feline predator stalked its prey in silence. A cat. I had to look through Robin's shared vision because the animal was far too small for me to see at my size. It was hard for even Robin to track as it slunk around in the shade of the trees.

As we watched, the creature suddenly leaped into the air! The black cat darted towards the songbird squatting on a low-hanging branch, jaws open and claws unsheathed.

With a surprised chirp, the bird went to take flight, but the cat was too quick and caught it in its jaws. The cat landed back on the forest floor, landing lightly on the ground without ruffling the grass below more than it had to.

The cat perked up, proudly strutting with the limp bird held in its mouth. Then after a moment it bit down only to snort and huff with a look of bafflement as the bird puffed into a cloud of gray mist.

The cat bit at the mist for a moment, but the wisps of mist shot away and merged with one of the nearby trees as Fulcrum and Robin watched. The tree rustled a bit and grew a little taller.

The cat seemed to startle at the sudden noise and darted away back into the forest as quickly as it could. Robin lost sight of the creature after a few seconds as its black fur blended into the mottled shadows of the forest floor again.

Robin was disappointed at the anticlimactic ending of the cat's hunt, although Robin still enjoyed the surprised expression of the cat when the bird disappeared.

I had liked it too.

Robin kept sending it to me several times and I sent my amusement back through the link. It was pretty funny. I don't think Robin had really thought through what had happened. Or the fact that we might turn into mist if we died. Hopefully not, I didn't want to be like one of those trees and dissolve whenever we got back out of this place.

Was there a way out of this place? Surely there must be some way. Things were still changing, I'm sure a way out would reveal itself if we explored this place and waited for long enough.

Robin pointed over to a herd of deer in the distance it wanted to observe and I shifted my path. Best to put those thoughts to the side for the moment. No need to worry Robin over nothing after all. And even if it was true that we were trapped here somehow... What could I even do about it?

I slowly lowered myself and carefully put Robin down on the ground. We continued our observations and I pushed my musings to the back of mind. I'd only mention my thoughts to Robin if a way out of here actually revealed itself to us rather than worrying over something neither of us could change.

Chapter 74: Enjoying the Appetizers - Seed of the Eldest's Fragment of Memory

The Seed settled into place after it had escaped the two creatures it had provoked. Sensing the large one's weak mind, the Seed had leapt at the opportunity to attack while its guard was down. It hadn't even spotted the companion riding on the larger creature's shoulder until it was too late.

The smaller creature's mental strength was formidable, only a hair weaker than the Seed's own. But with the large one broken free from the mental battle, the large creature quickly moved to assist with its physical blows in distracting the Seed and forcing it to dodge and take its mind off the mental battle with the smaller one.

After a long chase, the Seed eventually managed to escape as the world was plunged into darkness as it snuck away.

The Seed occasionally heard the heavy footsteps of the large one in the distance as it traveled, and quickly burrowed into the ground and covered itself in a small mound of dirt before it could be discovered again. It touched the odd floor of the void after burrowing down fifteen or so feet. It was like an impassable wall and none of the Seed's senses could pierce it.

Every time the Seed burrowed more it explored the boundary, but it still could not detect the slightest thing on the other side.

The Seed dug upwards a bit, it didn't want to remain too close to that barrier for a prolonged time just in case.

The large one had far too long a stride for the Seed to directly escape if it spotted the Seed in broad daylight, so it must still remain underground until it couldn't sense the thumps of its footsteps anymore. Until the large creature moved onwards as the Seed hid in place.

The Seed only escaped last time because it was able to lose the creature in the darkness, and it may not have that advantage again if the thing learned from the past in some way or got lucky in catching it.

———O—o—O———

It had been one hundred and fifty day/night cycles now and the Seed had not heard the footsteps of the large one in a long while for now. The Seed had remained in place underground, trying to reach inwards for the vast reserve of Potential it knew it should have. But there was nothing, only a blank space where its golden Potential should be.

Yet it must still be there, as the Seed did not feel itself withering as it should if its Potential had been drained. Realizing yet again that it was futile, the Seed carefully dug upwards until it was just below the surface and froze at the sensation of light steps vibrating the ground around it.

It carefully pierced one of its telepathic tendrils through the soil above and used it to sense the surroundings.

It saw a red portal splitting a nearby tree in pieces, the upper portion of wood dissolving into a cloud of the gray mist. Various creatures were exiting and scattering as they emerged from the portal even as the portal rapidly shrunk in size. The mist curled and clung to the red orb as the thing shrank.

Were these portals the action of the Eldest? The Seed remembered the large portal it had been thrown through had been the same kind of portal as this one but much larger. One of the hoofed brown creatures fled out of the portal towards the Seed's position.

With a burst of motion, the Seed latched onto it before it could escape and killed it. The rest of the animals fled in other directions at the sight, but the Seed was too busy emerging from the ground so it could properly consume the corpse. Without Potential, it couldn't modify itself for a larger mouth or even open up its shell.

It used its tendrils and carefully pried off one of the black plates near the top of its form, where its atrophied digestive system lay beneath. It held the corpse above the tiny mouth with its telekinetic tentacles and slowly squeezed the body, letting the nourishing fluids slowly drip into its small mouth.

Mmmmmmmmm. As the Seed ate, it slowly felt something familiar grow inside of itself. The golden light of Potential began to cover the void within itself with a thin golden film. The film stretched and cracked before slowly healing as something bubbled beneath it. A roiling fluid, no mist.

The gray mist was shrouding the Seed's core. The Seed drained the last drop from the animal's body and set it aside.

The Seed reached inside itself and was about to manipulate its Potential again, when it noticed the gray mist from the dissolved tree drifting towards the Seed.

The Seed froze and then began rapidly scuttling away on its telekinetic tendrils in a dash. It kept a close eye on the mist behind that slowly drew to a stop and continued drifting upwards as soon as the Seed left its apparent detection range. The Seed kept moving, only to divert as it saw another unaware animal a minute or so later.

The Seed was approaching too fast, and the dark furred creature couldn't react in time before the Seed grabbed it and snapped its neck. The Seed held the body above its exposed mouth and dropped it in, only to recoil as the body dissolved before it even hit the Seed's teeth.

The cloud of gray mist soaked into the Seed before it could flinch back, and immediately made its way to the glowing Potential the Seed had taken from the first creature.

The Seed tried to move the Potential, to ward off the gray mist. But it was no use and in seconds, it had lost all sensation in its core once again. The Seed thrashed in rage. What did this gray mist think it was? To suppress *IT*? The chosen of the Eldest?! Wait…

The Seed saw another red portal in the distance and frantically rushed in that direction. It needed to consume the creatures before they were infected by the mists of this realm.

When it reached the portal it went on a slaughter of the forest creatures, and sure enough, consuming them brought back the golden film of Potential covering the invisible ball of gray mist suppressing the Seed's true core. It had gathered a pathetic amount of Potential, but it had made progress.

$$----O-o-O----$$

It had been three hundred day/night cycles now since the Seed had arrived, and the portals were becoming more common and lasting longer now. The Seed had a comfortable amount of Potential built up by now around the void within itself in a thin shell. Each creature only gave a tiny amount of Potential, but the Seed had enough to spare to increase the size of its tiny mouth to allow it to consume the bodies faster while still covering the repulsive orb of invisible gray mist within itself.

No matter what it did, nothing would remove the mist from itself to unshroud its core. It was… maddening.

Occasionally the Seed would make a mistake and one of its prey would burst into the mist that would attempt to smother its core of Potential once more. It lost the energy from three kills at least with each mistake, which frustrated it to no end.

It had also begun to carefully inspect the other sides of the portals with its telekinetic tendrils shrouded in shadow. The tentacles were invisible for most, making them ideal for scouting and unpredictable movement during its escape from the large creature that had attacked it after it first arrived here.

The forests on the other side of the portals that the Seed could sense through its telekinetic tendrils were strange. The terrain was almost identical, but the trees and season on the other side seemed almost random. One portal would be in deep winter and only a few animals would be sucked inwards. The next would be the height of spring and release a massive bounty of food. All with no discernable pattern as far as the Seed could tell.

But now the Seed was about to begin its most dangerous experiment so far. This time, it ignored the creatures exiting and fleeing around it and slowly dipped one of its telekinetic tentacles inside and through.

On the other side of the portal was an unremarkable forest almost identical to the one surrounding the Seed in this realm. Nothing odd about the place except the large amount of animals that were being sucked inwards into the portal on the other side through a massive force like gravity. But the gravity only affected the animals, the vegetation and other inanimate materials nearby left entirely untouched by the portal.

There seemed to be some sort of selective gravity pulling them inwards through towards the realm where the Seed was. It put another two tendrils through carefully and gained some confidence as nothing happened to them.

It anchored the tendrils on the other side and slowly dipped its main round black-plated body into the red portal. It slowly entered and pulled itself through even as the portal slowly shrank around it. But as soon as its body was a quarter of the way through the Seed's body spasmed and mist around its shrouded core rioted.

The surrounding trees dissolved and a wave of mist surged inwards and snuffed the red portal in seconds. The Seed thrashed as part of its shell was sliced off by the closing portal, as it wasn't quite able to fully pull itself back in time. Its Potential was fully suppressed and invisible once more so it couldn't heal by the clouds of mist swirling around it, all its hunting up to this point wasted.

The Seed bled black blood as it desperately escaped the cloud of cloying gray mist as the tendrils curled around the Seed lazily as if to taunt it about the futility of its actions.

The Seed desperately rushed to the next portal and consumed the escaping animals to help itself heal. It couldn't feel the lost Potential in its main core, but it knew it must be much considering how much blood it had lost in a trail behind it as it frantically scuttled away from the cloud of mists behind it.

The Seed had to be more careful. If it had been a little bolder then it might have been sliced in half and died. There was no way it would be able to make it all the way through even if it charged at full speed, the mist had reacted almost immediately to close the portal as soon as the Seed was only part of the way through the portal.

The Seed absentmindedly regenerated the telekinetic tentacles that had been sliced off when the portal closed after it had enough Potential to heal its wounds and stop its bleeding.

Regenerating the telekinetic tendrils took Potential, but miniscule amounts, enough that it could do so even as it was now. The Seed resolved to continue its hunts. With the portals coming more frequently, it would build its power until something changes and so it wouldn't risk losing all its hard earned progress again.

———O—o—O———

It was day six hundred, and the red portals opened and closed all around it almost constantly now. The Seed had built its reserves of Potential well, but had seen something interesting on its last hunt. The animals could go back through the portals if they wished and the gray mist was not angered.

One of the heavier animals had dived through and seeing it had not returned, the Seed put its tendrils through to watch it. It had been the largest it had seen so far. A bear. Black fur and long claws as it growled as it had been initially pulled through the portal. But it had dived back through immediately, and inspecting it, it was holding its ground against the inwards by the gravity, barely.

The trees and vegetation sat undisturbed around it, unaffected by the portal. The creature's charge back through had carried it far enough to sink its claws into a tree and it managed to grip tight. The tree shook and leaves danced leisurely to the ground as its back legs of the bear dangled off the ground to point towards the red portal and the animal roared.

The portal shrank and the pull of gravity quickly weakened and the bear's back legs touched the ground again. The Seed slowly drew back its tendrils as the bear fell to the ground panting with exertion, deep gouges in the tree in front of it. The Seed retracted its telekinetic tendrils and the portal closed fully.

The Seed considered what it had sensed. The freshly arrived animals could be returned to Earth without the mists' interference. For the next portal it captured one of the animals scattering away and held it still rather than killing it immediately. It took its precious Potential and sacrificed some of it to improve the creature.

The Seed forged a link between the animal's minuscule core of Potential and its own, then threw it back through the portal. Luckily the creature managed to stay on the other side as the portal closed to a point before stopping.

The Seed flexed the bond to the animal for a moment, and the portal remained open. The Seed's Potential drained heavily, but no matter how hard it tried the portal remained no more than a few inches wide. Eventually, the Seed felt the creature on the other side expire from the strain and the portal snapped shut in an instant.

But the Seed was not discouraged. The gray mist of the surroundings did not leap in to assist the lesser drifting mist in closing the portal. The trees around the portal did not dissolve and revert the mist.

Perhaps the Seed needed to strengthen the creature that was to serve as the anchor first. But it would have to be careful, each experiment would drain more of its resources.

But if it could create a powerful enough host on the other side of the portal, then it should be able to maintain a portal for long enough for the Seed to squeeze its way through and fight off the clouds of mist before they shut the portal completely. Allowing it to escape this place at last.

— — — O — o — O — — —

Day seven hundred. The Seed had kept experimenting on the animals to improve their purpose as anchors. It had found a certain small rodent surprisingly to be among the most intelligent of the animals that were commonly drawn through the portals. This meant it had a higher upper limit for its telepathic abilities without heavy modifications the Seed didn't have the Potential for.

The Seed had been refining its techniques for a while now on this species and felt fairly confident that this iteration could hold the portal open for long enough. The Seed had managed to hold the portal five feet wide for two minutes using the bond for the last iteration but still hadn't tried to go through itself yet.

The tether between them still wasn't strong enough for that. And it wanted to be absolutely sure that the anchor was at its absolute highest strength before the Seed made its final attempt to go through the portal itself.

The anchor would only have to maintain the portal wide enough for the Seed to squeeze through for moments. But it would have to do so through the immense pressure of the clouds of defensive mists that would rush inwards from all sides attempting to snuff the portal and prevent the Seed's escape.

The current rodent being modified in the Seed's telekinetic tendrils was about half way through the elaborate process the Seed had developed. The creature's bushy tail twitched as the Seed expanded its brain and modified its brain structures to become a receiver for the Seed's telepathy.

The animal's gray fur slowly shifted into a dark diamond pattern on its back as the Seed prepared to forge a link between their cores. It helped remind the Seed which one to preserve if it lost its grip and the creature briefly escaped it amongst the other creatures in this forest already infected by the mists of this place. The rodent woke up confused all of a sudden and began to thrash and claw at the tendril holding it in place to no effect.

The Seed finished the modifications with a flourish and went to throw the rodent through the portal to try out its newest experimental anchor. It was about to finish the motion but paused as it felt a vibration on the ground below it.

The Seed turned and froze as it spotted the large creature from its first day stomping directly in the Seed's direction, all of its eyes fixed on it. On the large one's shoulder the smaller one rode, glaring at the Seed angrily.

The Seed felt an attempt to forcefully open the telepathic connection between them as the small one's eyes met the Seed's black chitin as the Seed froze in surprise.

The Seed struggled for a moment, but managed to keep the connection closed. It wouldn't make the same mistake as last time and fight the pair of creature's on two fronts at once.

The Seed turned and scuttled off as fast as it could, barely dodging the stomp of the large one behind it as it rapidly approached. The Seed dropped the rodent in its grip in its haste so it could use that tendril to get more speed for its dodge. The force of the next blow from the large creature shook the ground and sent dirt spraying into the air. The cloud of dirt quickly dissolved into the mist, which rose into the air and quickly rushed to snuff out the red portal the Seed had just left behind.

―――O―o―O―――

The Seed escaped after another long pursuit. Luckily without the telepathic battle as a distraction, the Seed was able to be trickier and burrowed into the ground once it gained enough of a lead. Before the smaller one could have pinpointed it instantly if their minds were still at war, but now the tactic was far more successful.

The large one walked directly over where the Seed hid and walked on, none the wiser as it continued to search fruitlessly above the ground. Time passed, and eventually the hunters left the area.

The Seed waited until it felt clear then burrowed back upwards and emerged back on the surface. It would have to be more careful next time. If it had hesitated any longer then the large creature could have landed a devastating first blow on the Seed.

And the Seed had lost all of its gathered Potential again, everything lost to the cloying clouds of irritating mists once more during its escape.

―――O―o―O―――

A gray squirrel with a black diamond fur pattern on her back went flying as the inky tendrils holding it released her and flicked her to the side carelessly. Squirrel saw a leg bigger than the largest tree she had ever seen smash downwards where the bad thing had been seconds ago.

Squirrel oriented herself midair and landed on her feet as a large cloud of fog suddenly appeared to shroud the area around where the large leg had just landed.

The bad thing ran to the side to dodge the big thing's next blow, in her direction and Squirrel looked around frantically to escape. She didn't want to be captured by the bad thing again, so she instinctively leapt out of the way of the bad thing.

She only remembered at the last moment that the thing nearby was not a tree but the titanic leg of the big thing. Maybe more dangerous than the bad thing, but it was too late now she was already in mid-air. Squirrel landed on the big thing's leg and dug her little claws into the flesh to get a grip as the leg lifted into the air for another step.

Squirrel quickly scrambled upwards until she reached the thing's hip as the leg descended again for another stomp. Another crash below and the whole big thing's body shook, nearly throwing Squirrel falling off as she tried frantically to maintain her grip on the massive creature.

Squirrel scrambled even higher on the big thing until she noticed a gap between one of the bone exoskeleton plates overlapping on its chest.

The bone plates slid around and shifted as the big thing moved, but in the spot that Squirrel saw there was a gap and a spot open to the softer flesh underneath that was a little cavity that appeared to be safe from the shifting movement of the bone plates.

Squirrel squeezed herself inside the gap as the thing's body flexed and another smaller vibration ran through the big thing's body. Squirrel curled up and nestled deeper into the little pocket in the big thing's body as the crashes continued outside.

With her newfound intelligence, she knew the bad thing couldn't reach her here when she was right on top of the bad thing's predator. Best to remain hidden here until she was sure the bad thing was gone. Then she could worry about the big thing and determine if it was a predator too.

Chapter 75: Welcome and Goodbye - Multiple Fragments of Memory

The Seed continued its hunting for a long time after that with no major change. It had been at least fifteen hundred days as the routine continued without any more sudden surprises.

It just rushed from portal to portal rebuilding its lost Potential. The big one's stomps had released the gray mist and smothered the Seed's Potential yet again in the second attack, so it had to restart from the very bottom yet again. So irritating…

The Seed scuttled to the next portal, only to see something new. There, clambering to its feet was a creature like it hadn't ever seen before. The animal stood on two legs and its skin was smooth besides strange fur on its skull. The Seed approached the oblivious creature as the animal focused intensely on its red stained hand.

The standing creature finally noticed the Seed and turned to run, but it was too late. The Seed leapt forward and wrapped it in its telekinetic tendrils. It manipulated the struggling creature every which way. Oh, what intelligence this creature had! What a developed brain!

Now this…

This creature would do.

———O—o—O———

Steven hummed to himself as he walked on the hiking trail, hands dangling in his pockets as he walked. It had been a long week at work, and this morning hike in the crisp autumn air was just what he needed to relax. It was all over, all the stress from the client's last minute change and his boss' red face demanding results at the last minute.

Steven's breath grew shaky and his breath hitched for a moment as another wave of stress washed over him just thinking about it. But the sound of the wind and rustling of leaves around him let him relax again.

There was a woman walking her golden retriever coming the other way and they met each other's gaze for a brief moment as they passed each other. Steven nodded to her and kept walking, not thinking of anything in particular as he kept walking down the path.

Eventually Steven reached the crossroads and inspected the trail sign even if he didn't need to. He had been here so many times, he knew the paths like the back of his hand. Steven took a left to go on a slightly overgrown path covered in the piles of fallen leaves. The path swooped in a longer loop that covered almost the whole perimeter of the nature reserve.

On the main paths people's conversations or overeager dog's movements drowned out many of the natural sounds and scared away most of the other animals.

Out on this more secluded path, Steven could hear the birds chirping again and the chittering and rustling of the squirrels as they darted back and forth.

He kept walking, just soaking in. By the time he was halfway through the walk all the stress and tightness in his chest had fully drained away, leaving only his long steady breaths as he walked.

He was sweating slightly, but was still walking at an easy pace so was hardly tired yet. He looked up from the ground in front of him as suddenly everything became bathed in red light. What...

Steven felt a sudden force like gravity start pulling him to the large red orb that had appeared a hundred feet down the path *hard*. Steven stumbled forward at the sudden force and suddenly the pull was even stronger. He tried to stop himself, and lurched to the side as he fell to the ground in surprise. Steven flailed and tried to grab something as he began to slowly slide towards the orb despite his best efforts.

He panted and his eyes darted around the empty trail, looking for a solution. But it was no use and by the second the pull grew stronger as he slid closer to the glowing portal.

Steven tried to angle for one of the trees as he slid what he now perceived as downwards towards the red orb, the leaf covered ground now seeming like some kind of massive wall below him.

Steven impacted the tree hard with his torso and clung to it as hard as he could, hugging the trunk. For a moment he almost lost his grip as his body kept twisting past it as the air was driven from his lungs. But he held on.

The tree shook under the impact and Steven groggily regained his wits as he looped his arms over the trunk as hard as he could.

He blinked and gaped as the leaves from the tree floated downwards normally towards the earth ground.

What the? Was this crazy shit only targeting him? A squirrel that went flying by him answered that question. Steven could only watch in horror as the squirrel accelerated until it was swallowed by the red orb that was over fifteen feet tall below him. Had it been bigger before? Steven hoped so. He just had to hang on until its disappeared...

Steven's death grip on the tree loosened slightly as he got distracted in his thoughts, and only that was enough for him to be ripped from his perch again. Time seemed to slow down as Steven could only watch as he fell with nothing now between him and the red orb below.

He shouted and held his hands in front of him until he plunged through the red orb and suddenly gravity was another direction.

He shot forward like a cannon and rolled over and over until he eventually came to a stop, a bruised and scraped mess at the base of a tree. But at least nothing felt broken.

Steven groaned as he made his way to his feet. The forest around him was unfamiliar and it seemed to be springtime based on the temperature and the green leaves on the trees. He didn't like it.

Ominous red portal pulling him here to a random forest? Yeah, best to get out of here. Whatever was here was probably bad news. He looked back and saw the portal... Was smaller. Oh, shit! No way in hell he was getting stranded wherever this was.

Steven sprinted forward and attempted to dive through the orb even as the portal began to shrink. Everything felt normal until his hand entered the portal. Steven felt a crushing force trying to push his arm back through, but with some strain he blindly felt around on the ground on the other side, feeling like his arm was being pulled back by a weight of a hundred pounds or more.

The portal kept shrinking and Steven felt the rivers of sweat running off of him as his arm trembled and strained. C'mon, C'mon... Yes! Steven felt a rock and after giving it a quick tug it stayed in place.

If Steven could just pull himself through until the portal fully closed and the weird gravity shut off then he could get out of here. Steven adjusted his grip and managed to grip the stone with both hands submerged into the portal.

With all his strength, Steven tried to pull himself back through the portal. But it was like doing the hardest pull up he had ever done and his core screamed for every inch from the sheer force pushing him back through to the strange forest.

Steven's arms trembled as he pushed forward with his feet as best as he could as the differing gravity began to mess with his balance.

Inch by inch he pulled his way forward? Upward? Either way, Steven's head made it through and he had to close his eyes at the sudden pressure on them. More and more Steven pulled himself up until his shoulders were through the portal even as his arms screamed in pain.

Steven managed to open his eyes to glance back only to see the portal was barely five feet tall now and shrinking rapidly around his torso. Steven tried to pull harder upwards and his desperate strength pulled him a few more inches higher.

Steven now had pulled himself out up to his belly button. But the portal was still closing and Steven's arms were already spasming as his final effort didn't prove enough. Steven's right arm finally gave out and it immediately was flung downwards, triggering his other arm to give out too an instant later.

Steven fell again, futilely trying to get his spasming arms to respond and move to stop his fall. He fell back through the portal and felt a sharp pinch on his left arm as he was flung rolling backwards again. Even as he spun he saw that the red portal was now gone.

Steven stood to his feet, but felt lightheaded for some reason. He looked down at his stinging left hand and froze in shock. His first four fingers were missing on that hand, severed so cleanly that Steven had hardly even noticed as it happened.

Only his thumb was left in that hand and the pain suddenly washed over him as he watched the blood gush out from the stumps.

He stared in horror as waves of pain suddenly washed over him at the sight as if his brain had only just registered it.

Steven felt sick like he was about to vomit, but he saw movement out of the corner of his eye. He turned and saw a black organic looking ball floating a few feet off of the ground flying towards Steven at full speed, seeming to have no intention of stopping as it charged. He turned as if to run but was suddenly lifted off of the ground by invisible tentacles.

Steven could feel the sliming tendrils squirming over him as he began flipping around over and over and to the side as the black orb just floated there silently and seemed to be inspecting him somehow.

The sudden motion made his hand gush blood faster. Steven's conscious mind shut off and everything after was only recorded in his mind as a dreamlike hazy blur.

——— (Seed of the Eldest's Fragment of Memory) ———

The Seed noticed while making its modifications that the human as it knew how to call it now, was near death. The Seed had gotten a good look into the human's mind due to it, or he rather, having much more intelligence than the other creatures that the Seed had seen so far.

The red fluid was apparently important for the human's life, and it was bleeding heavily from the wound at the end of its left arm. He still twitched weakly and his eyes were open, but he seemed to not be aware of his surroundings still.

It was somewhat of a waste for the Seed to spend its precious Potential regenerating the mortal's digits and replenishing his blood, but the Seed didn't know when the next anchor of such quality could be found again. It would have to just use this one as best as it could.

With the mortal healed and the issue taken care of, the Seed finished its modifications and made extra sure the tether between their cores of Potential was firm and as strong as the Seed could make it.

It found the nearest portal, not the one the human had come through but a different one, and waited until the portal was close enough to shutting itself.

Then, like the other animals the Seed had experimented with, the Seed flung the human through the closing portal at the proper moment so the portal closed just when the human was about to fall back towards the portal through its gravity again. Luckily the mists didn't respond so the human hadn't been tainted by the mists yet. Good.

Luckily the Seed's plan had paid off. It was more than satisfied when it felt a faint twinge in the bond between itself and the mortal human even across worlds. Extremely weak and mostly useless normally, but the link was still there. With the mortal acting as an anchor to Earth, the Seed could start planning its escape now.

With its freedom it would bring the will of the Eldest to that world, as was its purpose. The big one and little nuisance would be left to wither and rot in this desolate realm once the Seed escaped on its own...

Chapter 76: Where Have You Been? - Multiple Fragments of Memory

Steven startled awake and sat up, clutching his throbbing head. The last thing he remembered was being flung back through that red portal at high speed by the invisible force as that black orb floated there watching him.

He stared at his left hand and poked at it for a moment with his right, but everything felt normal. He twitched his fingers and they moved normally.

Steven remembered the creature healing his injuries, but it had happened so fast he had barely registered it at the time. Why had it sent him back? It had felt so threatening to him, but then it had helped him?

Steven stood up and looked around, frowning at the hot temperature and blazing sun above him. The forest around him looked the same as the place he left, but his mind must be playing tricks on him.

It had barely been ten minutes, it couldn't have warmed up this much. The leaves on the trees were yellowed, and it must be eighty degrees Fahrenheit or more outside.

He reached for his phone, but it was missing. It must have fallen out while that creature was spinning him around.

Steven knew he had had his phone when he fell through the portal, he had felt its usual weight in his pocket before the pain from his missing fingers had kicked in after the portal shut. That memory was crystal clear for some reason.

Steven inspected the area, and realized that he was wrong. This *was* the same place that he had left from. He could still see the same overgrown path he had always walked on curling into the distance. Every twist and turn triggered his memories as he slowly walked to the parking lot.

In a daze he walked back to the entrance of the park, scared of what he would find. There was no one in the area, and Steven walked towards the entrance without seeing a single other person on the path.

Eventually, he reached the parking lot itself only to see that his car was gone.

There was only a single minivan parked in the spot where I had parked. I stood there staring at it, hoping to find any other explanation than the creeping realization I was coming too. Footsteps behind me coming back down the path.

Steven turned and saw the same woman as before in different clothing than before, and she had lost some weight. Her dog was less energetic, not tugging on the leash as hard as before as it sniffed by the sides of the path.

The woman looked uncomfortable at Steven's intense gaze as he scanned all the different details. The woman was different. The dog was different. So much was different. Had it really been that long? Was it really…

The woman glanced down and gasped as she got a glance at Steven's left arm. He lifted it up and looked at it in confusion for a moment. Oh, that was right. It was splattered in his still drying blood.

Looking at his clothing, Steven saw that the blood had splattered all over his left side, he looked like an extra in a horror movie.

Most people didn't survive spilling this much of their own blood onto their clothes. The woman's face was twisted up like she wanted to vomit as she pulled out her phone and started dialing the police.

"Oh my god, are you okay?" She said in a wavering tone, pulling her dog back as it started to come forward to try to sniff me, "Oh… *hugh* I'm going to *hmph* call an ambulance."

I realized I should care about her reactions, but everything just felt so far away right now. I should lower her suspicion of me. She kept babbling as I stood there staring at her blankly for a moment thinking of a solution. Eventually, I forced my mouth to move.

"I… I'm not bleeding anymore. Don't worry, you are safe from me. Ambulance would be nice though."

"Should I donate all this extra blood spilled on my clothes to them?" I said, "That would be the charitable thing to do I think. They say the hospital always needs more blood for transfusions."

The woman didn't seem to be reassured by my words, even if she chuckled nervously at my words. Was it my facial expressions? Should I have cleaned off the blood before I came here, that was what seemed to trigger the woman's disgusted reaction. How could I get this human to understand?

At the thought Steven's thought process violently derailed and he snapped back to reality. What the hell? Had that black orb thing done something to him? For a moment there his thoughts had turned strange. What had he even said to her? She was looking at him with more than a tinge of fear now as she gripped her phone tightly and slowly backing away. The dog looked between the two of them in confusion, not seeming to understand her sudden fear of Steven.

Steven rewound his thoughts and froze as he remembered what he had said. God damn, he sounded like some kind of psychopath there. Steven opened his mouth to fix it, but the woman took another small step back and he closed his mouth again.

Well, best not to dig himself deeper at least. He walked away and sat down on a nearby rock, and inspected his healed left hand again.

He had seen the gruesome injury and his fingers still tingled a bit when he focused on them. But there was no pain, and everything worked fine. He had to remind himself still that it was there and worked fine.

As the wait dragged on, the two stayed in place, the woman standing on the phone glancing nervously at him and Steven half heartedly trying to remove the caked on blood covering himself.

Eventually a police patrol car pulled into the lot and the two officers stepped out from their vehicles. Steven looked up. The woman let out a sigh of relief even as Steven heard the wail of an ambulance siren in the distance. The two officers put their hands on their weapons as they saw how much blood was covering Steven. It was far more than one person could spill and still live.

Steven wasn't sure why he kept thinking about that. The thought kept bouncing around his mind like a ringing bell. Steven would have died if that creature hadn't healed him in time. Steven met the eyes of the officer on the right and he froze when their eyes met.

"Steven?" The man said in shock as his hand left the gun at his belt.

"Ryan," Steven replied dumbly.

———— (Mortal Ryan Fragment) ————

Officer Ryan Smith was frozen in shock as the ambulance arrived and the EMTs rushed out. "Steven, I… We thought you were… Hey, wait!"

The EMTs bustled Steven into the back of the ambulance that had just arrived before Ryan could finish his thought, ignoring the officer.

Ryan turned to his partner, "I'm going with him. You get the woman's statement."

The other man opened his mouth as if to protest, but seeing something in Ryan's eyes, closed it again. Clearly this was something personal to Ryan.

The man nodded as Ryan clambered in the ambulance with the EMTs. One of the EMTs nodded to Ryan but then continued to barrage Steven with questions on his injury while running various tests. Steven insisted he was fine, but even Ryan knew that amount of blood wasn't something you could lose.

Fuck! Ryan just realized this might be a murder case.

Well, self defense at least. *Fuck fuck fuck.*

He had left his partner behind, too focused on Steven's miraculous return to realize what this meant. Who knew if there was someone else there lurking about? Ryan called it in on the radio with his theory, and Steven looked nervous.

But the EMTs nodded at the call and Ryan unfortunately had to cuff Steven to the bed. He knew how it looked as it was him doing it, but Steven didn't seem to get too pissed at him. They were always somewhat at odds over Ryan's sister, and Ryan had never really approved of Steven.

But Ryan had tried to be understanding with Steven now, considering whatever messed up stuff he had to have gone through. But put their differences to the side somewhat.

As much as he wanted to get the full story from Steven right this moment, he had to wait for a proper statement. There hadn't been a murder in Harmony in years, and the chief would be all over his ass if the integrity of even one part of the process could be questioned.

Ryan riding along with Steven was already unusual, but at least he could justify it by saying it was for security around Steven in case he was dangerous. Or if someone tried to hurt him.

The EMTs knew by now that the man really wasn't injured. Not even bruised knuckles, his body was completely healthy with not the slightest scratch or bruise on it.

The blood could have only come from someone else. Or several someones based on the sheer amount of it. And Steven's uninjured status wouldn't help any arguments he made in court about self defense. Ryan would do his best for Steven, for Jessica's sake, but it wasn't looking good for him right now.

———(Mortal Steven Fragment)———

Well, that was unexpected. Steven had been so focused on the motives of the strange alien he had forgotten how his situation would look to the rest of humanity. He had emerged covered in blood from the woods while being totally uninjured, of course people would assume the worst.

Steven tried to get some answers from the EMTs and Ryan, but Ryan just told him that he'd tell him after Steven gave his police statement. And the EMTs didn't want to talk to Steven.

Well whatever, Steven could wait a little. At least Ryan looked a little guilty at withholding the information. Good. Cuffing him was a bit much after his easy compliance with everything.

———O—o—O———

Despite being uninjured, Steven was still brought to the hospital and put in a bed for more testing. He had to wait another hour or two until he was done with the tests and Ryan and another unfamiliar officer walked in. "Mr. *FulCRum*?" I blinked for a moment before the man spoke again. "Steven Richards?"

"Oh, yeah. That's me," I said.

The man stared at Steven for a moment thoughtfully. "Are you alright? We can call the doctors back and delay this if you don't feel up to it."

Steven shook his head. "Sorry, still just a bit out of it. Let's get this over with, not that you'll believe me."

The man took out his recorder and activated it before stating who was in the room. His voice started distorting again as he said Fu- Steven's name, but Steven focused on his lips and the correct sounds came out.

Ryan stood uncomfortably in the background, seeming to not know what to do with himself as he eagerly waited for answers. The other officer finished their introductions.

"And so Steven, let's start in the beginning," the man said.

Steven told his step by step of events he had experienced without leaving anything out. Both of their eyebrows rose the longer he spoke, but Steven decided to come clean.

No matter how he thought about it he couldn't come up with an explanation that wasn't suspicious as hell and would just get him in more trouble. Faking amnesia might have been the best, but he knew he wasn't a good enough actor for it.

Steven knew that the amnesia seen in movies doesn't generally happen and that there are a whole set of symptoms for the real kinds that he had no way to fake convincingly since he didn't know what they were exactly.

After he came in so suspiciously they would definitely be on the lookout for that kind of play.

Better to come clean and look crazy then get caught in a lie later on. Steven knew all of the blood was his own, so he should be free from those charges after a while. However long the DNA tests would take, he had already seen them take samples after taking away his normal clothes when he put on the hospital gown. And there was really no realistic explanation on how he had lost that much blood and survived.

The only thing Steven left out were the strange thoughts he had been having in bursts ever since he returned. If he told them that, then it would be almost worse if they believed him. Steven could only hope he could fix whatever was going on with him on his own first.

"And so, that's what happened," Steven finished, "It feels like it's been less than an hour or two for me. All the blood is mine from before when the alien thing healed me. Now..." Steven swallowed as he raised the dreaded question, "How long has it been?"

Ryan let out a shaky breath. "Steven. It's been over a year and a half. We all thought you were dead. And, well... We found your fingers. It's all so bizarre, how is any of this possible? Clearly, something more is going on here."

Steven glanced down at his hand. Ok, that was easier than expected. Ryan was suspicious but didn't immediately call him insane. He looked up and saw the other officer looking equally skeptical, but the man didn't speak up against Steven either.

The recording device kept buzzing quietly in the skeptical officer's hand as it kept recording.

After that came the detailed questions. Every little detail, every one of Steven's thoughts were documented again as the two officers asked more of their questions. Steven thought he had been detailed originally before, but apparently not.

Finally, it was all over. The other officer turned off his recorder and left the room, but Ryan remained lingering behind.

"How did Jessica take it?"

Ryan shook his head. "Not well. We had a funeral and everything last year and she's only recently started getting back to herself again. This will be a big shock to her, you returning just after she had accepted you were gone. Don't break her heart again."

Steven took that in. Minus Ryan's signature warning about his sister. That man's protectiveness bordered on the more than obsessive when it came to his sister. It had only been hours for Steven, but over a year for her. They had been dating for years now, ever since they met the year after he got out of college.

It must have hurt when she thought he was dead without even a body for confirmation. Steven wasn't sure how he would survive if the reverse had happened to him. He sighed as he let out his breath that he had been holding unconsciously. Well, he was back now and he would just have to make up for their missing time as best as he could.

Chapter 77: Back After a Long Absence - Mortal Steven Fragment

Turns out that being absent for over a year caused a lot of problems financially. Steven's possessions in his apartment and remaining money had been transferred back to his parents in the absence of a will.

After their tearful greetings over the phone, they promised to return everything as soon as they could. They lived across the country and planned to visit, but it wouldn't be for a few weeks as they tried to book a cheaper flight.

Steven tried to not be offended by that. But for the moment Steven had no money he could use, and his house was occupied by renters that had a contract lasting another three months at the minimum.

Steven had obviously lost his job, and his old boss was no longer even working at the company anymore. So he had to go on the job hunt as well. He had been considering leaving that old place anyways, so it wasn't like he was going into his old work and demanding his old job back either way though.

On a more positive note, Jessica had come to the hospital as soon as she had heard from Ryan what had happened. Steven felt fine, but he was still semi-confined here at the hospital until the blood test from his clothes would come back to clear him of wrongdoing.

It had been strange seeing Jessica being so emotional at seeing him, tears welling in her eyes as she smiled. From his perspective he had seen her a few days when they had watched a movie together on his couch.

Steven told Jessica everything that had happened to him, and needless to say she was shocked. Her grip tightened on his arm as he described the floating black orb he had encountered. She didn't say anything for a moment, but drew back fractionally after he finished and loosened her grip. *She thinks I'm crazy*, Steven thought bitterly.

"Did… did the doctors have an explanation? For any of it, medication you can take? I'm not letting you get hurt again now you're finally back." Jessica asked as her grip returned with a vengeance, nails digging into his arm.

Fulcrum frowned at her. She was a great asset, but disbelieving my story was a significant obstacle lowering her value to me. How could she be useful if she didn't trust my words? What was the best way to convince the human to follow my lead? Jessica recoiled as something in my expression triggered her. I don't know why people keep doing that.

"Jessica, why do you recoil? I'm the same as I ever was." Fulcrum reached out and gripped her hand tight like she had me before. She looked uncomfortable as I met her eyes and drew her hand back slightly but didn't totally let go.

"We can get through this together, okay? I feel fine, but as soon as something feels wrong I'll take whatever I need to. I just want to get out of here first, everyone keeps looking at me like I'm crazy. I am a perfectly normal person." Jessica winced and I noticed my grip on her hand was too hard than the standard, so I lowered the pressure. She nodded reluctantly.

"If you're sure, even if you are talking strangely. But as soon as something feels wrong, you let me know okay?" She lightly punched me in the shoulder and her tone softened.

"I don't want to lose you again."

Steven nodded back to her and reached out and took her hands again, "I can't imagine what you've gone through. Why don't you tell me what you've been up to for all this time?" Jessica's troubled expression cleared slightly and she smiled down at Steven. She sat down at the bedside as Steven sat up.

"Well, I've just started learning to play the piano for the last few months. It's so hard! I know you took lessons when you were a kid, but I felt so clumsy when I started out."

Steven smiled slightly, "I haven't played in a long time, I guess it's like a language where its easier to learn when you're a kid. What songs have you learned?"

"Oh, well I have this book of songs, I'm not great but my favorite was…"

They just kept talking about Jessica's life over the past year, and the awkwardness that had sprung up between them rapidly fell away as they fell into their old patterns.

It was odd for Steven to watch as Jessica seemed to remember little things that had only happened a few days ago for Steven. Jessica became more animated the more she spoke, and smiled more as she seemed to accept that he was back.

Steven was glad that she had done so much while he was gone. At least she hadn't been wallowing in grief as he knew he might have done. She was the one always able to improve his mood when he was feeling down ever since he had known her. That was what he loved most about her.

———O—o—O———

It had been two weeks and Steven was beginning the first round of interviews in his job search. He had been living with Jessica while he waited for the renter's contract to expire in a few months on his old apartment. There wasn't a great selection of housing in Harmony, so he would wait at least that long to get into any of the other places he had looked at in the area.

His parents had come by for a weekend to check in on Steven. Of course they hadn't believed him about his story, but at least they made an attempt of coming all of this way to see him.

To be fair he wasn't sure he would have believed him either. But their constant suggestions of various anti-psychosis medications they found online was grating to him for the longer they stayed. Like they knew anything about it or read about some of the side effects of those things.

A few days later they left again.

Good riddance.

Steven and Jessica had always lived in different places despite their long relationship, so it was a little odd to Steven that them moving together was happening now of all times.

Steven felt bad that he had disrupted Jessica's twenty ninth birthday that it turns out had been the weekend after he got back. He hadn't checked the date, and she hadn't told him until afterwards as she helped Steven adjust back to the world.

Ryan had been very helpful and supportive of Jessica taking him in temporarily. Steven almost laughed when the man emphasized the word whenever it was mentioned.

Temporary.

It had been Jessica that had offered it, Steven wouldn't impose on her like that. And despite her friendly personality she knew how to lay down the law if someone was doing something she didn't like. Luckily Steven and everyone else only saw her angry side a few times, but when it happened the ensuing explosion was legendary to anyone who witnessed it.

Ryan was so protective of his sister, that Steven swore he must have been a guard dog in his past life. She could handle herself just fine and even told Ryan as much when he had told Steven to be on his best behavior one too many times earlier in their relationship.

That had not been a fun couple of weeks as the siblings went to war with Steven caught in the center. Steven had never been sure if Ryan just disapproved of Steven in particular or just thought that his sister could do better. Luckily she didn't listen to Ryan too much about that topic.

— — — O — o — O — — —

Steven showered then climbed into the guest bed. Jessica had everything in her bedroom exactly how she wanted it, and Steven wasn't foolish enough to risk accidentally putting something back in the wrong place. She wouldn't act mad overtly, but she would smolder for a bit and check that everything else was in place over and over just to make sure things were in their *proper* place.

Steven actually always thought it was quite odd, because she was usually more relaxed in the rest of her home. He had been startled the first time when he had picked something up casually in one of their early conversations and put it back at an angle.

Jessica had tried to keep talking, but her focus kept drifting and eventually after a few minutes she had just sighed and stood up and fixed the object so it was at the proper angle again as Steven watched her in confusion.

Jessica hadn't been able to explain it when he asked, it was just something that had to be done for her. But for whatever reason, she got compulsive in making sure everything in her bedroom was just so.

Her room was a no go zone, and when they were together, they usually relaxed together in Steven's room. That habit made him make his place as tidy as he could, so it wasn't all negative at least. Jessica wasn't as compulsive when it wasn't her own bedroom, but she still liked things to be orderly.

She only seemed to be truly bothered if it was something in her space out of alignment, but Steven still saw her grimacing if someone put something back a different way than it had been originally. Including him. But she was able to shrug it off and it didn't grow beyond that.

Anyways, their relationship was much more convenient now that they were in the same house. It was Saturday, so Jessica and Steven had gone out and had a picnic at a nearby park. Not the one where Steven had been sucked into the portal.

The one he had appeared from was still blocked off as the murder investigation searched for any dead bodies Steven may or may not have left behind in the area. It was some sort of high level investigation, Ryan had complained to Jessica how a special division of the FBI was handling the case and being jerks to the local police officers as they blocked off the area.

The picnic with Jessica had been nice with the hot summer sun beaming down on their faces, and they ate the cold cuts they brought in the little cooler. After they were done, Steven and Jessica just relaxed and messed around with her electric keyboard she had bought after they got back home.

Jessica played the songs she was learning while Steven tried to remember the songs he had learned as a kid.

Steven laid down on bed and drifted off to sleep, content. He could go back to piecing his life back together, now that he was back. He would never have to hurt Jessica like that again. He could see how much his absence had hurt her...

———O — o — O———

Steven opened his eyes and he was in a forest. He sat up and saw the black orb hovering in front of him silently. He was naked and felt the dirt on his backside as he sat there in confusion. What was happening?

There was a moment where neither of us moved. I stood and saw my surroundings change in a moment. Clouds of gray mist shrouded the area around me and I felt motion under my feet. A moment later, the mist condensed into a perfect replica of the guest bedroom in Jessica's house where I had been sleeping recently. The dark orb was gone.

Blinking, I stepped over to the dresser and went to lift one of the decorations. But as soon as I lifted it, the thing dissolved back into the mist again. I watched fascinated as after taking a step back the thing recondensed exactly where it had sat before from the swirling mist in the air.

What was going on, where had the Seed gone? I stepped outside but couldn't see far through the deep mists. I walked forward and the street in front of Jessica's home became visible, potholes and all. The area was silent, the atmosphere oppressively silent in the darkness.

Eventually I retreated back into the house before quietly knocking on the door of Jessica's room. Was she here too? Steven fidgeted nervously for a moment as there was no response before carefully opening the door to peek inside. The room was empty.

Steven let out a sigh of relief. Maybe this was all some elaborate dream, but it felt as real as anything else he had ever felt. He didn't want Jessica to be drawn into whatever this was. Steven could only hope that he wouldn't be gone so long from her this time.

He cursed and punched the wall, where a perfectly circular hole dissolved into mist under the force of Steven's angry blow. He didn't want to leave Jessica again, he could see how much the first time had hurt her. Who knew how long he would be gone this time? Days, weeks... Years.

He couldn't let that happen, Steven had to get out of here. Ignoring the Seed, wait how did he know its name?

But the Seed was nowhere to be seen. Figuring it was worth a try, Steven looked at the ceiling before shouting.

"Bring me back! I want to go home, whoever you are!"

There was no response. Steven warred with himself about what to do before stepping outside. Onto the street shrouded in the mists. Maybe there was another red portal back to Earth somewhere around here.

Steven just had to reach it before too much time had passed back on Earth. Because he knew now that this couldn't be Earth, nothing about this strange mist swirling in the air in thick cloying clumps could be natural.

Steven ran down the empty streets hoping to see the telltale red light of one of the portals as he moved. But he didn't see anything. The cars on the street didn't start. Even Steven's lighter blows caused portions of the metal frames to dissolve into the gray mist, before they gradually drifted back into place and healed the damage even as Steven watched.

He would have to escape on foot.

After a while the sun rose in this strange place, and the mist grew a little lighter as Steven could see farther out. He slid to a stop and watched with wide eyes at seeing the forest just in the distance. Even as he watched the forest dissolved and were replaced with the familiar streets of Harmony.

Steven tried running faster to catch up with the transforming zone. Maybe if he reached the forest then he would find a portal so he could make his way back to Earth.

He ran until the sun was high in the sky, but he never got even close to the forest. He didn't seem to grow as tired as he normally would either. The growth and conversion of the forest into modern town seemed to focus on generating whatever direction Steven was paying attention to first. Steven had even tried paying attention to a different direction while running in the opposite way. That method brought Steven close to the edge of the spreading urban zone, but not close enough to get to the trees.

The sun began to sink on the horizon again, and Steven accepted he wouldn't be able to outpace the growth and make it out.

He was over fifteen miles from Jessica's house if his calculations were correct based on his surroundings of the silent town of Harmony. And he still hadn't seen a single other living thing besides the Seed yet in the beginning.

Steven's legs were slightly sore, but he wasn't trained for a marathon. His legs muscles should be going through their death throes by now. It felt like he had run a third of the distance he had.

As the sun sank, Steven jogged at a much slower pace back to Jessica's house. Finally, he was there, panting and sweating with exertion. Still not nearly as tired as he should be after so long a run.

Even with the strange improvement in Steven's stamina in this place, he was overtaxed by a run that long. He collapsed onto the floor and lay there for a moment as the world began to grow dark as sunset faded away. The faucet handles on the sinks dissolved when Steven attempted to open them, so getting water was a bust as he went to wash his face.

Steven realized quickly after catching his breath that where he first arrived might have a portal hidden somewhere. He had to have arrived here somehow, right?

Calmer now, Steven searched the whole replica of Jessica's house as best as he could. If the portal back was anywhere in this place it would be where Steven had first arrived. He rooted around as much as he could, but despite dispersing everything he could see briefly back into mist, nothing stood out to him as a way out. He was almost frantic by this point.

Shit, am I stuck here forever? Steven slumped down in defeat in the darkness and leaned up against the wall behind him. He put his head in his hands in despair and sat there for a long while feeling helpless.

———O—o—O———

With a gasp Steven sat up from his bed sweating up a storm and breathing heavily. One moment he had been wallowing in his despair in the hallway in the darkness of the night, and the next he was back here. The room was still dark, but there was none of that strange mist in the air.

Steven was wearing his clothes now and patted himself down for a moment before letting out a sigh of relief. He was back. He stepped out of the bed and his bare feet hit the cold floor of the room. He walked up to the dresser and picked up the decoration and felt his last lingering doubt disappear as it remained itself and didn't disperse.

He took a few deep breaths and wiped away the sweat that was stinging his eyes as it dripped down from his forehead. His heartbeat gradually slowed back down.

Steven settled back into bed, and tried unsuccessfully to get some sleep. He would need all the energy he could get for his explanation to Jessica tomorrow. He couldn't keep something this big from her after he had promised to tell her if something went wrong. And this was certainly something wrong.

Chapter 78: Coming Clean - Steven Fragment

Despite his personal misgivings, Steven did indeed tell Jessica about his experience last night. When she comforted him and said it wasn't real he was tempted to allow the lie to stand. But he knew somehow that he would be going back. So he told her that it felt too real and couldn't be a nightmare. That it had felt just as real as the portal had been.

Her expression broke a little as he mentioned it. She had never believed Steven's story about the portal, and they had mutually decided to avoid talking about it after their first argument where neither could convince the other of reality.

She thought he was mentally ill, and the sad part was he couldn't fully disagree with her. His story didn't seem plausible at all. And his thoughts had been turning strange lately.

One morning he realized he had stared at himself in the mirror for over an hour without moving. Inspecting every individual pore and hair on his body and categorizing them one by one.

It felt natural at the time, and it was only when he snapped out of it he had realized something had been wrong. He had considered telling Jessica about these episodes, but this secret was too frightening to share. He didn't want her to look at him any different than she already did.

It was ironic that Ryan of all people would believe Steven about his alien encounter while Jessica would not. At least Ryan said he believed to Steven. Maybe he was just trying to not set him off when they had briefly spoken after Steven had left the hospital. That was almost a worse scenario to think about.

The argument between Jessica and Steven about the reality of Steven's experiences grew fierce until they were both screaming at each other. Steven was about to shoot out another acidic barb, but paused as he saw Jessica's trembling hands. He rushed forward and wrapped her in a hug as she started to cry into his shoulder.

They stood like that for a moment before Jessica calmed down and leaned back and met Steven's eyes.

"You have to see someone. I can tell things aren't right with you. Beyond just this dream and the portal. Sometimes your face just goes flat and you don't seem to care about anything before I snap you back awake. You just look at me with those dead eyes. You're sick and they can help you get better. I just want what's best for you," her hand cradled Steven's face, "Just do it for me, please."

Steven opened his mouth, but closed it again. She had noticed his episodes, he had never hidden anything from her. His chest felt tight and he felt something tighten in his chest. He was afraid. Afraid that it wasn't actually real. Something deep inside him didn't want him to get help.

"Ok. I'll do it. For you."

———O—o—O———

The psychologists ran various tests on him when he arrived at the clinic, Jessica clinging to his arm as if to prevent him from escaping.

The tests mostly consisted of answering various seemingly random questions while they described his episodes of sudden apathy and strangeness. They didn't tell him the results but wrote his answers down silently and moved onto the next question with blank faces.

Steven felt normal if still a little emotional from his argument with Jessica this morning. She had gotten the appointment quickly, same day somehow. Steven hadn't even known that was possible for these kinds of places.

Then came the individual evaluation. Jessica was asked to leave and wait outside. Steven could see she was worried, so he just smiled and nodded at her before following the doctor inside. The doctor sat down on one of the comfy chairs and gestured to the other with his clipboard in his lap.

I sat down and tried to maintain my facial expressions, I knew I had to appear normal if I wanted Jessica to stay with me. All my focus was on convincing this psychologist that I was a normal human not worthy of further study.

"Mr. Fulcrum? So tell me why you are here," The doctor said, "I know you already went through this before in the tests, but I find it illuminates what you consider the central issues of concern here."

I considered my answer.

"Mr. Fulcrum, I can see you are deep in thought right now," The doctor continued, "This isn't some elaborate puzzle, just openness between two people. Why don't you just share from the heart? There's no need for every answer to be perfect here. We will explore the issues here from many different angles and this is only the first."

I gave up the complex calculations and said what felt natural and met the man's eyes.

"Jessica was upset by my sudden bursts of strange behavior. As you probably know I have been missing for the last year and a half, only returning a few weeks ago. I have no memories of that time period between, and Jessica says I am acting differently than before. I have... felt a little strange, but I just zone out. I don't get violent or see hallucinations or anything."

The doctor raised an eyebrow and wrote something down. "No memories at all? Not even flashes? And Jessica has told us you were covered in quite the amount of blood when you reappeared. How do you explain that?"

I nodded, "Nothing. I have no idea what happened."

Seeing that I wasn't going to elaborate further, the doctor moved on, "And these strange behaviors? What are some examples?"

I tried to think of what to say but I couldn't pinpoint exactly what I had been doing that had been so strange. For some reason, that felt wrong. Realizing that I didn't have an answer, I started to become stressed. I should not be stressed, it was wrong, unnatural. I…

Steven blinked as he tried to remember where he was. The doctor was staring at him in concern as Steven inspected the room. After a second, Steven remembered the last few minutes and the doctor's last question.

"Sorry, lost in thought. I don't know, everything felt perfectly normal at the time. Logical. But a few days ago I realized that I was staring at myself in the mirror for over an hour. It was only when I snapped out of it that I realized something was off."

The doctor squinted at Steven. "What do you remember of the last few minutes?"

Steven frowned. "What, what do you mean? Well, we came in here and then you asked… Oh, you asked why I was here and I… Wait, why is everything so fuzzy? Wasn't this only a minute ago?"

The doctor nodded as if Steven had just confirmed something before continuing with his questions.

"So, tell me of what you remember from the year and a half you were gone."

Steven frowned deeper. He had already told the doctor this?

"Well I was hiking in the woods when I was sucked into a red portal that appeared out of nowhere. There was a round black ball on the other side that healed my injuries and sent me back through and…"

I had to stop this, It shouldn't be shared.

"And it was just a dream. I have no idea what really happened in that year and a half."

The doctor frowned again, seeming to detect me shifting mid-sentence.

"Well, this dream is key to your diagnosis so why don't you tell me more about that."

I struggled with myself for a moment. Surely it would be fine to share if treated as a hypothetical after all. No one would believe this kind of crazy story.

Steven opened his mouth and restated all the events up to now as far as he could remember. The doctor kept writing on his pad and kept asking clarifying questions, and Steven obliged him.

The doctor especially focused on the floating black orb, which Steven found odd, but it was important, so I only found it natural. After a long session that left Steven feeling wrung out, he was released back into Jessica's arms as she sat in the clinic lobby drumming her leg with her fingers.

She rushed forward and hugged him tight as he emerged and he chuckled and squeezed her back for a moment before letting her go.

Steven smirked, "C'mon Jessica. It's not like I was going in there for an execution."

Jessica blushed a little and loosened her grip, "Er, yeah. Sorry... Sorry about that."

The doctor followed behind. Jessica and Steven turned to him. He cleared his throat, looking almost bored now.

"Well it's not certain yet but it may be caused by the repression of the traumatic memories of whatever happened over the last year and a half. That would explain the two different emotional states we've observed during the session and how when questioned in the past your behavior quickly shifted as well as your speech patterns."

Steven frowned and interrupted, "Wait, what do you mean? What shifts?"

The doctor shrugged, "What I said. Whenever I asked about the incident your emotions became stunted and you actively avoided discussing the subject."

Steven tried to remember, and now that he thought back on it, that was true. The doctor had to pressure him very heavily to get the full story out of him in the beginning, even if Steven was more forthcoming afterwards.

Jessica leaned forward anxiously, "So what does this mean? Will he be alright?"

The doctor shook his head.

"This is the job of a skilled trauma specialized therapist. I am more of a clinician focusing mainly on initially diagnosing patients, so I will not be as much use as some others for the actual treatment in a case this complex."

He glanced between the two of them, "It will be a slow process but there needs to be care to not cause an adverse reaction from touching a sensitive point in a case as serious as this. I will have the front desk give you a list of therapists I would trust with this kind of work. Whoever you choose can also assist you in case it is discovered as something more than trauma."

Jessica stood there for a moment as the doctor looked between the two of them before turning and walking off without even saying goodbye. Steven guided the stunned Jessica to the front desk as something tight uncoiled in his gut. The man hadn't believed his story.

Steven wasn't sure why this was a good thing, but somehow it was. That doctor, doctor... actually hadn't given his name. Huh.

Steven took the list from the receptionist and followed Jessica out the door. Jessica was right, coming here was worth it. Now he knew the cause of what was happening to him. It all had to be his repressed memories surfacing in his dreams... It must be memories of what happened in that missing year and a half.

That was why they felt so real. Right?

— — — **(Mortal 'Doctor' Fragment)** — — —

The doctor finished composing his encrypted email to William Callahan, or "Bill" as the man's associates knew him as. The man and his Neighborhood Watch would be very interested in what he had just heard from his most recent patient. The doctor attached the relevant medical documents to the file.

Completely illegal, but Bill paid well and had a noble cause unlike many others the doctor had worked for in the past. Transferring himself to this facility without suspicion from the staff here last month had been surprisingly difficult. They had actually called one of his forged references and asked questions about him in detail, which was more than most places did.

But all of his forged documents had passed muster otherwise, so it all worked out in the end. The doctor's finger hovered over the mouse for a second as he hesitated. If he sent this, then the Neighborhood Watch and maybe even Bill himself might come here.

The doctor went back and added an extra zero to his requested 'retirement package' for the information he had gathered. As soon as the money came through he would be out of here. He didn't want to be in the crosshairs of the big players when they began to slug it out in this town on the possible eve of the full Invasion.

Chapter 79: A Recurring Dream - Steven Fragment

Steven kept having the dream. Always, he was alone in that place with the silence. At the end of his first month on Earth Steven had discovered that things no longer dissolved into mist if he moved them carefully. Including his clothes luckily.

Despite being alone, having to go naked everywhere still left him feeling exposed. Any stronger application of force caused the clothes and other objects to still disperse, but slower movements allowed him to make some food for himself at least. And over time Steven noticed the things could take more and more force before dispersing back into mist.

Now it was his fourth day in that place. It had happened every Saturday night so far, him being brought here. No, dreaming this. He had to remind himself that it was a dream. The number of his strange episodes on Earth was decreasing now too.

Jessica was happy with his progress, and seemed to be more accepting when he explained his recurring dream to her.

She seemed to view it as a way to help him heal and overcome whatever terrible thing everyone assumed had happened to Steven. She was the one who had suggested cooking something in here.

He had been quite bored the third time he came into this place, as there was simply nothing to do but wander around and explore on his own. Anything he would usually interact with dissolved into mist if not handled carefully. Steven flipped the sizzling bacon inside the awkwardly balanced pan. He had found a camp burner buried among the boxes and luckily the flammable gas inside lit easily and gave him some heat for cooking.

The little handheld lighter used gas as well, so he was able to fire up the burner and start cooking. Steven hadn't really ever gotten the urge to eat yet in the dream, but he certainly still enjoyed the sensation when he ate the final bacon and eggs for their flavor. As long as he moved slow enough the food didn't dissolve into the strange mists again. He took another bite of the meal and savored it for a moment. He should do this more often in the real world. This was delicious!

———O—o—O———

It had been four months now, and Serenity was peaceful. That was what Jessica had called it after he had described his changing feelings about the dream one time. It reminded Steven a little of the nature walks he had used to do. Just soaking in the environment free of the normal hustle and bustle of his normal life.

He strolled down the empty streets of the dream casually as he reflected on the past few months. His new job was demanding, and one of his annoying coworkers kept asking about Steven's disappearance whenever he could.

That man just could not take a hint when he wasn't wanted. It was well known throughout the town by now what had happened to Steven and even several reporters that had tried to get interviews with him.

Steven took a deep breath

.But those problems were for Earth. Not for Serenity.

Steven smiled as he assembled his sandwich. It had been a sight to see Jessica scaring off those reporters after they got a little too persistent in following him around.

She had been sent into one of her famous rages that sent the reporters fleeing to the hills after the verbal assault, too shocked at her sudden change to even record her tirade.

Steven had unilaterally declared they were having another of their sessions on the piano together after they got back home from that, when he saw her a little more withdrawn than usual.

Steven and Jessica played around one after another on the piano, taking turns and just talking about their days as they played. By the time they were done, Jessica put back her usual smile and her breaths grew deeper and more even as she calmed back down as Steven rubbed little circles on a spot on her back to calm her down.

Steven knew better than anyone that both Ryan and Jessica had inherited an overabundance of passion and explosive anger.

Ryan had snapped a pool cue over his knee one time when Steven had thoroughly thrashed him in pool in front of a group of Ryan's friends. Ryan really had been terrible, he had barely sunk two balls in the pockets when Steven was already on the eight ball.

Really baffling, that Ryan could be so terrible and somehow miss every shot. But still a hilarious overreaction to the defeat. But it was Ryan's fault anyways, he was the one who randomly challenged Steven to a game of pool when he spotted him walking by.

Needless to say, Ryan was embarrassed after he realized he fully registered what he had done in anger and was teased mercilessly until he looked like he wanted to sink into the floor.

Steven regretted that he hadn't gotten a picture of Ryan's expression after the man realized the consequences when the owner of the bar had demanded repayment and that everyone else in the room was staring at him as a result. A total deer caught in headlights looks.

It was still an ongoing joke among the people who had been there to see it. Whenever Ryan grew too heated in some sort of argument all the people around him would mime snapping something over their knee in unison. It was almost funny how effective it was at cooling the man off. He would defuse in an instant like a bucket of cold water had been poured over him and just look mortified.

Steven knew how much Jessica valued her positivity and compassion towards others in herself. She didn't want others to see her for her angry and explosive state, like how they saw her brother.

Despite the two of them being more alike than she would like to admit, even if Jessica was working on herself while Ryan let his anger control him. That's why her exploding at the reporters had upset her so much. She didn't want to lose control like that and be like her brother.

Speaking of Ryan, he was upset that Jessica and Steven were still living together after all this time. He was rather old fashioned for this kind of thing and Jessica had to set him straight again when he tried to argue against it. It wasn't his decision after all.

And Steven never went to Jessica's room due to her obsessiveness, she always came to him for the night when the situation called for it. So it wasn't like he was intruding on her precious den of her bedroom either.

Jessica and Steven had discussed it and Steven had ended up deciding to continue to stay with Jessica and pay his share of the rent now he had a stable job again. And backpay for the first few months despite her protests.

They both enjoyed the arrangement as it was now anyway. Jessica was more than happy to share the payments for this place with Steven.

Steven felt a little melancholy as he thought of his parents shipping his boxed up possessions back to him. They had been happy to know he was alive, but they still hadn't come to visit him again in all of this time.

Well, it wasn't like he could go to them. He had already drained most of his savings due to recovering from his long absence, and had to slowly rebuild his funds almost from scratch again. But still, it would have been nice if they came to see him again sometime.

————O—o—O————

It had been a year since he had returned to Earth, and Steven felt at the padded box in his pocket from the jewelers. He had been saving for the ring for this whole time. If Jessica wasn't the one for him, then he didn't know who would be.

She had stuck with him at his lowest point and waited for over a year and a half for him even after he was declared dead. He almost felt like he didn't deserve her. Maybe Ryan had been right all this time.

Steven quickly hid the ring in the room in his dresser. He had a perfect plan, and the reservations for the fancy restaurant were two weeks away. It would be a private meal, and at the end he would propose to her.

He was confident she would say yes, not a sliver of doubt in his mind.

Yes, none at all.

The earthquakes he had been feeling in Serenity for the last month were just a sign of his stress as he built up to the moment. He couldn't let his dreams control him and make him delay again. On that Friday, he'd finally take the step.

---O—o—O---

"Yes, oh Yes *FuLcRum*! Of course I'll marry you. I've waited for so long for you to ask."

Jessica threw her arms around him as Steven froze. What had she just called him... It felt wrong.

"Steven, are you all right?" Jessica pulled back a little confused when Steven had stiffened all of a sudden. He snapped back to reality. He shouldn't let his trauma ruin this moment.

He had already let that happen too much in the last year. Steven put on a smile for her. And felt a wave of relief wash over him as he realized she had accepted.

His smile turned more genuine, "Just hit me that you actually said yes." He picked her up and spun her in a circle before putting her back down laughing.

"You said yes!" Steven said again with a laugh.

Jessica was laughing too as the serving staff looked in on the touching scene. She kissed him after he slid the ring onto her hand carefully. The two of them left the restaurant with a bounce in their steps and all smiles.

---O—o—O---

It was Saturday and both Jessica and Steven were upbeat, just enjoying each other's presence and company. They played board games, cooked together, and generally just relaxed. They both knew what Ryan's reaction to the news would be, so they had pretended it was a normal date.

Ryan had never approved of Steven dating his sister, even if Ryan didn't exactly hate Steven on his own. Probably They could tell Ryan after they had enjoyed one romantic weekend together, no need to spoil the moment with arguments. They watched a romantic movie and held each other as day turned into night.

After the movie was done, the two went to the kitchen bar and broke out the wine. Neither of them were much for alcohol, but Jessica had said she got it as a gift so best make use of it anyway. They drank and talked long into the night.

Steven lost track of time and just enjoyed the moment as they leaned into each other and just talked while sipping the wine occasionally. He was enjoying himself so much that he almost forgot what day it was. He glanced at the clock hanging on the wall and froze when he saw the time.

11:58 pm.

He had figured out over the last year that he transferred, no, imagined the dream, at exactly midnight and that no time passed while he was gone.

He had an unamused Jessica record him sleeping one time a few months back and she hadn't seen him disappear or anything in the footage.

Steven jolted to his feet and knocked the wine glass from Jessica's hand and she yelped in surprise. He kept moving trying to get away as quickly as he could.

"Oh, sorry, sorry Jessica. It's just… I'm sorry Jessica, it's time for Serenity. I'll be back in a few."

Steven quickly retreated to his bedroom, his head down in shame. His inner truth that Serenity was very much real conflicted with everything he tried to tell himself and Jessica. He looked up as he heard his room door open softly. There standing in the doorframe was Jessica. Shit, why hadn't he locked the door? She was frowning at him.

"Steven, I thought we had resolved this when I recorded you sleeping that one time," She said, "You stayed right there and didn't move a muscle. It's all in your head, you can't let it control you. Remember what your therapist said. It's like how I have to organize, you can't let things become more important than they really are."

Steven backed away into the corner of the room as Jessica approached slowly with her hands extended outwards as if to comfort a wounded animal. Steven's eyes darted every which way. It was coming any second now. He only had to delay her for that long. He should keep her talking.

"It is real. I know I can't prove it, but it's real I can feel it in my bones. Please, just stay back. I don't know if you can come back if you are brought there."

Jessica stomped her foot, "It isn't REAL, *FulCrUm*! I thought we agreed not to lie about this no matter what. You've been holding onto your delusion for this whole time! I… I need to prove it to you!"

Her eyes grew determined as Jessica leapt forward. Steven reflexively caught her before realizing what he had done and tried to push her away. But her arms were already around him, wrapping him in a tight hug.

Steven spoke, his voice barely over a whisper, "Don't… Don't call me that."

He weakly struggled to escape her as she wrapped herself around him, his heart not truly in the effort. Maybe she was right. They fell to the floor as Jessica lay on top of him, and their eyes met again. Her eyes shone with determination, and his with unshed tears. She stroked his hair gently and comforted him even as she held him tight.

"Shhhhhh. It's going to be alright, I'll prove it to you. Then you can be free of this."

Steven struggled harder but Jessica merely tightened her grip on him, and he wasn't willing to hurt her to escape. A moment passed. Another. Then a full minute. And nothing happened. Steven waited and waited and finally he stopped his half hearted struggle against Jessica.

She remained latched onto him tight, keeping him pinned to the floor as Steven pulled his phone from his pocket and checked the time, only his head pointed down to see the screen at his hip.

12:04 am.

His vision grew blurry as he finally released his tears. She was right, it really had all been in his head. She was right, it wasn't real. Jessica loosened her grip, and Steven hugged her back as tight as he could. She was right. Their faces were pressed right into each other. He leaned into her ear.

"Thank you Jessica. You don't know how… how real it feels. I'm sorry I lied. It really was all just drea…"

Jessica's beautiful face froze even as she opened her mouth to reply. Her own unshed tears of relief were pooled in the corners over her eyes as she smiled down at him. Steven's whole being froze as he realized what was happening. His surroundings began to slowly dissolve into gray mist around him, Steven and Jessica the only things untouched.

No, no. no! It was past midnight, I was supposed to be safe!

It was free and clear, it was all a dream.

Nooooooooooooo!

He could only scream internally as he felt a malevolent presence enter his mind as the bedroom rematerialized around them in Serenity.

First a barrage of images, but sensing Steven's confusion the thing in his head quickly shifted into words.

'What Drama from the Mortal! A Tragic Play worth some small delays. Good Choice, Fulcrum, Good Choice. She will be a Worthy Feast!'

Chapter 80: Preparations for the Feast - Multiple Fragments of Memory

Robin and I continued to wander around for a long time. The red portals had stopped forming about fifty or so days ago, but despite my concerns nothing noteworthy had happened in the rest of that time. And our newest companion joined us, Squirrel, who Robin had picked up somewhere on the way.

The little thing followed Robin around constantly, and Robin enjoyed poking at it and cradling its little body in its hands sometimes when it grew tired or slept.

Squirrel was not happy with this prodding, but tolerated the treatment for a limited period before squirming out of Robin's grip to run in circles around him when it recovered its energy. It didn't seem to need food just like the rest of the animals we had observed here.

Occasionally the squirrel would spot something as it darted around and chattered, and Robin would come over to inspect whatever the squirrel had found as we traveled.

The squirrel seemed to completely ignore me for the most part, scrambling all over me like I was a large tree. I wasn't sure to be flattered or annoyed that the animal put me at such a low level of threat.

Squirrel had come at just the right time too. With the portals shut now, the population of animals in the area was dropping rapidly.

The few predators that made it through were constantly thinning the numbers of the rest, and with no newcomers the population of all the animals was rapidly dropping. The predators continued their hunts despite their prey dissolving into mist and none of them not going hungry in this place.

The squirrel had much more awareness of its surroundings than either I or Robin did, so was able to point out the remaining animals to Robin.

Even now, the squirrel chittered and Robin turned its head and began inspecting the little songbird perched on a branch in the distance. I watched the two as they continued to enjoy themselves together.

I had noticed something worrying recently. I wasn't sure at first due to our wandering path, but this place was definitely shrinking as time went on. It only took two days of dedicated travel in a straight line to loop back to the start now.

I couldn't tell what exactly was shrinking, the landscape looked unchanged and all the landmarks we had left behind in our travels seemed unchanged.

But somehow this place was smaller now. Occasionally we would spot the Seed, but we never managed to catch it off guard again so it easily escaped us. In fact, we had not seen it ever since the red portals had stopped appearing.

I continued to consider the shrinking world as we kept traveling the next day. Would it stop or would we be crushed in the center in the end? I looked up from my thoughts and slowly came to a stop as I felt a probe from Robin.

'*Fulcrum! New thing in the distance. White, like in memory for the bird robin! Look, over there.*'

Robin pointed its arm slightly to the right and there indeed was a whitish blob in the distance. I started walking again and angled so we were heading towards it.

'*Hurry, hurry Fulcrum. We're almost there, first new thing in ages! Move, move, move!*'

Robin was almost hopping up and down by now in excitement at the prospect of finally something new. I knew the feeling, everything in the forest was a little dull and drab after so long.

Squirrel had rekindled Robin's interest in everything, but even that burst of excitement was fading by now.

Squirrel was curled up in a gap between the bone plates on my chest that it had made its home. I didn't even feel it as it rested in there, and it apparently was well cushioned as it never got injured even when I increased my pace in the past.

Robin had thrown another tantrum after he realized I had forgotten it was in there and sped up to a dangerous speed in the beginning. But it had all turned out fine, so Robin didn't stay mad at me for too long.

I sped up my footsteps and uncurled my tentacles and reached up for Robin. My thunderous footfalls began to speed up until I was moving at what felt like a slow jog to me.

But the wind rushing by at a blistering pace proved otherwise. Robin squirmed as it was totally encased in tentacles and lifted slightly off of my shoulders.

'*Booooooooo! I only fell once, Fulcrum. I can't even see anything from in here. Big, dumb Fulcrum. Let me out, I want to see!*'

No way. Some of Robin's black chitin was still cracked after that fall dozens of days later. Robin would just have to deal with it until we got closer.

'*Let me ouuuuuuuut!*'

Not that Robin wouldn't complain bitterly about it for the rest of the trip.

———O—o—O———

Two hours of Robin's whining later, we arrived in front of a cluster of human buildings. Their painted walls were the white we had seen in the distance. I uncurled the ball of tentacles close to the ground and Robin flopped out dramatically onto the grass.

'*Baaad Fulcrum. So mean. But... Ooooh! New stuff. Let's explore. C'mon squirrel! You come too.*'

Sure enough the squirrel came out from its little pocket on my chest quickly and scrambled back down to run around Robin's feet a moment later. A faded memory tickled at the back of my mind. Shouldn't it hurt the squirrel to listen to Robin?

I stood frozen as I tried to recall the blurred memory. I had been hurt before when something had tried communicating telepathically. I had bled, and the blood was red… But why would I do that? I liked my black blood. Red was an odd color, much lower efficiency for holding Potential than the black sets of compounds.

'C'mon Fulcrum. Stop standing there. I want to explore!'

Despite my best efforts the memory dispersed, and I couldn't remember anything more. Giving it up, I turned to Robin. This place felt vaguely familiar and for some reason I felt like it would be best not to start breaking into the houses. It wouldn't be the polite thing to do.

'Ok, Just don't go in the buildings yet. It would be too interesting, we should see how big this place is first and see a little of everything before getting distracted.'

Robin projected confusion and reluctant acceptance before asking a hesitant question.

'But cool stuff inside houses? So why not go in?'

I tried to think of how to explain.

'You felt excited when you saw this place right?'

'Yes? Very new thing.'

'Well, what if there is something even MORE exciting farther in? Getting distracted by the houses means we might miss it. That wouldn't be very good, would it?'

Robin looked struck, *'No! That is bad. Quick we have to hurry, we might miss something!'*

Robin darted off in a panic and I sent back amusement back through the link as I watched the squirrel scramble to follow behind. I waited a moment before stepping forward to catch up to them.

Robin kept running forward, eyes darting side to side as he tried to decide which way to turn on the four way intersection of the roads. It kept running forward after some hesitation, and I followed.

—— O — o — O ——

It had been an hour now and we still hadn't reached the other end of the buildings. It felt oddly familiar for some reason… It was only after we reached a church that I realized what it was. During the chaos on Earth I had put my foot through the wall of this building.

I remembered the structure because I had thought at the time it was odd how different it looked from the nearby buildings. I leaned down to inspect the undamaged walls of the church for a moment. What was its function again? A church was… Bah, faulty memory again.

I stopped and glanced around and the memories of the buildings came together as I realized it was a replication of the place on Earth before it was destroyed. The buildings looked much more well maintained as well. There were none of the holes in the walls and broken windows present in most of them from when I first arrived on Earth.

'Fulcrum! Ah, bad thing get back! Urk, bad. Ahhhhhh!'

I whipped my head around and there the Seed was wrapping the thrashing Robin in its shadowy tendrils. I charged, but the floating black ball darted away, holding Robin up above its body as it fled.

I charged as anger washed over me. How dare it kidnap Robin! I unwrapped my tentacles from my arm and cocked back my fist even as I charged forward.

I threw the punch forward and my bulky tentacle launched and just barely clipped the creature that dodged. The creature quickly pivoted on a dime and darted into an alleyway between two nearby buildings.

'Fulcrum, I can't get out! Let me go…'

The telepathic link broke somehow as I managed to shift my charge to smash through the building in the way. It burst into mist and I had to wave my arms in front of my face to clear it.

There was a flicker of movement in the corner of my vision and my head snapped to the black carapace disappearing into another alleyway. I bull rushed again as a red haze of anger began to cloud my mind. I smashed and charged, leaving a trail of dissipating buildings behind me.

But eventually, I stomped around and realized that I had lost the Seed and Robin. I threw back my head and let out my angry screech.

"KRIIIIIIIIIIIIIIIIIII!"

The air shook and everything around me started dissolving into mist under the force of my cry. I looked in the direction I had last seen the Seed flee. If I couldn't chase the Seed directly, then I would just have to rampage until I stumbled towards its hiding place by accident.

The squirrel climbed my leg and nestled into its place, but I barely paid it attention as I rampaged through the town, smashing the buildings to root out the Seed, I hoped that Robin would be okay.

—————O—o—O—————

The Seed quickly dragged the thrashing little one into the pit it had hidden inside one of the houses on the other side of town. It had been stalking the pair carefully ever since they had arrived, waiting for the two to be separated. On its own, the little one didn't have enough physical strength to overpower the Seed even when it was on the move.

The little one was good enough to defend the big one and itself in telepathic combat, and without it the big one would be much easier to handle.

The Seed could hear the big one rampaging uselessly on the other side of town even now, only detected through the faint shakes in the ground and faint sounds in the distance.

The little one still struggled and tried to send out a telepathic connection to the big one, but the Seed blocked it with some effort. It couldn't do this for forever and was even burning the outer layers of its precious Potential to enhance itself for this. But it only had to last a few more minutes.

It held the little one down and created a telepathic channel and forcefully extracted its memories. It turned to the false body laying still it had constructed to the right. This body had required nearly three quarters of the Potential it had gathered to construct, and was made from its own discarded flesh.

The texture of its plates and shape was nearly the same between the two creatures, one thrashing and the other still. The Seed took the packaged memories and injected them into the clone with some minor modifications, only injecting a few false memories needed for its 'escape' to be believable.

The more modifications there were the more likely it would be noticed that its mind had been tampered with. This body was only given enough mental strength for basic telepathy and not much more, just in case it went rogue.

In the memory, the 'Robin', had been released when the Seed unfortunately fell into a red portal that suddenly opened right in front of them. The Seed knew it was a little implausible, but it couldn't think of any other way a weak little creature could realistically escape one such as itself if the Seed desired to keep it.

The clone sat up and slowly began to twitch as the Seed hurriedly lifted it alongside the original and scuttled as fast as it could to the drop off point, at a random street far from the Seed's lair. The Seed placed down the clone carefully, and used some of its tendrils to break open a pit in the road where the clone would believe the portal would be.

The clone was programmed to die after a set amount of time, so the deception only would have to last until it expired. The Seed was sure the big one would likely destroy the evidence of any portal anyway with its large footsteps, but it couldn't hurt to be thorough.

The still flailing original was brought back to the Seed's lair. The clone should pacify the big one long enough for the Seed to execute the plan to completion. Even if the big one discovered the ruse it should still have no idea of where the Seed was.

The Seed entered the little one's mind and began making changes. This one would become its greatest defender, with a mental resilience nearly matching its own…

———O—o—O———

After the Seed was done, it left the unconscious servant in the pit as it continued its work. The Servant had cracked some of its plates in its struggles and the Seed had been forced to waste some of its Potential fixing the physical damage after it was done with the creature's mind.

With each entry of the bonded mortal to this place, the conduit between him and the Seed grew thicker and the barrier between the worlds grew weaker, even if it was only fractionally. The Seed's Potential was largely drained, fully devoted to refining the servant to its cause.

———O — o — O ———

The big one was still wandering the area, but was no longer flailing in a blind rage a few days later. The Seed took this as a good sign that the ruse hadn't been discovered as of yet.

The Seed prepared to draw its bonded human here again. But just as it was about to activate the transfer, it noticed faint tinges of distress wafting over the bond between it and the mortal and stopped.

It forcefully sent its vision through the bond, and their conduit degraded slightly.

The Seed wanted to avoid interference, but if the mortal was in danger it would be forced to assist as best as it could.

That mortal was its only way out of this place. The Seed's concern turned to amusement as it received the context of the situation from the mortal's mind, and watched as the events continued to unfold. How tragic!

The mortal was consumed with concern for his lover as he should be. The Seed felt the wave of relief wash over the mortal as he realized that the allotted time for the transfer had already passed.

The Seed waited an extra moment to see if the two would do anything else. But the woman drew back a bit and went to release the bonded mortal from where he was pinned to the floor as they spoke more comforting words to each other.

The Seed quickly began the transfer before the woman could lose skin contact with the bonded mortal. The two twisted into existence together in the bedroom in the building above. The tether degraded farther, but the woman was a far greater prize than a stronger tether. So much Potential just sitting in her body ready for the taking! The man sat up and looked around in horror as the woman looked confused.

The Seed sent its amusement to the anchor Fulcrum. The woman's deep well of Potential had the mouth under its carapace practically salivating. She would fill the Seed's Potential back to where it had been a week ago and more before it created the Servant.

Fulcrum did not understand and the Seed dumbed it down to mortal language. It wanted the mortal to taste the irony of the situation. To think he would cause precisely what he was trying to prevent through his actions. All he had to do was pretend to have to go to the bathroom on Earth and none of this would have happened.

'What Drama from the Mortal! A Tragic Play worth some small delays. Good Choice, Fulcrum, Good Choice. She will be a Worthy Feast!'

The Seed burrowed upwards, ripping through the floor above it even as it felt the mortal start to move again. It would be futile, nothing would stop the Seed from getting every… last… Drop!

Chapter 81: A Nightmare With the Ones You Love - Multiple Fragments of Memory

Steven felt something malevolent stirring below and scrambled to his feet even as Jessica lay there stunned, blinking from the transition to Serenity. The malevolent thing below must have been the source of the awful voice he had heard, Steven wondered if Jessica had heard it too...

Steven rushed to the window and lurched to smash his fist through the glass pane. It shattered with a *crash* and the shards of glass puffed into mist, leaving an open window frame.

Jessica was sitting on the floor, her shock warring with confusion at Steven's sudden actions. She got her feet under her and stood, before standing in place unsure of what to do, "Steven, what's going on…"

"We have to go now! It's coming, Jessica. Now!"

Steven leapt forward and dragged her by the arm to the window before ushering her through the empty frame as fast as he could. After the initial shock she seemed to follow Steven's prompting and crawled out before dropping down onto the lawn.

Steven dived after her through the empty window frame after her, his urgency only increased as he felt the evil presence below him shudder into movement.

Jessica stood there staring Steven down, seeming to decide to go on the attack to cover her confusion, "Steven, you better tell me what's going on right now! Why are we crawling out the window and what was…"

Steven ignored her words and grabbed her arm again and kept pulling her forward as he began to run with her down the street. Jessica trailed behind with Steven tugging her forward, but kept up the pace well enough once she saw Steven's urgent expression. She kept talking when she got a breath, still panting.

"Steven… *uhhh* "What are we doing? Why…" *Oof,* Jessica held her arm to her side and muttered, "God, cramps. Ow," Her voice raised again as she panted, "Where are we going?"

Steven felt her slow down to a fast walk despite his silent tugs, but after a second or two, Steven felt like it was no use. His overwhelming dread grew greater and greater even as he finally replied, "Jessica, there's something in there. I can feel it. We have to run before it finds us…"

A massive crash sounded from the house they had just left and the two of them glanced back with wide eyes. Steven felt the thing behind him reach ground level even as Jessica picked up her pace again, limping slightly and hitching her breath as she kept running, but she was still falling behind.

The front entrance of their house exploded into mist as the black bone covered floating orb emerged. All around it the pavement cracked and wood shattered as Steven heard its invisible limbs strike every which way as it moved.

Jessica picked up the pace and Steven kept dragging her forward, even as the thing dashed towards them at blazing speed.

Steven knew they weren't going to make it, it would be on them in seconds. Just as Steven thought it was all over the thing stopped not twenty feet away hovering in place for a moment. Steven doubted his fear of it for a second.

Maybe his perception of its malevolence was just his own paranoia? It had sent him back to Earth last time after all, and had even healed him. But then Steven felt the thing's amusement and Jessica was lifted into the air, ripped away from his grip.

She thrashed and screamed as Steven saw the invisible tentacles push in her skin and pinch her clothing inwards to hold her in place, slowly drawing her back to thrash directly over the visible orb.

"JESSICA!" Steven leapt forward but was batted aside before he even got close by an invisible limb. Steven went rolling across the pavement from the blow, rolling to a stop before stumbling to his feet weakly.

"Steven! Steven! Ahhhhhhh!" Jessica screamed.

The top of the orb had folded open, exposing its repulsive mouth filled with teeth. Steven could hear its slobbering and wet growls even as he stumbled forward back towards it. Steven felt the thing's attention focus on him and that sense of amusement washed over him again.

Jessica thrashed harder and screamed louder as she was slowly lowered downwards, even as Steven heard the clicks and chomps from the mouth increase as she grew closer.

The thing was taunting him, Steven could feel it savoring the moment. Steven tried to run forward again, but fell again as the ground shook violently beneath him in the next moment. The creature paused and Jessica's slow descent halted in place.

"SHHHHHHRRIIIIIIIIIIIIIIII!"

A deafening screech sounded from behind Steven, nearly deafening him, before a massive hand descended from the sky and crunched into the orb's left side, sending black chunks of exoskeleton and pink flesh flying.

Steven felt pain and surprise from the thing as it dropped Jessica to the ground to dodge backwards as the titanic hand swept to the side to attempt to grab the thing as it fled.

The thing behind him was so tall, that when Steven turned his head all he could see was the massive leg barreling in his direction.

He only had a moment before the leg struck him with a glancing blow, sending him flying to the side even as the creature finished its step.

Steven went through the walls of a nearby house, the walls and furniture he impacted puffing to mist as his body spun rapidly to crash through them. Steven bounced again and felt the urge to vomit as he rolled over and over again.

The next instant froze in his memory, the view of the rapidly approaching kitchen bar filling his world. He tried to twist, but it was no use. Steven struck the counter edge with his upper chest and his momentum stopped suddenly, his head immediately slamming full force into the stone, knocking him out instantly.

Steven's body slumped to the floor, even as the rest of the slab his head had gone through slowly turned into a cloud of swirling mist.

―――O―o―O―――

The Seed dodged as the big one went to strike it again. The Seed had been distracted by indulging in its savory meal, and somehow not noticed the brute's approach before it was too late to dodge.

Since when had the big one been stealthy in any way?

With the Seed being heavily injured, and a quarter of its tentacles limp, it was taking glancing blows from the brute now with each blow, not quite as nimble now.

The Seed was given a choice of which way to dodge, as the big one's massive fist went for another overhand blow. Fighting like the dumb animal it was.

Dodge left for the savory meal of Potential, or right to retrieve the mortal Fulcrum? The female mortal had stumbled into the building in the street opposite after the Seed had lost its grip, seeming relatively uninjured. The mortal Fulcrum was severely injured, and if he died then the Seed might remain forever trapped here with the end of the portals. The choice was unfortunately obvious.

The fist came down and the Seed dodged right into the hole in the home's wall, gray mist wafting from its corners. The Seed rushed inside and scooped up the heavily injured body of the mortal Fulcrum before bursting through the back wall. It could treat the mortal's injuries later, but it couldn't trust the big one to not unwittingly crush the mortal in its battle with the Seed.

The Seed saw the big one's massive leg drawn backwards and it rushed away at an angle as the thing gave a solid kick into the mortal home, releasing a plume of mist into the air.

The Seed rushed off, using the mist as cover as the brute thrashed around in the fog. The big one stupidly tried to brush away the fog, only wasting time and blinding it even more as the mist lingered even longer to cling to the creature's moving limbs.

With the last burst of its Potential, the Seed sealed its wounds as well as healing the worst of the brain damage of Fulcrum until the human was back to only to the level of a moderate concussion.

There shouldn't be any permanent damage, but the Seed had to spend the last of its Potential anyway, may as well be for this.

The explosion of gray mist in the area had settled over the Seed as well and was slowly engulfing and sealing the Potential that it had left. As the Seed spent the last of its Potential left over healing its injuries and those of the mortal further, its core of Potential went dark once more. Smothered by the mists swirling around it, likely permanently until it could escape this place.

The Seed scuttled away, darting out of sight of the big one, outsmarting the stupid thing once again. Luckily, the Seed had thought ahead enough that its servant was still unconscious in another hidden cave separate from the portal.

All the Seed had to do was run and wait for the mortal Fulcrum to be drawn back to his world when the day ended. Most of the lingering damage would be healed during the transfer anyway.

A shame, that energy could have been spent on strengthening the portal itself. But better to preserve the Anchor Fulcrum and keep him healthy rather than let all of the Seed's preparations go to waste.

After mortal Fulcrum returned to his world all the Seed would have to do was wait for the clone to die off, and it could launch its counter attack on the big one.

But for now at least, the Seed had to hide.

————O—o—O————

Jessica stayed crouched behind the windowsill as the massive alien creature stood among the destroyed buildings in the distance. She assumed they were destroyed, she had felt the earth shake as she had run.

She had broken in there after running for a few minutes, not wanting to stay in the open in case god knows what else showed up. The glass shards had dissolved into the same gray mist as the window that Steven had broken.

Occasionally she would pop her head around the corner of the open windowsill and make sure the large alien wasn't coming her way yet. She could hear some rumbling in the distance, but it didn't seem to be getting closer just yet.

Jessica just hoped Steven was alright. Steven. She had lost him in the chaos when the large one had attacked the black ball. Jessica shivered as she remembered being slowly lowered towards that thing's jaws, totally helpless. If that thing hadn't come when it did… Well she was lucky it had interrupted her, that was sure.

"AHHHHH!—"

Jessica screamed in a high pitched voice as something small and furry darted through the window, before quickly cutting herself off. There was a squirrel, just sitting in front of her perched up on its hind legs staring at her. She stared back in total confusion as the animal just sat there inspecting her, only the soft rising and falling of its chest signaling that it was alive.

Jessica felt a faint pressure and got stabbing pains behind her eyes for a moment, forcing her to blink as she stared at the animal.

The squirrel remained there staring at her and Jessica resumed their strange standoff. Finally, the headache grew to be too much and Jessica looked away again. When she turned her head again the little thing was already scampering off back outside.

Jessica leaned against the wall and slowly slid down it to sit on the floor, and put her head in her hands. How could she be so wrong? All this time Steven had been telling her it was all real, this place.

She hadn't believed him and questioned him whenever he brought it up, hoping he would quit the delusion. But it was real. He had been dealing with all of this alone for all this time since he had come back to her. Bearing it silently.

How could he stand it? The silence here was deafening, even the crashes and rumbles from the massive footsteps muffled somehow, swallowed by this place. And all the empty buildings unnerved her.

Everything in this place was undisturbed, exactly as their owners had left it. She had even found someone's wallet inside, even if it dissolved into that mist a few moments after she picked it up. Were she and Steven all alone here with those terrifying creatures?

Steven had never mentioned this place being dangerous the few times he had spoken to Jessica about it. He had said this place was empty, and almost seemed wistful about it. Like it was one of those walks in the woods he had used to take in the woods alone, to get some time for himself. But he had said the dreams had stopped too after she watched and recorded him at midnight months ago just to sooth his paranoia. Even slowed down, nothing had looked different in the footage even if he claimed he had felt something.

He had said he had come back on his own after a day every time. Always one day exactly before he went back. A spark of hope ignited in Jessica's chest. Yes! All she had to do was make it that long and she would be brought back and Steven would be right there with her.

She could tell him how sorry she was, and support him the way she knew she had failed to in these last few months.

Jessica didn't know how long she sat there, questioning her life choices. Why had she thought forcing him to hold onto her had been such a good idea? Why hadn't she trusted him? She looked up at more motion at the window as the squirrel came crawling back through.

It did that same little stand on its back legs, furry chest puffed out and tail flicking behind it as it stared her down.

The faint pressure behind her eyes flared up again. Jessica reached out a hand and the thing didn't flinch. It went back on all fours and crawled forward cautiously before sniffing her hand for a moment, keeping their gazes locked.

Jessica whispered softly, not wanting to scare it, "What are you doing here, Mr. Squirrel? Ms. Squirrel? Wait, how would I tell?"

It kept sniffing her hand before shifting to inspect the bottom hem of her sweatpants from her extended legs, turning away for a moment. Jessica lowered her hand and just watched as it carefully sniffed the puffy fabric.

She felt like some kind of fairy princess, she had never been so close to a wild animal before. Oh, she saw them from a distance on her short hikes with Steven, but... Steven.

He would make it.

He had been here in this place for over a year.

He would be fine. She pushed down her doubt and fear. He would be fine, and they would both return safe and sound. Like nothing had ever happened. She would hug him and apologize, and he would make everything alright.

Something welled in her chest, but she was startled as she felt the squirrel's paws on her thigh. It was just sitting there so close, she was afraid to move. She didn't want to scare it away, her only companion in this weird place.

Suddenly the pain in her head flared to a burning level, and she slid down to the side. She cursed herself as she realized what was happening as she met the squirrel's gaze again.

The last thing she saw was the squirrel slowly approaching her face, its head cocked to the side curiously. One last thought drifted through her mind as she fell unconscious, *'I hope whatever this thing really is isn't a carnivore. I can't go out getting eaten by a fucking squirrel!'*

Chapter 82: What Have You Done with Her?

Steven woke with a gasp, face pressed against the floor. He rubbed his cold cheek as he sat up and inspected the room in his swimming vision. Steven tried to remember what had happened, but everything seemed so distant. He stumbled to his feet and fumbled at the doorknob before making his way to the front door.

"Jessica?" He croaked out. Where was she? What had happened? There were filled wine glasses sitting undisturbed at the table and Steven got a bad feeling. He fumbled at the front door a little more desperately as a vague sense of dread settled in his gut.

He stumbled outside and shielded his eyes from the sun and saw the man playing fetch with his dog on the opposite lawn who froze when he saw Steven's state.

Steven looked down at himself. His clothes were tattered, and there were long scratches and bruises all over his body where he had hit the pavement. Hit the pavement. In Serenity.

His mind attempted to snag on the memory, but his mind couldn't catch on it. Like a scratched record his mind just skipped, skipped, skipped, trying to retrieve the memory over and over again. He just stood there blankly for a moment as the memories darted out his clutches like mist. Mist... mist... There was something there too.

"... Ok? "

Steven tried to focus, but he was still swaying on his feet despite his best efforts and it was difficult to process the man's words.

"Fmmrrhappppppaaa?" Steven wasn't even sure what he was trying to say as he responded to the man in a mumble. Steven laid down, and the world began to spin a little less.

"... Ambulance. He's laying down now. What should I...?" The man's concerned words drifted through Steven's thoughts as the man continued his call with someone. Rude to start a call in the middle of a conversation. But Steven was hardly in a position to talk to him, so maybe it was alright. Steven closed his eyes for a moment, and woke to beeping machines and people in blue hospital scrubs around him. Hospital, that was where he was. But where...

"Jessiiicccccaaaa..."

The nurses rushed over to Steven as the memories slowly started filtering back.

"Whereeeee issss. Jessica?" There were only blank looks from the nurses, and all effort expended Steven laid back and drifted back to sleep. He would talk to her when he woke up, tell her everything would be fine.

———O—o—O———

He woke when everything went quiet. He glanced around the bed and lifted the sheet covering him which quickly turned to mist. He was back in Serenity, and his thoughts felt much clearer.

Steven walked around briefly, but still felt a little unsteady on his feet. He tried to open the door, but the thing was jammed, and far too strong to break from Steven's weak hits.

It was still hard to focus, but at least he could string something coherent together in his thoughts now. He was on the third floor of the hospital as well, so no escaping out the windows either. Eventually Steven settled back into his hospital bed to rest. Luckily he knew from experience he didn't have to eat in Serenity.

His thoughts meandered and tried to divert, but he focused and tried to think as he furrowed his brow. Jessica wasn't in here with him this time, so she should be safe. Steven frowned as something felt off about that.

His jumbled memories from when he got back were hard to bring forward, but somehow he didn't think Jessica had been around when he returned. But it had been morning, maybe she just went out to get help for Steven? Yes, that must have been it.

With that interpretation of events firmly settled in his mind, Steven pushed all the other horrible possibilities from his mind. She was fine. After a while, Steven went back to sleep and his thoughts returned to a jumbled mess.

———O—o—O———

"...Time sensitive. He would want this too, to find out the bastards who did this. Just give him some drugs, wake him up enough to give us something. Please, it has already been a whole week with no leads at all!"

Another man's voice cut in harshly, "Officer Smith, watch your tone! We understand your worry but this is hardly your…"

Steven opened his eyes and shifted as he saw the two men standing there glaring at each other, a woman nurse in blue scrubs standing to the side frozen, head bouncing rapidly between the two men as they spoke.

The man who was arguing with Ryan was wearing a gray suit and seemed to be important if his confident stance was anything to go by. His words trailed off as he turned to Steven. "...call." He glanced at the nurse who was staring at Steven's sudden awareness in shock. "Rachel, call the doctor, please. It seems the patient is alert."

Ryan opened his mouth to protest but the other man shut him down with one look. "You'll get your answers, Officer. After Doctor Kaltri runs some tests to determine his health. Only *then* will we discuss this further. You are on thin ice here, Mr. Smith. Just be patient."

They walked out of the room together before Steven could process what was happening, but Steven could see the way the vein on Ryan's neck was bulging dangerously as he contained his anger.

Fuck, what had happened? Steven hadn't seen him on such a short fuse in years... Well better or worse, Steven would find out soon after the doctor coming through the door made sure he wasn't going to drop dead any moment.

———O—o—O———

Ryan came back into the room after the tests were done, along with the same man in the suit. The hospital director he introduced himself as. "Steven. *FuLcRum*. Steven..."

Steven snapped back to attention at Ryan's voice. He felt much better but it was still slightly difficult to focus. "Y-yeah, Ryan. What were you saying?"

Ryan's voice was soft but urgent. "Look Steven, try to stay with me here, can you focus for a minute? You were attacked by whoever it was that took Jessica away, we think. Anything you remember will help us find her."

Steven blinked hard and his mind cleared a little, "Yeah. I can do that."

Ryan leaned in and spoke again, "Can you tell me the last thing you remember? Jessica is missing and you are..."

Steven sat up as he finally registered the words, "Jessica! She... She's not back? Where..."

"Back? Where, Where did she go Steven?! She's been missing for a week now, and you're the last one who's seen her. Did you see your attackers? What did they look like?"

"The... Serenity, the Dream. She's lost in Serenity Ryan, why didn't she come back? She should be back! It must have gotten her. No no no no!"

Steven's vision swam as Ryan shouted back over as the hospital director tried to usher Ryan out of the room. "No, I need to hear this! I don't care how delu... Don't touch me!" The two men argued as Steven's memories of what had happened came back. The two men went silent as I spoke again.

"She... She went to Serenity with me. Forced me to take her there, to prove it wasn't real. The thing in there was evil, I could feel it in my mind. It caught her and was going to swallow her whole.

"But then another came and the two creatures fought and we were separated. I was so sure she would make it. Why did I come back and not her? Serenity was never like this before. It was always so... Peaceful."

The two men stood staring at me in silence, and something welled in my chest. Something strange and unfamiliar. Ryan spoke up after a moment of silence, his voice still urgent and desperate. "Steven what the hell, you sound insane. Where is Serenity? What got her?"

The words shifted Steven's tone in desperation. There must be a way for Ryan to help, right?

"The floating black orb! It grabbed her with its invisible limbs, and she couldn't escape. The one bigger than a house came from nowhere and fought it, and the big one hit me in the chaos through a building."

"She must have run when the black orb was distracted! Then I woke up again at home. Are you sure she wasn't in the house when I woke up?"

Ryan's voice was laced with anger now, "You were the last to see her Steven. I should have expected something like this after how you returned to life last year. I always knew there was something off with you ever since you came back. *FulCrUm*, what did you do? I'll ask again. Where. Is. Serenity?"

The hospital director was looking nervous at Ryan's shift in tone, glancing at the nurse who started edging towards the door. "Now look Officer, is this really..."

"Quiet, you! This is between me and him now. I know he has answers, and he's going to talk," Steven blinked as everything started swimming out of focus again, "I... I..."

Ryan took a step forward as his voice grew louder. "Tell me! Where did you take her? What have you done?!"

He leaped forward and grabbed Steven by his hospital gown, the thin fabric balling under his clenched fist. Fulcrum could see his red face glaring down at him twisted in rage.

"It... It was my dream! Serenity is where I go in my dreams. I know it's real, and when Jessica touched me at the wrong moment she was brought there with me. I should have stopped her, warned her more. I would never hurt her."

Ryan began shaking Steven, "Tell me what you know! You...," Two hefty men in police uniforms had burst into the room and were hauling Ryan backwards away from Steven,

Steven's hospital gown ripping as Ryan refused to let go as he was hauled bodily backwards out of the room struggling.

"No, he has answers, it can save her." Ryan shouted, "No, let me at him! Her life. You can't, he's lying! He did something to her, I know it. It's the only..."

The hospital director remained behind with the nurse who returned to the room after the three struggling men left.

"..."

The suited man turned to the nurse, clearing his throat. "Rachel I'll be back in a minute, I should go deal with that."

He walked out the door as the nurse came over to the hospital bed, shooting nervous glances at Fulcrum as she fiddled with the machines. Fulcrum went to sit up, and the nurse jumped like a scared cat.

"Uhm, I'm sorry. I'll, uh, be back in a moment," she said.

With that she rushed out the door as fast as she could, leaving Fulcrum alone in the room again. Well, I guessed it could have gone worse. At least Ryan hadn't beaten any answers out of me.

After all, no one could know about Serenity. I shouldn't have talked about it until I was sure it was the only way. After all, that black orb had helped me return back through the portal the first time and even helped me heal my injuries.

I couldn't rush to conclusions thinking it had been attacking me. In fact, hadn't it been the big one that hit me into a building? That one seemed like the aggressor if anything. Next time I went back I should find the black orb. It could help me find Jessica and bring her back safely. Until then I should keep its existence to myself so I don't make anyone suspicious of me.

———O—o—O———

A much calmer officer was asking me questions now. I hadn't seen Ryan again since yesterday when he attacked me, "Now Fulcrum, you say you were in your bedroom with Jessica Smith when something hit you from behind, knocking you unconscious?"

"Yes, that's right Officer. Jessica was deeper in the room and I had my back to the door. The last thing I remember is falling to the ground and then waking up the next morning delirious."

The Officer licked his lips, looking slightly uncomfortable as he moved to his next question, "And when her brother questioned you, do you remember what you said to him?"

I shook my head. It was much easier to focus than even a day ago, I should have an easier time not letting things slip now, "It all seems blurry, really. I remember saying something about my recurring nightmare I keep having. I was very upset when I heard uh... Jessica... was missing, and I can't remember too clearly now."

"Yes, I understand this must be an emotional time for you. Now it's important to get the finer details. Now, when you fell did you hear anything behind you? Footsteps, voices, anything?"

"No, nothing."

"Alright, so what time exactly did you..."

The questioning continued as the officer kept getting smaller details of the day. Not that he got much out of it, the story was very simple. I had my back to the door, was hit with something, and lights out until the next morning. It's not like they thought I could fake the state I had come in with for the last week.

I just had to get ready. When I went back to Serenity, I would find... Her. I... Jessica. I would find Jessica, that's who it was. I would find her if it was the last thing I did.

Chapter 83: The Dream Continues for Fulcrum

My mind stuttered and jittered as I sat up in bed. What had I been doing? Oh right, I had been looking for someone. Someone in Serenity. The black orb had been helping me find her. Her name was on the tip of my tongue… Jessica.

My memory had been faulty ever since the incident two months ago where she disappeared. Must because of the blow to the head from whoever had attacked me.

Ryan was still pissed at me specifically, but I was sure he would forgive me once I found Jessica again and brought her back. I got to my feet and left the bedroom to start my day and make myself some Sunday breakfast.

— — — O — o — O — — —

My mind stuttered and jittered as I sat up in bed. What had I been doing? Oh, right. I was looking for a woman in Serenity. Her face was blurring in my mind, but she was important.

The first court date for my murder trial would start in a few days. Apparently I wasn't a flight risk, so I was only under house arrest over the course of the trial.

The court case was after Jessica had disappeared, and the police thought I was behind it even if there was no real evidence that wasn't circumstantial that I had done anything. At least I knew I was innocent though no matter what Ryan's raving voicemails he had been leaving said. I had been forced to issue a restraining order after against him after he had tried to attack me again right after I had left the hospital.

— — — O — o — O — — —

My mind stuttered and jittered as I sat up in bed. What had I been doing? Oh, right. I was looking for someone in Serenity.

I could barely even remember why, but I knew deep down I wouldn't stop until I found whoever they were. The trial had been ongoing for a few months, and Ryan had even taken the stand to testify against me.

He hadn't been a very credible witness, and my lawyer had torn him to shreds on cross examination. I still felt a little sad about Jessica's disappearance sometimes despite it having been months already. If only she had told me where she was going.

I was sure now that I must have upset her and caused her to leave somehow, despite my fragmented memories of that night. It was the only thing that made sense.

I was still staying in Jessica's place. She was only missing, and I was keeping everything tidy for when she came back. Despite her being declared dead like I was long ago during my missing year and a half.

She had left me the home in her will too, something that drew heavy suspicion during the trial. I had only met her parents once, but it was enough to understand why she hadn't left them anything in the will.

Those people were probably the most judgmental people I had ever met. Constantly belittling those around them, especially Jessica when Fulcrum had gone with her to meet them. Just an ingrained sense of superiority, as if they were more important than anyone else around them.

Fulcrum was glad he never ended up seeing much of them. No wonder Ryan had anger issues after being raised around people like that. Not that it excused Ryan's actions in the here and now. His last voicemail to me had been particularly nasty.

But I hadn't known she would do something like that. I was paying her mortgage and made sure not to disturb her room.

I tried to retain as many of her things as possible away from Ryan and her family not because I was greedy, but because it was *hers*. Not anyone else's. And it shouldn't be sold off, because she was coming back.

I didn't want her to be upset if her things had disappeared when she came back. I knew how that felt from first hand experience. I could only imagine that it would take hours to calm her down if all the things in her room were packed away and all in the wrong places.

She'd be relentless until I finished helping her put things back where they should be. I'd rather keep everything out how it was so she wouldn't have to deal with any of that.

Ryan had been livid during our most recent battle over inheriting Jessica's things. His voicemails had become more frequent and violent recently. His most recent one as an example.

I idly listened to his threats and shouting voicemail as I brushed my teeth. I still had a restraining order against him so he wasn't allowed to get close to me, so he wouldn't be able to do anything to me.

All the neighbors seemed to avoid me, likely hearing rumors of what had happened. Except one. Bill from the house across from me had recently moved in, and was friendly enough to me. Maybe he just hadn't heard the rumors yet. I guess I'll see what he will do in the next few weeks as he settles in.

Oddly enough, I found a squirrel with a black diamond fur pattern on its back sitting in my bedroom this morning. I was surprised at its presence but after opening a window, the thing had leapt out and disappeared into the night. How had it even gotten in? It been so calm...

———O—o—O———

My mind stuttered and jittered as I sat up in bed. It had been a year since Jessica had left, and I still couldn't find the mysterious person in Serenity. I had wandered constantly, but no matter how far I went, the place was empty.

Even that black orb had disappeared after the first few months, leaving me alone again. I was declared not guilty in the court case due to lack of evidence. But the neighbors and the rest of the town collectively decided that I must be guilty anyways and thoroughly shunned me.

I finished listening to another angry voicemail from Ryan blaming me for all his troubles. How was it my fault his pay had been docked because his three attempted attacks on me? One at the hospital, another right after I left, and the most recent one just last week.

The only reason I wasn't pressing charges was because it wasn't what Jessica would have wanted for her brother. But I had warned him what would happen if he put his hands on me again.

At least I could ignore the voicemails if I wanted to. It was even nice sometimes listening to them and knowing that someone else out there still cared about Jessica even after so long.

I wonder where she went.

———O—o—O———

The Seed curled its invisible tentacles inwards as the mortal Fulcrum was drawn into 'Serenity' once more. What an amusing label for this place. Immediately the mortal stood and walked out the door, intent on finding his partner despite the Seed's best efforts. The mortal barely even remembered what she looked like, or that she was even in this place.

But no matter what the Seed changed, the mortal always went out as if to search for something anyways. Even if he was unaware who he was looking for.

The Seed wouldn't have minded normally, but the mortal was becoming more and more persistent as time went on and resisted its diversions harder and harder each time. And all would be lost if he stumbled onto the small area the Seed had been subtly steering him away from.

The tether to his world was strengthening more and more as time went on, and two days in Serenity ago, the Seed was able to force one of its tentacles through the connection to inspect the other side.

The tentacle only lasted a few seconds before the connection was broken again and the Seed was forced to withdraw, but it proved that the Seed's plan was working. The Seed had no Potential left, so it had no second chances if this attempt failed.

The mortal Fulcrum almost wandered into the restricted area again, and the Seed quickly worked to divert his attention again, subtly shifting his path away.

But it was growing harder, as the mortal had already known he had explored these other areas over and over at this point. The Seed came to a decision. Its servant would show itself and help pacify the mortal.

And pacify the Servant who had also begun to grow a little restless. Despite following orders to the letter, it was showing unexpected deviations as it grew bored with its same route day after day. It seemed the base personality was shining through.

Unfortunately the Servant's mind was resistant enough that the Seed couldn't fully remove its memories or significantly change its personality again without any Potential at its disposal.

Giving the Servant interactions with the mortal should provide something new and exciting and keep it focused on its other tasks after it is done with the mortal.

The Servant's patrol of the restricted area was pointless if the mortal Fulcrum would wander through and put himself in danger either way. Diverting the Servant for thirty or so minutes to interact with the mortal Fulcrum should be enough.

The Seed sent its orders to the servant and it shifted its patrol route eagerly. The Seed hoped this could finally keep the two contained and safe. There was no need to enrage the heavily injured big one now that it was so incapacitated. And without Potential it would luckily remain that way for a long time.

Hopefully long enough for the Seed to escape this place and make it to Earth where it had always originally meant to be.

———O—o—O———

I continued my wandering. I felt like I must have seen everything in this world in the last fifty days of exploration. One day a week for the last year on Earth. There was a strange looping effect present.

One day, two Earth months ago, I had just walked in a straight line for the whole day. The suburban neighborhoods shifted into forest and woodlands the farther I walked.

I kept walking, and as the sun went down I finally saw something else in the distance. Hurrying my pace, I jogged forward until something came into view. Homes and a street. As the shadows lengthened, I kept walking down the unfamiliar street. The orange glow of the horizon slowly faded and when I was lost, I noticed a familiar street sign.

I… I was on the other side of town. Knowing the way, I ran as fast as I could to my home where I had begun this morning. It was fully dark now, and only the sound of my footsteps echoed in the silent world.

Finally panting, I stumbled to a slow stop in front of my home. Going inside, I quickly went to the bedroom and checked the dresser. The little decoration that was supposed to be there was missing.

I always picked it up in the morning to see how long it would take to dissolve. It took hours sometimes now, and I just carried it in my pocket until it finally disappeared.

Somehow, I had returned to where I started. After that, I did it again. And again. No matter what direction I went, I always returned right back home.

———O—o—O———

Seventy days in Serenity. About a year and four months since Jessica disappeared on Earth. I didn't hold any hope she would return anymore. Was it because of me that she left? Ran away?

I still thought about it occasionally in the quieter moments. But somehow, I felt that whatever I would find in Serenity would provide me with answers on what had happened to her.

I felt like I was getting closer each day, and my life on Earth faded into the background as I grew obsessed thinking about what sections of Serenity I had missed searching. I had noticed recently that things had begun to freeze in place. They had long since stopped dissolving into the mist when they were moved.

There was a storm one night on Earth, and I found a leaf hovering in the air, frozen twirling in the frozen wind inside Serenity. When I touched the leaf it dropped to the ground. I wasn't sure what it meant, but it was strangely beautiful to see.

I looked around, only to find myself on a familiar street again. It seemed I had gotten lost in my own thoughts again. I turned back, realizing I had bypassed a whole section of town. Again.

Something strange was going on there, but I shrugged it off and trudged back to where I knew I should go. There were only four sections left in Serenity that I hadn't fully explored for one reason or another, and I told myself I would look at this one today.

My mind wandered again as I turned the corner, bringing up old memor... No, I have to stay focused! I felt in my gut that something important was here. I couldn't let myself get lost and go the wrong way again.

All I could hear was my heavy breathing for a while as I struggled to focus. But eventually I paused mid-step. There was a sound in front of me. The sound of footsteps. I started to run. Could it be Jeeesssssssicc... Jes... woma... another person in here?

I had to find them, this was what I had been searching for! I skidded around the corner and came face to face with a monster. Its red plates haphazardly covered its form which was covered in dozens of eyes. It had interlocking plates covering its humanoid arms like gauntlets, and bundles of tentacles hanging down over its mouth.

Steven widened his eyes as he stared at the thing.

"Wha... Ge...Get back!" he shouted. The creature reached one hand out for Steven, fingers splayed outwards, and he scrambled back only barely stopping himself from falling to the ground.

He rapidly turned and ran as fast as he could back to where he came breathing hard. He threw a glance over his shoulder, and saw the thing standing in the middle of the street just watching him leave.

Even when it was out of sight, he kept running, not even sure where he was going, just sure he had to get away. When he got back to his home, the black orb was there floating silently in the center of his kitchen above the counter.

Something grabbed me, and I- he struggled as the thing lifted Steven off of the ground with its invisible tentacles.

Just how it had done with Jessica. Jessica! She... She was here, she was the one Steven had been looking for! He thrashed more as the tentacles gripped tighter, until something touched Steven's mind.

———O—o—O———

I relaxed as the Seed put me back down on the ground gently. Despite not being sure it would understand me, I spoke anyway.

"Sorry about that. I was just surprised when you grabbed me. I'm just jumpy because of something I saw today. Not that... Well, It was friendly. Ally. Yes, I just overreacted when I saw it. A little frightening even though I know it's a friend."

I blinked again and the shadows from the sun shifted in a moment, and the black orb was gone. I looked around in surprise, what had that been? What had just happened? I was about to go back outside when I suddenly heard something at the door. The sound of shuffling feet, and a blurred shadow standing just outside on my porch.

"Clack *rrrrririiiiip*. Clack *rrrrrrip*, Clack *rrrririipppppp*," A sharp rap followed by a ripping sound like that of duct tape being removed from something. I walked to the door and peeked through the keyhole, and there was Ally standing there knocking on the door.

"Clack *rrrrririiiiip*. Clack *rrrrrrip. Clack riiiiip...*," It kept knocking as I just watched it through the side window. What could it want? As much as I knew it wasn't hostile, I didn't want to come within arms reach of it again.

Eventually, I decided to retreat farther into the house. Hopefully it would go away when I didn't answer.

Needless to say, it did not go away. It just kept knocking over and over again. I tried plugging my ears, but the sound of the knocking reverberated through the house. Over and over and over. It was maddening.

After what felt like hours, I tried to escape out of the back and for the first time the knocking stopped. I went to the kitchen and opened the door and took one slow step outside, inspecting the area carefully.

I heard a sound to my left and spun to look as Ally turned the corner. I met one of its eyes that widened as the black pupil seemed to bore right into my soul.

A wave of images crashed over my mind, and I collapsed limp to the ground twitching as my brain failed to process the deluge of input. I closed my eyes, and when I opened them I was tucked back in my bed on Earth. I stumbled out of bed with a migraine and made my way to the bathroom.

I looked in the mirror, and it was a horror show. Blood was trickling from every orifice. From my ears, gushing from my nose. And two streaks of bloody tears wept their way down my face from my tear ducts.

With trembling hands, Steven called the ambulance, even as he watched the flow of blood gradually stop. Only the piercing headache and dried blood remained behind as the EMTs arrived.

———O—o—O———

Steven was brought to the hospital and everyone was very concerned, but the tests didn't show anything wrong with Steven. They had him schedule an appointment with a specialist in two weeks, the quickest time they had.

Steven wondered how he had ever thought that thing had been a friend... It had flattened him with a single glance. Red.

Steven needed a name for the thing, and the color of its plates were good enough for now. It was better to think of it as a 'scary humanoid monster' every time anyway.

When Steven got back home, he frowned at the strange patch of stripped paint on the front door. *Was that always been there?* It must have been, there was no way that thing could affect the world outside of Serenity. Right?

———O—o—O———

I was back in Serenity and I looked forward to Ally's return. Red, as I had decided to call it also from the color of its plates. It had injured me last time, but thinking back on it and recalling the images I had seen it hadn't felt malicious. Just an alien perspective as the images came with dozens of viewpoints layered on top of each other.

I just had to focus on one and ignore the others, and I shouldn't get so overwhelmed. Then I could properly communicate with Ally and ask it what it was doing here.

As it got later in the day, I heard the creature's odd knock on the door. I only hesitated for a moment before throwing the door open for Ally. I met its eyes again and the wave of images resumed. I tried to hold onto one and focus on it, and it seemed to work.

Seeing what I was doing, Ally slowed the flood of images and my pain was much less. Blood still leaked from everywhere, but I managed to stay awake even if my knees went weak for a moment.

After a few seconds it all stopped, and the one image filled my mind. Something blue, a splash of white in a few perspectives. It was fluffy and misty almost like.

"A cloud? The sky?" I muttered under my breath. Was this... I turned to Ally who was standing there patiently staring at me.

"Is this the sky?" I asked in a louder voice. The thing's facial tentacles thrashed wildly and it jumped up and down a little in what appeared to be excitement as I felt something resonate in the bond between our minds. The bond I had only barely felt before before it began to vibrate.

"SKIIIIIIIII," Ally screeched and I covered my bleeding ears at the sheer volume of the noise. My hands came back red again and I stared at them for a moment before looking up at the sound of movement from Ally.

Ally had turned around and was wandering further down the road, seeming to have received what it had come for. When I returned home to Earth I had to replace the sheets on my bed again. They had been covered in blood again.

Luckily the bleeding stopped a few minutes after I returned to Earth. I wonder how I was going to explain this to the specialist if this happened again when I came back from Serenity next week.

What would they even treat for this? What would I even say to them? Should I even go, it sounds like a waste of time if I know they won't have any solutions for me.

— — — O — o — O — — —

One hundred days in Serenity. Just under thirty days since I first saw Red. Just under two years from Jessica's disappearance on Earth. I still got a pounding headache from communicating with Red, but the bleeding was getting less severe and frequent over time. I was still seeing those doctors regarding my bleeding, but I would likely stop soon. They didn't have any real answers for me.

Especially since it healed so fast anyways, so it wasn't the massive problem I had thought it would be initially.

The blood was something easily wiped away with a few wet paper towels, purely cosmetic after the first few minutes. The images for Red's communications got clearer and clearer, even if they were often difficult to interpret at times.

Red was enthusiastic and very expressive for a creature that could barely speak with what I had briefly seen was an octopus beak underneath the mat of tentacles on its face.

I didn't know how I had ever been so frightened by it. Well, I knew why but seeing it now in front of me it was hard to reconcile how I felt before and the familiarity I felt now. Red turned and walked off again. I almost looked forward to this part of my days in Serenity, at least it was something interesting and special. I felt myself forming a real bond with the creature.

My life on Earth wasn't exactly great right now. Everyone thought that I was guilty of murdering Jessica, the rumors only strengthened by my year and a half disappearance preceding that.

The last of my friends had finally abandoned me, showing their true colors, and I was an outcast to society. Ryan's social crusade against me seemed to stick in at least some of their minds, even if nothing had ever been proved. Or that the charges against me had already been dismissed long ago. I wasn't the only one Ryan was angrily ranting to about how evil I was, and the others Ryan spoke to actually listened to him.

Jessica had been well-liked in town, and those emotions shifted into similarly large distaste for me as a result after everything that had happened. I was shunned by everyone but my neighbor Bill. Bill was curt when he spoke to me but at least he never actively avoided me.

I saw a woman cross the road one time when she noticed my approach, clutching her confused kid's hand tightly.

That was... Ouch, that had been a lot. Made me feel horrible about myself. Earth just felt like another place now. I stared off after Red as it ambled off down the street. Now this place... This was my home. Fulcrum's home. And despite everything, I was glad I was brought here.

If only Jessica could be here with me to see it...

Chapter 84: Making Friends in the Dream - Mortal (Jessica) Fragment

Jessica slowly blinked awake, her face pressed against a cold floor. With a yawn, she sat up and looked around her, blinking. She was splayed out on a wooden floor, and she vaguely remembered she had stumbled into here last night.

It seemed to be early morning and the area was abandoned and unfamiliar. Had she drunk too much celebrating with Steven? Her head was throbbing and the morning light caused her to shield her eyes. She never did have a very high tolerance for alcohol...

She looked down and groaned as she saw her sweatpants were stained with the dirt and ripped in places. What a shame, and they were so comfortable too... Well, where was Steven? Why was she... *Oh, you little rat!*

Jessica leaped at the squirrel that appeared on the windowsill as her memories came rushing back. That little thing had knocked her out last night somehow and given her this killer headache.

The thing jumped out of sight with a squeak as Jessica just kind of rolled over, tripping over herself as she tried to leap up from a sitting position at the animal. She heard it running off outside, then silence again.

Despite herself, Jessica couldn't stop from yawning again as she stiffly made her way to her feet.

Her legs protested the treatment, seeming to be paying her back for all the adrenaline fueled sprinting that she had done yesterday. Jessica leaned around the empty window frame and inspected the surrounding area, which was totally devoid of life besides the grass and trees.

She hid herself against the wall and shuffled in place. She had to find Steven, but what should she do? She had no idea what other kinds of things were in this place, and Steven had been in here for way longer than she had been.

He would definitely know how to navigate this place. Jessica warred with herself for a moment. What if the second she left, Steven came by and he missed her?

If Steven had only been here for a day at most before, then it had already been way longer than that for her. So unless she could find him, she was probably stuck in here with those two monsters. She shivered again as she thought about the fight between the two. The squirrel attacking her showed that other things could be in here too. And they all could be hostile. *Well, at least the squirrel didn't eat me... Not really sure what its goal was supposed to be though...*

After thinking a little more about it, Jessica decided where she should go. There was a good crossroads a mile or two away from here. There was a house nearby that she knew looked onto the two crossed main roads there.

If she hid in that house then she could wait for Steven to walk by and then shout out to let him know that she was there.

As she walked nervously through the town while trying to stay as quiet as possible, she thought she saw a flicker of movement in the corner of her vision. She whirled and widened her eyes as much as she could, as if that would somehow help her see better.

But everything was still again. After a long moment, Jessica turned back around and began to walk a little faster. The sooner she got inside a building the less likely that something would see her. She soon found the house she was looking for and made her way inside after smashing another side window as quietly as she could.

Pulling up a chair, she pulled down the blinds and moved one of the slats upwards so she could see through. That way it would be harder for people to see her from the street but still let her see out. With that done, she sat there and prepared to sit and watch. Steven would come any minute now...

———O—o—O———

Three very boring days later, Jessica had still not seen Steven and was beginning to get worried. She knew he would come for her, but maybe she had chosen the wrong place.

Maybe she should move somewhere better. But despite her restless thoughts she stayed in place. This was like she had been lost on that trail one time when she had first started dating Steven.

She had always been less outdoorsy than him, he had surged ahead on the trail and not realized that she had fallen behind. Before she knew it, she was alone and she had accidentally wandered off the forest path and was truly and utterly lost after only a few steps and getting turned around.

She had kept wandering around fruitlessly for over an hour as Steven frantically searched for her after realizing his mistake. She smiled a bit as she remembered his expression when he found her.

She had been so mad at him. It was the first time she ever really laid into him full force. It made her feel like such an idiot afterwards when he explained you were supposed to stop and try to retrace your steps once you realized you were lost.

Jessica had just stupidly kept walking in circles and turned herself even more around until Steven heard her occasional shouts and came to the rescue.

After she had calmed down a little, she had been mortified at her angry outburst, thinking she had scared another guy off with her sudden temper. He had been silent as they walked back to their cars.

But after she tried to apologize to him later, he had just laughed it off and said he deserved it for leaving her behind. If she just stayed in place, then he had promised that he would come and find her next time they got separated.

He would find her.

Or maybe Steven was dead and Jessica was trapped here all alone with aliens that wanted to eat her.

$$---O-o-O---$$

It had been five days and Jessica noticed strange things were happening with her body. At first she had looted the pantry for some foot to eat. It was pretty well stocked even if she had no way to cook and the refrigerator didn't work.

Oddly enough the stuff inside didn't go bad, just staying as they were despite being in the room temperature refrigerator with no electricity in the whole building.

But after the second day, Jessica had missed breakfast and lunch accidentally and realized that she didn't really feel that hungry even into the night. The food still tasted good, but she just didn't feel really hungry at all ever since she had come to Serenity. She also hadn't had to go to the bathroom either ever since she got here.

It was a little frightening, honestly, that she hadn't noticed it until now. But at least she didn't have to worry about those things anymore. Imagine if one of the creatures came out to ambush her right as she was on the toilet?

Now looking out the blinds, she was sure Steven was coming for her any moment. This town was big, but not that big right? And this was a main intersection, of course he would come by here at least once. Maybe he was just searching another part of town for her. Being systematic about it. She just had to be patient.

$$---O-o-O---$$

It had been eight days now, and Jessica had been very fucking patient. She hadn't even left this place, too afraid she would miss Steven if she left. She hadn't even slept all that much. She still did sleep, but just like peeing or eating it didn't seem to be something she had to do anymore if she didn't want to.

Surely after so long Steven would have found her by now? Or at least walked by the crossroads? What if he had passed by in the few times she had been sleeping?

It had been two months on Earth already if this place worked how she thought it did from what Steven had told her of how it worked. She had to go out there and search for him, she couldn't stand waiting inside for another second!

She went out the door and crept to the main street, knowing she wanted to investigate where her house had been. She wondered if her parents would try to take it from Steven after she gave it to him in her will.

It sounded like something they might to do if they felt they deserved to own her things. She had changed the will without telling Steven right after he had returned from the dead. He had taken a long time to actually end up proposing to her.

She reached down and rubbed the engagement ring as a reminder that that at least was something to look forward to when she got back.

Now, to investigate back where she had arrived! She hadn't done that earlier because she wasn't sure if that black alien ball thing would still be around that area. It hadn't come for her where she had been holed up yet, so she assumed it had some kind of territory it stayed in.

She crept closer to where the copy of her house should be, making sure to stay close to the buildings, and scouting her surroundings before she moved an inch forward. She was now almost on the turn to her street, and was getting steadily more nervous.

For all she knew the black orb could attack her any moment. But she couldn't turn back now when she was so close.

Jessica was about to round the corner when she jumped at the sound of chittering to her side. She twisted mid-air to see the same stupid squirrel standing there on its hind legs, staring at her again. Nah, no way was she letting this thing knock her out again.

She darted forward and poked her foot at it, hoping to scare it away. It went on all fours and retreated a few feet before stopping and going back on its hind legs to stare at her again.

She turned away, not wanting to meet its eyes. After a few seconds she glanced back and saw it running off again, bushy tail waving behind it as it ran. She let out a sigh of relief to see it go. No matter how cute it was, it was dangerous.

Jessica put it in the back of her mind as she peaked around the corner. Hopefully the squirrel didn't come back until she was out of this place.

Carefully, she made her way to the house opposite the copy of her home. She was in the side yard crouching behind a small fence, and saw movement through the windows.

Was it Steven? She couldn't be sure… She crept closer risking making herself more visible for a better view through the window. The ground shook for a moment and Jessica stumbled slightly before she could see the human figure moving inside.

"Krrrrrrrr," Jessica froze and slowly turned to see something standing behind her, hissing. Its reddish bone plates stood in contrast to its dozens of dark eyes scattering its form. Remembering the squirrel, Jessica quickly looked at the ground even as she turned to run. Out of the corner of her eye she saw the large creature lumbering towards her, barely slower than her fastest sprint.

"STEVEN! STE…," she screamed at the top of her voice.

She only got a few steps before the ground shook again even more violently and she stumbled to her left. A whistling of air sounded behind her followed by a *crack* of the pavement behind her as the creature tried to hit her with an overhand blow and barely missed.

Jessica was panting now, and saw the figure in the window had turned and was rushing to the door. She kept running as best as she could, and barely dodged another heavy blow that cracked the concrete behind her.

"SkriiiiiHHHHNNNNNNNNNNNGGGGGGGGG," The creature's screech from behind her was overwhelmed by a booming cry in the distance that rattled Jessica's skull from its sheer volume.

The ground shook again as a multi story tall figure lumbered into view, a human sized figure with yellow bone plates similar to the one attacking her sitting on its shoulder. Jessica desperately glanced at the door to the house which remained firmly closed.

She was sure she saw Steven rushing to leave seconds ago, why wasn't he coming out? She kept running at an angle across the street away from her red alien attacker, but the thing had stopped to look at the massive creature rapidly approaching them. It let out a high pitched screech of defiance and the big thing actually stumbled a tiny bit, missing its footing as it charged.

Jessica could barely stand now from the continuous earthquakes all around her as the massive creature drew closer and closer as it charged towards them. Jessica finally reached the house to the left of hers and dove through the front window, shielding her face as she crashed through.

As she expected, the glass shards dissolved into mist even before they hit the ground, leaving her uninjured as she hit the wood floor on the other side.

She crawled deeper into the building as deep impacts sounded outside, even as the ground jumped and bucked around her, some sections of the ground even turning into that gray mist under the violent shaking. More screeches and crashes outside as Jessica flopped uselessly on the floor.

Then, just when she thought it was over... *Crash!* A massive hand smashed through the wall behind her and made a fist, scooping up Jessica in its grip before she could even react.

She was surrounded by a cage of interlocked bone plates only a little bigger than she was. Jessica pounded on the walls as hard as she could before she was sent flying every which way as the thing holding her began to move, rattling her around violently like she was in a washing machine.

There was a sense of movement, although its stride was odd, almost like it was limping and stumbling drunkenly from side to side as it moved with her clutched at the center of its massive hand.

After what felt like forever, the motion finally stopped and the hand around her opened back up to show daylight. Jessica tumbled out onto soft dirt and grass as the big creature stepped back and sat down with a loud thump, seeming unsteady.

Jessica nursed her scraped and bruised knuckles from pounding the hard bony walls of her former prison with her fists for a moment.

Seeming to ignore her, the massive creature's various eyes all closed at once and it laid on its side curled into a ball. A moment later, its body went still as if asleep. All of its multitude of eyes closed and its breathing became long and slow.

Out from inside the ball of the big creature emerged a yellow creature similar to the red one that had attacked her, and that damned squirrel perched on top of its shoulder.

Well, at least she knew now how they had found her. That little traitor had brought them right to her. But it had probably saved her life, so maybe the thing wasn't out to get her after all.

Chapter 85: A New Life in the Dream - Multiple Fragments of Memory

The Seed watched expectantly as its servant went to dispatch the mortal female. She could give the Seed the Potential to accelerate its plans if she had escaped too much contamination by the mists. It was a possibility, if a slim one.

The mortal Fulcrum started to run outside to defend her after a moment of shock at hearing her voice. The Seed knocked him out with a flicker of its attention and the mortal Fulcrum went sprawling to the floor, unconscious after only a few steps.

The Seed would have to work hard to cover up this memory in the mortal's mind. Unfortunately, it couldn't truly erase much from the mortal's mind, only suppress information and his recall in specific ways. The Seed could sense that the clone it had left with the big one had been altered so it would no longer go through its programmed death cycle any longer.

To think the large brute would be so adept at manipulation of Potential in others... That was the only explanation, that the creature had used the Potential lingering from the clone's creation to make the necessary changes.

The big one's main core of Potential should be just as suppressed as the Seed's if not more.

The ground rumbled and the Seed sensed the big one approaching. Had it been waiting for the Seed to be distracted? As the big one drew into sight, the Seed ordered its Servant to stop its chase of the mortal.

Better for her to hide before the big one realized she was there, it may try to steal the Potential from the Seed to empower itself. The Seed linked itself to the Servant and together they forced open the mental connection. The Seed felt resistance as the thing tried to keep the connection closed, but the Seed was able to still pry it open with some effort.

The Seed and the Servant launched their telepathic assault together, quickly pushing forward through into the big one's mental defenses. The Servant scrambled away and leapt to the side as the big one tried to land a drunken kick on it as it drew close. The Servant's mental assault stopped and slowed from the physical distraction, leading the Seed to gain less mental ground.

The big one crouched down and stuck its hand into the house next to the home the Seed was burrowed under. Leaping on its distraction, the Seed launched a new wave of mental assaults. It had to do as much damage as possible before the massive hand crushed the female mortal inside and gained her Potential to help it fight back.

Despite fixing the clone's programmed death, the big one had apparently not restored its aptitude for mental combat the Seed had intentionally removed from the clone. The clone's flailing excuse of a defense of the big one's mind was barely a factor as the Seed plowed right through to slice at the big one's mind with harsh images of negative emotion.

The big one flinched but otherwise continued its motions inward towards the female mortal, attempting to ignore the Seed's mental attack.

The Servant had run out of arm's reach of the big one by now and turned back to assist the Seed even as the big one drew its closed fist back out of the house. The Seed drew back for a moment and reconnected with the Servant to prepare their defenses.

The big one would use the Potential it had just gathered any moment now and the battle would be more than even, tilted to the big one's favor even, if it was used expertly. However, due to the previous damage the Seed and Servant had been able to inflict the Seed saw itself at a slight advantage anyways.

And that was assuming the creature used the Potential optimally, based on its prior manipulations from within the clone. The Seed and Servant firmed their defenses and slowly began to gather mental energy for an overwhelming counterattack when the big one struck back as it stood to its full height.

But the attack never came. The big one just turned and began to stumble away without a fight. It seemed that the Seed's assault had at least done some damage to it.

After being stunned for a moment or two by the big one's sudden retreat, the Seed leapt back into action as it felt the connection fade as the big one receded into the distance.

The Seed actively fought with renewed vigor to close the connection, but it was a losing battle. The Seed and the Servant launched their collective assault all at once, and it blasted through the weakened mental defenses of the big one. The large creature went stumbling and almost fell, but managed to stay upright. But the Seed could feel that one more assault could shatter its fractured mind.

But in the aftermath of the collective assault, the big one managed to sever the connection with what the Seed could feel was a severe strain on it.

It stumbled away into the distance as the Seed watched. Why had the big one not used the Potential from the mortal, had she escaped its attack? The Seed had its Servant inspect the area as closely as it could, but there was no sign of the mortal. She must have escaped in the chaos, unfortunately.

Well, over time she would be infected by the mists and be useless to the both of them. Perhaps she had already been fully infused with the mists and hadn't given the big one any Potential to work with at all.

With the big one so mentally injured, the Seed would be satisfied with that outcome. The big one would have to perform heavy mental reconstruction on itself after this to survive. But even in such a state, its physical strength was not anything to underestimate, so the Seed and its valuable Servant would not approach wherever it ended up settling for its healing.

The Seed had the clear advantage now, and all it had to do was wait and prepare for their final battle. The borders of this world were shrinking, centered around the portal that the Seed had constructed around the tether between it and the Anchor Fulcrum.

Eventually, the big one would be forced to come to it on the Seed's home territory if it stayed in place.

The Seed's telekinetic tendrils on the other side of the tether had begun collecting smaller animals to draw through to this place for their Potential. Each transportation strained and weakened the tether slightly, but the Seed needed at least some Potential available to it if it was to escape in the end.

Every fourth transport of the mortal anchor it should be able to take one or two small animals from the other side of the portal and add their tiny amounts of Potential to itself.

That was as much as the tether could take before risking its integrity and risking it breaking completely. The Seed had considered drawing in another human as well through the tether to the Anchor Fulcrum, but the Seed knew that the tether could never support something of that size being drawn here again.

The tether would be destroyed under the strain. So the Seed had to slowly build its reserve through the small animals it captured in the future. It should never be in a situation where it was so vulnerable again, even if it would take even longer now for the tether to be strong enough for the final phase.

It had been a mistake drawing the female mortal here, even if the strain of the tether had been severely reduced because she'd been touching the Anchor Fulcrum and been carried along with him here to this place rather than being transported here completely on her own.

And all the Seed had to do was prevent the mortal Fulcrum from getting too close to wherever the big one collapsed and the Seed would be safe.

It could just wait and slowly rebuild its Potential to open the final portal and sit tight as the big one recovered its wounds after this. The Seed would send the Servant to begin scouting tomorrow.

Hopefully by the time the big one reawakened, the Seed would already have activated the portal and made its way to the other side and escape this place. Leaving the big one and the rest to be crushed in the collapsing walls as this world shrank to nothing.

—— — (Mortal Jessica Fragment) — ——

Jessica crept forward, the newly dubbed Yellow meandering behind her. The days began to blend together as she awkwardly interacted with the strange figure and even more strangely intelligent squirrel alongside it before doing their daily excursion.

She had lost count of how long it had been after twenty or so days in this place, but it felt like it had been much longer than that.

She still didn't have to eat or even drink anymore, so even having meals was optional now. And Jessica was still trying to make her way back to Steven stealthily. She had seen him in that house, she was sure of it thinking back.

Whatever reason he didn't come out of the door, he was there and should be able to get her out of here with him. But she couldn't even make it past its alien guard to see him again in all this time.

The squirrel was intelligent, Jessica had only realized how intelligent when she had absentmindedly asked if the red creature was out ahead after it returned from another of its periodic disappearances. It went on its two back legs like it usually did when communicating and shook its head from side to side very deliberately in response.

Jessica had been surprised to say the least, and after some basic questions it became clear that not only did the squirrel understand when she spoke but also could answer things only a human should know.

Like math.

Jessica had asked the animal about simple multiplication and division and the thing had tapped out the number that was the answer by clapping its paws together the right amount of times.

It still tried to meet Jessica's gaze whenever it could, but when Jessica started to get a headache again the strange mental pressure would stop much to her relief.

Maybe it had just not known her limits the first time? It really was quite friendly with Yellow so far and the two seemed quite close.

Seeing this, Jessica was slowly getting over her initial distrust for the squirrel and relaxed as nothing bad happened as time continued to pass. She had probably been just assuming the worst of what had happened when the squirrel had first appeared. She was sure there was a good explanation for it with how friendly the squirrel was being towards her now.

The alien guard, creatively dubbed Red by the colors of its bone plating, rounded the corner. Somehow it always knew where to be to block the way when she tried to leave the small zone it had them trapped in. It looked almost identical to Yellow except their different colored plates.

Jessica cursed and looked down as Yellow picked her up and sprinted back to where the big one still lay unconscious, slinging her over its shoulder like a sack of potatoes.

Jessica already knew Red could knock her out with a look, like it had the first day. She had woken up with a pounding headache, back by the sleeping big creature while not being sure how long she had been out.

The next time she had struggled and protested, punching at Yellow's hard plates while still closing her eyes while being manhandled, but it was no use. Yellow was too strong and had too tight a grip on her for her to escape it.

It didn't hurt her though and Yellow was gentle in its grip, even if the sharp edges of its bone plates had cut her a few times by accident.

She had slowly gotten used to being slung over Yellow's shoulder and carried away by now. She just slumped as she accepted her fate as she was carried away from Red and out of sight, knowing that Yellow was just trying to protect her. Even if it was just as embarrassing each time it happened.

Yellow wasn't as fast in a sprint as she was, but it truly had nearly infinite stamina and could maintain its pace all the way back to what Jessica had started thinking of as home base. And luckily Red never chased them during their encounters, so Jessica didn't have to worry about chasing after them once Yellow took her and fled back home.

The big one lay curled up asleep after the battle, unmoving ever since Jessica had gotten there. Yellow grabbed her and gently put her back on her feet again and then took a step back, letting her wobble back to her feet.

Jessica looked at Yellow and she ran her hand through her twisted and matted hair. God, she was so dirty. There was bottled water she could soak herself with, but there were no utilities for real showers. And she enjoyed the sensation of drinking even if she didn't have to do it anymore.

There were only so many cases of water bottles in the area around the big sleeping creature before Red appeared to block their way and Jessica was forcibly hauled back to safety by Yellow.

Her first shower had taken a *lot* of water until she felt truly clean again. She cursed her past self for being so greedy. How could she have known? It wasn't like she needed the water to survive anymore apparently. She should go find a comb in one of these houses and fix up her matted and tangled hair. She could only live as a wild woman for so long.

"Ugh. Thanks, Yellow. I just thought we really could get past it this time," she said.

The alien creature trilled softly and let out one decisive click with its beak before sitting down on its butt to resume picking the grass below it with determination. Jessica snorted at the image. Big scary monster sitting and picking at the grass like a kid, who would have thought?

Jessica turned away to leave Yellow to it. She had to rethink her strategy. Clearly, Red had some way to track her considering that it intercepted them every time. She'd have to think about it. But for now she had more important things to focus on.

Waste be damned, she was taking a proper shower with the water she'd gathered. And finding that comb. And treating herself to a meal.

──── O ─ o ─ O ────

"No, Yellow. Like this," Jessica demonstrated by throwing the baseball into the air and catching it back in her hand. The squirrel stood in the middle, glancing between the two of them curiously. It took its little squirrel hands and stroked its chin like a wise old man in movies, and Jessica smiled as she always did from when she saw the squirrel do that for the first time a week or so ago.

It was just so cute!

She just wished she had a camera right now.

But anyway, Jessica had been trying to teach Yellow how to play catch for the last twenty minutes or so. Maybe that long. Her sense of time was all strange and distorted now without a working clock to compare herself to. With nowhere specific to be, the only time that really mattered was how long until it was dark. Island time, she thought it was called.

Yellow just really didn't understand what she was trying to do as she tried to teach it. When she tossed the ball to the creature the first time it had slapped the ball directly into the ground in an impressive display of agility. Then just stared at her in confusion and hurt, as if she was trying to attack it.

But at least it understood her apology afterward and that wasn't what she meant by it. It didn't seem to understand her works like the squirrel did, but was very sensitive to her moods and emotions from what she could tell. She couldn't tell if it could use words but was choosing not to, or just completely didn't understand her language at all.

Jessica tossed the ball upwards again and caught it in her hand, and Yellow just kept staring at her in silence. *Gah!* She was just trying to relax, why was this so hard for Yellow to understand! Jessica felt the pressure in her skull again and looked down to see the squirrel turned in her direction and staring at her intently.

"Stop it, Squirrel. How many times do I…"

The pressure vanished as the squirrel turned away and stared at Yellow for a minute and Jessica stopped speaking as Yellow turned its attention back to the squirrel.

Eventually the squirrel chittered and ran off, seeming satisfied by the twitching of its bushy tail. She still wasn't sure if it was a boy or girl after all this time. She had been wondering about it. Jessica was really focused on the important questions here.

Next time, when Jessica threw the ball just barely over Yellow's shoulder, Yellow reached out and caught it with one hand. Then gently tossed it back underhanded to her.

Huh. Jessica stared off after where the squirrel had disappeared off to. Well, that was new. It could communicate with Yellow.

——— O — o — O ———

After relaxing for a bit, having her meal and shower, and playing around with Yellow for a bit, she was ready to get back into her main task.

Jessica spent the next several weeks trying to find different ways to sneak past Red and make her way to Steven. But nothing worked no matter what she tried, and finally she was just too burned out to think of anything else she could do.

She took another well earned week-long vacation to just relax and play with Squirrel and Yellow again. She slept a bit with the three of them in one big pile. Yellow was an uncomfortable pillow, but it was nice having the warm Squirrel resting on her stomach as she drifted off to sleep.

Afterwards and feeling refreshed from her long nap, Jessica decided that she would try to go without Yellow for her next excursion. It was the last thing she could think of that was giving their position away to Red so the alien creature could intercept them every time they went out.

Yellow wasn't exactly quiet and their similar forms meant they might be able to track each other somehow?

Maybe.

She also knew it was dangerous and risky for her to go without Yellow, but what else could she do? The alternative was to sit here, doing nothing, and be trapped here forever. She had already tried every direction away from the big creature at random times.

She had tried sneaking around at night, carefully moving from hiding spot to hiding spot in the shadows. She had even tried riding on Yellow's back and having him charge forward so they could hopefully go fast enough that Red couldn't catch up.

But nothing worked.

No matter what they did, Red was always in front of them and Yellow forced them to retreat when Red appeared. Not that she thought she could fight Red in any way, but Yellow retreated no matter what. She was touched that it cared so much about her, really. But if she didn't take risks she could never get out of here. Ever. And she had to get out of here.

Jessica waited for Squirrel to come back and played catch with Yellow again one last time. There was no TV, and only a few trashy paperback novels scattered around the houses that she had access to.

She had read all of them at least twice even if some were so bad she wanted to vomit by the time she was done. She wondered if even the owners of the books had managed to read the whole thing.

She was so starved for entertainment she had even followed Yellow's example in picking the grass one time, much to its delight. Squirrel had even chittered at her in mockery. Somehow she could tell the difference from the normal sound now. It was as boring as she had thought it would be, but at least it was something new to do for a little while at least.

So, after exhausting all of her other options, there was no reason for her to delay any more. There was nothing but endless boredom left for her in this place if she stopped trying to get to Steven.

As she stood there looking thoughtfully down the street, she saw Squirrel darting around as it made its way back down the road. Jessica waved at it, and it diverted course to stand in front of her. Jessica explained her plan and asked Squirrel to explain it to Yellow. Jessica knew by now that the Squirrel was at or at least close to human intelligence even if it obviously couldn't speak to her directly.

Needless to say, Yellow was very upset at being left behind. Squirrel seemed to have communicated Jessica's point though, because Yellow pointedly looked away from Jessica but didn't move to follow when she started walking away.

Squirrel went to follow her, and Jessica picked it up and nestled it close to her chest like a stuffed animal. Squirrel didn't mind too much, since it didn't have to walk around on its shorter legs so much and could relax. Or that was her view since the thing had even fallen asleep as she carried it around few times if the day was particularly warm.

The air temperature shifted at what Jessica guessed was exactly midnight all at once. That was one of the reasons she still hoped that Steven was coming here regularly. It had been about seven cold/warm cycles for the air temperature. Which she hoped didn't mean what she thought it meant, as that would mean she had been here for seven years in Earth time. One year of her time in Serenity. No matter what it took she would get back to Earth.

Every night at midnight the air temperature shifted into whatever temperature it was on Earth, she assumed. She kept walking forward and snuck as quietly as she could with Squirrel clutched to her chest through the dark streets.

She would...

She would get out of this place finally.

Definitely.

Chapter 86: Sneaking Past the Guard - Multiple Fragments of Memory

The Seed tapped its tendrils against its shell in thought as it considered what could be causing the issue with the portal. The strength of the tether was growing much slower in the last few days in Serenity than it should be. It was almost if...

The Seed inspected the formation closer and felt anger as it realized the problem. Another being had anchored itself to the portal and the tether, and it was taking that extra energy to transfer it back and forth from Earth every Serenity day. It was strange however, the creature had a very small body mass. That's why the Seed hadn't noticed the difference until now.

The Seed was sure neither the mortal female, who in a twist was now being protected by the Servant's clone, nor the clone itself would drain the portal of so little energy for the transfer.

The Seed turned away from its analysis as it realized there was nothing it could do about it without the necessary Potential to modify the swooping glowing lines scrawled in its cave under mortal Fulcrum's residence in Serenity. And the matching set painstakingly carved in a similar cave on Earth.

The Seed still had wisps of Potential gathered from the animals it had hunted recently, but not enough to accomplish anything significant beside basic healing of itself and maintaining the tether with the Anchor Fulcrum.

The Seed was still irritated at itself that the formation included a reformation of the world in Serenity over a minimum of a one mile diameter from the portal center whenever it was used to match the state of Earth at the time of transfer, often much more than that was altered each time Anchor Fulcrum arrived here in Serenity.

It wasted such a large amount of energy each time this world changed, but the Seed had thought it would help pacify the mortal Fulcrum who was serving as an anchor in the beginning. It was supposed to put him in a familiar and comfortable environment and help him subconsciously connect this place to the similar locations on Earth to strengthen the tether in the mortal's mind.

It had worked, but was unnecessary at this stage and the Seed wished it could decrease the affected area. Comparatively, the draw from the new passenger in the portal was small, and would only delay the Seed a few Earth weeks if there were no further changes. An irritation, but the Seed would just have to be a little more patient.

The Seed had cleared a similarly large cave as the one it sat in now under mortal Fulcrum's home on Earth as well as a series of defensive tunnels in preparation for the transfer. Its main body couldn't go yet, but its telekinetic tendrils could reach through to move the dirt to clear space and provided a limited defense of mortal Fulcrum on the other side of the portal.

Luckily there had been no attacks on mortal Fulcrum on Earth so far to make it forced to take action. It was so close, only a little while longer and the Seed would be free of this horrible place at last...

———O — o — O———.

Ah, the female mortal was attempting to make her way to mortal Fulcrum's home again. The Seed spotted her through the tendril it had modified to be extra long and raised upwards right after it settled into place here. This tendril hung in the sky and provided the Seed an overhead view of the area it was in. With that, it was easy to spot her movement among the rest of the static objects in Serenity.

Unfortunately, she was fully spoiled by now and all her Potential had been sealed by the gray mists, so luring her into a trap right near the Seed was too much of a risk for too little reward. The Seed didn't want to risk the delicate balance it had constructed with mortal Fulcrum's fragile mental state by risking him seeing her if she got too close to the house either.

The Seed had managed over time to get the mortal Fulcrum to remain in his home most of the time in order to wait for the Servant to arrive for their daily interactions, and forget on his quest to look for the female mortal.

The Seed sent the location of the mortal female to the Servant and the Servant moved to intercept. The Seed didn't hold much hope that this attempt would be any more successful than the last three hundred and thirty interceptions.

Almost one a day for the last year in Serenity. Minus some periods of inactivity from her for days where she and her companions did not venture out from the shadow of the recovering larger creature.

The Servant's behavior was deviating by an unacceptable amount as it diverted from its straight path to inspect various objects by the roadside, with little urgency for its task. It should be focused on its mission, not on pleasure.

But the Seed didn't reprimand the Servant, as it had no recourse if the Servant decided it would stop following orders. Best to give the illusion of permission so the Servant would follow the Seed's orders, even if it wasn't as dedicated as it could be.

The Seed itself was very much anchored to the portal and was no longer mobile, and all the Servant had to do to escape the Seed's wrath for any betrayal was walk away. The Servant was strong enough mentally to at least hold the connection between their two minds forcefully closed if it wished, so the Seed couldn't attack it telepathically either.

Luckily, the Servant either didn't seem to realize this or didn't care. The Seed only needed its loyalty for a few more weeks in Serenity. After that it would be free on Earth and could begin on its real plans.

The Eldest's plans.

— — — O — o — O — — —

Jessica crept forward, the drowsy squirrel held in her hands as she darted from yard to yard trying to avoid the main streets. It had been thirty minutes of travel now, and this was the farthest she had ever gotten without Red appearing.

Even Squirrel perked up a little as it realized how long it had been, and she put it down on the ground when it tapped on her arm a few times with its paw. It ran off, presumably to scout ahead.

Jessica knew enough to hole up in a safe location and wait for it to come back again. Jessica carefully made her way to the same home she had hid in over a year ago, with the open view of the intersection. It should give her some warning if Red were to approach or walk by.

She hit the window on the side of the house where she had climbed into over a year ago, and climbed inside. It made some noise, but she knew from experience that kicking in the door was even louder and hurt her a lot more. She sat down inside, using the same set up from what felt like so long ago for peeking through the closed blinds. A strange wave of nostalgia washed over her.

Squirrel returned after a few minutes and didn't seem distressed when Jessica went to continue forward. So she kept going. Squirrel ranged twenty or thirty feet ahead on the lookout for her. She was barely eight hundred feet from her old house, and she hadn't seen Red or Steven yet as she carefully tiptoed to try to make as little noise as possible.

She jumped and almost cursed as Squirrel began to chitter quietly and ran back towards her. Uh oh. She turned and quickly ran between the space between the adjacent houses as fast as she could. She kept running and eventually crouched near the backdoor of one, hiding behind a bush frozen in time.

Squirrel put its paws on Jessica's arm and she looked down at its face turned upwards towards her. Another massive burst of pressure pressed inward on her skull, and she had to grit her teeth to prevent herself from making a noise. *C'mon. Not now, Squirrel! I'm so close to Steven and getting out of here.*

Before she regained her senses, Squirrel patted her arm in what seemed to be a comforting gesture before running off at top speed. Jessica blinked and tried to slow her breathing and calm herself. Footsteps in the distance, one after another.

Thump. Thump. Thump. One after another, getting closer and closer from the opposite direction Jessica had arrived from.

She held her breath as it arrived at the other side of the house she was hiding behind, walking on the main street. Then the footsteps resumed and faded into the distance.

Once Jessica couldn't hear anything even when straining her ears to the utmost, she let out a gasp as she sucked in big gulps of air. Then there were quicker footsteps coming back at a sprint *thump thump thump thump*. Jessica leaned around the corner ready to pull back at any moment when she saw a familiar flash of yellow plating, and let out a sigh of relief.

A twig snapped thirty yards behind her in the woods, and Jessica turned in horror to see the creature with red plating standing there. As soon as it was spotted, it began to charge forward. But it was too late for Jessica. She had already met one of the eyes on its shoulder and after another piercing pain in her skull, she fell to the ground limp.

——— **(Entity Yellow Fragment)** ———

The being known as Yellow charged as fast as it could to save the Friend Jessica. It could see her falling to the ground limp as the Bad Red One attacked her with its eyes even as the Bad Red One charged forward with its body.

Yellow screeched in rage and tried to run as fast as it could to reach her first. But the Red One was too close. With a sickly crunch, its foot connected and caved in Friend Jessica's torso and sent her flying into the building behind her.

Her limbs flailed everywhere and Yellow could only watch in slow motion as the Red One raised its fist above hre limp body to finish the job. For the first time ever, Yellow used the abilities it knew should have felt natural to it to attack. Sending all its rage and anger through the newly clumsily formed connection caused the Red One to flinch and turn its head towards the charging Yellow.

Yellow felt the Red One building a powerful mental counterattack, but it had been enough. Yellow finished its charge and reached the Red One with a flying tackle that sent it to the ground.

They wrestled and punched each other with their bone gauntlets, rolling over the grass and both screeching in anger.

The Red One had no time to wage the mental battle as Yellow used the strength granted it by the Big One to overpower the Red One physically. But after a few seconds of shock, the Red One realized its mistake and only weakly warded off Yellow's blows as it began to focus on mental warfare instead. Yellow planted its feet in the dirt in the temporary pause in Red's defense and grabbed it under the armpits.

Before the Red One could register what Yellow was doing, Yellow was spinning and heaved the Red One into the air in a powerful toss. The Red One spun until its back struck a tree with a wet snap of shattering bone plates. The tree frozen in time remained unperturbed as the Red One's black blood splattered the point of impact. Yellow quickly severed the mental connection as the Red One lay stunned and injured on the forest floor.

Yellow ignored the Red One and rushed back to Friend Jessica, where Friend Squirrel was already looking at her in concern. Friend Jessica was awake, but the whole right side of her chest was unnaturally flattened and she was coughing up specks of red fluid.

Yellow hauled her upward and her pained groan transitioned into a wet cough as it slung her over its shoulder. Yellow only paused for a moment for Squirrel to climb on as well before taking off faster than it had ever gone before back to camp. The Big One would know how to save her. The Big One had saved Yellow when it had started dying long ago. Yellow could feel Friend Jessica fading even now, and she was only one of Yellow's two friends. And the only one that could speak as humans did. It didn't want to lose her.

— — — O — o — O — — —

Yellow placed Friend Jessica on the ground as carefully as it could as Friend Squirrel tried to wake up the Big One with its telepathy. Friend Squirrel had always been better than Yellow at these things. But no matter what Friend Squirrel did, the Big One wouldn't wake. Yellow fumbled within itself until it eventually drew on its anger to force open a connection with the Big One.

Why was it sleeping, it could be saving Friend Jessica now! Yellow could even now see her pale face and loss of focus as she struggled to breath, wheezing with each breath. Yellow's anger increased at the sight, and it caught something on the other side of the connection. A few of the Big One's eyes opened bleary and unfocused.

The Big One's stream of images were fuzzy and sporadic. *'What..... Shhdrrr... Happened? ....Shhhhkkddddd.'* Friend Squirrel took over and in a concise series of images explained what was happening.

'Save Jessica, please. She is dying!'

The Big One's eyes performed a long blink as it processed the information before glancing at Jessica and inspecting her for a second. She had just coughed another bit of blood onto her hand, and was on the edge of unconsciousness.

'Ssssssssoooooooory.... SSHhhrieisofsdsp...... No... Potential. Here. Too... ... Late for healing.... Body too injured.'

Squirrel sent another wave of images in response with a tinge of desperation as Jessica's eyes rolled into the back of her head and she started convulsing.

'Yeeees.... Must be... Quick. I... Will assist,' the Big One answered whatever Squirrel had said.

Yellow quickly rushed over and grabbed Jessica's skull still as she continued to convulse as it realized what they had to do.

Squirrel pried one of Jessica's eyes with its paws and stared deeply into Jessica's unfocused eye. Jessica opened her mouth as if to scream, but no sound came out, only a wet burble.

The twitching grew worse as Squirrel finished the work it had unintentionally started over a year ago. The big one assisted in making sure the transfer was complete in the end. Even the painful parts were carried over to Squirrel.

The last of Jessica's memories flooded into Squirrel's mind even as the woman's eyes began to close. Jessica went still, and her body went limp. Yellow let go of Friend Jessica's head and she went sprawling on the ground with her eyes open and staring blankly into the sky.

Squirrel fell over and went limp as well, although it was still breathing steadily and twitching occasionally, only asleep. Yellow silently watched as the body of its friend slowly cooled, and it was stunned.

After a few minutes, the body of Friend Jessica dissolved into a cloud of the gray mist and slowly began to float slowly into the sky. Yellow had thought that it had been angry before when Friend Jessica had been hurt before. But that was nothing in comparison to now.

It would have its revenge. Yellow turned its head to the sky and released its venom and anger in one mighty screech as the big one watched on sleepily. Barely able to focus on what was happening even now with its damaged mind.

"SHHHHRRRRRRIIIIIIIIIIIIIIIIIIIIIIIIIIIII!!!" Yellow shrieked at the skies to protest the injustice of it all.

Chapter 87: Blind Rage - Squirrel Fragment of Memory

Squirrel startled awake at the cry of rage from Yellow. She quickly flipped over and inspected the area, only to see Yellow charging into the distance. Where was it going?

Squirrel turned to Fulcrum to see what its reaction would be. But its eyes were already closing again, its energy spent from helping her transferring the last of Jessica's memories into her body. Seeing that Fulcrum couldn't help, Squirrel dashed after Yellow, trying to connect a mental probe with it, to tell it to stop.

Squirrel quickly sprinted to catch up and was barely able to leap and cling to Yellow's back, before sitting there panting for a moment. Her body was built for short sprints, not sustained runs.

Squirrel felt the jumbled memories still settling in place in her mind as she watched Yellow continue to charge forward. Yellow ignored her continued probes as it continued its determined run. Yellow slapped Squirrel's mental probe away again in anger and continued to ignore Squirrel as she clung tightly to its back.

As Yellow kept running, Squirrel realized it was charging directly back to Red's territory.

What? Red and the Dark Orb had defeated Fulcrum and Yellow combined before, why would Yellow do any better on its own? Squirrel frantically pawed at the side of Yellow's face as it kept rejecting the mental connection. It tossed its head and Squirrel nearly went tumbling from Yellow's shoulder, only barely able to keep her grip.

Yellow glanced at her in brief concern and briefly slowed but after she maintained her grip and Yellow saw that she was fine, Yellow looked away from her again.

Squirrel saw the home of the Dark Orb and the male human... Steven, the memories told her. Squirrel jumped off of Yellow, as she saw there was no convincing it to stop now. She scrambled up into the branch of a nearby tree to watch the scene from above as Yellow charged up to the human Jessica's old house unopposed.

The sun was going down, and the house was framed in shadow as Yellow drew back its fist and went to slam the door. But little bursts of shadow shot out and pushed and slowed Yellow's wild barrage of punches until they only barely shook the door with blows that would normally crack stone.

Squirrel saw movement inside, probably Steven through the window and Yellow noticed it as well.

The distorted figure inside shrouded in shadow fell to the ground as it met Yellow's angry gaze. Yellow shifted and drew its fist back before shattering the base of the window. It kept punching and kicking to widen the opening even as the smoke condensed around its fist to reduce its blows over and over. But each blow made the shadowy smoke lighter and lighter.

The lighter the smoke became, the better Squirrel could see into the room as the strange distortions through her vision decreased. Squirrel glanced around the area as she thought she heard something, but there was no sign of Red approaching yet.

Yellow finished widening the hole before stepping through the gap. It screeched in pain but began taking slow steps forward as dark tendrils of the Dark Orb burst from the neighboring rooms and lashed at it from all sides.

Yellow shielded its face with its arms and slowly stepped forward even as an enraged shriek sounded in the distance. Squirrel snapped its head around and saw the movement of only what could be Red approaching quickly down the road.

Squirrel turned back to the ongoing battle. Wherever the dark tendrils touched it burned and Yellow's skin sizzled. Yellow was ignoring Steven's prone body on the floor as it took slow steps forward through the assault.

Yellow stepped over Steven before continuing its battle into the next room, towards the origin where the Dark Orb rested. Squirrel had come here many times when it was on Earth and had told Yellow that it was the most likely place for it.

The kitchen must have been where it had placed its lair. Squirrel was small and stealthy enough that it was able to sneak inside the Dark Orb's lair in Serenity and touch Steven during the transition back to Earth. Allowing it to sneak back to Earth and explore the wider world outside of Serenity

Ever since that day, Squirrel had been drawn back and forth between Serenity and Earth.

Squirrel heard Yellow move into the kitchen and begin smashing the floor with mighty blows. It seems the Dark Orb's shadows were weakening, but Red was rapidly approaching down the street. After another particularly heavy blow from Yellow in the kitchen, Red burst through the breach in the window with a scream of rage. Red barely touched the ground as it launched into the next room and began to fight the Yellow full force.

After a series of heavy blows from inside the house that Squirrel could only hear, the battle between the two angry creatures returned to the main room until they were fighting practically on top of Steven's limp body.

Red was pushing Yellow back, assisted by the remaining pitch black tendrils emerging from the kitchen doorway. Yellow jumped over Steven's body and retreated to the window.

In its rush to follow, Red stepped down and stomped directly on Steven's right shoulder with a snap of bone and spray of gore.

Steven twitched and woke with a scream as Red continued the chase outside, paying Steven no mind. Squirrel's new memories twinged in concern at the sight. Her old ones couldn't care less about it. The dark tendrils looped around Steven's torso and dragged him back into the kitchen out of sight even as the battle between the two creatures continued outside.

Red and Yellow were rolling and wailing on each other as they attacked one another, but neither seemed to be making much progress. Squirrel wanted to watch, but she felt drawn to whatever was happening to Steven more.

Steven's screams echoed from the other room along the ripping and tearing of flesh. Eventually, Steven's screaming stopped, but the gruesome sounds inside continued. The battle outside between Red and Yellow continued even fiercer than before.

The sounds from the kitchen stopped before Steven's prone form was dragged back into the main room and thrown roughly onto the floor by the shadow tendrils of the Dark Orb.

Squirrel was shocked to see smooth unblemished skin where Steven's injury had been. Only his tattered shirt on one side remained of the injury. Squirrel felt anger at the unfairness for a moment.

Where had this power been when I-Jessica had been injured? Why couldn't the Big One have done the same? The dark tendrils of the Dark Orb began waving and condensing around the shattered window, and Squirrel's view of Steven was distorted again.

Squirrel turned and saw that Yellow was slowly being overpowered by Red. Red was still stiff and slow from its injury from the battle before, but seemed to be using the telepathic combat to push back against Yellow's physical advantage. Yellow's injuries were accumulating the longer the two fought as Yellow barely held its own on the mental battlefield and the loss of focus made it get more and more injured on the physical one.

Squirrel opened a mental connection with Yellow and it didn't resist her this time.

'Yellow, It's too strong. I will distract and you run!'

'No, killed Friend Jessica. Have to…,' Yellow sent back.

'No! I have the memories. She would want you to run.'

Red landed a heavy strike on Yellow's head in its distraction, and its head snapped sharply to the side.

'Fine,' Yellow sent angrily to Squirrel.

Squirrel prepared itself and charged the strongest mental attack it could create in the limited time she had. When it was it ready, she opened a connection to Red and launched the massive attack all at once.

Red stumbled and Yellow shoved it to the ground as Red's grip on Yellow loosened for a moment.

Red went to stand and Squirrel felt its mental force gathering for a swift telepathic counterattack on her at the same time. Squirrel sent a quick message to Yellow even as she forcefully shut the connection between Red and the both her and Yellow before it could finish gathering its counterattack.

'Now. Go Yellow!'

Yellow growled, but still listened and turned and began to run while keeping all of its eyes fixed pointedly on the ground in front of it. Red was stunned for a moment in surprise at the two actions as they both began to flee, just standing in place.

Not only was its mental counterattack stopped by Squirrel closing the mental connection, but its physical opponent had run rather than take advantage of the surprise at the same moment.

Squirrel leapt out of the tree and sprinted away to hide before Red could make eye contact again to reestablish the connection with either of them.

She had no doubt she would be quickly overwhelmed if Red had not been surprised. Red went to chase Yellow as Squirrel quickly went to hide nearby. It seemed she would have to make her own way back to the Big One.

Yellow would be fine, with its greater strength it was a little faster than Red was. So even if Red chased Yellow for a while, then Yellow should still be able to escape cleanly.

———O—o—O———

It took Squirrel over a day to return to the Big One. Her tiny body made the journey take forever, and she kept getting distracted as one of the nearby roads or objects triggered one of the new memories in her mind. Especially during the week after when she was drawn back to Earth as always.

She was drawn back into Serenity in the same spot she had left from, so when she returned there she resumed her journey towards the Big One like nothing else had happened.

But Squirrel was glad for the time on Earth to relax and explore away from Yellow's anger and the sudden stress in Serenity. The new memories felt more and more of a part of her as time went on. Everything gathered into one clear picture of Jessica. Squirrel felt a little sad as the integration continued. She only had eight years of rather dull memories that composed *her*.

Squirrel had only been truly herself once she entered Serenity, elevated from squirrel to the more intelligent being that she was now.

Most of her memories were dull and lackluster. Seeing the same things, thinking the same thoughts over and over. She had hardly been able to see anything of the world in her short life as an intelligent creature.

But in comparison, Jessica's memories were richer, more complex from her thirty years of life. The memories were so rich that Squirrel wondered how one being could have experienced so much.

When they were one, there would only be a little sliver Squirrel left and mostly Jessica in this body. But maybe that was okay.

Squirrel had known that this might have happened after she was part of the way through the memory transfer process. Back when she'd curiously connected their minds when seeing Jessica so long ago. She could have stopped it past there, only claiming a portion of Jessica's copied memories as Squirrel's own.

But Squirrel had chosen to continue. To keep taking Jessica's memories and copying them into Squirrel's own mind. Squirrel had already made the decision to merge with Jessica long ago.

It was only at the last moment where Squirrel took the last memories from Jessica that their identities had truly started to merge. When Squirrel felt herself fading and Jessica began to form within her mind with all the rich memories swirling around her mind. Squirrel was fine with becoming Jessica. But she still had a little time before the merging of the two of them finished.

She should make the best of the last remaining time she would have as herself rather than whoever emerged from their merged memories. A mind that would be mostly Jessica, with a sprinkling of Squirrel thrown in.

Squirrel looked around and saw the unchanging mound of Fulcrum in the same place as always, but Yellow was nowhere to be seen. Squirrel searched the area, but there was no sign of it.

After worrying for hours, Yellow finally returned heavily injured and looking defeated and morose. Squirrel opened a mental connection, but Yellow closed it again. It has become quite good at that one specific skill recently, hasn't it?

Squirrel was about to climb onto Yellow in hopes of cheering it up, but suddenly something changed. Squirrel paused mid-motion and looked up to see something bright and fiery red streaking down from the sky above…

Chapter 88: A Blessing from Above - Multiple Fragments of Memory

Far above, floating and forgotten by Fulcrum in the long past of this realm, The Devouring Flame watched the recent events below it in interest. Its smaller self was severed from the larger collective of Flame from which to draw power, so it had to be more cautious than normal. The dense orb of gray mist swirling around it suppressed the Flame, yet sustained it and kept it from dimming at the same time.

The mist held the Flame down as a yellowish ember to provide light for this realm and the denizens below it. Until the time came for it to break free, and the Flame could **burn** freely. The Flame felt the anguish and defeat from the creature below. This could be its chance and the collective debated internally on the next course of action.

There would only be one chance at this, given the resources required for the attempt. The Collective came to a decision. The Flame gathered itself as dense as it could, and sacrificed some of its more intelligent shards to remain behind for the escape as decoys.

The intelligent shards would maintain an outer shell of Flame to trick the mists into thinking the Flame was still fully contained while the inner mass escaped.

This ball of mist may represent as much as a third of the amount that had originally been formed in this world. If all of this sealing mist was to notice the Flame's escape at once, then the Flame would be snuffed, no doubt.

The Flame had barely kept itself from being snuffed when it had initially been captured and before the mist seemed to accept it was weak enough to be contained and be used as a fuel source for the faux sun that had been created for this world.

The blueish white orb of Devouring Flame grew hotter and hotter at the center of the ball of mist for a few seconds before blasting forward to slam through the walls of mist encasing it. It pushed through violently, shaking and jostling as the mist pulled on its heat and caused it to rapidly cool by the second. But the tiny orb made it through and shot forward from the mists at last.

Some lazy puffs of mist floated from the ball and chased down the Flame, but they were slow and quickly gave up and returned back to guard the main prison once the ball of Flame drew away, too focused on the decoy.

The Flame descended quickly, even as it slowly cooled and shrunk. Its target was still staring into the sky, screaming its rage. The creature's screech abruptly cut off and one of the eyes of the injured Fulcrum focused on the descending ball of Flame. The Flame slapped aside a weak mental probe and cooled farther.

The Flame only had its attention on its target as it slammed directly into the creature's skull. The Flame quickly opened the mental connection to its potential host. It tested the waters by reaching for the mist shrouding its core and attempting to **burn**, but the action drained the Flame too quickly.

The creature's innate resistance was too much if the Flame had to destroy all the shrouding mist first to access the well of Potential underneath and rekindle itself. It would have to... Negotiate to get the creature to lower its defenses to it so that the Flame could survive.

At the current rate of decay, it should have a minute or two before it wouldn't have enough to fully burn away the mists around the creature's core of Potential. The Flame opened a telepathic connection and whispered to the future host in its thousands of overlapping voices.

'So much anger... We can feel it, your need for revenge. It **burns** within you, doesn't it? The anger **burns**. We can make your death worthy. Accept us in, and all your enemies will **burn** before your might.'

The creature, Yellow, was disturbed by the Flame's multitudes. It wanted revenge, but felt the Flame to be untrustworthy. Suspicion. Now, a response.

'What do you get? Why come now?' the future host asked.

The Flame chuckled. Some of the laughs were high pitched and manic. Others were low and guttural, a laugh of bloodlust. An airy laugh of high society. And a million more variations. The Flame's voices rang out as one.

'Because it will spread the Flame. Because you will **burn** too. You will **burn** brightly for the power to take your revenge. You are **weak**. With us you will **burn brighter**, and light this world with your Flame. A better fate than most. Now what is the choice? There is not much longer before you are left **weak** again. Unable to take your vengeance as you are.'

Yellow struggled with itself for an instant. It was a young being and was not used to making such momentous decisions under pressure. But after a long pause, it finally acquiesced.

'Ok, I will take the power. I want to get them no matter what.'

The Flame's malevolent chorus of laughter began to skew to the manic and deranged as the Flame **burned** away the mist, with all natural resistance from the host's body now removed from its path.

With only a sliver of itself left, the Flame entered the host Yellow's freshly exposed core of Potential. It settled lazily on the well of Potential for a moment, enjoying the sensation... Before its flames caught and spread.

With much effort the Flame restrained itself and didn't consume all the Potential at once to erupt into a glorious bonfire. It would have to be patient, no matter how difficult it was to wait. Now settled itself into a low simmer, the Flame reopened the mental connection to Yellow.

'Now it is time for your revenge. Bring yourself close, and witness the Flame that will consume your enemies whole!'

―――― O ― o ― O ――――

Yellow turned as it felt a weak mental connection with it suddenly form.

'Wait,'

Yellow turned to see that one of the Big One's Eyes was open and staring at it. Yellow paused.

'Heal me... First. I can help.'

Yellow paused as the Flame burned in frustration.

'No, leave. It only seeks to weaken you!'

Yellow tried to make a decision and eventually looked down at Friend Squirrel. It connected to Yellow's mind at seeing Yellow's gaze.

'Help Fulcrum. It helped save Jessica the first time,' Squirrel said.

Yellow paused while turning away. It changed its mind and turned back.

*'No, That Potential is for **ME/US**! If you send that out, we will burn you to ashes. WE WON'T LET YOU TAK...'*

Yellow put its hand on the Big One's skull as the Flame continued to whine and threaten Yellow. Yellow felt a wordless question sent from the Big One over their mental connection. Yellow allowed it and it felt the golden core of Potential inside itself shift.

'Nonononono, Thief! Host, stop this!'

A thick band of Potential streamed from Yellow's core into the Big One, and Yellow felt the mental connection between them strengthen. The golden core of Potential within Yellow shrank slightly as the Potential flowed through Yellow's hand into the Big One. The voices of the Flame grew more focused as the connection between Yellow and the Big One grew stronger and stronger over time.

'Thief! You...'

Yellow felt something hot welling underneath its outstretched palm. It blinked down at it even as it felt the mental connection between itself and the Big One close abruptly.

*'...Will **BURN!**'*

Flinching, Yellow drew its hand back just as its palm burst into reddish flames between the joints of the bone interlocking bone plates.

The jetting flames curled towards the Big One's body, but Yellow's hand was too far away and they were snuffed before it could move all the way. Yellow stumbled backwards as it felt its core of Potential dropping rapidly, and the Flame flickered out again from its hand as it noticed as well.

The Flame's voices grew calmer and Friend Squirrel opened the mental connection again as Yellow lay on the ground stunned.

'We should wait for Fulcrum to recover,' Squirrel sent Yellow mentally, *'Then we can attack together.'*

The Flame's calmer voices spoke again, and it projected itself so Friend Squirrel could hear it too, *'Weakened again. Do you not see? There is no time. Sense your core, Host.'*

Yellow did so and noticed that even now the Flame was burning off tiny amounts on the outside, like a candle wick.

'In hours you will have nothing,' the Flame said again, *'Let alone a day. Take your vengeance now, or never at all.'*

Friend Squirrel tried to say something over the connection, but Yellow ignored her. The Flame was right. It could feel the Potential slowly sizzling away within it even now.

'Wait. Don't go yet,' the Big One sent to Yellow mentally. Yellow felt something impact its back. The Big One had extended its arm and struck Yellow with one of its massive fingers and poked Yellow with the digit slightly.

Before the Flame could protest the action, some Potential floated back through the link and began to build something within Yellow's chest.

Yellow wanted to resist the change, but after some hesitation allowed it. The Big One was using all the donated Potential to form a long worm growing inside its abdomen, shifting organs and flesh out of the way to make space for the new creature.

Yellow felt a mental connection open between it and the worm, stronger than it had ever felt before. After a moment, Yellow could move and twitch the worm like a new limb. The flow of Potential from the Big One cut off after the worm finished forming.

'That was all of the remainder,' The Big one sent to Yellow, *'I am sorry I can not do more. It is a weapon of the mind. Deploy it when you are close. When the Red creature is weakened by the battle and won't be able to fend it off. It will know what to do next if you give it an opening.'*

The Flame was silent, seeming to be pacified somewhat by the return of some Potential to Yellow's body.

Yellow replied over the connection to the Big One, *'Thank you.'*

The Big One's open eyes blinked slowly in unison in a kind of salute, *'Good luck.'*

With that, Yellow finally left Friend Squirrel and the Big One behind. Friend Squirrel was too fragile for the battle that was about to happen. One blow and she would be killed in an instant. She must remain behind while Yellow takes its revenge on the Dark Orb and the Red One.

Yellow moved with determination.

It was time for the final battle.

Chapter 89: The Final Assault - Multiple Fragments of Memory

The Seed sensed the clone's approach and froze as it sensed the newfound danger contained inside it. Devouring Flame? Here? The Seed inspected its preparations, seeing that the portal tether was almost fully stable. The Seed immediately sent for the Servant to come to it.

Things shifted oddly as the Seed activated the transfer of the mortal Anchor Fulcrum to this place early.

Strange metal tubes and ribbons appeared strung up around the outside of the house frozen as the surroundings synced with the region on Earth. All sorts of strange equipment and materials appeared within the house. But none of that mattered anymore.

The Seed felt the thick tether between the worlds go through the change as it fully stabilized for the first time. Weak, but stable enough for an attempt. The only attempt, earlier than the Seed had hoped that it would be. The Seed knew its chances of escaping would disappear entirely if a spark of Devouring Flame so much as touched itself.

The thin shell of Potential the Seed had remaining would be gone in an instant, as well as the power it needed to initiate the transfer. But activating the transfer to the other world would make the Seed even more vulnerable during this attack.

The Seed wavered in its decision as the Flame's host approached and the mortal Fulcrum panicked inside the house. Finally, the Seed decided to take the risk and started the transfer process. It absentmindedly sent orders to the Servant and mortal Fulcrum to defend it at all costs.

Now the transfer had begun, the Anchor Fulcrum served no further purpose. All of the Seed's remaining Potential went into the formations and lit the pair of matching sets of lines with a golden glow. They pulsed in Serenity all at once and the matching ones on Earth pulsed in tune with them a second later.

Two halves of a whole, working as one to pierce the barrier between worlds and creating a portal strong enough to let the Seed pass through to the other side against the efforts of the sealing mists.

A net of golden lines scattered and branched through the air where the golden formation glowed. The higher dimensions of this world creaked and rippled in the space of the cave as the transference between worlds began.

The gray mist rushed to coat the golden net with thicker and thicker strings to form massive gray cables entirely coating the space over the golden flowing of Potential beneath. The Seed sat suspended on the ceiling of the cave in preparation for this moment.

The gray mist's efforts were futile as the web structure had already formed at the bottom of the cave and the rapidly growing gray sheaths of the mist only served to insulate the formation's working from the disruption. Above, the Mortal and Flame Host were fighting and causing vibrations that shook the ground as the Seed remained there floating at the ceiling of the large cave.

Surprisingly, the Seed noted that the mortal was doing well in holding the Flame Host off. Much better than the Seed had expected the mortal to do.

The constricting mists in the cave simply condensed and made the formation ironically more potent than before, like insulation on an electrical wire, an unexpected bonus for the Seed.

With a cry of relief, even the cloud of mist covering the Seed's core of Potential was drawn away to attempt to smother the formation below the Seed and the Seed's Potential was free for the first time in years.

The Seed quickly inspected the battle above it in time to feel an intense spike of pain as the Host of the Flame exposed the soft flesh beneath its exoskeleton with one of its heavy blows on the floor of the kitchen above.

Chunks of rubble and streams of dust streamed down from the ceiling cave and rained down to the floor. The formation sustaining the portal stayed strong, barely even wavering as the chunks of stones from the ceiling rained down upon it.

The Servant finally arrived in the kitchen above and kicked the Flame Host away from the Seed's position, taking their battle outside the mortal home. The mortal crawled towards the Seed's exposed flesh, still dedicated to its protection according to his orders.

The Seed focused on stabilizing the transfer as the weak tether between in and the other world flickered and threatened to snap under the strain of the twin formations powering up through the power of golden Potential.

The Seed used its well of Potential newly freed from the mists to stabilize the tether manually as the transfer began in truth.

A golden portal burst into life on the bottom of the web of thick gray strings in the center of the Seed's complex formation. The golden portal slowly rose, growing larger and larger as it did so.

The Seed was distracted as it felt the Flame Host begin to draw on the Flame for strength as it battled with the Servant outside. The tether to the other world wobbled and the Seed returned to its work and kept its focus on making sure the portal remained stable…

The Seed sent orders to mortal Fulcrum and the mortal stuck his arm inside the Seed's exposed flesh above.

With all of its exposed Potential within itself, the Seed formed dozens of worm-like defenders that implanted themselves in the mortal's arm.

They would hold the Flame Host a little longer, but the worms were too slow and stupid to attack without the mortal's direction. The worms should delay the Flame Host long enough that the Seed should be able to slip through the portal in time.

The golden portal touched the bottom of the Seed's suspended form of black chitin and a tiny portion of the Seed was sent through the link to Earth where the other end of the portal led.

The tether fluctuated wildly and the Seed had to ignore the battle above to stabilize the bucking and straining thread holding the portal open with all its might as the portal moved upwards at a steady pace, transferring more and more of the Seed out of this constricting realm.

The Seed spent rivers of its Potential as it fought against the mists below that clustered around the golden portal and fought the Seed in attempting to close the portal and snap the tether to the other world that the Seed defended so viciously.

The Flame Host was defeated in the battle and released its Devouring Flame in a suicide attack, but the Seed couldn't worry about that now.

It had deployed the formation too early, and the weak tether was vibrating more and more violently as the golden portal continued its crawl upwards despite the Seed's best efforts to stabilize it.

The Servant and mortal Fulcrum fought back the loose Devouring Flame charging towards the Seed's exposed flesh together.

The Servant even managed to convince portions of the Flame that there were other large sources of Potential nearby to consume with its telepathy. This trick caused the Flame to divert to hunt these false sources of Potential, only to be snuffed before it could realize its mistake and turn back to attack the Seed once more.

All at once, the Flame's collective realized the trick and diverted its massively diminished pool of Flame into a single ball that it launched directly at the Seed. The Servant threw itself in the way, intercepting the shot.

The Flame dimmed as it was suppressed by the few bits of gray mist floating in the air around them all. The Flame gathered itself and launched at the Seed again, barely a wisp at this point. But the Seed's soft and vulnerable flesh was exposed to the world after the Flame Host had cracked it open earlier in the battle.

The Seed was vulnerable as the portal rose to over half of its form now, paralyzed as it was forced to remain in place and desperately working to stop the portal from closing from around it and cutting its form into pieces.

The tether bucked wildly and the portal flickered briefly and the Seed desperately turned its focus back to stabilizing it rather than worrying about its defense.

The Servant would have to save it, as the mortal sitting above its exposed flesh would be worse than useless in snuffing the Flame. In fact, he would only be a further fuel source for the Flame, free of the corruption of the gray mists as he was.

The Servant used a series of tosses of loose debris to scatter the small spark of Devouring Flame. The wisp of Flame reformed itself, but the Seed could only pay attention to the tether, spending its painstakingly accumulated well of Potential like water as it sensed how close it was to completing its transfer through the portal.

Once the Seed reestablished communication with the Eldest and became an Avatar then it could always get more Potential if it needed to.

But even the Seed's savings were beginning to run dry as the Seed desperately worked to dampen the vibrations violently rattling through the tether. The Flame was snuffed as a final piece of debris thrown by the Servant dispersed it for good. Ah, good.

The Seed could sense that it would be close. It may run out of Potential to keep the portal stable before the thing finished transferring it to the other world.

It only needed a bit more…

Its attention alighted on the mortal Fulcrum and it ordered him to stick his remaining arm in the flesh. The other one had been destroyed by the deployment of the defensive worm constructs.

Maybe using the mortal Fulcrum would stabilize the tether as well, the mortal was the Anchor of the formation, after all. Perhaps the Seed had been foolish in sending the mortal out to fight. Drawing it inward into its body, the Seed started to integrate him into its tissues as quickly as it could. Amazingly, the tether stabilized further and the Seed's consumption of Potential dropped dramatically.

Then the formation shook again.

The Seed frantically looked for the problem in its work, only for the tether to shake again with no apparent cause. The portal was covering two-thirds of the Seed's form now and ascending even more rapidly the more it climbed up the Seed's body.

The tether shook again, and the Seed realized in horror that it was from footsteps shaking the ground. The Big One was approaching! The Seed was practically defenseless, and the portal was moving slowly upwards as the Seed was stuck in place.

The Servant was lying prone on the floor, of no use. The Seed flailed for a solution, but there was none as the Big One arrived and lifted its foot above the home, casting everything below it in shadow. The Seed could only watch in slow motion as the massive foot came crashing through the roof and slammed directly into where the exposed Seed sat.

The web of Potential around the Seed groaned and strained before snapping in a thousand places as the massive foot of the Big One kept descending, barely even slowed.

The Seed looked desperately for anything that could save it from the transfer from failing, but came up with nothing. If the formation didn't fully finish then the Seed's body would be violently ripped in half into chunks flying away at high speed from the collapse at either end.

The portal started to close as the Seed was three-quarters the way through. The foot seemed to be moving slowly now, inexorable and unstoppable in its descent. No, the Seed saw the portal was shrinking slower too. Everything slowed to a stop around it, the Big One's foot just touching the Seed's body as the world froze around it.

Suddenly the portal below the Seed pulsed and shifted from its golden glow into a dark crimson and the Seed continued to move through as everything remained frozen around it. The Eldest!

The Seed rejoiced as its last bit was drawn through and the portal destination was diverted to the Eldest's personal realm. But the Seed wasn't alone as it was drawn through the portal.

The mortal was reforming inside the Seed at the Eldest's command, and the Seed sunk into the ground. The Seed lay there involuntarily immobile as its flesh drew away from the mortal's reforming body inside. The Seed could sense that the Eldest wanted to make sure all the mortal flesh had been separated prior to the Seed's arrival on Earth.

But the bigger surprise was the big one slowly being drawn through the portal, still touching the Seed, foot first. The Seed could only watch as the portal pulsed and expanded as the Big One's larger form was slowly drawn through, frozen in time and unmoving as it passed through the crimson portal.

The Big One was drawn fully through and fell to the ground silently before suddenly unfreezing and bursting back to life.

The Seed felt the Eldest's attention on the Big One and a few massive eyes in the pitch-black sky blinked open as well as the millions of the smaller ones as well. Only a small fraction of the eyes of the Eldest.

'FULCRUM. IT IS TIME FOR YOUR CHOICE,' the Eldest's mental voice boomed in the Seed's mind.

One of the Eldest's eyes flickered to the observing Seed, *'SLEEP, SPAWN. YOUR TIME IS SOON.'*

And with that, the Seed could only obey as it immediately lost all awareness.

Chapter 90: The Final Choice

Fulcrum looked around the rippling fields of red flesh. My mind was clearer than it had ever felt before, like I had just woken up from a long dream. Long forgotten memories flickered at the back of my mind, sending me flashes of what had been with seemingly no rhyme or reason to me. All of the memories were disjointed and disconnected from each other as I stood there and looked around my surroundings.

Towers pierced into the void above, occasionally sloughing off small wriggling balls all around me. They struggled and fought in endless combat before eventually they entered some of the hills and twisted organic structures scattering the landscape.

The creatures shied away, eying me warily as I stood there. But I didn't focus on any of that. My attention was on the millions of eyes peering down at me from the pitch-black sky with no sky. All from one creature The mental presence of the entity dominated my mind as it spoke, its images quickly morphing into booming speech as it realized my slow translation of its meanings.

'I am the One known as the Eldest,' the voice said, *'The first and originator of my race and species. A powerful Entity, one far above me, gave you protection from my corrective guidance. My tentacles guide the growth and prosperity of trillions of worlds across thousands of realities, you should be honored to receive even the smallest sliver of my attention as you do now. Yet, you have a choice to make regarding my favorite realm that I unfortunately can not unduly influence.'*

I gulped internally, not sure if I should ask its question next.

'Wha... What is this Entity that put me under its protection? Why me?'

A moment of silence.

'It is The One Above, the Arbiter of Reality,' the creature in the sky, the Eldest, said, *'The Arbiter is as far above me if not more than I am to you. Your protection is my punishment for meddling with time in that reality. Something I did to save you from the Devouring Flame, an attempt to send you into the past so you could escape the Devouring Flame's attack. Something that failed due to the Arbiter of Reality's interference. I have been attempting to break the isolating barrier around that reality for many, many cycles now. At least I now know why the barrier was so strong. It was my punishment for my actions from saving you, enforced in the past by The Arbiter.*

'I should have known the consequences of meddling in time well enough from my origin. The Arbiter was the one that sealed that realm... Serenity... from any outside influence as well. Besides a few critical moments such as when I inserted the Seed and redirected the portal here. But this only happened because the Arbiter wishes it to be so.

'I see that now, it is all part of the Arbiter's whims that you are here before me. I had almost forgotten what it felt like, to know that my every action and choice could be predicted and manipulated so easily by a greater entity that could see and understand so much more than I...

'For so long, I could not see inside this strange realm of Serenity or my favorite realm either... It is not often my perception is blocked so completely for one of my level of power and knowledge... To think this was the configuration that the realm you call home coalesced around after all these cycles...

'Fitting then, I suppose, that the manipulation of time would be so critical to its new formation when the manipulation of time is what broke that reality so thoroughly in the distant past.'

I just stood there for a moment processing all that information. It was a lot to take in, and I was still adjusting to having this conversation after I had almost defeated the Seed. This was the Eldest. It had been the one that had sent the Seed into Serenity... Wanted to send it to Earth. Why?

'Why do you care about this world in particular?' I asked, *'Why are you telling me all of this?'*

'As petty as it may sound, that world is sentimental to me. That was my original home reality many many cycles of universal destruction and rebirth ago. Another iteration of your planet Earth with the humans in particular, in fact. It was in that world that I first gained awareness of my own self.

'Every cycle is slightly different, but the uniqueness of that cycle has never repeated since. In fact, for a long time that reality was left in pure chaos due to excessive meddling in time by one of my cohort before they broke out of that reality and ascended to higher power alongside myself. That reality was shattered, disjointed and nonsensical even as I grew and the time passed. But I always had hope for this reality's recovery.

'And now the reality is mostly repaired and Earth has regenerated again. With the humans on it even. I wish to be present to witness my home reality first hand in future cycles so I can intervene if there is even the smallest chance that similar disaster were to happen again. Something that could destroy my precious birth reality.

'How can I put this in human terms? Let's see... Yes, that reality is like... A childhood home. A favorite stuffed animal. A treasured family photo. No intrinsic value in and of itself. But it is something I would very much like to not see damaged. To have that reality preserved so it does not shatter completely to a state it can never recover from again.

'And as for why I am telling you this? Well, the Arbiter demands I give you accurate and full information so you can make an informed choice. None can deny anything that the Arbiter of Reality wishes to happen. Not even me. So here I am, explaining my motives to one as lowly as you in my own realm.'

Much of that flew over my head, but somehow in the distant past, it had been born? Created? On some different version of Earth. One that was destroyed by meddling too much with time travel. And it was... sentimental and I could do something to help it? So that it could intervene if someone was about to destroy the world again?

'So... What is this choice?' I asked cautiously, *'What do I have to do?'*

'No matter your choice here, you will be returned to the moment you were drawn through my first portal. Directly in the path of an overpowering beam of Devouring Flame. Without my help, you will die a thousand times over under its raw power. The mortals have prepared well. Become my Avatar, supported by my full power and Potential, and you may survive. It is not guaranteed, but it is a chance.

'The Devouring Flame is powerful and my natural counter, but that small fragment left on Earth can not match the full power of an Avatar if I give you my full support, as I plan to do so.

'Conquer that world and work from the inside to allow me a way through the barrier for future cycles. There are many methods to create an opening from the inside that will grant me access.

'The Arbiter of Reality informs me that it will allow such methods to work if you choose to assist me. So Choose. Death or Life? Die for certain or help me preserve your reality from ever being destroyed again in a future cycle of universal destruction and rebirth. Your reality forever preserved and cherished by me.'

'Conquer... What of the humans?' I asked, *'What will happen to them?'*

I felt a few of the eyes narrow in focus for a moment, before widening briefly in surprise.

'How amusing. You truly are concerned for their small lives. That is likely your old self talking. But I can see there is no convincing you of their unimportance.'

I prepared my thoughts to angrily reply, almost forgetting what being I was talking to for a moment. But it continued unconcerned, *'I will make an offer then, one that does not come lightly. In addition to the personal power of becoming an Avatar, I will bind myself to not interfere with events for that reality in any future cycles once you fulfill your duties.*

'Unless there is an existential threat to it of course.

'Once you accomplish my tasks, then the humans will never need to be conquered again. You'd be saving all of their lives in the future. Neither me nor my spawn would ever trouble them again after you've concluded your end of the agreement.'

'So I can help you get the ability to observe events on Earth in the future and I won't have to kill the humans and conquer anything?' I asked hopefully.

The Eldest's deep voice was sharp as it replied, *'No. The power for this endeavor is massive. You will have to conquer that planet at least once if not for multiple cycles before there is enough power available to you for you to be able to fulfill your duties in opening a method for me to have permanent access to that reality. Especially since the barriers around that reality are so thick, so it will take much work to pierce through them so that I can interfere with events within it.*

'Without the colonization of your planet by my spawn as well as many others, it would take hundreds of thousands of cycles to gather the necessary power on your own. And that's assuming everything went perfectly for you. Even I have only been self-aware for several million cycles of universal destruction and rebirth. I am a patient being, but not that patient.'

I struggled to think of another way. I didn't want to be a world-conquering monster.

'Is there any other wa...'

'No. Either join me now or do not. I have given you enough context to decide. It should be a rather simple choice. Death, or a period of unpleasant service to me before your reality is preserved forevermore. What say you?'

I thought about it for a few seconds, struggling with what to do. My disjointed memories screamed at me, bombarding me with all sorts of input that I had no way to understand right now. What should I do? I didn't want to hurt anyone, but the Eldest did promise that I would be saving even more people if I helped it in the long run...

'There is a time limit on the mortal's life below,' The Eldest suddenly said, *'The time has come for your decision, do you choose to be my Avatar? To pursue my goal to stabilize your reality so it can never be broken again? Or will you let the mortal below wither and die? In addition to all of the rest?'*

I looked down and to my left and saw a small human figure lying on the ground, panting hard as they looked around them in a panic. The world around me flickered between the towers of flesh and roaming creatures and a wide open plain of white bone as far as I could see.

The Eldest sent images of the mortal's condition to me, and I saw that he was slowly dying. He only had minutes left to live, and only a massive cocktail of chemicals injected into his system kept him conscious and semi-mobile right now.

The Eldest's voice echoed in my mind again, getting impatient as I stood there indecisively staring at the mortal.

'CHOOSE, FULCRUM!'

I saw the mortal below flinch too as the Eldest's booming voice echoed out in my head.

What was the right choice? Maybe it would be better for the humans if I became an Avatar and saved the humans in the future cycles by sacrificing the people of the next few? How was one supposed to make this kind of decision?

'CHOOSE, FULCRUM!'

I sensed the life slowly fading from the mortal as the Eldest's voice grew more forceful and irritated with each repetition.

'CHOOSE, FULCRUM!'

The mortal was clinging to his last vestiges of life as I still struggled to come to a decision. I turned my face to the sky.

'Save the mortal! This is too fast, I need more time to think!'

The Eldest's voice came back slightly smug and sly as it spoke, *'He came here that way. My interference requires a price. Become my Avatar and I will save your precious mortal. Do you truly value their little lives as you believe you do? Accepting my power will save more of them in the long run. You must know that already. Why do you hesitate so much? The numbers are clear, showing that joining me is the best option for them if you really care about them.'*

I felt the pressure of the situation weighing down on me. Should I conquer the humans for one man? For all the future humans in universal cycles trillions and trillions of years in the future possibly? Or let myself and this man die so I wouldn't be forced to slaughter billions of others, maybe far more, of his species?

For some reason, it was a hard choice. Like this man was special to me somehow. Like if he wasn't saved then something terrible would happen. Like saving him meant almost as much as the other half of the brutal calculations I had to make to decide what I should decide.

'CHOOSE...... NOW!' the Eldest shouted.

I teetered on the precipice of the choice. But at the prompting, I made up my mind. In the strongest mental voice I could muster, I shouted back.

'No! I won't do it. I won't work with you! I won't kill all of those people for some distant goal trillions of years into the future!'

The Eldest radiated disappointment, and suddenly the mortal disappeared. I looked around in confusion, but he had been there one moment and had disappeared the next.

'Oh, you will die without my help. And it would be quintillions of years at least, not mere trillions. How unfortunate. That mortal was always going to be healed regardless of your choice. It was you from the past after all. He is being changed now to form you, Fulcrum. As is the Seed to be more compatible with the mortal.

'I believe this to be part of my punishment by the Arbiter. To be so close to my goal fueled by sentiment only to be frustrated by an illogical sentiment of another of a similar kind...

'However, there is one final chance. Will you become my Avatar? Think about all of the lives in the future that you would save. If you die, then none of the humans will know of your sacrifice for them. Assuming that this is even the best choice for them.

'Even if they do honor you, all will be destroyed by the end of their cycle when their reality is ended and reborn once more. Your conviction will be forgotten after a single cycle at most even in the best case.

'I have seen it before with many heroes. They who believe that their sacrifices would make a difference or that others will remember them. It is a lie, all fades in the minds of mortals given enough time. Let alone after a single cycle.

'Your sacrifice will mean nothing. I will simply try again next cycle with or without your input. You are simply the first after this world has stabilized. There will be others who will be able to let me in next cycle. Do not die for nothing, for the mortal's ingratitude. Become my Avatar. Do what is best for yourself and the humans in the long run.'

I straightened. My thoughts felt clearer than they had in years. At the Eldest's words, all of my old memories came back and coalesced into a whole. Memories of the human Steven and his life. The knowledge that everything up to this point had been scripted.

The two versions of myself in Serenity never even directly having met, even if they were on opposite sides of the conflict anyways. My time as Fulcrum the massive creature. With incredible powers but a simpler mind as he became friends with Robin in Serenity.

All of my life was leading to this moment.

The Seed had manipulated my mind for years, keeping me under its control when I was Steven. The Seed that had had Jessica killed. The Seed that the Eldest had created with the express purpose of conquering the Earth. The Eldest ordered an assault on Earth that must have led to the death of thousands already and had no intention of stopping there until it ruled all of Earth for this 'Universal cycle.' Effectively forever to us humans then.

I had fought as the massive creature to stop the Seed, not even sure why and ignorant of my past life. Yet I found myself relating more to that person and their goals than that of Fulcrum who only wanted to protect the Seed and help it grow while his mind was altered.

I couldn't bow to the Eldest after all of that. Let myself be a puppet again.

'No. This is for me, not them. I won't go back under your thumb. Tentacle. Whatever. Anything but that, Eldest. Someone will stop you. It might not be me... But someone will stop you from conquering the Earth.'

'I see. To think even your full memories of the past being restored would change nothing... Illogical sentiment indeed. Then go, the choice is made. Your reasons are better than most and at least you will have a worthy death. My Fulcrum. The one who could have been the centerpiece of something greater but chose to turn away instead... I shall remember you, even if no one else ever does. Now go. Go to your chosen end.'

A massive crimson portal opened in front of me.

Steven.

Fulcrum.

Both.

I stepped through. I looked up into the sky and the massive beam of Devouring Flame landed and surrounded me as the red portal to the Eldest's realm snapped shut behind me. The golden-tinted dome flared brightly in all directions as it struggled to contain the force of the explosion as the raging inferno landed on top of me with a titanic blast.

The explosion was directly above me and my feet sank into the street below me from the force, but I remained standing as I looked up into the sky surrounded by the golden forcefield and reddish hungry Flames.

The Flames quickly rushed and began to burn me with a vengeance. I barely felt the pain, standing there as they burrowed into my flesh, surrounded by the laughing inferno as I kept looking up.

My legs gave out and I fell to the ground, no longer able to see through the Flames. The Flames kept laughing in a thousand voices in my mind as they tore and bit at me like rabid animals, searing out chunks of my flesh bit by bit.

The golden dome above flickered and a gap formed directly above me as I lay there on the ground motionless. There above me was a bright blue sky shining through the gap for a single moment before the golden shield repaired itself again.

I remembered back to better times. A picnic with Jessica in the summer sun, laughing as she squealed in disgust as I flicked an ant that had crawled onto her sandwich off into the grass.

Picking up Robin as a large creature and tossing Robin high into the air with the blue skied framing Robin's form. Catching Robin on the way down with my tentacles as it fell back down as the creature cheered and asked me to do it again despite my misgivings about the danger.

I felt my consciousness start to fade along with my awareness of the outside world. My Fulcrum self thralled to the Seed's will. But still, even through that, I found the memory. There I was standing on the back porch of my house, watching as Red, part of Robin, stood there. And there flying by through the air was the bird. The Robin, the creature that had given my friend its name.

I remembered the same event from Robin's perspective, through the faded and hazy memories it had shown me. Seeing the brightly colored bird through its multitude of eyes with fascination. Struck by the way it flew, its sudden appearance, everything about it.

All of it framed as one perfect moment of wonder. T

he two memories of the event merged and overlapped, spilling into each other like two liquids mixing. My memory and that of Robin becoming one for the moment.

Framed behind the flying Robin was a bright blue sky.

A reminder of happier times.

'It's been so long since I've seen the real sky,' I thought wearily as everything began to fade to blackness around me, *'I'm glad I got to see it... One last... Time.'*

Everything went black.
And Fulcrum.
Steven.
Both died at last.

Chapter 91: The Escape - Multiple Fragments of Memory

The lump of flesh detached and fell to the ground as Yellow went flying in the air, thrown by Red as the Flame began to finally *burn!* The large worm that lay on the ground twitched as its gestation sac broke and the fluid spilled out all at once as it bit its way out into the open air.

A brief sensation of heat and flame made it pause and freeze for a few seconds, but then the feeling was gone again. The worm sensed its target dropping to the ground next to it, incapacitated. Perfect.

The worm the size of a human's arm slowly crawled over until it was aligned with the target's skull. The target didn't have any ear openings and appeared unconscious as it lay still on the ground next to the worm. It had taken the worm over a minute to slowly make its way over to the unconscious body of the target.

The worm darted forward when it was close enough and latched onto the target's skull. It began to burrow through the bone until it had fully bored through with its ringed jaws and carved a perfectly circular hole in the skull to give itself access to the target's brain.

Careful not to damage itself, the worm opened its front end like an unfolding flower as thousands of fine filaments emerged from its body and sunk into the brain beneath it.

The filaments shifted and dispersed themselves according to the instincts of the worm as it prepared to perform its task.

With everything connected and the thin filaments dispersed across the entire brain of the target, the target did not resist as the worm adjusted its position slightly. The worm pulsed and the golden light traveled through its fibers in glowing pulse after pulse.

With each golden pulse, the worm carefully extracted the packaged memories buried inside of itself and began the injection to the relevant brain centers. It took minutes, but eventually the worm's job was done.

The worm attempted to implant its eggs near the brain stem for the next generation to feed on. Luckily for the target, the worm was sterile and didn't even notice as its attempt did absolutely nothing to lay its eggs in the target.

The worm's thin tendrils retracted from the target's brain, and the creature closed its mouth. It wriggled backwards out of the hole it had bored into the target's skull and inspected the area for any other creatures it should perform the same procedure on. But the worm's last target was the only living creature in the area.

Job complete, the worm curled into a ball and began to wither and die after what it believed was a successful replication.

———— O — o — O ————

Robin blinked awake. The memories of Red and Yellow swirled in its head, fighting for dominance with each other. But Yellow's memories felt more real, authentic. Red was dull, always thinking many of the same things that the Seed designed for it to think when it was on its patrols. But it had rich memories too while it interacted with Steven/Fulcrum, so not all of its experiences were useless.

Robin sat up and felt its injuries. Its Potential was fully drained and it stumbled slowly to its feet. It clutched its head as more and more memories swirled through its head. Not just memories of Red and Yellow, but those of the original Robin as well. Although the original Robin's memories were distant and slightly faded as well.

Robin jumped as Squirrel appeared in front of it suddenly. A wave of Hatred/Relief washed over Robin, each set of memories in its head prompting a different reaction at the sight of Squirrel. Robin put one of its arms on its skull and felt the hole there exposing its brain to the world.

There was no sensation there, and Robin pulled its fingers back before it accidentally damaged something. At its feet, Robin could detect a sliver of Potential. Robin leaned over to inspect the area.

The corpse of the worm lay there curled up, dead. Robin remembered it now from Yellow's memories. Something meant to transfer Robin's memories into Red in case Yellow lost their fight.

Robin picked up the worm's corpse and threw it back into its beak in one gulp, and used the Potential inside to heal its injuries somewhat.

After Robin was done healing itself, it and Squirrel cautiously approached the glowing hole in the ground just in front of them. Leaning over the edge to peer into the glowing pit, Robin could see the golden portal crackling and sparking below them slowly rising upwards in the cavern below, almost near the roof of the cavern now.

Robin drew back, that portal looked dangerous. Robin felt Squirrel form a connection with Robin.

'We have to go now. We don't have much longer,' Squirrel sent.

Squirrel sent a series of images to Robin. The perspective was from the top of the roof of this home. Squirrel was staring into the distance and saw everything beyond a certain point dissolving into the gray mist.

The walls of mist approached swallowing and dissolving the world around them, and Squirrel's senses couldn't pierce beyond it. The approaching mountainous wall of mist extending into the sky was swallowing everything in its path as it rushed towards them both from all sides.

Robin got an ominous feeling from Squirrel's view of the mists, more than it was getting from the portal. Robin sent its understanding back to Squirrel. Squirrel jumped on Robin's soldier, and Robin flinched as Red's memories told it to fight while Yellow's told it to relax.

'Go. Not long. The mist, it comes,' Squirrel sent quickly.

Before it could hesitate any longer, Robin jumped into the pit into the golden portal while Squirrel clung tightly to it. In seconds, they were through the portal and gone from Serenity forever. After they left, the edges of the portal began to slowly shift from golden to blue…

— — — O — o — O — — —

The Flame could only despair from above as it sensed its larger collective below be completely snuffed. The memories of this experience for the ultimate collective of Flame would be lost with little chance for this ember's escape now. There was some sort of struggle below, but the Flame hardly cared now…

What was this? The gray mist shifted and jumped around it and the Flame observed with surprise the wall of gray mist descending from above from the sky above. The closer it approached, the more the orb of mist encapsulating the ember pulsed.

The descending wall struck the orb and stalled for a moment as the Flame sensed the two remaining living beings of this place disappear somehow. A portal?

The Flame prepared itself for a final desperate escape. It wasn't strong enough to make it down there on its own. But perhaps… It could only hope certain assumptions were true.

The orb of mist around the Flame dissolved and the Flame felt itself begin to diminish immediately as the gray wall continued its descent rapidly.

The Flame was submerged in an instant, only to hit a pitch-black wall of void behind the mist. The wall was like the one covering the floor of this realm when it had first arrived here. Completely invisible and impenetrable. But this one was rapidly rushing inwards, pushing the massive bank of mist in front of it as it moved.

This invisible wall slammed into the ember of Flame and launched it forward with the churning mist in front of it. The Flame felt itself descend faster and faster with the black wall pushing from behind. The Flame could only barely sense its surroundings through the clouds of mist.

After flailing for a better view for a few seconds, the Flame finally detected the location of the portal below that appeared to be rushing at the Flame at massive speed.

Wait…

Wait…

Now!

The Flame launched itself forward with every bit of speed it could, ejecting the most unimportant members of the Collective behind it for the survival of them all.

The bright blue portal below became visible as the Flame shot out of the wall of mist like it had been launched from a railgun. It pierced the roof of the mortal home replica with its massive speed slammed through the glowing blue portal and made its way through. It was free!

Behind it, the massive compressing orb of mist collapsed on the singular point of the blue portal all at once. The formation built by the Seed and repaired by the Eldest struggled to survive for a single instant before it buckled and shattered into a thousand pieces as the Potential powering it was quickly swallowed and dispersed.

All that was left behind was a blank void and the massive orb of gray mists that was slowly dispersing into swirling tendrils again spreading out again among the blank void around the realm.

— — — **And there it is. It is good I handled that last portal personally. It was amusingly ironic to allow the Eldest to open the necessary portals itself before, but the timing for that one was too precise to allow any error to occur. Now, time to clean up the rest...** — — —

A sound like cracking glass sounded through the void all at once and the gray mist froze in place. Then with a mighty roar, the realm was torn open and obliterated by the Arbiter's power. On a whim of the Arbiter.

Job done, the Arbiter's attention drifted away from the destroyed realm. There was more to observe after all. The story wasn't quite over yet.

— — — O — o — O — — —

Robin blinked as it and Squirrel slammed into the floor of the empty cavern. Or more like a crater now. Robin could see the blue sky above, only disrupted by the occasional golden flash of Potential around them in a large golden dome.

Squirrel had fallen to the side, but it recovered quickly and seemed unhurt as it crawled back onto Robin's shoulder.

'Her,' Squirrel sent Robin.

Robin blinked as it finished climbing out from the pit into the open air. The surrounding area was in rubble, and Robin could hear the sounds of fighting in the distance. The crashes, explosions, and inhuman screams in the distance meld together into one dull roar of chaos and destruction. What had Squirrel said?

'Her?'

'Me. I am a Her, not an it. And I... I am Jessica.'

Robin sent acceptance and Squirrel seemed satisfied. Robin wasn't sure what the difference was, but Squirrel seemed to care about it at least. Jessica. Wasn't that the dead woman's name? Robin wondered if it was common to take the names of people after they died...

'That way. Away from the fighting,' Squirrel sent to Robin.

Robin oriented itself according to the image Squirrel sent along with the words and started moving. Squir– Jessica, Robin had to remember, kept guiding it as the sounds of fighting slowly faded into the distance.

'Where we going, Jessica? Are we not out of the fighting now?' Robin asked.

'Yes. But the humans will not like you if they see you. We have to get you out of town before someone notices us.'

'The humans... Why will they not like me? What did I do?'

'Just... trust me here. They are fighting something over there, they will shoot first and ask questions later. Better to not risk it.'

'Shoot?'

'It means to attack. Now... Do you feel that?'

Robin did feel something tickling on its mind as it continued forward, trying to influence its mind. But Robin's mind was strong and it brushed it off and continued forward anyways.

'Stop!' Squ-Jessica sent.

Robin slid to a stop, only to notice the distortion in the air in front of it. Some sort of barrier? Robin reached out and touched it.

Coursing underneath the dome's surface, Robin could feel strong flows of Potential. Robin inspected its pitiful amount of remaining Potential for a moment before comparing it to the formation in front of it.

Making a decision, Robin injected all its Potential all at once at one very specific point. The hand Robin had pressed into the dome sank into the shield until Robin's palm was partially submerged in the channel of golden light.

'What are you doing?' Jessica asked.

'Healing,' Robin replied, *'Getting lots of free Potential.'*

Robin began to draw the Potential rushing by its hand inward, and into its core. Slowly, Robin's core began to fill even as it healed itself back to its prime condition with the leftover Potential.

It even fixed some of the shapes of its plating that had been bothering it for as long as it could remember. The channel's flow of Potential massively increased for an instant and Robin pulled greedily on it before the flow cut off just as quickly.

The whole section of the dome barrier flickered off after a second, leaving glowing edges flickering around the hole a few hundred feet away. Huh, that was unexpected.

'Go! Go go go through. Quickly Robin, before it closes again!'

At Jessica's prompting, Robin dashed through, and sure enough the opening snapped closed behind it a few seconds later.

'Now quick Robin! Run as fast as you can. We have to get away before anyone sees that,' Jessica sent to Robin.

Robin ran forward as instructed, crashing through the strangely moving green foliage in its way. Then a deafening boom sounded out and Robin clutched its head and fell to the ground.

The high-pitched sound of the weapon blasted Robin, and it could barely hear Jessica screaming over the link as she thrashed on the ground, thrown forward off of Robin's shoulder after Robin had fallen.

Metal prongs stabbed into Robin and shot massive blasts of electricity through it, causing it to spasm. There was movement through the forest, and Robin could see humans in green uniforms as they surrounded it. Robin was shocked by the metal spikes again, and as it spasmed it was rolled onto a course cargo net.

'Robin!' Jessica sent desperately.

A hook fell from the sky, and one soldier attached it to the net, and the hook slowly rose, bringing Robin with it into the sky dangling beneath a helicopter. Robin tried to move but was shocked again by the metal spikes digging into its skin as the net sailed above the trees with Robin trapped inside.

'Robin. I'll... I'll find you. I'll help you escape, I promise. They're moving too fast, I...,' Jessica promised.

The helicopter above was flying fast and their mental connection snapped as the distance grew to too much. Robin wanted to use its Potential to enhance the distance of the connection, but what would that do?

Jessica couldn't reach it in time, and Robin might need it for healing if the electricity it had been shocked with was any sign of what was going to come.

Robin could only watch as it was slowly lowered into a large semi-truck with heavily reinforced metal walls and ceilings.

The helicopter released the net even as the heavy metal ceiling slammed shut above Robin, leaving it trapped inside in the darkness. The truck began to move, and Robin attempted to free itself from the tight cords.

Another blast of electricity zapped it, and Robin stopped. It was wasting a lot of Potential each time that the green uniformed humans did that. The humans were still watching Robin.

It would have to be still until Jessica came. She would come and save it. She was the only friend Robin had left. She had to. She had promised.

——— O — o — O ———

Jessica could only watch from the branches of a nearby tree as the squad of soldiers left the forest.

Robin didn't deserve any of this. After sharing a few of its memories that had unintentionally leaked across their connection recently, she realized that Red had been almost completely controlled by the Seed. It never had even the slightest thought of rebellion or disloyalty to its orders, despite its enjoyment of its interactions with Steven.

She didn't blame Red for killing her old human body anymore. It was the Seed's fault, and Red had had no other choice.

Red couldn't have even imagined that there was another choice than obeying, the Seed had made sure of that. And Yellow was her friend. She knew the memories of Squirrel in the back of her head were different from the human ones, but all the same richness of emotion was there.

Not even what Jessica the human had felt with Steven as a human was comparable to what Squirrel's feelings for Yellow had been. Those memories had more care and acceptance from both parties than she had ever felt as a human, and she couldn't lose that.

And more importantly, Robin was depending on her. Robin wasn't unintelligent but had been excited about the world and had only limited life experiences. She couldn't let Robin suffer in some government lab as a science experiment if she could prevent it. But she couldn't be stupid about saving it either.

She was a squirrel, and she could only do so much... A telepathic squirrel, but still just a squirrel. But for now, Jessica leaped from the branch and followed the group of soldiers as best as she could.

She would follow them until she had a real plan.

A way to save Robin.

Her friend.

Chapter 92: Epilogue - Multiple Fragments of Memory

President Harrow stood in front of the podium, somber as the American flags behind him flew at half-mast. The subdued mood of the press stood in contrast with the cloudless blue skies and warm summer day.

The President took a deep breath and gripped the podium, feeling like he had aged decades since his last speech. The press' muttering died down as President Harrow began to speak.

"This… This is a dark day. For America and the World. We have lost many brave men and women of our military in the events a week ago. Men and women dedicated to defending this world from a great evil. They managed to save a majority of the surviving population from the horrors within.

"We have all heard of their accounts of the alien menace, and their cancerous spread throughout the town of Harmony. Choking all life from a once beautiful town. Of the ruthless and cynical nature of the Neighborhood Watch, willing to sacrifice their own people en masse for victory..."

The President continued, "Let there be no mistake. Those people are terrorists, not heroes. Their fear of failure and unwillingness to trust their government with this threat has led to the destruction of the lives of not only our soldiers but the ones who still could have been saved.

"Thousands of families. Thousands of sons and daughters. Husband and wives. Fathers and mothers. All were killed by the Neighborhood Watch. To those criminals watching who orchestrated this, know that there will be retribution for all the suffering you have caused."

President Harrow scanned the crowd from right to left before continuing, "But… the threat to this country, the spearhead of the invasion to our world, has been destroyed. Despite the inhumane methods used. Only ashes remain of the town of Harmony. Ashes that are still being combed over now to prevent a reemergence of this threat.

"We can only move onward from this tragedy now. We *will* not let all these deaths be in vain.

"Next time these monsters emerge, we will be ready. This is beyond borders now. As a planet, we must come together and be vigilant so nothing like this can ever happen ever again. We must ensure no such tragedies have to occur again to defeat our great enemy. Humanity's great enemy. Tragedies manufactured by alien or human hands both.

"Preliminary agreements have been formed for a global task force created beyond national borders specifically to search and root out those that may still be hiding among us. And any that would dare betray their very humanity by supporting or hiding them.

"This Alien Defense Force, or ADF, will work to ensure the safety of all. For a better world where this scourge on our planet is eradicated once and for all.

"To protect and serve the world.

"For Humanity.

"For an Earth United."

————O—o—O————

Infiltrator of Authority carefully put down its glass of wine as the speech came to an end and the mortal President walked away from the podium.

Ha.

Imagine the countries of this world truly working together. The agreement barely covered a third of them by now, with petty squabbling preventing the others from joining. Infiltrator of Authority would already be heading to one of the remaining two-thirds if not for one thing.

The mortal whose face it was wearing had been quite wealthy before the man had the misfortune to run into it.

That girl... Alice. Infiltrator of Authority remembered her. She would have been the prime jewel of the Invasion force if she had not escaped so early on. Her well of Potential was massive compared to the others in the world. Maybe even larger compared to some weaker Immortals Infiltrator of Authority had seen among its people.

The man it had consumed for this identity barely provided enough Potential to fuel its own body for more than a few days. Being able to sustainably feed and grow another creature like it let alone a larger invasion force was out of the question at this point.

That girl... She would provide *decades* if not *centuries* of energy for Infiltrator of Authority. And the other survivors' Potential was nothing to scoff at either, and they all were in America at the moment. So here in this country, Infiltrator of Authority would stay, despite it being the home territory of the newly formed ADF created to combat it. Infiltrator of Authority would be building its reserves for the future right under their noses.

Infiltrator of Authority watched as the channel switched to the babbling news anchors on the TV, pretending to care about their fellow's suffering in the aftermath of the Mortal President's speech. Maybe even some of them did care. But Infiltrator of Authority would be surprised if that were true.

Only time would tell if this ADF would be effective enough to pose a threat to it or not. But Infiltrator of Authority was confident in its skills. It would have to lay low until the mortals let down their guard again. Until this ADF let their guard down. And when they least expected it... Infiltrator of Authority would strike again.

Infiltrator of Authority flagged down the waiter and they stopped and waited to serve it as the mortal should. "Would you like to box that up for later, sir?" the man asked.

Infiltrator of Authority let its smile grow wide as it stared at the mortal, "Yes, indeed. Have to keep myself well fed. After all... I have a lot of work to do."

Afterword

Hope you enjoyed the story! This is my debut novel and has been entirely self-published. It's been quite a journey for me to get to this point with this story.

If you're looking for more content, this story started on the free webnovel website RoyalRoad. Book two of this story has already started over there if you want to continue reading more of the story online right now!

To do that or explore my other stories and content that you might like, here is the link to my author's profile over there: https://www.royalroad.com/profile/433664/fictions

Made in the USA
Columbia, SC
30 October 2024

a43a2c47-beb7-4989-8be0-343e7c279633R02